Between Life and Death

By David Pyle

Between Life and Death. Copyright © 2014 by David Pyle.
All rights reserved. Printed in the Unites States of America.

Second Edition

Library of Congress Cataloging-in-Publication Data has been applied for.

ISBN-10: 0692306234
ISBN-13: 978-0692306239

Revised and Edited by david@pentwist.com
Designed by david@pentwist.com

www.pentwist.com

This book was originally published in the United States in 2009 by Publish America which is currently *Out of Print*. Any reproductions of original or revised versions are strictly prohibited - First Edition
Library of Congress Registration: TX-7-320-338
ISBN-10: 1-60836-244-2
ISBN-13: 978-1608362448
Between Life and Death. Copyright © 2005, 2009 by David Pyle.

"…this kind of thing's too awful, here this time of night with witches and ghosts a-fluttering around so. I feel as if something's behind me all the time; and I'm afeard to turn around, becuz maybe there's others in front a-waiting for a chance. I been creeping all over, ever since I got here."

---*Mark Twain, "The Adventures of Tom Sawyer"*

Between Life and Death

PROLOGUE

Monday, June 6ᵗʰ, '77

When I was very young, I believed that all women could read minds. At least all the women in my family and their friends could. At some mysterious age, this gift was passed on and all of the female gender kept this well guarded secret from the male population at large. They seemed to know just what I was doing or thinking at any moment and of course, I would get into some kind of trouble for whatever I was planning… or had already done. So, the dilemma was how to keep my thoughts mundane while in the presence of any female.

Oh well, I know that's not possible.

Somewhere along the timeline of my 17 years, I dismissed this notion, along with the Tooth Fairy and the Easter Bunny.

However, incidents over the last few days have driven me backwards into a reevaluation of my logic and beliefs. My childish beliefs about the boogey man, hidey behinds, ghosts and the unknown are all subject to scrutiny.

Right now…, this second, the small hairs standing up on the back of my neck are governing my belief system.

So, why am I standing in the dark, outside, in my boxers and t-shirt, listening to something that I thought I heard? Something that I thought I glimpsed out of the corner of my eye?

Silence escapes me.

All I hear is the beat of my heart pounding in my ears and every breath I take sounds like a cow in labor.

I've heard that it's adrenaline…, I think its fear.

Nevertheless, I'm beginning to see things that aren't there, out on the edge….

Chapter 1

The gentle currents of the Mississippi night air pushed the faint scent of locust blossoms through the sheltered back yard. The sound of a lone cricket, scratching its legs, matched the ebb and flow of the leaves in the huge cottonwood near the tool shed.

Behind the large frame house, one silent witness stood frozen, back sticking against its clapboard siding, listening intently.

A scratchy click, click, clicking sound coming from nowhere in particular, that didn't match anything in a library of memories, had become a nightly irritation.

Last week, James Earl Williams made his annual flight from New Jersey to visit his maternal grandparents. This had been uneventful enough, but this year *normal* ended somewhere over the Mason-Dixon Line.

Since his arrival in Deep South Mississippi, a nightly sound, somewhere between the back porch and his bedroom had broken that subtle routine of the body and mind. At 3:00 AM, when most people enjoy their deepest sleep, James was busy with a begrudged nightly inspection.

Without the aid of the familiar light-polluted radiance of the Jersey skyline, James had only a mix of glow and shadows from the single streetlight standing far in front of his grandparents' home.

The dark seemed ridiculous.

He shook the silver-tube flashlight once again and the dim yellow light reappeared. It was more of an irritant than aid.

James stood still, thoughts churning in a desperate attempt to prove his theory that this was something common in nature. He had never been the type who needed a nightlight or ran whining into his parent's bedroom from a nightmare or some imaginary monster under the bed. Spooks and monsters were reserved for cheap horror movies and novels and of course, what he dispensed to his younger brother Sam. It was a wonder that *Sam* could sleep at night after fifteen years of their old neighborhood coupled with his sibling torment. Maybe this was karma making its circle.

The sound disappeared about as quickly as it started with the same nightly shuffling sound followed by dead silence. Even the lone cricket and air movement died away as if on cue.

Beyond the beat of his heart, James heard the solitary sound of distant thunder with its gentle rumblings and flashes of orange heat lightning along the horizon. His damp back sticking to the outside wall and fingers digging into the clapboard siding like a rock climber had produced its regular migraine. With a slow practiced exhale he let the tension in his body ebb away.

Maybe this was only an exaggeration of the mind and none of it was real. After all, he was taking on a new life, and stress was known for pulling the purse strings a little too tight. Reality would be the raucous alarm clock that would wake him in a couple of hours. What could have changed since his last summer in Natchez, Mississippi?

For now it was back inside, back to bed, back to the steady drone of the ceiling fan and then pray he would get a few minutes sleep.

Journal - Thursday, June 9ᵗʰ, '77

Ever since I arrived at Gramma and Grampa's, I've spent my best sleep time of the morning, investigating inside and outside, with my ear against the wall. There's this ticking noise and it's driving me crazy. I know it's just a bug or something, but I want it gone.

If I had a stethoscope, I would use it, find it, kill it.

They do have a cat. Gramma's monster Siamese. "Tommy", takes care of mice with his creepy ability to zero in and make a meal of anything that moves especially moths and crickets. But the last few days he's been out being a tomcat.

Both my grandparents have dismissed the ticking as "house settling." Yeah. Like a miniature jackhammer.

You know these old houses settle for years. -That was what Gramma Ames told me- They just wear out like the bones in us old folks and start creaking.

I like the way she puts things in perspective. I took that as an answer the first few nights, but it just won't quit.

Okay. Here's the part I don't want to admit, not here on paper, in case someone reads this.

I've started seeing these things…, not just things…, faces, glaring at me. Just faces. In the daytime…, in the morning, in the evening. It's not like I can tell anyone.

So…, it's like I'm daydreaming about something, anything…, and out of the corner of my eye, in a pattern in the floral wallpaper or in the furniture arrangement or even a bush or tree outside, there's a face staring back at me.

Now before I'm labeled completely crazy, or over imaginative, or psychotic, the faces don't go away when I look their direction.

They aren't happy faces either, of course not.

Some sad, some angry, or just plain pissed off, but never happy.

I asked my Gramma Ames if she saw one last Friday morning. She just stared as I went over to the collage of vases and flowers on her curio trying frantically to help her see, until I noticed the desperation of boredom come into her eyes.

I never mentioned it to her again for fear that she would think her grandson was kooky. Was I? Am I?

James Earl Williams, average white boy, ready for the loony bin at age seventeen. Is it the trauma of moving halfway across the country from my usual Jersey City life, to Mississippi where there are only three local channels on TV?

These people don't even have cable. Most of our neighbors only have a bunch of twisted rusty metal poles strapped upside their houses with arrow shaped antennas dangling from the top.

And it doesn't help that I'm going stir crazy, already.

I like visiting my grandparents, but when it became a forced visit, part of my probation, it took away all the usual feelings I normally had from being around them.

But this is my last summer to be under that thumb and I'll be free!

Really free.

It's hard to believe that five years have passed since I was sentenced to stay here during my summers, away from my parents and brother, but more importantly away from the "bad influences" of the neighborhood.

I don't know where I'll be going, but I'll definitely be gone.

Or will I? I can't make up my mind. I'm really starting to like the slower pace and the people here. At least work at Earl's Garage with my Grampa keeps my mind off my troubles.

Now if I can only figure out what's making the ticking racket.

Chapter 2

It was finally Sunday morning at the Ames household and after two more nights of desperation with no sleep to speak of, it was time for church.

Family Southern tradition in the Bible Belt.

The grandparents, Martin and Maime Ames, were cornerstones of the small Holiness Cathedral Church in the community. It wasn't a question of whether they were all going, or if they would be on time. It was which clothes they would wear.

Holiness Cathedral Church had seen many changes over the last thirty years. Several face lifts, a steeple and cross as well as a parsonage added onto the back. Its stained glass windows created a turquoise glow inside indicative of the peace of heaven.

The most controversial change being that its congregation was *integrated*. This still wasn't a very popular word in the Deep South among some circles.

Noise of Klan activity in nearby Greenville, Mississippi still frequented the local Radio and TV stations from time to time along with some demonstrations. Just people looking for more ways to hate.

However, this little community east of Natchez was close knit and cared about each other no matter what the color.

Pastor Arnie Milton, the new minister and ex-war protester, seemed to be more "up with the times" than the recently retired hell-fire and brimstone preacher. The new Pastor Milton had a simple message directed more to love than fear. Attendance was up and money coming in when they passed the collection plate, so no one seemed to be complaining.

The one thing that James could depend on was a good ten-minute nap somewhere during the pastors steadily droning voice and a good jolt in the ribs near the end from his grandmother to wake him up.

Today's Sunday morning service was no different.

On a last minute whim, James Earl decided to hang around to meet the good pastor and maybe ask a few non-committal questions.

His gramma was pleased to see that he had taken an interest by the fact he was lingering, so she and her husband of almost forty-five years started home to begin Sunday dinner.

After an eternity of shaking hands, his dispensary of "God bless you" and "Come again" began to run out and the pastor's acceptance line shortened to a few die-hards. These were the few that always seemed to need "special attention" or prayer as it is with most close-knit congregations. James knew he was in for a long wait and didn't really know how to bring up the subject of his lunacy anyway.

After forty minutes of watching the clock it became evident that there would be no questions answered today. He decided to walk the few blocks to his grandparents' house. James Earl could already picture the fried chicken, mashed potatoes, homemade biscuits, and brown gravy that would be awaiting him.

As he moved toward the double-door exit, a familiar voice called him out.

"James Earl...? James Earl, is that you?"

James recognized the dusty voice as one of the oldest people on planet earth. Granny Smith must have been around when they dug the foundation for the church or when God made the dirt under it. At 87 years of age, it was a miracle she was breathing.

"I'm so glad to see you, young man."

She urged on toward him with a two-handed grip on her sturdy aluminum framed walker.

James groaned as he pictured cold chicken and skimmed over gravy the closer she got.

"My, my, you done turned into a man for sho'. James Earl..., you been on my heart. Yes you have. I heard tell that you were back for another summer with Brother and Sister Ames. They always have such good thangs to tell 'bout you."

She hugged him up as best she could and held his hand, patting it gently for a few moments. Her dark brown skin had acquired a dusty sheen over the last few years, but that was something James never noticed.

"Yes Ma'am," he answered, in his best polite voice. "Glad to hear it..., I was just...."

"Yep, good thangs," she interrupted.

He had forgotten Granny Smith couldn't hear it thunder on most days and puffed a quick muffled laugh.

Over his shoulder he glimpsed the pastor disappear with a young couple toward the pastors' chambers....

"Come set a spell over here with me."

James gave up all hopes of getting home before dark. Whatever pieces of the errant sermon he'd napped through would usually be updated by his aged friend.

"Like I said, you been on my heart lately. I still have my regular prayers at night, you know? I don't sleep much any more the older I git. Wake up at the crack of dawn."

James watched expectantly as she wandered off in thought for a few moments, darting her tongue in and out and licking her parched lips.

"Old habits…, but I wanted you to know that if there was anythin' that you need or wanna pray 'bout, you just let me know. Seems like that's all I'm good for any more. Too old to git 'round and visit or cook like I used to. I miss bein' about the Lords work."

Another certainty James could rely on was that Granny Smith could keep a secret. She already knew about most everything that he'd gotten away with, and some he hadn't, for the last five or six years. Ms. Smith kept many detailed secrets of his life during his summers in Natchez including the anvil of probation hanging over his head. Somehow, she always found her way over to have a "talk" and he'd get diarrhea of the mouth and tell all.

Over the years he had developed a deep respect for the wisdom and unconditional friendship that Granny Smith had chosen to show him.

She never condemned James and somehow, together, they always agreed on a solution of how to make whatever the circumstance might be, turn out right without alarming the community.

So as was his customary duty, James mentioned that he had been having trouble sleeping and about the ticking noises. He didn't mention the faces for fear that she would say he was possessed of the devil.

"I remember tell of a story similar to yours…, been many, many years since…," and she drifted quietly back off into her silent thoughtful state, closing her eyes.

If James hadn't known better, he'd have called for someone to help revive her.

"Back in '23 I think it was, there was somethin' like what you're describing, happen' to a friend of mine. I don't rightly remember all the details. My mind ain't what it *use* to be."

Her dry voice was straining as she was caught between talking and concentrating on her subject.

"I do know one thang though, if whatever it is been robbin' your sleep, it ain't from God. If it's a tormentin' you, it ain't from God. Ole scratch comes to kill and steal. All he good for…, yep…, all he good for."

James could tell from her pained expression that her aged body was tired and her sermon was over.

"Thank you for listening Granny…," said James with a genuine hug.

"I know more how to pray 'bout it now," continued Granny.

A worried expression crowned her face for a moment. "Best remember, sometimes thangs get worse before they get better."

She put an iron grip on the back of the pew they were sitting on and shakily struggled to rise from her seat.

"You best be gettin' on to your Gramma Ames. If I know her, she got a table full of good vittles that'll be getting cold shortly."

James said his goodbyes while helping Granny down the steps to the sidewalk. She only lived a little over one block away, lived there for years.

The Sunday afternoon sun met him square in the face, brightening his mood. James left feeling lighter, but still confused about what he was supposed to do about the strange visitations.

At least somehow he didn't feel as alone any more.

Journal - Monday, June 13, '77

Eleven years of this journal and I haven't been able to put it out of my life yet. I know the shrink requires it and that it's a good way to deal with the hell I went through in our Jersey neighborhood all my life.

Funny how I always seem to be looking back - maybe that's what all this writing is about. Some of the past wasn't bad I guess.

I didn't know you could grow 6 inches taller over night. Thank God for puberty and hormones. Back when I was little, I'd already learned to hit back at The Hand, *the biggest neighborhood gang, but growing meat on my skinny bones was my great equalizer.*

I found out that I'm pretty good at fighting back too. It's better than being run over and I guess somehow I started to like the feeling of power a little too much. At least that's what my shrink tells me. She likes to tell me a lot of things I don't really agree with.

Sorry if you end up reading this, but it's true.

I've done my best to turn the tables on those that made me feel weak and useless and made me the fall guy for every criminal thing they forced me into.

Revenge and retaliation were not traits that my mom and dad wanted me to pick up or teach to my little brother Sam. Hey, its hell being a role model and I never asked for the responsibility.

They've always worked full time jobs and Sam and I were taught to be self-reliant, mostly to make up for their absence, I think.

But all of that changed when a Judge - with a few nods from my mother's aunt - decided it was in my best interests to spend summers where I was born, here in Natchez, Mississippi. The attitude adjustment seems to be working, I guess.

Now, the complaints of parents, storeowners, and law enforcement have started to fade away. I can tell they still remember me by the looks on their faces, but the hate is fading with time.

My parents don't really know who and what I've become. I don't think they ever listened or believed the stories I told them about the neighborhood or the stuff that happened to me at school. They were always too busy. Or blind. I'm tired of reliving that old story.

One thing I learned to do was run. I did like Football in High School and at 6'2" and 178 pounds; it was a good choice at the time. But my heart was never in it and nothing I wanted long term. I felt like my life had other destinations instead of kicking around on a football field.

Anyway, school's out for me and it doesn't matter anymore. It feels so strange to say that. High School is finished. Wow, I need to clear my head.

When I come here, I can breathe. It reminds me that the whole world isn't like the people in New Jersey. Always in a hurry, pushing or being pushed, using the weak. Mom says that the people are as cold as the climate. I think she misses her home in Mississippi, but she'll never admit that to dad.

My "roots" she calls it. "Don't forget your roots."

I guess it's worked out good for me. I see the people here in Natchez and wonder why everyone can't get along like they do here. Everybody knows everybody else; they stay on the sidewalk instead of dragging their feet across the neighbors neatly trimmed lawns. Black, White, it doesn't matter. There's still those few that cut eyes when you walk past, but those people will always be around no matter where you go.

The little kids are almost the same here, ornery, full of meanness. I know some kids will always have a cruel side, but not like that hellhole back home. It's like they were bred to it. Always looking for something just a little more evil than the last to scare the hell out of their "slaves" or put the fear of the devil in the other gangs. Someway to break you down. It's hard to admit, but I guess I have a little cruel left in me too.

I'm doing it again…. It's a different culture. I'm glad I found my way out.

"You either thrive or die on the vine," my Gramma Ames says.

Gramma was always the one with thundering rolls of advice and opinion up until she started to mellow out. My Grampa was the quiet one - Reserved.

Now the older they get, she seems the quiet one and Grampa taking over that role. I've seen some of the looks he gives and he still wears the pants in the family.

My momma's folks have lived here pretty much all their lives. In a big white frame house in an old neighborhood on the east end of Washington St., a dead end outside the city limits. With their chickens and a little garden out back, it's like going back in time.

Grampa's owned the same gas station and garage near the "tracks" for as long as anyone can remember.

I've spent plenty of hot summer nights alone on their front porch swing, looking through the moss in the trees at the moon, listening to the sound of the train wailing and hammering its way to and from Natchez.

Grampa taught me to fish, swim, and drive…, pretty much everything a guy is supposed to know. Something my dad never made time for.

Earl's Garage. Now that's where I learned to work on cars and trucks. Got my first car when I was 15. Grampa picked up an old '67 Mustang that needed work. It became our summer project these last two years. It runs great now, so when I come here I not only have a nice ride, but a fast one too. Another reason I like summers here in Mississippi. It doesn't hurt that the girls are nicer here too.

Now that I'm out of High School, mom and dad want me to go on to college. I'm thinking about going to the Natchez Community College in the spring, so I can stay here.

I've never been close to anybody. I've always felt as separate as that noisy train from the real world. I can't really explain it. All I know is that thanks to my shrink, my journal is the only source of letting go of crap that likes to cling. Linus and his blanket.

It's a ball and chain, but I still come here and spill my guts on paper.

Girls would probably call this a diary….

Chapter 3

Every man needs a sure thing every now and then. It keeps him going. When the sure things run out, like fidelity in marriage, a steady income, or even the usual reassuring smile of a steady friend, then evil can be born.

Hope is also a fickle partner, it can make a man walk across a desert with nothing and somehow survive.

Hope can also kill a mans soul, while he holds onto something that's dead, expecting it to somehow revive, all the while knowing inside that it's over.

Life can be that way....

Some people can deal with it; others seek out things of superstition or the supernatural to pull them along.

Billy Don Poole stood quietly rehearsing some childhood bible verse about having a choice..., "choose life or death." Lately he wasn't so sure about life. Things hadn't been going his way for quite some time.

It was like a dark cloud hovering over his head, following him around. He felt it there. Hot. Sticky. Swallowing up his thoughts like a fog. Decisions that used to be so easy weren't clear any more.

Sallee Mae Poole wasn't sure she wanted to be his wife any longer. It wasn't so much what she said, but how she acted when they were together.

His boss was tired of the same old excuses of why he was somehow always late for work. Over and over giving him one more chance to straighten up or he was gone.

Bills over his head....
Thoughts..., so many thoughts were swimming around inside his head like so many voices, pushing him under. Almost like drowning....

Yeah. He needed a sure thing to pull him through. Some people used alcohol, like his dead father. Others..., dope or the Army; that seemed pretty much the same thing to Billy. It seemed like drugs and wars were the only things making news nowadays.

Billy chose a different route. He had higher hopes than to die a worthless alcoholic in a ditch outside of town or a ditch in Saigon.

As Billy stepped out of the bleak darkness of the remote shack and into the bright early summer sunlight, he felt lighter. Despite the heavy sweltering heat and humidity of the Mississippi River weighing him down, things were sure to change now.

He had himself a *mojo* bag.

A charm.

He didn't ask what was inside it. Didn't care. As long as that little red bag worked its magic and eased his troubles.

An ancient voice croaked from behind him, "Careful with what you brang me, you hear?"

He nodded and stepped away, down a hardly noticeable trail, with a feeling that everything was looking up again. Quickening his pace, Billy remembered the day he met this old woman in the mouth of a little cove out on the Mississippi riverbank. The way she spoke to him let him know it wasn't simply chance, and that they would cross paths again. It had been the start of a strange but fruitful relationship between them.

She needed a good strong man to do certain favors for her and was willing to pay good money for his services. All it had cost him was a little time and a few favors for the old lady. Something he and a couple of friends could easily do.

He stepped out from the cover of a thicket of young slash-pines onto the Mississippi River levee road and noticed that several miles to the south there was a dark storm rising.

Yep, life was going to be good again, ...at least he *hoped* it would.

Chapter 4

Clik. Click-Clik. Clik-Clik-Clik...

Darkness... black... suffocating black... like swimming through crude oil. In the distance a yellow flickering began drawing and pulling at something inside James Earl, as if his insides were on a kite string.

The feeling was nauseating, dizzy.

Click. Click..., Click. Click.

A hard crash of thunder shook the ancient structure of the Ames house, jolting James Earl awake. Thank God. It was only a dream.

Clik-Click Clik...

"Awww, not *you* again...," James whispered to himself.

A flash of blue light scorched the retina of his eyes as the instant boom of thunder finished shattering his nerves. An onslaught of rain began pelting the windowpane nearest his bed driven by a howling wind.

The pain in his eyes slowly subsided and he lay listening once again. There was a shuffling sound for a few moments that he attributed to the deluge outside and overhanging limbs above his roof. Drifting back off to sleep, James noticed something on the ceiling near the foot of his bed. The outline of a face as if peering down from above, looking at him. He rubbed his eyes and another flash of lightening cleared his vision.

Nothing. Imagination.

Then another earth-shaking rumble retentioned his nerves.

"Well at least the thunder can drown you out tonight," James said aloud, turning over to rest on his right side facing the partially open door with his back to the window.

Just as he faded to sleep, there was a sharp sound against the floor near the end of his bed that yanked him fully awake once again.

Shocked from his dreamy state, he lay affixed, as cold fear walked into his thoughts, freezing his eyes in a blank photographic stare waiting for some other movement or sound to relieve the anxiety.

His mind would not tell him what had alerted him this time, but he was sure it was a noise inside his room and he dared not move. Slowly he closed his dry burning eyes listening intently for sounds below the noise of the downpour and intermittent throaty rumbles of thunder.

He was rewarded with the sudden thump of a heavy footstep on the end of the bed that shook the boxed springs, sending the bed into a shiver.

James was frozen with fear and for reasons unknown could not force his eyes to reopen. He lay as still as he could without breathing, a slow rumbling growl stepped its way up from the foot of the shaking bed toward his pillow, growing louder. The weight shifted and flopped heavily against his back.

Sweat gleamed on his brow as he peered over his shoulder to where the heavy weight was pressed against him.

"Tommy…," he whispered in an exasperated relief. James reached behind him, giving the old cat an appreciated scratch on his furry belly, "Oh God, am I glad it's you."

The twelve-pound giant of a Siamese cat had chosen his bed for the night. He exhaled deeply and fell back into place staring into the shadowy darkness of his room. An exhausted sleep finally overtook him with the comfort of the rumbling animal guarding his back.

Chapter 5

Red-eyed and wrinkle faced, James walked into the big kitchen where breakfast was waiting for him. Ham and eggs, biscuits, and appropriately, a bowl of red-eye gravy, sat waiting around the table.

"Mmmm, smells good," said James. "Mama cooks good, but you're the best."

"You look rough this morning, did the storm keep you awake?" asked his gramma.

"Nope, it was the best sleep I've had in a week," James lied, yawning and stretching. "Tommy kept me company."

"He must have come in out of the storm," she said, fussing with the last of breakfast.

His grampa had ignored the conversation and was frozen in his seat at the table, glaring at the morning Gazette.

"I can't believe this. The old family graveyard's been boogered with," said Martin Earl Ames, thumping the front page. "Our church's graveyard," he said, looking up at his wife, Maime.

The cemetery behind their church had been vandalized. A grave dug up and the bodily remains taken. No traces or tracks.

"Just as well, the rain last night probably washed everything away," he mumbled on.

"Who would do something like that?" asked James. "That's too weird."

"Well, it's the third grave robbery in Natchez since February and I'm sure our brilliant sheriff hasn't got a clue," said Martin.

As soon as breakfast was consumed, the two men started out the door to open up Earl's Garage while his grandmother hummed and put away the dishes.

"Speak of the devil," said Maime, peering out the kitchen window. "Look who's pulling in the driveway."

The sheriff and one of his deputies started crawling out of their Adams County vehicle, about the time James and his grampa walked out the kitchen door.

"Mornin', Sheriff."

The spring on the screen door screeched painfully as it pulled the door shut with a loud WHACK.

"Mornin' Martin. I see you made it back in town for the summer, James," said the sheriff, nodding at each of them.

James was thankful that the sheriff didn't act as though their few hours together each summer entitled some sort of friendship.

"What brings you way out to this end of town?" asked Martin Ames, cutting him off.

"Have you read the morning paper? About the vandalism in Heaven's Gate Cemetery?" asked Sheriff Howard.

The deputy was nervously switching his eyes from person to person without moving his head. James instantly became amused, watching his piercing gaze turn into an imaginary ping-pong match inside the deputy's head.

With the sheriff's drawl and the deputy's antics, it was all James Earl could do to keep the grin off his face.

"Yep, as a matter of fact I have, …evil thing it was," agreed Martin Earl.

"Well, we're going through the neighborhoods to the closest *prox-imity*."

James choked back a laugh and turned away. Did he even know the meaning of "proximity?

The sheriff's eyes sparked darts toward James and back to Martin.

"As I was saying, I'm asking everybody *close by* if they saw anything suspicious yesterday. Anybody or any vehicles you don't normally see."

"We're pretty isolated out here on a dead-end street," said Martin. "I doubt that anyone would be using our road for an escape route."

"Well the rain last night did a number on anything that might have been remotely judged as evidence. It seems they were real careful," said the sheriff.

He ducked his head and scratched the back of his neck, obviously bothered about something he wanted to discuss.

"We're grasping at straws on this one. The other two, uh, occurrences happened up in the Natchez City Cemetery, but this one, well…."

As if he'd finally gathered his scattered thoughts, he finally stepped closer to Martin Earl and lowered his voice.

"Mr. Ames, I don't know how to tell you this, but it seems the grave that was robbed was a relative of yours. Syrus Earl Ames, one of the oldest graves inside Heaven's Gate cemetery."

Martin Earl was suddenly quiet.

Gramma Ames stepped out the side kitchen door onto the small porch, listening closer.

"Grampa, are you all right?" asked James.

"Sheriff Howard, what the hell are you telling me? That was one of our family graves that was dug up?"

"Martin… Earl… Ames!" said gramma. "Watch your tongue…."

She must have seen the quick glance from her husband and shifted her look elsewhere.

"Sorry I had to be the bearer of bad news Martin, but I didn't want you to find out from town gossip or worse, tomorrow's Gazette," said the sheriff.

"I understand," said Martin. He looked apologetically around at his wife, quickly cooling off.

"Any ideas on who might be responsible?"

The sheriff lowered his head, "We have a couple of very thin leads, but no hard evidence as yet. If we hear anything, I'll drop by your Garage or leave a message here at your place. I'm real sorry about all this…," he said turning to leave.

"Let's go, deputy."

Sheriff Howard stopped and lifted his hat, dabbing at some early morning perspiration on his brow.

"Oh, and James, I assume we will keep our usual arrangement?"

James nodded a stiff but thankful approval as the sheriff turned to leave. At least the sheriff had the decency not to make a big deal about being his interim probation officer.

Chapter 6

Earl's Garage opened a little later than normal that morning. There were the usual customers already waiting for gas at the pumps, some heading out to work, or farmers up north to their fields. James quickly took care of them while his grampa opened up the shop for business. Earl's Garage was also one of the last remaining full-service stations in the county; something the older list of patrons seemed to appreciate.

As soon as the early morning rush cleared out, the spit and whittle club arrived with their dominoes and parked themselves on their usual bench under the shade of an enormous live oak beside the garage.

James and his grampa had settled down in the office area for a short break and a cup of fresh coffee.

"This business with the cemetery ain't right, James," said Martin thoughtfully. "I mean, more than just robbing a body and being a member of our family, there's a feeling I get about it. No good's gonna come out of this."

Storms in life come and go. Mostly go. Some are worse than others. Preparation is usually the key, but it's those surprises that always seem to get you. Life in Natchez had mostly been a laid-back ordeal for the Ames family. Something with the weight of a premonition pressed down on Martin Ames all that day, warning him that change was in the air.

About a quarter before ten that morning, the clear blue sky began to cloud over again from out of the southeast. It wasn't long before deep rumbles of thunder began to creep closer to the busy farming community.

"Looks like another downpour headed our way," someone declared.

Grunts and mumbles of agreement came from four wrinkled farmers, slapping down dominoes.

Life east of the Mississippi almost guarantees a person to be nearly drowned or electrified by thunderstorms when they decide to move up along the *Mississippi Delta.*

"James, you better go pull down the overheads before it hits. Looks like this one could be nasty," said Martin Earl.

The wind instantly arose as leaf twisters danced across the pavement before thrusting high into the air with other loose debris. A few large drops of water started dotting the pavement and the domino club grabbed their domino hands and headed inside the garage. Rays of sunlight gleamed through the dark rain bearing clouds as the storm pushed in.

"Devil's beatin' his wife," declared one of the most wrinkled of the foursome.

"Mmmmmf," grunted the rest as they hurried for shelter at their breathtaking pace.

Six or eight more customers, three hours of solid rain, wind and lightening and it was time to close up shop for the day. The weather served as a needed distraction for the two men, their thoughts mulling over separate recent events.

The phone rang and Martin Ames picked up the receiver to the familiar voice of Catherine Williams, his daughter. He spoke in soft tones for what seemed about a half hour. Then he set the handset down on his desk and walked out into the garage where James was tinkering with his Ford Mustang.

"James, your mama's on the phone," said Martin.

James quickly put down a handful of tools to pick up a red oily cloth. Wiping his hands briskly, he trotted toward the office.

Their conversation was cheerful and light as James related some of the recent events. She was concerned about his not sleeping well and James played it down, not to worry her. He changed the subject by asking how dad and Sam were and what they were up to.

Sam had a summer camp to go to in a few days and afterward would be joining James near the end of his summer stay. Dad says "Hi," and that he had been promoted to second in command of some other corporate position, which to James meant there would be even less time at home and with family; if that was possible.

"Mom must be lonely," he quietly thought, as she chattered on in dialogue.

Catherine agreed with him, urging her son to consider enrolling in the local community college for the coming fall session, to get his basic courses while there in Natchez.

His parole agreement would be complete in a week or two and only the sheriff and his family knew about that situation. Of course, this would mean staying with his grandparents instead of flying back to New Jersey after summer was over, which hit James squarely in the chest.

Catherine assured him that ample money was already there for him when he made his decision. James knew where that money came from..., his mother's wealthy aunt. He could probably stay in school for the rest of his life and she'd pay for it.

His Mother was in the middle of explaining that he would need to list his grandparents address as his primary residence and the conversation fell into silence.

Catherine Williams was homesick to see her family and the current events that her father relayed, only served to remind her more of how time was getting away. Her parents were getting old, her son turning into a man and leaving home. She was half-way across the nation from her parents and oldest son.

James picked the conversation back up and assured her that he could take care of registration and that he would go next week to get information in Natchez.

A few I love you's and James hung up the receiver.

James stood in emotional silence, looking at the sudden cost of both freedom and change and suddenly felt lost and alone again.

Journal - Wednesday, June 15, '77

What are the chances that I'd be born in a scratched out hole like Natchez Mississippi?

I often wonder what the odds are that a person is born to this or that family, in this country instead of some obscure village in China or a tribe in the Congo, or little village in Brazil. In this year, this month. Rich, poor, middle of the road. Good looking, ugly, skinny, fat, ...or different. Gramma always says that we have a lot to be thankful for. I guess she's right. So many questions, so few answers, and so little time.

I suppose it's these strange questions always on my mind that make me want to read and investigate. I need to find out what, why, who we are and other minor details. I hope that someday all of the dislocated gibberish of knowledge will somehow put itself together in my mind and congeal into something that is logical and makes sense. Yeah, right....

Like getting the hell beat out of you every day for living on the line between two violent street gangs. Now that makes perfect sense.

Mom's right. I need to stay in school, but what a bomb that was. I never expected her to agree with me. I'm not ready to write how I feel about that yet. Almost like telling me it was time to get out and move on, but not really.

...and how am I supposed to study?

I'm so damn tired of this clicking crap, every night, then the sorry ass faces appearing in everything, and now that weird dream.

I'm going to find out what you are and what is going on with me if it's the last thing I do.

...I miss my family.

I hate this stupid journal. You never answer my questions. You only create more questions.

Chapter 7

Suppertime with the elder Ames family was usually one of light chatter, discussing the day, guests dropping in and great Southern cooking. Today was no different, except the conversation seemed chalky and stressed.

There was no re-reading of the Gazette, no rehashing the front-page news or mention of the Sheriff Howard's visit. This evening was filled with choppy conversation and comments about how unusually powerful the thunderstorms had been the last two days.

Gramma spoke up after several moments of uncomfortable silence.

"Hope nothing is brewing out in the Gulf. I haven't listened to the weather in a week. By the way, I was talking with Elberta today…, about that clicking or ticking James has been hearing in his room."

James Earl inhaled and nearly choked on the half-chewed sweet peas in his mouth. He hoped his coughing would provide a quick detour from this new conversation.

Elberta Straw was the strange next-door neighbor that never weeded her flower garden, which blanketed her entire front yard. She rarely came outside except to harvest a few items from her herb garden or to pick a few tomatoes off the vine.

"Now Maime, you know that I don't like you talking to Elberta about personal stuff," croaked grampa. "That old woman is weird enough as it is with out getting her started on some subject like that. *Ms. Bonnet* likes speculating on stuff she has no understanding of, and more important, she likes to gossip about what she invents."

Gramma quickly defended her position, "I know, I know, she's a strange old widow woman, but she told me about a distant relative near Atlanta, Georgia that had something similar in their house 20 or so years ago. She seems to think it's a bad omen."

Maime Ames quietly trailed off her comment while observing the unflinching glances that her husband began giving her.

"Omens, Bah," scoffed grampa. "Superstitious bullcrap. You're letting your Gypsy side flair up."

Gramma blushed and her eyes darkened at her husband, "Well, I still think that if some noise is keeping James Earl up at night, we should get rid of the problem instead of ignoring it."

Her eyes flamed as she tried to appeal to her husband's logical side. Evidently, Catherine had called earlier that day and talked to her mother

28

before calling Earls' Garage.

"Especially if we want James Earl to be spending the summer with us. If it's the house settlin' - that's one thing. We should look into getting the house leveled, but if it's a rat, we need to root it out and get rid of the vile thing."

"That's what Tommy's for," chided grampa, taking another bite of food.

There were a few minutes of silence as Martin waited for his wife to cool her quick temper.

"But if that worthless cat ain't doin' his job…," Martin trailed off. "Me and the boy will look into it."

"Thank you, *Honey*," she cooed somewhat sarcastically.

"Just don't be letting that witch next door put ideas in your head."

"Martin Earl!" scolded Maime, gazing toward the kitchen's screen door, at a few golden rays of sun creeping in. "She's only an old woman with weird ideas. Besides, you shouldn't be calling our neighbor names, she might hear."

Grampa rattled his half-empty glass of iced tea, drowning out the last of what his wife said.

"I talked to mama today," said James, a desperate attempt at changing the subject. "She said to tell you hello and that she misses you. She also told me to check into starting at the community college in Natchez this fall instead of next spring. Do you think you could put up with me while I go to school in town?"

"Why that'd be wonderful, James!" said gramma. "We'd love to have you stay here as long as you will. Fact is, I was hoping that you'd stay awhile now that you're out of High School, so that works out even better. Did your mama say when she or Sam would be coming to visit?"

James began to wonder if his mother had actually called his gramma considering this odd question.

"She only mentioned that Sam would get to spend the last couple of days of his summer vacation with us, but that was about all," said James.

A knock at the door abruptly ended the train of thought. It was one of the church folks dropping in to say hello and since every one was through with the evening meal, James excused himself to his room.

This felt like a new beginning and his first steps to independence as James readied himself to make a trip into Natchez in the morning. First order of business, he wanted to check out the local campus and surroundings, but there were other concerns.

Summer trips into town with the Grandparents had educated him as to where everything was located, but with freedom came the price of the unknown.

Even more important now, it was early and he still had a little daylight; a good time to investigate his room and the outside wall to the house. If he intended to stay here, there would have to be some changes.

The rain had previously ceased its fervor and the sky was displaying a few clear blue patches. Cool evening air, damp with haze met his face. The air smelled of sweet ozone. Cool drops of rainwater were slowly descending from leaf to leaf on the huge cottonwood out back.

Suddenly the clean feeling of early summer fled, replaced with a heavy sensation of being watched. He imagined his familiar nightly path in the dark along his side of the house and how differently it looked in the last vestiges of daylight.

The old huge house was built up high on solid blocks and Bois d'Arc stumps for a foundation, well above the ground. He shook and bumped the flared skirting around with his hands and carefully bumped around with his feet, but couldn't get it to move. It seemed planted in the ground like cement.

James scratched at a small hinged door built into the skirting, used for access under the house. Flashlight in hand, he released the hook latch and raised the door to peer into…, complete blackness.

He stuffed in the flashlight with its already yellowing beam, along with his head, into the darkness to get a better view.

"Yep, bunch of tree stumps," he said, his voice becoming a flat echo.

A clean dirt foundation…, dry…, a few spider webs, two glowing green dots….

Without further delay, two reflective eyes jumped through the access door yowling and clawing its way to freedom, right across James's face and chest.

He fell backwards into a puddle of rainwater, soaking his rear and adding to the misery.

"What in the world got up you!?" yelled James, as he wiped stinging blood off his cheek and forehead.

Tommy became a blur in the distance.

"How did that tomcat get under the house? Maybe he *has* been trying to do his job," thought James.

"What happened to you?"

Gramma caught James at the side kitchen door and made a fuss over the array of fresh whelps and scratches.

"I'm okay; it was only the cat."

James gently tried to fend her off until he realized the futility of arguing with someone her age.

His grandmother made a fuss of daubing alcohol and *Monkey Blood* (her name for some red-dye antiseptic) over his wounds, turning his face into streaks of savage war paint. After he managed to escape her attention and changing into a pair of dry blue jeans, James went back to the opening under the house to take one last look. He didn't see any loose floor boards hanging down, floor joists were stock solid. So, he gave up this part of his search, closed and re-latched the trap door.

"Find anything?" asked Martin.

James was half dragging, half carrying a heavy old wooden ladder from its resting place beside the tool shed.

"Tommy," said James, sharply.

His grampa twisted his head in an awkward position looking at his grandson's face, with a widening grin.

"Got you pretty good. I see your gramma helped you out."

James stood in yet another silent inspection.

"What you plan on doin' with the ladder?" he inquired.

"Just thought I'd look for loose boards on the side of the house or under the eaves," said James.

"Probably a rat scuttling around inside the wall space." said grampa. "This old house isn't insulated very well. If you want, we can check the attic later. By the way, I'm glad you'll be staying on with us while you're in school."

He paused for a moment.

"I could tell your mama misses you. She's bad homesick. She'd be here if she could."

He looked at James thoughtfully. "I think for her, with you being here, it's like a part of her being here too."

"Thanks grampa. That means a lot."

"Well, you don't need me for this. I'm about to throw some scratch out for the chickens," he said before wandering into the shed.

After all was said and done, there appeared to be nothing out of place. The house was well maintained and in excellent shape for its age, which didn't exactly help identify the problem.

James put the ladder away, scratching his head and grabbing a tight handful of his long black hair, wondering what to do next.

He looked at the western sky, which was clearing and was displaying the last stage of a beautiful peaches and orange sunset. A few puffy clouds hovering around....

Another face. In a small white cottony cloud.

Angry? No, pissed off. Then as fast as it appeared, it was gone. James shuddered in amazement.

Whatever happened to the days when he would lie on his back looking at the clouds go by and imaging horses or rabbits or other would-be animals? What the heck was this about? Did the whole world suddenly go nuts?

Chapter 8

A gentle breeze was blowing the fresh peach scent of Mimosa blossoms through the open back bedroom window, along with the cool humid air. The storms had brought cooler weather, although everyone knew that it was only a temporary relief from the summer swelter to come.

A few moths were beating the last of their wings off while desperately trying to get inside to the light, and making soft thumping noises against the window screen. James finished reading the last few pages of a novel brought with him from home and switched off the light.

All was quiet, the gentle whirring of the ceiling fan, and the thoughts of getting to stay here for the next few years lifted his spirits as he drifted off to sleep.

Tick. Scratch....

Clik...

Click...clik. Click. Clikclikclik.

"You're early tonight," said James, aloud.

He silently rose from bed, went to the hall bathroom, washed his face and returned to search this out once again. He reached into his room from the hall and switched off the bedroom ceiling fan, which slowly swung to a complete stop. The air became suddenly dank and heavy, the curtains by the open window hanging dead and lifeless.

He entered his room as silently as possible, stood in the doorway and listened. That damnable steady clicking was still there. He turned to the left and an inch from his own face was a stark white pale face.

James jumped backwards hitting his head against the doorjamb as his gramma said, "It's me. It's me. Easy son, I'm sorry."

"You scared the..., well never mind what you scared out of me," declared James palming his throbbing head.

On her face was a pound of white face cream that made her features scream in the dim light coming from the distant hall bathroom.

"I heard you get up and thought I'd see if I could help," she said in a hushed tone.

After their combined inspection, they discovered that the sound was similar to a bird pecking at something and it was coming from the wall and attic at the same time, both places echoing each other. Maybe that was just it. Maybe it was an echo from something outside. Then contented that it had its audience completely disturbed, it quit all commotion.

James felt satisfied that at least he had a witness to his visitor.

A few hugs later and they were both in their beds asleep.

James Earl was once again floating in something that felt like warm oil, comfortable, but nauseous. There was that same familiar pulling sensation on the inside of him. Like something soft and invisible tied to a part of him just inside his navel. In the black distance was a flickering yellow light. No..., several lights. A steady rhythmic melody was soothing him onward.

It was almost hypnotic.

He felt akin to a fish on the end of a line being reeled in, to be gutted and cleaned at the hands of something..., some faceless terror.

Then from somewhere near his head came a steady beep, beep, beep..., as his god-awful alarm clock sounded.

Any other time he would have wanted to chunk it to the floor, but this morning it had freed him from an awful, fearful place.

James lay quietly thinking, "There has to be some relief. Some explanation. Somewhere."

Chapter 9

An early breakfast. No discussions were offered about the late night rendezvous with his grandmother or their expedition. The two men went off to the garage in Martin Earl's pickup.

James wanted to retrieve his car from the shop and hurry into Natchez as early as possible.

When they arrived at Earl's Garage, they opened as usual and grampa ushered James over to the storage room directly behind the double bay garage. Inside was a stack of four new tires with a makeshift bow from a red cloth tied to the top of the stack.

"Well, if you're going to drive that thing back and forth, you'll need something substantial under foot," grampa said.

James yelled an instant, "No way!" loud enough for the arriving customers to hear.

It was the last piece of hardware the '67 Mustang needed to make it truly roadworthy.

Forty-five minutes later James was tooling down Highway 555, the "Triple Nickel", as James called it, into Natchez. Windows down, music up. One step closer to the freedom of manhood.

There was only one good Rock Station on the radio, but one was enough.

"If this isn't a chick magnet, there isn't one made," blared James out the window. He realized how stupid he sounded…, then let out a clear laugh, "Who cares?"

He found downtown Natchez quiet and slowly awakening. The clerk in the College Administration Building informed him that it was too early for regular admissions, but he managed to get all the information about the school and the list of things he needed, including how many times he went pee that last year.

Even with his exceptional grades, transcripts from three different High Schools should be interesting to explain. Then there was the embarrassment of a probated sentence and its explanation….

That always seemed to get raised eyebrows.

After a few phone calls, his multiple transcripts were on their way. He looked at his watch and it was a quarter 'til eleven. He had expected to spend most of the day rambling through admissions applications and possibly entrance exams.

Time to do some research.

Natchez wasn't exactly information central, but it had a ton of history and a decent public library.

James drove around lost, without asking for directions, and eventually found the archaic building. He couldn't help noticing the beauty of an era gone by everywhere he looked in the town. Nothing there resembled the concrete jungle, the congested brownstones or cramped houses, or the smell of sewer from his old neighborhood.

He ambled up several steps into the somber quietness of the library. It was the beginning of summer and only two other people visible in the entire building.

"Might as well get a library card; this will probably be a regular stop when school starts."

The librarian was not the typical dusty pre-posthumous, gray hair in a bun stereotype, but a middle-aged sensible looking lady. After about 15 minutes, a smile, a question about the scratches on his face and a deposit, he was busily browsing the card index looking for…, what exactly?

What exactly do you look up when you do research into weirdness?

It was for sure, he *wasn't* going to ask the *Librarian*.

Religions, Mythology, Folklore….

Folklore. As good a place as any to start.

Hauntings, another hit he was considering - *Superstitions*.

He quickly scribbled down the locations for a couple of maybes.

Occult…, the jackpot of strangeness. It was the mother-load of weird crap - in fact, way too much weird for a library in the middle of nowhere this far south.

His life was always unsheltered and he had already been through more evil than some adults in one lifetime. However, the few volumes in front of him suggested evidence of an alternate reality.

The long section of the occult was unbelievable and matched the shiver down his spine. He quickly jotted down another ten or twelve titles along with their Dewey Decimal locations; ones that seemed like they might have related information. Just as he was about to close the card file another subtitle sprang into view: *Grave robbers*.

Two large stacks of books surrounded the top of his table, discouraging any would-be visitor from asking any embarrassing questions.

Time passed with notes galore. He discovered terms about a totally different world and wished he hadn't. Were these people from a different planet?

"Pentagrams" – weird.

"Incantations" – strange.

"Voodoo" – hairy!

"Witches" – got to be kidding, only in movies.

"*The Exorcist*" or "*The Omen*" were glorified versions of the "*Creature from the Black Lagoon."* All were exaggerations of someone's imagination. Witchcraft, Voodoo people…, it was ridiculous. Surely people didn't go around trying to act out this stuff they saw in Hollywood fantasies.

James's face must have been as tightly screwed as his internal emotions not to have noticed the person standing behind and looking over his shoulder.

Deep in thought, James squinted at the current page displaying the image of a rotting cadaver with accompanying fine print below.

"That's a very odd collection of books you have…."

James almost came out of his skin.

"Do you always sneak up on people and…?" he asked loudly, his voice trailing off.

A young slender girl shifted to the edge of his table, unflinching at his outburst.

"Is that your usual greeting to strangers?" she asked with a smirk. Her voice was low, soft, and had an unfamiliar non-Southern sound to it.

"Well no…, I just…, I didn't hear you come up behind me and…, I was somewhere else I guess," James stuttered aimlessly.

"I wouldn't have bothered you, but I saw the stack of books you were collecting and I need *Devils and Demons* you have in your stack over here. Looks like you already met with a few stray spirits yourself," she grinned, while scrutinizing the fading red paint on his cheek and forehead.

"Are you through with it?" she asked.

James had become fixated on a pair of bright blue eyes and wavy dark hair, a slender face, olive complexion….

"I said…, are you still going to use this, or are you through with it?" she asked again, her voice tinted with frustration.

James came out of his stupor and said, "Uh, no, I mean yes, I'm through with it, you're welcome to it. Take it. It's too weird for me. In fact if you need any of these, help yourself," he shrugged, waving his hands frantically over the amassed group of books. "I don't really know what I'm looking for anyway."

"For someone who doesn't know what he wants, you sure did pick a strange collection of books," she mused. "I haven't seen you here before. Are you new?"

"No, I mean yeah, kind of. I come here every summer to visit my grandparents," said James.

"Do you live here in Natchez?" he asked hoping to keep the conversation going.

The librarian cleared her throat and motioned for the two of them to quiet down, as if there were anyone else in the entire building that cared about their conversation.

James had a voice that carried, so he probably sounded like a foghorn, and by now he likely had the room's undivided attention.

The strange young girl picked up the book and one other of his odd collection, sauntered over and sat down at the table directly behind James.

Great. Just Great. That was smooth as sandpaper.

"I didn't get her name or anything," he thought angrily.

He slumped back down in his chair, looking back over his notes, unable to think of anything except blue eyes and long soft black hair. He'd never been shy, so why was he acting so weird now?

He got up his nerve to turn around and ask her for her name; he shifted and eased his arm over the top of his straight back chair, and..., she was gone. There was only the stack of books still on her table.

"Crap," he hissed. "Smooth move, James."

He was already poised to bolt toward the front of the library and then rush out the front door when someone tapped him on the shoulder, making him jump.

Uncontrollably he pushed his chair over backwards with a loud echoing smack on the hard floor.

"Are you always so jumpy?" she asked.

"I was just..., do you *always* come up behind folks and scare them silly?" asked James. Then quickly setting the chair upright, he looked for a way to turn this awkward situation around.

Instead..., "Do you mind if I sit at your table?" she asked. "It's easier to share these books than to wait for you to decide if you're going to use them or not. It seems that you have about half the books that I needed. Isn't that odd?"

"By the way, I'm Jolie Dimanche," she said with a mock courtesy. The tiny smirk she added went completely unnoticed by his glazed eyes.

"James. James Williams."

He thought how ridiculously close his introduction sounded to "Bond, James Bond" and he cringed, putting away the hand he was about to offer. No one his age shook hands. What was he thinking?

Once again, they had drawn the attention of the Librarian who was hawking them over the top of her reading glasses.

Jolie circled around to the other side of the table and sat down directly across from James who eased into his chair as quietly as possible. He quickly shuffled his notes so that his research would not draw any more ill attention than he had already received.

As if reading his mind..., "So..., what are you researching?"

Jolie was peering over her own notes, glancing up at him.

James, flushing, stalled, looking for some excuse as to why he was looking into things that were weirder than anything he'd ever imagined. Oh well, when in doubt, use the truth. He'd probably already struck out anyway.

"Just personal stuff," James mumbled quietly. "I don't really know what I'm looking for exactly."

"How will you know when you find it then?" replied Jolie, her eyebrows almost perfect arches.

James still taken in by those mesmerizing blue eyes, managed to repeat that he was staying with family east of the city and there was something out of the ordinary going on there that he wanted to find answers to.

James looked at the clock on the wall of the library about the same time his stomach growled embarrassingly loud and saw that it was 2:05 in the afternoon. He was about to cave in.

"I'm starving; can you tell me some place that has good food near here?"

No pain, no gain.

"If you're hungry, you're welcome to come along," he said, casting his lure. "My treat."

"Might as well eat. You're hogging all the information," chopped Jolie. "There's a good place a block from here; they won't rob you either."

She stood, gathered her few personal items, including an extremely worn notebook that looked ancient. Jolie then walked up to the front desk and politely asked the Librarian if she would leave their books where they were, explaining that they would be back shortly.

The dusty light of the library was no match for the blinding summer sun and increasing heat.

Jolie walked on ahead, leading a fast pace. The white spaghetti strap top and blue jeans she was poured into had James Earl hypnotized within moments.

Jolie was mostly quiet as she led the way across the busy street.

This wasn't happening, not to him. After a somewhat closer inspection, James decided that she was really a mirage. Meeting someone of her beauty had been the furthest thing from his mind. He was either extremely lucky or she was destined to disappear forever after today.

Her lazy stride had him playing out scenarios in his head, thinking of a way to get a date with her.

The blaring of a car horn brought him back to reality. He realized how juvenile he was acting and tried to start up a conversation with Jolie.

"Did you say you live in Natchez?"

"No, I didn't," she answered, as she continued on at a brisk pace.

He was met with more irritating silence.

Ok. That was a dead end.

"Here we are," she exclaimed softly as she walked through the door into the blissfully refrigerated coolness of a Cajun restaurant. A little hooked bell jingled as the door opened and closed.

Someone across the room chimed, "Welcome to *The Cajun*."

Jolie took a seat at a table nearest the door, by a window, not waiting to be seated by the hostess.

An attractive older waitress came and took their order. Her mannerism was authentic, as was her slight Cajun dialect.

"So, how long are you staying in town?" asked James.

"I live right across the river in Vidalia," Jolie said sipping at her melting glass of iced tea. "But I come over here most every day."

Her blue eyes darted up from another sip of tea, then her lips creased a grin.

"So, you're planning on going to the community college..., what exactly do you want to be when you grow up?" Jolie asked tauntingly.

James stiffening his posture defensively, "I haven't decided yet, but when I do, I'll be glad to let you know."

James suddenly remembered that he hadn't mentioned anything about attending community college, or did he? She could have told him she was from Timbuktu and he probably wouldn't have remembered.

With very little small talk, their food came and went as they both sat picking at the remaining pieces of the best blackened catfish James had ever eaten.

James' mind drifted back to his notes and trying to figure out what it was he was looking for. It was probably futile and he doubted any library would help.

"So, why don't you tell me about the strange stuff that's going on?" asked Jolie.

"Do you always do that?" asked James."Do what?" asked Jolie, innocently wrinkling her brow.

"Nothing...," sighed James, feeling stupid at his outburst.

Was he really that transparent?

"So..., are you going to fill me in or will I have to read your mind?" asked Jolie.

"I think you should read my mind. You've been doing a pretty good job of it so far," said James.

Jolie laughed. A bright smile spilled across her face.

"She's an angel," thought James as he smiled and a flush of color rushed across Jolie's cheeks.

"Okay. Like I already said, I'm living with my grandparents..., for now. It's an older house, you know..., kinda big and..., well this is really going to sound stupid to you. I come down every summer to help out at Earl's Garage. East of town?"

He waited for some hint of recognition in her twinkling eyes, but received none.

"This year has been..., so different. Every night since I've been back in town, I get a wake up call from some bug or animal or something "ticking" in the wall or somewhere. At first, I thought it was the house settling. Or at least my gramma said it was, but now I'm not so sure."

James realized that he was droning on.

"I knew you'd think this was stupid," James said standing up and stretching.

"Relax, sit down and finish your story," said Jolie.

James eased back down in his chair, and their waitress came back by and refilled their tea glasses. After taking her time looking James over, she strolled away from their table.

"Well, you have to understand, I'm not the skittish type. I can sleep through a train wreck," James braved on, measuring his words.

"So..., something else must be waking you up, dreams or something," Jolie encouraged him on.

"Yeah, as a matter of fact...."

James saw where this was heading and if he was going to get a real date with this girl he had to find something that they had in common, instead of his "problems". Maybe it was already too late for that. She seemed more interested in picking information from him than getting to know him.

There was an uncomfortable silence as he mulled over his long list of errors.

"So, what were you researching?" asked James.

"Don't change the subject," Jolie smarted back. "You're definitely not from around here or you'd know what that ticking is...; it's common local superstition. It sounds like a little ticking bug called a *death-watch*. It's rumored to be some sort of a warning device to let you know of a possible death in the household. You need to find it and get rid of it pretty quick. That is..., according to local superstition," she added quickly.

James sat dumfounded, looking over at Jolie, again mesmerized by her eyes. Deep in thought, he remembered looking everywhere to find the source of the ticking.

"You said you visit here each summer. Where do you visit from?" she asked.

"New Jersey..., actually we moved a few months ago to Tinton Falls, nearer the ocean, but nobody's ever heard of there. So, I usually tell people it's New Jersey. My dad's job kind of tells us where we'll be living next.

I'm planning on staying here for a couple of semesters of school, and then decide what I'm going to do."

James started to feel a little more comfortable, now that the conversation was away from the topic of problems.

"Oh! So, you're a transplant!" Jolie said with a grin.

"Not really. I was born here in Natchez. My mom and dad lived here for a couple of years near her folks until my dad's job forced us up north,"

James said, looking nervously at an old round clock hanging near the door.

"So, that's why you don't quite sound like the local color," Jolie mused using a fake local accent. "But you don't exactly sound like you're from New Jersey either. So I guess that makes you more of a graft, doesn't it?"

James saw her teasing as relief from the twenty-questions they were playing.

"What's your story, you don't exactly sound like you belong on a fishing boat either?" said James, grinning.

The waitress walked up and asked if they needed anything else.

James arose reaching for his wallet and the waitress said, "That's okay, it's on me."

James stood gawking, completely dumbfounded at her generosity.

Jolie stood and hugged the waitress, "Thanks, Aunt BeBe, the food was great. We're going back over to the library for a while. Oh.... This is James...."

"James Earl Williams, Ma'am, and the food was really good," he added.

BeBe's eyes searched James from head to toe for a second and turned to walk away, "Not bad, Jolie. Not bad."

James could feel his entire body sink in a rush of heat.

Jolie only grinned and started out the door, "Coming?"

Journal – Friday, June 17, '77

What a day. For once in my miserable life something good happened.
Jolie Lefleur Dimanche.
Lives in Vidalia.
Personality as crisp as cold lettuce.
Drop dead perfect.
I met her at the library in Natchez…, to heck with all that.

I'm meeting her again tomorrow, Saturday morning at the library. She said that she had a few personal books that I could look at and make some notes from. Some info that I wouldn't find in any library. If it can answer some questions and get rid of my nightly visits it'll be worth the trip.
It'll be worth the trip even if I don't.
Jolie Lefleur Dimanche. Mystery girl.
Her name is as pretty as she is. I haven't felt this good since…, ever.

Ok. This is not like me, but this is not like my usual luck. I've dated a few lookers but most of them are overrated and don't have many brain cells to match. Which probably makes me a complete jerk for saying that, but after the pretty wears off, what do you have left? Something like talking to a fruit stand.
What's inside the tootsie roll pop?
On the other side of my world…

The ticking sound eased off some last night, but that same dream came back, over and over. I'm beginning to doubt my reasoning. Is it just me? AM I going crazy? What bad timing.

Out of the corner of my eye just this evening, driving home, almost dark. I was staring at the road, minding my own business and passed a mailbox on the side of the road, then all of a sudden, it was a person, or the silhouette of a person. I looked in the rear view mirror and it still looked like a person for a few seconds, then it… I don't know… It was gone. I see things move out of the corner of my eyes all the time now. When I turn and focus, nothings there. My intuition tells me that it's always been there and I'm just now noticing it. But what's caused me to become so aware and start attracting this weird crap? When I'm here in Natchez, I normally live the dullest life on the planet, well…, up until today.

I'm a homebody. I work hard and come back to my grandparent's house. I haven't been anywhere special. New Jersey isn't special, just different; the hurry up and wait, come home to TV, books, homework, baseball with Sam and…, the gangs, lets not forget The Hand. I don't see anything special about me - unless it IS a mental problem. I wonder if there's a history of mental illness in our family. Somehow, I'm going to bring up the subject and ask Gramma about it. She'll know. Mom would only worry.
I'm wasted. No more of this tonight.
I'm getting sleep tonight even if I have to plug my ears with cotton.
As a matter of fact, I'm taking the couch tonight. Gramma won't mind, only for one night.

Chapter 10

What wonderful music! A soothing rhythm…, and that voice…, soft, like a mother whispering the words in his ear…, like a baby cradled in arms.

Floating in the water and relaxing…, the quiet water is pulling…. Like learning to swim, start shallow, gradually going farther out, barely over your tiptoes in the sand…, peaceful and quiet…, clouds in the blue sky…, warm sun….

Dreaming again.

"This is a dream," thought James relaxing.

Faces formed in the clouds…, family faces…, his mother…, others…, unknown family, but family still…, taking turns talking, whispering…, explaining things…, indecipherable things that he can't seem to understand…, warnings…. All was peaceful as he drifted back into nothingness.

Then he was floating again above the ground in the air…, flying low…, under trees…, moss in the trees…, brushing the skin softly.

Below are big rocks, no…, square stones, some with shapes.

Gravestones. Head stones. An immense necropolis rocked and swayed beneath him.

Then there was nothing but darkness.

"I want to wake up now," he thought struggling against his paralyzed body.

A voice began calling. Growing darker again…, blackness. A familiar pulling from inside him. Being reeled in like something dead. Nauseating.

The beat of some distant music like sticks began to pervade all other sounds. Sticks clicking together…, and a soft drumming.

Click…click… tick.tick.tick.

Click. Click. Tick.tick.tick.

The rhythm. The pain….

Everything began to revolve around him as he gasped for breath.

James woke with burning acid in his throat, unable to breathe in and about to heave his guts out.

Jolting up, nothing looked familiar and he didn't know where he was. The room was spinning. James slid off the couch onto his all fours and closed his mouth breathing desperately through his nose, redirecting air into his lungs. As soon as his burning lungs were full of air he coughed out the burning gag stuck in his windpipe.

Drowning in your own vomit; surely not the most pleasant way to die.

As soon as his breathing cleared to a steady burn, he cupped his hands over his mouth tightly and gagged. The burning bitter taste and smell in his throat fed the nausea.

There was a faint light in the hall and he remembered that he was in the living room. Everything was muffled. Cotton. He stuffed cotton in his ears. He pawed at both of them and cleared his head.

Tick.tick.tick… Click. Click. Tick.tick. Click.

Not again! The insanity of it. How did it find him here?

James jumped up, feeling his gut wrench again with the vertigo.

He walked as quickly as his rebellious legs would take him to the hall bathroom. He hit the floor on his knees as dry heaves twisted his stomach and diaphragm, but there was no offering for the porcelain god, not this time. He reached around and closed the door not wanting to wake up the whole house.

After getting his senses in order, he nabbed a wash cloth, soaked it in cool water and masked his face, breathing through the cool fibers. After repeating the process several times, he began to feel better. What was that all about? Something he ate?

He sat down on the closed toilet seat remembering back when he was a kid and had a mild food poisoning. This was almost as bad, but that lasted for days. A few minutes later, his head cleared along with all his symptoms, despite a throbbing headache.

He made his way back through the hall to the couch, where a cool breeze was wafting through the windows pushing the thin curtains from side to side.

It was only a couple of hours before sunrise; a couple of hours before the sun would come screaming through those clear glass windows.

The ticking had stopped. He fell into the blanketed cushions of the couch and fell fast into a dreamless sleep.

Chapter 11

A small fieldstone wall embedded with wrought-iron fencing surrounded Heaven's Gate Cemetery. The entrance was only a city block behind the Holiness Cathedral Church and at near capacity, it was decorated with some of the oldest graves in the state of Mississippi.

The gently rolling land stretched lazily into the distance, with its back directly against undeveloped wilderness. Heaven's Gate belonged primarily to the Holiness Cathedral Church and a handful of board members. Though little management was necessary, it wasn't maintained to the best of standards.

Lately a few spotty patches of weeds had squatted on the front of the property giving it an unkempt appearance. Nevertheless, sunrise can make even the most cold and dreary of places seem warm and inviting. The sun's rays began to erase the last wisps of ground fog hovering over its captive audience.

Most of the "late" members of the church and many generations of local community were permanent residents. The scattered monuments and tombstones were a mixed garden, proof that death does not discriminate against victims of past wars, diseases, and old age. The earth freely accepts all comers into its folds.

Over the entrance was an ornate arch that once displayed the expert handiwork of a master iron artisan, now embellished with dark flakes of rust.

A love vine crowded one encrusted side of the arch and gateway, entangling itself tightly in a grip of life throughout the metal façade. The other side was also on its way to summertime obscurity with the beginnings of a morning glory vine. Profuse violet blossoms were opening in expectation of the rising sun.

Noble aged Live Oaks and odorous moss hung thickly, blocking out all but a few rays of early sunlight from the unkempt grounds.

On the back wall of this blessed land of the dead, was a small section undermined by one of the largest Live Oaks in the cemetery. The powerful roots had lifted and ruptured the stone wall, grasping the earth with giant fingers while supporting the massive bulk of the expansive upper growth. Yellow crime scene tape haphazardly spat from tree to brush to headstone, marking the desecration of a sleeping soul.

Strewn dirt. Splinters of decayed and rotted pine. An overturned headstone. Evidence of a morbid visitation.

The flattened stone read:

The Mortal Remains of
Syrus Earl Ames
Beloved Brother
Rest In Peace
1780 – 1824

Most of the rainwater had subsided, but clouds of mosquitoes were rife and appalling in the thickness of the dank humid air, all vying for access to the hole full of brackish rainwater.

The quietness and peace dissipated as invading footsteps squished through the hole in the fence. Nearby, two tiny black eyes watched lazily as the pair of grimy mud caked feet came nearer and stopped a dozen paces short of the open grave.

Out front, at the main entrance, another visitor hurriedly pressed through the arched gate and vines. Light tan uniform, gray Stetson hat, holster with a tight gun belt and a badge.

Slowly with determination, the uniformed man advanced toward the back through the multitude of gravestones in the direction of the other living visitor, making frequent stops and looking cautiously in all directions.

Upon reaching the open gravesite, he slowly made a circle around it looking at the depressions in the soil, disturbed leaves, any signs of who had been excavating the dirt from the resting place of the ancient Syrus Earl Ames. The officer heard a soft squishing of wet grass behind him, slowly unholstered his weapon and turned to find…, Billy Don Poole.

"Good God boy…. I almost shot you," said the uniform. "Are you crazy, coming here so soon after the dig? I already cleaned up after you once, but this ground is a recording device now that it's soakin' wet. Anybody with good eyes or a good dog could sift you out in a heartbeat."

"I came back to make sure you did your part of the job, *and* you did want to get paid didn't you? Here's something for you," Billy said, handing the uniform a small envelope. "I'll have one more 'lil something for you to do in about two weeks. There'll be another storm, a real floater. Not much reason to pay you, but it's always good to have the law on your side."

The officer looked at Billy strangely, wondering how this stodgy guy thought he could predict the weather.

"Pleasure doing business with you," said the uniform, ignoring the slight. It was good money for keeping his mouth shut and misdirecting evidence. "Now you better leave while I'm here so I can cover your tracks."

There was the low rumble of an engine at the front of the cemetery. Idling, then stillness. The faint sound of a car door opening and closing.

"You better leave now…, go!" said the uniform.

He picked up one of the abundant broken branches nearby and vigorously swept the ground behind the slick footprints. Careful to trample in the footsteps left by Billy, then quickly disposed of the branch over the fence as he heard footsteps swishing through the deep grassy path of the graveyard.

Slowly a young man in a pale blue t-shirt and jeans determinedly made his way in the direction of where the uniform was waiting.

He was holding a piece of paper and making frequent stops to see which direction to navigate. He spun, getting his landmark and turned back toward the open grave. Now with more intensity, he focused on what appeared to be a hint of yellow in the distance. In a few moments, he closed the gap, when he heard a voice.

"Hold it there, son," said the uniform.

"Deputy? Is that you?" asked James Earl.

"Who are you?" asked the uniform.

"Don't you remember? I met you the other day when you and Sheriff Howard came by my grampa's…, *Mr. Ames house*?"

"What are you doing disturbing a crime scene? Do you see this tape? That means you shouldn't upset anything in the area or you could halt our investigation…," he began to ramble.

James listened to him drone on while looking around. The deputy reminded him of some boring old sit-com officer from TV.

"Are you listening to me?!"

The deputy raised his voice in pitch to a whine.

"Yeah, I'm listening. The sheriff asked me to come by here to inspect the site for my family. You know? Mr. Ames? I'm supposed to see how much damage was done and report back for the family. Here's the piece of paper signed by the sheriff with the directions to the grave. So, before you get yourself all worked up, you need to check in with your Boss."

"He didn't say anything to me about any family coming here disturbing the crime scene," argued the deputy, snatching the note.

He immediately recognized the sheriff's handwriting and personal stationary.

This cop was exactly like every other flatfoot that he had endured from his old neighborhood. No respect for anyone and guilty first. Of course every cop back in his Jersey neighborhood was also on the take to one extent or another.

"Nothing changes," mumbled James.

Again, he ignored the deputy, stepping under the yellow tape to make a survey of the gravesite. He stooped over and looked at the fallen marker reading its etchings, pulled a pen and pad from his pocket and took a few notes. There was some slight shivering movement under the stone that went unnoticed as James tried in vain to tilt the heavy granite monument.

The gravestone wasn't defaced, broken or chipped and despite its age the huge block of granite was in good condition. The inscribed words were worn thin only from time and erosion from the elements.

He put the pen away, looking around at the area. Dirt was now scattered splotches of mud and washed flat from the previous rain. He saw a dark spot over near the cemetery wall and headed for it.

"Hey, where are you going?" asked the deputy.

"Just over here, it's not inside your precious yellow barrier," replied James.

The deputy snorted and stomped clumsily through a vine to where James was walking. James reached the wall first and found the broken down opening and a gigantic root from the huge overshadowing oak wedged in the base of the fallen stones.

He stepped through and noticed a few footprints in the mud. Slick soled footprints. Really big feet.

A few broken limbs littered the immediate brushy area and then nothing but bramble beyond. Poison ivy encroached the entire area like a plague. The deputy closed the gap between them and stopped at the wall.

"Hey, what did I tell you? You aren't supposed to be back here. The sheriff may have sent you to look at the gravesite, but that's all. You need to finish up and get on back there," spat the deputy.

"You should tell that to whoever owns these slick soled shoes," James said, pointing down at the ground in front of the deputy.

"It was probably some sightseer. We can't keep a guard day and night on this place; we took note of everything important the morning after all this happened. Now you should leave."

"Yeah, I need to get back to the station and give this to your boss," said James. "Oh…, can I have the note from the sheriff back?"

The deputy crumpled it into a wad and tossed it to James.

James shook his head and picked up the note, "Thanks for your help."

As James walked away, the deputy decided immediately that the boy was going to be a nuisance.

Minutes of disgruntled waiting…, a car door closed…, its throaty engine came to life and quickly drove away.

With a tight smirk, the deputy selected a large rock fallen from the border wall and smashed the back of Syrus Earl Ames' gravestone cracking the aged slab of granite in half.

The two beady-black observing eyes bolted from its dark secrecy underneath the tombstone, whipping its serpentine body toward the deputy, making its way like lightning through the uncut grass. The deputy stumbled over backwards and fell against an iron marker, barely regaining his balance as six feet of water moccasin rushed past him into the darkness of the undergrowth. Shaken and pissed off, he picked up his Stetson out of the mud pasted grass. It was going to be a long day.

James met the sheriff at Earl's Garage, letting them know the condition of Syrus Ames' gravesite and that the headstone was okay and wouldn't have to be replaced. There wouldn't be any need for permits and red tape to re-close the grave, but the few remaining relatives would have to be notified.

He mentioned that the deputy was there and that he seemed to have a problem with controlling his temper as he handed the wadded up paper back to the sheriff. He also made mention of the shoe prints outside the back wall in the mud and the trail into the vine thicket.

The sheriff looked puzzled at the news of his deputy's presence but passed it off as good investigative follow-up.

"Oh, by the way, James," said the sheriff. He presented a large envelope to James Earl from the top of his grampa's desk.

James only stood and glared..., perplexed. Never had an officer of the law given him anything that turned out good.

"Well, are you just going to stand there?" asked Sheriff Howard.

James slowly took the envelope and saw a familiar address stamped on the face, *New Jersey Dept. of Corrections.*

"You are officially free, young man," he continued, looking over at Martin Ames. "As your interim probation officer I want you to know that I've really seen a change in you over the last few years. All for the good. It's all noted there in your dismissal. You shouldn't have any problem getting the records expunged."

The grin on James Earl's face slowly spread into a tight smile.

"You can come by the office in a day or two and sign a few things in front of the judge to make it legal."

A couple of hours later, James had finished up a brake job on a '68 Chevy truck, tuned up a carburetor - or at least sprayed all the gunk out with cleaner, and was now cleaning himself up to leave for Natchez.

"You emptied out both bays in a big hurry, didn't you son?" asked grampa.

"I, uh…, I guess so. I need to go to Natchez to finish up some research I started and I didn't want to leave you with a bunch of stuff to do," said James.

"Research…."

There was a short pause.

"What's her name?" grinned Martin.

"What…?"

After a few moments of deafening silence, James answered.

"Jolie. How did you know?"

"Are you kidding? Maime and I were watching you after you came home. You looked like someone put a light bulb in your eyes. Only a couple of things I know can do that to a man. Why don't you invite her to come over for Sunday dinner?"

"Well, I don't know her that well yet, so I can't promise she'll agree to that or not, but I'll try," said James.

"Git yourself by the house first and clean up good," frowned Martin. "That gasoline and oil cologne you're wearin'll run most girls off…, at least the ones you want to keep anyway.

"Go on. Git! I'm closing up as soon as these two vehicles are picked up and gone," said Martin Earl, walking back to the office.

Ten-fifteen in the morning, James was speeding down the road barely over the limit, wind in his hair, and music blaring on the radio. The one good station on the radio was screaming out a familiar tune by the *Rolling Stones*.

At a quarter to eleven, James parked at the library and found a seat on the stoop out front while waiting for Jolie to show.

The morning shadow continued to recede from the looming two-story building as the seat of his jeans ground further into the hard front steps.

"She said about eleven this morning," mumbled James.

Thoughts and scenarios played through his head, wondering if he had made a wasted trip. His beautiful mirage was probably a no-show. It figured she would stand him up.

He got up to walk inside the library and check to see if she was already there, hoping he had only missed her somehow.

Two blue eyes intently watched James Earl as he fidgeted nervously around the front of the Public Library. His coal black hair was chaos, violently whipped from the wind on the highway as his fingers combed through it in futility to make it behave.

Tight jeans. V-shape. Solid arms. Jolie decided that she had seen worse. Her mind played a few scenarios of its own.

She had told this strange boy when to meet her, even had a heated discussion with her aunt, but now she had stopped to look and listen, and to make up her own mind. This was a big chance she was taking after all.

While standing frozen three steps up the front library steps, a sharp finger tapped James Earl on the shoulder.

He jumped inside as he turned to see.

"That your car?" asked Jolie.

"You have a talent for coming up behind me and…. Yeah, it's my car," said James. "Sorry, didn't mean to bite your head off."

"I'm the one who's late, I got caught up in some family discussion," said Jolie. "It's nice."

"Wanna go inside?" asked James.

"Not really. I have a better idea," she answered.

Jolie assembled the small bundle she was holding, walked to the passenger side of his car and stood waiting.

James woke from his stupor and walked over, opening the door before she slid in.

Jolie stared at him for a moment after he fell into the driver seat.

"What?" asked James.

"Looks like one of those cat scratches are going to be there for awhile," Jolie said, sounding amused.

"Cats love me," spat James. "Where to?"

"The Gardens…, it's where I like to go and think," said Jolie.

"You'll have to show me where it is," said James cranking the Mustang.

As soon as the engine caught, the radio blared at near full volume. He jerked for the knob turning it down.

"You actually listen to that?" asked Jolie.

"It's all there is to listen to down here," said James. "It's either that or some of the weird local stuff."

She took James the long way around town to the garden area of the city park. As they pulled in, James noted the amount of green everywhere. Nothing like the pavement view he was used to back home.

Jolie led him to a quiet area with benched seats, sat down and placed her books beside her. James managed to sit as close as he could comfortably next to her, glad that she didn't protest.

She shuffled through two old books and a newer one trying to decide which one to open first. She lifted the one that looked as if it would fall to pieces at the slightest breeze.

"I guess we can start here," said Jolie.

The book turned out to be a family ledger and was like no other that James had ever seen. Its onion-skinned pages contained detailed accounts of family members long past, with a birth to death record of events. For several generations, it listed where each person lived, who they married, where they worked, who they worked for, their children, who befriended them, who their enemies were, …even how they passed on.

Some entries had far more information than others did. Some had photographs, some older ones had inserts of etchings and hand drawings that were very detailed. Jolie flipped through the book, back a hundred years or so and stopped.

"Look at this one. I found a similar incident that happened to a relative, where they were having a ticking sound, like the one you told me about. The only difference was one of them was having precognitive dreams and visions of some kind that were driving them crazy. You know…, really paranoid stuff."

"Really," said James dryly. "What kind of dreams and visions?"

"It's not clear about the visions, because they kind of went…, well…, they didn't handle it well and the notes are a little vague," said Jolie. "The two dreams they recorded were really interesting though. Each account describes the effects of a *drawing spell* to lure the spirit or soul of a person."

"*Drawing spell?* And you believe that kind of stuff about spells and dreams and visions?" asked James in disbelief.

Great. If it wasn't for those startling blue eyes drilling a hole in his heart, he would have stood up to leave.

"Not completely I suppose, but I try to keep an open mind," said Jolie. "But they certainly did. Not everything is black and white, especially when a family is prone to the *gifts*."

"Gifts?" asked James. "What gifts?"

"Our family has a few, uh…, people," she stopped and looked at her new friend's expression and slowly continued, "…that have had unusual gifts or abilities from time to time."

Jolie seemed to be transfixed, holding her breath, waiting.

"Okay, I think I've heard enough," said James.

That was why Jolie was digging through the same sort of information at the public library. He felt his heart sink.

"I don't really believe in all this hocus-pocus type stuff. I know that there's a God and a devil and all that stuff, I believe in the Bible, but this…, this is only somebody's imagination gone off its rocker."

"I know it's hard to accept or understand. I'm not trying to convert you to believe anything. You asked me if I could tell you what might be going on with you at your grandparents' house," said Jolie. "That's all I'm trying to do. Just…, help."

They sat in silence a few moments, looking past each other. Jolie held her breath, waiting for any hint that James was about to make up some excuse to leave and drop her off somewhere back in town. She knew she had moved along too quickly, but there was no other way. Until he understood what was going on, she wouldn't be able to help him.

"I didn't mean to make it sound like I thought you were a weirdo or something," said James finally. "I'm sorry. It's because I've had so many…."

"You've been having the dreams and visions too," said Jolie.

"And that!" fumed James. "You're constantly telling me what I'm thinking, or already know what I'm about to say."

He stopped his rant and sat forward a moment. He was about to throw some stones he couldn't pick back up, despite the fact that she was right.

"Yeah, I have been having the dreams," he answered. "I guess it wouldn't be a problem if you weren't always right, and you are."

He sat thinking for a few seconds.

"Who's the lucky person in your family with gifts now?" asked James.

A longer silence ensued.

"Me…," said Jolie. "And my Aunt BeBe too. I'm still hit or miss right now, but as I understand it, over time they become second nature."

James felt himself swallow a dry lump in his throat. It was now or never. Stay or leave. Could she really help him?

"So, what do these books have to do with it, or do they?" asked James.

"Someone got the bright idea that we could predict who would be endowed with abilities by tracking our family's history. Personally I think that's still debatable, but the older relatives swear by it," she half grinned, shaking her head as she thought back through that very morning's argument and why she was late getting to the library.

"Anyway, I've been handed the family journal to keep, and update all the records. It's kinda like passing on the torch, if you know what I mean. If you want to bolt and run, you can. I'll understand completely. Heaven knows you won't be the first."

She closed the book and looked at James steadily, waiting for his final decision. He had considered some excuse to leave, but something she didn't understand was holding him there.

"So, me finding you at…," started James.

"…at the library? No, it wasn't an accident. I was there waiting for you," said Jolie. "I had the same dream for three nights with you in it and knew that I had to meet you."

"So, I'm what…, some experiment or a good deed you have to perform… or…," James said. "Am I going to be another entry in your family's journal?"

"No, well maybe," said Jolie. "We just…, know things…, we don't have to do anything or get involved…, it's just that…,"

Jolie reached over, pecked a kiss on James' cheek, and sat back. Her face flushed red with sudden heat. She didn't know what made herself react so unexpectedly, but mostly she feared he would think it was only an impulse. It was…, a strong impulse; one she gave into as soon as she accepted the real reason he didn't leave her standing there alone.

"I like you and I only want to help," said Jolie. "Isn't that enough?"

James sat staring off into the moss-burdened trees for a few minutes thinking about everything that was said. He stood and walked a few steps down the narrow path from where they were seated wanting something to make sense. His mind told him that this was way too weird, but his heart, well…, it was singing a different song.

She only wanted to help and he had to admit he was about out of options. How many more nights like last night could he survive? What if he had actually choked last night?

James gathered his courage and finally sat back down beside Jolie. He looked in her eyes, remembering what brought him back to her in the first place.

"So, you read minds, and dream stuff," said James. "What else?"

"Let's leave it at that for now if that's okay with you," said Jolie. "I'm new at this too. My gift is only that, a gift, I have no idea how deep or wide yet, so to speak…."

Another silence ensued.

"Am I going to go nuts?" asked James. "I mean because of all the weird crap that's been happening to me. I know what'll be said if I go see a shrink. They'll put me under observation, or medication, or worse."

"No, you aren't going nuts…, there's a strong possibility that you have some gifts too," said Jolie. "You see, we never tell anyone about our family's gifts or abilities unless they have some type of gift themselves. Otherwise, we work completely neutral…, as anonymous as possible."

"Then you really messed up this time," said James. "I'm no mind reader. Trust me…, if I was a mind reader…."

Jolie smiled, but turned the conversation back quickly.

"Has anyone ever discussed anything like this with you from your family? Your mother or father? About you hearing and seeing into the spirit world?"

"No, of course not…," James trailed off…, trying to remember something faint from his childhood. Almost a dreamlike memory forced itself to the surface.

"You do remember something don't you? Something that you can't quite put your finger on?" encouraged Jolie.

"Yeah," said James. "My mom…, but I don't remember it exactly. A conversation, when I was about five, between mom and her aunt a few weeks before my younger brother Sam was born. My mom was telling her something like…, '*It can skip them. We moved away from all that….*' I never knew what mom was talking about. What am I saying? I still don't."

"That might explain why I had the dream about you," Jolie said, wrinkling her brow.

"This is too much for me," said James. "I mean, I like you and everything, so don't get me wrong, but I don't know if I understand all this or even want to. I only want the crappy dreams to go away and especially that god-awful ticking bug thing. And if the ticking means something bad, I have to find a way make it go. What does it say happened in that book, what did they do?" asked James.

Jolie carefully opened the book back to where she was reading from and sighed.

"They had to clean the house to make it go away," said Jolie. "But before they did, the oldest family member died."

James thought of his grandparents and panicked. He couldn't bear the thought of something bad happening to either of them. Maybe he should get away from the house and see if this 'death-ticker' or whatever it was, would leave with him until he could find a way to get rid of it. But even that would break his grandparent's heart if he left right now.

"What do you mean, clean the house? I'm not slow or stupid but I know you don't mean mop and sweep. Can you, or do you know how to 'clean' a house?" asked James.

"Yes, but I'm not the one that has to do it. You are..., or someone else in your family that is prone to the gifts," said Jolie.

His mind pictured a vivid enactment of his grampa scowling at his gramma over their next door neighbor..., calling Elberta Straw a witch.

"I don't think anyone in my family would be as open minded as I am on the subject. The only reason I am is because I'm the one with the creepy shit driving me crazy. If there is anybody with more than the gift of gab in my family, I don't know about it."

"I can help with that...," she said. "But it may have consequences. Let me explain. I can tell who has abilities most of the time, but I might reveal my own to them, which could be bad."

"My grampa said I..., uh, well I uh, I was going to ask you to come to Sunday dinner tomorrow at my grandparents'. That might be a start," said James.

"What time?" asked Jolie.

"Huh?"

"What time do you want me there?" she asked. A thin smile slid across her lips. "Didn't you ask me to come for dinner?"

"I can come pick you up around noon," he said.

"What time do you want me there?" asked Jolie, placing her hand on his.

"About one or one-thirty is pretty close, about an hour after church is over," said James taking her hand in his.

"I'll have one of my family drop me off, if you can bring me back home," said Jolie.

"Do I need to give you directions or do you already know that too?" asked James.

Chapter 12

Saturday, precisely two-ten that afternoon, an Adams County vehicle parked silently on the edge of Hwy 555. A few miles ahead was a southbound intersection, leading to the railroad tracks east of Natchez.

Deputy Floyd received a call concerning a certain maroon Mustang that had left downtown Natchez several minutes earlier. The overheated engine in his patrol car was making a tinkling sound as he waited in anticipation.

Sheriff Howard had been tightlipped when the deputy casually asked about the teenager his boss had such an interest in. That was immediately after the sheriff had all but interrogated him over his presence at Heaven's Gate Cemetery.

One way or another, he would find out who this smart-mouthed boy was…, and get some measure of revenge while he was at it.

James Earl was on the rollercoaster ride of his life and he knew it. There was never a time in his life growing up that was anything close. Sure, there were the beatings he took as a little kid from the neighborhood gangland trash, later there were the beatings he delivered as the neighborhood bad ass. Memories flooded his mind about where his life had been going; the neighborhood parents' complaints, counselors, including several police calls and arrests.

Arguments with his parents pursued him every step of the way.

Finally, he was free from all that and his life had begun to level off. He was gathering a new perspective since his annual commute to his birthplace in Natchez, Mississippi.

But this? Everything was turning upside down and right side up at the same time.

How could he be so lucky to have met anyone like Jolie?

She was sharp, sweet, pretty, soft, everything a guy could want; then there was the hell of only getting a couple of hours sleep each night, the dreams, all of it.

Up. Down. Up. Down.

His heart began to pound in his chest and his breathing became short and erratic. He had to quiet his mind. After a few slow breaths he began to relax. He was way too young for a heart attack.

A juniper tree on the right side of the road in the distance seemed to be luring his eyes toward it. He glanced in short bursts in its direction.

A face. Not angry this time, but following his eyes. He swerved to keep the car centered in his lane and slowed down.

The face looked familiar somehow.

"Okay, Jolie. If you're right, this isn't necessarily bad."

At that thought, the face peacefully dissipated.

James recovered enough to start looking for the southbound turn onto Wilson Rd. leading to his grandparents, when he saw flashing red and blue lights roaring up from behind him. He quickly looked at the speedo…, 58 MPH, in a 55 MPH zone?

He slowed down, thinking the law was headed toward an emergency farther down the road. It wasn't. It wanted him.

The Adams County vehicle pulled right up on his bumper, close enough to tap if James applied the brakes too quickly.

The Officer behind him removed all doubt with a gravelly blast from a loudspeaker.

"Please pull over to the shoulder and stop your vehicle."

James panicked, realizing it could be an emergency with his grandparents and this was the only way they could find him.

James stopped. Turned off the motor. Rolled down the window and waited.

The officer got out, came ambling up to the drivers' side, and peered inside at James through black tinted shades.

"Can I see your license and registration sir?" quoted the officer.

"Deputy? Is that you?" asked James. "What's the problem?"

"I need to see your license and registration please…."

"What's this about?"

But James was thinking…, "Just what I need."

Handing him his license, James asked, "Is this about my grandparents, are they all right?"

"Please remain seated in your vehicle, I'll be back in a moment," ordered the deputy as he stalked back to his vehicle.

"What the heck?" thought James.

A few minutes later, the deputy returned with his efficient clipboard and pen.

"Mr. Williams, the reason I stopped you was for speeding, I clocked you at 65 mph in a 55 mph zone," said the deputy.

"There's no way," said James. "You know that's not right."

"Tell it to the Judge," smarted the deputy.

"I will," said James. "Don't you have anything better to do than follow me around?"

Deputy Floyd shot a few hidden daggers from behind his sunshades, but didn't reply.

"Please sign here; this is not an admission of guilt, merely a consent to appear in court…"

Blah, blah, blah... his voice trailed off in James' mind.

The deputy got back in his car and blasted off around James onto the highway turning back toward town.

James threw a few choice words at the "To Protect and To Serve" emblem on the door of the vehicle while he sat there in silence.

Feeling angry and beaten, James drove around for some time before aiming his car toward his grandparents'. It wasn't his first traffic ticket, but it was the first one he didn't deserve.

The only consolation to all his confusion was his newfound friendship with Jolie. James remembered the face in the tree...; he knew it wasn't only coincidence. What if he hadn't slowed down? What would the great lawman have charged him with if he *had* been speeding? Why did the deputy lie about how fast he was driving?

The more James thought about what was happening, the more questions arose in his mind. James crossed the railroad tracks and pulled into Earl's Garage. He parked by the gas pump and looking for a diversion, decided to put gas in his car. He opened up the station with his keys and turned on the breaker to the pumps. The smell of gasoline drifted in the air as his mind filled with the days events.

Things weren't getting better, they were decidedly worsening. He made a note of the reading on the pump, added it to the daily record book and laid down some cash for the gas. After locking up *Earl's Garage*, James propped on his car, thinking.

His sleep deprived mind would no longer focus for the first time he could remember and his forced efforts were getting him nowhere.

It was time to drive on home. Home. His grandparents' home. Where was his home? He was about to turn down their familiar road into the neighborhood, but something was pulling him on..., further down the road. He switched off his turn signal and kept going straight another couple of blocks.

Several left and right turns carried him through more familiar neighborhoods. He passed the Holiness Cathedral Church and began thinking about what happened at the cemetery that morning. What about that back wall? The broken limbs that wandered out into the abyss of brush, thorny vines, and poison ivy.

Where did that trail go? James whipped his car at the next road and turned by the front of the cemetery. As he slowed to a stop, James realized how many hours he'd killed already. It was starting to get late and was almost dusk.

In the back of the cemetery, where the wall lay broken, it would be almost dark by now from the thick cover of trees. He drove farther down the narrow lane looking for a road he seemed to remember, one that led around back, outside the perimeter of the cemetery. He saw the caretaker's road a few feet from the front and knew that was a dead end, no one had been there in years, so he slowly crept along.

Just ahead there was another dirt lane he finally recognized from long rides on his bike when he was a kid. Back when life was simple and the sweat and dirt was something that could be washed off with the cold water from his grandparents' sun-crackled water hose.

Sure, he remembered. It wound itself around for miles and was used as a farm road. He had never followed it to the end that he could remember.

James slowly turned down the road and eyed the few mud puddles lined with crawdad monuments, freshly rebuilt after the foul weather. His car was made for smooth pavement and speed, not mudding. He decided to drive as far as he could and then walk a little farther before it turned dark. His efforts had taken him only a hundred yards down the twisty dirt trap road, when he saw that he couldn't afford to drop off into any one of the potholes. His grampa would say that some of them were deep enough to fish in.

James backed up into a clear sun dried spot and turned his car around, seesawing back and forth. As he was leaving, there was movement in his rear view mirror.

Back in the far distance, two barely distinguishable figures pushed their way out of the thicket and began walking the opposite direction from where he was. He twisted, watching, with his engine idling for a few moments until his neck was aching from the awkward position. It was an impossible task trying to see out of the nearly horizontal back window of his Mustang Fastback. The only thing distinguishable was a dingy white baseball cap one of the figures wore pressed to his head, then the overgrowth and encroaching darkness took its toll and James gave up.

Probably only two people walking. No one in their right mind would come back here right after vandalizing a grave.

"No one in their right mind would rob a grave," mumbled James.

He slowly pulled forward still avoiding the ruts and slowly rolled left onto the gravel lot in front of the cemetery. Soon his tires gripped the pavement of the real world, the one his car was designed for. It was time to find his way back home.

Even though James felt there was still something that wasn't exactly right he forced himself away. So much for his intuition or "gifts", as Jolie had called them

As he drove away, a familiar car, marked "To Protect and To Serve," silently sat observing his movements from its concealed location.

"James Earl Williams…"
"Yes."

"Seventeen year old male Caucasian, Black Hair, Green eyes, About 6 ft. 2 in. tall, medium build, 180 pounds...."

"New Jersey Drivers License ...4667... Uh, huh."

"Really..., that bad? Oh, I see."

"Thanks, you've been a great help."

Deputy Floyd hung up Sheriff Howard's personal extension and quietly walked out of his senior officer's private office, making sure that nothing was moved or ruffled.

This young parolee was going to be trouble.

James walked slowly into his grandparents' house. Everyone was sitting around the kitchen table drinking coffee and talking to someone. Gentle laughter arose above the conversation from time to time. Feeling the total sickening defeat of the day, James decided to ignore his hunger and ease silently to his room.

"James? James Earl? Is that you, Hun?" asked a familiar voice from the kitchen.

Busted. He felt that quick tightening of the gut he used to get when trying to sneak back in the house unnoticed.

He obediently spun on his heel, destination kitchen, not feeling much like visiting with anyone, not feeling much like existing.

As he walked in the kitchen, he noticed the familiar face of the person they were talking with. It was his Great Aunt Martiel, his mother's aunt and grampa's younger sister.

Now there were very few people on James' private list of lovable people, and Aunt Martiel was definitely on it. Near the top. She always seemed to treat him like an equal and understood what he was talking about. They had always hit it off.

She always made sweet iced tea, exactly the way he liked it. Come to think about it, she did most everything the same way he did.

Her frequent telephone calls to New Jersey kept his family apprised of the entire goings on of his grandparents and local events. Hers was never gossip, but a gentle and sometimes colorful reminder of how life in Mississippi was progressing.

"Hi, Aunt Martiel!"

"Oh, come here!" his aunt shrilled her thick Southern drawl.

After moments of hugs and small talk they all sat back down around the table. Without even recognizing it, her entrance had momentarily whisked away the dark cloud following James around.

Seemingly in record time the subject came up about Jolie – is she cute, is she this and that, and about her visiting the next day.

Eventually the grilling session and laughter ended and silence eventually fouled the air. With the quiet, James returned to his previous dank memories of the deputy.

"So, how was the rest of your day?" questioned gramma.

"Oh, that," said James. "Well it didn't turn out as great as the first half."

Reluctantly, James shared details about the drive home and his encounter with the sheriff's deputy. Grampa's face grew a little more tinted after each minute listening to the account of what happened.

Gramma was watching his expression and muttering, "Oh, my Lord", under her breath.

When James was through, Martin got up without a word, walked over to the phone and quickly dialed a number. After a few seconds…, the room was suddenly still and quiet.

"Sheriff Howard, this is Martin…, Martin Ames."

"How are you?"

"…yes. Fine, thanks."

"The reason I'm calling is because of your deputy and his attitude problem."

"Well, I'm *NOT* so sure about his motives…," he raised his voice.

"Excited? You haven't heard *or* seen excited yet.…"

The first few minutes on the phone with the sheriff were tense.

"I didn't know grampa knew the sheriff personally," James said quietly. In all the years he had visited, Martin Earl's conversations with the sheriff were little more than random events.

"He knew Sheriff Howard's older brother," answered his grandmother. "They were the best of friends before he got killed in an accident."

Martin had obviously calmed down, but was still not too happy about the circumstances as he hung up the phone.

"The sheriff promised me he'll look into what the deputy is up to," said grampa. "After the way he treated you out at the cemetery the other day, I would have thought he'd try harder to improve his attitude."

Aunt Martiel chimed in, "There's more?"

"It's a long story," said James. "I'm not sure it's even worth the telling."

"Sheriff Howard says that the deputy is his model officer, compared to the last couple of recruits that were in his command," grampa said mockingly. "You're absolutely sure you weren't speeding James?"

"Yes, Sir. Positive. Ten miles back was a different story. I was probably going six or eight miles over the limit, maybe more at times. But when I…, I uh…," his voice trailed off. "When I was three or four miles from our turn-off, I thought I saw something on the side of the road and slowed down to the limit. It was right before the turn that he stopped me."

The whole conversation was about to erupt all over again and all James wanted to do was go find a place to hide.

"I'm tired of the whole thing," said James.

"Yep, let's have a change the subject. That'll work itself out and be old news in a day or two," said Maime.

"Martiel, how long are you going to be in town?" she continued.

"Well since I'm still guardian of the family trust and the family plots over at Heaven's Gate Cemetery, it's my duty to stay and make sure that they get the grave closed back up. The health department has to get involved and you know how slow bureaucracy is to get off their collective rear ends. So..., I have to stay until the whole thing is paid for and settled.

"What has me puzzled is why someone would do such a thing in the first place?" said Martiel in her sing-song voice. "What would some hooligans want with a bunch of dead man's bones?"

Martin nodded at his little sister. Evidently she sensed the same dreariness over the situation that he had.

"Why don't you please stay over here with us?" he asked. "We have plenty of room and we need a canasta partner for next Thursday's social at the church."

"I might stay one night or two, but you know I need to spend some time over at the old home place and see if it's in any disrepair," said Martiel.

"Well which is more important?" asked Martin.

"I wouldn't miss a good night of canasta!" she laughed. "I still don't understand why you two don't pick up and move over there and live in the old estate," she continued. "It has all new furnishings downstairs, better plumbing, its way bigger...."

"We like it just fine here," said both the Ames at the same time.

They all laughed at the union of their speech.

"I'm close to my garage," said Martin.

"...and I'm close to the church," said Maime.

"It's easier here. I can't imagine having to move all this junk, especially at my age," said Martin.

"You know how ridiculous that sounds don't you? It wouldn't cost a drop in a bucket to move you, without either of you having to lift a finger," said Martiel. "You know there's more than enough money in the family estate to take care of you both.

"In fact, you don't have to mess with that old garage, Martin. If y'all don't like it over there at the home place, you could move on into Biloxi near me, ...with me!" Martiel continued on. "I guess I could look into selling the old place...," she muttered quietly, then shivered at some unknown recollection.

"Now Martiel..., Martiel..., we've had this conversation more times than I can remember," said Martin. "We like our life here. It's a simple one, but I like giving back to the community and serving the community. We like giving to the church and all the good people there. They don't know who gives them the secret help and it keeps the spirit of miracles alive in the hearts of God's people."

"Have I ever told you two that I love you?" Martiel said with watery eyes.

"We know, and you've been good to us too," said Maime.

Martiel fanned the air, waving away a sudden rising of emotions, "Enough of this sentimentality. James Earl, why don't you come and spend a night or two with me over at the old home place, so I won't have to be alone over there while I'm in town?" James looked back and forth unsure of what to say.

"Now don't you go taking James Earl away from me," said Maime. "I finally talked him into staying with us while he goes to school this fall over at the college."

"Your momma and daddy must be really proud of you," said Martiel. "What's that ornery brother Sam doing these days? Why isn't he down here with you this summer?"

James redundantly explained things back home in New Jersey, how their life still rotated around their dad's job. Sam at summer camp. Their recent move. He found a stopping point when his stomach growled like an animal.

"I'm about ready for a snack," said James.

Chapter 13

Voices…, soft voices all talking at once. Comforting yet direct…, telling him….

Telling him what? It was right on the tip of his mind, but he couldn't quite make it out as the multitude of words slid off into the distance….

James was walking over a small rise in a meadow. There was a gentle breeze blowing across his face and hair. Walking over the crest of the meadow, he saw a wide river down below the placid sloping banks, the Mississippi River no doubt. There was hustle and bustle far away along the banks.

A large majestic white boat with…, a huge round paddlewheel at the rear, was docked on the shoreline. A riverboat. He looked down at the ground to watch his step as he descended a worn footpath and noticed his feet. Button-eye clasp, boot looking things, and white of all colors. As a matter of fact, he was dressed in white. As he looked down, he noticed…, he also has a beard! No, a long goatee and he ran his fingers through its salt and pepper gray, feeling the tug against his chin.

He laughed at how comical he looked. Like a masquerade.

Suddenly he noticed that there was a lady walking at his side. Beautiful by any standards. James remembered seeing pictures of a Southern Bell from school. A lovely face. Long flowing black hair. High cheek bones. Dark brown eyes. Her dress could pass for a wedding gown, low cut in front exposing lots of cleavage.

He felt himself blush as he saw the rise and fall of her breathing and laughed at how he could blush in a dream.

This is a dream. This IS… a dream. She twirled her parasol, and laughed beautifully at some unknown comment that he made.

Her voice was melodious in tone and he found that he was drawn to her deeply.

Suddenly the dream changed as they walked arm in arm across a boardwalk onto the front of the riverboat. He guessed that it was the same one he'd seen in the distance.

Someone bleated, "Welcome to the Goldenrod," while another mentioned Fort…, something….

They introduced themselves, some jumbled names, indiscernible to his dream addled mind. Friendly people, obviously with money, littered every available space of the decks. There was dining, dancing, drinking and laughing. A live group of minstrel type entertainers wandered from one end to the other in the dining hall, playing unfamiliar tunes he found himself humming to.

The scene changed again and now he was comfortably seated at a table with five other gentlemen in costumes similar to his, one in particular smoking an enormous cigar.

Soon there was a heap of money and personal items in the middle of the table. He was holding a hand full of cards and very nervous. There was a show of cards and he won.

He knew he would win. He couldn't believe it. Somehow, he couldn't lose.

He's shaking, he's so nervous. One of the gentlemen, a large contributor to his fresh heap of earnings, was visibly angry.

"One more hand…," he demanded. The others pushed away from the table only observing and a crowd of people began milling around the table, looking on.

Soon there were a lot of legal looking papers stacked on the table…, and more money – it looked like play money – except for the gold coins, more than he had ever seen.

They lay down cards. He WINS!

"Drinks all around!!" he yelled, causing an uproar of cheers.

The other man jumped up and screamed obscenities as he bang-stepped to the bar. James Earl or whoever this dream person was…, scanned his winnings, unbelievable, the money, titles and deeds.

"Never count your money at the table," comes to his mind from somewhere…, right before a woman screams…, blood curdling…, shrill.

The other gentleman was staggering drunk…, swinging his arms through the crowded room, knocking everyone from his path.

Outside and over to the rail, he hurled himself overboard…, over the side of the riverboat…, into the dark eddy currents of the Mississippi.

James watched on as this dream man frantically collected his earnings into a leather bag…, there was screaming and yelling as the lights slowly went dark on the boat.

Then he was suddenly floating…, and it became darker…, this seemed so familiar…, a cooing voice drawing him, pulling him. That spinning nauseous feeling…, a soft something tied to his insides, pulling him…, a soft beating sound…. In the distance, yellow flickering lights appeared…, darkness still all around…, he was swimming in it…, getting closer to the lights.

There were candles in a large circle…, something white and wiggling…, no. Not wiggling…, writhing. A white dress. It was a black woman with a white wrap or a white dress of some kind, writhing on the bare dirt ground in a circle of candles. The blackest black woman he has ever seen. She shines and has a distinct beauty about her face that lulls him closer.

She begins calling him…, it's some language he doesn't know, but her calling is urging him on. Every time she repeats that sing-songy name, he gets a steady pull on his insides…, pulling him to her, to the center of the circle.

Sticks are tapping that incessant beat, sticks clicking together.

Click… click… tick.tick.tick.

Click. Click. Tick.tick.tick.

The rhythm. The pain feels like his body is trying to turn inside out.

AWAKE! OH thank God….

Lying on his back, heaving in breaths, his heart was racing.

Click. Click…. Clik.Clik.Clik.

The bed shook and there was a moment of relief. Tommy must have awakened him again.

James looked up into the dimness of his room.

A shadowed figure was looming over his headboard looking down on him from behind.

Wait.

Behind? There's a wall behind his headboard.

Click. Click. A clawed hand was tapping the wooden ball on the headboard of his bed. The face on the figure was grinning a huge toothy smirk….

That's all the incentive he needed.

James Earl Williams, all 180 pounds of him, was instantly wide awake and standing in the middle of his bed, springing for the door.

The coil springs in his bed groaned and screeched as he jumped to the floor with a thud. He opened the door and was met with a bright hall light and the figure of his Aunt Martiel swiftly walking toward him.

His aunt followed him to the bathroom down the hallway.

"I heard you talking in your sleep and then give off that awful sounding groan. It woke me up and I had to see if you were okay," said Aunt Martiel.

"It…, It was only a bad dream…," croaked James, shutting the bathroom door behind him.

"Must have been a doozie," said his aunt, through the door. "Wanna tell me about it?"

"Not really, I want to forget it, but I'm taking the couch for the rest of the night."

There was the sound of running water from the sink as he splashed his face.

"What's that ticking sound I hear in there?" Aunt Martiel asked, looking toward his room.

"Wait, don't go in there," said James, snatching the bathroom door open. "I mean, I have clothes on the floor, you might trip."

Martiel stood waiting patiently.

"You have a light don't you? I've seen clothes on the floor before, and I'm sure I can step over them."

James stared for a moment, at a loss as to how he could stop her from joining in on his terror.

"What's wrong with you, James?" she asked, looking back into the darkness of the hallway.

Chapter 14

Breakfast scents of coffee, buttermilk pancakes, bacon, and quiet murmuring, was flowing from the kitchen.

"Morning already," thought James.

"Why didn't you tell me about this before now?" asked Martiel in low hushed tones.

"I didn't think it was anything to worry about," said Maime. "James didn't let on to us that there was anything scaring him."

"You know our family history.... I'm worried about you and Martin now," sighed Martiel.

They each took a sip of coffee.

Martin walked into the kitchen, fresh shaven and anxious for the day.

"Good Morning Martin Earl, sleep well?" asked Martiel.

"Yeah, but it was really stuffy last night, hard to breathe," he said. "I should have switched on the air conditioner."

The two women exchanged glances.

"I miss something?" asked Martin. "This happens every time you visit, Martiel."

His wife Maime got up from her seat at the table and decided to wake up James for Sunday breakfast.

Martiel took the opportunity to exchange a few hushed words with her brother after she left the kitchen.

"That boy don't look so good," said Maime walking back into the kitchen. "A good hot breakfast ought to fix him right up."

Breakfast was mostly silent with persistent glances toward James as he picked lightly at his food. Almost on cue, everyone stirred from the table to begin the ritual of getting ready for Sunday church service.

After about twenty minutes of useless effort, James knocked on the grandparents' bedroom door.

"Gramma?" called James.

A muffled, "Yes, Hun," came through the closed door.

"I don't think I feel much like church today. Would you be offended if I stay here and rest?"

The door cracked open slightly.

"Are you going to be all right son?" asked Martin.

"I didn't sleep very well last night and I'm kinda frazzled," said James.

"Well you're gonna have to watch the roast I put in the oven while we're gone," said his gramma from somewhere in their room.

"By the way. You have company coming over today, remember?" she continued.

James had completely forgotten Jolie. What a night. Anything that could make him forget her for an instant had to be bad.

"I'll keep an eye on *anything* you leave cooking," said James jokingly.

"It better still be here when we get home too," said Martin.

The family left for the Sunday meeting and James ran into his room, grabbing his journal as quickly as he could, looking around nervously. He walked out onto the front porch in the fresh air and plopped onto the swing to think.

The moist morning air filled his lungs and seemed to clear his head as he listened to the birds singing close by. The sun beaming up from it's hiding place on the left end of the porch.

The rest of the world seemed to be going on fine and dandy everywhere around him.

Why was he was in hell?

His mind swam over the last few days events. He didn't know where to begin his Journal, it was too much.

Journal – Sunday, June 19, '77

There have been so many things. I'm going crazy. I can't tell anybody. Dreams are eating me alive. Even the ones that aren't bad don't make sense.

Now I know what the ticking sound is and it's not a little bug or the Easter Bunny. The faces aren't so bad any more compared to last night's visitor. Whatever the hell that thing is.

Well, at least I know what's doing the ticking. Oh God, what do I do? I'm not going back in that room again, not by myself.

But what do I tell them? How can I explain? They'll put me away, I know they will. It seemed so real, …but what if it wasn't? What if all of this is only in my head? It can't be. I know it's not, I can feel it inside me. I have to find a way to get this thing out of their home.

Aunt Martiel asked me to spend a night or two at the family's old home place while she's in town. That will be a first.

I don't ever remember spending more than a few minutes there at any one time. I hope she asks me over tonight, she has to. What am I saying? What if this thing follows me and goes there? Then I'm responsible for bringing danger to her. What if it doesn't and stays here? I don't know the right thing to do.

And now that deputy has his underwear tied in a knot about me. Something about him definitely isn't right.

I'm so confused. God help me.

The roast!
James fell from the porch swing and ran inside.

Church was as usual again. The music from the swaying choir was exciting and anointed, after which a young couple came and dedicated their lives to the Lord.

In his usual banter, the pastor drummed on with some slow flowery sermon that nearly put everyone to sleep, to the dismay of several of the regulars.

Dismissal prayer was finally spoken and everyone began to make their way to the door.

"Mrs. Ames?"

"Mrs. AMES! Glory be!" said Granny Smith.

"Morning, Ms. Smith," said Maime Ames. "How are you?"

Maime hugged the aged wonder and sat down next to her.

"I be just fine," said Granny Smith with her usual glowing smile.

She seemed more excited than usual, looking around where Maime Ames was seated.

"Where is that James Earl this morning? He ain't gone back up north already has he?" asked Ms. Smith.

"Oh. No, of course not. He's decided to stay with us for a while and go to school here in Natchez," said Maime Ames proudly.

"Is my James Earl here? Can I talk with him for a spell?" asked Ms. Smith, looking around again in earnest.

"He stayed home this morning. He didn't rest well last night and..., well, he's had an awful lot of things happening to him lately," said Mrs. Ames.

"Just as I spected, as I spected," said Granny Smith. "I had myself a talk with James Earl last Sunday. I know a little 'bout what's botherin' him. It's almost like a curse or sump'n evil trailin' him. I've been laying down some serious prayer for that boy all week. It's an attack of the devil, I tell you. And there be a two-legged one after him too," she finished, her dry voice trailing off to a whisper, as if someone there might hear her secret.

"When you see that James Earl, you tell him Granny Smith need to talk to him, soon as he can," she stressed.

Mrs. Ames sat there staring at Granny Smith for a few uncomfortable moments.

"What you're saying is true, Ms. Smith," she began. "James has been having an awful time since he came to visit this time. I don't really know how to help him."

"Prayer, Mrs. Ames. Prayer, that's the answer," she said quietly. "You remember to tell that young man that I needs to talk to him, will you?" Granny Smith pleaded.

"Can you tell me?" asked Mrs. Ames.

"Noooo..., least not here," she whispered. "There be too many ears that knows too many people. You make sure an' tell him to stay as far from the law officers...."

"Well, Hello Mrs. Ames!" said a young woman, interrupting their conversation.

Mrs. Ames turned around to see a bright-eyed young blond woman and wondered how long she'd been hovering near her private conversation.

"Sallee Mae, is that you? How in the world are you? Why I haven't talked to you since your wedding, right here in this church!"

"I gots to be goin'," said Granny Smith, a little begrudgingly. "You take care now, ya hear? Remember what all I said."

"G'bye, Granny, we love you, and thank you for your prayers," said Mrs. Ames.

Granny stood and started shuffling off with her walker toward a small group at the church doors.

Turning back around, Mrs. Ames picked back up her new conversation.

"Where are you living now, Sallee Mae?"

Maime Ames had tidied up the house and was putting the finishing touches to her Sunday meal, when she saw a strange car drive up.

"James?"

"Got it gramma," said James, eagerly bolting toward the front door.

A light blue Chevy Caprice pulled into the driveway and stopped. James walked out onto the front porch and stood for a few moments after recognizing Jolie's face through the windshield. He stepped off the front porch and walked slowly toward the car, as Jolie got out of the passenger side and walked around to meet him. James noticed that it was her Aunt BeBe driving.

"You take real good care of my baby girl," said BeBe out the window.

"I will, I promise," said James. "Why don't you come inside and meet my family while you're here?"

"I will next time," said BeBe. "I have to go take inventory of my stock so that I can open early tomorrow. You can bring Jolie by the restaurant tonight when ya'll are through with your visiting."

"Yes Ma'am," said James.

With that settled, BeBe got their phone number, backed out of the driveway and left.

James thought she was a little over protective but Jolie was her niece and she was responsible for her.

As they started back to the porch, Jolie took James' hand and reached up to give him a quick peck of a kiss on the cheek.

"Didn't think I could get away with that if I waited until we got inside," said Jolie.

"I missed you too," said James with a dumb grin on his face.

"It's not quite one o'clock, am I too early?" she asked.

"Not at all. I've been here all morning, while they went to church. I didn't exactly have a great night to tell you the truth."

"More dreams?" asked Jolie.

"Way more than just dreams," said James.

"Ya'll coming in the house or staying out on the porch all afternoon?" piped someone from inside the house.

Just inside the screen door stood both his gramma and Aunt Martiel taking turns getting their first looks at Jolie.

James and Jolie walked inside and James attempted introductions.

"Everybody, this is Jolie," said James. "This is my Gramma Ames..., this is my Great Aunt Martiel, and over there on the couch is my Grampa Ames."

Martin stood and hurried over, extending his hand.

Gramma spoke up, "Well Jolie, James has had nothing but good things to say about you. Somewhere along the way, he failed to mention how pretty you are."

Aunt Martiel chimed in, "I agree, you are a little doll."

Jolie was obviously teased, but not shy. She casually looked around at each of James' relatives and sensed nothing out of sorts. Was it possible that she had completely misread all the years of compiled information in her family's journals, or was one of them hiding something? It didn't matter. She instantly fell in love with each of them.

"I can see I'm going to get along with your family just fine," said Jolie laughing.

"Ya'll wash up, dinners on the table and almost ready," said Gramma Ames.

"Oh my, this looks good," said Jolie stepping into the kitchen.

The table was lined with pot roast, mashed potatoes, home made brown gravy, corn on the cob and a feast of other selections.

"You want iced tea, lemonade, or Coca-Cola, water...," Maime said, voice trailing off softly.

"Is the tea sweet?" asked Jolie.

"Is there any other way to drink tea?" asked Aunt Martiel.

"Iced tea," said Jolie.

They sat down and for the next few minutes Gramma Ames fussed about with the last of the food placement. Finally, she sat down as well and they said grace over the meal, Grampa Ames presiding. Small talk kept them busy for almost an hour during dinner.

"James says that your aunt owns a restaurant downtown," said Maime. "Is it the one near the town square beside that line of shops?"

"Yes, Ma'am, The Cajun. It belongs to my Aunt BeBe, but she has a lot of help from cousins and other family," said Jolie.

"We've eaten there lots of times," Maime said, nodding over at Martin. "The food is really good there. Small world."

"Oh my Lord, can we talk about something besides food," said Martin Earl. "I've eaten enough for all of us and I'm going to have to get away from this table or pop."

"Wonderful as always," he muttered and reached over to give his wife a peck on the cheek.

He picked up his plate and raked what little was left into a scrap pan set aside for the chickens.

"How did you do that?" asked Jolie in a low voice.

Both women stared at each other with questioned faces.

"What?" asked Aunt Martiel.

"Train a man to clean up after himself," grinned Jolie.

"I can't claim any part of that, this one came housebroken when I got him years ago," said Maime. "I guess that's one of the reasons I kept him."

Laughter finished up the afternoon meal.

"Your family is really sweet," said Jolie.

"Thanks…, my grandparents have always been good to me," said James.

They strolled out onto the tall front porch overlooking the lawn. It was still a young afternoon but a cool breeze was lifting the early summer weight.

"Would you like to sit out here for awhile?" asked James.

There was a supernatural energy stronger than the lack of sleep keeping James awake as they sat and exchanged family stories and childhood memories.

He learned that Jolie's parents were divorced when she was ten. No brothers or sisters, but plenty of cousins to run with. Her father had moved to the east coast a year after the divorce, and mysteriously offered no more concerning him. Her mother lived somewhere in California, near the southern coast. Joint custody allowed her to know both of them, but she was tired of bouncing from coast to coast. Both had eventually become reattached to new partners she didn't care for and as a result Jolie didn't want to live with either of them. When she turned seventeen, she moved to Vidalia with her Aunt BeBe.

It seemed obvious that she was holding back more than she was telling, but James didn't pry. And it explained a few things. Such as, why she never answered some of his questions about family or didn't want him to see her home. He only assumed that she was an overtly private person, which wasn't the case at all.

She was content to go wherever her extended family did and worked with her Aunt BeBe. Still unsure about college, either parent could afford to send her, so money wasn't the issue. Her roots were here, she decided to hang out with her family in Vidalia until she knew more about what she wanted to do.

They were both living away from parents, with other family, far from their normal surroundings.

Maime brought out iced tea to them at one point and spoke fondly over her small patches of flowers in the front yard.

James shared information about his life since leaving Mississippi as a child. The different schools he went to, delicately touched on the trouble he fell into and out of. About his brother Sam, and tormenting each other as well as depending on each other and what close friends they had become.

A little about his parents surfaced, and their strained relationship, but his part had devolved into a distant friendship instead of a family bond. He was closer to his mother, because she was in his life more than his father. Not that his father was abusive, quite the contrary, he was almost absent - never time for baseball, fishing trips, or anything personal always working, consumed by career. Without detailed explanations, it was obvious he was more of a parent figure to his brother Sam.

He began to ramble lazily on with whatever came to mind. Jolie seemed more like family he was getting reacquainted with, instead of a new friend.

Hours passed pleasantly in conversation.

Nothing about the stress of problems and decisions facing James surfaced. All was sanity and peaceful. James enjoyed looking deep into Jolie's eyes as they talked, memorizing the expressions on her face. Very little escaped his inspection, her soft skin and the thick locks of wavy black hair. It was the first chance that either of them had to really get to know each other.

Family traffic began to pick up as Martin Earl revived from his nap and began tinkering with the lawnmower out on the lawn. Minutes later he pushed it past where they were seated toward the tool shed, grumbling about rainwater in the gas tank.

Maime made another appearance and asked if they wanted to join in on a game of canasta. They both agreed that their seats were getting sore from the hard porch swing and came inside.

Everyone busied around the cleared kitchen table and lightly chatted as they scrambled four decks of playing cards and dispersed fifteen cards for each.

"We play to get 2 red canastas and 2 black canastas," said Maime. "We don't play by most peoples rules, but you'll catch on. You two can be partners."

The conversation was light and cheery and after three or four rounds it was clear that Maime and Martiel had played the game once or twice before.

After another thirty minute session, the center stack of throwaways began to form a heap and had collected most of the wild cards, so all four were tensely watching every card they gave up.

The seating rotation had placed Jolie before Aunt Martiel and Jolie was out of wild cards to block with. Hand after hand, Jolie seemed to know exactly which card not to give up, so as not to give away the coveted stack to their opponents. James was somehow able to do the same thing, but wasn't as relaxed as Jolie about the situation. Finally the stack was becoming obscenely large when Maime dropped the ball and gave the game winning cache of cards to Jolie. They easily completed their sets and in a couple of hands went out.

Jolie smiled over at James and winked. He missed her intended inference and her secondary purpose for visiting his family.

James asked, "You losers want another try?"

Chides of good-natured ill-will ran around the table, as the hoard of cards were shuffled and reassembled for the play.

Another half-hour into play and a similar situation started building.

James was grinning profusely at the way the game was stacking up, incessantly taunting their opponents.

Suddenly Aunt Martiel had an epiphany; an expression of slack coolness came over her face. She reached and placed a hand atop the nearest of Jolie's, patting it softly.

"I see that we have a lot in common, you and I," smiling coyly.

Jolie had her answer and tried to hide her grin, "Why, whatever do you mean? You know, this game is a little like life.... It's only a matter of who leads and who follows."

"Well spoken," said Aunt Martiel, squeezing her hand sweetly.

James and his gramma looked questioningly at each other and then back at their cards.

"Whose turn is it?" asked James.

The hand finally went to Maime and Martiel and they all decided to call a truce, when someone knocked at the door.

Elberta Straw was peering in through the single glass pane of the front door, impatiently waiting for someone to let her inside.

"Oh Lord, do you have to let her in?" whined Aunt Martiel. "She's a fruitcake."

"Sssshhh, she might hear and put a curse on us," Maime said with a grin.

Jolie looked over at James with a big questioned expression on her face. James quickly explained that Elberta Straw was the next-door neighbor and was somewhat of an aged know-it-all and gossip. She also considered herself versed in the "arts" of precognition.

"She's been giving my gramma advice for years and most recently about the noises in the house. And she's driving my grampa nuts in the process," he said rolling his eyes.

"Hello Mrs. Ames, how *are* you today?" began Elberta. "I see that James Earl is home."

"Why..., yes, he is...," Maime Ames said.

"Good, good.... Sometime this evening, I'd like to have a word with him. I think I may be able to help with his sleeping disorder that we discussed."

"Well, he's...," Maime injected, trying to diffuse the situation.

"Hello Martiel!" exclaimed Elberta, interrupting Maime. "I didn't know you were here, how have you been? Here for a visit? Shame about that graveyard business. And it was one of your own relatives t'boot. What a crazy world this is turning out to be. Are you staying at your family's old mansion? I don't see how you can stay out there in that big old monstrosity by yourself."

One efficient breath of air fed the flood of interrogation. Gossip central was trying to gather enough information to keep her going for the next month or two.

Whatever Aunt Martiel didn't say was construed as a secret and Elberta would fill in the blanks with supposed knowledge. It was one of those situations where you're "danged if you do, danged if you don't."

Even if Martiel told her the truth, by the time it was repeated by Elberta, all factual information was lost.

James took Jolie's hand and nudged her out into the quiet muggy night of the backyard. Fresh dew had already fallen and the grass crunched like lettuce under their feet.

"It's safer out here for the moment," James said in a low voice. "I know she's only an old woman with nothing else to do, but I can't stand her."

"Sometimes it's easier to let someone like her talk themselves out," said Jolie. "I'm sure she's lonely and wants attention."

"James? James Earl..., are you out there?"

Elberta's grainy voice rang out into the evening air. The indoor light forced her dark silhouette of shadow to rush across the yard, bringing with it a crash of dread and memory to James.

James reached over and whispered in Jolie's ear, "We didn't run fast enough."

"Be there in a minute, Elberta," said James reluctantly.

They both walked back inside the house, James ready to take his medicine.

"James Earl. Thank you for joining us," wheezed Elberta.

She had talked her vocal chords into trauma in the short time since she had arrived.

Gramma and Aunt Martiel stood in the background, shrugging their shoulders, as if to say, "We tried."

"I think I know a way to find out the source of that ticking," Elberta continued, wasting no time.

"Oh, nooo...," James was thinking.

"If you have a few minutes, I'd like for you to come on over to my house; you can bring your friend if you like, to take notes."

In the last 20 years or more, no one, at least no one from the Ames household had ever been inside the home of Elberta Straw.

Both of the Ames women were speechless and James was not pleased with this new turn of events.

Begrudgingly James Earl walked single file behind Elberta as she trudged across the street, through the weed-laden gate, and up to the door. Jolie was all but snickering at the look on James' face as Elberta fiddled with the screen door and opened the inner sanctum of her home.

Surprising to James, the house was clean as a pin and well kept. Her home was nothing like the yard and the surrounding growth that perfused the rest of the property.

There was a hand-sewn quilt folded and draped over her couch, other custom woven articles lined table tops and such. Each contained unusual and colorful patterns.

She also had a curio corner with an enormous crystal ball and other odd looking artifacts lining its shelves.

In her dining room, a bright multicolored cloth covered her table and a single candle sat waiting, ready for use.

"Let's get right to it, if you don't mind," said Elberta. "Please sit down. I'll go get what we'll need to root this out."

She returned mere moments later with a board covered in a cloth and a matching cloth pouch.

She revealed her treasure to be a OUIJA board and *eye*. Placing it on the table, she arranged the board and candle, then handed a pad of paper with pencil to Jolie.

The board looked relatively new, but the planchette was obviously a well used antique. The board had a Yes and No in opposite corners, the alphabet written in an arc across its face. The numbers 0-9. Sun and Moon, etc…, and some other symbols….

She sat down across from James and explained the rules.

"This board has been in my family for several generations," she explained. "It can help us. Now, this is a called a Ouija board. It's used to communicate with the spirit world. All we have to do is…."

James interrupted, "I don't see how this is going to help me stop the house from settling."

Trying to downplay the nosey old woman's reasoning was an exercise in futility.

"Just try to relax and keep an open mind. Place the tips of your fingers on the eye…, and don't press down hard. I'll put my fingers on this side and then we wait. Just let it move on its own. If you feel it start to move, move with it. Don't try to stop it or make it go yourself."

Elberta tapped a finger on the table near Jolie.

"Young lady, if you'll kindly note anything you think is important?"

Jolie nodded as Elberta lit the candle, but didn't seem too happy with her job.

"Now focus on the candle and its light and let me do the talking."

James looked over at Jolie and shrugged his shoulders, but did as he was asked. With candle lit and eyes focused, she started.

"Spirits. Spirits. We call you to us. Can you hear us?" Elberta chanted.

Jolie's expression changed and she looked at James to get his attention.

"James, we shouldn't…," Jolie tried to say something as a heavy cloud of oppression began to press into the room.

"Hush child, concentrate," corrected Elberta.

"But…," said Jolie, wide-eyed and looking around in the shadowed gloom.   She sensed that this thing was something the old woman had invited into her home on many occasions, something very *familiar.*

"Spirits…," Elberta was about to start again.

The eye began to jiggle and move. James looked up and tried to tell if the old woman was causing it to move.

It started off slowly and slid in circles smoothly. It felt as if it were pulling James fingers and arms with it. It slid over to "yes".

"Can you help us?"

Again, the eye moved in a circle and landed back on "yes".

Elberta was obviously pleased with herself.

"What is the source of the ticking in the Ames house?"

The eye swung erratically in circles and side to side coming to rest on "E" then "V" then "I" and "L".

Jolie hissed, "Evil."

"Can we rid the house of this evil?"

Again, the eye moved over the letters, "N" and "O", spelling it out instead of using the "No" on the board, as if in emphasis.

Frustrated, Elberta said, "But we must, is there no way."

The eye started jittering and circling, then stopping on the letters:
N, O, T, T, H, E, H, O, U, S, E - then it stopped dead still.

Jolie whispered, "Not the house."

"So it isn't the house that has the problem, is that right?"

Once again, the board answered, "Yes."

Then the eye started moving in its frenzy again. It began moving without waiting for the next question. It yanked their hands so quickly that it was almost impossible for James to keep his fingers on the eye. The old woman was having a hard time also and was looking accusingly at James.

It started spelling again. "W H O A R E Y O U W H I C H W A K E S T H E D E A D F R O M M Y S L U M B E R"

Jolie muttered, "Who are you which wakes the dead from my slumber?"

"T H E R E I S O N E W H I C H W I S H E S T O S P E A K T O Y O U"

Jolie wanted to protest, but their hands were flying too quickly around the board to do anything other than jot down the letters as they were selected.

"There is one which wishes to speak to you."

Even more violently the eye was moving side to side nearly falling from their hands.

"I H A V E F O U N D Y O U"

Jolie repeated, "I have found you."

"James…, I don't like this…, let's go."

Still her hand was writing down the letters from the board.

"Y E A R S I S E A R C H E D A N D N O W I H A V E Y O U"

Jolie shook her head, "Years I searched and now I have you."

"James?" Jolie said quietly.

The candle sputtered and began to burn like a propane torch straight up. First blue then mutating into a blood red flame. Spewing and spitting, wax hurriedly fell down its rapidly declining taper. The *eye* suddenly jumped from under their fingers and started moving on its own.

"NOWIHAVEYOUNOWIHAVEYOUNOWIHAVEYOU"

The aged wooden eye swam up into the air and slammed itself back down on the board disintegrating into pieces. The board warped and twisted itself from all four corners beyond the point of breaking. All of them moved back from the table's edge, as the OUIJA board slammed back down and skidded into the wall, wounded.

The three of them sat in stunned silence as the candle burned a horrid red flame and spewed until it was gone.

Then there was silence and inkwell darkness.

Jolie said, "James lets go, now."

"I'm with you," said James, jumping up from his chair.

Light filtered in from the outside street as their eyes slowly adjusted to the gloom.

The old woman still sat frozen in terror, eyes fixated on the two of them and finally back to what was left of the board.

The table started shaking and the table cloth rose as if lifted by a string in its center. The now empty candlestick holder toppled over and rolled off the table onto the floor with a loud metallic clank, clank, clank.

The sculptured shape of a human figure filled out the table cloth from underneath to reveal the supernatural effigy of some disgruntled spirit.

An arm with a pencil thin finger reached out and pointed at James. Directly at James.

An airy hissing voice emerged from underneath the cloth.

"hhiiiii ffffoouuuund yoouuu" "hhhhhaaaaa" "haaaatt llaaassst"

"What do you want spirit?" croaked Elberta, strangely reminding James of Ebenezer Scrooge.

The fingered arm spun around and pointed at her.

"fffaaake!" "ddonnntt ghheetttt hhiiiinn mmyyyy whaaayy"

"iiii whiiillllll deeeeestrooy ahlll whooo oopoooossse mmmmeeeeeeeee"

There was a gentle breeze as the table cloth drifted to the floor, followed by a thunderous POP!

Complete silence amplified the last horrendous noise.

"Get out…. GET OUT!!! GET OUT OF MY HOUSE!!!" Elberta roared. "GET OUT and NEVER COME HERE AGAIN!"

James and Jolie were only too glad to oblige. They were at the door before the end of the first set of orders and to the gate by the end of "…AGAIN!"

Elberta slammed her front door. Turned on all the lights and could easily be seen from the street, rushing from room to room like a mad woman.

Aunt Martiel and Maime met them at the front door of the Ames house.

"What was that noise?" they both asked in unison.

"Something popped in Elberta's house," James said.

"What in blazes…, what in the world is Elberta doing?" asked Maime.

"You kids look like you've seen a ghost," said Aunt Martiel.

"Oh, it's a little more than that…. That old woman's crazy. Let's go inside and we'll tell you what happened," urged James.

Jolie gave him a sharp glance.

She grabbed his arm hard, digging in with her nails to get his full attention.

"You heard what that awful thing said. Do you really want to involve them?"

"I'll white wash it, but I have to warn them somehow," whispered James.

"I've got to hear this," thought Jolie.

James described the OUIJA board and some of the antics "performed" possibly by Elberta to impress them. Then something happened to the table cloth and the candle went wild and rolled off. It was a miracle the house didn't catch fire.

According to James, Elberta was giving them the evil eye when something loud popped in her house and she freaked and told them to get out.

"Basically she's old and weird and really freaked us out," said James.

"James, it's starting to get late and I promised my Aunt BeBe that I'd meet her at the restaurant before she left there. I don't want to make her wait too late," said Jolie.

Jolie wanted to get away as soon as possible. How could she tell them that the old woman next door was trafficking in familiar spirits? A practice that, according to her family history, always led to destruction. She had to swallow her thoughts when she saw a look of agreement on Martiel's face.

"You're right. If you intend to come back over and beat us at canasta, you better get home at a decent hour," said Maime. "I'm so sorry your visit ended on such a sour note."

"It was so good to meet all of you. You're exactly like family and I enjoyed dinner and visiting and…, well everything except Elberta," said Jolie laughing a nervously convincing laugh.

Elberta's lights were still on in every room with loud knocking and banging emanating from different parts of the house.

"That old kook is really losing it," said Aunt Martiel.

On the highway, the cool night air rushed in the car windows. Jolie slid over as close to James as the center console would allow, leaning on his shoulder.

"I'm going to have to talk to Aunt BeBe about everything that's happened tonight," said Jolie. "This is way over my head."

"Tonight was only the icing on the cake for me," said James. "Last night was just as bad."

James explained what happened in the past night's dream. Then carefully explained his visitation. How he already knew what was causing the ticking. Or at least what it wasn't. It sure as heck wasn't some 'death-tick' bug, unless that's what the creature leering out of his wall was called.

Jolie related to James that it was his Aunt Martiel which was endowed with some type of supernatural abilities. Jolie giggled as she described the look on Aunt Martiel's face when she began to understand what was going on during their card game. Once she knew what was happening, she blocked her thoughts and it became almost impossible for Jolie to see the cards Martiel was holding in her hand.

She told James that she could also tell that Aunt Martiel was itching to talk to her openly since it was so rare to find someone with similar talents and they seemed to have some kind of common bond.

"Probably James," thought Jolie.

"I don't know what I'd do if I didn't have you to talk to about this," admitted James. "I don't usually let others know my problems. I always try to deal with them myself."

Jolie hugged him close.

James didn't want the drive home to end. It meant the end of this short piece of sanity and going back to a list of questions and possibly another night of horrors.

Jolie suggested that they drive by the City Gardens before dropping her off - reading his mind or yielding to her own wishes.

At the entrance to the park, James took Jolie's hand and they walked a short way down the lamp-lit path together. They shared vivid thoughts without conversation, listening to their feet crunching in loose gravel. Even though the night was still muggy, promising the usual onslaught of summer weather, neither of them seemed to notice. The sounds of the night air and distant muffled traffic from the city passed between them.

James suddenly understood that none of his thoughts of affection toward Jolie were hidden - indeed never had been hidden - which made him somewhat uncomfortable, but at the same time reassured him that she possibly felt the same for him.

As Jolie stopped, James leaned down and kissed her waiting lips.

Instantly lost in the moment; time stopped and all life ceased to exist. Never had he felt the electric music playing on the nerves of his body from only a single kiss. There was something special about Jolie, more than physical. How could a kiss turn him inside out? A simple hug followed for a short moment in time. Jolie led them over to one of the park benches and sat down, pulling him beside her.

The bold fragrance of rampant flowers swept past, carried on a breeze as they held each other, learning each other. Jolie heard her heart thumping in her ears and she knew that she had to get to her aunt's or risk.... "Risk what?" she thought as her mind melted into a puddle of longing.

His lips slid across hers once again, her cheek, the scrim edges of her ear, then back once again, driving her to shivers.

She cared for James, but giving into her own desires, both their desires, would be a disastrous mistake.

James cared for her, it was no secret. There was an immediate bond between them that was present when she first dreamed of meeting him in the library. That was her secret to keep.

"One thing at a time," Jolie thought. "One thing at a time...."

Screeeeeeeeeeeeaaaaaaaaaahhhhh!!!!

An ear piercing noise sounded near them, echoing from all directions.

Their moment of passion was doused sending shivers over James.

He stood and spun looking everywhere at once to see what had made the noise.

"Its okay, James," giggled Jolie. "It was only a screech owl. You *are* a city boy."

He could have sworn that he saw several man-sized shadows scattering into the darkness around them. James stood looking at Jolie seated calmly on the park bench, as he tried to calm himself.

"What?" she asked finally, looking confused and becoming frightened.

"My nerves are shot," he said as he fell in a slump on the bench beside Jolie.

He made a sad attempt to regain his shattered ego and took her hand in his.

"Thank you for coming here with me. You don't know how much it means being able to talk to you."

She turned him back around and they held each other for a quick last kiss.

Jolie felt the seriousness of James' distress and silently wished that she hadn't laughed at his fright.

"We should probably go. I need to have a serious talk with my Aunt BeBe ...tonight. This may be one of our all-night sessions."

"I know we should leave, but I don't want to," said James, turning to face the graveled walk leading back to the park entrance.

"I'll probably go with Aunt Martiel over to the old house tonight. If what you said is true, maybe I can talk with her too."

He looked nervously around as they both arose and slowly walked arm in arm back to the car.

James let his mind wander, reliving the evening. His family really liked her and he had never felt this way about anyone before.

Jolie listened in to his thoughts, silently, and worried that this was exactly what she was feeling warned about; yet now it was exactly what she wanted. She was beginning to hunger after his attention and this was distracting James.

On the way home, Jolie brought him back to his senses reminding him that there was something evil after him. Specifically him. Whatever this entity was had determined to get him, whatever that meant.

The two of them arrived at *The Cajun* around nine o'clock. The lights were still on in the front window, even though it was closed.

Jolie walked to the front door of the café and opened it with the key draped around her neck.

Inside were the lingering scents of various foods and strong black coffee. The chairs were turned upside down on the tables, surrendering to the imaginary *café gods* and the bare hardwood floor gleamed up at them. Quiet rumbling and scratching sounds bounced from the back of the café and became louder as they locked the front door behind them.

Aunt BeBe was busily taking cans out of some boxes and arranging them on her pantry shelves. She looked up when she heard them come in the stock room.

"You two look like you either had a really good time or a really rough time..., or maybe both," said Aunt BeBe worriedly.

Her eyes darted accusations between the two of them waiting for an account of their time together.

"Both," said James. "But probably not what you're thinking."

"He's right," said Jolie, quickly dispelling the squinting eyes of her aunt.

Aunt BeBe stood up fully, stretching her back and her eyebrows rose in a profound questioned look.

"Since when do kids admit to having a really good time?" she asked, turning to start another regimen.

James offered to finish emptying the boxes and put all the items on her shelves. The offer was gladly accepted. Jolie tugged her aunt back into the front of the restaurant and filled her in on some of the more interesting events of the evening.

"You really know how to pick-em, babe," said BeBe. "James needs to isolate himself from his family until this is settled."

"But how?" asked Jolie. "Without telling them why? Doing that will put them in just as much danger."

"What about you, Jolie? What kind of danger will you be in?" asked her aunt, trying to make her point more obvious.

Jolie hadn't really thought about herself as being in any danger until that exact moment.

"We'll talk more when we get home," said BeBe. "It's time you let your friend go home and try to get some rest if he can. I can tell this a lot harder on him than you know."

They locked up the café. BeBe gave James a quick hug thanking him for his efforts with the rest of her canned goods. She began a list of motherly suggestions, that he be very careful where he went, and who he talked to the next several days. In addition, she advised him to stay as close to home as possible, even if it meant not seeing Jolie.

And seeing the instant look of desperation shock his face she added, "Just for awhile. We do have a telephone you know."

Standing at the curb outside, BeBe took off a necklace she was wearing around her neck; a gold chain with an interesting medallion on it. She put it over his head and around his neck.

"Don't take it off," she said smiling. "I want this back soon, okay?"

The Mustang roared to life and James started his long route back home. Down the street, an older model car quietly inched from the darkness and followed him out of town, staying a convenient distance behind him.

Chapter 15

James drove home wondering how fate could have placed Jolie in his life; how he could possibly have fallen for her so quickly.

Well, at least that much was a no-brainer, but her attraction to him began equally as fast and that wasn't something he had expected.

"Maybe I'm blinded, but not dumb," he mumbled to himself. "I've only known her a couple of days and yet it feels like I've known her a lifetime, like I want to know her for a lifetime."

Learning to trust his newfound instincts, James took a familiar detour when he neared the neighborhood by his grandparents' home.

Heaven's Gate cemetery was once again drawing him closer.

He slowly cruised past the arched iron gates and couldn't help but wonder if all this had something to do with the vandalized grave of the ancient Syrus Earl Ames. It was that same feeling again.

Two other cadavers had been stolen from the old Natchez City Cemetery, far north of town. The sheriff mentioned they were remarkably old graves too. Probably not related..., but that same uneasy feeling wouldn't go away.

He made a mental note to find out the names of other robbed graves. Stolen corpses, maybe only skeletons, were probably nothing more than dust by now.

He drove on past the front of Heaven's Gate to the twisty dirt road that ran along the side of the grounds into the thicket. As he idled slowly past he saw a faint light down the road and stopped his car. He put the Mustang in reverse, backed up a few feet and killed the engine. The Mustang's throaty exhaust was not the quietest car on the road, especially after the improvements he and his grandfather had installed.

He quietly got out and walked next to the walled outer edge of the graveyard's barrier. Looking down the dirt road, he saw two dark figures, barely silhouettes. Again, one of the figures was wearing a glowing white cap on its head.

"Unbelievable..., looks like the same people," he thought.

There was barely enough ambient starlight to illuminate their movements in the darkness. He crouched down and watched patiently as they walked back into the thicket opposite the graveyard. He heard the soft thud, thud, of doors closing and an engine came to life. Their vehicle pulled from its stealthy parking spot and headed..., right for hi

"Oh, crap," said James.

He walked quickly back to his Mustang and slid in. Thankfully, it was back far enough in the rough that they might not see him.

In a few minutes the vehicle, a mud caked and rusty looking 4x4 pickup truck, pulled out of the darkness and rolled up the dirt road, stopping briefly in the shadows of the intersection. The two figures inside were arguing over something that sat between them.

In the dim light, James got the last four digits of a Mississippi license plate ...4PHR before the truck and its occupants drove slowly away. He quickly wrote down their license plate numbers on the only thing he had available, the back of his journal hidden under the passenger seat of his car.

Martiel and Maime Ames were waiting out on the front porch as James pulled into the driveway. He got out and noticed that Elberta's lights were still on in her house and there was still some noise coming from over there. Over three hours had passed; not a good sign.

Walking up to the porch where they were, his gramma patted the space between them on the porch swing and ordered him to sit.

The chains on swing creaked their protest, but held, and suddenly he felt like a trapped rat.

"Did you have a nice drive?" cooed Aunt Martiel.

"See any flying table cloths on the way?" asked Maime.

James said nothing.

"We went over and had a nice chat with Elberta after you two left," said his gramma. "You'd be surprised what you can learn from a blathering scared old woman."

"She told us a slightly different story than the one you described," said his Aunt Martiel.

"But, you don't understand, I...," James was cut off. Gramma raised a hand signaling him to be quiet; it was too late for excuses.

"We know why," she said calmly. "It may be admirable, but not very smart. You see, that's how any enemy works. He separates you from the pack, gets you all alone, and pounds your head in."

"There's strength in numbers," they both agreed.

James didn't know what to say. He sat silent for some time trying to decide what to tell and what to keep to himself.

"You might as well tell us everything," said Aunt Martiel.

"Oh God, not you too...," groaned James.

"Too...? Ahhh... Jolie," said Aunt Martiel. "And you aren't only protecting us; you're worried about her too."

James collapsed, emotionally exhausted, covering his face in his hands. Hot tears formed that he quickly pushed back inside.

James started from the beginning and gave them the short version of everything that happened to him since he arrived for the summer. The nightly dreams getting worse each night. The faces, and how the last one seemed to have warned him of a coming event…, which turned out to be a traffic ticket.

The visitor over his bed he kept to himself; they weren't ready for that terror.

He mentioned that he drove by the cemetery, a couple of times, and how he had felt drawn there. He had part of the license plate numbers of a truck carrying two strange men in the dark. It was a stretch, probably nothing, but more than the authorities had done so far.

They finished up and Aunt Martiel said, "You're staying with me tonight. A change of scenery for a day or two will do you good. Now, go get some of your things together and let's get on over to the old house before it gets any later."

Suddenly, there was more loud rapping coming from inside Elberta's house.

"Poor old woman, she shouldn't play with the dead - she might actually wake them up," thought Aunt Martiel.

Chapter 16

The Estate

James followed his Aunt Martiel roughly fifteen miles north on Highway 555 to Ames Heights Road, to the old family home place.

All was dark and quiet. A single ornate lamp, nested beside a blossoming magnolia, illuminated the lawn in front of the massive two-story mansion. A plush green carpet of St. Augustine blanketed the entire grounds visible in the dim light. Streaming arches of moss flowed from the regal Oaks and Pecan trees surrounding the estate.

A shadowed porch wrapped and outlined the front of the house, as well as both the north and south sides, corner to corner. Several huge pillars supported a veranda twinning the first story below.

James grabbed all their belongings and made one cumbersome trip inside. The leaded glass in the front door threw shards of colorful welcoming light as Martiel threw the key into the lock.

"James?" Aunt Martiel said softly. "Someone's been in the house."

"Was it the caretakers?" asked James. "The place looks really trimmed and clean."

"I don't think so," she said. "Look…."

She stood in the open doorway pointing down at the polished wooden floor, several scruffy marked footprints trailed inside. The trail came in, stopped, advanced a few steps, turned and walked back outside.

"Doesn't look like they stayed long," they both agreed.

"But, how did they get in?" asked his aunt. "They would have needed a key and the locks are new. There are only a handful of people in town that have a copy. One to the caretaker, one to your Grampa Ames, one to the family lawyer, and one that the sheriff keeps in case of vandalism," she said, concluding her short list.

"The sheriff keeps a key?" asked James. "Isn't that a little weird?"

"Well, considering that I live in Biloxi and the fact that my brother isn't getting any younger - don't you repeat that - that way the sheriff can search the premises without waiting on me or Martin Earl to get here. There are some very valuable antiques stored in almost every room in the house."

Her last remark came out with the sound of uncertainty.

"Lock the door and let's take a quick inventory," she said matter-of-factly.

They flipped on lights and skimmed through all eight bedrooms, as well as the old servant quarters, kitchen, library, sitting room, etc., until they were satisfied that nothing had been vandalized or removed.

"It was as if they were testing to see if they could get in, so that they could come back later and clean house," she said.

"Or, something spooked them," said James. "The place is a little creepy without any lights on."

Clean House. There was that awful term again. It shocked James back into reality.

"Uh, where do you want your things, Aunt Martiel?" James asked nervously.

"If you don't mind, I'd like them in..., up here...," she muttered, leading the way upstairs.

The upstairs bedroom door opened, revealing one of the larger bedrooms with two full-size, four-poster beds already arranged with clean linen. The contents were well dusted, unlike the remainder of the house. She walked in the bathroom and turned a knob on the sink, making sure the water was left on as she had requested.

"You can put your things over there, if you want," she said. "This is the only room they prepared for me and if it's all the same with you, I'd rather you stay here in the same room...," she said, her voice curling into a question.

"I was hoping I'd be someplace close by or maybe in the next room," said James. "You know this is the first time in my life that I've felt skittish about nighttime?"

"Well, after the experiences you described to me and your grandmother, I'm surprised that you sleep at all," she remarked. "Those things are NOT normal, James. Most people would have already run screaming to a nut house."

"If it hadn't been for Jolie...," he blurted, about to reveal his true feelings. Thankfully he shut off the claptrap.

"Yes, Jolie's a remarkable girl, James, remarkable," she said. "She seems much older than her years..., much more mature. As a matter of fact, so do you, James. I'm quite proud of you as I'm sure your mother is also," she went on, searching for some delicate way to describe what she wanted to say.

"Jolie..., seems to have..., I don't know how to put this."

"Gifts.... That's what she calls them, Aunt Martiel."

There was no need to try and skip around the truth. James started looking for a place to hang his clothes to offset the uncomfortable feeling that was building.

"Gifts..., what an appropriate term," she agreed. "I noticed them today at the card table. I also noticed something else, James...," she added, a little less politely. "If I didn't know better, I'd say she is deeply infatuated or maybe even in love with you. She's probably not even aware of her own feelings as yet. Women can be a little stupid like that sometimes."

James felt a rush of heat from head to toe. Love wasn't a word he'd attached to any girl he'd ever known until now. Was Jolie really in love with him?

"And...," she sighed..., "I see that you are in no better shape than she is. James, until you figure out this business with whatever is attacking our family, namely you, please go slow.... I'd hate to see either of you get hurt. That little girl is a lot more delicate that she acts. Most of that bravado is a façade to impress you and to hold herself up by her own bootstraps."

Martiel unpacked the rest of her clothing and placed them nervously about, waiting for everything she was saying to sink in.

"I'm guessing that Jolie's parents aren't in the picture much," she urged on.

"You guessed right," said James.

Thankful for a change of topic, he began to ramble on, hoping his aunt would tire of their conversation.

"She's living with her Aunt BeBe. I think she got tired of being bounced back and forth between her parents. I don't know how much she would want me to tell you about her personal life..., but.... I don't think she came here only to get away from that, but I guess, searching, you know, what she wants to do with her life. Well, I'm sure it's more than that too."

James remembered some of the talks with Granny Smith and that sudden feeling of runaway mouth.

"Just shut up, James," he thought to himself, as he continued on beyond where he intended to stop.

"She didn't know what to do about certain changes that she's going through."

"The gifts, you mean," said Aunt Martiel.

"Right, the gifts," said James, inwardly kicking himself.

There were a few minutes of silence with James biting his bottom lip to shut his outward flow of secrets. After all, Jolie had mentioned that his aunt could be the one in his family that was like her.

They finished putting their clothes away and got ready to retire as it was getting extremely late.

Aunt Martiel opened the bedroom windows to let in the fresh cool night air. She flipped a loud clicking switch and the silent whipping ceiling fans came to life.

They were both about to turn out the lights, when....

"James?" said Aunt Martiel. "You'll have them too."

"I'll have what?" he asked.

A thousand things ran through his head in unison.

"Gifts," she said bluntly. "Our family has a sort of legacy, and it looks like they might fall into your lap."

"Oh God, no way," thought James. Jolie couldn't be right about that too.

"What if I don't want them," he asked. "I mean…, I *don't* want them."

"Not much choice in the matter," she sighed. "I should know; I'm burdened with them myself. Apparently, one of yours is to see into the spirit world. Quite easily it sounds like. Problem is, sometimes, they see right back. That might prove to be what's causing all your troubles."

Without another word, she turned out the lights and slid into her bed. Now he was silent, but at least he had someone to talk to that might understand.

"We'll talk tomorrow," she yawned. "I love you, James."

With a hundred unanswered questions, he echoed the rote, "I love you too, Aunt Martiel."

Chapter 17

Monday morning, six sharp, Deputy Floyd walked into the Police Station. A few items from his hands dropped onto his desk, when the sheriff followed over, pausing at his cubicle.

"In my office in five minutes, deputy. Go ahead and get yourself some coffee. We have a couple of things to discuss."

Sheriff Howard hurried away, flipping pages on a clipboard he was carrying.

Floyd shook his head. "I hate Mondays. It's always the same old story, playing catch up. Someone probably ran over a dog and the owner got in a fistfight...," the deputy was thinking aloud as he stirred the soupy mixture in his coffee cup.

He walked in to the sheriff's office and his boss peered up from the notes he was scribbling, motioning for Floyd to take a seat in front of him.

"Exactly what is this?"

The sheriff was displaying a 6" x 8" piece of paper.

"Looks like a traffic citation," answered the deputy, sipping attentively at his steaming cup.

The coffee must have not kicked in yet, because the sheriff was not amused at the short answer or his refusal to look at the particulars of the document on display.

"Why, yes it is," he said, forcing the paper toward the deputy.

"Yup, I remember this one well..., kid was speeding, gave him a ticket," said the deputy, stirring his cup with a swizzle.

"Deputy, you do know that you can't let personal feelings toward our citizens sway your judgment when performing your duty. I understand that this boy, James Williams, may be a little bit of a smart mouth. I do. But, our public image is at an all time low right now with the unsolved grave robberies up north of town, and now this new one east of town. Do I need to remind you that an Ames family member is one of them?"

"But...," the deputy was about to get wound up with explanations.

The sheriff stared at him blankly in protest.

"Hear me out, deputy," said the sheriff. "The Ames family has given a tremendous amount of time and money to this community. They stood up for us in the budget meetings. They've lived here for generations. It would be extremely bad press if it became public knowledge that you targeted this kid out, because of some personal reasons."

The deputy stood, red faced, staring at the sheriff.

"Sheriff, I give you 110 percent and follow your orders to the letter," he barked. "I can't believe that you would think that I…"

"Before you get too sanctimonious, deputy, can I ask you a couple of questions?"

Deputy Floyd halted his rebuttal, nervous waiting for the inevitable.

"What time does your shift normally end on Saturday?" asked the sheriff.

"Two o'clock, unless there is an emergency," replied the deputy. "You know that, sheriff. Saturday's have always been my short shift."

"Would you read to me the time that is recorded on that ticket, written in your own hand?"

"Two-fifteen, but I was…," the deputy began another protest.

"Deputy Floyd, for the last six months, every Saturday, at precisely one o'clock, you have been sitting at that desk right out there, filling out reports, and watching the clock, ready to get out of this place, which I don't blame you for that. Why is it that on *this* Saturday, at two o'clock you happened to be parked, on this particular road, and happened to have caught this alleged speeding offense? And, I won't dare ask you how you knew that this young man would be traveling that route because I will not stand for personal conspiracies in my department."

The deputy fell blank and silent.

"That doesn't mean that he wasn't speeding," the deputy protested.

The sheriff shook his head in disgust as he held up the ticket, placed it on his desk, wrote "Void" on it and signed his name to it.

Floyd felt his eyes draw to slits and couldn't seem to move.

"Would you be so kind as to hand this to the clerk on your way out?" asked the sheriff.

"Yes, sir," Deputy Floyd said curtly.

"And, by the way deputy. I received an unusual phone call this morning from the DMV, up in some little town outside of New Jersey proper, wanting to know if I required any follow-up *family* information on a *James Earl Williams*. You wouldn't know anything about that, would you?"

"Haven't a clue," he answered, nervously turning his face to the door.

"If I ever hear that any officer of the law under my jurisdiction is abusing his sworn office for personal reasons, there will be severe repercussions. Do I make myself clear?"

Floyd was visibly angered, barely able to breathe.

"You've been my best officer for almost a year now, Deputy Floyd, by working hard, following orders, never complaining, even about the awful hours. Please don't tarnish your good reputation with this department, over some juvenile conflict."

The deputy nodded with his back to the sheriff, and walked out of the office, throwing his hot cup of coffee in the trash outside the door.

"The little bastard," he crunched between pursed lips.

Sunday night was uneventful for James and his aunt. James slept in until eight that morning, barely moving and snoring slightly. His Monday morning trancelike sleep was interrupted by the echoing sound of Aunt Martiel downstairs, talking to someone at the front door.

James stretched and rubbed the cornbread out of his eyes as he sat on the edge of the bed. No dreams…, he couldn't believe it, no dreams at all. No ticking. No monsters. No shadows, no nothing. A night of peace. Maybe, it was all over.

One single shard of panic pursued him. What about his grandparents' house? He had to find out.

He heard the front door close and the footsteps of his aunt making her way to the kitchen. He hurriedly gathered his day's clothes and rushed to the bathroom.

After his morning ritual, he walked downstairs to the kitchen to find a fresh pot of coffee and some doughnuts on the table.

Aunt Martiel was on the phone talking busily with some unseen cohort.

Hanging up the phone, Aunt Martiel said, "That was your gramma. I had to find out how things went last night at their house. She said that everything was quiet as a mouse at their house, but it seems that wasn't the case with Elberta. About 2:00 AM, they heard an awful clatter over at her house, loud enough to wake them up. It seems that something spooked old Elberta and she turned all the lights back on in her house and there was more beating and banging the rest of the night. Your little excursion to her house may have been a good diversion, like a wild goose chase so to speak, to whatever has been bothering you.

"I suppose it wasn't that good for Elberta, but let's not forget she did everything but drag you across the street."

Martiel shuffled a large sack on the counter.

"Oh, I forgot to apologize for the doughnuts. You see, I never was much good at preparing food. I never really paid much attention to my mentors when I was younger. I usually eat out or…, well, actually I eat out a lot…," she finished, laughing.

James had already eaten one and was well on his way through the second by the time she finished her explanations.

"I was lucky to get donuts or cereal, back home," smiled James. "We're always in such a rush. Sam and I would *fight* over something like this. It's always hard for me, after my summer visits down here, when I have to go back home. Gramma always spoils me rotten."

Martiel looked preoccupied after plucking one of the donuts from the box on the counter. She made several trips to the pantry and another to the refrigerator, then she shook her head dismally.

"Well, I suppose we should get this day started."

She made a pass around the kitchen, picking up the remains of their morning while James finished his coffee.

"Do you want to go with me? I have to go by the law office to sign a few papers and cut them a check. They're handling the Health Department and the work crew to get old Syrus Earl Ames' grave closed back up. That shouldn't take more than an hour. We won't need to go by the gravesite since you've already inspected it."

"I should really go by and help out grampa at the garage," said James.

"Goodness no!" she grunted. "He said to tell you to take today and try to get some rest. Oh, I almost forgot. He said that the little matter about the speeding ticket was taken care of. The sheriff called him this morning and assured him that there would be no more incidents from *Deputy Do-Dah*."

She grinned, all the while sensing that there might be more to the problem with this deputy.

"Well, that's one thing off my list," sighed James.

She gathered her keys and took one more sip of coffee before plotting her day's travels.

Chapter 18

A tall mud crusted pickup truck fought its way down the single lane dirt and mud road that followed the Mississippi levee out north of Natchez. From the looks of the vehicle, this was its breeding and testing ground. The deep treaded tires threw dirt and mud at sundry times from the front, as well as the rear, caking a sticky substance on the barely viewable windshield.

There were miles of levee access roads, not really meant for the casual citizen, and usually reserved for official use. This didn't seem to phase the forward progress of this collection of metal, rubber and glass. The truck made a turn from the rarely traveled route through a thick stand of young pine trees into a small clear-cut and stopped. Two seemingly inseparable teenaged boys dumped out of the truck at the same time.

"It's yor turn to talk with Miss Lyda," the driver said, circling around the front of the truck.

"Hail no…, she makes mah skin crawl," said the other. "You go an' talk to her. She *likes* you."

"You don' mind the gold pieces she pays you and me," continued the driver.

"Ain't doin' it this time," said the passenger again, fiddling with his mottled cap. "I'll take m'chances street-beggin' first."

The driver reached behind the passenger seat and pulled out a bottle of courage and took a long drink. Jack Daniels was his favorite, but the cheap stuff still did the trick.

"We done some weird she-it fer this ole hag, but meetin' up with her has got to be the worst part," agreed the driver.

He reached and grabbed a large cloth bag sitting in the middle of the seat and clutched it carefully.

"Day-uhm!" said the driver angrily, stalking off toward the shack. "Stay here and keep your eyes on the truck."

The early daylight folded over into bleak darkness there in the thickness of the moss laden trees. No matter how many times he made this trip, he hated this very walk. He'd never admit it to his partner, but his knees shook as he walked toward the shallow porch directly in front of his path.

"Rather face a crazy man with a rusty knife then walk inside this doah," he thought.

The boy pulled up his baggy pants, hoping that the old woman wasn't there, and was about to knock on her door.

"Where's yo' paht-na?" wheezed a dusty set of vocal cords.

His insides wobbled like jelly as the voice oozed from the darkness.

"He's… a keepin' a look out back at the truck, Ma'am," said the young felon.

"Speck he is, speck he is…," huffed the voice in a poor excuse for a laugh.

"In mah' day, a man that didn' walk up to the doah, weren' no man," she scoffed.

"No Miss Lyda, reckon not," he agreed.

That S O B was definitely making the walk next time. His bladder was about to collapse from fright.

"Billy said give you this," he blurted out. "He said it was important."

Trying to get his business over with and nervously digging in his pocket, he pulled out a piece of paper and another little bag. It was the moment of truth, where he had to man up and step forward. He walked on inside the shack inspecting his steps carefully.

The creature seated beside a makeshift table and chairs was barely visible. He carefully placed the large heavy cloth bag on the table with a noisy clump. There was a slight breeze and he felt a hard chill inside the cabin as his eyes adjusted to the gloom.

This old woman had easily seen a century pass and probably wouldn't recognize the civilized world. Her only contacts were probably by word of mouth.

She eased herself from her chair. Her body was tall, even when crumpled over, "poor-thin" like some starved animal, despite the food spilling from the open pantry.

A shock of white-gray hair that looked like a halo crowned her head, contrasting her dark skin, the peak almost bald.

The boy slowly extended his left hand with the other contents to her open palm. Her hand looked like greased whitleather, fingernails black and yellow streaked, from age or other pursuits.

She reached up and latched onto his hand as quick as a snake. The boy flinched, but didn't dare break and run. He had experienced what this old voodoo woman was capable of. Her other hand took the contents from his palm, never letting go of her claw like grip. Then she carefully took a fresh hold of his calloused hand.

"Hmmm…, seems you betta' watch yo' back," she wheezed as she felt the creases and cracks of his palm.

Closing her eyes for a moment or two, she continued to rub the skin around his hand.

"There be a fox on yo' trail," she whispered.

He was getting itchy to leave when he remembered, "Billy done said you needed us for some other kinda errand. Will you still be needin?"

"Mmmm hmmm," she began slowly, with a far away look in her rheumy eyes. An odd expression crawled across her wrinkled face in the dim light. Dropping his hand, she shuffled from the room slowly and pushed aside a black and white checkered sheet. The thin cloth hung loosely over the doorway separating the room they were in from the one adjacent.

She disappeared into the still darkness and he could hear her slowly moving objects and mumbling. He listened stiffly at the tinkling of glass and a scraping, scratching noise.

Strange scents met his nose, until his eyes found the cold fireplace with its few embers smoking from the night before.

The teenaged boy tuned out the subtle noises, thinking of the money he had hidden that would soon take him far away from the Mississippi Delta, but for now, this was his life.

A loud noise woke him from his hope filled distraction and he snapped back to this present situation. Raw fear kept his feet planted, again watching the wispy smoke rising from the ashes in the fireplace as she began her shuffling back into the room.

"Yo' errant is this…," she began, handing him a small clay vessel about the size of a hen's egg, a cork stopper in its top.

"Take this, put it in yo' pocket and don't open it for nuthin' nor nobody."

"Whas in it?" he asked.

"Never you mind…," she wheezed and took a few labored breaths.

"We gonna lay a little trick, thas all."

He did as he was told and she shuffled on over to the table.

Slow as cold molasses, she sat down in one of the chairs. Her hand reached across the table to a small piece of paper, and after folding it in half, handed it to him.

"Now listen up, and listen up good," her voice croaked and squeaked. "Take that there jar in yo' pocket, go to the place where that paper say's so, an sprinkle it all round the door, on the door, an inside on the *flow*." She took a few moments to gather her breath before continuing.

"Do it quick like, now. You hear? Don't take so much as a single breath whilst the jar be open. Bury the jar, and put this…," she said as she stood up, reaching in her apron pocket, "…put this under the front steps or under the porch …close like.

"Now when you leaves that place, go and wash yo' hands in lye water three times, and burn the clothes you wore. Iffen you want to live to spend your payday."

He nodded profusely, "I'll do it exactly like ya said…, to the letter."

Her eyes seemed to gloss, her breath labored and tired from her discourse.

"Since you be the only one with his manhood still attached betwixt yo' legs, listen up. I gonna give you a little somethin' to tie you over, for a week or so. When you done wit my working, find yourself a hidey way an stays there. You be keepin' yo' mouth shut about *all this*. Hear?"

Her scratchy voice was worsening.

"Turn round!" she ordered.

He heard shuffling and scooting and a few other noises. His feet were already pointed the right direction and he thought about leaving…, as quick as his legs could take him.

"Turn back here," she ordered a second time.

She dropped six pieces of gold metal coins in his hand.

"This be for you, an you alone."

"That sissy partner of yours gonna get hisself ketched. Let him…. Leave him be. He won't be doing any talking, for sure. You give him *this* coin."

Reaching in her apron pocket, she pulled out a little piece of cloth with a coin carefully wrapped inside.

"Make sure you put it in the middle of his hand, rite hear."

She made a stabbing motion with her crumbly fingernail on the center palm of his hand.

"Make sure you don't touch it."

Her hand was beginning to quiver from the stress of dealing with the pale skinned young boy.

"Now, iffen you go yella, an flap yo' gums, ole catfish'll be eatin' yo' nuggets before the weeks out."

He stood there unable to move, while she continued to stroke his hand, with four kinds of terror crawling up his skinny backbone.

The old woman looked down at the floor as if seeing something, then reached up again with her other hand and spit on her index finger. She took that same finger and rubbed the clear spittle in the palm of the hand she was holding, then closed his fingers over it.

"Memba, I hear yo' tongue if you say anythin' about me."

"Yes Ma'am," he replied, his voice quivering. "Ah'll be keepin' my mouth shut tightern' a frogs-aice."

"Rightly so…, rightly so…, now…, there's gonna be a thunderstorm, a real whistler. Don't you be comin' back this-a-way til after that storm is done an past. That's yo' sign to come out of hidin' an pay me another visit," she wheezed with great difficulty.

She turned around and sat back down heavily at her table, wiping her hands slowly on the thread bare apron she wore. Her eyes glazed over, ignoring him; his notice that she was through with him and he could leave.

Once he got his feet in motion, he didn't slow down until he was touching the tall hood of their truck with both hands, his breath heaving. There was a small wet spot on the front of his pants, evidence of his past experiences with what this old woman was capable of.

"How much we git?" asked the boy with the cap.

"Two slugs-a-gold, as usual," said the driver shakily, lying through his crooked teeth.

He handed his partner the coin wrapped in the cloth exactly as she had ordered.

"You're a goin' next time."

He watched closely as his partner opened the cloth and took a breath to speak, to tell him to wait, but fear of the old woman's threat tightened his lips and he looked away. The guilt and betrayal sank inside him as he hurried back in the truck. The other boy wasn't much of a friend, but he was the only friend he had in the world.

The boy with the white cap dropped the gold piece in the palm of his hand and smiled a crooked toothy grin. He held it up and eyed its pretty yellow shine in the morning sun and bit down on it gently. It was a museum quality gold piece.

"Time to celebrate," he said happily, jumping in the truck.

Chapter 19

James Earl and his Aunt Martiel spent a busy day taking care of business at hand, but as with all good things, the day came to an end. After a quick stop by the grocery store, then his grandparents' home, they drove back to the Ames family estate.

As they arrived, James listened to the crunch and pop of the tires pushing through the orange hued pea-gravel pavement of the driveway. When they neared the circle drive beside the house, there sat a man on the front steps in an extremely strange looking set of clothes.

The stranger was dressed in black slacks, a peculiar white derby hat, white jacket and vest with a lavender shirt beneath.

"Aunt Martiel?" questioned James…. "Who's that?"

Martiel nearly gasped. Her nephew already had 'the vision' and didn't even know it. Her father had been there to explain things to her, but James had been struggling through his changes all alone.

"Why don't we pull on up to the garage and bring the groceries in at the kitchen door?" she suggested quietly, looking off to the side.

"I'll go and see who that is while you put this stuff away, alright?" she finished.

It took James several trips to bring in the brown paper bags and stack them on the kitchen table; quickly distributing all the groceries inside the empty pantry shelves.

Aunt Martiel had busied herself with whoever the visitor was and after a few minutes sprang into the kitchen from the same outside door. She fumbled around first in the pantry, then under the kitchen sink throwing various things from side to side clanking and banging. She came out with some thick rubber gloves, a spray bottle, and a small sack of dry white powder.

"Do you need some help with something?" asked James.

"N…no, no, I can get this," she grunted as she carefully poured some of the white powder into the bottle and cautiously filled it to the top with water from the sink. Many things were swirling around inside her head. First the shock of what was happening with James Earl, and now this.

She grabbed an old cleaning towel from inside the broom closet and set her attentions back toward the inside of the house, shaking the spray bottle vigorously as she went.

James finished with the groceries and sat down at the table. The squish, squish, squish, of the water bottle attracted his attention along with other noises associated with cleaning…, something.

Curiosity finally got the best of him and he walked over to the sink where she had left the sack.

"Powdered Lye," said James to himself.

He started to go find his Aunt Martiel and observe what she was up to, when suddenly he heard the front door close. He decided to go out the kitchen door and follow the porch around to the front of the house and see exactly what was going on.

There was his Aunt Martiel with a scarf wrapped around her face, rubber gloves on, and that infernal bottle squishing every which direction on the door and all its surrounding fixtures. She then scrubbed diligently with the cloth until it looked as if her efforts would remove a couple of layers of wood.

"Aunt Martiel? What is going on?"

She jumped in surprise at his appearance from around the porch, but said nothing. There was a horrid stink booming up from where she was squatted down, vigorously working. She stood finally and stepped back admiring her handiwork.

"There..., much better," she said cheerfully, then looked at his questioned expression.

"Bird droppings or something on the door," she said. "Never can be too careful," she mumbled, shifting her eyes as she walked around to a burn barrel out back of the house.

James stood at the corner of the porch and watched her throw in the cleaning rag, remove the scarf and throw it in, and finally remove the gloves and throw them in.

"That's weird," he grunted. "Really weird."

He walked back over to the door, which had already dried to a dull smeary finish.

What a stench. He saw some yellowish powder on the door-facing beside the doorknob. He slowly poked his finger at it and came away with a fine powder on the tip. He cautiously sniffed it....

"Holy..., crap...," said James aloud. The stench was so bad that it made James a little dizzy and nauseous for a moment, then he wiped his finger on the bottom of the cuff of his pants and backed away to get some fresh air before he gagged.

Aunt Martiel stepped lively around the corner of the porch towards the front door where her nephew was backing away.

"So, who was that at the door?" asked James, still trying to rid the smell of the sticky yellow substance from his finger.

"Oh. That was..., the caretaker coming by to collect," she said as she walked inside the house.

He didn't ask any more questions....

The remainder of their evening was spent together, wandering from room to room in the huge old estate, while she educated James as to several generations of legacy and history pertaining to the Ames family.

He settled down in a room upstairs with an old family register dated to the early 1700's, which his aunt affectionately referred to as the "antebellum" era. Aunt Martiel left him to read and explore and went back downstairs to "hunt for supper" as she put it.

The old book was bound in dry-rot tan leather, but had obviously been taken care of during the previous generations. The cover was oil stained from various hands that had folded open its covers to maintain the contents. There were other undetectable stains, which looked something like dried burgundy wine or maybe even blood. This thing was easily 200 years old and it was amazing that it was still in one piece.

He thought it particularly interesting that every first-born male from every recorded generation had the blessing of the name *Earl* as a middle name. He was destined to be the last one in their branch of the Ames family that carried on that tradition, even though "Ames" was only on his mother's side, since she was an only child. If he or Sam didn't pass the name on, then the Earl moniker would die out forever. So it was up to Sam. He sure as heck wasn't naming any of his future kids "Earl".

Generations….

More generations….

Did any of this have something to do with all his confusion?

Aunt Martiel had said that the attack was "against their *family*, namely him."

Chapter 20

James continued to hammer at thoughts that might forge themselves into something viable. The spirit or whatever it was that made itself known to them at Elberta's kept saying something about "I found you" and pointing at him.

Of course that didn't make any sense.

With only a few years of his entire life lived in Natchez, it made even less sense and even so, why now? He could possibly move back to New Jersey, but what about Jolie?

Was he willing to leave and give up on her?

No.

Was it all about his so called gift or new abilities? He sure didn't want them. Not if it meant that every night of his life was to going to be spent outwitting some unseen spirit.

Well…, NOT unseen any longer.

This must be Hell, that's the answer. It was some sort of torment leaking out of some infernal pit. If it hadn't been true, it might have been funny. The only thing missing from his personal psychodrama was the *Wicked Witch of the West*.

His mind wandered back to all the other events of late, wondering if he could somehow tie them together. The last details of his life before he stepped on the jumbo jet in New Jersey were nothing remarkable to speak of. His first week in Natchez was even droll and boring. There was no switch he remembered flipping that might have opened up something as weird as this. What he wouldn't give for dull and boring right now.

He must be losing it.

That was only paranoid thinking; he didn't do anything to cause any of this to start happening.

What about the other grave robberies at the old Natchez Cemetery north of town? Maybe he should find out who they were and see if…, see if what? See if they had anything to do with his family? That was a very old graveyard but how could those strangers possibly be connected?

His grampa's, Great, Great…, Uncle Syrus was probably the oldest in the Heaven's Gate historic cemetery. If the successors of Syrus Earl Ames were buried in the same private graveyard, and they weren't messed with…, then what?

"Somebody's not telling all that there is to tell. There are too many pieces missing," thought James. "But why me? Why…, me?"

Just more questions and the sudden dizzy of a migraine was inching upward. He'd look at the old family register again tomorrow.

His forehead drooped over to rest on his forearm as he sat still, trying to relax his overworked mind and emotions. With a slow turn of the head, his eyes wandered around the room and it was really a sight.

Every piece of furniture was from a different era, but looked as if they were recently delivered and set in place. A traditional four poster bed. A huge multicolored cedar wardrobe. Fully stocked bookshelves covered an entire section of wall. His mind drifted, thinking about what it was like when this house was occupied and in its prime.

As he drifted off, on the verge of sleep for an instant, he heard soft laughter....

James sat up slowly expecting to hear Aunt Martiel's footsteps coming up the stairs and down the hall to where he was.

Nothing.

While wiping his tired eyes with his knuckles, again he heard soft laughter and mumbling voices coming from somewhere. It all felt so dreamlike in his tired mind.

Then there was whispering, "He's family, I see the resemblance."

"Who said that?" asked James, snapping his head around.

Whispering - "We did.... Your family.... Well mostly...."

More mumbling ensued, some sort of disagreement taking place.

James stood up, looking around the room for the source of the sounds.

Whispering - "We're all right here.... Don't get too excited...."

James scuffled backwards into a wall and braced his back against it, looking frantically from side to side. Should he run for the door?

Whispering - "Now, now, don't be afraid.... Look, you scared him...."

"Who are you?" asked James again.

Whispering - "I do so hate repetition.... Is the boy addled? Didn't we tell you we're family?"

The voices were getting clearer the longer James listened.

"What do you want?" James asked, sliding slowly toward the open door.

Whispering - "Don't be leaving us now...."

The door began moving on its own, picking up speed until it slammed shut and the latch clicked of its own accord.

James slid the rest of the way to the door and reached the door knob with his right hand. Locked - Of course. James couldn't help but think this was exactly like one of the tricks he'd played on his brother Sam.

"Ok, you have me, now what?" he asked.

Whispering clearly - "We are here to help you, of course...."

"Help me, how?" asked James.

The room started swimming in front of his eyes and he suddenly felt dizzy.

He remembered this same feeling…, like his dreams.

"Not while I'm awake too," choked James and he squeezed his watering eyes shut.

Whispering - "Breathe young man…, breathe. Focus on your breathing."

James was watching the air in front of him swimming, no…, shimmering like a quick breeze on the surface of a still pond.

He could smell the cedar from the tall open wardrobe standing across the room from him. The smells and scents of years trapped in the pores of the room were amplified until they were all almost indistinguishable from each other. Then slowly he could smell sweet Jasmine perfume…, then it faded…, then sweat from an afternoon of heat and humidity…, other odors familiar and unfamiliar.

Whispering - "Good, you're breathing…, the dizzy spell will pass."

"You want to help me? Help me how?" asked James.

Whispering - "Teach you to control your gifts…, and your dreams…."

"I'm listening," said James cautiously.

Whispering - "Good. First you must always remember to breathe. Open your mind and focus on your breathing like now."

He had to admit, he did feel better, even though the shimmery air was still present.

"Is…, is that you I'm seeing?" asked James carefully, squinting his eyes toward the apparition.

Whispering - "No…, it is only a door between our existence and yours. Our world is as a vapor to the untrained or ungifted eye. Soon, you will be able to see into our world as easily as we watch over you."

"Soon? What do you mean soon?" asked James anxiously, frightened.

Whispering - "Learn to use your gifts in your world, lest you join us…, in ours. Does he understand we only want to help?"

It was another voice this time, more masculine, deep concern in its voice.

There was a bumping sound from below in another room.

"Go…. Look under the front porch steps. Rid yourself of the accursed thing."

The shimmering faded…, the door clicked softy and opened on its own accord.

There was a sudden empty, dead quiet.

"Shit," said James.

"James?" a voice arose from downstairs, breaking the silence and making him shiver all over.

Frozen, he came to himself, still stuck to the wall by the door. Drenched in sweat and now gulping for air. His black hair clung in ringlets to his forehead and face.

"James?" called Aunt Martiel. "Supper is ready! Such as it is," she finished with a mumble.

James hurried out the door and down the hall and finally his feet were skimming down the staircase. Should he tell her? Of course, he should. He would…, and right now.

James shot into the kitchen, looking around for his Aunt Martiel, now hovering by the kitchen counter near its sink.

"Why James…," she said with a start. "Oh Dear, you look like you've seen the devil himself."

"Would you settle for heard?" asked James.

"Oh…," her voice trailed off. "I see you've met the family."

She stood there, matter-of-factly, staring at James, wiping her hands with a small kitchen towel.

"What?" spat James. "You left me up there and you knew that this place is…, what…, haunted? What am I saying, haunted? Inhabited, is more like it."

"Inhabited is right, but they're also a bit stuck," said Aunt Martiel. "Oh, the timing is never good for stuff like this."

She turned around and made a fuss over two glasses of tea destined for the table, her mind frazzled at how to explain what was happening.

"How do sandwiches sound for tonight?" she asked, apologetically.

"Sandwiches? I'm not sure if I want to stay here," said James. "How can you be so calm? Why didn't you tell me that my whole family was candidates for the nut house?"

"That's exactly why," she said. "Only you and I in our entire family truly know about the "gifts" and now of course, the inhabitants of this old house. This knowledge is kept from every other member of the family and only I, …and now you, are entrusted with being the "caretakers" of the estate. As you can see, the "estate" is more than simply managing the family resources and investments. We kind of become…, messengers and helpers ourselves, until it's time for the next in line to get the responsibility. Sure the others know that there are 'goings on', but that's all," she concluded.

Her explanation was almost dreamlike, romanticizing the insanity of all she tried to describe. As if this was some introduction into a high calling or majestic honor.

"Oh, this is great," said James as he sat down heavily at the table. His favorite Great Aunt Martiel was fruit-loops and dragging him into her dementia. Suddenly he was feeling his pocket for his car keys, falling into a panic. He did NOT want this.

"You really don't want to pass up your turn," Aunt Martiel said. Her remark was as *matter-of-fact* as telling him it was his turn to ride a bike.

"I already have a life," said James. "This hasn't got anything to do with it. Isn't there any other way?"

"There is only one other way that I know of and you won't like it," she said quietly. "The responsibilities are only passed on fully by the death of the prior recipient. In other words, when I die you will have full possession of…, well…, the family estate. Until then, I have the responsibility to make sure that you are taught, educated, equipped as it is, to handle…, everything."

She gestured with her hands sweeping around.

"You basically have to…, pass on…, to get rid of the job. It's also not really healthy for the other living family members to know too much either. In fact it's pretty much a secret, need-to-know kind of thing. Surely you understand…."

They sat in complete silence for a few minutes.

James figured he would play along until he could find a way out of this…, if it wasn't another one of his dreams or some wild hallucination. He'd heard that some of the drugs on the street could do this kind of thing to a person. Maybe there were gasses trapped in the upstairs bedrooms; the house was always closed up. But how could he and his aunt have the exact same delusions? Was this all real?

"Okay," said James. "But for the record, I don't like it."

"Neither did I…, at first," Aunt Martiel admitted.

The phone rang, catching them both off guard.

Aunt Martiel took the call and talked for a few moments while James ate a few tiny bites of tasteless sandwich.

The conversation seemed light and pleasant when….

"Why yes, he is. He's sitting right here. Would you like to speak to him?" she asked.

Handing the receiver to James she mouthed, "It's your mother," and motioned for him to smile.

She wandered off into the deeper parts of the house and left him alone to the privacy of his phone call.

"Mom?" asked James quietly. "It's really great to hear your voice…."

After more conversation, James sat back down to his evening meal and only picked at its contents. He could still smell the foul odor on his finger where he had touched the yellow junk.

Disgusted, he went over to the kitchen sink and washed his hands vigorously, until he couldn't smell the stench of it any longer.

He finished his sandwich and other items in silence, repelling any thoughts that tried to enter his mind. He remembered the demand from the invisible voices, to go to the front steps, actually under the front steps, to remove "an accursed thing".

He sat there in rebellion as the memory pressed like a heavy weight.

Then the room sighed heavily, as if it was breathing.

James jumped up from the table. The chair he was seated in exited in a slide backwards and tipped gently over, pivoting ever so slowly, and slammed on its back with a..., WHACK!

James spun, now running toward the front door, to anywhere outside those walls. He exited the house, heart hammering in his chest; he then sat down on the front porch after a few moments of restless pacing. The late evening air was cool to his clammy skin and began to calm his nerves.

He remembered the evil of his early childhood, of tortuous escapades of cruelty from the neighborhood gang.

He was back in it all again. If only he were there. He could beat his way through any of the old gang now. He was *the man* there now, with scars to prove it. He earned that reputation the hard way.

But he wasn't there now, he was here.

How could he fight a dream or the air? This was something that he couldn't even touch or really see. Had these "things" already been around him all the time and he couldn't see or hear them before now?

His head was swimming again with a rising dull ache.

James looked up to find that he was sitting on the front porch steps where his new benefactors had instructed him to look.

It was almost pitch black outside. The porch light was off and the large front lamp along the drive was beginning to ignite.

He eased himself down to the bottom of the fourth step and peered around the side underneath. There was lattice trim covering both sides of the steps barring his entrance. The left side looked as if it had been pulled loose recently. He felt around under the thick planks, imagining spiders and snakes lurking in the coolness. He snapped back his hand in frustration and pulled the lattice back further. With the thin decorative barrier out of the way, he pressed his face where he could get a better look.

Black.

Nothing, not even shadows.

Aunt Martiel had heard the calamity in the kitchen and decided to make her way downstairs to check out what was happening.

As she was about to make her way to the kitchen, she noticed that the front door was standing open; the only exterior door on the house without a screen door. She flipped on the porch light and walked quietly, peering over the edge of the porch at a new noise.

James was bent over with only his rear end and legs visible from where she stood.

"James?"

There was a muffled - BUMP!

James, startled by the intrusion into the silence, bonked the back of his head under the heavy planks of the porch steps.

He cautiously eased himself from under them rubbing his head.

"Oh, what a perfect evening," James thought.

"I'm here," he said, as he rose up, still rubbing the back of his head.

"Should I ask what you are doing?" asked Aunt Martiel.

"I'm looking for the *accursed thing*," said James, flatly, as if everyone in the world should know exactly what he meant.

"Oh, you've been given an errand," said Aunt Martiel, almost cheerfully.

"I'm in Hell," thought James. "I... am... in... Hell...."

He looked up at Aunt Martiel with blanched eyes as if daring her to say one more thing.

She caught his mood and deciding to take another approach, walked a few steps back to one of the porch swings and took a seat. The swing creaked slightly from the weight of the first living family that had sat in its cradle in possibly a year.

"Oh, my...," said Aunt Martiel suddenly thinking aloud. "He didn't tell me about any cursed objects."

"Who didn't tell you about what?" asked James angrily. "Let me guess..., the visitor on the steps when we got here. So, it wasn't the caretaker. I should have guessed."

He felt himself wilt as he contemplated the true extents of this expanding insanity.

"Just another friendly family spook to brighten up our day!" he said loudly, turning and walking off into the heavily shadowed front yard.

Aunt Martiel got up and went inside and reappeared some ten minutes later. James Earl was still walking on the lawn mumbling incoherently to no one in particular. The large lamp by the drive was casting oddly shaped shadows of her nephew as he paced the evenly shorn grass. James composed himself somewhat and walked back up to the front steps when he saw the expectancy of his aunt's expression.

Martiel held out a dimly lit flashlight, "Here, they gave *you* the errand, *you* should look."

He grabbed it from her hand without a thank you and peered cautiously once again under the steps.

There. Just back there..., almost in the center.

Got it. Pain.

James jumped back as if bitten by some venomous creature.

There was a spot of blood dripping from one of his extended fingers. Angered, he snatched back the fractured lattice onto the lawn and gingerly grabbed the object of his "errand" - a little colorful doll made of twisted sticks.

"Is this some kind of joke?" he asked, attempting to hand the doll to Aunt Martiel, who quickly moved her hands in refusal of the effigy, letting it flop to the ground.

"It looks like some kind of poppet," said Aunt Martiel.

She picked up a small stick from the ground and prodded it like a dead rat. Cautiously, she reached and pulled at it with her fingernails and produced a long pin.

"Here's what got you," she said looking worried.

"I know I don't want to know, but what is a poppet?" asked James, squeezing blood from his ailing fingertip.

"It's only a doll of sorts..., it's..., it's hard to explain. I barely remember my daddy talking about such as this."

Martiel inspected the object, turning it this way and that with the stick. Rolling it carefully like a dung beetle with its prize.

"We should burn it," she said, thinking out loud..., then changing her mind. "But if it's a voodoo doll, we shouldn't burn it. Oh..., I wish I could remember; these things are so confusing. Could you bring me a knife, James?"

He reached into his back pocket and flipped open a pocketknife as if it had already been open in his hand.

She looked at him a little startled.

"We need to talk about that," she drawled.

She took the knife carefully and sat down on the front steps.

"If it's a curse doll from a witch, it'll have certain plants and things inside or only stuffing."

Her breath quivered as she continued, "However, if it's some sort of hoodoo or voodoo, it will have..., other things inside."

She took the knife and proceeded as if dissecting a frog. Slowly and carefully she plucked the point of the knife down the middle of the back along hand sewn threads.

Martiel squealed and jumped back, dropping the knife with a thump.

James looked on in horror as maggots dropped out in clumps, from eating a meal of unknown origin inside the doll, which now wreaked a vile odor.

"Let's get all of it and take it up to the creek and throw it away," she said quietly, covering her mouth with her sleeve.

"I take it that this is a voodoo something or other? Is that bad?"

"It's certainly not good..., let's do it now," and she rushed into the house.

She came back moments later with a dustpan and broom and a small brown paper sack.

Together they gathered the remains of what looked like a rotting finger from a cadaver, other unspeakable items and a host of living creatures designed to eat away the remains of the dead.

Chapter 21

That same evening another type of battle was forming. In the dim light of a back room, a solitary soul was kneeling by her bedside on a thin pillow.

"…and Lord, I thank you for all yo' blessin's that you brung me all these years. Thru every trial, every burden, you been with me every step of the way…, oh, hallelujah, Lord.

My time be drawin' near, oh God. I can feel you callin' me home to my family and my reward. I done outlived all my kin, except my granbaby, Lilly.

I'm ready, Lord, to go.

Before I go, I has this burden for one last soul, oh Lord. You know who I'm talkin' bout Lord. This James Earl. He a good boy.

His family been good to me and mine over the years too. They listened to yo' voice when I was in need and blessed me many, many times, even tho' they didn't know I knowed it was them.

I see in my spirit Lord that there be a mighty evil that want to destroy this boy. Way bigga'n ennythin' I ever had to face.

There has to be someone standing in the gap for him, Lord. If'n I'm gone on home, who be there for him? Prayer, and standing with him, the onliest thang that saved his life up to now. Ole scratch been tryin' his best to douse the flame left in James Earl's life. Only prayer done put a hedge round about his life for now. Blockin' his enemy from takin' the most precious thang he owns…, his soul. Lord…, thank you for listenin' to me."

A dark shadowy object slowly invaded the privacy of the corner in the room and made itself known. Something old and evil hearted.

"He's mine. I've looked a long, long time for him and I aim to have him…," the evil whispered.

Granny Smith didn't move or shake at the sound of the words. She looked over for only a moment and buried her face back in her hands, the same as she was before.

"Lord, I thank ya' that we be given power to tread on them serpents an' scorpions an' all the power of the enemy."

Her prayer suddenly stopped, "Lord, my work finished."

"LOOK AT ME!" the spirit wheezed loudly.

"I done seen all of yo' kind I ever wanna see. I been fighting the likes of you since I be five year old, ain't nuthin' you got to say that I ain't heard before…, nuthin' but lies," Granny answered peacefully.

The spirit screeched in rage, rattling the old loose windowpanes in the bedroom.

"Best you can do, I see…. There be a place waitin' for the likes of you…. Best you be gittin' there," Granny said quietly.

A blinding white light flooded the room, completely clearing the air of her unwanted visitor. Quiet peace where there was tension.

A soft gentle voice spoke from seemingly everywhere….

"Wema Smith?"

"Here I am, Lord," said Granny.

"It's time for you to take my hand. I have someplace for you go now, something better for you to see…. Someone I want you to meet…."

"Yes, Lord," she said, reaching out her dry weathered hand.

Elsewhere, far away in a dark, damp room, lit only by a candle in a cold fireplace, something very, very old ran screaming into the wall and fell down covering it's face, uttering curses and growling…, "Mine…, Mine…, Mine…."

James went to bed Monday night full of the day's events. Sleep resisted him until late in the night. Aunt Martiel had been fast asleep for hours in the bed across the room. Somewhere between asleep and awake he understood that unless he relaxed, this tension would turn into another migraine and keep him awake all night.

James lay under a thin sheet, tossing, eyes roving nervously behind the covered sheath of his eyelids. Sweat glistened on his forehead in the dim light of the late risen moon outside, despite the pleasant cool night air filling the room.

Running…, he was running, from what he didn't know. His horse had fallen dead from exhaustion, with him in the saddle. Some terror was right behind him, black, moving like a shadow attached to his heels.

"Baka!" - the word spoke loudly inside him.

Somewhere in the far distance a screaming voice hurled words, pelting him like stones.

He was near insanity. Stopping for only a moment to catch his breath, he ran his fingers through salt and pepper hair badly in need of a trim. He looked tenderly at the small cloth package he clutched carefully under his arm, fighting back a gut wrenching sob.

Running along the banks of a river, *The River*, the Mississippi River, had drained all his reserves. He had to get back to town; the lights were glittering right around the next bend in the distance, no more than a mile or so. His heart beat in his chest like a drum as his mind reviewed the scenery from the last several months. Life had been looking up for once. He'd won thousands of acres of this coastal land. Slaves. A sea going ship.

But there was a rumor of war; civil war was near on the horizon. With the future uncertain, he sold all the possessions had won and converted it into gold. He hid it all. It was now in his brother's possession. He was rid of that terribly heavy burden. The only things he had truly wanted in life were dead…, one wrapped under his arm.

But he was still being chased and tormented…, by what?

Baka! The word hammered him in the back again, throwing him forward.

James somehow understood that this awful place was yet a dream…, then he remembered to breathe. He was reliving some event, someone else's event. Who was this?

A voice whispered loud in his ear and, "Ssssyrus…," escaped his sleeping lips.

Syrus!

There was a rustling in the reeds along the bank of the river and he was off again…, run…, run…, bolting through the loose dirt and debris along the banks.

Then, everything changed, and he began to float and rise up into darkness…, pulled away.

Music…, wild music filled his ears. A nonsensical beat.

The beat was fierce. James became more lucid, but he still had no control of the dream no matter how much he fought or carefully he tried to breathe.

The beat picked up, discordantly. He could hear a mix between *"Walk this way"* and *"Black Betty,"* in the tempos, not that *Aerosmith* and *Ram Jam* would *come together* to do something like that. His mind wandered and began flowing with the beat, absorbing its energy, letting it uncontrollably fill him.

"Oh God," he thought. There was that nauseas feeling again…, that pulling of his guts while on a leash.

"Breathe… Breathe…," moaned past his sleeping lips.

It didn't help. Nothing helped.

There was no way to control his breathing with that awful clapping, drumming beat. No ticking this time.

His breath was ragged as he slid toward the same ring of yellow lights…, candles…, he'd seen in another night terror. There was the beautiful black woman in a white dress, writhing on her back, someone calling to him, over and over.

Was it her? Was that her urging him on?

He saw a fleeting glimpse of someone standing in the dark.

There was a skull on a wooden pedestal, a candle burned on top of its bleached white surface in the shape of a hand, each fingertip on fire. There were lidless eyes in the skull looking maniacally in every direction in a silent scream.

Some hellish leash pulled him right up to the circle and the black woman rose to a seated position…, stiff as a board on a hinge. He met her stare face-to-face, nose-to-nose!

Oh God! Those eyes…. Her eyes…. Those horrible huge empty eyes were glaring at him. Like portals right straight into the pits of hell.

Now he was helplessly heading for them, right into the circle.

He hit the edge of the circle like a brick wall.

And he stopped.

Everything stopped.

"Noooooooooo!!!!!!!!!" the woman screamed…, in anger!!

James screamed…, in terror!!

As his eyes snapped opened, his Aunt Martiel was grasping his shoulders, shaking him awake.

"James! James! Wake up!" she yelled.

The lights were on in the bedroom and Martiel was frantically trying to break the hold of his dream.

He had the necklace that Jolie's aunt let him wear in his palm with a grip so tight his hand ached.

He folded up and Martiel hugged him tight. Together they sat for a few moments until his thoughts cleared.

"Gawd, what a scare!" she said, her own heart pounding.

"James, what was that all about? One minute I'm sound asleep and the next you wake me up talking in your sleep. I…, I thought I saw someone's shadow standing over you, but when I turned on the lights…," her voice trailed off.

"You said a couple of things that I could make out, but none of them made any sense. *Syrus* and what was that other? It sounded like *Baka*, and then you screamed bloody murder. Thank God we don't have any close neighbors or we'd have the police on our doorstep in the next few minutes."

Aunt Martiel sat up with him until the burden of exhaustion overcame the two of them and they were both asleep, minutes before sunrise.

Chapter 22

"Ring-Ring..., ring-ring..."

The sound of the double ring of the phone reminded James of when his grandparents could only get a "party line" from the phone company because of where they lived on the outskirts of Natchez. One ring was the neighbor about a mile up the road, double ring was their closest neighbor, three rings was them. That was back when eavesdropping was an art.

Quietly pick up the phone and you could listen to one of your neighbor's conversations and ease the receiver back down. Everybody knew it was happening, but cold stares when you met people in town confirmed your suspicions. Of course that probably depended on the conversation, but things get twisted so easily. That was when James wasn't even old enough to go to school, back when he and his mom would visit for the weekend at her parents' house.

"James?" called Aunt Martiel. "It's for you-u."

"Oh..., God it's early," mumbled James looking at the clock.

James jumped from his morning slumber and forced himself downstairs to the kitchen phone, dragging a shirt on as he went. There had to be other phones in the house..., somewhere.

He could tell by the grin on Aunt Martiel's face who was calling.

"Hello?" answered James.

"Hi James, its Jolie. I went by your grandparents' and they said you were staying over at your aunt's. I hope its okay to call there," she drawled, letting some of her heritage show through.

"Of course, it's okay. It's great to hear your voice," said James as he walked around the corner with the long stretchy phone cord.

"I should have called you and let you know where I was. Things were getting too weird for me over there...," he said remembering last night was almost a repeat.

"James, are things any better?" she asked softly.

A moment of silence told her what she probably already knew.

"I was talking this whole thing over with Aunt BeBe and she doesn't think we're looking in the right place for our answers," Jolie continued. "You see, if it's witchcraft of some sort, you might have some scary stuff happen for a while and gradually fade away, depending on how strong the conjure."

Conjure came out sounding like "con-ja", mimicking BeBe, but of course James thought it was cute.

117

"Aunt BeBe thinks this is something else way beyond that," said Jolie, her voice becoming serious. "You might be in real danger James and not only from nightmares."

"What do you mean? What does she think it is?"

"We need to get together today or tomorrow and talk," said Jolie.

"Today," said James. "Last night was…, not something that I want to repeat. I'm worried about my family now. If I don't find a way to make this stop, I'm afraid…, well I'm afraid something might happen to them. It's only a feeling."

"You don't go anywhere, James. I'll come to you this evening, after work here at the cafe."

"Thanks Jolie… I…," stammered James. "I'll see you then."

James stood holding the phone in his hand long after there was only the steady buzzing of the dial tone. Finally, his stupor broke and he walked back to the kitchen in silence.

"Ring-ring…, ring-ring…"

The phone made both of them jump in a repeat performance.

"Must be the lack of sleep," said Aunt Martiel reaching for the phone. "Hello?"

There were a couple of wrinkled looks, a few "oh, nooo's" and an "I'll be sure to tell him", right before she hung up.

"What?" asked James.

"Granny Smith passed away sometime last night…."

A numbness set in that grayed the rest of the morning.

James made himself a tall glass of iced tea and went outside through the kitchen door, lazing onto the porch. As the screen door slapped shut behind him, he felt the day heating up already.

He yawned thinking of the cool nights and hot days heading toward another hot steamy summer. He walked from one end of the shady porch to the other resting against the banister at different intervals looking at the beauty of this old home place.

Out front, close to the gated entrance stood the single ornate lamp that illuminated the drive, far from the front of the house.

The enormous magnolia tree now in full bloom looked like a Christmas tree out of season, with its lowest branches encroaching the base of the lamp. A wooden split rail fence drew a border around the immediate property with the southern portion washed in flowering wisteria, the hum of bumblebees fighting each other for rights of occupancy.

Although the landscaping was rather plain, the foliage and trees turned the scenery into a shady masterpiece.

He walked back and sat down on one of the porch swings at the front corner of the house. There were empty hanging pots every few feet down the length of the porch in every direction, a few sprouting grassy weeds. Nothing had been planted in them for several years evidently.

Despite the beauty, he was beginning to understand why he never visited this house before now. It never crossed his mind that there might be a reason the family had no desire to live here in a relative mansion. Then it also made sense why Martiel had never sold the place.

James sat and rocked the swing silently for some time, his mind wandering from Jolie, to Granny Smith, and back to his personal torment.

He hated that his life had become so self-centered. Never had he been the type that needed the world to revolve around him and now it seemed that every thought was focused on himself.

The rising temperature, the steady drone of the cicada's and other summer insects lulled him off into drifting quiet.

As he gazed out across the lawn he saw a couple dressed in formal attire like something out of *Gone with the Wind*. They faded in and faded out as he rubbed his eyes sleepily. Then there were more of these strange fading people in various modes of walking and conversation.

The pots hanging empty a few moments ago were bursting with growth, some with ivy, greenery, and ferns, while others spilled over with petunias bursting with color and fragrance.

The spectral gathering appeared to be a garden party of some sort. There was a table laden with food under a large oak on the side lawn.

James rubbed his eyes again and sat back closing them for a moment. When he opened his eyes they were gone. What took its place forced James back in his seat from surprise. It was as if he were seated front row in a pitch black movie theater.

There were two men digging in the earth with a shovel and pick axe. They were young kids his age. Both skinny, with long brown matted hair, one wearing a smudged white cap. It was as if the noon sun had forgotten its duty and the brightness of the scene continued to dim. It was obviously late evening where this was happening. He could hear the mumbling and complaining of the two boys as they struggled and labored.

"Ya'll push that rock outa the way..., won't be doing him no good no more," said a third voice.

An older man, short and stocky walked up to them and helped them push a large oval stone from where it stood. A headstone.

It all looked so familiar.

James sat forward in the swing, never before had he experienced anything like it. It had to be from the lack of sleep or another hallucination.

He saw the writing on the stone as it rolled backwards, face up, and out of the way of the busy crew. It was the grave of Syrus Earl Ames.

As they neared their goal, the older man said, "Be careful, they ain't gonna be much left."

There was a loud "clank" from a shovel and one of the kids groaned, "There's a crypt. It's got a rock coverin' it."

"Great," said the older man. "Dig around it and lets get it off."

The three of them struggled at pulling a rock slab from off the top of the casket. Even though it fought with its weight, the three men managed to move it off the top of the sleeping corpse.

There was a rumble of thunder that got all three's attention.

"We best hurry or we'll be swimmin' our way outa here," one of them said.

Leaves began blowing every direction and thunder sounded again, much closer.

"There's our next payday!" said the kid with the cap.

They lifted the paper rotten casket from its resting place. Light as a feather compared to the slab of rock that had been covering the surrounding crypt. With no effort whatsoever, the casket's lid came off cracking like an eggshell, exposing its contents.

The clothes on the cadaver had mostly turned to dust, but the bones..., yes the bones were still together and the skull was almost intact. They carefully retrieved the contents into a long slender sack. As they lifted the skull, the slack jaw fell from the place where sinews and muscle once stitched, and it snapped and fell apart.

James jumped backward at the sound which played its role in harmony with the vision.

The skull appeared to have eyes, lidless eyes, roving in mad confusion like a trapped animal. It too was set carefully into the cloth bag.

Huge drops of rain sounded in the tops of the trees around them and slowly began pelting the ground. The three men hurriedly gathered their tools and headed out through the back wall of the cemetery.

The kid with the cap turned around and gave the casket a swift kick. The rotted wood, centuries old gave way, showering the air with dust and splinters. He then ran laughing to meet the others and together, they climbed into a tall mud-covered truck and drove off.

James' eyes were burning and watering from staring without blinking at the scenery before him.

Everything came back into focus at once and James was left perched on the verge of the swing; bugs and birds singing, and a quiet hot breeze tugging his hair around.

"What was that!?!" James stood, his legs failed and he fell back down where he was, bouncing the porch swing.

Head swimming, he picked up his glass of tea from the rail and took a long drink closing his eyes.

"Why me?" asked James.

James was still on the porch swing, sprawled out over its full length, passed out asleep when Aunt Martiel drove in. She carried him a pillow and he remained that way most of the day.

While stuffing the pillow under his head, he remembered her saying something about Granny Smith and the funeral as well as something about Elberta Straw gone missing. It was all a haze.

Aunt Martiel woke him again at four o'clock. They were scheduled to go to his grandparents' for their evening meal. Jolie called while he was asleep and promised to meet him there around seven.

Rejuvenated by his long nap and the thought of getting to see Jolie, he rushed to get up and hit the shower.

In twenty minutes he was washed, clean-shaven, and dressed; both of them hurrying out the door, looking forward to a home cooked, family evening meal.

Aunt Martiel and James made the most out of the fifteen-minute drive across the countryside with conversation.

"Aunt Martiel, I had another one of those strange things happen to me today," said James. "I had some sort of vision or daydream or.... I don't exactly know what to call it."

"A vision..., really. Tell me about it," she said.

James described in vivid detail, the day's private afternoon matinee that played in his head.

"That's some vision," quipped Martiel. "I've had something similar happen to me before, but they were always short and they helped me with future events, or major decisions pertaining to the estate. Yours is obviously a past event about the grave robbery of Syrus Earl Ames."

"Okay..., well, you have to explain what's happening to me, where I can understand it," said James. "What else is going to happen to me? I don't like all these surprises."

"Basically, you should be able to read the minds of those who don't know how to guard their thoughts; you'll have premonitions or hunches and feelings about the eminent future. You can see into the spirit world. I didn't get this list supernaturally; it's only what you've been telling me. Our family has had a variety of these abilities from way back; as long as our personal recorded history. You're obviously starting out with a few more variations of the same theme," she commented questioningly.

"So..., what does that mean?" asked James. "Is there some spell or chant or incantation you do to start and stop them?"

Aunt Martiel laughed refreshingly.

"We aren't witches," she said matter-of-factly. "We don't do *magic* exactly, we don't do spells, rituals, or incantations as you put it. It's a natural talent as far as I know, passed on genetically or spiritually. Think about it; have you done a ritual or a spell of any kind?" she asked. "Did you attend any kind of ceremony or sacrifice a goat?" she continued. "Of course I was only kidding about the goat."

"No," James said quietly. "I guess I see where you're heading with all this. We didn't do anything to get the abilities, so that's why you call them gifts," James concluded.

"Very bright," said Aunt Martiel. "There are those that use spells and incantations, potions and call themselves witches. Honestly, most are fakes. It's hit or miss with them."

"Well if you ask me, it's been hit after hit with me," said James. "I'm tired of getting hit too."

"That's what has me worried," she replied. "You see, there are those that work outside the confines of mere spells and rituals, James. They dabble in death and the dead, spirits and such. There have been a few times where our ancestors have played cat and mouse with them, but no one has ever had an encounter this strong or this direct. We usually turn on our senses as much as possible and stay out of their line of fire."

James remembered the dream about Syrus and wondered if everything was correctly recorded in the family history.

"Then what?" asked James. "Will they just go away? They seem pretty determined to me. And how can I hide from my own dreams. I have to sleep sometimes and that's when this person or thing finds me."

"Very true…, we have to find the connection and break it," she said thoughtfully.

James thought silently – "What if I'm the connection?"

"Well, we're here. Thanks, Aunt Martiel; at least I know I'm not a witch or something."

"You're not a witch for sure…, a something…, now that's up for debate," she grinned. "We'll talk more, later tonight." v

Supper was everything James hoped it would be. His gramma should get some sort of an award for home cooking. He gained five pounds every time he sat down at her table. At least his appetite wasn't affected by the recent events.

"James, I'm sorry that I'm not much of a cook," said Aunt Martiel. "But at least I know where to find one."

Maime and Martin Earl were in their usual cheerful mood and the evening was turning out to be the best diversion from evil James could wish for.

"It's such a shame that Granny Smith passed on," said Gramma Ames. "I so dearly loved that old woman."

"We have to be careful who we call old now a days," said Martin looking at his wife. "She was only about twenty some-odd years older than us, you know."

"Why…, you two have lots of years left in you," said Martiel. "But we women don't divulge that sort of information, so you better watch your tongue, Brother Dear."

"Yeah, we don't get older, only a little more wrinkled," he grinned and laughed.

"Speaking of old and wrinkled, did someone say Elberta Straw is missing?" asked James. "...or did I dream it?"

"Why yes, she went missing yesterday evening and they found her only a couple of hours ago," said Maime. "She was wandering up the highway half-dressed and babbling on about stuff that happened over 20 years ago like she was reliving it. One of our neighbors up the road found her and brought her back home, but she was too..., well, incoherent to leave by herself. Some of her folks came and picked her up and took her to 'Green Oaks', if you know what I mean. I didn't know she even had any relatives close by. No one ever came to see her."

"That only goes to prove that people shouldn't mess around with stuff they don't know anything about," said Martin Earl.

"You're one to talk," said Maime. "I've seen some of the cars you've worked on lately."

Maime giggled and patted her husband on the hand.

"Yes, and they were working properly when they left my garage too," he answered defensively.

"I kind of feel sorry for Elberta," said James. "I know she grates on everybody, but she *was* trying to help."

There were a few looks between all the older adults that may have indicated that they didn't entirely agree, but nothing was said.

"I hear you are having a visitor tonight," said his gramma. "Jolie seems to be a very nice young lady."

James had not forgotten.

There was an animated clock in the shape of a black cat on the wall beside the *icebox* - his grandparents name for the refrigerator. The clock was one with plastic jewels set in several places and wagging its tail while looking from side to side; squeaking and clicking as it moved. He'd been watching that cat-clock since supper began in anticipation.

The table setting was being dismantled and the conversation had dwindled to small talk over Granny Smith's funeral and the sending of flowers and that sort of thing. The clinking and clanking of dishes had almost subsided when there was a knock at the door.

James was the first to arrive, but was disappointed to find another face at the door with eyes other than the blue sapphires of Jolie.

One of the lone church members had dropped by to find out more about Granny Smith's funeral, the schedule, if there was to be a wake, etc. James feigned ignorance of the whole affair and invited them into the living room. Martin and Maime heard the exchange and quickly rescued James.

He went back to the kitchen while information was being shared of the dead. Sheer disappointment emptied his anticipation when he looked up at the clock; it was already seven-fifteen.

Was Jolie alright?

Suddenly he felt a tingling presence behind him and he turned to see Jolie's smiling face looking back at him.

"You're getting better," she grinned. "You never knew when I was there before."

"I missed you too," he said matching her grin. "I was getting worried about you, did you sneak in?"

They gave each other a hug and quick kiss before anyone else sought out their whereabouts.

"Your Aunt Martiel met me at the door and led me past your visitor in the living room," said Jolie. "I like her."

"Where is your Aunt BeBe?" he asked.

"Oh, you should know her by now, she's gone back to the restaurant to close up and do the books," sighed Jolie.

James told her about Granny Smith dying and what a good friend she had been over the years. Also about Elberta Straw being found walking half-naked and getting a one-way ticket to the nut house.

"Let's see if we can get down to the root of the problem," said Jolie. "I talked to Aunt BeBe for hours about this and she's sure this isn't witchcraft."

"Aunt Martiel feels the same way," said James. "She seems to think that it's something darker."

"I think we've narrowed the persistent contact down to my dreams," said James. "I can't seem to escape whatever it is, because every time I go to sleep, it's waiting for me, like some hound out of hell. And then there's the dreams about Syrus Ames," he continued. "Or, at least I think it's about him."

"Syrus Ames?" asked Jolie.

"Yeah, my grampa's great, great…, I don't know how many great's, Uncle Syrus Earl Ames. The one that was stolen from the cemetery a few nights ago. I've had dreams about him, as well as the bad things. Jolie…, I even had what Aunt Martiel calls a vision this afternoon. I watched three men dig up Syrus' casket and steal his bones. I can still remember what they looked like, they…," James stalled out.

"What?" asked Jolie.

"I can identify them," said James. "I know who they are, at least what they look like. It's the same two that I saw leaving the cemetery. That's why I had to go by there, instead of going straight home the other night. I wrote down part of their license plate number. I can describe their truck. It was the same one in my vision. I watched them push over the headstone and dig up the grave."

James had digressed into an excited conversation all his own, while Jolie looked on at his expressions.

"James, what are you talking about?" asked Jolie finally. "You're going on a hundred miles an hour and you're not making any sense."

"Jolie, in the vision I had today, I saw the faces of the guys that robbed the grave. One of them had on the same cap that I saw this guy wearing the other night by the cemetery, when I saw their truck. I have the last four numbers of their license plate. But, the sheriff will never believe how I know. I know I wouldn't. And that deputy..., he'll try to say I had something to do with it," James rambled on, thinking out loud.

"Do you still have the license plate numbers?" asked Jolie.

"Sure, why?" asked James. "Give them to me and I'll make sure that the Sheriff's Department gets an anonymous tip about the truck, and all the rest of the information," said Jolie. "Write it all down carefully, so I get it right."

"Great," said James. "That works, but there was a third man, short, looked like a bulldog – well not literally – you know what I mean.

"So my dreams have something to do with Syrus, something to do with the family and the family estate, like Aunt Martiel told me. I was too stupid to put it all together, until now. There must be some other connection somehow, that's what I'm feeling."

The other dreams didn't connect, as he forced himself to recall their details.

"Why am I always getting pulled to that circle in my dream?"

"A circle? Then that's what we need to focus our efforts on, tying the two sets of events together," said Jolie.

"I think you're right, but I don't see how some great, great, great, great, whatever Uncle Syrus and his past has to do with the other one where I'm dragged by my guts to this circle of candles...," said James.

"Oh," he said holding up the necklace for Jolie to see. "Tell your Aunt BeBe that I think this saved me the other night, in my dream."

"Saved you?" asked Jolie.

"I was at the circle in my dream, there was the same black woman in the white dress, already inside the circle, pulling at me somehow. But I hit the edge of the circle like it was some invisible wall..., she screamed..., and I uh..., I woke up," he sighed, neglecting to tell her of his waking screeches.

"Oh, and when I woke up, I was holding the medallion."

"So this is a spiritual attack, more than a physical attack?" asked Jolie.

"It looked pretty physical to me," said Aunt Martiel.

They both turned to see Martiel walking in through the kitchen door. "Sorry, didn't mean to alarm you."

Now in the kitchen, she refilled her drink, "Mind if I join you?"

Without waiting for either of them to answer, she pulled out a chair and scrunched closer to their huddle.

"James, did you offer Jolie something to drink, or some of your gramma's desert?" she asked.

"No, I guess I didn't think," said James.

"Just something cool to drink would be fine, thank you," said Jolie.

Martiel hurried away from the awkward huddle with her new errand, looking on at their new focus, "What kind of medallion is that, Jolie?"

"I'm not really sure. My Aunt BeBe has had it as long as I can remember. I think she said it was a *King Solomon's Protection*..., something or other. I don't know much about it other than my aunt wears it all the time."

"I think it helped me last night," repeated James.

"That's all well and good, but just the same, we need to find the origin of these particular dreams," said Martiel. "I believe that the ones about Syrus are from..., well..., a good source, but now the dream about the candles and all that..., that's a different story altogether," she finished sipping at her glass of tea and sat down.

Another hour of discussion around the kitchen table and the grandparents' company from the church started leaving.

"Well, I guess that's our sign. I think we have a good plan started," said Martiel. "Jolie will make an anonymous tip to the police...."

"Make sure it's Sheriff Howard you talk to," interrupted James. "I don't trust that deputy."

"We'll examine our family register more closely to see what we can find out about this Syrus Earl Ames character," continued Martiel.

"What about the other grave robberies up in the Natchez cemetery?" asked James. "I keep feeling I'm supposed to find out the names of the people that were taken, to see if they had something to do with this."

"We'll do that first thing tomorrow," said Martiel.

She looked over at Jolie and asked, "Would you ask your Aunt BeBe if she's ever heard of the word *'Baka'* or something that sounds like it?"

"*Baka*", said Jolie. "Where did you hear that word?"

"Oh, it was something James said in his sleep the other night," said Aunt Martiel. "It might not mean anything. By the way Jolie, does your aunt approve of you getting involved with all this? I can't help but feel like it's a bad idea."

"It's..., okay," said Jolie. "I want to help."

Tommy, the huge Siamese, marched in through his door and made a grand entrance, "Yeoll!"

"Guess somebody's hungry," said James standing up to go give him is usual meal of leftovers and cat food.

They all arose and readied to go separate ways.

"Hey, what's up with the cat?" asked James.

Tommy was standing in the middle of the kitchen floor looking up at the ceiling, switching his tail wildly. Growling and varying from ears back and ears forward; he moved his vision toward the hanging light fixture in the center of the ceiling. A few moments later a moth fluttered from the glass cover and began dancing on the ceiling, driving the cat into a wild frenzy.

They all laughed.

"Guess we're all a little bit spooked," said Martiel, hiding the fact that she felt something out of place as well.

No one saw the solemn silhouette of a face withdraw back into the ceiling just beyond the light.

James and Jolie walked outside the house and out on the front lawn.

"You know I really missed you," said James.

"I missed you too," said Jolie. "I..., I don't want anything bad to happen to you, James."

"I don't want anything bad happening either, to me, or anybody I..., care about." he quickly added.

Jolie gave him a quick hug and they started walking up the road.

"You know I always figured that I'd meet someone later on, from the west coast out where my mother lives."

Jolie fell silent gathering her thoughts.

"I never expected to.... I came to live with Aunt BeBe to kind of get my head on straight. I wanted to pick a road, so to speak. Decide what I wanted to do with my life, other than be the keeper of the family journal, that is. I was always so confused, with my parents always fighting, the divorce, and having to bounce all over the place. I only wanted to be a kid, you know?" she said.

"I guess I am only a kid...," she sighed.

There was a short silence while James collected his memories.

"My reasons were a little different for coming here. I was fed up with a lot of things at home. There weren't the open arguments like you had. We had our own personal cold war. It was more about what *wasn't* said than what *was* said, if you know what I mean. Mom was always sad, always seemed alone and empty, both of them hid in their work. My brother Sam's pretty cool, you'd like him, now that he's older, but I was tired of being his dad. We'll probably always be close because of it, but he was always hitting me with the hard questions. The ones that dad should have been there answering, instead of always being gone."

James scooped up a rock from the heated pavement and gave it a toss down the road ahead of them.

"Truth is, it was either come down here or pick a juvenile center as my next home. I was out of hand, and I know that now, my mom could see it, but she didn't know what to do to fix it. My dad pretty much ignored it. Coming here has been the best thing that's ever happened to me. Until now. You're the best thing that's ever happened to me," he said squeezing her hand softly.

He exhaled loudly, having finally found a way to tell Jolie how he felt.

"Now, if I can get rid of the part of me that I don't want…."

Journal – Tuesday, June 21, '77

Just as I suspected. Mom and dad are moving again. To Boston. That's the bad news. The good news is, mom decided to quit work and be a full time parent to Sam. She sounded excited but she also sounded tired.

Gramma said that Boston would be like a fresh start for her and Robert, but how many fresh starts do you need? I hope she's right this time, just the same.

Mom said she could tell something was wrong, but I didn't let her know that my mind was about to explode.

Too much is happening too quick. Too much weird crap is happening, period. There's no way to explain all that's happened to somebody that's never experienced it.

I don't know how much more I can take.

Granny Smith died. My best friend from church.

I don't handle death and funerals very well.

Granny was the only one, other than family, that I could trust with my problems and my soul. I think she had a special relationship with God of some kind. I wish I could have got her to pray this mess away from me. God help me. Someone help me.

My Gramma and Grampa are too old for this stuff. I can't tell them how I feel. They won't know what to do.

Then there's Jolie. Jolie Dimanche. I couldn't bear the thought of anything happening to her. That thing that talked to us from under the tablecloth said that any one that got in its way would be hurt.

I won't let that happen, I can't let that happen.

Her Aunt BeBe was onto something with this necklace thing. Somehow, I think it kept me from going into the circle of candles, in the dream, where that thing, that woman, was pulling me. I'm not sure what would have happened to me if she got me, inside the dream. Would I be dead? Or something worse?

If BeBe was right about that, then maybe she can really help me or find what I need to be free of it.

My dreams are wild now. If that wasn't bad enough, now I'm seeing stuff in broad open daylight. Talking to people I can't see right here in this house.

I feel sometimes like I should just accept it. Tell all the invisible crazies - Here I am! Come get me. Get it over with.

I used to laugh at people that saw ghosts or told tales of spooks and now.... I'm worse than anyone I've ever heard of.

I am so sleepy.

Chapter 23

James woke extra early Wednesday, the dreams, while similar, were less intense. He sat on the side of the bed trying to wake fully. The torment of being chased in his dreams had become his new demon. Constantly being dogged by something barely out of his vision, on the fringe of perception, but always there on his heels. And he was running, ever running…, all night long.

Although the night terror was gone for one night, he worried that paranoia was taking its place. Expectation was driving that runaway cab. It was as if whatever was attacking him was regrouping to come back in a full wave.

James stood and stretched, deciding that waking up tired was a thousand times better than waking up screaming – or not at all.

Aunt Martiel was still sleeping soundly and James looked over at the clock. It was five in the morning.

He quietly got up and managed not to wake her as he made his way from the bedroom, downstairs to the kitchen. After a quick inventory of grocery items, he decided to cook breakfast for Martiel and himself. The list of items in the pantry was better and he managed to put together a simple breakfast of French toast, fried eggs, and coffee.

Martiel needed no invitation as she eventually wandered into the kitchen, smelling food. She was as regular as clockwork and her built in alarm was set to six o'clock every morning.

"Well, I see you've been busy," she said with a yawn. "How was your night?"

"Better, maybe," said James. "I ran all night long in my dreams from something I couldn't see. I even caught myself looking around the corners coming down the stairs this morning and I almost tripped."

"Probably from the lack of sleep," said Aunt Martiel.

"Really weird, too," said James. "It felt as if something grabbed at my ankle."

"Well, you be careful with my favorite great nephew, …who cooks!" she laughed, as she sat down at the table.

For someone that didn't know how, or chose not to cook, Aunt Martiel certainly knew how to eat. It was beyond James how she could stay so slim, but he chalked it up to heredity. All the Ames family were tall, some a little plump, but all of them seemed to have no problem with burning off calories.

"Let's eat while it's hot. Lord knows we've got a busy day today," she sighed. "And you've got to wear your pretty clothes."

They finished up and hurriedly went their separate ways to get ready. James only possessed two suits and rarely had an occasion to wear them. Never had he placed them on his body while living with his parents. There weren't any activities of a formal sort, or informal for that matter. No church to bother with. He might as well have left them at his grandparents' all year long.

One suit was black and reeked of crime family pin striping which James loved, but had outgrown last year. He couldn't pass it on to Sam, as he had almost matched his stature despite being younger.

The other suit was an expensive dark navy Hugo Boss ensemble that his Aunt Martiel had lavished on him during a shopping expedition in Biloxi last summer.

It had been one of her infrequent "need to spend" binges in which "no" was not the acceptable answer. He knew it was too expensive when the tailor taking the measurements couldn't speak English.

"Things don't make the man," sighed James, shrugging into his shirt. "The person inside makes the man."

The jingle of BeBe's medallion brought James full circle from his mental trip of a much happier time in his life. He looked at the necklace as he was dressing. The gold chain was very delicate, and not wanting to take a chance on loosing it, he removed it from his neck. After all, he was going to be at church and awake at the same time. He'd keep his promise to wear it later that night.

One last look in the mirror....

"Are you ready to go?" asked Aunt Martiel.

James opened the door almost immediately after her voice chirped and echoed through the walls.

James was shocked at the lady which stood before him. She was wearing a midnight blue silk suit, pearl earrings and a small string of pearls around her neck as well. Simple but elegantly stunning.

"You look really pretty, Aunt Martiel," said James.

An expensive fragrance emanated from Aunt Martiel reminiscent of soft flowers after rain.

"I've been told I clean up quite well," she said sweetly.

She inspected him for a moment, turning him with a few nudges to his shoulders. "My, but don't you look the handsome young man."

She reached up and pulled a wisp of James' black hair from its perfectly combed array and dropped it just down his forehead.

"That suit fits you like a glove," she said, marveling at her own handiwork. "Now that we're through admiring each other, we need to hurry on out of here."

"Hello, Sheriff's Office, how may I direct your call?"

"Yes, I need to talk to Sheriff Howard, please," said a small childlike voice.

"His phone line is busy, can I direct you to the Chief Deputy or one of his other duty officers?" asked Jeanette, the desk clerk.

"No, I need to speak to the sheriff directly, it's about the grave robberies," the little voice urged.

"Can I take your name and number and have him call you?" asked the clerk.

"No, thank you, but I'll be glad to hold as long as you need me to," said the small voice.

Jeanette was waving anxiously through her window at the closest suit to come over to the phone. She wrote "information - graves" on a piece of paper and held it up for the first there to see.

"Send it over to my phone," the officer whispered.

"Just a moment and I'll transfer you," said the clerk.

With a few clicks, the call was connected to one of the desks in the cubicle maze right outside of the sheriff's own door.

"How can I help you?"

"Yes, is this Sheriff Howard?" asked the childlike voice again.

"No, this is his deputy, how can I help you?"

"I only wish to speak to the sheriff...," the voice repeated once again.

"I'm sorry, the sheriff is on his line at the moment, can I have your name and number, and I'll be sure to have him call you?"

"No, thank you, I'll call back later," the voice whined obviously growing tired.

"Who is this?" asked the deputy again.

There was silence.

"Is this a prank call?" he asked, his patience waning.

"My name is not important, but the information I have is," said the voice as if reading.

Jeanette heard some of the conversation and made her way to the window of the sheriff to get his attention. He hurriedly finished his call with the Mayor and walked to the door.

The clerk explained the situation about the same time the sheriff looked over the cube wall at his deputy.

"Who is this?" barked the deputy belligerently.

The sheriff was suddenly in front of his desk, extracting the receiver from the deputy's shaking hand.

"Sheriff Howard speaking...."

"Yes, thank goodness," said the little voice, smaller than before. "I have information about the grave robberies that you should know."

The sheriff couldn't discern whether the caller was a male or female, but it was obviously a child.

"One moment please," said the sheriff.

"Transfer this call to my desk please," he told the deputy.

"I'm going to put you on hold for only a second and I'll take your call in my office, please don't hang up."

The sheriff walked out of the cubicle as quickly as possible and punched the blinking light on the phone switch in his office.

"Hello, I'm here," said the sheriff. His door clicked shut behind him.

"I have information about the vandalized grave at the Heaven's Gate Cemetery, Sheriff Howard," said the voice.

"Why don't you come in and give us a statement? I don't have time for prank calls and I warn you if this is a prank call it is a serious o-ffense."

"I assure you this in not a prank call," repeated the voice tiredly. "Do you have a pencil?"

The sheriff fumbled with a pen and pad and said to go ahead.

"There is a big four by four truck in town, completely covered in mud, with these last four numbers on its license plate, a Mississippi license plate."

He scribbled the numbers down hastily and repeated the numbers back to the voice.

"You will find two young teenaged boys, one wearing a white baseball cap on his head," continued the tiny voice. "The truck was so caked with mud I couldn't tell what kind it was, but you will find all the evidence you need inside the truck and the mud on their tools in the back should be the same as the grave."

"If this is true, then why didn't you come in and give me this information?"

"The same reason I didn't give you my name, sheriff. You should probably handle this personally, and..., be careful who you tell inside your department, you should watch your back."

"Thank you...," he muttered.

There was a click before he could finish, and another softer click as he hung up.

Deputy Floyd suddenly had an urgent dispatch to handle and picking up his gear, walked briskly toward the rear door to station parking lot..., not without first drawing the attention of Jeanette and Sheriff Howard.

Howard sat quietly for a moment considering several obvious coincidences of late and finally decided to trust his instincts that this call was legitimate.

He hurried to the dispatch room and requested Allison, his chief dispatcher, to issue an APB on a truck matching the description of the vehicle. He looked out toward the parking lot for Deputy Floyd, intending to give him the partial license plate number to cross with the DMV, but remembering his quick exit, handed it over to another duty officer.

"Radio me *first* if this one turns up; I'll be in my car." v

All the regular church family was assembled at the Holiness Cathedral Church at two o'clock sharp. There were only two adult members of the family present to view the body of one Wema Smith. Her granddaughter Lilly Piers and husband Raymond along with their newborn child.

All the other relatives were either deceased, or too distant to make arrangements in time.

Granny Smith was not at a loss for friends however and the church and churchyard were packed with visitors.

Granny had befriended most everyone that crossed her path and at one time or another had turned a helping hand and a listening ear their direction.

The body would remain here in the sanctuary instead of the funeral home per Wema Smith's request and the chapel ceremony would be held inside her personal sanctuary, her church of nearly 60 years.

Funerals mortified James and gave him the creeps, but he had been charged with the duty of door greeter as well as the visitors' log book, per his friend Granny Smith's request.

Dressed in his finest, he reluctantly accepted his job. The only funerals he had attended growing up were from relatives that he barely knew. This would be radically different.

His first misperception had been expecting a small quiet gathering of pious observers around a dead body. What actually transpired was a vast amount of people and cars crowding around the church house, full of life and chatter.

There were several hundred people of all walks of life, that signed the visitors book and most every one felt compelled to tell a short little tale to James of how they knew Wema Smith, or Granny Smith, or Ms. Smith, or just plain Granny.

In those two short hours he received more of a lesson in dedication to God, than he had his entire life of going to church. He heard stories of *miracles*, of visions, of prayers…; a lifetime of service to what her faith meant to most all of the people that she met.

By four o'clock that afternoon he was exhausted, but filled with hope over his own situation.

There was hope. He felt it, somehow knew it. His view of church and its real meaning outside the church walls seemed to fall into place.

Swelling with buoyancy, he knew it was time to schedule a visit to see the pastor of this church where Granny Smith attended these many years; not to mention his grandparents. After all, if half of what he'd heard about Granny Smith was true, then maybe there was something more to this business of church.

After most of the visitors and help had dissipated from the church grounds, he made his way to find the pastor. He wasn't readily available because he was counseling a couple of members in the church at that moment.

He found his own family members and helped with arranging different items and preparing the place for a vigil over the body for that night. There were several volunteers and many wanted to stay and visit as the all night watch proceeded. There was a mass of food provided in the kitchen for anyone that wished to stay.

After an hour or so, the pastor emerged from his office and a young couple walking behind him exited by the side door.

James made his way over to the pastor to catch him before he was reeled into a conversation.

"Pastor Smith," said James.

"Yes," said the Minister. "How can I help you?"

"Oh, Lord," thought James. "What in the world do I tell him?"

"I…, I was wondering if you might have a few minutes to help me with some things that are…, bothering me personally?" asked James, not knowing how to proceed.

"Why, I'd be glad to," said the Minister. "If you'll see the clerk and fill out an appointment card, I'll make sure that I…," the pastor rambled on.

"Well…," James said cutting him off. "I really wanted to speak to you today…, now, if I could. It's sort of important. I promise I won't take up much of your time."

"In case you haven't noticed, there's a funeral yet to prepare, and several details to be attended to," said the pastor changing his tone. "I'd be glad to see you as soon as all this settles down. I've rescheduled all my appointments until after the funeral Thursday afternoon, so probably Monday or Tuesday next week would most likely be available."

"I understand," said James, frustrated. "I'll get a card and fill it out, thanks."

James walked away deflated and a little disappointed. He couldn't remember a single time that Granny Smith turned him away when he was having a problem, but the pastor was right after all, this was Granny's time to be remembered.

The pastor walked outside and mingled with some of the staunch members, which were lingering on the church lawn.

James walked back over to Gramma Ames and Aunt Martiel as they stood stuffing bottled soft drinks into several ice chests. James made sure that they wouldn't notice any difference in his attitude and quickly pitched in to help.

"Couldn't we find some of the other *fine church members* to help with all this?" asked Martiel suddenly.

Maime Ames flushed, cutting her an eye, and changed the subject accordingly.

"I was really moved to see such a good turnout for Granny Smith," said Maime Ames. "If I didn't know better I'd say that the entire community showed up."

"How many signatures made it into the register, James?" asked Martiel, picking up on the chill in the air between the two women.

"About 246, the last time I looked," answered James. "Most of the visitors have left."

James walked over to get another pack of soft drinks, turned and slipped on a handful of ice on the tile floor.

His feet went up, his head went down.

All went black.

Quiet.

"James…," said a soft voice floating from somewhere distant and quiet, peaceful.

"James, can you hear me?" the voice echoed again.

Lights started flickering in his field of vision and a thumping sound erupting in his ears. A cool moist cloth covered his forehead. It felt great. He thought he'd go back to sleep….

"James…," said the voice booming and amplified this time. "Are you with us?"

James opened one eye to a bright light and squinted it back shut with pain.

"What happened?" James whispered hoarsely.

"Just lie still…," said Maime. "You took a little spill, but you're going to be okay."

James quickly remembered what happened and groaned.

"How stupid," said James. The sound of his own voice rang like a bell in his head. "I slipped on ice…."

"It was only an accident," said Aunt Martiel. "It could happen to anybody."

An hour of stiffening his posture and declaring that he was fine did not persuade his family to believe him.

"I think you should at least see a doctor," said Martiel. "You could have a fracture or concussion. Would you let me take you?"

"I don't think I need to, I really don't want to," said James.

If there was anything that James disliked more than funerals, it was hospitals.

Ten minutes later he was planted in the passenger seat of Aunt Martiel's BMW, in route to the hospital in Natchez.

Jolie had spent all afternoon helping bus tables at The Cajun Café. She rehearsed plans to attend the funeral of James' long time friend Granny Smith and her mind was scattered over several subjects.

The main thought on her mind was James Earl Williams. How his black hair flipped to one side and always managed to get in the way of one of his bright green eyes. The way he *really* looked at her when he talked to her, like he could see right through her. Just who was this James Earl Williams with his strong arms, nice legs, nice….

Abruptly, she had a feeling of vertigo and had to grab a chair and sit down.

"You okay?" asked Aunt BeBe, noticing her from across the room.

"Yeah, I think so. I got dizzy for a second. Don't worry, I don't think it was the food," she said grinning. "I'm better now."

"Why don't you go clean up and take the rest of the evening off?" asked Aunt BeBe. "You've had enough excitement today. Did you get any sleep last night?"

"Not much, I guess," said Jolie. "I'm still worried about James."

"You were pretty quiet last night coming home," said BeBe. "You fell asleep before we got five miles down the road. Jolie…, listen to me sweetheart. I know you're old enough to make your own decisions and I don't really have a right to tell you what to do, but do you think getting involved with James is a good idea right now? That boy isn't going to run off anywhere."

"I think so," said Jolie defensively. "I mean, I believe I'm supposed to do something because of my dreams about him. Three nights in a row, I had the same dream, right up until the day I met him at the library. Right where I dreamed it would happen. You're the one that explained to me how dreams work."

"You know you don't have to get involved don't you?" asked Aunt BeBe.

"I don't know if I want to talk about this any more," said Jolie standing up.

BeBe sighed. Her niece already had it bad. She couldn't blame her. James was a looker, nothing like the local scrawny boys that followed Jolie around like honey bees.

"Okay, okay, sit down and relax. If you feel that strongly about it, I won't stop you, but at least let me help."

Forbidding her to see James would only push her away, at a time she really needed to vent to someone.

"Did you find out anything else about what's vexing James?"

"We managed to put a few things together," said Jolie hesitantly. "James had a vision of who robbed his great Uncle Syrus' grave."

"He had a vision?!" asked BeBe. "There is a lot more to that boy than I thought. How come you haven't talked to me about this?"

Jolie stared at her twiddling feet in silence and BeBe let her question pass.

"So did you find out enough to make sense out of any of it?"

"We wrote down all the details and decided to turn it over to the police," said Jolie. "I bribed one of the neighborhood kids give the County Sheriff an anonymous phone call. I was listening in…. I think James might be right. There *is* something wrong about that deputy. He didn't only try to hog the call before the sheriff answered; he got really hot. I know I wouldn't take a chance on losing a good tip because of my temper and it was almost like he wanted us to hang up. He really wanted to know who it was that was calling."

"Is that what your instinct is telling you or your feelings for James is telling you?" asked Aunt BeBe.

Jolie huffed out a breath, glancing up at her aunt's probing eyes, "I don't know. I'm a little cloudy on that subject."

"So I noticed," said Aunt BeBe.

BeBe had to hide her grin. This girl was head over heels and didn't even know it. She sure knew how to pick 'em.

"I almost forgot…," said Jolie. "His Aunt Martiel said she overheard James talking in his sleep during one of his nightmares. He said something like *Beka* or *Baka*, but I don't know if I'm saying it right. She wanted to know if you had ever heard of anything like that."

Aunt BeBe's face turned a lighter shade of its usual soft olive hue as she stared off into the distance.

"*Baka*…, are you sure?" asked Aunt BeBe.

Her hands were suddenly concerned with her long dark hair, clearing it from her face.

"Yeah, that sounds right, what's wrong? You know what that means don't you?"

"That could be bad, Jolie…, really bad," said her aunt. "I'm sure it would be better if you didn't see too much of James until this is all sorted out."

"What are you talking about?" asked Jolie. "I realize I've only known him a few days, but I feel like I've known him all my life. Besides, you already know how I feel about him, I want to help him any way that I can."

"Jolie…," said Aunt BeBe quietly. "A '*Baka*' is a demon sent by a dark voodoo priest or priestess…. It's like a *hound of hell* they can send out to do almost anything they tell it."

BeBe paused at Jolie's rounded eyes, wondering if she should tell her more. No, Jolie had to know all the facts.

"A *Baka* can track a person down, drive a person crazy, or…."

"Or WHAT?" asked Jolie. "Finish what you were saying, please."

"If the person sending it out is powerful enough…, it can kill a person."

"How do you know about this stuff?" asked Jolie. "I've never heard you talk about anything like this before."

"Speak of the devil…. It's best that it's never mentioned," said Aunt BeBe her voice still in hushed tones. "A *Bokor* can turn most anything into pure evil. Rumor is…, they can even tell when someone is talking about them.

"Voodoo is like most any other religion, with people that do good and some that do bad things with their know-how. The ones that are good don't really mix with the ones that use the dark arts. In fact, most of these that dabble in the dark arts don't mix with anybody. They're pretty much loners, guarding their secrets with their life."

"Aunt BeBe, this doesn't make any sense at all," said Jolie. "I'm inclined to side with James on this one. Voodoo is…, well that really doesn't fit. James may have been born here in Natchez, but he hasn't lived here since he was two or three years old. He's lived his whole life over a thousand miles away. How could he get on some witch doctor's hit list?"

"It could be a family thing," said Aunt BeBe. "Are you sure his aunt said *Baka?*"

Jolie silently nodded her head.

"You at least need to warn James and his Aunt Martiel. They need to know they could be in real danger. After that, I want you to keep your distance for a while…, and that is not a request young lady, it's an order. You can still be his eyes and ears, Honey."

"You're scaring me, Aunt BeBe. Please tell me that we can help him. You make it all sound like something awful has already happened to him."

"We'll sort this out," said BeBe. "There's always the chance that that his Aunt heard wrong, or he was only dream mumbling. In any case, you can help him better from a distance right now. If you get that boy's heart all distracted, he might be in worse danger."

The doctor flicked the light pen into and out of James' eyes repeatedly checking for equal dilation and response times. Then he checked for various other anomalies with the motor functions of the body. As most doctors do, he then disappeared for the next twenty minutes to some hidden sub-chamber, deep in the bowels of the hospital building, probably the bathroom.

Taking the x-rays of his head had seemed like some medieval torture chamber and now he sat alone in the freezing examination room, which reinforced his loathing of hospitals.

"It looks like you're going to live," said a calm reassuring voice as the doctor walked through the door.

"You do have a mild concussion, but the x-ray shows no fracture and there's no apparent swelling, so I'm going to let you go home. I want you to take it easy, get some rest, no more acrobatics."

He scribbled some indecipherable gibberish onto a piece of paper and handed it to James.

"This is a prescription for the headache you're going to have later tonight and tomorrow. If you have any problems, especially tonight, come back up here to see me or one of my emergency staff."

"Great, Drugs…," thought James sarcastically.

A nurse tapped on the door and motioned to let the doctor know he was needed elsewhere immediately.

"Thanks, Doc," said James as he walked out the door, more out of politeness than genuine appreciation.

He met Aunt Martiel out in the waiting room and complained as much as possible that the trip was totally unnecessary.

Aspirin and rest. He heard the same thing at football practice when one of the guys got hit and thought he could fly and ultimately discovered that he couldn't land any better than he could fly.

"Says here you should stay awake for at least the next 6 or 8 hours," said Aunt Martiel. "And this prescription is a far cry from aspirin. In any case, I have to go back to the church and help Maime. Now do you want to stay at the old house or go with me?"

"Go with you. If I go to the old house and take any of these, I'll be passed out and we both know what that means. God, my head already hurts."

"Lets get out of here, okay? We'll stop by the pharmacy and get you fixed up."

James started for the emergency room parking lot without another word.

"I'll take you by the estate and let you change clothes first…, at least you can be comfortable," she offered.

"I got my suit dirty," said James, sounding like a kid caught in a mud puddle with his school clothes on.

"We can get your clothes cleaned, for that matter we can get more clothes, but we can't get another you," she said, leaning over and hugging him up close.

Chapter 24

Sheriff Howard spent most of the afternoon driving around, thinking over so many different thoughts. To be a good leader you have to be aware of your team. Their needs, strengths, weaknesses, even personal problems. You have to know what pushes every button they have and which ones you can use and which *never* to push.

Sheriff Howard could only remember one or two other times that he felt as uninformed or unable to come to any conclusions about their caseload and his present resources.

He had left the downtown area of the city, ending up trolling through *Natchez Under-the-Hill.* There were a few bars and assorted colorful tourist attractions next to the river which usually attracted a more eclectic clientele. A riverboat was docked close by, accepting passengers for an all night excursion up the Mississippi.

It was getting late and the butter spot of sun was almost set. He told himself that he was going on a hunch, but actually he had covered almost all the surrounding area and this tourist area was all that was left.

It was like the joke that whatever you are looking for is always in the last place that you look for it.

"Where oh where has my little dog gone..., oh where, oh where, can he b...," the sheriff was mockingly singing a nursery song quietly to himself when he saw it.

Parked in front of a place called the "Oar House" was a muddy truck that looked like *Southern Fried Chicken.* Dipped in grease and rolled in batter.

"You'd have to hang your head out the window like a dog just to steer this thing," he thought.

He pulled past slowly to look at the plates. Impossible. They were completely mud caked. Nobody could read that.

At least that was a violation worthy of a citation that he could question the driver for and have himself a better look.

Instead of waiting for the driver to appear, he chose the shortest distance between two points and parked behind the truck. The closer he walked to the massive 4x4 vehicle, the bigger it appeared. The mud coating seemed to make it loom larger than life.

It looked to be a modified short bed Chevy..., about a 1970 model. Color? Only God could tell at this point.

He spit on his finger and made a swipe on the side of the truck which yielded..., a muddy swipe. He went back to his squad car and took out a paper napkin and revisited his muddy swipe. The previous attempt had dried into a smooth finger painted goo.

Scrubbing with the napkin, he cleared the spot to reveal rust brown primer paint. He tried another spot on the side of the hood..., dark blue. At least he had one real color.

He hurried back to the license plate and made a few half hearted attempts at clearing it off. The last three digits were..., PHR. He looked at his notepad - 4PHR.

He vigorously cleaned off the remainder of the plate and wrote down the entire number and stood from his crouch. How should he handle this?

If he waited for backup, the person could see him and run. He wasn't as young as he used to be, even though he was no slouch.

He chose his second option.

With his vehicle parked out of conspicuous sight of the front of the bar, the truck was still in plain sight. The sheriff then called in the complete license plate number for the owner information.

After what seemed like an eternity, dispatch called him back and informed him that the vehicle belonged to a Jeremiah Foster. It was registered as a 1966 Ford Fairlane - reported stolen.

With stolen plates, it was a good guess that the truck it was attached to was also.

Another five short minutes later, a Caucasian male, by his looks about 21 years old, shoulder length brown hair, thin as a scarecrow and wearing a stained white baseball cap, exited the front door of the Oar House.

As he was walking out, an older woman obviously very drunk grabbed him around the neck and gave him a drunk hug and a kiss on the side of his pale patchy face.

Everything fit except that the informant said his suspect was a teenaged kid.

He got out of his squad car, deciding that he would take the chance that the young man would be too drunk to bolt and run.

"Excuse me sir. Are you the owner of this vehicle?"

"Whoo wans t' know?" asked the kid yanking his key back out of the truck door lock.

The sheriff brought up his flashlight to the young man's face and discovered that he was obviously younger than first believed.

"I'm Sheriff Howard - Adams County. I need to see your license and registration for this vehicle."

"Shnot mine," said the kid turning around to walk away.

"I need to see your drivers' license all the same," argued the sheriff.

About that time, the kid glanced over his shoulder, hoping for an exit. He jumped off to the right..., at least in his mind he did. He hit the ground with the grace of a sack of potatoes.

"Don' hit me agin'," whined the kid, crouching. "I won' run."

"You're drunk sir, and you fell," grinned Howard. "The ground hit you, not me. Now that you're comfortable, can I see your driver's license, please?"

"Yeah…, lemme sit up," the kid said reaching around to his back pocket. "Didn' know there wuz a law ginst havin' a good time…."

The sheriff took one look at the license and almost laughed aloud, but being the professional that he was, he managed to keep it inside as they were starting to attract a crowd.

"Jimmy, whad-ju-do?" someone yelled from the gathering. "You been messing around in ole man Carter's junk yard again?

The group laughed a good drunk chorus of laughter. This was a good thing. At least the kid was a regular at this watering hole and some of these regulars would know him.

The drivers' license revealed the picture of a middle-aged black man by the name of Jimmy Brown.

The sheriff took his time arresting the young man he estimated to be 17 or 18 years of age, name unknown, for drunk and disorderly, …for starters.

The crowd dispersed after he had *Jimmy Brown* comfortably handcuffed and seated in the back of his cruiser. In only a few moments the boy's head was propped against the window, mouth wide open dispensing drool and fast asleep.

He walked back over to the truck and climbed up into the bed using the two-step trailer hitch. The inside bed of the truck was strewn with junk, a few rusty truck parts, a couple of obviously dead batteries and some tools.

There were a couple of shovels and a pickaxe, all of which were heavy with a thick coating of caked clay-like soil.

In about fifteen minutes the truck would be on its way to the county impound and Sheriff Howard guarded it while waiting for the tow truck to arrive.

He also made a call to a friend at the Liquor Control Board and gave them an anonymous tip that the "Oar House" was serving alcohol to underage clients.

It was shaping up to be the end of a good day, and it was about time for some good press in the Natchez Gazette.

Chapter 25

The Ames family arrived about fifteen minutes early for their watchful duty at the church. Their part in the all night vigil over the body of Wema Smith was from eight until ten o'clock that evening. There were several church members that would be there most all night to play cards or dominos and help the others not fall asleep.

It was a type of 'wake', but the church didn't like the idea of labeling it as such.

History had proven, it wasn't unheard of to find out that someone who was thought to be dead wasn't actually finished living.

The not-so-professional medical community of earlier years didn't notice any vital signs of a weak heart. So to make sure the dearly departed was actually dead, the person was laid out, usually at home while friends and family would gather around, and then wait to see if the person would 'wake' up.

No one expected to see Granny Smith sit up like some ghost story around a campfire on Halloween, but out of respect and love, scores of people volunteered. She would have liked the gathering.

James was bored beyond sanity and looking for any excuse to walk outside about every ten or fifteen minutes. The clock on the wall had gone on strike and wasn't moving in its typical fashion.

Basically, he was stuck.

When he sat, he became sleepy, when he walked his head pounded, despite the prescribed pain relievers.

Bottle of cold Coke in hand, he walked outside into the steamy night air. Summer was well on its way. It would soon be time to start relying on the air conditioning to hold back the heat like the levee along the banks of the Mississippi River.

He perched on the front steps of the church near the bottom and watched the occasional car drive by and a neighborhood cat moving stealthily from house to house in search of some feline treasure.

There was a gentle breeze pushing the sparsely mossy trees around and from the looks of the sky, there would be another bright moon tonight.

He thought of Jolie and wanted to call her, to see her.

"*Mr. Intelligent*," he groaned internally.

He should have taken door number two and stayed at the old mansion and spent his time in forced isolation on the phone with Jolie.

He attributed his fatal error in judgment to the smack on the head he received a couple of hours earlier. God, it even hurt to think. He popped it really good.

Somewhere in the warm night air, soft tinkling laughter drifted toward him, quiet and inviting. James thought of his encounter at the old Ames estate and shuddered.

He carefully rose from the church house steps and walked back inside the church, plopping down near his grandmother.

She was busy helping part out snacks for the few steadfast members about to start another round of some card game.

She quit the rigor of her chore and sat back close to James.

"How's my boy?" she asked, hugging him close.

James leaned his head over on her soft shoulder and breathed out. There was comfort from merely the touch of love. James recognized it and wished again for the presence of his mother. He sat up when he realized that in those few seconds, the comfort of her touch had almost lulled him off to sleep.

"Love you, gramma," he mumbled while getting up. "Almost dozed off."

If the gang back home could see him now.

Tough guy. It finally hit him that that part of his life was officially over and in his past. All that violence would never cross his path ever again. Maybe it really was the separation from the violence that was offering him back his good sense.

"I'm going back outside before I fall asleep," said James.

He wandered back over to the ice chest cautiously and grabbed another cold drink. The familiar burn from the first drink out of the Coke bottle woke him up enough to make one more hour pass.

He made his way back to the bottom step outside and finally another slow trip around the church grounds. The thick St. Augustine lawn was evenly cut and looked like expensive carpet.

James was tempted to take off his shoes and walk barefoot as he remembered doing when he was a little kid. With the humidity high, the dew was beginning to fall and his shoes and pants cuffs were getting wet.

The few streetlights cast slowly moving shadows on the ground in time with the slight breeze. Why couldn't his whole life be this simple and easy?

He heard that same soft sound again, but this time it didn't sound like laughter, it was more sighing or moaning. Only for a moment before it drifted away quickly as it came.

Was there someone in trouble or pain? His instincts came alive and he began to pay attention.

He looked around the neighborhood at the few houses. Most all had already turned out the lights for the evening.

Nothing was stirring, nothing but peaceful quiet and the steady murmur of the occupants inside the church house.

Was it those damnable gifts acting up again and letting him hear some specter? This was not the place he wanted to see spooks, so near the Heaven's Gate Cemetery. Even the mere thought of seeing some unknown at a graveyard made him cringe and turn away.

He settled back down to his rambling thoughts when he heard another sigh and soft muffled whimpering scream, and again, and again. Then silence.

Every night bug had ceased in their incessant chirping.

There was nothing but continued silence. He saw nothing, sensed nothing, and relaxed again. It had to be his imagination. Some over active tree limbs were probably screeching against one another in the night breeze.

Whatever it was, he had made up his mind he didn't want any part of it.

His feet turned and walked slowly back in the direction of the front of the church. It was a quick motion seen out of the corner of his eye that stopped him; a dark figure moved in the distance. Silently it moved, from one shadow to the next, starting and stopping, standing still.

Someone, prowling around the church grounds. He stepped quickly toward the spot where he last saw movement.

The shadow darted and sped up along the grassy edge of an alleyway and disappeared. He walked on over to where the person or whatever it was had been standing. There were impressions in the grass. The "whatever" was definitely a person, unless ghosts left small footprints. It was probably some kid out past curfew.

He turned quickly to go back and report his findings to anyone interested when he heard a loud…, Thump.

He saw speckled lights in front of his eyes and was on his knees for a few moments before reality set in. Now he knew first hand what he'd always heard about seeing stars.

A low hanging tree limb jutting out in the darkness caught him right on the forehead.

He stood back up as quick as he could manage, stunned for a moment and understood how vulnerable he was standing out back of the church in the dark with some prowler lurking about.

What an idiot.

His head was pounding like a hammer, his eyes bleary from a steady drip of uncontrolled tears.

He remembered the speech that different coaches told him back in school. If you get two or more concussions back to back, you might end up in a wheel chair with somebody feeding you with a spoon and wiping your butt for you.

The visual from memory lane made him want to go lie down and forget this entire day ever happened.

He walked carefully back to the front steps and made his way back inside. After depositing his soft drink bottle into an empty carton, he quickly brushed the dew and grass clippings off the knees of his pants.

He decided not to tell anybody about his encounter with the prowler or the bump on the head. His head hurt enough without spending the next thirty minutes repeating all that transpired, especially with the possibility of another trip to the hospital.

He stepped inside and walked over to the card table where some of the older people were visiting.

"James!" said Aunt Martiel excitedly. "Your head is bleeding."

Chapter 26

Martin Earl Ames eased out of bed Thursday and after his morning duties moved quietly to the front porch to retrieve the daily newspaper. He folded it under his arm and smelled the aroma of his wife's coffee already brewing in the kitchen. A fresh steaming cup was waiting for him on the table when he sat down.

Martin recalled the past night's adventures at the church and shook his head.

He took a sip of hot coffee and opened up the newspaper to the front page.

Natchez Gazette
Thursday Edition

"Suspect Arrested in connection with Grave Robberies"

He nearly dropped his coffee cup in his lap.

"Look here Maime," said Martin. "They caught one of those hooligans that stole Syrus from his grave. That moves Sheriff Howard back up a notch or two on the respect scale. Maybe now they can wrap up that whole business and get everything back to normal."

Martin scanned the page with a frown, "Why..., he's only a kid, it says he's only about eighteen years old! They don't know his real name..., and they put his picture here in the paper hoping that someone will come forward and identify him."

"Did they put the piece on Wema Smith in there about her funeral today?" asked Maime.

"Yep, it's right here on page three. They did a nice write up about her life, but...."

He rattled the paper and frowned angrily, "They mentioned that an anonymous donor paid for all the funeral expenses. I wonder who leaked that out? In any case, a good article might bring a few more people back to the church."

"You know why those few left, they told us plain and simple, the new pastor wasn't their cup of tea," said Maime. "They liked Pastor Baskin's style better, he was older, and they related to him better, that's all."

"I liked the old pastor better too, but he deserved to get to spend his

last days with his kids," said Martin. "A lifetime of service is admirable....
I don't know if I'd have that kind of dedication to give up that much time
from the family. I do wish the board could have taken more time to select
a better candidate for a replacement."

He dropped the paper and took another sip of his coffee, "Speaking of
kids, why haven't we heard from Catherine or Robert lately?"

"It's probably because they're still in the process of moving to Boston,"
she answered.

"Moving to Boston? Didn't they just get settled in that other little
town?"

"I must have forgotten to tell you," sighed Maime. "James told me that
Robert got another 'promotion'. Catherine is supposed to be quitting her
job and staying home."

"We've heard that before," grumbled Martin.

"Just the same, if it's true, it'll be good for Sam," said Maime. "It would
have been good for James too. Maybe he wouldn't have had so many
problems."

"You can't change the past, Maime. Catherine loves those two boys and
that's what matters. Besides..., James is turning out to be a fine young
man. All that anger and hostility disappeared since he started coming here
to stay with us. He never gives me a moment's grief."

"You're right, he's a different boy when he's here," said Maime. "And
since he's staying on, I think all of that trouble is in the past. I sure wish all
this other confusion would go away. It's like a curse. That's what Granny
Smith said the other day before she...."

Maime lowered her head, "I'm really going to miss her. She took to
James like one of her own...," she said staring off into space.

"Oh my, Martin..., she wanted to talk to James. I forgot to tell him and
I took it for granted that she'd simply be there the next service and she
could talk to him herself. You know, she started telling me that James
needed to stay far away the law officers, and that was right about the same
time he got that ticket."

"Started telling you?" asked Martin.

"We were interrupted or something, I don't remember," said Maime.

"It's time we got ready to go pay our last respects," Martin said standing
up. "I think all the arrangements are taken care of and everybody got paid,
I only need to make a few other calls to make sure. I don't want her grand
daughter and family to worry about any expenses."

Chapter 27

Vidalia, Louisiana. Historical home place and port to explorers such as Hernando De Soto, traders, and pirates the caliber of no less than Jean Lafitte. Prosperity also inevitably attracts connoisseurs of deception and thievery. The scales of justice are an everlasting teeter-totter to this effect.

This morning a cool breeze, naturally moist from the rising humidity of the Mississippi River, was blowing gently over Vidalia's sleeping inhabitants. The sun would soon peek over the River Cities Bridge only a couple of miles from where Jolie and her aunt lived.

A few hundred yards away was their nearest neighbor - an abandoned home place of about five years. The obvious malady for its vacancy was primarily the fault of the previous owners.

It was told that on a particular spring outing, the family went a few miles north up the river to camp and fish. While there, the youngest daughter found a peculiar vine with beautiful green scalloped leaves, with equally brilliant flowers about to blossom. She pulled a handful of the vines from the ground and brought them home and planted them against the trellis by the front door.

She was later to learn that the hearty vine was named Kudzu, which had been imported from Asia in the 1800's.

By the time the family learned exactly how hearty this vine was, it had already established itself as a part of the landscape.

Gasoline and motor oil served only as fertilizer to this alien invader. Eventually they moved for reasons unknown, but the house and the surrounding trees had become a mound of green growing fleshy vine. The trees were now dead from the lack of sunlight, house overrun from many years of neglect.

The place was virtually an uninhabitable snake pit and the perfect place for someone to park a car completely undetected from any one not specifically looking for a trespasser.

This Thursday morning, just such a visitor, made his way silently from the privacy of the overgrowth carrying a small brown paper sack under his arm.

With a quick check to make sure that the inhabitants of this home were still fast asleep, he stealthily made his way to the back of the lone vehicle parked out front.

When the bag was opened a five-pound bag of granulated, refined sugar emerged. In less than three minutes, the intruder was making a hasty retreat back to his means of escape.

All evidence of the visitation, save a few misguided sugar crystals, was gone.

"Why, it's a beautiful day for a funeral," said Aunt Martiel.

"Mmmmpf…" replied James, disgusted.

There was no need for nightmares or specters to do any dirty work in behalf of James. He had become his own worst enemy and his head was a steady reminder to that fact.

"Can you take aspirin for breakfast?" asked James.

"I don't think that's what they were intended for," said Aunt Martiel. "Are you feeling any better?"

"Yeah, I'm better. I got a double portion of stupid yesterday."

"Let's hurry on over to your grandparents' house, so we don't keep them waiting," said Aunt Martiel.

By nine that morning, Martin and Maime Ames had prepared themselves and they were going about their usual daily business. A few necessary calls to various church members and one last call to make sure that the gravesite had been readied at Heaven's Gate Cemetery for the graveside service of Wema Smith.

James and his Aunt Martiel had made their way over to the Ames residence. Jolie and her aunt were to rendezvous with them at around noon that day before the afternoon service.

At 10:00 AM, the phone rang and a distraught BeBe was apologizing that they were not going to be able to make an appearance at the funeral.

"I don't understand what could have happened to my car," said BeBe. "I had to go by the café this morning to make sure everything was running smooth before we left. I went back out to the car and it wouldn't crank. It's practically brand new and I take it for regular maintenance."

"I'm sure that Martin or James would be glad to look at it for you," said Maime Ames. "There's plenty of time before we have to be at the church for the funeral."

James overheard the conversation and was showing his teenage enthusiasm at the option of seeing Jolie, going to check on the car, or bringing them over to the his grandparent's house.

"James says he would be glad to come and pick you up if you like," said Maime Ames.

Martin Earl waved a passive hand in the air and spoke toward his wife and the telephone, "I can get the tow truck and bring her car to the garage."

"I don't expect you to put yourself out for us," said BeBe. "I can get somebody local to…."

"Nonsense," Maime Ames interrupted. "Martin's been a mechanic for as long as I can remember. They'll be there within the hour...."

BeBe Cavalier reluctantly agreed to let them come and rescue her vehicle.

"They seem like such nice people," said Maime looking at James.

Aunt Martiel shook her head and chided her nephew, "James, are you sure you feel like driving after yesterdays' ordeal?"

"I'd be shocked if he didn't have a miraculous recovery at the chance to see Jolie," said Martin hiding a grin.

"You did seem a little anxious James, is there something we should know?" asked Maime.

James stood open mouthed and disgruntled, unwilling to offer them any more ammunition to fling his direction.

"Come on, let's get on over to the shop and get the tow truck. I don't want to have to be cleaning up greasy fingers ten minutes before the service," said Martin.

James was glad that he didn't have to answer their questions and hastily walked toward the door shaking his head.

"Don't you think you should make a quick change of clothes before you leave?" asked Maime.

"You should probably take your car, James," said Martin. "If that car of hers is broke, they sure won't like it if they have to ride back in our smelly tow truck with their good clothes on."

"One more time..., what's your name boy!" demanded the sheriff. The skinny young man looked dumbly back at him as if he were completely alone in the room. In fact, he looked as relaxed as he did when he left the bar mere hours earlier.

"Am I gettin' through to you, son?" piped the sheriff, waving his hands in front of the kid's face.

"We matched the mud caked on the tools inside your truck to the mud from that grave you dug up over east of town."

The boy remained calmly silent.

"We found splinters from the wood of the casket in the toe of your boot."

Still he only stared blankly.

"Who's your buddy that helped you?"

"What did you do with the remains?"

The boy's eyes were fixed in a dead stare as if no one was home inside his troubled head.

There was no reaction to the sheriff's antics, but he slowly tilted his head to the side as if listening to some beautiful music off in a far away place.

Sheriff Howard threw up his hands in desperation, "I think this boy's all doped up or something."

The court appointed attorney shuffled to get in direct line of sight of the boy and spoke very calmly, "It will be better for you if you cooperate and let them know who you are. You're charged with a felony and they're going to try you as an adult. Unless you snap out of it and help me, you could take all the blame for this mess you've got yourself into."

The attorney looked away in disgust, "I've called for a doctor to come examine him. The boy doesn't look right."

Sheriff Howard parked his chair back under the table and hurried to the door, "I think we should put him back in a cell and let him sit there until we find out if he's messed up on drugs or not. This is getting us nowhere."

The Sheriff's Deputy was eagerly watching from outside the porthole window of the interrogation room door.

When the sheriff opened the door, he motioned for the attorney and one of the attending officers to escort the kid back to a holding cell.

Deputy Floyd stood silently by the door as they made their way past. The young man shuffled along dumbly and didn't offer as much as glance in his direction.

Looking over at the clerk the sheriff asked, "Did you get anything back on those fingerprints and photos yet?"

"A big fat zero so far," she replied. "He doesn't exist, no record in this state, but I've sent everything to our neighboring states."

"Good work. We might try running his picture by the Oar House and ask the locals."

"Well, I could send a couple of our men out there, but the Oar House has been shut down..., temporarily lost their operators license," said the clerk.

"Yeah, that's right," said the sheriff, his face flushing slightly. "Those same people have to get tanked up somewhere..., there're lots of places in the vicinity."

"We might have got some information out of those folks last night, but there was nobody available to take statements. After our suspect got his picture in the paper and all..., well..., they might not be as willing to talk, you know?" the clerk commented sheepishly. She didn't need to remind the sheriff that they were undermanned for the amount of territory they had to cover.

Floyd sat quietly nearby, throughout the entire process between the sheriff and his clerk Jeanette.

"Pull a couple of our duty officers in here before noon..., I want to have a quick meeting and bounce some ideas off them."

The clerk obediently walked over to the little closed room where the dispatch operator was attentively making entries in a logbook. A large reel-to-reel tape unit was slowly turning in the background. She barked an occasional comment into a microphone to an unseen recipient; mostly informal chatter at that moment.

Jeanette quietly closed the door behind her and sat down in the only chair in the cramped space of the radio dispatcher's office. After a few seconds, the dispatcher dissolved her trance and gave Jeanette her full attention.

Allison hated working dispatch and was extremely close-minded at having visitors in her tiny workplace. She had gone to an upstate police academy, placed in the top ten in her class, been accepted on the police force, got transferred to her hometown of Natchez, and was immediately shuffled away in a closet as dispatcher.

"A woman's job," to quote the sheriff, "and she has a nice clear voice."

"I swear…, that sheriff hasn't got a live brain cell in that head of his."

Jeanette's voice trailed off when she saw Allison's expression.

"Do you have something new for me or are we going to rehash our usual conversation about this place?" asked Allison sarcastically.

She handed Allison a note requesting two available officers in the field to report in for a noon meeting and special assignment.

"This ought to be good," Allison said, after reading the note.

"If we could only record it and sell it to one of those sit-coms on the television," said Jeanette.

They both laughed, lightening Jeanette's expression and mood at the same time.

"I've never seen someone so adept at shooting himself in the foot with his own revolver," grinned Jeanette. "Just be glad you're in here away from the insanity at my front desk."

"You forget, it all passes through me and my log book eventually," said Allison.

"And that deputy…? He gives me the willies," said the clerk with a shiver.

"Which one…? Deputy Floyd?" choked Allison. "Why, you don't know the half of what he's up to."

"Mississippi's Finest!" Jeanette snorted a laugh.

The door eased open and a voice mumbled for Jeanette to "please report back to the phone switchboard."

Jeanie jumped up and headed out the door, then spun and poked her head back inside.

"Let's go get some lunch today, ok?" pleaded Jeanette. "I don't want to be around to see this dog and pony show."

The squeal of the speaker of the dispatch radio transceiver interrupted them and Allison nodded profusely in agreement.

James and his grampa pulled in front of The Cajun Café a little less than an hour later.

Out front stood a slender young lady in a long black dress, its bodice covered in delicate embroidered lace, her slim arms crossed underneath her bosom. Her lazy pose could have easily been mistaken for a vogue model. Cascades of her long glistening hair lent a gothic air to her aura as she leaned against the ancient lamppost.

Most women aspire to natural beauty most of their lives, however in the eyes of James, Jolie had achieved this righteousness at an early age.

Jolie waited patiently in the cool shade, as if waiting for an imaginary photographer to make their next shot. Her mind had actively delved into rhetorical thought, nevertheless the illusion was there.

Martin Ames quickly gathered that he would be doing all of the work while James oogled the lithe figure of Jolie.

"What happened to your forehead!?" asked Jolie as soon as James stepped out of his car. Her hands were already reaching out for him as he stepped up the curb.

"It's nothing," said James. "You look incredible." He wanted desperately to change the subject as he hurried to greet her.

Martin stepped up on the curb to meet BeBe, and was also caught by surprise. "You look very nice, BeBe."

"Why, thank you, Mr. Ames," said BeBe. "I hate that you came all the way over here to rescue us. I'm never this helpless."

BeBe Cavalier had undergone her own transformation into loveliness. Her usual daily business attire was temporarily discarded giving evidence that Jolie had inherited the feminine side of the family's ability to shine.

"I'm sorry you're having trouble with your car. Is this one yours?" he asked. "You know, they never give you trouble until you absolutely have to be somewhere."

"Everyone that works here at the café either walks to work or share one family vehicle. They'll be short Jolie and I already," she said apologizing. "That's the only reason I didn't borrow another car. I still can't understand what happened to this poor old thing."

BeBe stepped down the curb to the street and kicked at the front tire.

"It's practically new and I treat it like a baby."

"I'll take a quick look to see if it's something minor, before I hook up to it with the tow truck," said Martin.

"The keys are in it, for all the good it will do ya," griped BeBe.

Martin Ames eased down the tall steps of the curb and slid into the drivers' seat and turned the ignition – clunk, clunk, clunk, went the starter.

"That didn't work, but it sure is trying," Mr. Ames said as he stepped back from the vehicle.

He popped open the hood, could find nothing obviously out of place, broken, or missing. He reached in his back pocket and pulled out a long screwdriver and touched it across the two poles on the starter.

Pop! – Grr-rrr-rrr! Then nothing.

"Starter's not frozen. It's acting like the battery's low, or it's not getting gas."

"I did spend a little too much time trying to start it," BeBe admitted.

He then checked the for the obvious offenders, but everything was full and already cool to the touch. He looked at a few other things and then at his watch, remembering where they had to be.

"Hmmm…, this could take a while to sort out…," he mumbled.

He fumbled with the accelerator pump on the carb…, nothing came out, not a drop of gas.

"It's not getting any gas, probably something as simple as a fuel pump or filter," said Mr. Ames. "I need to go ahead and take it to the shop where I can look at it. James, you want to gimme a hand?"

James only needed an introduction to put on a show, waving and directing the wrecker back to the bumper, hooking up the sling, and locking everything in place. When they were through, Mr. Ames got out of the tow truck.

"Jolie, I need you to come by the shop and stand around so I can get him to move like that all the time," said Martin.

Jolie hid her smile from James.

The joke went in one ear and out the other as James wiped his hands off on some red oil-smelly cloth from the back of the tow truck.

Disappointed that his joke missed James' ego, Martin Earl was ready to get home.

"This thing is the best you can get to haul around broken cars, but you should really ride back with James."

"At your service," said James.

"That bonk on your head has really made you the gentleman today, James," grinned Martin.

"What bonk on the head?" asked Aunt BeBe.

James tried to cover the discolored bruise with his shock of hair.

"Is that what happened to your forehead?" asked Jolie.

"It's a long story. I'll tell you on the way," James said gritting his teeth. "Thanks, grampa."

Martin felt appeased at his minor victory.

"My pleasure, James."

The particulars of a funeral are never truly pleasant due to the reason for the gathering. However, the eulogy and words shared by chosen members of the church and community elevated Wema Smith, known as Granny

Smith by all, to near Sainthood. Not a dry eye was found among the congregation, the flowers were overflowing, and music filled the air.

It was Granny Smith's express request that it be a happy occasion when she passed on, no sad faces or gloomy expressions.

"She has run her race and fought her fight for 87 years," said the pastor in finality. "We should all have her testimony."

Several quiet amen's later; the congregation was prepared to view the body one last time before the graveside service.

The group was within walking distance of the final resting place of Wema Smith and exited the church in a cluster, some holding hands and others talking softly.

James and Jolie were walking side by side with family, feeling the heat of the afternoon sun beating down. Some of the regular members had cleaned and trimmed a path to the gravesite in Heaven's Gate Cemetery.

"Is that the limb that reached out and hit your head?" mused Jolie in a whisper.

James decided not to answer as a matter of pride, but looked over in the general direction of where the mysterious visitor had actually been. Any evidence of a prowler was long gone with the tumultuous group that was passing through the area.

A shimmering outline, like water reflecting in the sun, caught James' attention over the wall of the graveyard, resembling a face and looking fiercely at the mourners.

"Do you see that?" asked James. "Over there…, right next to…," the swimming air shifted and vanished into what looked like black vapor, jumping from sight.

"Never mind," said James.

"Granny Smith will be two rows over from the Ames family plot," said Maime Ames, from behind them.

As they walked down the row, Martin Earl noticed that the gravesite of Syrus Earl Ames was not covered or sealed back up. Out of morbid curiosity, all their portion of the procession detoured toward the open grave. There was the hole, the splintered residue of the coffin, and a broken headstone without remedy.

"James?" queried Martin looking sternly over at him. "I thought you came by here and made an inspection."

"I…, I did," stammered James. "It was all in one piece when I left it. I don't understand what happened. I even lifted it up to look at it."

Aunt Martiel made a closer inspection and discovered a large chipped rock that was obviously the tool of choice to break the aged granite into two pieces.

"It happened after the fact, Martin," she said to her elder brother. "Look at this. Somebody pretty strong lifted this up and dropped it right in the middle of it…, the weight did the rest."

"Must have been that deputy," said James angrily.

"Now James, we don't know who did it, and they only have one of those hoodlums in jail," said Maime. "It could have been one of the others still on the loose."

"In jail?" asked Aunt BeBe. "They have one of them in jail?"

"Why yes," said Maime. "It was all over the front page of today's Gazette. The sheriff found him single handed over in lower Natchez."

Aunt BeBe, Jolie, James, and Aunt Martiel, all looked at each other's faces reading one another's expressions.

"Is there something I don't know?" asked Martin Earl.

"I know that kid didn't break this gravestone," growled James.

"Who said it was a kid?" asked Martin, glaring at James. "Did you read the paper this morning?"

"I…, I must have heard someone mention it this morning before BeBe and Jolie called," stammered James.

"Lets hurry on over to the graveside service," said Maime, ushering them on. "They're about to start."

"What a wonderful funeral," said Maime.

James looked over at her dumbfounded without commenting.

"There were plenty of folks that cared about her," said Martin.

"I'm glad that's over with," said Aunt Martiel. "Funerals are for dead people."

This earned her direct stares from everyone, including the ones that agreed.

"What?" Aunt Martiel asked. "Did I say something wrong?"

"I need to have a talk with our beloved sheriff again, about the headstone of Syrus Ames," said Martin, changing the subject.

"You need to let Martiel and our attorneys handle that, you have a vehicle to fix first, if I remember correctly," said Maime.

"You're right, it can wait, but I still want to talk to Howard about it," said Martin. "I'll get changed and see if I can get BeBe back on the road."

"You ladies come on back to the house while the boys take care of your car," said Maime.

Chapter 28

Martin Earl had been under the hood of the '75 Chevy Caprice for over thirty minutes.

"Try to crank it James."

Grr rrr rrr click, Grr-rrr-rrr-click.

"No more. Battery is almost dead, grab the booster," said Martin.

He began removing minor hindrances preventing a clear view of the engine. First went the bulbous air cleaner and he tied back some of the hoses. The engine was clean enough to eat off and everything was well maintained exactly as BeBe had described.

"Got to be something simple; usually is, especially on these newer models," he mumbled to himself.

James struggled with a heavy pull cart, wrapped with thick cables.

Martin checked the ignition system again, then the fuel one more time.

"No gas...," he muttered, repeating his earlier diagnosis.

He sighed a heavy puff of air – a clogged fuel filter or bad fuel pump.

"She probably buys gas from one of those stations that don't filter their gas."

There were boxes of filters in the storage room for the particular type carburetors and he unscrewed the filter and removed the fuel line....

"What is that smell?" he mumbled.

He slid his long slim body back off the fender and the cloth in his hand snagged on something sharp causing him to drop the old filter on the concrete floor of the garage.

Shop-light in hand, he reached to pick the filter back up when he noticed something glittering on the concrete floor by the filter.

He backed up and sat down on his work stool. The florescent light over the work bench delivered a cleaner light than the incandescent bulb inside his hand held light. He tapped the filter on the bench gently.... Out from the end of the filter came more shiny crystals.

Sugar. Granules of sugar.

"James, come take a look."

James had finished connecting the battery booster and set its timer.

"What is that?" asked James.

"Looks like our friend BeBe has picked up an enemy."

"I'm Doctor Ashton from the county hospital. I'm here to see Sheriff Howard about one of his detainees."

Jeanette turned around and rolled her eyes as soon as she believed she wasn't being observed. A quick glance through the adjoining window between offices told her that everyone was out.

"One moment," she said.

She punched the button on her switchboard to the sheriff's extension and could hear a faint ringing in the background of the quiet office.

Clop, clop, clop, clop went the familiar footsteps. Jeanette sighed. At least the sheriff was trying.

His voice blared out of her telephone receiver, "Sheriff Howard..., oh, it's you Jeanette. What do you need?"

In all their years of working together he had never been able to distinguish the difference from an inside call and an outside call.

"There's a Doctor Ashton here to see you," she answered.

"Send him back; I'll meet him at the entrance."

"Dr. Ashton, if you will follow this short hallway, the sheriff will meet you at the door," Jeanette said as pleasantly as possible.

"Hello Dr. Ashton, thank you for coming."

"Yes, well, I don't usually make these calls, but there was no one else available at the time," mumbled the doctor.

"Can you explain why you need a doctor to evaluate a..., uh..., who is this person, sheriff?"

"He's the person we arrested in connection to the cemetery vandalisms."

The sheriff had his back turned, already hurrying toward the interrogation room.

"If you will just follow me, I'll have the subject brought in so you can have a look at him."

"Those grave robberies?" asked the doctor nervously.

"Haven't you read the newspaper about the..., never mind," he said looking at the doctor suspiciously.

"Will he be restrained? There are all kinds of terrible diseases someone could catch from digging around in an old cemetery."

"No need to worry, Dr. Ashton."

"This is highly irregular, sheriff," continued the doctor. "We normally...."

"I thought you said you didn't normally make these calls," said the sheriff, with a disgusted look. "If you'll have a seat, I'll be back in a moment with the prisoner."

"Sheriff..., this prisoner isn't violent is he?"

"He isn't.... But actually I you need to make your own evaluation instead of taking my word for anything. I assure you that you will be completely safe."

"Yes..., safe...."

The door to the little room closed and left Ashton sitting in the cold silence. Being a physician for the county had good moments and bad. Right now Dr. Ashton was dabbing his forehead with a handkerchief and trying to remember one of the good times.

The door opened some five minutes later and two officers escorted an emaciated teenaged boy into the room.

"Jimmy" as he was being referred to, walked in peacefully, and sat down in the chair provided. He looked as relaxed as a child in his mother's arms, completely oblivious to those present.

"Are you sure you need a *medical doctor* for this evaluation?" asked Dr. Ashton.

After twenty minutes of checking vital signs and attempting conversation and reactions from his patient, the doctor concluded his preliminary examination.

The doctor stepped outside and met the anxious sheriff who had been standing waiting by the door the entire time.

"It's as I expected," said Dr. Ashton. "When I first saw the young man, I could tell that he appeared in reasonable health, but this is…, he is…, a very unusual case. His autonomic reactions are completely shut down…, he doesn't respond to any stimulus that I initiated…, in a word, he seems drugged or almost catatonic, but not in the usual clinical sense."

Ashton dotted his face a few more second with his kerchief, "He stood and sat and obeyed my simplest of requests, but otherwise appeared…, elsewhere - totally absent. I'm recommending complete blood work and a full psychiatric profile from a qualified psychiatrist."

"So…, basically, you don't know why he can't or won't talk and you don't know what's wrong with him," snapped the sheriff impatiently.

"What I'm saying is…, his mental state is beyond the scope of my professional boundaries," chirped the doctor.

The rushed impromptu meeting was not going as well as Deputy Floyd had hoped. His anxious phone call did get Billy Poole disturbed enough to rush to a hidden rendezvous.

"Y'all need to calm down some," said Billy. "He ain't gonna talk none. Not now, not ever. Besides…, them two boys don't know you from Adam."

"How do you know that? Are you willing to stake your life on it?" asked the deputy. "If my ship sinks, everybody on board goes down with the ship."

"I wouldn't go makin' no threats you ain't able to keep, now Floyd," Billy said brashly. "Anything happens to me…, something worse bad happens to the one that done the hurting. Plain and simple."

"If you're dead, you won't get to see what happens to me…, did you ever happen to think about that?" asked the deputy.

"I seen the results a time or two.... I'm still here," said Billy sullenly.

"Where's little *Jimmy's* partner?" asked Floyd. "You said he had a helper

"You need to quit your worrying, it's all in the plan, all in the plan," said Billy. "And you'll git paid just like all-us."

"I couldn't clean up anything from the truck," said the deputy. "The sheriff has it guarded pretty tight. He even seems to be watching me too close for comfort."

"Just sit back and relax, do your usual job, and let me and my sources take care of everything," said Billy.

"Your sources...," hissed the deputy. "I'd like to meet your sources."

"I ritely doubt that Floyd, yep I do," said Billy with a strange stare on his face. "There's times I...."

Billy's voice became hoarse and gravelly and he choked and coughed at the air for a moment. He spat on the ground looking around cautiously at the early twilit shadows cast by the heavens.

"Here's what you need to know," said Billy, going straight to the point. "In a few days there'll be another bad thunderstorm. There won't be much of a warning, it'll just happen," he continued. "But you'll know..., because I'll contact you."

Billy laid out details of what they were to do. The deputy's face grew cold and gradually a slim smile spread over his lips, turning into a sadistic grin.

When Billy Poole was finished, their two silhouettes parted silently into the darkness. In a couple of nights it would be difficult to hide in the shadows from the moon that was waxing near full.

"Sugar in my gas!" barked BeBe. "How could that happen?!"

The phone went silent.

"I don't know of a soul that would do something like that. Oh, no.... Does that mean I need a new motor?" she asked. "I don't know if my insurance covers that kind of thing."

"You're pretty lucky you didn't drive it very far," said Martin Ames. "It's a myth about sugar tearing up your engine..., at least right away. You see, sugar won't dissolve in gasoline. It *will* clog your filters and fuel pump and gas lines, but it looks like this just happened and you didn't drive it far enough to get it all up in the engine. It does tell me that whoever did this isn't too bright if they wanted to do some real damage. Now, if they'd mixed it with a little water first and dissolved it, or maybe poured something like corn syrup in the carb, now then were talking big money and a new engine. James and I can have your car back to you by tomorrow."

"I don't know how to thank you," said BeBe. "I really appreciate all your help."

"You can thank me by thinking about who might want to do something like this," said Martin. "You might not be so lucky next time."

"I'd tell you to report it to the Police Department, but I don't think that will do much good. We'll stay here a while longer and dump the gas tank, clean the fuel lines and I'll replace the fuel pump..., we should be done in about an hour or so. If you need to go before then, ask Maime for the keys to one of our cars."

After their conversation was completed, BeBe turned and explained the circumstances to everyone present.

"I don't know who would want to do such an awful thing," said BeBe. "We keep to ourselves and the restaurant."

"Maybe somebody didn't like the gumbo," Jolie said half-joking.

"Seriously," said Martiel. "Someone would need a pretty definite reason to go through the trouble to sugar your tank."

They discussed old acquaintances and patrons to the Café that might have a grievance big enough to do something destructive and dismissed them all.

"Speaking of food, I'm going to start supper for the men. They'll be starved when they get in," said Maime. "Would you and Jolie please stay and eat supper with us?"

"What about me?" asked Martiel. "You know I'd starve if it wasn't for fast food."

"You're not a guest. Besides, you're helping me cook...," said Maime.

"We'd love to..., and we'll all help," said BeBe smiling at Jolie.

Later, when James and his grampa walked in the door, both of them looked like raccoons that had been playing in mud.

"Looks like they used a whole bag of sugar," said James.

Martin tried to explain a little further, "We got it clean, but the fuel pump and filter were shot like I suspected.

"You two look a mess," said Maime smiling.

"The top of the gas tank is where all that road dust cakes and settles..., okay, you don't want an explanation, you're right, we're a mess." Martin agreed.

He took one last moment to address Jolie and her Aunt BeBe.

"It could have been a lot worse. I hope you figure out who might have done this."

"I can't tell you how much I appreciate you going through all the trouble," said BeBe.

"Something smells great," blurted James.

"Supper is almost ready..., you two go get cleaned up," said Maime.

They both excused themselves and wandered off to the back of the house.

Supper came and went with pleasant small talk and laughter.

Jolie and James passed glances at each other most of the evening and as soon as there was an opening in the conversation, they both excused themselves for a walk onto the porch. It was the closest thing to privacy that either of them would get with a houseful of relatives.

"What a day," said Jolie, sighing deeply. "These last few days have been a real strain. How does your head feel?"

"It's okay, it lets me know it's still there if I turn too quick," said James. "The medicine the Doc gave me makes me sleepy. So I have the option of being awake and hurting, or groggy and feeling no pain."

"I guess you figured out that we made the anonymous call to the Sheriff's Office yesterday," said Jolie.

"Yeah, and I noticed that he claimed all the glory too," said James.

"Did that surprise you?" asked Jolie. "Besides it doesn't matter anyway."

"I guess not, but it was a surprise that he caught one of them so fast," said James. "It was the one with the cap in my..., whatever it was..., vision."

"Today's newspaper said he wasn't talking," said Jolie. "He hasn't said a word, not even his name."

"One down, two to go," said James. "But you know what's even more frustrating? I still don't have a clue what they have to do with my dreams and my personal tormentors."

"I think you should let the law try and do the rest," said Jolie. "He'll eventually have to talk. They can take care of the rest. So unless you get another dream, I'd drop it."

"I didn't exactly plan on getting involved at all," said James laughing. He winced at the dull pain from his laughter, hiding it from Jolie.

"What about you?" asked James. "Are you doing okay with all of this? I think whoever is responsible for what's happening with me and my family is somehow responsible for your Aunt BeBe's car. It's only a feeling, but you heard the warnings too."

When she didn't answer, James suspected Jolie was hiding something else.

"Jolie, there have been other things that..., I'm not going to tell you about, that have happened," said James. "Not because I don't trust you, but because I don't want anything to happen..., I don't want anything to happen to you."

There was only one way to make her understand.

"So don't go reading my mind. I'm beginning to think that the less you know and the less you're involved the safer you'll be. Do you understand?"

"Yes..., but...," Jolie started to reply.

"Please...," said James. "And I'm not really used to saying please to anybody. Don't give me something else to worry about."

There was an uncomfortable silence.

"I think you know how I feel about you and I know this situation could get a lot worse."

"James, I want to...," Jolie started again.

"A lot worse, Jolie, do you understand?" he asked frantically.

"Are you going to let me talk?" asked Jolie.

Jolie sensed that James was breaking from the stress. The past few weeks had eaten away the protective coating that had taken years to grow around him.

"You've changed James..., just since I first met you at the library. Not necessarily in a bad way, but you are so much more tense now than you were. My Aunt BeBe agrees with you, that I should back off until all of this is sorted out and then...."

Jolie stopped mid sentence. She blushed slightly, her thoughts betraying her feelings. The evening darkness and shadows may have hid her feelings from James' eyes, but not his heart.

James put his arms around her and gave her a soft hug, pulling her close against him.

"See, that's exactly what I mean," said Jolie. "I feel who you are now, but I sense that you weren't always this gentle. I see something wild and hurt inside that I didn't before."

"Everyone has some kind of a past," James said, defending himself. "Mine wasn't anything to brag about, if you know what I mean."

"Don't you think I need to know?" she asked quietly.

"I'm not used to talking about me...," said James.

There were several moments of uncomfortable silence as James mulled over his options. Any confessions of his childhood could scar Jolie's image of him forever. Jolie was right though, she needed to know.

"Okay, you asked for it...," James said taking a deep breath.

"I explained where I lived..., up North..., well things were a little more mixed up than I told you."

"James, I'm not trying to pry about your family or anything personal," said Jolie.

"No you're right, and you have every right to know about my past. I don't mind getting personal, but I really do have an unpleasant past, Jolie. I had to deal with some pretty bad things where I grew up. It's been really good for me here, living with my grandparents. I had things happen to me that..., pushed me over the edge. My parents were always gone; they made lots of money, but never spent a dime for a nanny or a sitter. My dad said it would make me stronger, make a man out of me. In some ways it did, but it came with a price. That much you could have probably guessed."

James peered around looking for some help from the darkness around them, "Believe it or not it really started in first grade, so I guess I'll start there.

"There were a couple of gangs in the school. I mean, this is first grade. I wasn't stupid or naïve but I was barely six years old and I sure wasn't prepared for what came next.

"If you didn't belong to one of the gangs, you were screwed. I didn't and I didn't want to be, but I was scrawny, couldn't fight my way out of a bag.

"A couple of us guys stayed close all the time. I guess that we thought they wouldn't do anything to us if we stayed together..., but man were we wrong. The oldest kids in the school started what they called "initiations" the middle of the school year. It scared the hell out of all of us."

James and Jolie sat down in some lawn chairs away from the yellow glow of the house. They could hear soft chatter and some laughter as the night grew longer.

"So, most kids have to learn to take up for themselves in school. You could have been making too much out of it," said Jolie.

James sighed and continued as if he didn't hear what she said.

"It was more than shaking us down to get our lunch money," James continued, almost sneering at the memory of similar remarks from his parents. "They'd catch us on the way to school, or on the way home, take our clothes, knock us around at first. You know..., lots of threats. Told us that if we let anybody know, they'd do lots worse, but they did worse to us anyway. We were too young and stupid to know any better. We were just little kids..., we should have been playing baseball or hide and seek. Man, if I ever have kids.

"Anyway, the gang leaders were around fifteen and older..., it was their job to recruit us. They started giving us jobs. They'd take us in a store and they'd steal everything they wanted and put it in our pockets and under our clothes. Sometimes, if they thought they were being watched, they'd tell a worker in the store that we were stealing only to throw the suspicion onto us. I can't remember how many times my parents got a call from the police to come to a neighborhood store to pick me up for stealing. We couldn't tell or it would be worse the next day. I'd get grounded and made to stay away from my brother Sam, so I wouldn't be a bad influence.

"When I was eight, I decided I was going to tell my parents everything that was going on, but my dad said that I was trying to make excuses and not owning up to what I was doing. Then my mouth started getting me into even more trouble. I'll never forget the first time I cussed out my dad. Language spewed out my mouth that sent them both into shock. At first he went wild, then he started ignoring me. He said I was my mothers' child. My mom didn't know what to say or do. From then on I was *the problem child.*

"Jolie, I saw my friends beat up, tortured, molested, branded," James grew silent and pulled off the shoe and sock on his right foot. In the dim street light Jolie saw a scar of some kind, a raised whelp from a burn mark on the arch of his foot and she winced at how deep and painful it looked.

"I couldn't walk right for a week, then when it was almost better, they did it again. Over the weeks, well, they stopped when I didn't scream anymore."

"Didn't you tell your parents!? Didn't they know something was wrong with your foot!!??" gasped Jolie. "What if it got infected?"

"That's not the only one...," he said distantly. "Dad was only home two days a week and mom and Sam didn't get home until after eight in the evenings. I had a key to the apartment on a chain around my neck. Anyway, mom was always worn out and tired..., she'd ask if I got the supper she left in the fridge, or if I had any homework.

"I hid my scars from her, pretended that I was too old for her to help me with a bath or tuck me in. She took it as rejection and gave her hugs to Sam. Which was great for me at the time. The gang said that if I told, they'd hurt my mom."

"You believed them?" asked Jolie.

"Oh, I believed. I'd seen them do it before, some kid named Jarad..., his mom. They made all us younger kids watch as they pushed her down and ripped off her clothes..., there were a dozen of the older members. It wasn't pretty."

Jolie quietly searched James' mind to see if the unbelievable tales were simply exaggerations or even lies, but found him to be honest.

"I was nine when that happened, December 22, my mom's birthday. I never forgot...."

His voice trailed off as he ducked his head.

"There were so many other things..., but...."

James' green eyes turned a stale shade of gray in the dim light and Jolie shivered as she watched a look and feeling come over him she had never seen before. She sensed a deep coldness inside.

"You don't have to tell me any more," Jolie said softly.

"It's okay..., I think I need to," continued James. "Weekends, I hid in my room and read books, did anything that would keep me inside, anything that didn't make me have to go outside. I stayed there so mom wouldn't see any marks on me, or know anything was wrong."

"Then Sam started school, that same year.

"The *Hand* said that they would leave him alone as long as I did everything they said. I did..., everything they told me. I was their favorite puppet. I was the one that couldn't be caught most of the time, the fastest. So I was the one that picked up the drugs and delivered them. I took the blame for every time the fire alarm went off at school, when they carried off food from the store around the block, every call to the principal's office, every call to the police. It was all the time.

"Sam was scared of them, and at first he didn't understand what had been going on all those years.

"He tried to be tough and stand up to them and I'd take his punishment, while they made him watch. Sam caught on pretty quick; kept quiet and did whatever I told him. Then he'd get scared and try to tell mom or dad and the cycle started all over again.

"I learned to fight, scrawny as I was, I learned every dirty trick in the book, that earned some respect from the gang leaders after a while. I could tell Sam was afraid of me too, but he was more scared of them and I was his protection, so he stuck to me like a flea."

They were quiet for a few moments....

James knew that to venture on might end any chance of a relationship with Jolie.

"It's okay James," said Jolie quietly.

"The magic year was when I turned twelve. Things started happening to my body. My voice changed, I grew a foot in one year and put on weight. That was the year I wanted it all to stop and I knew I could make it happen if I was smart.

"I still remember the day that I made up my mind that I'd make it stop.

"Sam was going home ahead of me and one of the older gang members snatched Sam back into the alley. I just happened to see him. I always wonder how things would have been different if I hadn't seen....

"You have to understand, these guys were animals, they didn't care if you were a guy or girl and Sam was small like I was and..., well you get the picture.

"He had Sam pressed against the alley wall, groping around on him and I..., I snapped. I pulled him off of Sam and hit him, one time, square in the face with my fist, but I hit him so hard that his head bounced off the dumpster and he fell down and didn't get back up.

"I told Sam to run home as quick as he could. I knew if this piece of trash told any of the others what I'd done that I was dead. So I already made up my mind that I was going to end him. Sam and I were going to survive. I leaned over him, but I couldn't hear him breathing..., then somebody yelled....

"I ran..., but it was too late. He was in a coma for weeks. If it hadn't been for Sam telling the truth, I'd have gone to prison for the rest of my life. Even though they said it was self-defense of sorts, I was given probation for my long record of violent behavior. My past record caught up to me.

"My dad was mad at me and said that I should never resort to violence.

What a joke."

"So, did your parents believe you then?" asked Jolie.

"Not really, well to some degree I guess. They still thought it was an isolated incident and that I'd overreacted. Yeah, that was the word they used, overreacted. That was the year that the Judge sentenced me to probation here for the summers; away from the bad influence of my *friends*.

"They called them my *friends*," James laughed up at the sky.

"And that was when everything changed for me. It was the best thing that ever happened to me, Jolie. It wasn't until their perfect son Sam started having trouble that they started to believe some of what I tried to tell them.

"Years later dad got transferred, we moved and they kept us in private schools."

"Anyway, I was branded as trouble, and the rest is history. Summers here were intended as a punishment but were heaven to me. Even though I never made any friends here…, I was happy without friends. There was no one to tell me what to do or judge me.

"At first, I thought the whole world was like back there…, you know? That I'd be fighting my way out of trouble and be alone again.

"Grampa put me to work, taught me to repair things in his garage. I finally had chores and responsibilities that didn't involve punishment.

"There were fishing trips, expeditions along the river, and swimming in the Gulf at Biloxi, where Aunt Martiel lives. Life here was a reward instead of punishment…, still is. But it looks like all that has caught back up with me now.

"I remember all the talk in church about heaven and hell and the choices we make, well what about the choices we *don't* make? The ones that are made for us?"

"This isn't over yet," said Jolie. "Don't act like your life is over."

Jolie picked up her chair from where she had been sitting across from James and set it close beside him.

"You probably think I'm white trash by now," said James.

"You're only human, James," Jolie said and kissed his cheek. "You couldn't help what happened to you."

Jolie's mind fed itself multitudes of unanswered questions from scenarios and possibilities he had endured.

"Thank you for letting me talk," said James. "You're the first person that I've told most of that. I guess that's why I cared so much about Granny Smith. She knew everything there was to know about me, and loved me anyway.

"For the record, I'm not like that anymore…, not for a long time."

"Well…," she laughed nervously. "I'd share my childhood, but even with my parents' nasty divorce, its boring compared to yours."

"I'd trade a boring one for mine any day," said James.

He stood to his feet and walked a small circle on the lawn.

"Tell me about California. I've never been anywhere besides New Jersey, Mississippi and a plane."

He laughed off his diversion, hoping to change the subject.

They sat and traded small talk of a much happier subject level for another hour. She told him stories of the west coast and sandy beaches, never once mentioning her father or her visits to the east. It seemed enough that she had opened up at all after hearing the horrors of his past.

James had taken off his other shoe and was running his toes in the grass carpet of the front lawn. Finally relaxing, they laughed like two people without a care until the porch light flickered on and off. The screen door slapped shut a few times and James knew that was their reminder to come back inside for the night.

They said their goodbyes early and managed to steal a few quick kisses before going in.

"I so enjoyed their visit," said Aunt Martiel. "That BeBe is a mess."

'Mess' came out sounding like 'may-us', giving away her indigenous Southern lifestyle.

"We like them too," said Maime. "James, I hope you got a chance to visit and relax awhile."

"Yes Ma'am, I did," he agreed.

"Hey James. What's that on your cheek?" asked Martin. "It's not another bruise is it?"

James reached up and touched his face in an automatic reflex and blushed when he understood that it was the remains of Jolie's tiny mark of lipstick on his cheek.

"Now you lay off him, Martin," both women scolded.

"I for one am glad this day is over and I'm ready to get some rest," said Martiel. "Are you ready to go James?"

Before he could answer…, "Oh, wait a minute," said Maime as she hurried off back into her bedroom.

She came back in a few moments holding a small worn object in her hands.

"Granny Smith willed this to you James," she said handing him a well-worn Bible.

James carefully took it from her hands and held it for a moment looking at the Bible's tattered cover and worn pages, wondering….

Chapter 29

On the banks of the Mississippi River, some sounds can carry for miles; others are swallowed up and never heard. The wind and the water currents dictate most life near its powerful reach. In fact, many a soul exhausted their last breath of a scream fighting the deadly undertow of its dark waters, never heard. There are no tombstones for these souls, the missing, the forgotten…, the lost.

Rhythmic beats of sticks and drums with a soothing hypnotic pattern began offering up their call into the night.

Awakening…, drawing…, as the wick in a lamp draws fuel for its flame. Sleeping spirits were being pulled silently from their watery grave nearby. A calling of the dead to come, come and empower a lone practitioner of dark arts. This person was long lost to madness, after all desires, gifts, and abilities to help humanity fell into evil's shadows. Her strength now focused on selfish, evil pursuits of hatred, revenge, and greed. Revenge that was long sought for, but always just out of reach, was now coming into view.

A voice was calling, yearning, and chanting in a language and verbiage, in and out of this world. One by one, awakened and unseen entities unwillingly obeyed the pull of their masters' voice to come…, join in the revelry and become trapped in the snare prepared for them.

An open clay vessel sat prepared to contain what was left of their lifeless blood from the ethereal plane. In a swirl and wisp of misty vapor, each in turn rose with the nightly fog along the Mississippi yielding to the call. Each stringy wisp of vapor heard the call and found the cave along the riverbank, then entered an urn, their new home, their prison. Unable to resist, each were lost to themselves, becoming slaves to the will of their new master. This night several souls yielded to the beckoning call of the chant and melody, their sum total a force to be reckoned with, each collecting like many cells in a powerful battery.

Now a path of silent vengeance would be paved, using their power.

"The journal is wrong. It says that *Samuel* Earl Ames was the founder of the family legacy," said James. "That doesn't make sense. In my dream it was Syrus Earl Ames that won the family fortune gambling…, not Samuel.

"And there was something else. It was Syrus that sold all the property and I guess everything else he won, and converted it into gold. I don't remember everything, but it had to do with the civil war coming."

"I was never much on history," said Aunt Martiel. "You know how that stuff can get all muddled over the years. Only the winners of wars get to write the histories."

It seemed to James that his aunt was nervous and…, was she diverting the subject?

"Yeah, but why keep records at all, if they aren't true?" asked James. "Unless the records are meant to mislead people somehow."

"I heard that old Samuel Earl Ames kind of went kooky after his younger brother Syrus Earl died," said Aunt Martiel.

Was Martiel still trying to hurry him away from something she didn't want him to know?

"But not before he created the family trust in the Bank of Boston. The financial trust our family still lives under today; it was worth millions even back then."

The bed they were both sitting on screeched as James sat up to pay better attention. Completely forgotten was his argument to learn what she didn't want him to know.

"If the family has that much money…," said James.

"Why does everyone still live like regular folks?" finished Aunt Martiel.

"Yeah, I've never heard about any money or a legacy," said James.

"A lot of it got ate up when the country went to war, taxes, bad investments," said Aunt Martiel.

"Now don't get me wrong, not a single generation had to lift a finger to work, which was probably part of the problem. There were lavish parties, money flowed like water down the river; the ones that never had to work lost sight of what if meant to earn a dollar," she sighed.

"There's plenty of it left now too," she said casually. "About a hundred million or so, the last time I tallied it all up. Of course it's not all liquid assets you understand, it's in stocks and other investments too."

James almost choked at this new revelation, his eyes growing wide with interest.

"Your Great Grampa John Earl made some good investments and miraculously turned it all around, but at the same time, he passed down the virtue of a humble lifestyle to his successors. He tried to show the value of giving and helping those truly in need.

"He also enforced a few egregious amendments and stipulations to the trust. The rule of thumb is that each member of the family has to be gainfully employed or enrolled in a reputable educational facility to enjoy the benefits of financial assistance."

James was suddenly thinking of the couple hundred dollars in his wallet that he'd saved up the past two weeks. And while his mind was still spinning, he guessed that this was why his mother wanted him to enroll in college while he stayed with her parents.

"And this is what I'm supposed to take over?" asked James nervously. "I'm still a kid; I'm not ready to take on that kind of responsibility. This is all too much."

"That's what I'm here for," grinned Aunt Martiel. "Learning how to hang on to what you accumulate and make it grow at the same time is pretty tricky, but you won't learn it in any college. Oh, you'll learn the basics of how to place a value on it, and estimate its worth at different rates and such, but where and when to place your investments isn't covered in 'Life-101'.

"That's where your gifts will come in, you understand. Of course you can also rely on the judgment of your departed relatives if you are in some doubt."

She motioned around the house to remind James of his encounter with the family host.

"Imagine yourself at a bargaining table with two men," she said as she sat up straight on the edge of the bed. "One is an honest man, the other is a shyster. The honest man makes his presentation, which doesn't seem too lucrative. The devious man makes his presentation and it looks like a river of flowing gold."

"Who's telling the truth?" she asked, looking intently at James. "How do you know which is which?"

James shrugged and sat in silence, thinking this must be a trick question.

"That's when you rely on your ability to listen inside them and read them, like a gambler when he's playing poker, reading the faces of his opponent, so that he can tell who is bluffing and who is holding."

James sat back in shock. Not at the revelation of what his Aunt Martiel was trying to explain, but his dream of Syrus Earl Ames flashing before his eyes. That was how Uncle Syrus won at gambling and how he started the family money rolling. He could see into their minds and knew what cards the other gamblers were holding in their hands, while they were on the riverboat in his dream. Nobody could be that lucky.

"James, are you still with me?" asked Aunt Martiel.

"How do you do it…, how can you tell?" he asked, cautiously.

"Why it's as simple as falling off a log," she smiled.

Aunt Martiel went on to explain the joys of being able to use their natural abilities to see into people, their minds, their hearts and intentions, and tell which way to go.

"Relax and let your gifts do all the work. Lock on to the person and imagine what they must be feeling or thinking and a supernatural link just opens up to their thoughts. Then you can make a decision based on facts, not on guess work or face value. Sometimes making a choice to take the lesser gain will help the person that's in need and earn you more down the road."

James sat and listened for almost an hour, until it was getting seriously late. It wasn't until his eyes started watering and head was pounding that his aunt felt it was time for her to halt her primer into the supernatural.

"Enough for tonight," she said yawning. "I'm exhausted and I know you are too."

James understood that this was too much to absorb all at one time, but it was beginning to make sense. It was too easy. He went into the next room and put on PJ's while his aunt did her nightly ritual of facial creams and wonder ointments.

He came back in the room and literally flopped on his bed like a fallen log, trying to absorb all the new information. Even as he began to relax, an undercurrent of dread appeared in the forefront of his mind..., the threat of dreams.

He was drifting off into another world, when he remembered the Bible that Granny Smith had given him - *willed* him.

He reached over on the night table beside his bed and eased it over beside him. He flipped through it slowly. Its weight and the feel of the soft worn leather somehow gave him comfort. It fell open to a highlighted passage that read, "God has not given us a spirit of fear...."

His eyes watered from lack of rest and he gently closed the book. He was about to place it back on the night table, but instead found comfort with it under his pillow.

His head sank into the cushion and within a few seconds sleep found him.

In the stillness of the southern night, two bodies lay together in their bed of marriage. Small talk and touches after a time of intimacy.

"How would you feel if I was pregnant?" the wife asked.

"If that's what you want, we can have a kid," the husband sleepily replied.

"Would you want a boy or girl?" she asked.

"Don't make me no never mind," he replied. "Why you startin' up again about a kid, is there somethin' I should know?"

"I only wanted to know how you felt about it," she said, turning over and placing her back to him in a huff.

She laid thinking for a few minutes and said, "A little boy would be nice."

A giddiness arose inside her at the possibility. There was silence from the other side of the bed. She turned her head to hear the quiet snoring of her husband. Impatiently she lay in the silence of her solitary thoughts, for the better part of an hour, then she quietly slipped from beneath the sheets.

Walking to the kitchen, she took a cold beer from the fridge, then reached up on top and found her hidden pack of cigarettes and lighter.

The front door creaked slightly as she slid out to sit on the front porch of their small rent house. Lighting up her smoke gave her great satisfaction as well as the first long swallow of ice-cold beer.

She looked up at the stars in the sky contemplating their light, enjoying the warm muggy night. On the edge of the horizon a hard yellow moon was rising, starting another vigil, its blank eyes watching over all those beneath its path.

With the second cigarette extinguished and an empty bottle sitting beside her, she quietly walked back into the house. Peeking in the bedroom door, she found her husband in his usual trance-like sleep.

"The devil himself couldn't wake you up," she whispered to herself.

She showered quickly and put on a soft cotton floral dress, nothing underneath; almost smiling at the thought leaving her complacent husband on a routine visit to the other side of town.

Martiel lay sleeping soundly while James Earl was kicking his feet, pushing the covers to the foot of his bed.

Running, running, so tired…, if only he could stop and catch a breath of air. His lungs burned as he heaved in the crisp night air of his dream.

The dim light shifted in the room where James and Martiel lay sleeping and a silky darkness flowed along an already shadow filled path in the room.

Martiel Ellington stirred lightly from her sleep not knowing what had awakened her. She lay quietly as sleep drifted back over her. A light shuffling, scooting noise further awakened her from her twilight.

She saw movement at the end of James' bed and froze in horror. Then she relaxed and breathed deeply when she saw that all the commotion was James kicking his covers and mumbling softly.

She decided to wake him up and make him turn over so there wouldn't be another episode of him screaming from his nightly demons.

Quietly, she flipped on the light on the nightstand beside her bed, illuminating the bedroom with a soft warm light; all except for the wall nearest the foot of James Earl's bed.

She sat up with a start looking at nothing more than a shadowy form that refused to yield to the light from the glowing lamp beside her.

Not knowing what to do she leaned over, picked up one of her slippers from beside her bed and tossed it over at James hitting him upside his head.

"James," she said in a choked voice of fright.

His only reply was nothing but more light movement from his twisted and drooping covers.

"James," she dared a louder call and tossed another slipper.

She missed completely, hitting the wall immediately beyond where he lay. Her only weapon was in her purse downstairs.

The unyielding darkness moved over nearer the window, farther from where either of them lay and bumped into a chair, screeching its feet against the dry wood floor.

That was all the incentive Martiel needed.

"James!" she yelled as she threw back the covers and practically floated over the expanse from her side of the room to his bed, never taking her eyes off the intruder.

"You..., You get outa here!" she squeaked, waving her arms wildly, as if shooing away the intruder.

The darkness complied with her movement and drifted over into the other corner of the room.

Martiel became cotton-mouthed as she tried to call out her nephews' name once again. She jumped on top of the bed where James lay in his fitful sleep. Still, he didn't stir.

Martiel had her eyes transfixed on the corner of the bedroom, which shifted like a dark mist in a soft breeze. She began shaking James....

"James, James, James," she shook him violently.

His expression was still and peaceful as if the torment of his dream was turned into pleasantry. He actually smiled.

She pounced on him like a cat, one eye on him, the other on their unwelcome visitor.

Finally, he began to stir slowly from his sleep but it wasn't soon enough to please Martiel. She reached over to his nightstand and picked up the remains of a glass of water, stuck her fingers in the near empty glass and flung the spray at his face.

James sat bolt upright from his deathlike sleep with a shudder.

There sat a wide-eyed Martiel in the middle of his bed, glass in hand, and obviously scared to death.

James jumped from his bed and stood in the middle of the room looking at his aunt, trying to figure out where he was and what was going on.

Martiel scooted back to the wall where his bed rested and pointed to the corner mist of darkness that remained – watching and unwavering and unafraid.

James turned around and saw what she was pointing at, but didn't seem to understand that it was more than a mere shadow. To her horror and surprise, James walked over to the corner and waved his hand at the shadow as if it were smoky substance.

It yielded and moved once again, back to the corner of the room nearest his bed where Martiel sat perching, now clutching the knot of covers, horrified.

He walked back and sat on the bed without talking.

"James," whispered Aunt Martiel loudly. "What is..., that?"

"How do I know, you're the expert at this stuff," said James. "Looks like it's nothing but shadow."

The object seemed angered at James' obvious lack of fear and respect and shifted itself; slamming over the chair it had previously nudged, and then slowly took form before their eyes. Shorter than previously arranged, the solid black figure looked like a hound walking upright on its hind legs, with arms and hands at the shoulders instead of paws.

In a sudden moment of inspiration, James eased his way back over to where his aunt sat, still transfixed on the object. He slid his had under his pillow and pulled out the Bible that Granny Smith had given him and held it up.

The black form moved gingerly back to the other side of the room, knocking over other small objects as it went.

James said in a low voice, "Leave us..., get out of here," stepping toward the form with his new weapon in front of him.

The form shifted and transformed itself into a hideous face and exited through the wall, shaking the house and the very glass in the windowpanes.

"Well, that worked," said James.

There was a moment of silence as Martiel stared at her nephew in shock.

"You handled that better than I did," Aunt Martiel said with a quiver in her voice. "I don't know if I'll be sleeping any more tonight. Is that what you were running from in your sleep?" she asked. "Because I..., I can understand why you'd be running."

Martiel was beginning to ramble on nervously. James finally saw her state and tried to comfort her thumping heart.

"I haven't figured out how to deal with the dreams yet," said James. "But after my talk with Jolie tonight, I realized that all these things are exactly like the demons I had to fight when I was a kid. As long as you run, they'll chase you, but when you stand up, they don't know what to do."

"Why..., you've got more brass...," she stammered. "Uh, that is..., guts than I gave you credit for."

After several minutes of confessing her feelings of fright to James, Martiel slowly began to relax once more. It was a little after three in the morning and the day still too premature even for an early riser.

Together they examined the room and when they were satisfied that no specters were lurking, Martiel said goodnight once again and lay back down.

The light on the nightstand gave a faithful reassuring glow as she dug in under the covers on her bed.

James sat on the edge of his bed in silence, deep in thought....

Chapter 30

"You can't let me in the pound?" barked the deputy. "I need to take a look at the vehicle that the kid was driving."

"I'm really sorry Floyd, the sheriff ordered us. Anyone entering has to have signed permission with his name attached to it," said the officer.

"I'm still the Deputy Sheriff, Claude, besides…, if you still want me to get you tickets to see the Saints play, come September…."

"That's coercion or bribery or something isn't it?" grinned the officer. "All right, but only for a few minutes," grunted Claude. "The sheriff was really being a tight-ass about this. I can't afford to lose my job."

"Thanks," said the deputy.

There was a loud click as he bounded through the squeaking turnstile, "I owe you."

Moments later Floyd was circling the mud covered 4X4, which was parked under one of several dim overhead mercury lights. The unseasonably cool morning had fogged the air and covered the skin of the truck with a heavy coating of morning dew.

He grabbed at the tailgate and jumped up on the lower step of the bumper. His foot slipped on the goop and his shin crawled angrily down a rusty trailer hitch until the weight of his foot hit the ground.

Floyd moaned and cursed under his breath. His fingertips were covered in a slimy substance created from the moisture and the muddy cake. Once more, cursing the growing pain along his wounded shin, he carefully climbed up on the bumper and peered over the bent tailgate, taking inventory of the items not removed by the initial investigation.

There were various and sundry items along with dirt, rust, rotting leaves, and wood chips; all of which could link the truck to the scene of the crime and would take a shovel to remove.

More importantly, he didn't see anything that screamed his involvement.

He jumped down and looked at his watch, 5:40 AM, another ten minutes and he would have to leave or risk getting caught.

The driver side door of the truck opened and he eased forward peering inside at the shadows. The truck was much taller than it had appeared from a distance and the floorboard was equal in height to his upper thighs. He brandished his flashlight in and around the floor, and under the seat. Mostly spent beer cans and crumpled fast food sacks were all that littered the floor. He swished the items from side to side looking carefully, but seeing nothing of importance. The sound of the empty beer cans reminded him of his early career as a park ranger, foisting off raccoons from trash receptacles.

The floor was as dirt caked as the outside of the truck, but dry. He noticed the corner of a floor mat cemented to the floorboard, barely distinguishable from the wealth of packed earth.

One corner of the mat under the seat was loose and he cautiously pulled it up, popping dust into the chilled air as it released its hold from the floor. Underneath were several small pieces of paper and upon looking, they were only receipts from months or possibly years gone by. He lifted them out one by one and set them on top of the mat. They were almost illegible from the environment in which they had been encased. Then he tumbled them over singly, revealing places and dates, again mostly fast food or gas.

After he was convinced there was nothing of interest, he took all of the papers and pushed them back under the mat and it plopped heavily back down. The commotion forced a single slip of paper in the air, as if by providence, attaching itself to the front of his tan uniform blazer.

He brushed it off and in the motion noticed a smear of ink on the back. It was scrawled with "Floyd-2601". Tingles shivered his spine as he considered the thought of anyone else making that discovery. He hastily shoved it into his pocket, recognizing it as the last four digits to his pager number.

He was so busy with his new find that he didn't hear the familiar light squeak and click of the turnstile, the entrance into the confines of the pound.

"Did you find anything of interest?" asked a familiar voice.

The deputy spun on his heel to see Sheriff Howard looking at him just as a flashlight blinded his vision.

"Nothing in the paper about that little creep," said Martin Ames, sipping his morning cup of coffee and scanning the paper.

"I suppose I should call the sheriff and file a complaint about the gravestone being broken, for all the good that will do."

Maime had opened the oven to let some of the heat into the kitchen, revealing a pan of fresh biscuits.

"Does the paper mention anything about why it turned off so cool?" she asked. "I don't remember it ever being this cool here this time of year."

"I haven't exactly had my ear to the weatherman these last few days," said Martin Earl. "Besides, it'll probably be hotter than heck by noon. I'll be happy for a cool shop to work in this morning."

James Earl and Martiel ground to a halt the driveway, the deep rumble of the Mustang's engine going silent. Grampa looked up at the clock on the wall – 7:01 AM.

"About time," he muttered, looking back at his paper.

"Is something bothering you, Martin?" asked Maime. "You really seem uptight this morning."

She eased over and sat in the chair next to him for a moment, her hand sliding along his back.

"Yeah, I guess so," said Martin, with a sideways nod her direction. "It's not about us; you know I love you. We better talk about it later, Hun."

James and his Aunt Martiel sauntered in through the door, looking like worn, coarse sandpaper.

"Rough night?" asked Maime.

"You have no idea," said Martiel. "I'll save that little horror story for later.... I want to wake up some first."

"You ready to go James?" asked Martin.

"Now you let him get a bite to eat before you two leave," scolded Maime. "Earl's Garage and that car will still be there when *you* get there. I swear..., everybody is either uptight or worn ragged lately," she mumbled as she reached in the stove with her oven mitt.

"I can't believe how much sugar was in that tank," said James yawning and shivering at the same time.

"You still not sleeping?" asked Martin. "I was hoping that things would settle down for you over there with my little sister."

"Same old," said James, looking back at the pail of dirty golden granules.

He didn't want to alarm his grampa with the details of how physical his problem was becoming. He shoved his hands as deep as they would go into the pockets on his coveralls looking for warmth.

"You were right - the sugar didn't melt in the gas."

"Let's get busy and wrap this up," said Martin. "People don't seem to understand the *We're Closed* sign while the bay doors are wide open."

The Chevy's main gas line had been the hardest to clean and took over an hour to rid of its sweet parasite. Putting BeBe's vehicle all back together was the easy part.

They cranked the car and ran a mixture of cleaner to flush the engine of any possible residue. By ten that morning, Martin Ames was closing the hood.

"Another perfect job," said Martin. "Would you give BeBe a call and let her know that we're through?"

As James walked toward the office, his grampa added, "Let her know that I'll drop it off in an hour or so at her café."

"I don't mind taking it over to her," said James.

"I'm sure you don't," said Martin, his grin widening. "I don't want you driving. You need to go back to our place and get some rest. That's an order."

"You know, sometimes I hate it when you're right," said James.

When James Earl arrived at his grandparents' house, Martiel was fast asleep on the couch and Gramma Ames had left a note that she was at the church, helping clean up the facilities.

James had shed most of his grime with the coveralls at the garage, but scrubbed off the leftovers in a hot shower as soon as he hurried through the house.

Afterward, the house was still and quiet. James grabbed his personal journal and went timidly to the back room, where he innocently began this summer's visit with his grandparents. The bedroom was uneventful, but flavored with the love of his gramma's taste in décor. She had picked up, cleaned, and straightened up the room that had once been her daughter Catherine's before she married and left home.

He sat down in the straight back chair in front of a small square desk by his open bedroom door. After staring at a blank page, with pen in his hand for almost a half-hour, not knowing where to begin, he closed the cover.

"I think it's about time I put away some of my past," James said to himself aloud. "Time to be a man."

He quickly wrote, "The End."

James took his journal and tossed it into the waste paper basket next to the desk.

Feeling lighter, he walked over to the bed and stretched out across its soft white cotton spread.

The steady ringing of the phone in the outer office went completely unnoticed by Sheriff Howard and his deputy as they sat in the interrogation room with Officer Claude.

"Tell me again exactly what it was you were looking for," said the sheriff angrily. "You knew that truck was off-limits to everyone until it was gone over completely. Claude, didn't you explain to Deputy Floyd that no one was to have access to that truck with out my signature!?" he said slamming his fist down on the rickety table.

Claude looked the sheriff in the eyes and back down at the table. His eyes cut over to Floyd in a snap, expecting the deputy to own up, but neither said anything.

Sheriff Howard felt as if he were scolding two school boys, watching each of them shoot accusing glances at each other.

"Your silence answered my question," he continued.

Floyd cut his eyes sharply over to Officer Willis and quickly back to the table.

"I thought that I might see something that would help find the other people involved," said the deputy, which was only a partial lie.

The sheriff circled the two misfits, thinking.

"I guess I should have told you that I was watching the truck," said the sheriff. "I was hoping to leave it there under the light as bait to see who might be interested in its contents.

"Just the same, you still should have followed procedure..., both of you," he said. "Especially you, Officer Claude."

There was a long moment of uncomfortable silence.

"Alright, no harm done," said the sheriff. "The truck is still there and we'll keep up the watch over it for another day or two. I didn't expect to catch one of my own digging around in my trap."

"You might not be so quick to accuse me for trying to help next time," Deputy Floyd said, fully pushing his luck.

The sheriff looked at both of them for a moment, "What I expect out of you, both of you, despite your intentions, is to follow orders. If I can't trust my own men, we don't stand a chance making this office run. We don't need to be spending our time with internal problems while there are still more suspects on the loose. We need to work as a team.

"As much as I'd like to let this slide, I'm putting you both on report. Now, both of you get back to work," said the sheriff exasperated.

It was almost one o'clock by the time the sheriff was through scolding his officers, finally making his way past the front desk.

"Sheriff?" called Jeanette. "Sheriff, you had a visitor.... I looked for you, but...."

"I was in a meeting," said the sheriff gruffly. "Who came by?"

"Mr. Martin Ames came by and filed a complaint that has something to do with the Heaven's Gate cemetery incident."

The sheriff groaned and took the piece of paper offered him by his clerk. "What now?" he mumbled to himself.

He looked at the time and realized that it was well past his regular lunchtime, but decided on a cup of coffee instead. He ambled on, settling into his office and closing the door.

After he sunk down in his swivel chair, he rubbed his face with mildly calloused palms and fingers, wondering what could go wrong next.

After gathering his thoughts and a sip of old coffee, he picked up the form handed him and read the information penned by one of the communities more respected residents.

"Probably unrelated vandals," he mumbled to himself. "But Martin Ames won't accept that explanation. I guess I'll look at this one myself," he said changing his mind. "I need out of here...."

He pushed the button on his phone that connected him to the clerk.

"Jeanette, I'm going to go take a look at this complaint personally and grab some food..., do you want anything?"

Jeanette was shocked it was so out of his character. "Uh..., no, but thank you for asking. Already ate," came scratchily over the phone.

Chapter 31

The Chevy was barely moving from the idling engine, purring like a kitten.

"How much do I owe you?" asked BeBe. "My little car sounds like it did when it was brand new."

"It's already taken care of," said Martin Ames as he reached inside and switched off the motor to the car.

"I don't think so..., you have to let me pay you," she argued.

"I don't think it would be in good taste to charge *potential* future family members for favors."

BeBe stared at Martin's graying hair, "You're probably right about that. It is pretty obvious. Those kids *are* really stuck on each other. All we can do is let it run its course."

Martin shrugged, "They do look good together."

She grinned slyly, "Yeah, they do."

Martin chuckled and turned to leave.

"Well then..., thank you..., and James. At least let me buy you some lunch."

"I'd consider it payment in full," said Martin Ames.

"Well then, come on inside and pick a seat."

After ordering his food, BeBe sat down at his table cradling a cup of coffee.

"How is James?" she asked. "I know he hurt his head a lot worse than he told us."

"He's going to be fine," he said, after a sip of coffee. "I sent him home when we finished up so he could get some rest."

"He's still having trouble sleeping, isn't he?" she asked. "I have a friend that's a doctor and she happens to deal with a variety of disorders like James is having. I'd be glad to call her and find out if she has time to see him."

"After the incident with your car, you have enough problems without taking on more," he mumbled. "Did you ever come up with any idea of who might want to cause you that much trouble?"

"That's more than a nasty prank; in fact I think somebody is trying to send you a message."

"Not a soul. I don't have any enemies..., at least any that I know of. I have a policy of not throwing stones."

"Is there a possibility that it has to do with James?" asked Martin.

"Somebody jealous of him and Jolie maybe?"

"She doesn't really know anybody from around here," said BeBe. "Not that she hasn't had her regular share of offers, mind you. She moved here from out in California, right after she finished her school year, so she hasn't really had time to get involved with anybody. Anybody else, that is."

"Same thing with James," he replied. "Maybe I'm reading too much into it."

"I don't know either. We're both grasping at straws, because it isn't making any sense," BeBe said as she excused herself.

Before leaving the restaurant, Martin couldn't shrug off the strange foreboding he felt. Where he usually felt the relief of a completed job, there was the heaviness of some unknown. Something needed to be done.

"I gave your offer some thought about the doctor," he said. "I think it might be a good idea to get an outside opinion."

"Okay then, I'll give her a call and see if she can fit James in as soon as possible," said BeBe. "Of course we still need to see if James wants her help first."

"After the little I heard about last night, I don't see that as a problem," said Martin Ames.

The tiny scrim of moon from another time was on the horizon with a few wispy clouds scarring its glow. Cold February air was rushing past his dreaming ears, and into his heaving lungs as he ran.

Only a half mile further ahead, there would be people, someone, anyone who might help him. That is, if there was any help to be found.

There it was again, right behind him, pushing him, relentless and tireless. He never could quite get a look at what was on his heels, only a glimpse of shapes and movement.

Dry wispy switches, from winter sleepy limbs, were whipping at his numb cheeks as he pushed himself to the last of his strength.

His legs became rubbery beneath him, causing him to stumble and each desperately needed footstep to become unsure. More sure was his terror that this unseen predator would finally catch up to him and then what?

Unspeakable thoughts rolled through his mind of evils promised to be sent his way. His hand burned like fire, and the precious cloth burden became heavy in his clutches.

Was this thing sent to reconcile a life for a life? Why couldn't he remember? He had a faint memory of a fire, some lost love grieving his mind. He argued and plead that he had no part in what had happened, now months ago.

The gambler's drunken decision to jump over into the darkness of the Mississippi River was his own and in front of a multitude of witnesses. His only meetings with his adversary had been in horrid dreams. Now this judge, jury, and executioner - a black figure behind him – was refusing explanation and rigorously condemning him to some hellish finish.

But who could have sent it? Did someone know of his transgressions?

Syrus Earl Ames near exhaustion, lungs burning and sides in stitches, tripped on one of several cypress knees rising up out of the cold gritty sand.

The small inlet would have been a safe harbor to someone in a skiff, escaping a stormy river, but it served as yet another obstacle to a man running desperately along its banks. This was for his life.

He stood quickly from his fall, strength waning, tripped again, heaving in the cold night air.

A heavy weight landed on his back. With the last of his strength, he rolled over on his back to fight off his oppressor.

A dark figure, somewhat transparent to the brilliant stars in the sky, loomed over his body. Readjusting itself on top of Syrus as he rolled, centering its weight on his chest.

Syrus screamed until his throat burned. The weight was unbearable on his chest. He pushed and swatted at an enemy of mist dropping his precious package. It was like fighting the air in a storm with only fists as weapons. He couldn't seem to take in a breath from the weight and his chest was caving in from the pain.

As a last gasp of effort, he flipped and arose to his knees, again falling from the weight now shifted to his back. His face fell into the chilled waters of the Mississippi River and gasping for air, filled his lungs with muddy water.

When his last gasp came, when he understood it was ending, when it was almost over, he wept unseen tears into the dark unforgiving waters.

Syrus slowly slid from his body like butter on a hot plate into an oily darkness.

James woke up as he hit the floor in the bedroom, gagging and spitting up muddy water.

Real mud and brackish water splattered the floor as he coughed painfully. No dream could be this real. He was in hell. His head was pounding from yet another collision with the hardwood floor and his nose was bleeding.

In rushed his Aunt Martiel with a look of horror on her face. Instead of speaking, she turned and disappeared back into the hallway. She reappeared an eternity later with a wet towel from the bathroom. James managed to sit up on the floor with his back to the bed, with his face now buried in his hands.

"I don't want any part of any of this," blubbered James. "This isn't right, isn't normal, none of it. I've had all I can stand."

"Just close your eyes and let me wash your face off."

"Close my eyes? I don't ever want to close my eyes again," he croaked.

"Do you see this? Its mud and water. I just watched…, no I *FELT* myself, I mean Syrus, die with some black shadowy thing on his back and his face in cold muddy water. I *FELT* him drown and die. I *FELT* him die and slide right out of his body."

Aunt Martiel quietly washed the blood and something that looked like gritty dirt from James' face and mouth as he continued to spit.

"I've never seen or heard of anything like this," said Aunt Martiel. "We need to get you some help."

"There's no help for me," said James. "Where is it going to come from? No matter who I tell, they'll put me away, permanently."

Chapter 32

"I don't think it's a good idea for you go with me Aunt Martiel," said James. "I talked it over with BeBe and I don't think Jolie should come either. BeBe agrees."

"Well I don't think it's a good idea for you to be alone or without someone that can understand what you're going through," said Martiel. "That's not safe either."

A few moments later, a familiar car entered the driveway next to the Ames house.

"Now please, don't tell gramma and grampa what happened today. The less they know about what's going on the better, do you understand?" asked James.

There was a knock at the door and James stepped over and opened it to a familiar friendly face. BeBe stepped inside and said hello, giving a tired James Earl a much needed hug.

"I came as soon as I could," said BeBe. "I was able to make an appointment with my acquaintance for this evening. We have a few minutes before we have to go, but it's a long drive. Do you want to tell me a little about what happened?"

"Not really," said James. "Just another dream where I was Syrus Earl Ames, only he died…, I died or felt him die…, it's hard to explain."

BeBe looked first at James and then Martiel who only shrugged and nodded her head in agreement.

"You have another bump on your head, James," said BeBe, softly caressing James' forehead. "You're really getting beat up by all this, aren't you sweetie?"

BeBe stepped back and sighed, "Jolie wanted to come, but I didn't think it was in her best interest or yours, James."

"I agree," said James. "Jolie shouldn't be anywhere near me, nobody should. I think its best if only you and I visit your doctor friend."

"About that," said BeBe nervously. "I need to be completely honest with you about my doctor friend. She isn't a traditional doctor in that sense of the word."

"What do you mean, not a traditional doctor?" asked Martiel. "Is she some sort of specialist?"

"Let's just say, she is more of a "spiritual" doctor," said BeBe.

"A healer?" asked Martiel.

"Among other things," said BeBe. "She's a seer. She'll be able to figure this out and put an end to all of it."

James felt his head swim, "A seer? Oh, *hell no*, not more mumbo jumbo," whined James. "I've had about all I can take with the dreams and spirits and ghosts and Elberta's."

BeBe put up her hands defensively, "I know how you feel James, but I really believe she can help. She has helped me with bad situations before, maybe not as bad as this. I don't know of anybody else who would be more understanding of what you're experiencing without thinking you had gone off the deep end."

"Just who is this *friend* of yours?" asked Aunt Martiel.

"Her name is Dubois, Ms. Dubois, and she is a *Mambo*."

There was a long silence as BeBe let her revelation sink in.

"A what?" Aunt Martiel asked, flabbergasted.

James stood there speechless, suddenly wondering what his brother Sam was doing at that moment, and remembering that his mother, Catherine, had quit her job and was staying home nowadays. Wasn't he supposed to be installing new speakers in his car next week?

James slowly dropped down on the couch, realizing how insane his life had become.

He was in Hell.

With her wary passenger seated next to her, BeBe drove down the narrow two-lane clippity-clop highway to some obscure bend in the road in Louisiana that James had never heard of.

The sound of Aunt Martiel's voice was still echoing in his head. The two women had led him out to the baby blue sedan, the one that he and his grandfather had cleared of a sugar-infestation only hours ago.

Now he was going to see a witch doctor, a voodoo person.

"Life doesn't get any better than this," he thought, his eyes leaking salty drops of unspoken regret.

James looked at his hands, flexed his fists, watching tiny scars on his forearms shift, asking himself why his life had always been a curse. Just when he expected it all to get better, it all began to slide downhill.

Two hours of highway passed while watching vine covered trees and leaning telephone poles drift by, until they arrived at a small town with a tiny gas station and grocery store combined.

Its paint was a faded green and the small covered front needed some serious repair. The sky had become overcast gray the nearer they came to the Gulf Coast and the day seemed to keep getting longer.

James remembered the dread of his first trip to the doctor as a child for a tetanus shot and shuddered. If only this was that simple; a quick prick of the needle, a few pills, or some nasty tasting syrup, and a few days bed rest.

BeBe pulled next to an antique gas pump and got out of her car. James sat still, transfixed, staring at a decaying billboard advertising *Gulf No-Nox* gasoline. BeBe returned a few minutes later with two bottled Cokes and some snack food.

"We're almost there, do you need to stretch? Bathroom?" she asked politely.

James only shook his head and thanked her for the drink.

In another ten minutes, they were driving along a gravel road up to a nicely landscaped, large weathered home. Years of foul weather and little maintenance had worn the white washed paint on this once beautiful home place. The yard was littered with bordered patches of flower gardens. Neatly trimmed oleander bushes bursting with fuchsia blossoms accented each side of a flagstone path up to its porch.

As they parked, a woman in an intensely white dress and matching head wrap walked out onto the porch to greet them. Her dark skin highly contrasted the clothing and the beautiful smile that beamed from her face. She walked with the grace of any princess down the steps of a medieval castle.

James looked at her clothes and flashed a moment of dread. It was almost like the dream. Her face was different, but everything else about her was like some nightmare flashback.

BeBe prodded him onward, pulling at his stalled pace, her arm locked elbow to elbow.

"Welcome BeBe, and you must be James," Ms. Dubois said in a kind voice, obviously trying to put James at ease.

"Please, come inside," as she swept her hand toward her front door.

She gave BeBe a hug laced with comfortable familiarity and told her how good it was to see her again. As James walked past, her expression changed from her buoyant smile to one of deep concern.

"Please come into my sitting room..., would you like some refreshments?" she asked. "No? Well then let's get right to it then."

"James please come sit over here with me."

James looked around for a crystal ball and other items, but the room was as normal as his grandmother's living room. In fact, it could have been his grandmother's house. Everything was neat, clean, and normal, almost to a fault.

"I understand that BeBe gave you her medallion a few days ago, are you still wearing it?"

James politely said, yes ma'am, taking a seat in a soft wing back chair. Ms. Dubois pulled a similar chair in front of his, facing him squarely.

Reaching out, she took his hands in hers, closed her eyes only for a moment, and took a slow breath. When she opened her eyes, her soft smile was back and her pleasant features relaxed James somewhat.

"BeBe has told me most everything that I need to know, so you relax," she stated. "You don't need to feel as if you're being examined, even if you are."

She smiled again trying to calm his nervousness.

Her hands felt soft as a small child and just as gentle.

"I understand that you are about to come into some gifts of your own, is that correct? Just nod…, you don't have to talk."

James nodded yes, although he wished the opposite were true. He couldn't remember being this relaxed or peaceful in a very long time. She turned his hands over and back several times feeling his palms and backs with her fingertips. The sensation was so relaxing that James began to drift off.

"It's okay if you get sleepy and want to close your eyes. Take a deep breath and go ahead and close your eyes if you like."

James drifted off into a low sleepy state. Her voice seemed to come from some far away place.

"You don't seem to be especially happy about your new talents," she said.

James shook his head slowly from side to side.

"That's something you should be proud of under normal circumstances. It truly is a gift to be able to help others."

She then took James' right hand in both of hers with its palm facing up. She sat quietly for a few moments and James almost drifted completely to sleep.

Suddenly, Ms. Dubois sat back in her chair dropping James hand, causing James to open his eyes.

She sat trancelike staring straight ahead, yet seeing nothing but a far away place. Her expression turned to one of pain and a grimace across her forehead.

"You been marked," she said, her voice slightly different from before; almost having a texture to its character. She let out a long breath and took in another.

"Not you exactly, but it all comes down to you. These gifts have been handed down for generations in your family. It all started with a man and a woman many years ago; a deal was forged with dark magic. Now somebody wants your talents in a bad way and they want something that only the man knew," she continued. "His name was…, Syrus. I can only see so much, but the *Loa* see all and know all."

She took a breath and blinked her eyes and seemed to change again, relaxing. After walking over to a closed hutch, she reached inside and pulled out a round object covered with a bright yellow cloth.

Carefully, she set this new object down heavily on a small marble-top end table near them and shifted her chair more toward its direction. With the cover removed, James saw that it was a bust that looked like an African native, made of exotic, highly polished ebony wood. It was inlaid with gold eyes and gold teeth, but it's most striking feature were the eyes. They had protruding golden thorn-like objects as if shooting out rays of sunlight from them.

It was beautiful and yet frightening at the same time.

In a few seconds, her expression changed back into the alternate face it had been before.

"There is a *Baka* that has your scent and has been looking for you, chasing you. You have information Syrus hid and passed on to each male in your family. You have it in you even now, but it's hidden, from me and even from you.

The one which sent the *Baka* is dark, evil, the face is hidden from even me...," her expressions turned to those of pain as she spoke of the evil.

"You beat the evil with your strength and your faith and sent it back home, but it marked something of yours."

After a few moments of tormenting silence, she spoke again.

"Can I see the medallion, please?"

James removed BeBe's necklace and handed it to Ms. Dubois.

"Interesting. How long has it been smudged like this?" she asked BeBe and looking at James.

The necklace was deeply tarnished almost completely black on both sides.

"Why, never that I knew of," said BeBe and James confirmed the same answer shaking his head.

She held the medallion in her hand and faced the statue-like ornament. Once again, she was quiet for a few moments and laid the necklace aside.

"This *Bokor* is blinded and only knows greed and revenge. Very powerful. Very dangerous. Very determined. Whatever it is that is hidden inside you is very valuable to this *Bokor.*"

She became nervous and quiet as if listening to a voice only she could hear.

"The *Bokor* is preparing to send the dead, *voye lamo....*

Your life is in the balance. It can only retrieve secrets you have inside you if it can steal your spirit. It seeks to kill you and capture your *gwo bon anj*, your soul in a *govi*, a clay pot and make you *zombie astral*, a slave forever."

Ms. Dubois sat back painfully, as water dripped from her eyes.

"It must be stopped or you will suffer things worse than death."

Ms. Dubois broke off her communication with whatever source she was seeking and stood up and walked around the room.

James, by now, was wide-awake, watching and listening to everything she had to say.

BeBe sat quietly as if all of this happened every day. She spoke up and asked, "Can you tell us who or where this is coming from?"

"No, it is too dangerous," said Ms Dubois. "To seek the source is to invite its presence here. To call its name is to invite it here. It would be a summons.

"I will need to give you another medallion, BeBe. This marked one will need to be destroyed. It has not only been blackened, but marks James for the *Baka* to find him again.

"The *Loa* say that a trick was laid upon you, is that true?"

She drifted away again, painfully so….

"Yes, a worker came and marked your door, there was powder on your door. You touched it. Then you touched…."

Ms. Dubois gasped, "Oh no…, you put your blood on an effigy, an *ouanga*…, tossed underneath your front porch steps."

Ms. Dubois snapped back to reality, with James nearly in shock. How could she possibly have known that?

"James, you must not seek out this source. Your natural inquisitiveness has brought much upon you."

She quickly and carefully re-covered the bust with its cloth and placed it back inside her hutch, hiding it from sight.

"Let me see the hand that bled," she said.

James held up the finger that was stuck by the pin in the doll under the steps of the old home place. The tip was ugly and red.

"The yellow powder that was on the door, was that what you're talking about?" asked James. "It really stunk bad. My Aunt Martiel scrubbed the whole door with lye water. There was one little spot with this yellow stinky stuff…."

"You touched it with the same finger," she said. "Haven't you every heard that curiosity killed the cat?"

"How was I supposed to know?" asked James. "I don't know anything about any of this. How am I supposed to stop all this?"

"I can help you, little one," said a soft high-pitched voice from a doorway.

Everyone turned and looked in the direction of an adjacent room that had been dark and silent when they arrived. Ms. Dubois bowed her head as the little withered figure of a man nimbly walked into the room. He was dressed in brightly colored and decorated clothing from neck to bare feet and obviously older than he looked.

"This is my *Oungan*, Dominique, my mentor and wise one, also *Gran Met* to all who gather here," said Ms. Dubois, reciting some sort of rhetorical homage.

Dominique allowed her to finish before he entered the room and walked over to where James sat, stopping beside him.

He placed his hand on James' shoulder lightly as a feather.

"All is not lost. *Bondye* has looked on your innocence with favor. Because He has, so will I.

"This *Bokor* is not without weaknesses. This powerful one grows very old…, haste and greed may be its downfall. It is also the last; there will be no other to follow, if it is defeated.

"You must know that it has many eyes and ears and arms and legs that serve it without question. Do not let your affections snare your mind or you will continue this fight in death."

The little man became stiff and quiet, reflecting on the moment and frightening James as a tingling sensation flowed from Dominique's hand down through his shoulder.

"You must break the snare to end the terror or this evil one will grow stronger and go on without end."

James looked at BeBe as if Dominique were speaking Greek.

"Remember my words and save yourself *and* your family," said Dominique as he finished his oration.

He turned around and walked back out of the room through the same door.

Ms. Dubois stood and said, "We will make prayers on your behalf, but preparations must be made. It will take a few days. I also have presents for the both of you as my master wishes."

She walked out of the room and down a hallway to the back of the house. James and BeBe sat looking at each other in silence.

James started to speak, but BeBe laid a finger to her lips, motioning for him to wait.

Several minutes later Ms. Dubois reappeared out of the hallway entrance.

She had a small bowl and several items wrapped up in a cloth. Carefully she placed the bowl down and presented the rest to BeBe. BeBe ducked her head as she placed a new necklace and medallion around her neck.

Ms. Dubois placed another in BeBe's hand, "This is for your family member who insists on getting involved. She must not take it off or the snare will finish its work."

She turned to James and said, "The rest is for you, all you need to know is written inside."

She retrieved the bowl, "Please place your wounded finger into the liquid. It will purge the poison from your blood."

James looked into the small bowl, thinking of bad horror flicks with smoking boiling bats wings. He nevertheless obeyed Ms. Dubois and stuck his finger deep into the cool dark liquid. His fingertip felt much better for a moment then it suddenly began to burn like hell, even up into his hand and up his arm.

James jerked his finger out of the bowl, blowing on it frantically.

"Shit, shit, shit," he repeated as he puffed air on the end of his pointer. "Oh, I'm sorry," said James, embarrassed at his outburst.

"Your finger will be better before you get home," she said.

"Yeah, my aunt always tells me that it'll feel better when it quits hurting," he grunted angrily.

"It is time for you to go now. Follow the instructions exactly."

BeBe reached into her purse to pay for their services, but Ms. Dubois quickly placed her hand on BeBe's and stopped her.

"The *Gran Met* says that I am not to receive an offering for our services. The struggle James faces is for the good of all."

James felt as if the entire world had derailed and was wobbling aimlessly through space. He looked down at his finger and to his surprise the redness was gone as well as the throbbing pain.

"What was that bowl of stuff I put my finger in?" asked James. "And why were you so quiet in there? I didn't understand half of what was said by the Gramp Met..."

"The *Gran Met*," corrected BeBe. "He is sort of like the pastor of your church, or actually an apostle to several churches."

James wanted to ask how BeBe had come to know such strange people and dared a comment, "I've never seen a church like that."

BeBe nodded and turned the vehicle onto the highway, "Once, when I couldn't receive the answers I needed from my own prayers, I became impatient and found myself in a troubled place. That was when I chanced to meet my friend Ms. Dubois..., and she helped me through a very bad time in my life. You don't have to understand everything that was said, simply follow their instructions."

"Well I hope you took lots of notes and can translate it all to me," said James opening the cloth of other items.

James looked at the items and the care in which they were packed and wrapped with little individual instruction sheets for each.

After a few moments of silence and listening to the thump and hum of the tires on the road, James spoke up.

"I'm sorry for being such a rear and I appreciate everything that you're doing for me. I didn't mean to disrespect your friends either. I don't know why I'm losing it. I'm saying things I shouldn't say. I'm thinking things I shouldn't think. I....."

BeBe reached over, brushed James' cheek with the back of her hand, and smiled.

"We're all tired, James. It's okay."

Chapter 33

The condensed report was easily two pages long, with a more complete dossier on it's way through a fax machine.

"Got you now, you little bastard," said Sheriff Howard.

The file he held in his hands revealed the life and times of one Roger Mastyn escaped from Louisiana State Juvenile Corrections at age 15. He was a slippery little eel that had evaded the law for two years.

Father – unknown.

Mother: Louisa Mastyn – deceased.

"She died of a heroin overdose, big surprise," he mumbled.

Born in New Iberia..., wanted as a suspect in a murder..., liquor store robbery that went bad.... The list went on endlessly.

"Well, that's certainly more colorful than I expected for someone that young."

The sheriff pressed one of the intercom buttons on his desk.

"Jeanette, would you have a couple of men bring our new boy up front to the interrogation room? Oh, and call that attorney of his..., I don't want us to make any mistakes...."

Darkness had long filled the night sky as James and BeBe made their way back to Natchez, Mississippi. James had read most of the instructions provided before it became too dark to see inside BeBe's car.

He finally broke the silence that had hovered for almost an hour.

"I don't understand how taking a bath in this," he said holding up a small packet, "...and burning this or drinking this," holding some other items up for inspection, "...is supposed to help. Or..., this."

He held up a hand-sewn brilliant red and black pouch with interesting scents and fragrances spilling from inside it.

"Please don't think I'm ungrateful, but I don't understand any of it," said James.

BeBe assured him once again that if he would only follow the instructions to the letter, that things would start getting better for him.

"Remember, they will be praying for you too," she said.

James remembered the prayers that Granny Smith had made for him in the past. How things always seemed to work themselves out for the best. Her loss crushed him and he wished that Granny Smith was still around and fell into a deep quiet sadness. Darkness overtook his thoughts as he retreated into the previous hopeless silence.

If he could only tell his mother what was happening to him. That was a joke. His mother and father had already proven their support too many times in the past.

They never believed the things he told them when he was a little kid, fighting for his life right in front of their noses. Why should he expect them to believe him with something as wild as this?

He didn't believe this was happening to him, why would he expect them or anyone else with a rational mind to believe him?

He pictured himself in a nice white padded cell, with some doctor in a white suit quietly nodding to him as he described his insanity and scratching his own back inside the perpetual hug of a custom fitted straitjacket.

He was alone in this; as alone as he had been when he was six years old and got pummeled down to the ground while the teachers turned accusing blind eyes.

No matter how many people tried to help him, the fact remained, he was alone. To involve anybody would put them in danger. He knew this. He felt the certainty.

There was no need of some preacher or whatever to tell him; he was living this hell all to himself. James' thoughts drifted back to the present and he began dreading going to sleep again this night. Any night. He longed for someone to take it all away..., as the steady hum of the engine and exhaustion lulled him into light sleep.

The sheriff waited patiently, holding a file folder and sipping coffee outside the window of the interrogation room. He had been waiting for the young man's attorney to make an appearance and maybe get a few answers from this prisoner.

He peered once again into the room to see the exact same thing he had the previous four or five times. This Roger Mastyn was completely still in his seat and staring intently at the blank white wall in front of him as if it was a movie theater and the matinee about to begin. He looked about as threatening as a child with crayons.

"Murder suspect...," muttered the sheriff to himself.

It didn't seem possible.

The front door-sensor beeped, announcing that someone had entered the secure area of the building. In a few moments, the attorney along with Deputy Floyd entered the long hall, walking down to where the sheriff was waiting.

"I've been trying to reach you all day," whined the attorney in a high-pitched voice.

"I've been taking care of some internal business," said the sheriff, glancing tiredly over at Deputy Floyd.

"What was so important?"

"The blood samples came back from your John Doe. He's got some kind of drug resembling LSD in his blood, but it's incredibly potent and they can't pin down exactly what it is."

"Great, so he's on some kind of bad trip?" asked the sheriff.

"May be," said the attorney. "I have more bad news. Whatever he used was so strong, this could be permanent. He won't be able to stand trial in his current condition."

The sheriff handed the attorney the manila folder.

"Here, you probably want to take a look at this before we go in and try to talk to him. I'll need to make arrangements to have him moved to a medical facility."

The sheriff took another sip of coffee, watching Deputy Floyd and his every reaction.

"You should probably sit in on this one, deputy, since you have such an *unusual* interest in this case. You might pick up on something we missed."

"Roger Mastyn...," drawled the attorney. "Wow..., long sad history."

"Yeah, add grave robbery, trespassing, vandalism, public intoxication of a minor, grand theft auto, and drug abuse to the end of that sheet," said the sheriff. "Are you ready?"

"As I'll ever be...," said the attorney. "I must remind you that since it is doubtful that he can understand you or his Miranda Rights, the information we gather will most likely only serve to find his co-conspirators."

They walked in quietly, as if it would make any difference to their alleged felon. Mastyn sat quietly with an unassuming, peaceful look on his face.

The deputy folded his arms and propped himself in the corner by the door. No one seemed to notice the single bead of sweat on his forehead or the tiny nervous twitch of the muscle on his left cheek.

The sheriff eased in front of the prisoner slowly and bent closer to look him directly in the eyes.

"Roger? Roger Mastyn?"

The young boy twitched slightly and blinked his eyes for a moment.

"Son, are you in there?" asked the sheriff hopefully, noticing the first real reaction since the morning after he was arrested.

From somewhere deep inside him, Roger Mastyn stopped reliving an experience from kindergarten, and heard the teacher call his name.

The sound was coming from somewhere down the echoing hall of his mind and was getting closer.

"Roger, we only want to talk to you."

The boy's eyes seemed to clear and a few rows of wrinkles appeared on his forehead, as if waking from a dream.

He turned his head slowly toward the mirrored window, looked over at the deputy, then back to the sheriff.

"Wha..., What am I doin' here?" asked the boy. "I rememba..., I rememba...."

"You remember what?" asked the sheriff.

"I was...," and he seemed to gag and cough on something stuck in his throat.

He spoke again, but his voice had become raspy and painful sounding.

"I was jus gettin' good an drunk, and then...," he looked up at the sheriff. Floyd's arms came uncrossed and hung loosely by his side. The boy looked over at the deputy as if he was going to ask another question.

Roger Mastyn began to choke, lasting a full minute. He gasped for air and spat up foamy white bile. He regained his breath for a moment and started shaking all over as if a cold chill had filled the room, looking insanely around the bare room.

"I think he's having a seizure," whispered the attorney. "He needs medical attention now."

The Mastyn boy began to feel a cold darkness sliding in. The florescent lighting in the room became a dim green-yellowish color. A sensation remembered from when he was a kid, one of the many times he was ill.

He tried to speak once more, but his breath was shut off again. His hands went to his throat and he slid to the floor shivering violently.

"Deputy, don't just stand there go call an amba-lance!" yelled the sheriff.

With great difficulty, they straightened the boy out on the floor and the attorney rushed away to retrieve a blanket from a cabinet outside the door. The sheriff had seen the effects of drugs and drug-induced shock before, but nothing quite like this.

A few moments later both men reappeared and helped cover and cradle the young man's body.

A deep darkness had covered the mind of Roger Mastyn, and now he was in a painful place. Dark, murky, cold, and he could only see a dim light around himself. He tried to breathe, tried to speak, but was choked off by unseen hands. There was a dark face above him grinning and saying words he'd never heard before, "*eye-a, eye-a, som-o, so-a*", repeating incessantly.

In the fading dimness, he could see a small painted gourd rising and falling with a fevered pitch, a scratchy noise almost obliterating all other sounds in his ears.

He looked around, terrified and straining to see something normal again, then saw Deputy Floyd and tried to speak once again. All air shut off to his lungs and his chest heaved up and down trying in desperation to gasp one more breath of air. His eyes bulged, his face paled, then his eyes and ears began to hemorrhage. His nose and mouth finally bubbled out a stench of white foamy death as his heart thrust its final struggle.

Then all Mastyn saw was blackness and the toothy, grinning weathered face of death itself.

The look on his face was so desperate that the sheriff felt true sorrow for him and began to panic. No one had ever died inside the jurisdiction of his Sheriff's Office.

"Where is that damn amba-lance!?" yelled the sheriff.

In those few moments, Deputy Floyd gained a completely new respect for Billy's associates whoever they were.

Roger Mastyn, age 17 years old, bastard child of a drug-addicted mother, stiffened, shook and died while cradled in the sheriff's arms.

James was driving, the sensation was something beyond surreal. Jolie was in his car with him and they were driving blazing fast, even for him. It was like floating and the steering was as sluggish as steering a boat.

This was a dream. Breathe. Take a breath. Now wake up. Wake..., up. It was a dark night down a long empty road and the headlights of his car were barely exposing a few feet in front of him.

Faster..., the dashes of line in the road seemed to whip into a blur right in front of his Mustang.

Jolie was looking over at him with a smile. James was frantic as to why he was driving so fast. Why was Jolie smiling? Wake up. He was gripping the steering wheel like steel.

Up ahead the road ended with a multi-stranded barbed wire fence. It was either left or right, but which way?

He hit the brakes, but nothing happened. His foot hit the floor several times in desperation. His car flew through the fence and into a black nothingness.

James yelled and sat bolt upright gripping the dashboard of BeBe's car. BeBe instantly jumped out of her daze and almost ran off the unevenly paved and shoulder-less road.

"What the devil was that all about!" yelled BeBe.

James looked over at her, wild-eyed, and took a few breaths. Slowly he slunk back in the passenger seat, shaking and chilled.

"Dream..., it was only a bad dream...," he explained, and turned to the window looking out into the black sky outside. "Welcome to my world."

"Another fifteen minutes and we'll be back in town," said BeBe. "Will you be okay 'till then?"

"Yeah..., yeah, I'm going to be just great," said James.

"I wonder what's keeping them," said Martiel. "I hope nothings wrong."

Maime Ames asked again where BeBe had taken James and what the doctor's name was. Martiel hated lying to them about where and to whom they went to see. It was something she was not used to doing. Never before had she been forced into a situation where she was required to tell an untruth to her brother and his wife. She feigned ignorance, but it felt the same as an outright lie.

Martiel kept her thoughts and opinions close. She was also wondering what James was going to tell his grandparents about his trip. Where they went and what was said. Her imagination was running wild with possible scenarios.

Finally, a few minutes past eight o'clock, the headlights of a vehicle turned the corner at the end of their long dead-end street and James and BeBe pulled into the driveway.

Martiel gave a sigh of relief at their arrival and walked onto the porch to stave off the questions that her family would be in pursuit of. James got out of the car first and ambled slowly toward his Aunt Martiel.

"Well, how did it go?" she asked. "I hope you have something to tell your grandparents, 'cause they've been driving me crazy with questions."

"It was an experience I won't ever forget in a lifetime," said James quietly.

As he stepped up into the porch light, Martiel could see how much James had aged in the last two weeks and it frightened her.

She had seen presidents go into office and gain 20 years to their features in only four years of service to their country, simply from stress. Now that same stress was beginning to show on her seventeen year old nephew.

BeBe got out of the car and walked up to where James and Martiel were whispering to each other. She handed James a paper sack with all of the paraphernalia the "doctors" had given him.

"I thought this would look a little more official than the cloth they were wrapped in," said BeBe.

"Thanks," said James taking the sack. "I really appreciate what you're trying to do for me BeBe."

"I'm going to hurry on back home, if it's okay with you James," said BeBe. "It's been a long day and I want to check on Jolie. There'll be fewer questions this way. You remember, that if you need anything at all, call me."

"I will," said James. "Let Jolie know...."

"She already knows how you feel about her, James," BeBe said, giving him a hug.

BeBe backed out of the driveway as his grandparents walked to the front door.

"Hello James." The bright familiar voice of his grampa rang from the door.

James turned and went inside carrying his sack of rituals and herbs.

"How was your trip, James?" they both asked in unison.

"It was fine. I talked to two doctors. They gave me a bunch of stuff to help me sleep and relax me," James said, holding up the sack as evidence.

Dark circles appeared under his eyes as he stepped into the light.

"They said that the main thing I need right now is sleep."

Then he rolled down the top of the brown bag hoping it would be a hint to keep them from looking inside it. He then handed it to Martiel with a certain quick look of eye contact.

"Where was this place, James?" asked Maime.

"I'm not really sure, some little town outside of New Orleans. They all ran together and I lost track," said James truthfully.

"Do y'all care if I go on over to Aunt Martiel's and get some rest?" asked James. "It's been a long day and I'm really tired."

"Sure you go on ahead," said his grandmother. "You two come over in the morning and I'll fix you both a good hot breakfast. Maybe we can talk then."

"Do you think we should call Catherine and tell her about James?" asked Maime.

"Tell her what?" asked Martin. "We know as much now as we did before he went to see the doctor."

"I guess you're right. There's no need to alarm the settlement over something we don't know about."

The two of them sat and watched the evening news while crunched together in their conservative Victorian loveseat. Their relationship for these many years had been one of trust, giving and respect. Love and companionship had never suffered losses from rigid arguments or selfishness. They both gave and took with their own kind of balance.

At the end of the news, they began their nightly ritual of getting ready for bed.

Martin Ames was the first to lie down. He had opened the curtains over a screen covered window and flipped on the quiet ceiling fan. In a few minutes the light switch in their private bathroom clicked off and Maime walked through the soft light to the bed.

Soft murmurs of sleep could be heard from the two of them in only a few minutes of stillness.

Click. Click clik. Click. Click.

A restless sound was coming from the room that James had been staying in. Looking for its prior occupant, but somehow lost.

Click. Click. Click.

Maime woke from a restlessness she couldn't understand. She turned over and Martin was breathing quietly, deep asleep. She closed her eyes and was about to drift off again.

Clik Clik Click....

Maime opened her eyes again recognizing the familiar sound from her and James' expedition only a few nights past. The ceiling fan was probably still on in their guest room and the little tassel tapping against the wobbling light fixture.

After trying to fall back asleep, the constant noise wasn't going to let her.

She slid carefully from her side of the bed and walked barefoot as quietly as she could on the cool hardwood floors. She took a few more cautions steps and stopped to listen, pinpointing where the noise was originating, but didn't hear the whir of the ceiling fan. A few seconds later she decided that it was coming from James' room near the end of the hall, not the tiny guest room.

Click. Click.

She walked through the already open bedroom door and paused to listen. She could no longer hear the gentle breathing of her husband down the hall. For the first time since her and her husband of many years set foot in their house, she felt afraid. Some darkness seemed to rake cold fingers down the back of her thin cloth nightgown. Now, the quiet distant whirr of the ceiling fan in her bedroom and the clicking echo around her was all that could be heard in the dark hallway.

She started to go back and get Martin to show him the annoying clicking James had been hearing. She turned, but heard another noise from James' room and spun back around. Seated on the headboard of his bed was a dark silhouette, perched like a big bird.

The room offered no external light to that part of the room, which made her imagination run wild. She staggered back into the hall and stood quietly. Suddenly there was no clicking or ticking and her world began to spin.

She eased her head slowly around the door jamb to look back inside. As her eyes again adjusted to the difference, a hideous black toothy face met her gaze. Face to face. She screamed and fell backward into the hallway hitting the wall.

Her hands grasped for anything of substance to regain her balance. She grasped a large framed picture on the wall, which gave way as she slid all the way to the floor. The heavy frame fell on her, then to the floor, shattering the glass.

Light immediately flooded their bedroom, partially illuminating the hall where she lay. She was hurting all over and felt something warm on her arm. Martin Ames came quickly down the hall flipping on the lights as he approached.

"Maime, what happened?" he asked. "Oh God, you're bleeding."

Click. Click. Clik-clik.

He heard a sound from the room nearest him. He ignored the noise and picked up the small figure of his wife from the floor and carried her while grunting, to the living room couch.

He ran into the bathroom and got a wash cloth and towel noticing several drops of blood in a trail on the floor leading to his wife.

"Oh God, please don't let her die," whispered Martin.

He went quickly back into the living room and grabbed the phone on the way, slinging and fighting the long cord across several knick knacks as it followed him. He applied pressure to a fresh gash in his wife's arm and called an ambulance.

Click. Click. Click…, clik-clik…, echoed down the hallway.

James talked non-stop on the way home with his Aunt Martiel. He recited as best he could all that had transpired from the time they arrived at the *Mambo's* residence until they left.

His aunt showed neither surprise nor ignorance to most of the story and the information that he shared with her. When he had run out of information, opinions, and details there was finally an uneasy silence.

Martiel broke the quiet as they rolled up the crunchy pea-gravel driveway of her family's old estate.

"So the *Mambo* and the little man in the colored outfit, they told you that Syrus had some hidden secret that he passed on and that's what this devil-thing wants, is that right?"

"That's pretty much it," said James. "More surprises."

Martiel stood stretching and thought for a moment.

"Well…, why don't we find out what this secret is…, come on. Maybe the two of us can wring it out of our relatives."

"Aw, no. Do we have to?" pleaded James. "It's just that every time I hear or see something, another bad thing happens or everything gets worse."

"Come on, James," she urged. "I have a feeling that what we don't know *will* hurt us."

Aunt Martiel walked briskly up the stairs to the same room where James had previously heard his ancestors. They went inside and closed the door.

"Hello? Hello, we need to talk to you, now…, if possible," she said looking around the room.

Almost immediately, a cool breeze stirred the closed off room and the thin white curtains wisped slightly at the unseen passing of some specter. The air snapped with the sound of a rubber band hitting paper. With the room full of static charge that both of them could feel, they instantly turned to look at one another.

A portal appeared in the center of the room for a moment, as a shimmer in the air, the same as it had before, then another snap and it was like looking through a clear glass window.

"Well, that's new," said Martiel, frightened from the intensity of the changes that were taking place; spiritually speaking.

The face of a long ago relative peered at them. Somber, quiet, pained.

There was that nauseas, swimmy, feeling again that James had felt the first time he experienced the inhabitants of this house.

"Breathe, breathe," he remembered and the sickness quelled almost immediately.

"We need your help."

Martiel spoke up softly, almost a whisper.

The specter-apparent only looked at her, with still lips a voice spoke, in a powerful thrust, "You have no time for this, your family needs you now…, not everything is as it appears. Now hurry!"

The surface of the mirror-like portal regained a shimmery texture to its surface.

"But, we only need to know a few things", Martiel pleaded. "Someone is trying to *kill James Earl*…."

The apparition faded with a barely noticeable crackling in the air.

The phone was ringing incessantly from somewhere below in the house. An uncomfortable moment of stillness filled the room as the two of them looked at each other.

"Who would be calling this time of night?" grumbled Martiel.

Chapter 34

Billy Don Poole heard the rumble of distant thunder as he lay in bed. He was awakened earlier by the sound of the front door closing. Reaching over in the bed, he had found the spot where his wife Sallee Mae usually filled, cold and empty.

Billy kept still and listened as his wife quietly walked through the house. After a few moments in the bathroom Sallee had very carefully pulled the covers back and slid into bed and fell fast asleep. This wasn't the first time she'd sneaked out of the house without him knowing when she left.

Billy could smell the light fragrance of her cologne, the familiar scent of her perspiration, and a feeling he couldn't quite put his finger on.

Rough stubby fingers grasped the *mojo* bag under his pillow again and he listened. He was sure this time; it was thunder he was hearing. Remembering his instructions clearly, Billy rehearsed them once again in his mind.

He slowly got out of bed and silently got dressed. He knew it was time to meet with the old woman despite the hour. There could be no mistakes. Today was the day that everything would be put right for the old woman.

James hated hospitals with a passion and now he remembered why. The smell of disinfectant and bleach water seemed to scorch his nasal passages as he walked through the emergency room doors.

Almost an hour after the phone call from his grampa, James was pushing thoughts of death out of his mind. Aunt Martiel close on his heels, they walked in to find Martin Earl fidgeting quietly in the waiting room area with a paper cup of coffee in his shaky hands.

He arose quickly when he saw his family approaching, anxious to be free of the trap of his mind, where he had been entranced in memories. Memories of a lifetime with the woman he loved and depended on for so long were haunting him.

"Martin Earl, what happened?" asked his sister. "Is Maime going to be okay?"

He cried softly for a moment, as he looked in his sisters' eyes, "She lost a lot of blood. They're having to do emergency surgery, trying to repair the damage to her arm."

"There was something in the house, Martiel" he said quietly, as others in the waiting room turned their gaze. "She said she saw something in the back room. Then she passed out and I thought…, I thought…."

He was quiet for a few moments.

"I called Catherine. She insisted on flying down tomorrow evening," he said. "She wanted to be here and said she would stay as long as we needed."

James looked up in surprise to the fact that his mother would be there soon. Mixed feelings of desperate need and desertion overwhelmed him.

They sat quietly in conversation, shielding their information from other listening ears.

Several other patients were sprinkled around the room, caught up in their own troubles in the early morning hours. Each sat numbly staring or reading year old magazines of far away places they would never visit and recipes that they would never cook.

Another hour passed slowly as Martin had exhausted any further information of the night's events in their ears, and regressed back to the thoughts of his wife lying in a cold operating room.

Before he could fall back into the abyss of his worst fears, a doctor walked into the waiting room door, looking around.

"Mr. Ames?" he called out. When he saw the family huddled together, he approached where they were seated.

"The damage wasn't as bad as it looked initially," he began. "The hardest part is over and she's going to be fine."

James remained standing as brother and sister slumped into nearby seats. The doctor described how a shard of the broken glass had entered her arm in a "V" and cut a main artery in her left arm, missing the tendons and muscle tissue by fractions of an inch. They had repaired the damage to the blood vessels and had to give her blood. He gave further instructions as to Maime's personal care, reminding Martin Ames that his wife would be weak for several days from the blood loss, but didn't anticipate any permanent damage to her arm.

The doctor's voice trailed off as James walked slowly away and made his way to the exit doors into the darkness of cool damp early morning air. Relief washed over him.

James walked slowly in the lamplight of the hospital grounds with his arms folded across his chest thinking of how his very presence was causing this danger to his family. And what if he was back home up in…, where? Boston now?

Yeah, that's where the others were moving.

What then? He'd have absolutely no one to confide in except Sam. Would it be Sam in the hospital right now if he had been there instead? Or his mother?

And what about Jolie? She jumped into his life from nowhere, filled his heart and now she could be in the same type of danger.

"I should have left," he said aloud.

Or would this thing, this *Bokor* follow him all the way across the country, to extract some mystery bullcrap out of him that didn't mean anything to James.

And it was determined to kill him to do it. Would it have been able to find him? He'd gladly GIVE up this thing inside him to whoever this was, just to be left alone, but the only way to give it up was to die.

There had to be more to it than that. There had to be a way to fight back.

The more he thought about it, the angrier James became.

James swore and swung his fists in the air fighting an unseen evil, "If you were here, I'd…, I'd…."

After a few minutes of unorthodox exercise, he was even more frustrated.

"I should have left. Maybe there's still time for me to get away from my family."

Chapter 35

At 5:30 AM, the skies over Southern Mississippi were clear, but angry rumblings could be heard and seen in the near distance.

Deputy Floyd had received a page, 5-5-5 and 5-3-0, from Billy almost an hour ago. The buzzing-beeping pager had demon-danced on the night table until it fell onto the floor beside his bed.

The number signaled him to meet Billy Poole for an early morning breakfast at a local truck stop on Highway 555.

Now he sat somberly at the table stirring a soupy concoction of coffee, sugar and cream. If Billy didn't hurry, he was going to be late for work.

The sound of the spoon tinkling on the sides of the cup had already progressed in tone from a high pitch to a low clacking sound.

Floyd was deep in thought when Billy slid into the empty booth in front of him.

"Is everything set?" asked Billy. "We don't wanna mess this up, if ya know what I mean."

"Yeah, everything is set for this evening," said Floyd.

"That boy in yer jail, he's dead, ain't he?" asked the grinning mask of Billy Poole.

"How did you know?" asked Floyd.

"Just know," glowered Billy.

"Hey Billy, you were right…. I don't want to meet your people," said Floyd.

"Ya don't wanna piss 'em off either," warned Billy. "If ya know what I mean."

"I know what you mean, for sure," said Floyd, repeating Billy's inane script. The memory of the blood, gore and stark terror of the Mastyn kid, was still fresh in his mind. It was still a mystery how Billy's people had reached out to Mastyn while still in the confines of the Adams County jail cell.

"Aren't you going to tell me what happened?" asked Jolie furiously. "First you won't let me go with you and now you won't even tell me anything about James."

"It's for your own good," said BeBe. "Please trust me Jolie."

"It's not a matter of trust, you know I trust you," argued Jolie. "You know I'll find out even if I have to go see him myself."

Jolie sat and steamed, holding tight to the golden medallion her Aunt

BeBe had given her that morning. Alternately looking from it to the road outside the car, she was imagining the worst possible scenario.

And after the exhibition they encountered at Elberta Straw's house…, well…. James could have grown horns and a tail for all Jolie knew.

"Please don't be mad with me Jolie," BeBe said quietly. "Let me think on it and I'll try to tell you as much as I can. I suppose you can call James on the telephone, even though I don't like it. I shouldn't have to keep reminding you to stay apart from each other until this passes."

BeBe thought that a phone conversation couldn't hurt anything if James could show some restraint and keep details to himself. It was being in the same physical area of James that seemed to be the mark of danger.

"Ms. Dubois and Dominique both talked with James and…," said BeBe.

"They *BOTH* talked with him?" asked Jolie. "Now I know it isn't good. From everything else you've told me, Dominique never gets involved with singular problems."

"Now Jolie, he happened to be in the next room and heard what was said and he wanted to help," said BeBe, chewing out a little white lie.

"You might be able to fool somebody else, Aunt BeBe, but you should know I can tell when you aren't telling the whole truth," countered Jolie.

Angry silence ensued until they reached downtown Natchez. They parked directly in front of The Cajun Café, where the car could be watched the entire time by either BeBe or her family and helpers at the restaurant.

While at home, she had been parking the car up next to the front door of the house, which was right next to her bedroom window, every night since the vandal had tried to destroy her car.

They both got out in heated silence and walked together up to the door. BeBe turned and placed her back to the entrance, reaching out to her niece in one final plea.

"Jolie honey, I'm not going to apologize for caring about you."

"And I'm not going to apologize for caring about James or calling him this afternoon and getting the whole story either," said Jolie storming inside past her aunt.

The medallion she had clutched during their conversation had somehow slipped out of Jolie's hand and into the passenger seat of her aunt's car.

With no sleep to speak of before the trip to the hospital, James and Martiel reluctantly left Martin Ames in the room with his wife. After they had moved her into a private room near daybreak, Martin would not leave her side and they brought him a reclining chair, a pillow and a blanket.

The two *gifted* members of the Ames family did not feel so gifted at the moment. Both felt utterly helpless and other than relying on the wiles of *Mambo Dubois* and her teacher, they had not consulted or found any other resource.

"I need to call a few of their church folks and let them know what's going on with Maime," said Aunt Martiel. "I also need to make arrangements for picking up Catherine at the airport in New Orleans."

"Grampa said that she was getting a rental, so nobody would have to do that," said James.

"Your mother is so thoughtful," said Martiel. "I for one will be glad to see her and I know you will too, James."

"Actually, I don't know what to tell her," said James. "She doesn't know crap about what's been happening here. How would I even start to try and explain even one thing that's been going on?"

"She's your mother, she'll understand," said Martiel.

"No, she won't," said James bitterly. "She never has understood things when there was a problem. She lives in her own little world and if anything tips it over she ignores it until it goes away."

"James!" bit Martiel. "How dare you speak of your mother that way!"

James cringed and looked out the window of her BMW, avoiding his aunt's scornful gaze.

"You know your mother loves you James. There's no reason to take your frustration out on her."

"Saying that you love somebody and actually taking care of them..., believing in them..., are sometimes two different things."

"I don't know where all this hatred and bitterness is coming from James, but you need to take inventory and settle all this in your mind before your mother gets here," Martiel scolded. "Your gramma is going to need all Catherine's attention and we need to make sure that any problems about this situation doesn't cause any confusion. Are we clear?"

James realized that he was doing it again. Where was this coldness coming from? He hadn't acted this way since he was 14 or 15 years old. Back when.... Back when he was being pushed over the edge.... Like now.

"Are we *clear*?" she repeated.

James jumped from her emphasis on "clear."

"Yes Ma'am," said James a little sheepishly. "I seem to be eating a lot of my own words lately..., and I don't really have a taste for them."

Several hours went by at *The Cajun* preparing for the lunch rush in downtown Natchez. The usual breakfast crowd had come and gone.

With its full staff of workers, the restaurant hummed in unison and harmony. This was something that BeBe was very proud of.

They had their weekly delivery to unload with a fresh catch of seafood and everybody was bustling with the crates and separating the different varieties into different small freezers to preserve individual flavors.

"We may not be the Ritz, but we aren't going to be labeled the greasy spoon," BeBe had said more times that once.

With everyone busy, Jolie secretly walked into the small office and picked up the phone. She dialed the number to where James was staying with his aunt. The phone rang several times with no answer. She was about to hang up and try his grandparents' house when....

"Hello?" asked a groggy Martiel. "What time is it?"

"It's almost ten o'clock," said Jolie. "Is James there, please?"

"Is this Jolie?" croaked Martiel.

"Yes it is..., who is this?" asked Jolie.

Martiel sat up in bed realizing everything that she needed to accomplish that day and what time it was getting to be.

"Oh, Lord, I didn't know it was so late," said Martiel hoarsely.

Jolie then recognized Martiel's voice and thought it was unusual for her to be sleeping in so late, but asked again, "Is James there?"

"Why yes he is sweetheart, but I'm sure he's still konked out," said Martiel, then she remembered that they hadn't thought to add BeBe or Jolie to the list of people they called earlier about the calamity late last night.

"Oh, Hun. I'm so sorry I didn't call you this morning," said Martiel

"Everything happened so sudden and we were at the hospital all night last night. Why..., we didn't get home until almost six this morning."

Frustration mounted like a spring-loaded trap in Jolie's mind.

"What happened so sudden?" asked Jolie. "Is James all right? Tell me something, please?"

"Just hold ya horses and let me get my mind working here," said Martiel. "His gramma was injured last night at their house. A picture frame fell off the wall in their hallway and the glass broke and cut her arm pretty badly. She lost a lot of blood, but they managed to patch her up real good. She's going to be fine."

"I'm so sorry, is she still in the hospital?" asked Jolie.

"Yes, she'll be there probably most of today and maybe tomorrow..., I really don't know. They had to repair a major artery in her left arm.... Emergency surgery and everything," said Martiel as she yawned.

"I was so worried about James. I assumed something awful. I hope I wasn't mean...," Jolie said.

"No you weren't," said Martiel. "It's Okay. I'll see if I can wake up James. I know he will want to talk to you."

After what seemed like an eternity; Jolie could hear the distant sound of a toilet flushing and water running.

"Jolie?" said James almost whispering. "Hello?"

"Hi James," said Jolie tearfully. "I just heard about your gramma. I'm so sorry, James. When I called, your Aunt Martiel said that y'all were at the hospital all night and I assumed the worst."

"Everything's going to be fine, Jolie. In time, it's all going to work out."

"James, do you want to tell me what happened with Ms. Dubois and Dominique the other day?" asked Jolie.

The last thing he wanted to do was let his mouth begin to run wild after only four hours sleep and deferred his answer to BeBe's judgment.

"Didn't your Aunt BeBe fill you in on the details?" asked James.

"Well, she only told me a few sketchy..., aw, no..., I'm not going to lie to you. She didn't tell me jack!" whined Jolie.

"I'm afraid I'd need an interpreter to tell you everything that was said," James puffed, through a well deserved yawn. "They basically told me everything I already knew, which was pretty strange in itself, but they let me know that whoever is causing all this crap intends to kill me," James blurted out without thinking.

"Kill you!" squeaked Jolie. "She didn't say anything about that."

"Aw, crap. I didn't mean to tell you about that either. I guess I'm not as awake as I thought. Jolie, everything will be fine, you'll see."

"Is there anything else you aren't telling me?" she asked angrily.

"Probably, but right now I can't think of anything to hide from you, I'm so wiped out. I can't remember any time that I was ever this drained. I don't want you do get involved in all this."

"Involved?" fumed Jolie. She was sick of everyone trying to be her protector. "It's way too late *not* to be involved."

James was quiet a few moments, "Jolie, I don't want anything to happen to you, ever. You know..., I'm beginning to think you put some spell or something on me. I've never felt this way about anybody before now. When I'm with you or even think about you, this empty spot inside seems to go away."

"I know," said Jolie quietly. "I feel the same way."

"You need to know how much I care, but for now, I think its best that we...," James breathed deeply, trying to force himself to push her away. "I really want to see you, Jolie."

"I want to see you too, James," came her soft voice.

James changed the subject.

"Did my Aunt Martiel tell you that my mother would be here later tonight?"

There was quietness on the phone line for several moments as Jolie composed herself.

"Jolie, are you still there?"

"Yes, I'm still here."

James could tell that she was covering up an emotional breakdown by the texture of her voice.

"I'd like to meet your mother, whenever you think it's safe for me to come around," she said almost sarcastically.

"If you happened come by to visit my gramma at the hospital and I happened to be there at the same time with my aunt…, well…, maybe….."

"What time?" she asked.

A frustrated sheriff paced the floor of his office. It was about time for him to go home for the evening.

The coroner had taken the remains of Roger Mastyn away last night, his only real lead to solve an embarrassing string of unsolved graveyard vandalisms. Now to add to the embarrassment, his only suspect and witness was dead. All of this was about to make the AP and statewide attention - front page news.

And Mastyn had died right in the sheriff's own jail, right in his very own lap. Why hadn't he put that Mastyn kid in a hospital? He had seemed so calm, so sedate.

He was empty handed once again.

The night crew of officers had arrived and everything was quiet except for the unexpected appearance of a storm front. The weather bureau had issued a severe storm warning and hinted that a tornado warning might follow before the night was over. He felt as if he could sleep right through it, but knew that wouldn't happen. The quiet of the office let him know that nothing else of importance would be accomplished tonight. It was time to get some relief from the many hours of overtime he'd put in over the last several days. He grabbed his jacket and left the building.

Chapter 36

A reddish sky was lowering over Natchez and a brisk wind was pushing discarded paper products, along with other human artifacts, from one side of the street to the other.

In the distance, a constant rumbling could be heard.

The police vehicle impound was occupied by someone other than Officer Claude Willis. He had purchased a small stack of paperback books to occupy his idle time.

"Another night in solitary confinement."

He looked off to the southwest and could see flickers of what was brewing on the horizon. Silently, he begged it to go another direction. The last thing he wanted was to be sitting practically exposed, in this little glass and metal, six by eight room, in the middle of a wild storm. Especially like the ones lately.

It was going to be a long night.

Crack! Boom!

The officer dropped to his knees immediately and ducked under the tiny desk as the cannon of all thunders rattled the little shack he was confined to.

Feeling a little silly, he crawled back up from below the window line of the guard shack. A heavy power line flowed from a transformer down a succession of posts ending right next to the metal turnstile where he sat.

"Perfect," he thought. "Solitary and the electric chair all wrapped up in one."

He picked up the phone in his little hut and phoned the Sheriff's Office. He was informed that the sheriff had already left for the day.

"Damn," he muttered, looking back up at the lowering sky.

All he wanted was to lock all of this down and get somewhere safe.

The night clerk informed him of what he already suspected; that there was a real "frog floater" on its way and possibly dangerous. He told them that he was locking up and heading over there with them before it hit.

Craaack! Boooom!

"Enough of this, I'm out of here."

He walked in a stoop out to the turnstile and gate with a heavy chain and lock designed to render the two immovable. As he was running them through the designed openings, he felt a sharp pain through the back of his head and then nothing.

Billy carefully carried the officer back into the confines of his post of duty and tossed the heavy chain and lock on the floor beside the body.

He pulled the uniformed man up into the chair, ramming the body underneath the desk. With the officers' hat on his head, he folded his hands on his chest as if asleep.

He wiped a smear of blood off his gloved hands and quickly rambled through the box of keys, finding one that looked familiar. Like the one for a big mud hog of a truck sitting parked under the nearest pole and lamp.

He pushed the gate open as far as it would go and ran inside as a few drops of rain began to pelt down.

He climbed into the big 4x4 truck and hoped that the battery had survived these several days while sitting dormant.

He placed the key in the ignition and the engine roared to life. Full tank of gas. At least the boys were always prepared.

In eight minutes flat, he had absconded with the sheriff's only other piece of evidence linking to the three morbid thefts.

"Movin' right a-long," thought Billy as he flipped the radio up loud.

All was quiet at the old Ames Estate except for the frequent flash of lightning and rumble of distant thunder.

Its recent occupants had left to go visit a member of the family, still in pain and confined to Room 212 of the Natchez Memorial Hospital.

A dark silhouette moved quickly toward the Maroon 1967 Mustang, parked in the open carriage house. Carrying a small flashlight and hammer, a man crawled quickly beside the vehicle.

He tried to get underneath the front end only to find that his oversize body wouldn't allow passage. Lying as close to the edge as he could, he wedged his head under the cars body on the drivers' side, and used the flashlight to find what he was looking for. Fumbling with the hammer, he realized that this would not look much like an accident if there were obvious traces of metal-to-metal contact. He looked around on the ground outside and found a fist sized stone.

Then he systematically proceeded to beat the brake lines, which ran along the frame, to a flattened pulp. When the two lines were badly mutilated and creased enough to cause a leak under pressure, the muffled hammering ceased.

A good hard stomp or two of the brake pedal would produce the desired results.

Rock debris would serve as a perfect disguise. The car simply hit a pothole in the road and the body bottomed out on the pavement. No one would question a sentence carried out by the town of Natchez Mississippi's own fine street system.

He lay on the ground momentarily admiring his handiwork and making sure it was enough to do the job exactly as intended.

Craaack! Booom! A lengthy rumble shook him.

The stroke of lightening was too close for comfort; the black clouds of violent storm were almost on him. He gathered everything he brought with him and gave the borrowed rock a toss deep into the brush away from the side of the house.

It was time for him to leave and let time take its course.

The hospital was much quieter inside Room 212 as opposed to the hustle and bustle of the emergency room traffic down below.

James walked into the room to find his grampa dozing off in a chair next to his gramma's bed and holding her hand. Her left arm was supported and things were hooked up and beeping nice and steady.

Steady was good. As they entered the room, Maime turned her head and looked over at them with a smile.

"How's my favorite gramma?" asked James. "If you didn't like that old picture, I would have thrown it away for you."

His comment was meant to tease and remove tension. Instead a harsh darkness came over his gramma's face as she recalled why she was confined to a hospital bed.

"James, I..., I saw it," she whispered timidly, looking around the room as if something had trailed her to the room where she lay.

James tried to diffuse the tension in his grandmother's face as the timing of the steady beeps grew closer together, "Saw what, gramma?"

"*IT,*" she said, causing chill bumps to run up and down both his and his Aunt Martiel's body. "It looked me right in the face, James," she whispered painfully. "That's why I fell backwards..., it scared me."

"You won't have to be scared much longer," said James almost intuitively. "I'm going to make it go away. I love you gramma."

He hugged the small part of her torso unrestricted by the bed.

"James? Martiel?" said Martin waking up. "I must have fallen asleep. What time is it?"

"About seven," said Martiel.

James hid his thoughts from those present and sat down in a chair away from the sudden closeness of the room.

Aunt Martiel spoke up, "You gave us quite a scare Maime. Please don't do anything like that again. When do you think they will let you go home?"

Maime looked over at James and then her husband as if to say, "*I don't want to go back there.*"

Martin spoke up and said that the doctor was concerned with some odd escalations in her heart rhythm and that there might be nerve damage where the glass punctured her arm.

The doctor wanted to keep her there overnight and depending on her progress, possibly a few more days to be on the safe side. It would be easier to monitor the movement of her arm, administer antibiotics, as well as local pain medications.

A blue flash glazed the room through the window and there was a muffled boom of report. Even in the protective confines of the solid hospital building, the rumble could be felt in its structure.

The room became very silent for a moment and the phone rang. Everyone simply stared at it, as if it were a coiled serpent poised to strike. After the third ring, Martiel forced herself to reach and answer it.

"Hello?"

"Catherine! It's so good to hear your voice. Are you on your way?"

"Really…."

"Better safe than sorry."

"Well when…, tomorrow afternoon."

"Do you need me to pick you up?"

"Yes, your mother is going to be just fine, would you like to speak to…."

"Okay, Okay, I understand. We'll see you tomorrow then."

Martiel's nervous hand settled the phone back in its cradle.

"Her flight got diverted all the way to Atlanta because of this storm," said Martiel. "I guess you heard all the rest."

There was another flash of lightening with its crashing report. The lights in the hospital flickered slightly.

The duty nurse walked in the room to check on her patient. Her cheerful smile broke the gloomy moment that they were all sharing.

"Don't worry about those lights." said the nurse. "We have our own generator if that old storm gets too rowdy. You've got quite a crowd gathering here Mrs. Ames. Is this your family?"

After a few minutes of pleasantries and checking her patient's vitals, she exited the room.

James looked at the clock in the room and noticed that it was a quarter after seven. He was quietly getting anxious about the storm and for good reason.

There was a sudden surge in wind and the first huge drops of rain began to hammer against the small window in the room, which captured everyone's attention.

"Oh my, it looks like we might be getting wet on the way home tonight," said Martiel.

James was getting nervous from being in the small private room with so many people, even if they were family. He didn't really understand why, he'd never been claustrophobic before in his life. He and Sam had regularly crawled through an open sewer drain for several blocks to avoid confrontations with his former oppressors. The thought of that caused James to shiver and come back to reality.

"I'm going for a Coke. Anybody want anything?" asked James.

They all declined and James was glad that they refused his offer of politeness. He hurried to the elevator. The only vending machine he had seen was near the back of the hospital in the emergency room, which was down on the first floor.

The elevator doors opened and he started to step inside, but hesitated. Another closed, confined space. What was it with him and closed spaces all of a sudden? The door to the stairs was next to the elevator and he decided to walk instead.

He could hear the low rumbling of the storm tormenting the sides of the building as he descended. Halfway down the lights flickered and James froze. He took a deep breath of air and tried to relax. Maybe it was the lack of sleep or a hundred thousand other things working on his mind.

Bottle of Coke in his hand, he walked back into Room 212, to find two more occupants standing and talking around his gramma's hospital bed. James' spirits rose and fell when he didn't recognize the voices.

A couple of people from the church had braved the elements to come pay their respects and wish Mrs. Ames a speedy recovery. The visitors were listening to a washed down version of the events leading to the accident. Now the room was packed and it was time to take a walk to find a three year old magazine or go anywhere out of there.

He started backing out the door, when he felt a tap on the shoulder.

"This must be the right room," said Jolie.

He jumped and spun from the surprise.

"I always seem to have this effect on James," she said as she looked at her Aunt BeBe.

"Hey, you made it…. How did you keep from getting drenched?" asked James.

"We barely walked in the door when the bottom fell out," said BeBe. "Where are you going, James?" she asked, giving him a quick hug. Her hand offered a careful swipe down one side of his face as she examined his nervous eyes.

"Just out here in the hallway. It's getting really crowded in there," said James now looking intently at Jolie.

"Well, they'll have to move over and let us in too," said BeBe, walking through the door.

James and Jolie stood staring at each other for an awkward moment, then in unison they melted to each other in an embrace.

Her soft kiss was worth the wait and his emptiness fled like a shadow from the sunlight. He felt alive and well, as if plugged into a source of electricity, and for a few moments, there was peace.

Jolie quickly surveyed the empty hall of the hospital and finding no onlookers, pressed herself into James, along with another kiss.

Suddenly she broke off their kiss, "So you really did miss me."

James smiled and breathed in heavily.

There was scuffling from the door and they snapped apart straightening their clothes as it opened.

James spoke up and asked Jolie if she wanted anything to drink as the two church members walked out of the room.

"I think I should go in and visit your gramma for a few minutes first," she said with a sly grin.

The electrical storm had become so fierce that several areas of Natchez were already without power. Calls were coming in to emergency services across town for everything imaginable.

After paying their visit to Mrs. Ames, Jolie and BeBe made a hasty exit before the storm became any worse, to the dismay of James. BeBe had given the two of them a sly look as they were leaving as if to say, "You're so busted."

James and Martiel were now standing next to the covered emergency entrance, waiting for the slightest lull in the wind and rain.

Only minutes later an ambulance arrived, amplifying the roar of the rain as doors opened and workers scrambled outside. In a few moments they were wheeling in a police officer on a gurney with a bloody bruise on the side of his face, unconscious.

In walked Sheriff Howard, drenched to the skin despite the long yellow slicker, and following the hospital staff behind the hurt officer. He glanced over and spied Martiel and James, making a hurried detour their direction.

"I hope you aren't going out in that right now," said the sheriff. "The heaviest part of the storm has stalled over Natchez according to the National Weather Service. What are you doing up here at the hospital?"

"My gramma is here, she was injured in an accident at their house."

"Injured? Martin's wife? Is she going to be okay?" asked the sheriff, extremely concerned.

"She should be fine," said Martiel. "Martin's with her in Room 212 if you'd like to drop in and say hello."

"I certainly will," he said. "I hate to hear Mrs. Ames was hurt."

A nurse hurried over, "Sheriff? Could you sign these?"

"I've got to go," he said, turning around to follow her away.

He walked back to where the two were standing and asked, "Say James…, have you had any other problems with my deputy, Deputy Floyd?"

"No Sir, none that I know of," answered James a little puzzled.

"Thanks…. Thanks James. You be careful now," he said as he hurried away once again.

Chapter 37

Consequences

In the tempest of the storm, people are sometimes forced to stop and reflect on the role of humanity. Mankind still ran to hide from nature's most basic elements, its electricity, its floodwaters, its destructive winds; all culminating into one element - power.

Man's own struggles for supremacy have sometimes been disguised by greed, lust, envy, but ultimately seems to filter down to a desire for control.

In a cave on the east side of the Mississippi River banks, there was a celebration beginning. A conjure of the darkest order was in progress and a long awaited victory was within sight.

An altar set into the wall, with tiers of candles made of human fat, fried and crackled their light to display the sacrifices of fruits and rum that covered it.

A lone practitioner of the black arts was wrapped and adorned in her best black and red linen, and dancing around a moderate size fire. Her sacred *ason*, or rattle, was moving with a smooth rhythm and there was screeching laughter jounced by labored dancing of the corpse-like *Bokor*.

In her ceremony, she had once again rejected her alliances with any of the peaceful *Loa* and bound herself fully to the *Petro Loa*, or war spirits.

A slow transformation began to take place in her flesh and life started filling her dry weathered skin. The hunched, curved spine straightened; the revived posture giving her almost two additional inches in stature.

Sparse gray hair fell off her head as spent straw from a bird nest; new shiny black hair grew like worms crawling and covering its rightful places. Her dry breasts regained their youthful full appearance. The old crone gradually took on the fashion of a young, luxurious woman.

As her youth renewed, she slowly began a dance, a dance of possession around her *potomitan* or ceremonial post. This post stood in the center of her circle of candles, awaiting its sacrifice.

Outside the safety of the cave, the winds rose to a fevered pitch and lightening flashed over the city of Natchez, south of her hiding place.

A circle of white stones were carefully placed on the floor and inside this circle were markings in the earth, secret markings, recognized only by the spirits that were being called to and commanded.

There would be a fresh sacrifice tonight. The *nanm* - the spirits - of the generational descendants of Syrus Earl Ames would be summoned this night. The prepared *govi* or ceremonial clay pot was already present to receive them. She laughed deeply, knowing they would feel the pull and could not resist.

There appeared to be no cessation in the viciousness of the wind and rain, so James volunteered to run and get Martiel's car and bring it under the covered entrance.

Inside the car and on the way home, the two unlikely companions – bonded by friendship, blood, and now supernatural gifts - could hardly hear themselves think from the pounding noise of the rain.

The wipers beat furiously trying to remove the bleary vision of the road ahead without success. James drove slowly, both of them laboring to make sure they stayed on the road.

Lightening would flash and their eyes would have to readjust to the rain dimmed lights of the BMW.

"That was a pretty sad attempt to meet with Jolie," said Martiel loudly.

"What are you talking about?" asked James.

"You know exactly what I'm talking about. BeBe noticed it too," she said laughing. "You know, she'll still be there when all this is over."

James didn't reply, but thought to himself that it was more like IF this was ever going to be over.

"Now don't be thinking that way," scolded Aunt Martiel. "It can't rain forever."

"I guess I haven't got the hang of guarding my thoughts very well yet," he smirked.

The last familiar turn off the highway was immediately ahead and James was glad to see an end to this drive home.

As they neared the entrance to the estate, a set of tall headlights came on and a vehicle began moving toward them from up the private road. It was coming faster than James expected, but he managed to turn moments before it met them at their driveway.

Martiel grabbed the dashboard as they moved from harms way, "Who would be coming from down that way in this storm? Nobody lives down that way for miles."

"We're out in it," said James. "I guess somebody couldn't see the road and made a wrong turn."

James paused near the entrance, looking at the rain flooded yard and driveway ahead of them, trying to see the trail.

Behind him a somewhat corroded and rain-washed 4x4 truck eased past, having slowed down as James entered their property. In an instant he recognized it by the distinct rumble of its exhaust.

"That's the truck that I saw, Aunt Martiel! I thought it was in the pound after they arrested that guy. What's it doing here? What were they doing here while we were gone?"

He shot forward through the pond of water, hurriedly parking his aunt's car in the garage, and began fishing the keys of his Mustang out of his pocket.

"James, what do you think you're doing?" Martiel sputtered.

"I need to see where they're going," said James.

Rain was cascading off the edge of the open garage door as the storm continued to engage the outskirts of Natchez.

"That's crazy!" she said. "This weather is horrible and you don't know what they might do."

"Exactly," said James. "They are a piece of the puzzle of what's happening to me and I have to know. I'm wasting time. Would you call the sheriff and tell him we saw the truck here?"

Before Martiel could answer, James' car came to life and roared backwards into the pouring rain and took off into the darkness of the night.

"No James!" she yelled into the storm, deluded by false hope, waving her arms over her head.

She hurried inside the house, turning on lights as she went.

Nothing looked as if it had been touched and she felt somewhat safe that the truck was only a look-alike of the one that James had seen. But James had been absolutely sure, causing her heart to begin to race. What if James was right?

That gnawing feeling arose again, playing on her fears.

She took off her wet jacket and threw it over a chair in the kitchen as she flipped on more lights. On the table sat the paper bag that the two "doctors" had given James. Completely forgotten because of all the commotion from…, when? She had missed so much sleep she couldn't remember what day anything was happening now.

She sat down at the table for a moment and looked inside the bag. There were several things wrapped in a cloth, which she carefully removed and splayed on the table. As she unfolded the contents and saw the importance of each item, she whined, "Oh no, James."

She jumped from the chair, snatched at the telephone, and called the number to the Sheriff's Department penciled on the wall.

James' car gushed up rainwater as he cut through the driveway and slid sideways onto Ames Heights Road in front of the old Ames estate. His windshield wipers didn't quite keep up with the rain as well as his aunt's European model and the rain was practically sticking to the glass as he sped to catch up with the truck's dim taillights.

Finally, two tiny red dots appeared through the rain and James slowed down to maintain a safe distance. There was no hiding the fact that he was following them. If he stayed too far behind, the torrential rain would hide the direction they took; if he got too close they might bolt and disappear.

The truck stopped at the highway intersection and regardless of his intentions, James caught up with the truck. As it turned right onto the highway, headed southeast toward Natchez, James saw his worst nightmare.

His rain obscured headlights illuminated what appeared to be Jolie's face, contorted in pain and looking out the passenger side window.

The truck flew away up the highway with James casting a sluice of flying gravel hurrying after the truck.

"Oh, God… How did they get Jolie?" he wondered.

Had BeBe dropped Jolie off at the Ames Estate to see him? Had they followed BeBe's car from the hospital? Was it them that put the sugar in her gas tank? His mind was doing flip-flops.

"Please don't be hurt."

The rain was relentless and James' car was beginning to hydroplane. How could this truck go so fast on pavement and in the rain with those huge mud tires?

The wind rocked his car sideways, pushing the rain almost completely horizontal now, and the lowering sky flashed violently. His car began to fall behind and he power-shifted the automatic transmission into second gear, but the Mustang's engine and the driving wind, was too much for the slick highway.

Although he shot forward, he lost control and spun sideways toward the shoulder skirting the ditch by inches and spraying mud and gravel, obliterating his view out the passenger side of the windshield.

He noticed that his brakes were washing out from the deep rain gorged highway.

Madly flipping windshield wipers, along with the heavy rain, quickly cleared the muddy smear and he could see the truck getting away…, with Jolie inside.

He sped up again as much as he could control, watching for signs of where they might be going.

It began to hail.

Two chips in the windshield further hampered his vision.

"Shit, there goes my car," thought James. "Jolie…, Jolie…."

He slammed his fist into the dash.

The truck only drove a few more miles while weaving on the road from the storm and hail. It sped up and turned west off the highway, down the old Cemetery Road toward the river.

He wouldn't be able to follow if the road got rough but what choice did he have? He had to try.

A blind bend in the road came up hard and fast, but the truck went straight, breaking through a gate onto the levee road of the Mississippi River. They had to know he was following now.

There was no other choice; he was behind them, tires thumping horridly over a wide cattle guard across the gate's entrance.

Moments later the truck disappeared. It went completely out of sight. James drove cautiously up the road not wanting to get stuck.

After driving over several up and down slopes in the road, the truck was no where to be seen and he was having trouble keeping his car on the slick gravel and mud road. The hail ceased for the moment, but the rain persisted in blocking all reasonable vision beyond the hood of his car.

A flash of light blinded James and he saw the truck. It had been hiding somewhere in the dark behind him and was now riding his bumper. James sped up and nearly slid his car off into an abysmal darkness.

"Oh shit!" James railed; just as lightening revealed to him how high the levee road along the Mississippi River could rise. Then another flash of lightening illuminated his predicament fully.

He was high above the now raging Mississippi River flowing the last few miles to the Gulf of Mexico.

The 4x4 came up behind him in a bouncing blaze of headlights, ramming his car high above the bumper, crushing the tiny trunk and crumpling the back. The impact shattered the back glass and almost pushed him off the levee road.

Rain now poured inside his car and the roar of the truck amplified the noise of the storm.

James panicked.

He decided to try and deal with whoever this was face to face. As the truck raced the engine for its next intended battering, James slammed on the brakes.

They went to the floor.

Nothing!

He pumped the brake pedal in a frantic effort trying to get the brakes to do anything.

Wham!

His neck snapped backward as the truck connected with his car. The Mustang was trashed anyway…, why not go for broke?

He slammed the Mustang in reverse and hit the gas hard.

The car's huge engine screamed to life… four, five, six thousand rpm's on the tachometer…. Instantly it was pegged, bouncing past seven thousand rpm's. All three hundred and ninety cubic inches was going to explode any second.

His tires were on nothing but mud and sluice now and the truck, with its engine screaming, and mud tires digging, easily pushed him along into the night.

A vertical maelstrom of mud and rock flew into the open back of the car, pelting him in the back of the head. The only thing he could do now was attempt to slow the truck down and jump out of his car.

But what about Jolie?

He hit a patch of gravel and his tires gripped for only an instant. He snatched at the door latch and pushed…, but nothing happened. The impact from the truck had jammed the door shut.

He reached over and tried the passenger door.

Nothing happened.

His pride and joy vehicle was all but a ruin.

There was another flash of lightening and James could now see where they were pushing him. He had to get out.

There was another bend in the road not fifty feet ahead, straight down the levee and into the river.

James frantically started rolling down his window, but it would only drop a few inches. Apparently, the damage from the impact jammed the roller and slide, locking the window in place.

There was no time left.

"Oh, Jolie! What have I done?"

He reached over to try the window on the passenger side. Miraculously, it worked!

It was almost down and he started climbing over the console as his car slid forward, locked to the truck's bumper behind him. The truck engine screamed renewing its vigor at pushing him forward. Their headlights shining inside were showing his every move.

The road hit a hard bump and the chrome floor shift caught him squarely between the legs. James thought he would puke as he grabbed his crotch. The truck roared louder and the thrust of a new impact threw his aching body backward, the force breaking the passenger seat over backwards. He was now helplessly tumbling around in the car.

Suddenly the truck slid to a crunching stop.

But he didn't.

His car slid aimlessly down, down, its engine still whining in faltering bursts of speed and then it started rolling side to side, down to the waters black edge.

James bounced around in the car, hitting every part of his body several times until his head was splitting and then numb. His left arm was broken first and fell lifeless, flopping at his side. His knees ached and legs flopped limply as the car continued to tumble down.

It seemed a second and an eternity to James. The pain was unbearable and he cried out into the night.

When the car came to rest, upside down on the large rocks of the riverbank, it teetered on the edge between land and the deep angry waters churning around it.

The engine raced, sputtered and died. Only a single headlight was left shining out into the Mississippi River.

All James could hear was the sound of the storm and the water lapping angrily at the front end of the car.

His thoughts came in a painful flurry.

"This is what it feels like to die. Oh, God, it hurts."

Everything drew black as he felt himself swirling painfully in a thick black oily river. He fought it desperately gulping for air, as he snapped back to reality.

James lay there immobile, going in and out of consciousness for several moments that felt like days.

An absurd thought flew past his unreasoning mind, "This is what a chicken feels like coming out of its egg."

A dark figure of a man slid down the steep embankment to where his car was resting.

James noticed that the rain had slowed to a low roar and he could hear the rivers noises against the sides of the inverted car.

A faint metallic grit filled his mouth and he spit out a warm substance, along with several shattered teeth. He was having a hard time breathing; if only he could shift his weight and turn over.

Neither of his arms responded and he couldn't feel his legs or his groin that had just been uprooted by the gearshift.

"Jolie, oh, Jolie...," he remembered her bright blue eyes and soft kiss....

"Oh. GOD, what was that?"

Pain exploded from everywhere at once.

The car, resting on its crumpled roof, was rocking back and forth at the rivers edge.

James tried to speak, but only that warm liquid would bubble up.

Cold.... So Cold.... He could hear his gramma saying, "Come over here by the stove, Hun, and get your hands warm."

The smell of her hot biscuits inside the oven flowed into his mind as he remembered leaning toward the open heat.

"OH GOD!" he screamed in his mind, the car was rocking again, the pain shocking him fully awake.

He pushed his body to try and crawl and heard something in his back make a loud crunch.

Then nothing worked.

There was the muffled sound of someone cursing outside as the rocking stopped, then slowly it resumed with increased vigor.

The rocking efforts paid off and the car slid over forward, the frontend was almost covered by the murky water, the one unbroken headlight illuminating both the surface and river bottom below.

Cold water poured inside the car where James was lying crumpled and broken.

Water poured over his head.

The cold..., so cold.

He gasped for a breath and got only muddy water.

Gurgling like a catfish on dry land..., it was quickly over and the pain mercifully left his body.

Chapter 38

The storm raged on with torrential rains lashing the huge sides of the Ames Estate, while a fretful Martiel Ellington waited on pins and needles.

"Thank God, you finally called me back," said Martiel.

"What's the matter?" asked Sheriff Howard. "Tell me what's wrong."

"What's wrong is it's been almost an hour since I called your dispatcher and…," Martiel said, and then going silent….

"James is in trouble."

"Why don't you start from the beginning and tell me what happened?"

"There was this big four-wheel-drive truck; it looked like the one that was in the newspaper, the one that kid was driving? Well when we got home, it was sitting right up the road from my house. It turned on its lights and drove right past us.

"James shot out of here over an hour ago chasing it down the road to see where it was going or who it was. I told him it was probably another one, a look alike, but he insisted it was the same one. He said it sounded like it."

The sheriff remembered the distinct sound that the missing 4x4 made while it was running. He wondered how James would know its sound.

"Please, please tell me you still have that truck locked away and he's only out on a wild goose chase."

"The truck was stolen from the pound earlier this evening," said the sheriff. "In fact, the officer you saw at the hospital was the one guarding the gate. He was hit on the head from behind…, he might not live."

"Do you know which way James Earl went?"

"Why no, it would have been impossible to tell with the rain gushing down when he shot out of here. All I know is he went back toward the highway and I went straight inside and called your office."

The phone receiver went quiet and she could hear the sheriff moan in the background.

"Oh, James…," Martiel started sobbing and then broke down into silence.

The figure of a man stepped down into the edge of the water and looked inside the car where a crumpled James Earl Williams was lying. He could see James' swelling black and blue face turned on its side under the water, eyes open and staring…, lifeless.

"Yep, dead'ern hail," said the man, with an air of satisfaction.

He sloshed out of the river and grabbed the back bumper and tried to finish pushing the car down into the river. It crunched and screeched on the rocks below it but wouldn't budge any further.

Suddenly a blast of light flashed brilliantly around where the car was resting. An air horn blasted and the man began slipping and sliding trying to get back up the embankment of the levee. A barge was moving slowly toward the car from somewhere out of the receding storm on the river.

James felt cold, so cold, but the pain was gone.

He couldn't believe what had happened.

The pain, what had happened to the pain?

There he stood right outside his car in the driving rain and saw the raw carnage of his car. He must have been thrown clear somehow. He looked up as the figure of a man tried desperately to ascend to the top of the slick embankment toward the truck that pushed him down to the waters edge.

Then, inside the car he saw the unthinkable. A body was lying there blue from cold and blood swimming out of its mouth, nose and ears. It was his body.

The dash lights were still on…, and he saw little minnows swimming around his open eyes in the dim light.

His arms were twisted in some fantastic contortion, but it was the position of his waist and hips that made him snap away in revulsion.

"That's me? I'm dead?"

The thought reeled in his mind. He couldn't be dead.

"I'm still here!"

"Why am I still here?" James asked into the storm. It was against everything he had ever been taught as a child.

He looked back up the steep embankment again and started to walk there, but an instant later he was standing on the top of the levee. So…, James thought about this for a second.

"How did I get here?"

He thought about his dead body and suddenly he was back down beside the crumpled car.

"If I'm not dead, then maybe I can crawl back inside my body and…."

James saw himself lying there…, cold and still.

Then everything rational left him. He lunged in a frantic attempt to get back inside his broken body, regardless of the pain he knew would be waiting for him.

"It doesn't *fit* anymore," James thought frantically, struggling with his cold deformed corpse.

He remembered Jolie and willed himself back up the embankment to where the truck was parked.

The man had almost reached the big 4x4 and his feet were moving fast.

James looked inside and there sat a mannequin strapped into the passenger side of the truck with a wig of black curly hair on its head.

"Jolie? This isn't Jolie."

It was a trap. He had let his emotions drag him into a trap.

But how could this have been planned and why? What did he do to deserve this? He sat in the truck as a skinny man crawled inside. He looked vaguely familiar, but from where he couldn't remember at that moment.

Lightening struck somewhere near and his entire reality quivered in his sight for a moment.

The truck fired to life and began to rocket down the river road slowing at a secluded cove. The scrawny guy put the truck into low gear and got out. He then stood outside, holding the steering column through the open window, and guided the crawling truck toward the rain swollen cove.

It slowly moved downward into the slime until it was completely covered and finally the engine gurgled and died. The man hurried to another truck hidden only a dozen yards away, its driver a stocky built man. Both drove away – with some part of James Earl Williams sitting inside.

"No..., No...," groaned Maime Ames, tossing her head in a fitful dream.

Her husband Martin woke at her bedside and gently took her right hand, fading back to sleep.

Suddenly she sat up with a gasp that scared Martin fully awake.

"It got him...." She looked over at Martin, "It got James Earl."

"It was only a dream Hun. You lie back down and relax. James is at the old place fast asleep."

"No, you don't understand, it got him. My sweet little James Earl.... We have to go, Martin, we have to go home now, Martiel needs us. Oh, what are we going to tell Catherine?"

Martin Ames walked to the door and called, "Nurse?"

In a few moments, a nurse had given Mrs. Ames something to relax her and help her sleep, but despite the sedative, she tossed her head back and forth in a disturbed dream.

Martiel sat drying her eyes. Not knowing anything was just as cruel as plain facts. The phone wouldn't ring, and yet if it did, would it bring good news?

"James is on his way home," she spoke into the old house, her voice echoing blandly in her ears.

Surely the truck drove to the next town and parked in a driveway. Just mistaken identity.

The house seemed to come alive around her. There was a loud

rumbling, rattling noise from upstairs that sounded like furniture shaking. Was the storm about to tear the house apart, with her in it? There had been a lull in the storm, the rain had quieted, the hail had stopped, even the wind had seemed to die down outside. No, this new noise had nothing to do with the storm.

Martiel grew scared. Never before had she been frightened by the old home place, but now she was terrified.

Did she dare go upstairs?

The telephone rang and Martiel thought she would expire right then, where she sat.

She froze for a moment, letting her heart slow down, then yanked up the receiver, hoping for Sheriff Howard.

"Sheriff Howard? No, it's me, Martin. Are you all right Martiel?"

"Hell no, I'm not all right," blurted Martiel, as she started crying.

"What happened? What's wrong?"

"It's James. I don't know where he is. There was that truck, and James went to chase it, and I found out it was stolen, and that was over two hours ago…. Oh Martin Earl, I fear the worst has happened."

Martin had never heard Martiel lose her composure before, even after their parents had died. She was always the rock in the family pulling it all back together. It was like a talent or gift with her.

"Martiel, please calm down and tell me what is going on," he said

Martiel groaned in agony at having to relive the events once again for her elder brother. Her sobbing ebbed as she slowly retold the story about James, the truck, the sheriff, and the wounded officer.

"Why did you call me, Martin? You should have been asleep."

Martin didn't know if he should tell his sister the wild dream that Maime had, for fear that she would break down again.

"Maime. What about Maime?" she asked.

"I didn't say anything about Maime."

"You were about to - please tell me Martin."

"She had a bad dream and woke me up…," he tried to tell her.

"About James? Come on, spit it out Martin."

"Well, it wasn't much, she kept saying, 'It got him. It got him. It got James Earl'. It didn't make a lick of sense."

Martiel Ellington felt the very breath halt in her empty chest as she slowly breathed in a gulf of despair.

"It makes perfect sense," Martiel said as her tone changed to something dark. "I need to go, Martin."

She hung up the phone and looked around the room, "Why didn't you protect him?"

Everything seemed so familiar, yet so distant to James as he sat in the truck with the two men that only minutes ago had ended his life, his future, his love…. Jolie…, if it saved her life, then so be it. If it saved the lives of his family, so be it.

The permanence of the situation had not fully settled into James as he looked over at his assailants.

They sat completely silent, staring out into the drizzly dark in front of the truck, as they headed to some unknown destination. The stocky man reached in his blue jean jacket and pulled out a pack of cigarettes. He slowly tapped out a single smoke and pushed in the button on the trucks cigarette lighter. He acted as if he had just left work and was going home for the evening!

James became mad as hell and fury rose inside him.

The stocky man looked over at his smaller partner who had driven the truck which ran James over.

"Did you check an see?"

"Yep, he was a little over done, if ya ask me," said the thin passenger holding his left hand.

"What's wrong with the hand?"

"Just a scratch, don't worry none about it."

The unlit cigarette dangled from the driver's lips as he turned and stared blankly down the road. He reached back inside the inside pocket and pulled out a small red and black pouch. He lifted it to his nose and drew the scent in and smiled. He put it back where it came from, lit his smoke and started laughing.

James blazed uncontrollably inside.

The man seemed to glance over where James was awkwardly sitting in his truck and his cigarette dropped from his bulbous lip into his lap.

His attention was immediately torn between the smoldering ash on his crotch and something he was unsure of. Frantically, he swatted the sparkling red dot that had begun to smolder. The truck swerved erratically for a few moments, until his thrashing was completed.

"What the hails wrong with you?!" yelled the skinny man. The driver looked back over and saw…, nothing, it was nothing. Just his nerves.

This was interesting. Did this smug murderer see him? James felt somewhat pleased with his continued anger.

The truck took several side streets through town and stopped at a small, but clean looking house. The skinny passenger slid over and took the drivers seat of the truck and drove away.

When the man got out and looked up at the sky, it was still putting on a light show, with its scattered branches flickering high inside the thunderstorm and constant rumbling. The rain was still misting down, but had lost most of the fury.

The entire night was almost spent when he opened the front door and walked inside.

"Billy, where the hell have you been?" asked his wife, as he flicked the light switch on and off several times.

She was scrunched into a dingy armchair in their living room in the dark, clutching a bottle of beer.

"It don't work, stupid. The electricity is off. We had a storm, in case you didn't notice! I've been scared shitless," she ranted on. "Where were you?"

"Out there. Working. Just taking care of business," said Billy. "Y'all afraid of a little old thunderstorm?"

"Little hell! I thought the house was going to blow off, with me in it," she whimpered on, nearing the point of tears.

James had perched himself on the arm of a couch and was watching the show.

"I know them," he thought.

"You could have called me, or something," she said as she got up and walked into their bedroom, still shaking from her unspent anger.

"Calm down Sallee Mae," said Billy, following her into the room.

"Where have I seen them?" James wondered.

He could still hear bitter arguing coming from the next room and getting louder.

"I know what'll calm you down," said Billy. "I made a chunk of change tonight working out in the weather and all. Ya, know? Hazard pay."

James' ears snapped back to attention at the revelation.

"We might can get one of them houses you like over on the other side a town," offered Billy in a singsong voice.

James sat in the darkness of their home for several minutes recalling the last half hour of his life.

James remembered the unbearable pain he felt and the accident. The vertigo from tumbling and being beaten to death inside the metal rolling cage. He thought of the ruined Mustang and how scared he was..., then of Jolie.

Then..., in that same instant, he was there, standing beside the wreckage. There was a big boat anchored in the river and shining several floodlights on the scene, as the white-capped water beat against its side.

The word "Shadrach" was painted on the bow of the boat.

"Mah, Gawd," said the Captain. "Take a good look at that."

There was a radio on the boat and it was crackling badly from the lightening as someone was trying to communicate with the Natchez Port Authority.

A large black man wearing fishing waders jumped from the boat and walked over to the drivers' side of the car, holding a large powerful spotlight.

As he pointed the blinding light inside the car, he turned quickly away and gagged at the sight of the already bloated face of its occupant hovering under the surface of the water.

"It looks like a kid..., he's dead," said the fisherman. "Poor soul. Lord have mercy...," he began to pray.

"Too late for prayer now," thought James as he hovered around the car.

Speaking of that, wasn't he supposed to be somewhere else right then? Was there some sort of time delay that was broken?

There was screeching laughter echoing in the darkness. At the peak of the violent storm, the sacrifice was made. The work was completed, the words were cast, the *Petro Loa* appeased.

A scrying bowl of black liquid sat at the base of the *potomitan* where the *Bokor* watched on as the events unfolded exactly as planned.

The broken body of the sacrifice was twisted and destroyed from the focused hatred of generations of waiting.

The skull of Syrus Earl Ames sat on a pedestal, a *hand of power* candle mounted on the center top; each finger burning and wax dripping down the surface into the empty eyes.

At her command, swirls of mist, one by one, came and filled the urn that was prepared in the circle. Ancestors with their hereditary gifts of the Ames family leapt into the open mouth of the urn, each snared like a rabbit. Now each member had become unwilling participants to a summons that could trap them forever and unleash a torrid force of evil.

There was only one more soul to catch.

Chapter 39

The airport in Atlanta Georgia redundantly announced canceled or delayed westward bound flights almost by the minute. People were stacked in every restaurant, lounge, and available space.

Catherine Williams had bought a magazine from one of the cubbyhole stores along the gallery to occupy her time. After finding a somewhat comfortable table in the back of one of the rampant nameless restaurants, she avoided her worried thoughts. As long as she kept ordering coffee and tipping well, this would be her solace and refuge.

Her Delta Airlines trip had been diverted in-flight because of a massive storm front moving through the Gulf Coast region. It had been the earliest available flight to where her mother lay in a hospital.

Catherine was anxious to see her family once again. Seeing her son was an added bonus. She missed him in a way only a mother could miss a part of herself. James Earl had been a troubled boy for as long as Catherine could remember, but these last few years had molded and formed a young man out of him. One that could achieve most anything that he put his mind to. She longed to tell him how proud she was of him.

Her husband Robert had never wanted children, but to placate her, he had agreed that they would have at the most two as time and finances permitted. Robert was a proud man and even though his wife had enough financial backing to have provided for a house full of children, he resented the thought of taking her "family charity."

Catherine had not anticipated the life that she now led. Vulnerable was too weak a word to describe the feeling of quitting her career job. The agency she had worked with for over ten years was the zenith of both vertical and horizontal career moves. Now, the feeling of being manipulated or controlled into her current unemployed condition was ever present.

Robert's age-old argument about the man being the breadwinner and the fact that she made twice his salary loomed over his head, and was a constant thorn in their marriage. Nevertheless, it wasn't about the money with Catherine. Her thoughts were of togetherness and family get-togethers, and holidays with friends.

There never seemed to be time for any of these events with Robert. The magazine article she was subconsciously reading, "What Constitutes a Marriage" was listing prime examples of her frustrations.

With a sudden frown, she pushed the magazine aside and began watching people, as well as the time on her Gucci wristwatch, wondering what each passing stranger's life consisted of.

It was well after midnight and the schedule for her flight had been shifted to 3:00 AM, which did not allow her the time for a hotel or even a short nap.

Her silver, double chiffon skirt and paisley brocade jacket had survived the trip gracefully so far, but was not ideal for the extended time she was spending at the airport.

The waitress came by once more and refilled her cup with a smile. Catherine had chosen her alcove well to avoid the usual unwanted advances from men with teenage hormones. Admittedly, she could easily pass for someone ten years her junior, because of her petit build. But the thought of even the most mundane of small talk with someone on the prowl repelled her. She made sure she flashed her wedding rings to any would-be Don Juan which managed to troll past her booth.

Catherine had a moment of vertigo and shifted in her seat, looking at her coffee cup, she dismissed it as stress. The feeling passed quickly, but her mind wandered back to the circumstances surrounding her mother's accident. She'd experienced another similar mysterious vertigo only minutes before the phone call from her father explaining the details of her mother's injury.

She pursed her lips and looked down again at her watch, wishing the minutes forward.

The early morning sky was bright and clear. The air seemed fresh and softly chilled, but that would change quickly as the sun made its way above the horizon.

Several emergency crews were already working steadily around the city of Natchez restoring power to various neighborhoods. Leaves and small limbs littered the streets and yards for the fortunate areas, but others were looking at whole tree limbs protruding from the roofs of their houses.

Hail damaged cars littered driveways for the unfortunate residents without a garage.

Martiel pined away the remainder of the night in her empty house unaware of the havoc of the storm or even that the electricity was off in the estate. A worse darkness had filled her mind with worry and despair. How could she have allowed James Earl to take off like that? Why didn't she try harder to stop him? Had she lost her mind?

She was losing it now…, waiting.

A wrecker with three extra lengths of twisted steel cable had backed up to the levee where the "Shadrach" was docked during the night's storm. The wrecker had anchored itself so that it would not end up where the crushed vehicle was lodged near the rivers edge below.

Its operator was feeding the steel cable down the slope and was looking for something substantial to tie on to.

Alongside the wrecker sat the county coroner's vehicle and several Adams County department vehicles.

It was too early for Deputy Floyd to come in for duty and no one had been able to reach him all night. His home phone only gave a fast busy signal, phone lines down no doubt.

Sheriff Howard had requested help from the neighboring county during the night to handle the excess calls and emergencies.

After the distraught call from Martiel Ellington, he had been monitoring the emergency dispatcher. During the night he had noticed the description of this particular car and winced, praying to himself that his hunch was wrong.

Now…, he had been up all night and was not prepared for what he was now seeing.

The sheriff and a detective from the next county circled the trashed vehicle looking for anything that might point them toward what caused this tragedy.

With the help of a cutting torch and pry bars, the county coroner and his helper had extracted the mangled body of James Earl Williams from the wreckage. They also found his identifying wallet still in his torn blue jeans hip pocket. His drivers' license announced that he was a little over a month away from being 18 years old.

The sheriff had told the coroner that he wanted a full and detailed autopsy of the remains, as he knew he would have the full cooperation of the family.

Every member of the investigative team had been sickened at the sight of the broken, bruised, and bloated remains of James Earl.

Now Sheriff Howard had to go make some difficult phone calls to the boys' family.

The specter of James Earl himself, sat legs folded on top of the upside-down Mustang watching everyone trying to make heads or tails out of what had happened. He figured out pretty quickly that no one could hear or see him and communicating was impossible.

He also knew who had done him in…, but didn't have a clue as to the why. That only added another question to the stack hovering in James Earl's thoughts.

"Looks like it rolled at least 7 times down the 120 foot drop, the rocks and the fall did the rest," said the detective. "There are some footprints back here behind the car, but the rain washed it down and…," -looking down a notepad- "The fishing boat crew that found the wreck could have made them. I'm going to need their statements."

"Make sure that you get pictures of everything, including where it came off the road up there," said the sheriff. "Those ruts are deep, and they're probably dug by that 4x4 from the pound."

James agreed to no one and everyone present, "Yep, and its right up the road in a slime pit. I can take you to the house of the guy that did it too."

"This is useless!" screamed James to himself. "Why am I here!?"

"How are you feeling this morning, Hun? asked Martin Ames. "Did you get any rest?"

Maime Ames was propped up with a stack of pillows and looking at a breakfast that she couldn't stomach. Her hollow eyes looked over at her husband and couldn't answer him at first.

"I kept having that same dream over and over Martin," she said gloomily. "Have you heard from Martiel or James?"

"Nothing," he said. "She doesn't answer the phone, but I'm sure that's because of the storm."

"No. There's something wrong. Did you call the sheriff?" she asked.

"He's not there at his office. After his visit here late last night, I didn't want to call him at home and wake him up," said Martin. "You know there's nobody else there at his office I trust."

BeBe and Jolie were driving into Natchez, wowed by the damage from the night's storm along the way. Vidalia, Louisiana had mercifully been spared the brunt of the storm.

"I hope *The Cajun* is still there," said BeBe.

Jolie sat quietly, her mind on things other than the café. It had been a fitful night of strange dreams, unexplainable feelings, and horrible dread…, followed by a sudden emptiness in her chest that wouldn't go away.

"That's what it is," she thought, "dread."

They drove up to The Cajun Café, to find a power company truck parked next door with a group of her employees standing out front, arms folded, talking. A long-armed bucket was inching its way up around several obstacles, causing the heavy truck below to quiver at every nudge.

She parked the car and hurried up to the group.

"What's everybody doing out here?" asked BeBe.

Then she noticed that the usual customers normally sifting in were not there. In fact nobody was around except a few store owners cleaning up broken items, glass windows and trash.

"Powers off," chanted several of the group.

BeBe looked up at the service truck and in a few seconds she saw the problem. A melted and mangled bicycle frame was suspended across two of the power lines and had blown the circuit to the surrounding area. It was then she noticed that everything was dark around the square.

"How long before we get the juice back on?" she yelled up at the workers.

"Wicked witch of the west dropped her bike," joked the older of the two men in a work bucket. When he saw that she wasn't really amused he said, "Give us about fifteen more minutes and you should be up and running."

"Thanks," said BeBe.

"Everybody on the square is shut down for the day," said one of her family, hinting that she should follow their example.

"City workers got to have some place to eat today," said BeBe blandly. "If everybody else is closed, we'll be swamped, so we better get busy."

There were a few groans among the troops.

"All right, if it doesn't pick up by noon, you can all go home," said BeBe feeling like a pushover.

Jolie had already unlocked the front door and was taking overturned chairs off the tabletops and placing them around tables. The rest of the employees moved to help, out of guilt or boredom.

In ten minutes, the café looked as if it had been open for hours. The gas grill was well on its way to blazing and a rack of homemade rolls sliding into an oven.

BeBe had changed the small blackboard with the "special of the day" by the door, to their two fastest and easiest items to prepare.

BeBe said, "Jolie, why don't you try and call James.... See if they are all okay."

Jolie had already started skipping to her aunt's small office before the suggestion was cold in the air.

She called James' grandparents' house and let it ring a sufficient number of times without answer. Then she thought that James might be with his Aunt Martiel at their old home place.

She dialed that number with no way of knowing that its ringing fell on deaf ears. As a last resort, she dug a piece of paper out of her pocket with the phone number of the hospital and room number on it.

It rang once and the phone was answered so quickly that Jolie jumped.

"Hello?" said Martin Ames.

"Hi Mr. Ames," said Jolie. "How is your wife this morning?"

"Oh, hello Jolie," he said, his voice downcast. "She is much better thank you. The storm and all kept her awake most of the night, but she's okay."

"You haven't by any chance heard from James have you?" asked Martin.

The phone was silent for longer than was appropriate.

"Jolie, are you still there?" he asked.

"Yes, I... I'm still here," she stammered. "I was going to ask you the same question. I haven't heard from James. I had a feeling he would call me this morning. I was getting worried."

"Me too," said Martin. "I'll have him call you as soon as I know something. Are you at your house or...."

"I'm at the café here in town," said Jolie quietly.

"Okay, now you don't worry, and tell BeBe to keep a plate hot for us. If they let Maime go today we might stop by for some real food."

"I'll be sure and tell her..., and thank you Mr. Ames," said Jolie.

As Martin hung up the phone, they both knew that something wasn't right.

"Hold on a minute!" yelled the detective.

He and another officer walked over to the wreckage that was still upside down.

"Look at this...," he said, pointing to two silver tubes running along the frame of the car.

"Yeah, brake lines, so?" asked the other officer.

There was a noticeable amount of fluid around the area next to the wheel well.

The detective ran his finger along the edge of the frame and smelled it furtively.

"Brake fluid, it's everywhere along the frame right here," he said pointing to the edge of the underside.

"It took a hell of a beating coming down here, probably hit the rocks," the other said.

"This is fresh fluid and it looks like it was pumped out in a spray..., look here at the lines..., under here, they're crushed flat and broken. See how much fluid?"

"Probably pushing the brakes trying to stop going down the hill," said the officer.

"With a shattered spine? Did you see that boy's hips how they were twisted in half? He wasn't near the brake pedal going down the hill," said the detective.

"Could have happened while he was being pushed down the road," offered another officer.

The detective waved over at the photographer, "Take a couple of pictures of this..., all along here and here where the lines are smashed," he said pointing instructions.

"Can we pull this thing out of here?" yelled the driver of the wrecker from up the hill. "I got another call to go to."

"Hey Detective, you need to come take a look at this!" said another officer from up the hill. "I think I found the truck we're looking for."

The detective looked back up at the driver of the wrecker service, "You're going to be late...."

Sheriff Howard walked into the hospital entrance with the dread of death on his face. He pictured the young boy that he'd mentored for the last five summers as interim probation officer. His memory flowed forward to the image of the same boy while being dragged from the mangled wreckage of his car.

How could he tell his deceased brother's best friend that his grandson was dead? Not only dead, but murdered. Assailant or assailants unknown at present.

He stopped by the restroom and washed his face and hands looking in the mirror. His bedraggled clothes and hair was witness of over twenty-four grueling hours without rest.

He had this one last duty to perform before he quit the day. He had overturned the impersonal idea to phone them. As hard as it was going to be, he felt he owed them an explanation to their face. But he had none.

There was no excuse for what had happened. Why would someone want to kill a young boy like James? He knew the hard past James had suffered, but this was a good kid. He had grit, a kid he would have been glad to call his own.

He punched the button on the wall for the elevator and rode the empty car up to the second floor. When the door opened, he was looking at Room 212 immediately to his right.

He swallowed hard, wishing at that moment that he had chosen some other profession rather than law enforcement.

"Come in," said a muffled voice from inside the room.

Sheriff Howard tried to make his face as pleasant as possible without making too much eye contact.

"Sheriff, it's good to see you. We were just talking about you," said Martin Ames.

"How are you feeling this morning, Mrs. Ames?" asked the sheriff.

"Much better, thank you," she said.

"Mr. Ames..., Martin, would you like to step outside for a moment? I need to talk to you about something," said the sheriff.

"It's about James Earl isn't it?" asked Maime Ames. "Something has happened to my James," she said fretfully. "I knew something happened..., please tell us."

Sheriff Howard looked questioningly at Martin Ames, wanting to know what to do.

Martin sat back down by his wife.

"Why don't you have a seat sheriff and tell us both," he said.

The revelation of James' death aged Mr. and Mrs. Ames by years in barely a moment.

His mother was on her way there, no way to contact her. They were responsible for James. He was still only a boy growing to manhood in their eyes.

What would they do without him?

"Could you do us one favor, sheriff?" asked Martin.

"Anything," said the sheriff, a broad statement which he meant completely.

"Would you send somebody by our old family home? We haven't been able to get a hold of Martiel. She's been there for hours and she doesn't answer the phone."

The door closed quietly and the two of them sat in grieved silence together holding each other's hands. What would they tell Catherine?

Catherine Williams fought the early morning traffic out of New Orleans. Her redeye flight had delayed her arrival until after seven that morning, but she was still going to get to Natchez before the time she estimated to her family.

The rental car was pathetic and reeked of cigarette smoke. Burnt holes in the pale blue vinyl seat and some nameless odors began drifting from the back seat as soon as the sun came in the windows.

In a couple of hours, she would be home.

Home.

She longed for the reality of that word. The place where she was born, both her children were born: James Earl while they lived there, Sam by choice. She remembered the flight back home only a week before Sam was born, against her doctor's recommendations.

She wanted a piece of her heritage to be planted in her children; to always bring them back to where her parents had lived, and she had lived out her childhood. Went to school, dated, fell in love....

Love. Now there was a word she needed to work on. Something both her and Robert needed to work on.

He was not a native of Mississippi, but his parents had moved to Biloxi while she was in High School. Roberts's father was a roughneck on an oilrig located immediately offshore and had followed the oil boon. He went from one jobsite to the next wherever he could get work.

She remembered the summer that she went to stay with her family in Biloxi and met Robert. They were on the beach most every day that summer and simply hit it off. They liked the same things, food, music, clothes, goals.... No one bothered to tell her that every persons preferences change at least two or three times in their lifetime. She and Robert had not been the exception to that rule. Now their lives had grown so different and apart, she didn't know who Robert was. She didn't really know who she was any more.

A pothole in the road brought her back to reality and she looked at her watch and hit a button on the radio for a change in music.

Martiel sank deeper into the living room sofa. The bottle of Southern Comfort on the end table beside her was almost empty.

It had been years since she drank anything alcoholic, as least more than the single, social, watered down variety. Now she didn't even need or want a glass; the open bottle was perfectly fine.

Three hours she spent upstairs in an empty room talking to ancestors that refused to answer.

Couldn't answer.

They weren't there.

The house was empty, truly empty now. She felt more alone than she had ever felt. More so than when her husband, Jonathon Ellington passed away, now five years ago.

Something was terribly wrong. She could sense James as before, but something was terribly different, inexplicable. She had so much more to teach James. He was finally on the cusp of beginning to accept and understand his future role for his family.

Now…, she wasn't sure if there would be a family to govern.

She reached for the bottle and spun the lid off. It fell from her sluggish hands and she watched it as it ran doodling across the polished hardwood floor.

Then there it was again, that unbearable silence.

Another turn of the bottle and it was empty. She dropped it on the floor and went ambling slowly to a mahogany cabinet in the sitting room. Once there she faced fully stocked shelves with a variety of alcoholic vices.

She chose a larger, more "fashionable" bottle, a Brandy that she had saved for special occasions. The trip back to the couch was more labored than before, but after a few baby steps, and catching herself on the camel-back of the sofa, she managed to follow its edge to her comfortably numb warm spot.

There was a knock at the door.

"Who is it?" she slurred.

There was no answer. She removed the lid from the bottle and took a sharp sip of the contents. It was old, bitter and dry. Just like she felt.

Another pounding on the door, more persistent this time, roused her anger at being disturbed. James had a key; somehow, she knew it wouldn't be him.

"Just a damn minute," she swore. "I'm coming…."

She heard footsteps on the porch walking to one of the many windows and back to the door. The house seemed to be moving under her feet, but she managed to find the doorknob.

"Who is it?" she asked again straining angrily to form her words.

"Sheriff Howard, can I come in?"

She struggled for several seconds with the door lock and pulled open the door to a bright morning sun blasting her directly in the eyes. All she could see was the silhouette of a hefty man, until she stepped to the side of the door facing, which blocked the fury of the light.

Sheriff Howard took off his hat and walked through the door. Martiel shut the offending door to stifle off the early blast of heat, started back to the couch, and stumbled.

Sheriff Howard caught her misstep and after smelling the reek of alcohol didn't ask any questions.

"Hello Martiel, maybe this isn't a good time. Should I come back later?"

"No, No, by all means no," said Martiel. "Would you like something to drink?" she shrilled, waving her arm toward the open decanter of Brandy.

She sat down heavily onto the couch. There was something she was supposed to ask, but couldn't quite remember. James. That was it, James Earl.

"Have you heard from James, sheriff?" she asked.

"I saw James Earl a little while ago," he said, not knowing how to explain.

"Well he needs to learn to use the phone. I've been worried shick, uh... sick," she corrected her self.

"Your phone isn't working Martiel," he said. "Your brother Martin has been trying to call you for several hours. That's actually part of the reason why I'm here."

"Hasn't rang!" she boomed. "It's right in there."

The sheriff looked at the telephone beside the sofa where she was anchored, then followed Martiel's wavering arm. She pointed back through the dining room and into the open kitchen door.

"It's on the wall. I used it a little while ago," she said.

He walked into the kitchen to find the receiver dangling on the floor by the tangled coil of its leash.

"Why am I so cold?" thought James, standing in the sunlight, watching what was left of his car being hauled away up the levee road. The twisted metal creaked and groaned as it bounced clumsily on the back of the wrecker.

"Okay, so I'm dead..., but I'm not. I'm not in hell..., I don't think. This sure isn't Heaven. The only person that will know what I should do is Aunt Martiel. I need to find her, but what if I go there and I'm trapped like all the others there? I don't want to wander around with a bunch of people I don't even know in a house I can't leave. I guess don't have any choice. I have to go there and find her."

He concentrated on the house and…, nothing happened as it did before. He tried to close his eyes to help him focus, and found that he couldn't….

He couldn't close his eyes.

"This sucks," he said as he started walking the long hike back to the old Ames Estate.

The more he walked the madder he got, the madder he got the faster he walked.

He reached the highway in a matter of a minute, not realizing that the walk was a lot longer than that normally. Once at the highway he stood and looked at the empty road. Dirt and leaves washed up on the pavement as far as he could see from the flood of the storm. He thought of the miles he had to walk and how nice it would be to look over and see the mailbox at the end of the drive. He took a step and found himself standing at the end of the old Ames Estate driveway. Vertigo overtook him for a moment, but no feelings to concern himself with.

"Cool. If I have to be dead, at least I can travel fast."

He walked up the gravel drive and found the sheriff's car parked in the driveway.

Martiel was still in a stupor, but was coherent enough for the news of James' death. The sheriff thought that her current condition actually might help buffer the bad news, if he went ahead and told her.

"What kind of news about James?" Martiel choked out. "What were you just thinking?"

The sheriff looked at Martiel strangely.

"I was considering telling you some news of James. How did you know?"

"Long story," Martiel said as she lolled her head back against the couch, eyes rolling toward the ceiling.

She reached for the bottle of Brandy, but decided that it would be rude to drink in front of the sheriff and dropped her hand.

"There was an accident last night Martiel," the sheriff began. "James was…."

Martiel cut him off, sitting bolt upright, looking around her.

"James, is that you?" she asked. "Where are you?"

James nearly jumped from excitement that someone, anyone could hear him.

"I'm right here, Aunt Martiel, but I got hurt," he said, not knowing how to explain it to her.

Martiel was spinning around as if she were a crazy woman. The sheriff fell quiet, scared that the woman had lost her last marble over this sudden tragedy. He had known Martiel most of his life and had never seen her act this way. She was the sophisticate, a woman of money and prestige, not a drunk talking to the air.

He stood quickly.

"Martiel, maybe.... I think I should come back a little later, when you've had some time to sober up."

"NO, no, ask him to stay," said James to her spiritually attuned ears.

"Wait sheriff, don't go," she said and seemed a fraction more coherent than before. "Please sit back down and tell me what happened."

She put the lid back on the bottle of alcohol and sat it determinedly away from her own reach.

"You and James were right about that truck last night," he began. "It was the one that we had locked up. After James left here..., it looks as if he followed it all the way to the levee road. From what I can tell, that truck somehow managed to get behind him and..., and pushed him down to the river bank, almost into the river."

"James is dead," said Martiel in her semi-drunk revelation. "My heir is dead."

The sheriff sat silently letting his words soak into Martiel's marginally cognizant mind.

"Have you told Martin and Maime?" she asked.

"I just left the hospital, that's the reason I'm here. Your brother asked me to come by and check on you when he couldn't get you by telephone."

"Aunt Martiel, I don't know why but...," said James. "I know who killed me and where he lives."

"Thank you for coming by, sheriff. I need to get some coffee in me and..., well, you know.... This isn't like me. I was just so worried, not knowing and all."

"But, Aunt Martiel!" said James Earl. "I...."

"Hush James," she turned and whispered a short command into the air.

The sheriff turned his head and looked in the direction she had spoken.

"Uh, yes.... I see what you mean. I'll be going now. If there's anything I can do please let me know. I'll be back later to get a statement about what you saw last night. Don't forget to call your brother at the hospital."

"I will, sheriff, and thank you again for coming by and letting me know," she said ushering him to the door.

The door closed behind him as he ambled down the steps of the front porch.

"That was weird," he said to himself. "No, that was wall-eyed crazy."

The door closed and Martiel spun in a dizzying circle.

"James!" said Martiel. "Please tell me you aren't a spirit, please. Please be the alcohol talking!" she whined, as she broke down into a sob.

"I'm here," said James somberly. "I don't know what I am. One minute I was underwater and tasting muddy water and the next I was standing on the bank of the river freezing. Oh God, Aunt Martiel, it hurts to die that way."

"What happened to you, James?" she managed to ask through her semi-drunken wailing.

James recanted what transpired from the moment he left the driveway until the moment he lost consciousness and died.

"Something else has happened here too, James," said Martiel. "The house is empty..., that is except for you now."

"What do you mean empty? You mean the spooks that were living here are all gone? Wait.... I'm one of those spooks now. Awww this is messed up. How did I get left here, Aunt Martiel?"

"I don't know. I really don't. What about this person, the one you said..., killed you."

The words hurt her as she spoke them, how insensitive they seemed.

"I rode in the truck with him to his house. I can show you where he lives, right over on the other side of town. His name is Billy and his wife is Sallee something..., one of those sing-song names. Mae I think, yeah, Sallee Mae."

"Slow down Sherlock, you don't know what it was about, or if someone hired him to do it, or why...."

"I know that I've seen them somewhere before," said James. "Something's wrong with me. I can't seem to remember things as clear as before."

The bright sunlight now flooded the living room where Martiel sat.

"Let me see you James?" she asked. "I want to see you again."

"What do you mean, you want to see me? I'm dead, remember!" he said angrily.

"Just calm down, come with me."

Martiel walked a careful drunk pace to the stairs. She looked up and stood there for a moment trying to decide if she should attempt the mountain of steps in front of her.

She grabbed the banister firmly and took a few steps at a time. By the time she was half way, most of the alcohol was burning out of her system and her footing was a lot surer.

She entered the room that she had previously spent half her night in, beseeching her ancestors for an audience. After closing the door, she made sure that the drapes were pulled closed.

"Okay, James? Are you here?"

"Well..., yeah, as much as possible."

"I see you haven't lost your smart mouth," she said. "I'm glad you haven't.... James, I..., I'm so very sorry."

"Don't be sorry. Show me what you brought me up here for," he said calmly, trying to avert another emotional outburst of crying.

"Alright, this will get easier in time, but you need to get emotional," she said. "Any emotion will do as long as it's extreme. Angry. Sad. You know, emotional!"

James couldn't think of anything off hand, at first. Then he focused on the face of the bulging eyed man that ran him into the river. He wanted..., he wanted revenge. His anger flared. The thought of the way he drowned and how cold it was.

"That's it James, you're.... OH GOD!"

Martiel turned and closed her eyes, and covered her mouth with her hands.

James looked the same as the moment when he died. Mangled, torn, blue, blood gagging bad.

Martiel began another bout of uncontrollable sobbing.

"Oh, James. My sweet little nephew. Oh, I'm so sorry."

She stumbled over to the vacant bed in the room and fell onto it.

"What's the matter, Aunt Martiel?"

"Just don't look in the mirror."

Which to James meant, look in the mirror and you'll know what's wrong. He glanced at his reflection and saw a transparency of himself that was putrid and dead. The shock made his emotions flare wildly and he became even clearer.

James looked away and asked, "Am I always going to look like that?"

Martiel regained her composure and dried her eyes.

"It was what you were thinking about. Next time try and remember your face..., maybe right after you shaved. Do you have a picture?"

"Only my drivers' license..., oh, wait.... The police took that off my dead body," he said gloomily. "This is depressing."

"Well you certainly look better," she said after carefully glancing back his direction.

James took another peek in the mirror and saw his old self again.

Chapter 40

Deputy Floyd sauntered in at his usual time. He had a line of excuses prepared for why he hadn't answered his phone, including the tree limb that had knocked down lines in his neighborhood; even though his had merely been off the hook.

Actually, he had slept like a rock, ignoring the storm.

"I have a dozen messages for you," said Jeanette. "The sheriff is looking for you, too. There was an accident up north of town on the east riverbank that he's been working all morning."

She handed him a stack of memos.

"Allison needs you over in dispatch too," she said as she picked up the phone and answered another call. "Sheriff's Department...."

He wandered over to the small window that separated the dispatch officers' room from civilization and tapped on the glass, which he knew Allison hated.

She was busy on the radio and scratching a notepad furiously with a pencil. She looked up and saw who was rapping on her window and frowned.

Allison reached into a basket and grabbed a handful of slips of paper. The window slammed open, the stack hit the outside shelf.

"Prioritize these, I need 'em back an hour ago," she said bitterly.

The window slammed back shut before he could give her his usual offensive morning remarks.

He casually picked up the stack and walked to his cubicle out in front of the Sheriff's Office.

After falling in his chair, he looked at the stack of backed up calls, a few break ins, power lines down, mostly storm related items - apparently some people will use a storm to try to cover lots of stuff.

He shuffled and sorted the deck quickly and suggested a few specific officers to handle certain items and walked back to the window. Rapping on the glass, he opened the window, dropped them in the basket, and shut the window without expression.

Time for coffee and a road trip.

He walked past Jeanette, coffee in hand.

"I'll be out for a while, reach me on the radio if you need me," he said waving the stack of notes in the air.

His first call of business was payday. He waited anxiously for a page with a certain obscure number. Each number had been prearranged between himself and Billy to know where to meet. The one he found the most amusing was "007", a dive located at Natchez Under-the-Hill.

He was also anxious to hear how a certain accident was handled and if it was the same one the sheriff was working. It was best that he busy himself in other places as much as possible. The less he knew or was involved with the investigation at first the better.

A new face was addressing a small group of officers, thinking out loud and pointing toward a bulleted list on a chalkboard.

"So, what we have so far is…,

- Roger Mastyn, teenager dead from some strange drug OD.

"Never talked and his accomplices still at large."

- Officer Greene, near death - Attacker unknown.

"Considering it was Mastyn's truck that was stolen from the impound, it was likely one of Mastyn's accomplices."

- James Williams, another teenager, murdered.

"His attacker is yet unknown, but there are too many coincidences not to be related, considering it was Mastyn's truck identified as the murder weapon."

- Chevy Truck recovered from the cove, murder weapon.

"Does that about sum it up?"

The detective on loan from Jackson Mississippi was scribbling frantically on a chalkboard in a mad attempt at making sense of all the connected evidence. All the evidence fitted into a very neat validating timeline.

There were nods and mumbles from all around the table.

"Has anyone established a motive? How is the Williams boy connected to the Mastyn case? Was he involved or simply in the wrong place at the wrong time?"

"Mastyn and his accomplice robbed an old, old grave of the Williams boy's family," said the sheriff. "The truck that belonged to Mastyn, the one that killed Williams, was involved in the skullduggery. It's possible that James…, uh, that is…, the Williams boy was playing junior detective and got himself killed."

The detective quickly scribbled - *grave robberies*, at the bottom of his list.

"Could this be a cult? Or do you think it could be drug related?"

Sheriff Howard shook his head, "We're not sure of anything. Except for the few items retrieved from the truck at the time it was impounded. We're back to square one. But all that evidence we collected was related to Mastyn and the grave robberies."

"Would you mind if I looked at those items later?" asked the detective.

"You can look at them now, if you want," said the sheriff. "I'm missing something about all this and I want you to take lead on this case if you can. I'm too close to the situation to be objective."

He sighed and sat back in his chair feeling the pangs of exhaustion. The sheriff thought back on the futile efforts of investigating the grave robberies. It was as if the perpetrators knew exactly what someone would be looking for, to try and catch them or…, it was covered up.

As County Sheriff, he couldn't fathom the idea that someone within his organization was involved.

"I'll see if my Captain will let me stay on for a few days, but I can't promise anything," said the detective. "By the way, sheriff, you look wiped out, you should take a few days and get some rest…."

"What do I do with myself?" thought James.

His Aunt Martiel had passed out on the bed and was fast asleep.

The one person he longed to see was off limits. He didn't dare try to find Jolie. Even if he did, all he would be able to do is look at her and wish things could have turned out differently.

He wanted to ask Martiel to tell Jolie what had happened before she found out what happened somewhere else. This wouldn't be in the newspaper until tomorrow morning, but that was all the time he had, unless Jolie called his grandparents.

He needed to act fast, but Aunt Martiel, the only person who could hear him, was in a drunken sleep.

Nervous energy filled him as he deliberated.

The book of their family heritage was sitting on the nightstand and James wished that he had read it in more depth. He was at a loss as to how to do much of anything in is present state. After all, he couldn't pick up the book or turn the pages, although he seemed to have constant daytime no matter what kind of light source was around him. Even in total darkness, there was a contrast of images that made everything a kind of black and white. No, it was more of a bluish gray and white.

It didn't matter what it looked like, he argued; the fact was he could see clearly in the dark.

With nothing else to do to occupy himself, he wandered around the house looking at each room in depth, even the most insignificant items.

One room was almost entirely Victorian in its décor, another Early American. All authentic. The house was an eclectic museum.

He bored quickly from his ramblings and went straight back to check on Aunt Martiel. He had no idea how much time had slipped by.

She was still passed out.

Why would she let herself get in this situation? She needed to be at her best right now, not sloppy drunk.

He had to know what was going on, what he was, besides dead.

Then he began to wonder if all doors were open to him?

Could he go anywhere, anytime he wanted to?

He could wait for Aunt Martiel to wake up or....

Martiel could be out for hours and his patience was fading fast.

Then there was Jolie.... Once again that desperate longing to see Jolie swirled back to his thoughts. He couldn't even think of going to see her.

How was Jolie going to handle this? This change was not good. Who was he kidding? This wasn't change, he was dead. All he could do was ask his Aunt Martiel to let Jolie know..., that he had loved her, still did love her.

Should he do that? That would be even harder on her.

Too much thinking, no action, he moved downstairs and out the front door. James decided to go to his grandparents' house and see if his gramma was out of the hospital yet.

Now. How to get there? He needed to learn how to do this moving around without all the trial and error.

Concentrating didn't work. Was it the emotional thing again?

He thought of the warmth and love in their house. The memories of when he was a child visiting for Thanksgiving and Christmas. The living room couch on Christmas morning wrapped in one of his gramma's blankets.

That quick swimmy vertigo produced itself and he was there!

He looked cautiously through his grandparents' house and almost called out for one of them before remembering that they wouldn't be able to hear him even if they were there.

No one was home. That silence, he was going to have to learn to deal with that or change it somehow. It was deeply irritating, pervasive, like the cold that had seeped into him.

Why couldn't he get warm?

The hospital; he'd go there.

🦇

The dark cave was dimly lit now and the revelry was replaced with a certain placidity of knowing the job was well done.

Decades of work, planning, all culminated in one night, well orchestrated. Now it was time to use some of the newly acquired power. The lineage of the Ames family was at her disposal.

Her youth still manifesting itself, Miss Lyda began a slow chant and entered a trancelike state. She began to speak to the *nanm* inside the urn, to command them to arise before her. As one whole entity, they appeared, obeying..., listlessly charmed into submission.

She held the skull of Syrus Earl Ames in her left hand and gently rolled the *ason* in her right and spoke into the skull.

"Where is it?" she asked. "Where is the gold you *hit* for yourself?"

"Where you *hit* it?!" she demanded, her voice echoing throughout the cave.

A breath only, barely detectable, wisped from the skull.

"Hid from you."

"Where!!!?" she demanded. "Or your darkness be forever!"

"One sack left, you got the other."

"Liar!" she screamed.

"Can't lie…," the answer drifted forward.

"Show me where it is!" she demanded again angrily.

"This cave, hid here before, before you killed me."

"This cave we in? All this time, right hear? You a liar!" her voice rose in anger.

"Can't lie…," the skull whispered.

"Where 'tis. Tell now," her voice lowered.

"Follow the stream inside to its mouth, look up."

"The spring water inside hear?"

"Yes…"

"If you lying, you be my slave forever!" she cursed, all the while knowing that she would never willingly set them free.

She carefully placed the skull in a small sack and rolled it on the ground into the sacrificial circle. There was only one oil lamp lit and she picked it up and walked several hundred feet back into the narrow recesses of the cave.

Deep in the back was a small stream of spring water that was constantly bubbling along the floor to another underground exit. She followed it until she had to crawl over sharp rocks along a crevasse. There she held up the lamp and could see a coin sized hole that appeared to be a fountainhead.

Above it was…, nothing. Nothing she was promised.

She looked all around the opening where the steady stream of clear water was emerging and could not see any place remotely large enough in size to contain a sack of gold that should be there.

She sat down and looked up once more.

The opening had receded a couple of feet over the course of time since Syrus had died. She looked up and saw a cleft about seven feet up where some one might reach up to. She placed the lamp down firmly and climbed up as much as she could.

Nothing….

Angered, she screamed, "Liar!!!"

Her voice echoed and died flatly in the confined space.

Lyda noticed a strap of leather, the same color as the rock face, hanging down further along the cleft. She pulled on it and it broke from age rot and fell crumbling into her hand.

The walls were slick and wet so that if she were to climb, it would be easy to slip and fall. Desperate to see, she hurried all the way back to her makeshift altar room. She was about to fashion something that might be able to reach over the ledge when she heard a noise.

"Dat my boy?" she called out.

The only noise for several moments was a drip, drip, drip of water back deep in the cave. Gentle shuffling noises came nearer to where she was and a voice called out.

"It's..., It's me..., don't do nothing rash now, ya hear?" begged a small voice echoing slightly.

"I hear," she answered back.

Timidly, a stocky built man walked in from the mouth of the cave into the flickering candle light.

"Billy, you done good," she said excitedly.

"Wh..., where is the missus?" he stuttered. "Where is Miss Lyda?"

"Why, right hear, it's me," she said.

"But?" stammered Billy.

"What? I ain't no scraggly ole hag?" she said as she laughed.

"No Ma'am," said Billy cautiously. "I mean...."

"It's all right. I know what old look like," she said. "I seen it most my life."

Billy stared at her uncontrollably for several minutes, at her youthful appearance.

"Come back here," she said turning. "Follow me."

Billy couldn't believe what he was seeing. The old crone was now much younger and actually fairly attractive from what little he could see of her in the dim light.

He jumped into step behind her, back into the bowels of the dark cave. She stopped short of a spring of water and pointed up.

"Can you climb up there?" she asked.

"I'll try."

He looked for any type of footing and managed to hang his slick soled boot on a sharp snag in the rock face.

"Feel around up there for a sack," she said.

Billy ran his hand carefully back and forth and felt a lump of some kind. It felt soggy and when he pulled on it, whatever it was tore like rotten skin. He jumped back and slid down from his foothold, looking at his hand in the light.

The *Bokor*, Miss Lyda, quickly grabbed his hand and held the lamplight next to it, inspecting his fingers.

"Rotted cloth," she said excitedly. "Stay here."

She ambled off back toward the opening of the cave leaving Billy standing in an inkwell of complete darkness. Billy was beginning to get frightened by the sounds of the spring and its echoing, not to mention the pitch black. He had started inching his way back, feeling his way along the walls of the cave, but remembered lots of sharp objects and stopped.

In a few moments, the light began appearing along with a shuffling of feet.

Billy was relieved by the blinding light of the lamp as it entered the chamber where he stood clinging to the wall.

An empty wooden crate was swinging from her other arm and she quickly set it down, near the place Billy had felt the moldy cloth.

He pushed it around until it was firm and stood on the box.

Billy reached up over the ledge, which was well within his reach now and felt a good-sized cloth sack.

He scooped under it to pick it up, but it was stuck. It rattled as he removed his fingers from underneath it.

"It's stuck," he said. "I can get my hands under it, but it won't budge."

She seemed very pleased at what he said.

"Its heavy, fool. You gots to use them muscles," she chuckled.

He tried again and managed to pull the sack forward toward the edge of the jagged ledge. It felt as though it was falling apart in his hands and was much larger than he thought, but it was still moving his way.

As it came over the edge, the cord tying the mouth of the bag fell apart and a shower of gold coins pelted Billy's head.

At 10:00 AM, the duty nurse came in and checked on the patient in Room 212. The adjacent rooms were empty and quiet.

Martin Ames had not left his wife's side during her entire stay, except for a quick trip home to gather some clothes.

They asked the nurse early that morning to find out from the doctor when and if they could leave; the sooner the better.

She took Mrs. Ames vital signs and inspected her arm, which was still an ugly bruise from the ordeal and the surgery. Maime carefully moved all her fingers and thumb, which was a good sign that there was no nerve damage.

The doctor entered in the room and the nurse handed him her chart. He told them that if they could guarantee that she would keep the arm relatively immobile for at least a day or two more, she could go home. He went on for several cautious minutes explaining what he meant by immobile, until he felt they understood.

Later that morning, they were wheeling out the back door with Maime's arm in a sling. Martin had a handful of instructions and prescriptions with the memory of several more stern warnings from their doctor.

Becoming desperate to find his grandparents, James thought of the hospital and its pervasive noise and clatter, the stringent odors. Then he tried memory of the nurses' face that had come in the room where his gramma was confined…, nothing happened.

"I guess I could walk there."

The front door of his grandparents' house was closed; maybe if he went outside he could travel freely. Waves of fear that he would be trapped inside this old home began to overwhelm him.

He stepped up to the door and…, pressed through. The sensation was like silk sliding over him, all of him. Inside and out. It was strange but not bad.

He tried again to simply *will* himself to the hospital, then tried everything he had before, but couldn't move from the front porch.

Fine. He'd walk.

He stepped off the front porch and the next thing he knew he was back in the living room of his grandparent's house.

"What the heck?"

After hurrying back to the front porch, he looked out at the morning sunshine. Standing on its planked edge, he cautiously put one foot on the ground.

So far so good. Slowly he put his other down beside it and he was now standing there on the ground.

Great – it was only a catch of some kind. He walked off toward the street and right back into the living room of his grandparent's house.

Oh great. This couldn't be happening. This could NOT be happening!

Visions of being trapped in his grandparents' house overwhelmed him. Was he trapped exactly the same as the other ancestors had been trapped in the Ames family estate?

Dead *AND* trapped.

Back inside the kitchen, he looked at all the familiar sights. A would-be fresh pitcher of tea still sat carefully covered on the counter by the sink. He could almost taste it.

Taste. He leaned over the pitcher and sniffed…, nothing…, no sense of smell either!

So he had only sight and sound…. This was getting worse and worse, not to mention the fact that he was *DEAD*. Maybe this *was* some kind of limbo hell.

If that was true, where was everybody else? He knew of a few others that should be here with him.

He only *thought* he was bad off before. That is, before this happened. There would be no more home-cooking….

Suddenly, he felt hunger or something akin to it.

No more fried chicken or buttermilk biscuits or that wonderful homemade gravy. This was becoming torture. He needed to focus, to concentrate on what was important. If he dwelled on what was gone he would go insane in no time; an insane dead something….

He walked out through the kitchen door into the driveway without thinking and stood looking around at his childhood summer playground.

There was the pecan tree that he used to climb in and shake pecans from during Thanksgiving visits. The garden that he helped his grandparents' plant was still there, although most of the vegetation was hammered flat from the past night's storm.

James looked on in shock as he walked toward the back.

The huge old hackberry, that he and Sam used to pull green knots off of and throw at each other, was lying over on its side. A huge ball of roots and a cavity in the ground was all that replaced where it once stood. Their favorite shade tree.

The largest limb rested on the main utility power line, flat on the ground. James noticed some more debris and a splintered chunk of the house. The transformer was dangling upside down from its base on the utility pole.

As James moved closer, he got a wavy, swimmy sensation from his vision and body. He somehow "felt" clearer, or sharper in details, memories. He looked down at the rainwater still standing in the grassy yard and moved back out of the area suddenly understanding the hazard to his family. There was still electrical current present in the soggy grass.

Then he saw past the massive fallen tree to the house….

The power meter, a slab of the house, and the breaker box -normally on the inside of the enclosed back porch - was pulled in one big piece from the house. There was a hole…, a multitude of wires torn and hanging free where all these pieces used to fit.

"As if they don't have enough to deal with."

He walked out to the road without another thought, down the street away from the house. Railroad tracks crossed the road up ahead of him before he remembered the trap behind him. The trap was only in his mind; his fear had become his trap. At least some of his anxiety over the situation dissolved.

Fear was his enemy.

Still anxious to see her family, Catherine felt the adrenaline inside turning into fatigue as she passed the Natchez City Limits sign. In a few moments, she would be home.

Remembering that her mother was probably still in the hospital, she decided to stop there first. The Natchez Memorial Hospital was busier than she remembered, but her tired eyes hadn't noticed the trashed streets or the sparse utility vehicles still at work on her way through town. Her mind was fixed on other things.

At the front desk she asked for directions to Mrs. Ames and found that her mother had been released only half an hour before she arrived. So, she would go home, see her family, rest and change clothes. She looked forward to her jeans and pullover top.

Fatigue was transforming into exhaustion and Catherine thought of her son James as she walked out the door to find her rental car. Looking around, she couldn't get past that overwhelming feeling that she was being watched. The pervasive feeling halted her a few times in the parking lot before opening the door to the car. She decided that her parents' house would be the next logical destination.

Inside Catherine's rental car sat James. He had arrived at the hospital and felt drawn to the one person that any person is most bound to in life. His mother.

Catherine had been standing in the lobby of the hospital when he arrived, looking like an angel to him.

He had wanted to wrap himself around her and feel her kiss on his cheek and warm hugs. It was overwhelming.

He reached over again touching her hand, which could not feel him. He was afraid that she would feel the cold inside him and stopped his attempts at grasping it.

He inspected her chestnut brown hair, shining in the morning sun, her perfectly arched eyebrows and the soft eyes that used to look right through him. Now they couldn't even see him.

Somehow the anger of their past relationship slid away and only the sadness of his current state came to rest inside him.

He sat there beside her and drowned himself in self-pity all the way back to his grandparents' house.

Chapter 41

Martin and Maime Ames drove through downtown Natchez for about an hour looking at a few oddities that had not been cleaned up and pondering their unknown personal loss. Two days in the hospital made them want to see what the rest of the world was doing and appreciate being alive.

"Would you like to get some of that Cajun food downtown?" asked Martin.

"It's a little early isn't it?" she asked.

Then Maime understood the real reason he wanted to stop by BeBe's café. They owed them the truth, especially sweet little Jolie.

"Sure, you're right, that's a good idea Martin. It's the right thing to do."

Martin parked as close to the front of the café as possible. Downtown was almost empty and most of the shops had closed.

Martin helped his wife out of their Buick LeSabre and noticed a few dings here and there on the hood and top.

"Look at that Maime," he said rubbing his hand over one of the warbled dings. "Looks like that one was big as a baseball."

Then he recalled what the sheriff had told them, that James had been driving in the hailstorm when…, when it happened.

"Let's go inside Martin. I still feel a little light headed."

BeBe met them at the door, "Why I don't believe my eyes. I'm so glad to see you got out of that awful hospital."

She seated them at a quiet table where they could talk. The waitress came to take their order, but BeBe waved her off, telling her to bring iced tea for them.

"How is your arm feeling?" asked BeBe, but before either of them answered, she picked up on something else. Something they needed to talk about.

"You're not just here for our great Cajun food today are you," she stated more than asked.

"Oh, were here for the food," Maime smiled, but her smile didn't quite make the trip past her thin lips.

Jolie, looking for BeBe, saw the three of them sitting in their reserved section, and hurried over. She quickly greeted them and sat down as close to Maime as she could get away with.

"I'm so glad to see you doing better," she said cheerfully.

BeBe quickly asked Jolie if she would go tell the kitchen to fix the day's special for their guests and Jolie reluctantly hurried away to place their order.

"Something's happened," said BeBe. "Is it bad?"

She looked at them earnestly.

"It's James," said Martin. "We didn't know how to tell Jolie, but she can't find out from gossip."

"He's hurt?" asked BeBe, not fully picking up on their meaning.

"He was in an accident last night, if accident is the right word," said Martin, looking over at his wife. "He was out in the storm last night, chasing some truck..., and..., somehow..., he ended up north of town up along the levee. The truck pushed his car down the levee. James Earl is..., dead, BeBe."

Maime Ames looked intently at BeBe with water in her eyes. All their friend could do was return their gaze, while in the throes of unbelief.

"I don't understand.... That's not possible. It can't be true. Jolie.... Oh my God, she's going to take this bad. Really bad."

"We know, that's why we're here," Martin said. "You know her best. Do you want to tell her later?"

"We're going to close the doors at one o'clock. I'll let the crew close out and lock up. Maybe it would be best if we talk to her together?"

Jolie came bouncing back to the table, "Foods almost up - be here in a minute.... Iced Tea!" she said handing glasses around the table.

The young girl was antsy for the customers to clear out and give her a chance to talk to the Ames family and ask about James.

"Would you bring them some silver and extra napkins, Jolie?"

BeBe sent her on yet another errand to distract her insatiable curiosity.

"James told us..., last night..., that his mother is on the way here. Does she know yet?" asked BeBe.

"Not yet..., there's no way to contact her. She won't be here until later this evening," said Maime.

"It's not easy on anybody is it?" asked BeBe rhetorically. "Poor James."

"We'll talk about it later then," said Martin as Jolie and the waitress brought food and set it around their table.

Deputy Floyd's pager went off right about the time that he expected it would. Floyd had taken several calls and handled them as quickly as possible. Two small vandalism reports, mostly for insurance purposes, a power line across a road needed someone to direct traffic and get yet another emergency truck on the scene.

Looking at the numbers on the pager, it read 123, the city park. Payday.

Billy Poole was already waiting at the back entrance of the city park. His normal fidgety composure was gone. He didn't even appear agitated at

Floyd for being late as usual.

"Billy," said the deputy nodding his head.

He looked around in all directions and walked into the lush greenery of the park to a more secluded area.

A few moments Billy joined him.

"Sure is risky for us to meet in broad daylight the day after…," said the deputy.

"Ssshhh, keep your mouth," said Billy. "It's now or a month from now when everybody is watching for anything strange. Which you want?"

"Now's good," agreed Floyd.

He handed Floyd a little wooden knife box with a slide top.

It was heavy.

Floyd took it and frowned, "A knife? That's what I get for…."

"Ssshhh, keep it down, I tole you. Look inside," said Billy.

Floyd opened the sliding lid and four stacks of Spanish gold coins gleamed back in his face.

Twenty gold coins easily worth about $1000 a piece to a discrete collector.

Floyd smiled. "Nice, Billy. Hardly seems fair since I got to enjoy getting rid of a problem to earn it."

"Fate smiled on us both," said Billy. "Time for me to go. Be about a month, unless something comes up before then. I give you a call." He looked nervously around. "Pleasure doin' business with you."

Billy walked away with out another word or glance back over his shoulder.

Catherine Williams knocked on her parents' front door. She noticed a multitude of leaves and broken limbs on the ground in the front yard and on the porch. She stepped around to the side of the house and peered in the kitchen entrance by the driveway.

She pulled the screen door open to get a better look through the glass windowpane of the door. Dark and quiet. They could be asleep, but the windows were closed the central air wasn't on. The heat was already becoming unbearable with the rain soaked humidity.

She remembered the key her parents used to leave in the bird bath under the tree in the back yard. She turned the corner and saw a huge mess that used to be the back of the house.

"Oh, no…," she exclaimed as she walked around a huge overturned hackberry, her feet squishing in the plush grass like a sponge. Staying clear of a fallen power cable she looked in the clear rainwater of the birdbath. Nothing there.

"They gave it to me," said James to her unhearing ears. "It's in my wallet."

Catherine walked back to the kitchen door and twisted the door handle sharply from left to right and pulled up on the handle. The door almost opened.

"Neat trick!" said James.

Of course Catherine would know every trick about the old house, the place where she grew up.

Once again she performed the exact combination and the door popped opened.

"Whew," she said, wincing as she walked in the kitchen. "This has got to go."

She grabbed the sack of garbage by the door and carried it outside to the trash can. She left the door wide open to vent the stench and building heat. With the power off, the refrigerator would be starting to thaw about now. She opened the door and winced. It was a mess. The milk had started to spoil, while items in the upper freezer section were melting along with different meats wrapped in white butcher paper.

She shook her head. She had wanted to look nice when she saw her parents. Oh well, so much for first impressions.

Back to the car she hurried, dragging out one of her luggage. Ten minutes later, in jeans and pullover, she was sacking up, carrying out and dumping food stuff from the kitchen. If her mother came home to this..., well she couldn't let that happen. Where would they go? They couldn't stay in this mess.

"Not over there, for sure," she said aloud, thinking of the old Ames home place. "Daddy never liked that place."

But where else was there to go? She picked up the telephone to dial the number written on the wall. The same number it had been since she was a child. The phone was eerily silent and she returned it to its cradle.

James sat unnoticed in the kitchen, amused at the speed in which his mother had cleared out the entire house of spoilable foods and leftovers. He remembered how neat and clean their house had always been even though she worked long hours. She was a good mother, he thought, forgetting a few more of his prior grievances.

Catherine was carrying out the last sack of trash when Aunt Martiel drove up in the driveway.

"Catherine!" squealed Martiel, and hurried to give her a lingering hug. "I'm so glad you made it. You're early. How was your trip?"

"Awful," said Catherine, pointing to the putrid rental car. "But, at least I'm here now."

"What ever are you doing?" asked Martiel.

Catherine motioned and walked her aunt to the rear of the house, which explained everything much more concisely than a half hour of conversation.

"Where are my parents?" asked Catherine. "And James...."

Martiel looked as if someone had hit her with a brick. She walked on into the kitchen and sat down at the table without saying anything.

James was parked on the kitchen counter, something that his gramma would never allow when he was alive, and listened to see how Martiel would handle this.

"Martiel? Are you feeling all right?" asked Catherine.

"No, I'm not feeling well at all, Catherine," she answered. "You see, several things have happened while you were on your way here. There was a horrible, horrible storm here last night and…. Oh, God help me…."

Martiel burst into tears. The weight of responsibility was sitting squarely on her shoulders and it was breaking her.

"Its okay, Aunt Martiel," said James. "I'm here, you'll be fine."

Martiel sat bolt upright and looked around the kitchen. Catherine looked at her aunt as if she had heard something that she didn't.

"What is it Martiel?" she demanded. "You have to tell me."

"I know I do," she said. "Only I don't know how…. James was in an accident last night. He was driving in the storm…," Martiel stopped her story to stand and face Catherine.

"James is dead, Catherine. He's dead and it's all my fault."

Martiel fell limply back down into the kitchen chair.

Catherine stood unmoving, shocked to her core at what she heard. Quietly she walked to the open kitchen door and looked out, seeing nothing. She sat down on the steps of the little porch of her childhood and wept bitter tears.

The restaurant was cleaned and cleared and the doors locked. Martin and Maime Ames sat alone talking with BeBe. Jolie would join them from time to time while she had been helping close up.

Now that everything was finished, Jolie sat down at the table with the others sipping a glass of iced tea. Her usual happy smile and bounce seemed to dampen after a few seconds.

Everyone got quiet and looked at each other and Jolie pretended that she didn't know something was wrong. She had been picking up on bits and pieces of their thoughts. But if what they were thinking was…, well…, her antenna, or whatever it was that picked up others thoughts, was broken.

"Is someone going to tell me what's wrong?" asked Jolie suddenly.

"You sound exactly like Martiel," said Martin Ames. "She does that to me all the time."

Maime Ames spoke up, "Jolie, James was in an accident last night…."

"He's dead…," Jolie whispered, then…. "No. He can't be dead. I don't believe it. I would know. I would have felt it…, or something."

She slapped both her tiny hands down on the table, spilling her tea. Maime and Martin looked at each other in astonishment.

"This is all wrong..., he was..., he was.... He *CANT* be dead!"

BeBe hurried around the table to Jolie, placing a hand on the girls' shoulder.

"Get *OFF* me!" yelled Jolie, swinging her arm in a wild arc. "You told me that everything was going to be okay, that whatever it was, trying to get him.... You told me.... You promised...," she started blubbering aimlessly, bubbles forming from her nose and mouth.

Blank and beaten, eyes bloodshot, she whined at her deepening loss, "You wouldn't let me be around him."

Oblivious to the others staring at her she raised her voice to a near scream, "If I'd been with him this wouldn't have happened! I know it wouldn't!"

"You might have been killed too, Jolie," said Maime Ames, as calmly as she could. "The sheriff thinks James was murdered."

"Thinks? He thinks??!!! That's a first. I know he was murdered. That damned deputy had something to do with it. I know he did!"

Jolie's voice boomed throughout the empty dining room.

They all three looked on quietly, stunned at Jolie's sharp accusation.

She pointed a quivering finger at them, "I'll find out who did it.... I'll find out.... You'll see...."

She wilted to the floor, down to her knees....

"You'll see...," she whispered.

Chapter 42

The Buick LeSabre inched into the drive near to where Catherine was still seated. Cold dead eyes, cried out and empty, she hadn't moved from the steps of the back door.

Happy greetings were embittered by the fact of their loss. The only one that placed any visible blame was Martiel, and that was on herself.

The family assembled in the Ames bedroom where Maime reluctantly agreed to lie down, however she watched every corner in the house as she went inside.

Catherine and Martiel gathered as many of their necessities as possible to take with them over to the Ames Estate. It was, after all, the logical thing to do.

James watched his grieving family silently, not wanting to add to the stress of Martiel who had already sensed his presence. Martin Earl walked out onto the back porch and saw the gaping hole and eased carefully back into the doorway. The porch was not stable and had become spongy under the weight of his foot.

"What a mess," he mumbled. "It's all a mess."

Covering the hole was far too big a project for him to even think about, especially now. He slipped back to telephone someone to get their home repaired. As he hung up the useless dead receiver, he realized that it was Sunday.

They had missed church for the first time in almost nine years. He didn't feel the necessity to add that news to the group, as he was probably the only one that had lost track of the day of the week.

Martin walked back out to the front porch and kicked at the heap of wet leaves left from the storm. He sat heavily in the swing, feeling useless. Wife hurt, grandson dead, house unlivable, how could things be any worse.

For him, going to that old house…, that was worse. There had been numerous times that he had visited the Estate since childhood. Strange things that he had explained away as a child began to resurface. Haunting things filled his mind and he considered a hotel…, but that was foolish.

He cleared his mind as best he could and thought of his business…, it was time to close his garage…, for good. He wanted no part of it; everything there would remind him of his grandson.

Feeling old and tired for the first time in his life, he went back into their room, pulled out some large empty luggage from the closet, and began to help with the move of their personal necessities.

"One of you needs to help me find that worthless cat," said Martin.

James sat in the car with Martiel, every available space in both family cars and his mother's rental, were loaded with clothes and items that the Ames did not want stolen or pilfered through by vandals.

"James?" said Martiel quietly.

"Yes Ma'am, I'm here."

"You have to know how sorry I am, James."

James sensed that she was about to break down again and couldn't bear it.

"Aunt Martiel, please stop that, I don't blame you. It wasn't your fault. I know who was…, or at least two of them, and I know where one lives."

"I'm listening."

Martiel pulled in behind the caravan in the quiet neighborhood. Water had already formed in her eyes once again.

"You have to get past the grief, all of you do."

"Jolie knows," said Aunt Martiel. "Your grandparents told her earlier."

"I know. I heard," James said silently, not knowing how to respond. "I want to do what is best for her, even…, even if it means not letting her know I'm still here. Have you told anybody that I'm still here?"

"Oh heaven's no!" said Aunt Martiel. "Why, that would drive them right over the brink! They don't even know about me or…, what you could have been.

"Quit reminding me about the dead thing please. I haven't really accepted whatever this is yet. Anyway, back to what I was saying earlier, they need to get past the grief."

James was quiet for a few moments, thinking.

"I want you to tell my mother about…, well…, everything. All of it. My journal is in the trash in my old bedroom. Would you mind getting it and giving it to my mother? I want her to know what happened before, the *not so great* gifts, and that I'm still here. Then, I need to talk to her. I want you to help me talk to her."

"James, I can't do that," said Martiel. "Why, if…."

Martiel fell quiet for several long moments as her car came to a stop.

"I guess I can," she finally understood the implications. "There's nobody left at the old house to tell me what I can and can't do. But, remember this James, there were good reasons why they didn't want all the family to know."

"Well, shouldn't that be covered somewhere in that family book? I can't exactly open it or turn the pages or I'd have already looked it up myself."

"I know how frustrating that must be, James," said Martiel. "I've heard all that before many times from the…, well, the ones that are gone now."

"Yeah, but where did they go, and how?"

"I don't know. I just don't know," said Martiel as she quickly turned around to retrieve his journal from the house.

Martin and Maime Ames were the first to arrive at the Estate. Martin slowly cut his eyes over toward the porch and back several times. He was relieved to see everything looked normal, there was no unexplained movement in his periphery. He brushed the thought out of his mind.

The gravel drive was above the receding water, but the yard was still somewhat water logged and the plush carpet of St. Augustine lawn looked as if it had grown two inches overnight.

The ancient house was huge and with eight bedrooms, there was ample room for everyone and then some. Tommy was the first to exit the vehicle and began exploring.

He and Martiel parked inside the first bay of the carriage house, which had been converted into a garage many years earlier, while Catherine's rental was left outside.

As they entered the house, each had their own memories of the home place, both good and bad.

Martin expected to *feel* the same uncomfortable eyes watching him from everywhere, but something had changed. The house seemed blank, empty, quiet, and void of the phantoms from his youth.

He relaxed for the moment and started emptying the cars of their heavy-laden contents. Some, the trinkets and keepsakes, stayed in the garage in the oversized storage room.

Martiel arrived, parking in the next bay, watching all the movement of her brother and Catherine. With a heavy sigh, she hurried over and helped Maime into the house, as Catherine followed laden with a laundry basket full of clothes.

Martiel knew the drill as well as Catherine, both heading to the phone to make the appropriate calls to the rest of the family and such.

Maime chose a bedroom downstairs to put their belongings into and went to lie down on the couch while the others sorted and hid clothes inside their appropriate places.

Martiel instructed everyone to only do the bare necessities, that she had house keepers coming first thing in the morning to dust and clean. It felt like old times to her. The family together once again; at least most of it.

"May I speak to Robert?" asked Catherine.

"Robert..., Williams? I'll see if I can find him for you," said the polite feminine voice. "Can you hold?"

Before she could answer, there was a click and dead silence.

Thirteen minutes later....

"Who are you holding for?" asked another female voice.

"Robert Williams, this is an…."

"Hold please," and dead silence ensued once again.

Catherine was primed to kill the next operator through the telephone line.

"Hello, this is Robert, can I help you?" came the deep resonating voice.

"It's about time," said Catherine. "You need different secretaries."

"What's so important?" said Robert. "I'm in the middle of…."

"You're always in the middle of something," she bit, then remembering the somber news she had to deliver.

"If you only called to argue, I need to get back…," argued Robert.

"It's James…," she interrupted. "There's been an accident…."

"Sam? Oh, good!" said Catherine. "How are you?"

The camp counselor had taken almost twenty minutes to find Samuel Earl Williams.

She wasn't going to tell him about James. His best friend and brother. Not there by himself. She might even wait until he arrived in Natchez.

"How is gramma?" Sam asked. "Is she doing better?"

"She is going to be fine," said Catherine. "We're all staying over at the old place, remember it?"

"Cool!" said Sam. "I always liked looking around over there, but grampa never takes us over there, at least not very often. I guess he thought I might break something."

"Sam, I hate to make this call short, but your father is going to be there tonight to pick you up."

"Awww mom…," came the whine she expected.

"You two are coming here, Sam," she said as cheerfully as she could.

"I thought you said gramma was doing okay?" questioned Sam. "If she's okay, then why are we both coming there?"

Catherine didn't have a quick enough answer. She managed to delay a direct response by saying nothing more than they were going to have a family get together.

As soon as the phone hung up, Sam said, "Something's happened to James."

Night at the old house was strained at first.

Everyone settled into a room downstairs, except Martiel. She stayed in her regular room where she and James had spent the last several days together.

Catherine volunteered to go get groceries after looking at the bare shelves of the pantry; there were only a few eclectic items scattered about. The mix of groceries did not constitute creating anything that would represent a family meal.

Maime Ames was fast asleep on her bed and Martin had found a suitable perch on one of the porch swings outside.

Near twilight, a solitary whippoorwill sang a lonely song, the only break in the silence. No traffic could be heard from the highway, which was buffered by several stands of trees and over a mile of distance.

Martin sat quietly enamored, by the peace in the middle of turmoil, as the porch swing creaked.

James silently moved from room to room watching each member of his family with the understanding that he would never get to feel the warmth of their touch or solace of their voice mentioning his name again.

The cold…, the awful cold was still with him. If he could change only one thing, besides the death itself, it would be that.

He looked on as his gramma lay in bed gently breathing. Then on to his grampa on the front porch swing. James stood behind him and placed a hand on his shoulder as he stared out onto the many acres of land belonging to the family.

Martin Earl stood abruptly, leaving the old swing emptily rocking, while looking around, and James reluctantly moved back into the house.

Had his grampa sensed his presence? James peered through the doorway to watch him turn left and right and then rub his shoulder where James had placed his hand.

He did. He would have to be especially careful around his grampa. He couldn't imagine adding a heart attack to the list of misery his family was going through. This was probably why his grandfather never liked coming to the old house! Even though he wasn't the one with the gifts, he was still probably sensitive….

Wait. Why was Aunt Martiel the one with the gifts and not his grampa?

A valid question for his Aunt Martiel, but it probably wasn't important anyway.

Not wanting to startle his grampa any further, James went back inside up to Martiel's room. There were things to do, people to see, actually…, to spy on. He had to find out the root of this.

Martiel was folding and putting away laundry she had left from several days prior. The housekeepers would have their hands busy with the rest of the house tomorrow. They didn't know what they would be getting themselves into, showing up Monday morning. It wouldn't be the easy "sit and drink coffee and dust a few things" this time. They would earn their money. James entered the room and shivered Martiel from the mundane.

"James? That you?"

"It's me," James sounded sad. "Just thinking, do you want me to go?"

"No, for heaven's sake," said Aunt Martiel. "I'm used to a houseful of spooks; it was getting quiet in here. Oh, James I'm sorry. I didn't mean to refer to you as a…."

"Will you quit apologizing for everything you say and do, Aunt Martiel? I would be saying the exact same thing if it was me."

"You'd call me a spook?" Martiel chuckled, trying to offset her embarrassment.

"Probably. And a few other things. After all, I am the one that's in limbo here."

James' entire body shook and quivered in front of his eyes. His hands went in and out of focus for a few seconds.

"Aunt Martiel, something is happening to me," he said in a panic. "I'm kind of fading in and out here, wha…. What do I do?!"

"Oh. You're getting a call…, uh…, someone close is pulling you to them. Think of it like a telephone call."

"How do I tell who it is? Do I have to go? What if I…." rattled James.

"Slow down, slow down," she tried to calm him. "You don't have to answer, unless they have the power to summon you. Then you don't have a choice. It'll just happen…. James? James?"

James was in a small bedroom with a single candle sitting on a table. The silhouette of a lone person was seated with their back to him. It was a woman. She shivered as he focused in on where he was.

A kind voice was saying, "James…, oh, James…," and crying softly. "James Earl…, if you're still here, please."

Against his better judgment, James moved around in front of where she was sitting and waited. There was so much hurt and love in her eyes. Those beautiful drowning blue eyes. Water was streaming like a faucet from them as she sat staring at the candle.

"Oh, James. I failed you. Everyone failed you."

"No you didn't," he answered.

Jolie's head snapped to attention and she looked around, but then lowered her face into her hands.

"Can you hear me, Jolie?"

Jolie looked up frantically in every direction.

"James? James is that really you?"

"You can hear me?"

Jolie jumped up from her seat, looking around in a spin.

"Yes! Oh yes! I can hear you! I thought it was my imagination, oh James."

James was thinking…, now what have I done. I'm only torturing the both of us.

"Please sit Jolie. I have a lot of things to talk to you about."

For over an hour James repeated the incidents of the previous night and its consequences. He told her about the two men, where the one lived with a woman.

Jolie sat and listened intently at the unbelievable story she was hearing. How they had baited him into believing she was in the truck, held hostage.

"Jolie, you have to promise me something. Promise me that you won't try to get involved with what's about to happen. I'm going to try to find out who is responsible and why they wanted me dead so badly. If you get too close you could..., you could end up like me, Jolie. I want you to have a life."

"I can't promise that James," argued Jolie. "I want whoever did this to you punished."

"I know. I understand how you feel, but it won't bring me back and you might get killed," warned James. "That big guy, Billy, with the cigarette acted like it was just another day as usual and even laughed about it. It was as if he did this kind of thing everyday."

"I can't sit back like nothings happened," she whined.

"I'll keep you informed of everything that I find out, but you please don't get involved, Jolie. You have to promise me that or..., or I can't come back or tell you any more. You know that I love you Jolie. I loved you from the first day that I met you. I couldn't bear to see you get hurt or killed."

"I love you too, James," said Jolie. "I can't believe you're gone. What am I going to do without you? I had lots of plans for you."

"Plans for me? What do you mean?"

He heard himself laugh for the first time since his death.

"If you want to help me, help my mother get through this."

There was one thing that he could give her if he could remember how to do it.

"I need to get back, but before I go...."

James stood in front of her and remembered one single special moment with her as vividly in his mind as he could.

"I can see you James. How...?"

"I don't know. Aunt Martiel taught me how to do it. Jolie..., I have to go."

James faded from her view and prayed that he wouldn't have a difficult time returning to the old home place. It would be a long walk from Vidalia....

The food was almost done and Catherine was placing items on the table. It was a very late supper, but everyone would need their strength for tomorrow.

Martiel came down from upstairs, smelling the food like a bloodhound.

"Looks like you still remember your way around in the kitchen," said Martiel.

"I hope it tastes as good as you think it smells," said Catherine. "Would you see if mom and dad would like to come in here and eat?"

In moments, all of the present Ames family sat at the table, held hands and said grace.

James watched on hungrily as his family ate supper, tried to smell the aroma of the food, but was denied. Apparently this new thing he had become still remembered all his fleshy needs and desires.

It was time for some research.

James wanted to know if there was any hope of getting out of the state he was in or if it was permanent. The *Mambo* he had talked to meant well, probably, but didn't offer a lot of information that was in plain English. Aunt Martiel loved him and would do anything for him, but her information was tainted from listening to a generation of spooks that had been stuck here too.

He had tried to talk to the pastor before, but he had been too busy. Since he was a spiritual man and the leader of the church, James thought that would be a good place to start.

He decided to walk and think about what he would say if he could get the minister alone. It was after all Sunday night and the congregation would all be gone by now. The night was clear and muggy, but for James it was deathly cold, all the way through him.

Along the highway in the darkness there was little traffic. He rolled all the circumstances over and over to himself, replaying each person's role, all the way up to the end result.

He was almost up to the turn off to the road that would take him past his grandparents' house. There was the place where the deputy pulled him over to give him a ticket. He stood there in the road thinking about that deputy.

What did he ever do to piss him off anyway? Sure, he was in his face that morning at the cemetery, but the good deputy was acting weird and being a jerk too. Maybe it was..., maybe it was a lot of things. His temper flared at the culmination of memories.

From behind him came a blinding light, a horn blared as a car screeched and swerved to miss him.

"Well they needed to slow down anyway," he thought.

Had he been a real body, he'd be dead again. He *was* in the middle of the highway, in the dark of night. What did he expect?

He needlessly stepped to the shoulder of the road as the car stopped up ahead. He turned right and walked toward the road that led past the railroad tracks and into his familiar neighborhood.

Ahead was the Holiness Cathedral Church and the lights were still on, but all the people were gone just as he had guessed. He walked inside and through the closed doors. There were many memories here for him.

Sunday school, jabs to be quiet or wake up.

Summer Vacation Bible School.

All good memories. There seemed to be a soft glow about the church as he walked up the isle looking for the pastor.

In the study, he found the preacher sitting at a desk and talking on the telephone to someone. James had never really taken a good look at this guy before up close, but he was a lot younger than he'd noticed before. Maybe it was the prejudiced view from the pews that gave him the look of age and wisdom.

He took a closer look; it was something else. It was the hair.

It was combed to the side instead of swept back. James remembered seeing a more salt and pepper look to his hair, that was it, he had gray in his hair. But here…, it was probably only the light in here, or maybe the harsh light over the pulpit. His hair was a youthful, normal light brown.

Maybe it had something to do with his new vision.

Funny how people look differently up close. There were pockmarks on his brow and he had a funny way of lifting only one eyebrow when he'd make a remark to whoever he was talking to on the phone.

There was a knock at the door and the pastor told his party he had to go. He called out through the door and told them it would be only a moment. The pastor walked over to a bowl and mirror in the corner, sprinkled something on his hands and raked his fingers through his hair. He wet his hands in the bowl of water and back through his hair. Then, taking the towel, wiped off his hands before he ran a quick comb through his hair.

Viola! Gray swept back hair and ten years older.

James couldn't help but laugh to himself, but was enjoying the show.

James waited as he talked to someone that was relating the recent incidents with the Ames family members. A friend of his grandparents, James guessed. They began to discuss the morbid details of what had happened and he did not want to hear it rehearsed ever again, so he slid out of the room and back into the sanctuary undetected.

James became amused at himself for trying to be quiet while leaving the pastor's study, as if anyone could hear him. Time passed unnoticed while he sat in the pew where he had sat so many times beside his grandparents. He moved over to the pew where he and Granny Smith had shared many thoughts and secrets. A big part of his restoration from gangland was inside this place. A lot of good memories and prayers.

His thoughts were interrupted by the opening and closing of the study door. The pastor said that he would call the Ames family tonight and pay them a visit in the morning.

After saying their goodbyes, the front doors were locked this time and the pastor went back to his study, James behind him.

"If these people keep dying around here, won't be anybody left to pay my salary," joked Pastor Milton to himself.

Little did he or James know that his entire salary was paid anonymously, through the board of trustees, wholly by the Ames family, as it had been for many years.

It was finally quiet and James was having doubts about any help from Pastor Milton. James tested the waters to see if he was going to be able to communicate with the good pastor.

"Pastor Milton?" said James questioningly.

Nothing…, but louder this time.

"Pastor Milton!" shouted James.

Still no response other than the telephone ringing. The pastor looked over at the phone and started to pick it up, but it had only rang once.

"Weird," he said, frowning.

"Cool," thought James.

James watched over his shoulder as he put away a "Book of Sermons" by some noted author, personal notes, and pulled out a personal address and phone book. He flipped it open to the tab marked "A" and gave one of the numbers a call.

James listened in on a wonderful sympathetic oration of how sad he was for their loss, anything that he could do, and would like to visit with them tomorrow at their convenience. Naturally, he would notify the appropriate members and let them know…, blah, blah, blah.

After hanging up the phone, he started to put everything away, but stopped. He leaned back in his chair, looking into some far away place.

"Well, it was bound to happen sooner or later. The kid was nothing but a trouble maker. That family acts as if they run this church anyway…," and yawning. "I'm going to change all that."

James was smoking out the ears and backed over into a corner. He'd heard all he wanted.

The telephone rang; the pastor looked at his wristwatch and picked up the call. In about three minutes of the conversation, it started to sound like he was talking to his wife of many years, about bedroom matters. Interesting subject for a single man and pastor of a church.

James yelled as loud as he could into the nothing of his world.

The pastor jerked the phone from his ear and slowly put the receiver back up to his ear.

"Did you hear that?" he asked the would-be lover. "You're kidding, it nearly took out my ear drum."

James left, still angered, very disappointed.

Chapter 43

New Orleans Airport had slowly regained some regularity of their flights after the passing of an unusual tropical depression and a freak outbreak of storms.

Martiel Ellington sat anxiously at the Delta Airlines terminal, waiting for Delta flight 1012, arriving at two-ten Monday afternoon. The plane was unloading passengers, but none with the right faces had stepped off the airplane as yet.

Reluctantly, she had driven Catherine's shoddy rental car back to the airport and swapped it for a Lincoln, for Catherine and her family to use while they were in Natchez.

She was still musing over the sick, baby blue, vinyl front seat of the other car, when a familiar voice broke her concentration.

"Aunt Martiel!" chirped Sam. "Wow, I'm glad to see you!"

Martiel had heart palpitations for an instant at the similarity between Sam and his brother James. Sam could tell something was wrong as he looked at her ghostly face. She smiled quickly turning her attention on Sam, giving him a warm embrace.

Sam was almost a carbon copy of James now. She had not seen Sam in over a year and he was the same height and size as James was. Was..., reverberated over and over in her mind.

Robert met her warmth with a solemn look that only Robert Williams was capable of. Martiel looked past his handsome exterior and heard the harsh rambling going on inside him.

"What did Catherine ever see in you?" she thought.

"Hello Robert, I'm glad you're here," said Martiel.

Sam looked on with deepening questions, gathering on his face like storm clouds.

"It was a long flight…. Where is Catherine?" he asked.

"She's taking care of Maime. She is still pretty weak after her ordeal and the surgery."

"I see, well, it was very nice of you to meet us. I hate that we put you out like this," he said.

Martiel thought smiling, "Put you out? I'd like to put you out."

Struggling for some germane conversation, "It was no problem. I had to exchange that ghastly rental they gave Catherine anyway. It was just awful."

She grabbed Sam by the arm, which he had been using to rub his head strangely, and started walking toward their exit. She knew the drive back to

Natchez was going to be anguish on her good nature. At least she didn't have to stare at the cigarette burns in those awful baby blue vinyl seats.

Martin Ames strolled around his home once again, looking at the damage with an insurance adjuster. He had already contacted a local contractor to repair the damages, but they had been waiting for over an hour on the approval before they could start.

James followed his grampa as a matter of habit when he had left early that morning. He had ranted on almost all night with his Aunt Martiel about Pastor Milton until she fell asleep across her bed. Apparently, she was still not used to the lack of a time schedule of the dead. That was probably why she only visited the old place for a few days once a month. According to her, she only visited when she received financial statements or there was some sort of change to the family status quo.

Martin needed an escape from the atrocities of late and working with his hands had always afforded him some relief. Also, the army of house cleaners had arrived at the old Ames home place, driving him to a nervous jitter and he was relieved that his attentions were needed elsewhere.

Today the distractions of getting their home in order was not helping alleviate his distress. He was getting tired and wanted to get back to his wife and Catherine, despite the confusion awaiting there.

He couldn't believe how different it felt over at the Ames Estate. The shadowy feelings were all gone and it actually felt like a home to him again. That was something that he never expected to feel again about any dwelling.

The house where he now stood had been home to him and his wife ever since they had been married. It had been his home without incident, until Maime had seen something…, something that scared her. Scared her enough that it drove her stumbling into the hallway in the dark.

He didn't believe any of that hocus pocus junk that had been whispered about in his family for years. Life to him was cut and dried. He always kept it simple.

After getting the required signatures from the insurance adjuster, Martin opened up the house for the workers.

His first breath of air had an oppressive weight and odd musty smell to it. A moldy, tight odor was pervasive, probably because of the humidity creeping in from the gaping hole in the back of the house. Still something wasn't right and it gnawed at him. It was more than some odd premonition and it was evident that the contractor with his clipboard was feeling it also.

James walked to the entry door of the kitchen. Peering inside, it had a strange dim *texture* to the light in the house.

His nighttime bluish-gray vision didn't quite look like this.

Once inside the kitchen, he looked down the hall in both directions. To the left was toward the living room, and was fairly normal. To the right at the far end led toward his room, then past his door was the porch and washroom with the missing side.

In that direction, there was a gradual dimming of light, oily looking, strictly adhering to the darkest of shadows. It reminded James of some of the dreams he had experienced in the house. He walked cautiously in that direction.

"Curiosity killed the cat," swam back to his memory and he stopped quickly. It was almost a voice in his head. Who was it that said that? Ms. Dubois? Dominique? Well, that was true of the truck that hammered him. If he'd only left it alone and hadn't chased them. He should have known it was a trap. Who in their right mind would drive right where they could be seen, knowing that they might be caught? Unless they wanted to be caught.

He stood where he was, unmoving. The shadow on the walls seemed to consist of a dark film. He reached out as if he could feel it. He touched the door facing and although he couldn't feel it, his hand was immediately stuck to it. He looked around himself for a few minutes and made sure he wasn't touching anything else. Then he pulled. His fear grew and his hand stayed planted firmly.

"Flypaper for spooks?"

Suddenly he decided his quick wit wasn't funny. He pulled with his entire self, afraid that he would yank free and plant his entire body on the opposing wall from the force. If he pulled too hard, would he pull his hand off? What were the rules or were there any?

He yanked with all his might and as with any good spider web, the spider came looking. Apparently whatever left this shadow goop was waiting around for him to do exactly what he did.

"Why am I so predictable?" he screamed at himself. "I must be as stupid here as I was when I was alive."

His hand gave slightly, not enough to matter, but it *did move.*

Something was shifting around in his old room. He didn't so much hear it as feel it.

He screamed at his hand as loudly as his unheard voice could scream. His hand slid along the door facing in synchronous with his unheard blast.

A pair of white eyes set in a black vaporous body, peered around the door facing of his room down the hall. He needed no further inspiration.

He screamed bloody murder while pulling and yanking on his hand and..., slowly yanked free.

Cautiously James backed into the hall behind him, not taking his eyes off the predator coming out of the doorway. There was a definite decline to the black flytrap substance a few feet behind him and he moved there quickly.

The afternoon sun was shining through the living room windows and partly into that end of the hall. He backed all the way into the living room and watched this strange entity crawl out onto the wall and down it sideways. Its multi-legged form wisped in and out of vision the more it exposed itself to the ambient light of the upper hallway. When it saw that James was no longer attached to the inky trappings of the shadows, it stopped, blinked its eyes and slowly evaporated back toward the open door.

James left the building.

He waited and watched outside staying close to his grampa, until Martin was satisfied that the crew needed no further instructions.

James was never so relieved to get away from anywhere. He had to rethink everything. Now he knew he wasn't alone in this in-between place either.

Chapter 44

A sad but true story is one that tells of most family reunions occurring only at the death of a loved one.

At the Ames Estate, a house full of potentially close family members had chosen to take several opposing corners to mull over which way their family would turn.

The family tree, which had narrowed itself over the previous generations, had once again been pruned. Any gardener or horticulturist knows that pruning can sometimes make growth thicker and stronger, but if at the wrong branch, the wrong season, or too deeply, it can stunt growth permanently.

Martiel sat alone upstairs listening to the muffled sounds of talk below. Some of the chatter was not pleasant and she tried to ignore it. As in most old houses where wall to wall insulation was not a thing of priority when it was constructed, sound carried. She set her sights on a more remote room with benefits, namely the enormous kitchen.

Sam was rejecting the very idea that his brother was dead. He sat in his grandparents' room talking over good times, bad times and how James had always come to his rescue. The time Sam was caught in a storm drain under the street and James knew exactly where he was and got him out. He had a few dark dreams about that incident.

Sam neglected to admit why he was in the storm drain in the first place, which was hiding from the gang that was looking for him. Instead, he converted the incident into an exploratory escapade fit for someone his age after watching an inspiring old afternoon movie.

There were other less exacting stories of their bond as brothers, but there had been so many threats James had saved him from, that he couldn't think of any warm fuzzy instances.

His gramma steered the subject toward holidays and how Christmas was always special at their house with he and James.

Maybe it was time that Sam spent a week or two in the summer with them. Sam was having trouble concentrating now, mostly because he could still hear the indistinct conversation several rooms away.

"James should have never been here in the first place," said Robert.

"Why, so he could watch after Sam?" Catherine countered.

"No that was your job."

"And what was *YOUR* job?"

"Oh, so were back to my work again, *too many hours, you stay too long.*"

"It's true, you do, you never spent any time with James. You're doing the same with Sam."

"Someone has to earn a living between us."

"Living? LIVING! Robert, we could have comfortably retired five years ago and gone back to teaching."

"I have more ambitions than wasting my time trying to cram facts into the minds of college students that are more interested in their next party and what drugs they'll serve."

"It's not about the money; it's your ego, Robert. You never liked the fact that I made more money. Well now I don't. I finally quit my career for you."

"Oh, so it's back to that now."

Catherine began leaking teardrops....

"No.... It's about James," she blasted. "I've lost one of my sons and we're arguing about the same old thing like he never even mattered."

Catherine stood and walked out of the room hurrying to find some quiet part of the house.

Martiel and James were sitting in the kitchen, Martiel with a glass of iced tea, at James' request. He said watching her drink it would remind him of how satisfying the cold, sweet drink felt going down.

Catherine didn't expect to see anyone and kept her back to Aunt Martiel as she gathered something to drink for herself. The paper napkin holder was quickly losing its bounty as she stood in front of it. After she had purged most signs of tears, she turned to join Martiel at the table.

"I'm sorry, Catherine. I know how rough this is on you and Robert," said Martiel.

James had heard all of the same arguments time and time again. His father had given up on being a parent or in his opinion, being a husband to marry his career. But who was he to interfere?

"It's not the career, you know.... It's another woman," said Catherine in a low voice.

Martiel held her breath, silent with astonishment that her niece had finally had a revelation common to hers. James was inflamed.

"How do you know?" asked Aunt Martiel in an equally low voice.

"Phone calls that hang up, late hours, and..., other things," she blushed.

"Has he admitted it yet!?" asked Martiel.

"Please," said Catherine gesturing with her hand. "Keep it down. It's bad enough without everybody else getting involved."

James was ready to explode. Martiel sensed something building and blurted, "James."

Catherine looked at her quickly, "James, what?"

"We can't forget James in all this," she recovered. "After this week is over maybe, but now is not the time. We need to all pull together."

The front door came alive with commotion and muffled voices made their way into the foyer and living room. Catherine and Aunt Martiel both listened intently as more family members were introduced to their now fragile environment.

"Oh, God…, no," blurted Aunt Martiel, in disgust. "It's Bethany Monroe and some of her brood. It's these kinds of moments I wish there was another easy route upstairs where I could hide."

"Aunt Martiel!" said Catherine. "She's only an old woman and she's your sister."

"An old bitty!" said Martiel. "And a constant thorn in my side."

James laughed heartily at the sudden change in expressions on his great aunt's face, his angry moment abated.

"It's not funny!" she said looking around the room.

"I never said it was," said Catherine, frowning at her aunt.

"Ohhh…, nevermind," said Martiel, waving her hand and storming to the opposite corner of the kitchen.

"You'd think they would have the decency to find a motel room until they leave!"

Bethany Monroe and her youngest son Harold had come to "represent" their side of the Ames family.

Bethany, Martin Earl's older sister, lived in Washington State, on the outskirts of Seattle, touching the Canadian border. Her family had little to do with the "common" side of the Ames family. Her private family regime had become quite affluent over the years utilizing the Ames money to make investments and had quite often put a strain on Martiel's good nature.

Nevertheless, she had leveraged the available Ames financials to her advantage, with numerous requests for financial aid. Her husband, Moreland Monroe had hammered the capital into a lucrative shipping and export company on the west coast, whose assets would soon equal the Ames estate if all went well.

The years she spent arguing the fact that she should have had control over the Ames portfolio of investments instead of Martiel and how the "family" would have benefited manifold from their expertise emptied Martiel of any patience.

Only Martiel knew of the unscrupulous methods in which her husband Moreland had acquired his affluence in "creative" money management.

Her youngest son Harold, born to her late in life, had become somewhat of a pet and at 27 years of age had never married or held any viable position. His mission in life was to tend to the needs of his mother and live a very questionable lifestyle, barely outside of the radar of her inquiries, and on the family monies of course.

"Let's go pay our respects, Aunt Martiel," she nudged. "And be nice."

Catherine walked over to her aunt and locked her arm elbow to elbow, pulling her toward the living room.

"We can't let daddy bear all the burden of entertaining them," said Catherine.

"Sure we can, it's only proper," squealed Martiel as she was being dragged along on tiptoes.

Bethany's purposefully articulate voice enunciated every word with precision, having doused the flames of southern euphemisms.

"Oh, how do you stand the climate here?" whined Bethany. "It's unbearably muggy. Harold would you bring in our luggage?"

"Yes, Mother," he replied in his usual banal tone. The tall gaunt young man quickly disappeared out the door at her command.

Martin and his older sister had exchanged pleasantries for several minutes before anyone had heard the clamor of their arrival.

"I'm glad that you were able to make it here so quickly," said Martin. "Things happened so suddenly…."

"Yes, suddenly…," she said fanning herself furiously. "We made arrangements with our private jet as soon as we received your call."

Martin Earl closed the front door, allowing the cool air inside to propagate into the foyer. "We have the two front rooms on the north end set aside for you," he said.

"Mother's old room, how thoughtful of you," said Bethany.

"Hello, Aunt Beth," said Catherine, pulling a staggering Martiel by her side. She reached out and hugged the frail frame of her aunt.

Bethany immediately took a glance at Catherine down the sights of her pinched nose. "I'm so sorry to hear of your loss, Catherine. I know you must be desperately lost without James Earl. One never knows when our time is up, especially when we live a less…, *protected lifestyle.*"

The odd condolence hung uncomfortably long in the air until Harold blundered back through the door with a lazy man's carry of luggage, once again leaving the front door standing wide open.

"Hello Bethany," said Martiel with an outstretched hand.

"What, no hug for your old sister?" she asked mockingly, reaching forward to Martiel.

Martiel felt violated from the close encounter with her adversarial sister but hid her expressions as everyone migrated to the living room.

Harold took his place flanking his mother practically unnoticed and unspeaking other than cordial hello's.

Catherine had managed to ignore the cutting remark from her old aunt, but memories of the multitude of personality clashes began to rush in with a gathering coldness.

"Well, the old place hasn't changed a bit," said Bethany looking around.

"Yes, Aunt Martiel has done a good job maintaining it for posterity sake," said Catherine. "It's exactly the way I remember it also."

"Oh, really? I don't recall you spending much time here as a child," said Bethany. "Or Martin Earl for that matter. It was mostly *Martiel* who lingered until our father passed on. He always did seem to favor Martiel for some strange reason."

Martin Earl saw the course the conversation was heading; a familiar exchange that he did not want to relive.

"I know everyone must be tired," he said. "Let me show you to your rooms."

"Oh, Martin, you must be joking," Bethany said. "I think I can still navigate the home of my childhood. Follow me Harold…. By the way, what time will breakfast be served in the morning?" she quipped.

"I guess whenever I get up and make it," said Catherine.

"Hmmm, you don't employ a cook or a maid? How gauche," she said in her mumbling tone.

Moments later the luggage was being scuffed along the slick floor toward their rooms.

Martiel had said her few words and retreated upstairs to brood, with Catherine willingly by her side.

Soon all lights were out. The Grandparents were asleep and Catherine had taken some of their clothes and moved into the room with her son, Sam.

Martiel was in her usual state of unrest and awake in her room, distressed even more so by the arrival of her pompous older sister.

She sat quietly, listless from the events and assuming that James would begin some kind of entranced discourse - which he did.

James told his aunt of the day's events at his grandparents' damaged house, especially the large vaporous shadow creature that used shadows like flypaper to trap its victims.

She was shocked and had never heard of anything so sinister, yet she remembered a coldness when she had retrieved James' journal from the wastebasket in his bedroom.

"That might account for the reason I don't see any other…, others like me walking around," said James. "Maybe they're hiding or got caught by something like that."

Martiel seemed to move past her surprise and drifted back to her own thoughts.

"I want to talk to my mother," he said finally. "I need you to translate."
Martiel was instantly transformed back to the present.

"Oh, *NO* James, that's not a good idea at all," she protested. "That only cause's trouble. Besides, she doesn't know about any of the family gifts. What if Sam is next in line…."

She spun around realizing what she had blurted out.

"What do you mean by that?" asked James. "What was that about Sam being next in line? Next in line for what, Aunt Martiel?"

"Oh…, well I only meant…. Well, there is the chance, slim chance that the gifts that you…," she explained.

"No. It stops here Aunt Martiel. There's been enough damage to this family don't you think? I won't let that happen."

"There's no way that you could stop it James, its hereditary somehow, and always knows who should be next."

He hated it when she began to whine to make her point.

"Well they didn't count on me still being around either," said James angrily.

There was a quiet knocking on the bedroom door.

"Oh, no. What if someone heard us, uh… me, talking," she whispered. "Just a minute."

She ruffled her hair somewhat and frumped the covers on her bed to appear partially slept in.

"You be quiet," she whispered as she went to the door

"Aunt Martiel?" asked Catherine. "Were you asleep?"

"Oh, well no, not quite yet," she said, her palm covering a forced yawn.

"Who were you talking to? I thought I heard voices."

Catherine peered into the bedroom.

Martiel reluctantly opened the door and welcomed her inside.

"See, only me," said Martiel, feigning a smile.

"I thought you might be in a conversation with Aunt Beth," Catherine said smirking.

Martiel walked back over to her bed, "Please don't insult me."

"Tell her," said James. "I want to talk to her."

Martiel looked around and shook her head *no* sharply, trying to be secretive.

Catherine walked over and sat on the end of the bed and placed her hand where the covers were wrinkled. The bed was cool.

"Why don't you tell me about this old house, Aunt Martiel," said Catherine. "I used to hear all kinds of wild tales about haunts and ghosts here as a kid. Aunt Beth reminded me of a lot of things that used to go on here. My daddy was scared of coming over here and almost never brought me to see the place."

"Nothing to tell…," she said, her face flushing somewhat.

"Why did you decide to live in Biloxi instead of here?" she asked.

"I like the water front and the beach, you know that," said Martiel.

"Cut the crap, Aunt Martiel, tell her," said James. "I can make it interesting if you don't help me."

"Oh no," said Martiel absentmindedly.

"No, what?" asked Catherine.

"Last chance," said James.

Catherine and Martiel were faced off at each other, each not knowing what to expect, both for different reasons.

James began thinking about Christmas and the year his mother wrapped him in a blanket on Christmas morning and brought him hot cocoa, snuggling up close to him.

Martiel sighed and shook her head sadly.

"James?" Catherine gasped for breath and fainted on Martiel's bed.

Chapter 45

The free clinic was packed with a wide foray of needful, hurting, poor, and unemployed. The doctor scanned the test for the second time.

"I'm pregnant? You're sure?" asked Sallee Mae. "I mean…, I want to tell my husband, so I need to be positive about this. It ain't no false alarm."

"Absolutely," said the doctor. "You are about to be a proud mama. No more alcohol. No more cigarettes. We don't want complications, okay?"

"Oh, thank you!" shrieked Sallee Mae Poole.

Once outside the clinic, she rushed home to tell her husband the good news. She had wanted a child for over a year now. The question was…, how would her husband Billy react? She never really could tell when he was telling the truth or lying. Living with him had become a mystery.

She could live with his secrecy, since he paid all the bills. She couldn't really say that she loved him, but she could get along with him enough to make their cohabitation work. He hadn't hit her like her last boyfriend. Billy had even wanted to marry her, which was actually more than Sallee Mae wanted at the time, but what the heck. It kept down all the looks of scorn and the whispers behind her back and if it didn't work out, she could always divorce him, couldn't she?

When she got home, her little house was empty and quiet.

"Billy?" she called out. "Are you here?"

There was no answer. She sat down on the couch eyeing the worn material on its arms and the deep gouges on the coffee table.

Where was Billy? It was his day off and they were supposed to look at houses together.

She went into the bedroom and noticed that several items were scattered.

There was a note on the bed that read:

> Sallee,
> I had to go out of town.
> Be back tomorrow.
> Explain then.
> Billy

Not missing a step, Sallee Mae rushed over to the telephone, dialed a familiar number, and sat down.

"Hi, what are you doing?"

"I'm free tonight…, all night."

Breakfast at the Ames was rushed and uncomfortable. Aunt Bethany and company left early for breakfast in the city, much to the joy of those who knew her best.

Each member had their self-appointed duties lined up before James' funeral the next day.

Born on a Wednesday, buried on a Wednesday, thought Catherine. But, not necessarily dead. Catherine may have shown her weakness at the appearance of James, but she rebounded with a vengeance.

As soon as everyone scattered, she grabbed Martiel and went upstairs to her room.

"James," said Catherine upon entering the door.

"He's here," said Martiel with a frown. "I really disapprove of this for the record. Oh, I just know this is going to turn out bad."

"Really? Worse than James being dead?" asked Catherine.

Martiel rolled her eyes in disgust at Catherine's turn of phrase, which sounded exactly like James Earl.

"Now tell me everything…, and I mean everything."

"Here, you can start with this," said Martiel, handing Catherine the journal that James kept.

"Read this and when you're ready, I'll try to catch you up on the rest."

Three hours later, Catherine had a good basic understanding of what had happened and was as disturbed as James was, even with herself.

"I want to meet Jolie," said Catherine. "I know she'll probably be at the funeral tomorrow, but I'd like some time alone with her."

She sat thinking for a moment.

"It's really difficult talking about your funeral, while I'm talking to you here, James."

"At least now you see why I wanted to talk to you mom," said James, via Martiel.

"I don't want to make the same mistakes twice and I want to pass all the information through you, because I don't know if this is permanent or how much longer I have," he confessed sadly. "If I get trapped again and can't get away, you might not hear from me again."

"Make sure you stay away from that house," she said finally.

"Martin Earl, it's for you," said Martiel. "Telephone…."

She was sitting in the kitchen with a cup of coffee looking worriedly through the current month's highly guarded portfolio of family assets. The record was something that Bethany Monroe's eyes had never seen and would never see. Not as long as Martiel was alive and kicking!

Money wasn't the problem, it was where to get it and make the least impact.

"What do you mean, they quit?" asked Martin. "Can you get somebody else to finish up the work?"

"Well, yes, I would like to get my house back as soon as possible. Accidents? Is he going to be okay?"

Martin listened intently for several minutes.

"Okay…, do what you can and thanks for calling."

"That was the contractor, his crew quit," said Martin Earl, running his fingers through his hair.

"What was their problem?" asked Martiel, as she looked up over her coffee.

"It's a long story. The power company came out and repaired the transformer this morning. Whoever was supposed to secure the lines and put in the meter on the work pole, messed up. A couple of them got some burns from it. The porch shifted away from the house, so it has to be reattached and leveled to the house.

One of the workers refused to go inside the house to trace the wiring. Said he was scared of all things. Have you ever heard anything so crazy? You want to hear the whole list?" asked Martin with a genuine look of worry on his face.

"Funny thing is…, I felt a little strange when I was over there. Like I was being watched."

"Martin, you were spooked?" asked Martiel. "I don't believe my ears."

"I've been hanging around you and Maime too much lately," he said as he sat down. "I still haven't wrapped my head around what she says caused her to fall."

Her brother was about to delve into a conversation she didn't know how to repel. Her only option was to change the subject as quickly as possible.

"Now…, you want to see something spooky," said Martiel. "Look at this…." Martiel pointed to several items in a prospectus splayed on the table before them. "See these numbers…, this is the first quarter, this is the second that I recently received."

"These are a lot larger," said Martin. "That's good isn't it? So the price of gas going up isn't completely a bad thing?"

"It's not just good," she said containing her zeal. "Our oil, gas, and steel investments are up over forty percent across the board. We need to liquefy these earnings and put them…."

Martiel fell strangely silent.

After all the years of listening to the suggestions from a house full of dead relatives, she had been scared to make any decisions on her own.

Now that they were gone, she knew that what they had taught her over the years was still inside her. Suddenly, she didn't feel alone.

If she managed this correctly, the family was quite well off, beyond her imaginations. Even her cranky sister Bethany would be jealous of these figures.

"Put them where?" asked Martin. "You stalled out on me."

"Martin, keep this to yourself, but you and Maime need to help me spend some money…," said Martiel. "Why don't you close up that old house and if you don't like it here, we'll get something a little newer, anywhere you like. I need to make a few phone calls."

"I've never seen such a turnout at our church since we've been going here," said Martin. "I didn't realize we knew that many people."

The article in the paper had described James death as an "auto accident" to keep explanations to a minimum and not hinder the ongoing investigation into his death.

The church was not a small one by any standards, but it wasn't prepared for the potential amount of visitors tomorrow at the funeral. At the funeral home, the five hundred-plus visitors that came to pay their respects renewed Martins faith in people of the community and city.

People that James had served at Earl's Garage over the years as well as people that knew Martin Earl Ames sifted through. There was a viewing of sorts, but it was pictures only, the casket would be closed for obvious reasons.

"Catherine…, now that you know all the details, I need to ask you a question. Do you think that there is the possibility that whoever ended up with Syrus Ames's bones will come after James as soon as he's buried?" whispered Aunt Martiel.

"Before I talked to you and…, well…, James, I would have laughed at that, but now. I simply don't know," said Catherine. "I think it's very possible. Until we know what one thing has to do with the other, anything's possible I guess?"

"I have an idea," said Aunt Martiel. "If you'll go along with it."

"Okay, what do you have in mind?" asked Catherine.

"Not now, I'll tell you later," said Aunt Martiel.

"Where is James?" asked Catherine.

Martiel sighed heavily and looked around at all the milling faces, "Your guess is as good as mine. Just pray that he doesn't stir up more trouble than we already have."

James was hovering about the Pearl Funeral Home, noticing different faces. He remembered Granny Smith's funeral and how hopeful he felt while hearing all the good things that were told about her.

He also remembered the bitter feelings of rejection by the pastor when he asked for help, but now he understood the reason he acted that way.

Another more serious thought had attached itself to him; James wondered why he hadn't "moved on" like Granny Smith. She was certainly nowhere to be found. Why was he trapped here in some halfway house this side of hell?

Hundreds of people came by in the span of three hours, countless faces. Some he knew, most he didn't.

THERE!

It couldn't be. There was the woman. The wife of that big man that was driving the truck the night he was killed. What was her name? Sallee. Sallee Mae.

He quickly went to her and followed her over to the registry book, reading her signature, "Sallee Mae Poole." She walked up to his gramma and told her how sorry she was to hear about her grandson.

That's where he remembered the blond woman. From the church. She was one of the people that Pastor Milton had been counseling with her odd looking husband.

"Martiel!" said James excitedly, placing his hand on her shoulder.

Martiel nearly jumped out of her skin at his voice and something cold raced up and down her spine.

"Sh...!, don't you *EVER* do that to me again!," whined Aunt Martiel. She shivered and rubbed a sudden ice cold pain in her shoulder.

Catherine looked over at her aunt and asked, "What in the world are you talking about?"

"Later," she whispered, as she quickly calmed down.

"Aunt Martiel, do you see the blond woman talking to gramma? It's that woman..., the woman that's married to Billy Poole. The one...."

"Ssshhh, I remember," said Martiel and immediately started walking over to her sister-in-law.

"...and this is Martiel Ellington. James was her Great Nephew," said Mrs. Ames.

"How do you do, and you are?" said Martiel.

"Sallee," she said, sensing something was wrong by the probing look in Martiel's eyes.

"Please to meet you, Sallee. Thank you for coming."

Martiel continued hovering beside Maime Ames, observing, until *Sallee* finished her say and walked away.

"What was all that about?" asked Maime.

"How do you know her?" asked Martiel.

"She was married at our church two or three years ago," said Maime. "It was kind of a rushed wedding, if you know what I mean."

"You mean she was pregnant?" asked Martiel.

"Ssshh..., said Maime speaking low. "She miscarried about a month after the wedding, it was all hush, hush. They don't ever mention it from what I gather."

Sallee Mae stayed around until the last half hour of the viewing, although she didn't seem that interested in chatting with the other visitors or family members. When some unknown event transpired, she seemed ready to leave.

James followed Sallee Mae out of the Pearls Funeral Home and back to her car while all the other visitors were still mingling.

She drove from downtown over to an area familiar to him. The car stopped in the driveway of an empty house only a few blocks from his grandparents' neighborhood.

Sallee Mae got out of the car, trekked a few hurried blocks, and turned by the old Heaven's Gate Cemetery behind the Holiness Cathedral Church. James followed her, but didn't dare look over toward the cemetery. There were too many unexplained things he needed to learn, before venturing in there at nighttime.

She followed the cover of trees and shrubs along the back of the church and walked up to the back entrance to the parsonage.

After a few knocks, the door opened and closed quickly letting her inside.

James became the fly on the wall to observe and learn.

The pastor ushered her into his living quarters and she sat comfortably on his couch, patting the seat beside her.

"Well, you seem really excited tonight. Is there some reason that I don't know about?" he asked.

"Not now, come sit by me."

"I've got to finish writing the eulogy for that funeral tomorrow before I can relax," he said.

"I just came from the funeral home myself. The old man and old woman are real sweet, but the others are sort of strange. I met the kid's aunt and she was a real weirdo. She stared me down as if she knew me from somewhere. I don't remember her coming to church here."

"That family thinks the world revolves around them. He's nothing but a grease monkey and runs a garage over across the tracks for God's sake. It's about time they find out they're working trash like all the rest. Just because they're on the church board, they think they can rule the whole church."

"Well, I don't know about all that, but that aunt did give me the willies. Can't you do that a little later? Billy's gone again tonight?" she teased in a singsong voice.

"He's gone again? How does he expect to keep his beautiful wife taken care of if he's always running off somewhere?"

He walked over to where she was and sat down close beside her.

"I don't know if I can stand being all alone..., all night long," she cooed, placing her hand on his leg.

He smiled and they both laughed at each other's performances. Pastor Milton cupped her face between his hands and gave her a passionate kiss, which she returned eagerly.

In a few moments, it was clear to James the reason for her visit. This was definitely no counseling session.

He reached behind her, unzipping her dress as she fumbled hurriedly with the buttons on his shirt. It was becoming apparent that they had practiced these moves on many occasions.

A black lace brassiere fell to her waist revealing her bare breasts. Milton pulled her body close in a kiss as they continued to shed their clothes with their bodies intertwining.

In a few moments, there would be nothing left to the imagination. James had no intentions of being a *Peeping Tom* and was burning with fury that a charlatan was duping everyone.

His emotions flared, leaving him vulnerable to become a specter for ready inspection himself.

Sallee opened her eyes as she was pulling the slacks off her would-be lover and fell backward in a scream as the mood was temporarily broken.

James slunk away as soon as he knew what happened and receded into the unseen.

Sallee Mae covered her chest in a quick "X" of her arms, but whatever it was she thought she saw was gone.

Her partner fell tumbling onto the floor, with his trousers at his knees stumbling furiously to stand.

"What the hell was that all about!" he yelled, looking all around the room.

"I saw..., I saw..., I thought I saw something...," she said, embarrassed at what she had done. "Aw, baby. I'm sorry."

She sat back on the couch and took a deep breath. He sat beside her with his trousers at his ankles.

"Hmmm, I see a little excitement doesn't bother you," she said smiling. James left.

Martiel was weary from the day's adventures and all the rest of the family had begun their perspective nightly rituals.

The elder Ames had already retired, Robert and Catherine were passionately arguing. Sam was lying down with a pair of headphones plugged into a radio and staring at the ceiling.

Bethany and Harold had dined out in the city of Natchez arriving back late and going directly to their respective rooms.

It couldn't be called a typical family household by any stretch of the imagination, certainly not a desirable one.

"Aunt Martiel?" whispered James.

"Oh not tonight James, I'm so tired.... Is it important?" asked Aunt Martiel.

"I have some gossip for you," he said calmly, about to explode.

Her ears came to attention.

"Is it worth missing sleep over?" she asked wearily.

"You be the judge."

"Okay, but only for a few minutes," she yawned.

James told Martiel about following Sallee Mae to the church and the series of events.

Martiel was instantly awake.

"Why that sneaky bastard! He said that about the Ames family?!! Why, he has no idea what kind of hornets nest he's stirred up. This ones gonna light up his derriere!"

She had no idea that her voice was raised as her mind began to plot evil on the miscreant pastor. Actually, James wanted to hear her response as if needing permission to take matters into his own hands. It was possible he could do nothing at all, but....

"No, I want to handle this one," said James.

Billy Poole drove up the deserted road. It was almost two o'clock in the morning and he was bone tired. He had driven non-stop, to and from a private collector in Nashville that had a passion for old collectible gold coins. As usual, it was no questions asked and cash money for the exchange.

Billy was either too tired to care or getting used to the scary crap Miss Lyda Brown was capable of performing. Now she was young looking. She was also filthy rich.

Although the sky was brilliant with the last stages of a fat moon, he walked through almost pitch blackness of moss laden trees to the shack he had visited so many times before.

He recalled their first meeting while he was fishing up the banks of the Mississippi. She had scared years off his life back then and that had never changed, at least up until now.

There was a dim light coming out of the window of the shack and a drizzle of smoke from the chimney. The planks of the porch gave way under the weight of his footsteps, taking away any ideas of stealth he might have had.

When he visited in the past, he didn't know if he wanted to beat a pan to let her know he was coming or be quiet as a mouse so he wouldn't piss her off. Her moods always swung this way and that, each time he met her.

"Billy, that you?"

The voice wasn't as ragged as it had been in the past.

"Yes'm, it's me," he said clearing his throat.

"Come inside, hurry on. Let's see what you got."

"Beg your pardon, Ma'am, you sound different than you did before…," his voice trailed off wishing he'd kept his mouth shut.

"I been around lots of folks today. I picked up on their talk while I was out and about."

"Yes'm, I see you did," said Billy.

"Did you bring me something?"

"Sure did!" he said excitedly, holding up a brown paper sack. He opened the top and poured out over fifty thousand dollars in 100 dollar bills onto her table.

"Them little nuggets worth a lot more than I remember!"

She grabbed his wrist as he finished shaking out the contents of the bag.

"This all of it?" she asked digging in with her fingers.

"Yes'm, this is all it," he said, eyes bulging. "You only give me a handful."

"You wouldn't lie to me, would you Billy?"

"No Ma'am, I wouldn' lie to you. Truth is, you scare the hail outa me."

She sat down at the table and motioned Billy to do the same.

Billy helped her count out all of the money and made separate little stacks on the table.

She counted out twenty thousand dollars and handed it to Billy.

"Yours," she said and continued counting quietly.

Billy looked at the money in awe. He had never had that much money for his own at one time, in his entire lifetime.

"That's a lot of money," argued Billy, scooting it back at her.

"Baaah!" she growled. "Money ain't everything. You soon find that out. Real soon."

"Don't let that go to your head," she continued. "You keep your wits about you and there'll be lots more in time."

Her mood switched and she was quietly thinking….

"I ain't through with my working, you know," she said quieter than before, looking away.

"There be something better than gold that I want."

She turned her attention to Billy and looked him right in the face, her eyes glazed over.

"Voodoo tradition says I'm supposed to wait a spell before I can get…, this thing I'm after. I ain't never been good at following rules. I'm getting what I want real quick like. It's time for Miss Lyda to live again."

She finished counting the rest of the money in silence.

"You still got that mojo I give you?" she asked changing the subject.

"Yes'm, still got it right here," he said pulling it out of his waistband.

She snatched it from his hand and threw it in the smoldering hearth of her fireplace. It blazed and sparked for several moments.

Billy wanted to stop her. He had worked for that mojo bag and it seemed to be helping him.

"Don't you worry yourself none. I got something better than that," she said. "I'm gonna need you to do some errands for me. Time for me to move uptown, out of this shack!" she screeched in her old voice, scaring Billy backwards in a heap.

"Want you to git me a house in town. Something small for now," she said.

"You want me to buy you a house?"

"Nope, just let me a place to stay."

"You mean rent you a place?" Billy corrected.

"Rent me a place," she repeated. "I need to be in town, learn people. Somewhere near the river, close like. I been out here for so many years...," her voice trailed off. "Time to live agin'!"

"You be needing a way to git around, won't you?" he asked.

"Got that," she said. "My little Toad's gonna drive me where I need to go."

Billy knew that she was talking about the skinny kid that helped the Mastyn boy with his duties.

"You sure that's a good idea?" asked Billy. "I mean since...."

"Don't you go second guessing what I should be doing."

She shuffled another four thousand dollars into his hand and gave him a list of things she wanted.

"What name you be going by?" asked Billy. "Or should I use my name for you?"

"My name of course," she said.... "Lyda..., Lyda Brown."

"Lyda Brown it is," said Billy.

"How's that little honey you married to?" she asked, ignoring Billy. "She treating you right?"

"Spose so," said Billy questioning where the sudden turn of conversation was heading.

She put her hand on his and pulled it over, palm side up.

"She been a busy little girl I see, real busy. Wants herself a house of her own. You need to take care of that too. You be glad you did."

Lyda chuckled watching Billy's ever changing expression.

"She taking care of you in other ways?" she asked.

She reached out and placed her hand on the crotch of his pants feeling around lightly.

Billy's face went slack and turned a shade of gray. She had made advances toward him when she was an old crone that he had been able to avoid over the years. Now, he had no excuses.

"Uh, yes'm…," he stuttered, terrified of her awkward advances. "I…, suppose she is."

"Hmmm…," she stood and pulled him by the hand. "Come here with me. Like I promised, I got something better for you than that *mojo bag*…," she chuckled, as she dragged him into the back room.

Chapter 46

"**While we gather here** to remember James Earl Williams, cut short in his prime of life, let us also not forget the day to day service that he performed with his Grandfather, Martin Earl Ames for this community. A truly dedicated service to the all the farming and working class that keep our area and community strong.

Neither let us forget his aspirations for a higher education and to better himself in this life. We have to admire the drive and ambition of youth and the dream and desire to be more than you are...," Pastor Milton droned on in condescension.

Martiel was about to make a spectacle of herself, her black eyes were shooting darts over at her brother Martin as well as Catherine.

Robert Williams sat oblivious to the subtle demeaning remarks toward his son and his wife's' family.

Martin reached over and placed his hand on Martiel's and gave her a *'calm down, not now'* look. Sam was crowded in thoughts of disbelief that his brother was actually dead, pushing up closer against Catherine's arm.

James was hovering around the pastor and the casket that sat closed at the front of the church. He was wishing that he could re-animate his body and make it sit up and look at this fake, but he had more important items to attend to.

He wandered out among the mass that had filled the church to capacity. There on the front row sitting with his family was Jolie who had tuned out any words that might have been spoken and was filled with her own. Her expressions spoke volumes to James as he looked at her in silence.

His frustration and disappointment renewed his determination to make sure none of this ever happened to another member of his family or someone he loved.

He stalked the aisles angrily, looking. He saw many of his family's friends, Sheriff Howard, Deputy Floyd, other officers he didn't recognize. Friends of Granny Smith and regular church members dotted the mass.

There in the very back row of the church sat Sallee Mae and her husband Billy. James could not believe he was actually there.

The accomplice to his murderer was seated like the doting husband beside his *wife* at the funeral he was partially responsible for.

James moved in close. He placed his perpetually icy hand on Sallee Mae's back and rubbed up and down, focusing on his anger at Billy.

She shivered and sat forward and gave her husband a harsh glare. He sat there perspiring due to the closing tightness of the air in the church and the crowd. At two in the afternoon, the air conditioning was working overtime barely keeping out the hot, humid air from outside.

Sallee timidly shuffled nearer to Billy, who resisted, because of her body heat in the tight quarters.

James decided to take his torture one-step further, if only to make sure that everyone remembered seeing them at his funeral.

The time for being a gentleman was over.

James slowly placed his hand under the cushioned seat where Sallee Mae sat.

His anger blazed. His icy palm met the flesh where she sat.

Sallee Mae jumped to her feet and screeched loudly.

All eyes instantly trained on her as she angrily flapped a hand at the backside of her skirt. Her face flushed bright red and she returned to her seat, but the deed was done.

Deputy Floyd's eyes trained on Billy and they locked in an unspoken association. James watched for and saw the connection between them. It could have been a look that said, *'please, this is a funeral'* but James decided to keep an eye on him; maybe follow the deputy around for a few days. After all, Jolie still thought he had something to do with his death.

Other eyes on that same pew took more than a glancing look at Billy Poole and he became nervous. Just as the service ended, Billy grabbed the arm of his wife Sallee Mae, roughly pulling her from the church building. He didn't ask for explanations as to what happened to her, but melted into the crowd in the churchyard outside.

At the graveside service, the immediate family assembled under a framed awning. Martin and Maime Ames were silently thinking of their own mortality and realizing that this could have just as easily been one of them.

Maime was wondering when this evil would be satisfied. She had seen it. She truly believed that she had seen the thief that took her precious grandson from this life. She was undoubtedly frightened as she tenderly flexed the fingers of her left arm, remembering her own accident.

Catherine had made room next to her for Jolie to sit. She held Jolie's hand as the last words were being spoken over her oldest son.

Catherine leaned over and whispered in her ear, "I need to speak to you when we're through here, Jolie. Could you meet with me tomorrow or the next day?"

Jolie nodded and smiled slightly through her tears.

Near the back of the onlookers stood Billy quietly arguing with Sallee Mae trying to persuade her to leave. As Deputy Floyd was leaving the cemetery, he managed to step near Billy as if by coincidence.

"Why didn't you send up a flare?" whispered Floyd.

"Weren't me, was Sallee Mae got something up her butt," said Billy barely above a breath. "By the way, nice brake job."

Floyd flashed a grin, scanning the crowd, "We kicked his little ass, didn't we?" He twisted suddenly. "Gotta go."

Deputy Floyd hurried to his vehicle and left the cemetery.

Sallee Mae and Billy continued to argue about leaving, they had another "counseling" session with the pastor immediately after the last words were spoken.

James managed to hear it all. He was more confused than ever now. Who or why would anyone want to kill him? He barely knew anybody outside of his family and a few customers of Earl's Garage.

Nevertheless, Jolie's suspicions were true and now he was bound and determined to find out why. If they were willing to kill him, they would stop at nothing to hurt his family, especially if there was some hidden agenda.

Near the wall of the graveyard's fenced gate stood an elegantly dressed black lady watching the procession completely unnoticed.

She was mumbling something to herself, her lips moving in a quick gibberish of repetitive syllables.

The pastor finished his closing "…ashes to ashes, dust to dust" as the casket was starting its final descent into the earth.

The crank on one end of the lowering device jammed, the other broke from the shift of weight and the casket plummeted downward on one end.

There were gasps of breath as the casket dropped. The lid cracked and popped from the impact and slammed open.

Facing the crowd of family and onlookers lay the mangled and outstretched body of James Earl Williams, lurched forward with his swollen eyes bulging wide open, looking out on them.

Jolie fainted into her folding seat and the family turned away in horror.

The men standing nearest, hurriedly repositioned the cadaver and closed the lid, which now wouldn't shut properly. The casket was twisted and its hinge bent from the falling weight of the drop. It would have to be replaced.

"Another night above ground. Ain't that a shame."

The colored lady tipped her hat and chuckled as she walked away.

"Why in Gods' name did I listen to you and your family in the first place?" asked Robert. "The whole funeral was a sideshow and then that shoddy gadget destroyed the last sanctity of James' burial. We should have brought him home with us and…."

"Please Robert, not now," begged Catherine. "Isn't it bad enough that James is dead and then all this today, without us fighting too?"

"As far as I'm concerned, I'm through with the funeral. I have to get back to Boston by tomorrow evening and I can't wait around for these round-eyed swamp hicks to fix what they've broken."

"This is your son...," she said quietly. "Fine. I'll take care of it. I need to stay here for awhile and take care of my mother anyway."

"You do that," he blurted. "Let me know if you decide to come home. Sam and I will get our things and leave this evening."

"I'm not going, dad," said Sam.

He had been standing in the doorway listening to his father spouting hateful things at his mother.

"I'm staying here with mom," he said, tears in his eyes. "Until she's ready to come home."

Robert threw his luggage on the bed and started packing his things to leave as they stood around and watched.

Finally, he turned to Catherine.

"Another mama's boy," said Robert coldly. "You can both stay here as long as you like."

Catherine and Sam walked out of the room and left him to pack. No sooner than their feet rushed out into the living room, they were met with another barrage.

"I see there's still something to be said for good breeding," said Aunt Bethany.

Catherine bit her lip as a reminder to keep her composure. It was evident that Bethany had overheard the entirety of her supposedly private conversation. She couldn't expect Martiel to hold her peace while she delved into a rage herself.

"I must say, the funeral was somewhat of a charade, but I did enjoy the pastor's eulogy," she added.

Catherine was primed to unload on her dear aunt's rude insensitivity, when Martin walked into the room, catching most of the conversation. He didn't need to be psychic to figure out that there had been cross words spoken by the look of his daughter Catherine's clenched jaw and the smug coolness of his elder sister's face.

"I took the liberty of loading your bags in your limousine," said Martin. "I hope you enjoyed your stay in Natchez."

"You loaded our bags..., I don't understand. We had planned on staying a day or two longer to visit," said Bethany.

"I believe it's time for you and your *well bred son* Harold to be on your way," said Martin. "We've just buried one of my favorite relatives and we need some time alone to grieve."

"Well then, I suppose it is time for us to be on our way," Bethany said curtly. "We'll be in Natchez this evening and fly out in the morning should you change your mind."

Catherine was fighting back angry tears as she turned away to the waiting stairs. Martiel had been standing at the first landing of the stairs fuming. Catherine caught her arm and held her fast for a moment, but Martiel managed to yank free.

"Don't you dare stop me. It's about time for a hair pulling!" she yelled as she stalked down the stairs.

Robert walked past everyone with his two pieces of luggage in hand, never pausing to look up or say "goodbye" to the lit fuse burning in the living room. The door banged open and he disappeared leaving it open for the next set of unwelcome guests to leave.

"Harold! It's time to go son," said Bethany coolly, walking back toward her mother's old room.

James sat affixed to the end of his great grandmother's bed waiting and watching. His grampa had collected and removed the belongings of his estranged family, when James noticed that Harold slid virtually unnoticed back into the room behind him.

His distant cousin was busily pilfering through the drawers of a large mirrored dresser where several items, left to Martin and Martiel, were stored after the division of the Ames inherited possessions.

Several jeweled items had already been stuffed inside his pants pockets and he was busily examining other items for gold content.

After all the comments that were passed around in the home, theft was the icing on the cake.

Harold picked up a string of cultured pearls with a gold clasp and raised them up in awe, viewing their perfection with greedy eyes. The reflection in the mirror behind the pearls flashed with movement and he refocused to see a grotesque specter watching his every movement.

Harold spun and sat flat onto the floor gaping at an unrecognizable dead relative. His chest heaved and his vision blurred momentarily, nearly in a dead faint.

Harold prayed to faint, but unconsciousness evaded him as he scooted next to the dresser. James pointed to his pockets and made an angry face, his left eye protruding from its already grotesque position. Harold never let his eyes move from the visage as he dropped the pearl necklace he had in an iron grip, then quickly emptied all the contents of his pants pockets.

Trinkets of antique gold and jewelry spilled noisily across the hardwood floor, just as he heard his name being called from somewhere down the hallway.

James remembered that he could only scare him, but scaring him might be enough. He floated up, pointed toward the door, and mouthed a silent..., Go!

Bethany and her son met in the hallway, his face white as chalk. He spun her in the opposite direction as he half-dragged her toward the front door.

Martiel's feet had already hit the bottom stair step and her mouth was moving in language unlike her usual demeanor.

"Wait, come back here. I'm not through with you!" she yelled, as Bethany and son hastened down the porch steps.

"Let them go, Martiel," said Martin, closing the front door.

"Aahhhh!" his little sisters' scream echoed inside the house.

The funeral was past, the family relations were gone, and the house had finally become quiet after the untimely confrontation.

Everyone was drained, both physically and emotionally.

James was once again busy pushing the last of his Aunt Martiel's patience. All the other family members were asleep except for Sam, who was plopped on a couch watching a late night movie on television.

"I knew that deputy had something to do with it," said James. "I couldn't put them together until today. I still don't understand what's going on, Aunt Martiel."

"Neither do I," she said, trying to encourage him. "But give it some time. Look how much you've already put together in such a short time. By the way, what was all the commotion with Sallee Mae during the funeral?"

"Something that you taught me," said James.

"Something that I taught you?" Aunt Martiel asked cautiously.

"Put out your hand," said James. "I'll show you."

Martiel held out her hand and James placed the palm of his hand on hers. He concentrated a moment and she drew back her hand quickly.

"My hand is freezing, James. Did you do that?"

"I did that to Sallee Mae. I wanted everybody there to remember their faces, especially the sheriff and his bunch," said James.

"Why did she jump, James?" she asked again, pressing him for the truth.

"I can't really say. She must have sat on a cold spot."

"Oh Lord..., you won't do James," she said, her cheeks brightening.

"James I need some rest. I know you don't, but after today...," she sighed deeply.

Reluctantly James conceded to silence as Martiel pulled the covers down on her bed.

"Go ahead, I'll leave you alone. I can think of a few places I want to check out. Besides, as soon as everybody's asleep around here, I want to follow that deputy around."

Martiel was already in a deep sleep as James began his departing tour of the house.

Chapter 47

Catherine Williams welcomed Jolie inside the front door with a lingering hug as if she were her own daughter.

"Thank you for coming Jolie."

Jolie melted and cried softly once more. Catherine waited for her to regain her composure and led her into the living room. Catherine disappeared into their kitchen, reappearing with some iced tea.

Sweet of course.

Jolie was perched on an ottoman near the couch. Catherine couldn't help but notice how tiny she looked sitting alone in the room and carefully placed their drinks on the table between them.

"James told me a lot about you," she began.

Jolie stayed silent for a few more moments sipping some of the tea from her glass.

"I care a lot about James. I mean cared...," she quickly corrected herself.

"I know that you still care for him," said Catherine. "I also know how hard it is to let go of someone that you have such strong feelings for. Jolie..., I know about James."

Catherine let that sink in for a few seconds in case Jolie wanted to admit talking with James.

"It must be hard knowing that your son was murdered," said Jolie, fishing for her meaning.

"James told me that you somehow feel responsible for his death. You need to let that go, he was tricked into chasing that truck."

Jolie started to speak up, to refute the insinuation. She had an alarmed look on her face, but Catherine asked her to wait and hear her out.

"If it hadn't happened that night, it would have been some other night, or some other method. The people that were after him wanted him dead for some reason. The only thing that might have slowed them down would have been for him to come back home with me. But even then, it would have only slowed them down."

Jolie had tried listening for hints of Catherine's thoughts, but her own distress seemed to turn it all to gibberish.

"How did James tell you all this? You're not making any sense."

It was Jolie's last ditch effort to cast aside suspicions of something supernatural.

"Martiel of course," said Catherine, in a matter of fact way.

"Oh," said Jolie quietly, nodding her head.

"Oh, is right. He told me everything there was to know Jolie, including that he loves you very much," said Catherine. "But he believes that there is still an enemy that is after our family and even after him right now. You have to believe me that I wouldn't keep you from talking to him, loving him, or allowing him to be in any part of your life Jolie.

"However, I can think of three reasons why I don't think it's healthy for either of you. First, he is no longer here physically and you deserve to have a life and love with someone that you can touch and hold and can care for you that way.

"Even if you choose to continue, I won't object. I already like you if only from what James confided in me.

"The second reason makes the first reason conditional though. The fact that he is in danger even now and the fact that our family is still a target by some unknown person or entity. It could put your life in danger and your Aunt BeBe's also."

Jolie sat quietly while Catherine told her almost the carbon copy of what her Aunt BeBe had already said the day before.

"What if I don't want to let him go?" asked Jolie. "I can't bear not hearing his voice or seeing the look on his face when I surprise him or a dozen other little things...."

She stood up, walked over to a heavily curtained window and peered outside, not wanting Catherine to see her cry yet again.

"I know what you're telling me is true," said Jolie. "I know that by taking part in anything to help is dangerous, but I want to. I want to see whoever did this rot in jail or go back to hell, whichever it is...."

"There's another reason Jolie. My son's love for you could distract him again and pull him into another trap, something more permanent. You remember his dreams?"

Catherine let out a well deserved breath. She'd done all she could do.

"Well..., James is an adult, dead or not, and you are an adult Jolie. If you two agree to continue on as is; I want you know you have my blessing. I'd like both of you to check in with me every day without exception with even the littlest of information or..., anything that is out of the ordinary. Do you understand?"

Catherine looked around in the cavernous room, "James, do you agree?"

"He said yes," said Jolie.

"I figured that he'd be eavesdropping in on us."

"Thank you Catherine," said Jolie. "Thank you for giving me a choice instead of telling me to stay away. I would have done it anyway and felt guilty about it."

It was Catherine's turn to regain her composure.

"This isn't so hard sometimes. It's almost like having James on a conference call, except you or Martiel are the telephone system."

She was on the verge of another silent episode of grief.

"I'm going to miss having my son hold me or hug me. I'm going to have to treat it like he's gone to visit another country and this is the only way I can talk to him."

She turned and walked away, wiping the steady stream of water from her eyes and Jolie hurried over and held her.

They both shed their final tears together.

Sam came walking through the room at the exact moment Jolie was leaving and stared at her with a strange focused intensity. Jolie looked at Sam and gasped, almost losing her footing for a moment.

"This is James' younger brother Sam," said Catherine.

It took more than a moment for Jolie to compose herself once again, "I can't believe how much you look like James. I had to look twice. I guess my mind was too distracted at the funeral today to notice anybody around me."

They exchanged pleasantries for a few moments and Jolie let Catherine know that she would begin checking in with her that next day. Then as she was leaving, she took one last look at Sam and shook her head smiling.

As Jolie drove off in her Aunt BeBe's car, Sam followed his mother into the family library.

"Wow..., she's a *real looker!*" said Sam. "How did James find *her?*"

"I'm sure James agrees with you," said his mother, letting the present tense slip without noticing it. She quickly changed the subject before his fifteen year old, hormone driven mind, noticed the difference.

"Are you okay with staying with me for the rest of the summer?" asked Catherine. "I know it's asking a lot."

"I sure don't want to go back to that loser camp I was at."

"I thought you liked that camp."

"I liked it better than listening to you and dad fight all summer long. But I'd rather be here any day of the week. I've always been jealous of James getting to come down here all summer long, while I got prison camp."

Catherine sighed.... "Sam, you know that James didn't simply have an accident, right?"

"Yeah, I'm not deaf. Everybody kinda hid it, but I figured it out. What about it?"

"Well I need to set some rules while we're here. I hate to do this to you, but I'll explain as I go."

"Rules..., crap. I knew there was a catch," said Sam. "I knew it couldn't be that simple."

"Sam, one more thing, I'm sorry about the fighting with your dad. I don't know how to reach him any more."

"Are you kidding? He doesn't want to be reached, mom. I think he's starting the arguments on purpose so...."

Sam cut himself off quickly, realizing what he was about to say.

Catherine looked at him sternly for a moment and turned her back on him, while she thought. How could her fifteen year old son see something so obvious and it took her months to figure it out?

A different generation. Or.... She didn't let herself think about the possibility of his being gifted the way her aunt had described and forced it from her mind. She had already lost one son to a family curse her aunt called gifts. She couldn't bear the thought of losing her only other child.

"Rule number one," she began. "I don't want you going anywhere, anytime without you letting me know about it. No excuses, period. I know how Mr. Adventure you can be. Don't make me worry. Whoever is responsible for James' death is still around.

The police are looking for something that will lead them to who did it, but they haven't found anything yet."

"So grampa's right, they are a bunch of dumb-butts," chirped Sam.

"Sam? No more of that out of your mouth. Rule number two...."

"I just don't understand it," said the detective.

He sat alone and invigorated, despite the late hour.

Sheriff Howard had prepared him a little corner office which was not much more than a midsize storage room that had been emptied.

There was a large fold out table next to the wall in the room, now completely covered in small stacks of papers. There was a large chalkboard above the table covered with remarks and connecting lines, a timeline of events and lists of names and facts.

After running into one dead end after another he had decided to take a different approach to the investigation and see how the grave robberies might be related. He believed that they were also tied together somehow.

The problem was that the evidence, however slim it was, always ran off into open air. There were no suspects, no witnesses – alive anyway, everything hit a dead end.

It sounded as if someone could be cleaning up after them, they might have had previous law enforcement experience or they were very, very lucky. The sheriff had privately admitted that he had considered the possibility of an internal problem, then slyly withdrew the idea, intentionally leaving the seed planted.

He didn't believe in luck or coincidence.

"Start at the beginning. Always a good place...," he said.

After making a copy of all the notes, he took a cloth and completely wiped the board down to nothing except the timeline.

He wrote down the names of the three people that had been removed from their graves over the last six months. Two different graveyards, but were they somehow related?

James strolled from room to room in the house looking in on each member of his family. Both his grandparents were back to back, breathing softly, and seemed to be resting well. Catherine was asleep, but seemed to be enduring some fitful dream, more than likely a replay of her and Aunt Bethany or his father.

Sam was spread eagle across the top of his covers still in jeans and t-shirt with a pair of headphones lightly hissing in his ears. James listened closely to hear what sounded like the *Rolling Stones* and smiled. He sat for a while looking at Sam, his little brother, not so little any more. He was James' equal in size at only fifteen years old, but not quite equal in maturity. Sam was given the chance to be a kid, James wasn't. That was probably the difference.

Bored of wandering the halls, James went back to his Aunt Martiel's room. She had left the family history book open on a small table beside a lamp with its light still on, for James. He had read this at least twice, an hour ago and was getting restless, not knowing what to do with himself.

He thought back to the evening with the Mambo and her teacher. Some of the things that they said made sense to him now.

James had an unusually foul sensation. The prevalent cold that was always with him quavered somehow and James came to alert, listening.

Although he couldn't hear anything, he knew that something wasn't right. He looked at the clock beside his aunt's bed and it was almost three in the morning, an evil time.

Terror gripped him and shook him inside as his vision skewed and his senses tilted oddly.

He sat on the end of Martiel's bed still listening intently. He began to hear a soft familiar sound that reverberated inside him.

Where had he heard it before?

James felt a familiar yank..., and his senses came alive looking every direction.

Another yank..., pulling at his insides.

Another, pulling harder, this time there was pain. This was the first real physical feeling he'd had since he died.

James heard a sing-song voice calling, "Little Sy-rus.... Little Sy-rus.... Come here little Syrus."

As he listened, he actually felt himself being snatched away and screamed....

Martiel woke up with a terrified start, not knowing what it was she heard for sure. A silent scream seemed to be echoing in her mind.

She looked over at the clock. It was 3:00 AM.

"James?" she asked softly. "Is that you?"

There was nothing but odd silence.

"James?" she asked again in a normal louder voice. "Are you there?"

"James!" she said loudly. "Where are you?"

She jumped from the bed throwing the covers nearly into the floor. She bumped through the house and down the stairs to Catherine's room.

"Catherine..., Catherine..., wake up," she said softly. "We need to pray."

James felt exactly the same as he had in his dreams while alive. That soft hypnotizing voice was still calling him. Calling him "Little Syrus," but something inside him was answering to that name.

"Little Sy-rus, I gotta new home for you," he heard and felt a yank, hard on his insides, pulling him.

Down, down through black oily darkness. It seemed that he couldn't scream or ask for help. He was in that darkness again. There was an omnidirectional screeching laughter as he drifted farther and farther away from his place of safety.

The distance seemed so far away....

Then down, down, harder, being pulled harder, down.... The voice was getting clearer and sounded as if it was coming from the bowels of old shoe leather. He was being pulled deeper toward that awful terrifying voice.

In the distance was a light, a yellow light. Suddenly remembering what awaited him at the light, he fought it desperately, clawing desperately at the blackness that engulfed him.

Now he could see the yellow light was the circle of candles burning. Again, in the center of the circle was the beautiful woman writhing as if in the throes of some sort of erotic display. It felt as if he was sliding down now toward the light and he stopped. Just short of a circle of stones and candles.

A leathery voice boomed out of nowhere and everywhere....

"I been waitin' a looooong time for you boy. It be payday for you."

A corroded old woman was shaking a rattle of some kind at his face and body. She was holding a skull in her left hand and that tormenting rattle in her right.

Once again she started repeating a singsong phrase in some other dialect, but James could almost understand it. It was causing him to relax and float..., float on toward her. He had an uncontrollable urge to relax and do whatever she wanted. *Just obey and it would all be over soon.*

James looked at her face and somehow it wasn't the old hag, the face was..., younger..., enticing.... The young woman from the circle was gone.

He felt an overwhelming sense of belonging and being a part of something bigger than himself..., a whole. Finally, James was in her presence and she began leading him to one of several tall clay pots with beautiful symbols scrolled around its surface. His body was vibrating and shaking with something long lost to him.

Feelings! Physical feelings!

He had forgotten what it was like to feel anything but deep constant cold. James could suddenly *feel* the warmth of the fire that was burning, *smell* the rancid scent of the candles and the humid air. The smells were so overpowering that he could *taste* them in his palate.

Taste! It was almost like being alive again.

James snapped to himself only for a moment. If he could feel it, it could feel him.

She had him poised over that earthen jar, the earthen jar he wanted so desperately to enter and rest. Uncontrollably, he began to vibrate again, until he heard his name being called from far away.

"James Earl Williams! James Earl.... Come home James...."

James began to slide away into darkness, peaceful darkness....

The *Bokor* went wild, shaking her rattle in extreme swings of her arm..., and chanting loudly.

"James.... James Earl...," the call reverberated once again, louder stronger.

James began to recall who and what he was....

The woman shook her *ason* in his face and commanded, but he stood firm and resisted her.

He found his voice again.

"Why do you want me?" James demanded.

"You stole what mine, it belongs to me!" she yelled.

"I'm not Syrus," James said aloud, for his own benefit. "I'm not Syrus!" James yelled at the evil before him.

"You got what he took from me. I gone get it back now!" she yelled back.

"Whatever Syrus took from you, I don't have it," he blurted.

"Liar!" she screamed. "It right there inside you!" she said loudly. "I see it."

"If Syrus gave it to me, then it's mine, not yours," James said adamantly.

"James Earl...," called the voice once more.

"I have to go," said James. "You can't keep me."

"You mine forever!" she screamed. "I'll torment you forever!"

James reached out of his suspended stupor and knocked the rattle from her hand and into the fire. Her eyes became large, unbelieving of what had just happened.

With bare feet, she kicked at her instrument of power to remove it from the engulfing flames, in quick snapping motions. She quickly turned and placed Syrus' skull back on its pedestal to retrieve her rattle before it began to burn.

Finally, James yielded to the call of his name and began to leave.

She was bending down onto her knees, scratching at the handle of the *ason* in desperation. It was inching from the hot coals of fire as he started fading. The last thing he heard as he was leaving was the voice of an old woman screaming, "I'll get you. I'll git your bones and all you got will be mine…. ALL YOU GOT!!!!"

James somehow stopped where he was, somehow willed himself to stop. If he didn't stand now, he would be running and hiding from now on. His family would be running and hiding from now on. A continuation of the hell he had known all his life was following him into this version of an afterlife.

No, he had to do something now. He turned, trained on the flames of the fire. Reaching into the flames with his hand, he snatched the *Bokor's* tool of choice before she could attain it. He could feel the lick of the flames scorch what should have been his skin, yet without damage.

He spun the *ason* tauntingly into the dark voodoo driven eyes of his enemy. He could see both the old underneath and the young swimming on the exterior of the woman, all the while sensing something even darker within. Her disguise of the beautiful black woman partially shed each time he waved the instrument.

James remembered her short chant and the words and began to recite them back in her face. Apparently the old woman's rattle and her chant was not prejudiced to who was wielding its power.

She wailed and stiffened as she shrunk at his feet. James walked toward the circle where the jar had been prepared for him.

Beside it was a cap made of wood meant to imprison him inside.

He circled the lips of the urn slowly and continued the words of her chant to hold her at bay.

She writhed and spun in twisted gyrations, moving like a snake shedding its skin.

The old woman fell limp to the floor and the young rose with a demonic look of hatred. Controlled but not willingly, her essence swam and spiraled above the urn.

The powerful words of the *Bokor* directed the spirit and it began to fall as ash, sifting like sand through the neck of an hourglass, down into the bottom of the tomb which was intended for him. With his other hand, he fumbled endlessly, with the oak plug trying to make his fingers obey and finally capped the opening.

There was suddenly a deathly silence.

The old woman lay on the floor, powerless and unconscious…, or dead. He couldn't see her breathing.

James shook from relief and tossed the rattle on the floor.

There on the pedestal sat the skull of Syrus Earl Ames.

He picked it up and felt power coursing through himself, something completely foreign to him, but yet it felt natural. He remembered a similar feeling of power when he removed the gang member off the top of his brother Sam. It had been the beginning of the end of his domination then and he felt it could be again.

In the bleak silence, he heard soft voices calling for Syrus.

The cave was echoing their moaning cries and he followed the pleading to another urn that sat near the old woman's altar.

He placed his ear close to it and heard the voices clearer. He knew what he had to do. James tried to loosen the cap in the top but it wouldn't budge. He picked up a rock and watched it slip through his fingers. Angrily he tried again and while the stone remained in his grasp, he lifted it high before it fell once again, smashing the urn. A hole burst into the side with a loud pop.

The family he briefly met at the old house, wisped one at a time from the urn and thanking him, floated upward in final release – gone.

There were many urns here, but what did they contain? James shuddered and left them as they were. Fearful of what might have been trapped by the evil woman.

He felt triumphant and powerful. Had this been what the old woman was after? Power? Power to unleash a dark reign of terror on all others, including fellow Voodoo practitioners.

Hidden knowledge swam into his mind and he could see all the others that had disowned the *Bokor* since her beginning decades ago.

Some of that power that was now coursing through him…, this ethereal body without flesh. He looked around at the cave and the altar, the crumpled old woman. Something told him he would be back.

James Earl hid the skull in a recess high in the cave and yielded to a far away call, sliding away peacefully into silence….

Aunt Martiel and Catherine sat alone; an oil lamp lit the middle of the table before them. Their hands were joined and they were calling James by name repeatedly. The lamp light flickered violently before them and there was a sudden gentle breeze in the room. They both looked and saw James at the same time and broke contact with their hands.

"James! Are you all right?" asked Catherine. "We didn't know what happened."

Martiel looked dreadfully tired and remained silent.

"I met our family's enemy," said James.

"Oh my God!" said Catherine. "I can hear you James…, and I can see you too."

311

"How did you summon me?" asked James. "I was with that thing and she was about to trap me. I heard you calling my name and somehow that saved me. I was able to fight her."

"I can answer that," said Martiel. "The prayers of the living are always stronger than the summons of the dead."

"I.... She might be dead," said James quietly, as he recalled and described what happened inside the cave.

"You mean to tell me this witchdoctor woman was after something that's been hid inside us Ames' for..., how long?" asked Martiel. "That's bizarre. That makes me wonder what old Syrus Earl was really up to."

"You don't know how bizarre it is Aunt Martiel," confessed James. "I can feel..., and smell..., and touch now. And that awful bone chilling cold is gone from inside me. You can both see me. Here feel me," he said as he reached out and touched both of them.

He wasn't quite solid to their touch, but definitely not mist any more.

"I don't have to wait around for someone to get my killers now," said James. "I can track them down...."

His experience had left him power drunk. He was like a child with the keys to a bulldozer.

"No James, you can't take things into your own hands," said Martiel. "You don't know what you're saying."

"Aunt Martiel, I need to finish this, I don't want to be trapped here forever in this..., this..., whatever this is," argued James. "It's maddening. You sleep and you rest. I never rest. My thoughts never shut up. You can close you eyes and block out the world around you if only for a few seconds, but my eyes never close. You.... You're alive.... I don't know what I am."

"Please James, don't let these changes influence your thinking. That's not like you to want revenge," said Catherine. "Think about where it might be coming from."

"You don't know what I want," said James. "I only wanted to be left alone. You and dad never believed me when I told you what was happening to me when I was a kid. You always believed the teachers..., the cops..., the.... Here. Look at the brand on my foot, look at...."

James stopped realizing how cruel this was to his mother. He still bore the scars of his brandings even in death, still marked, still reminded.

Catherine sat silently and finally she spoke, "I thought...."

"I'm sorry, mom," said James. "I didn't mean to.... I didn't mean to hurt you. I'll do it your way, at least for now."

Aunt Martiel worried about the "for now" and was getting another bad feeling about these new changes.

"At least give us a chance to finish this so you won't have any regrets," whispered Catherine.

Chapter 48

War

Catherine Williams and her father were standing at the front desk of the Sheriff's Office waiting for someone to give them some answers.

Martiel left to take care of making "special" arrangements for the burial of her nephew's body since the incident at the funeral. It had to be a premonition, she didn't believe in coincidences. After last night's episode, it was clear that this person needed the remains of her nephew to complete some age old struggle with their family ancestors. James believed she was dead, but Martiel wasn't ready to bet the bank on anything James was *feeling* at the moment.

Martin Ames was getting impatient waiting for someone to show up.

"Jeanette, I know it's not your fault, but we deserve to know what's going on. We deserve an answer about who killed James Williams," said Martin Ames. "Isn't there anybody that we can speak to that knows something?"

"The sheriff is looking over the wreckage at this moment," said the clerk. "If you'd like to see for yourself, it's right out back. They haven't moved it to the evidence pound yet. I have to warn you though, it's really bad. If you'll sign here, I'll let you have all of James Earl's personal items."

Catherine signed and looked at the tiny shoebox of things her son had with him.

There was his wallet, keys, and key ring with a leather tag that Sam had made for him. Some small change along with a few hundred dollars from the wallet, admission papers to Natchez Community College. All were little pieces and reminders of past, present, and future hopes that were dashed.

Jeanette had one of the officers to escort them out behind the station to a secluded parking area where the remains of her son's car lay lashed to a flatbed trailer.

Both Martin and Catherine cringed at what was left of several years of James' hard work. Martin felt queasy as he looked on the reminder of James under the hood, grinning, covered to his wrists with grime, tinkering with his "ride" to make it a little faster.

The sheriff was with an assistant who was prying small areas apart in the hopes of revealing something that might have been missed.

Catherine remembered the look on her son's face the first time he drove the car up the block and turned around and came back.

James whispered to Catherine, "Tell them to look at the brakes, I heard

313

the stocky guy, Billy, telling the deputy something about a brake job."

Prompted by James, she inched around to the drivers' side of the wreckage, which was still upside down and chained to the trailer.

"I remember the other one rocking the car from behind, maybe there is a hand print on the bumper," said James.

"Ssshh," hissed Catherine.

"Hello Howard," said Martin grimly.

"Hello Martin, Catherine.... I know how difficult this must be for you to see where your son died."

He was standing with a clipboard and taking notes on even the tiniest details.

"Have you learned anything else?" asked Martin.

"I'm only making a few notes about some details, Martin. I've turned the investigation over to a detective on loan from Jackson Mississippi. He can answer your questions better right now."

"I assumed that you were in charge of investigating this mess...," began Martin.

"Martin, I'm too emotionally involved with James and your family to have a clear head. Just between you and I.... I don't know if I could act professionally if I found who did this. Right now, we're still trying to figure out how the grave vandalisms had any connection to James Earl."

"The brakes...," whispered James again.

"Dad, what are these two lines running under the car over here?" asked Catherine.

Martin walked over and looked at the smashed brake lines and at the amount of fluid in the area. There was something else..., where the lines were crushed was in a recessed area protected by the frame itself. A pothole would have only scraped the square-tube frame of the chassis. Even rolling down the embankment wouldn't have produced that kind of damage.

"Hey Howard, did you get a look at these brake lines?" asked Martin. "This looks like it might have happened before the accident."

"I think I saw some pictures of that area of the car from the crash scene," said Howard. "The detective said the same thing."

Catherine had already walked back to the rear of the car. She looked and could see no hand prints or even much of a place to put your hands to have pushed on the car with out getting cut on all the jagged edged metal.

Blood. There was some blood on the twisted trunk lid at the rear of the car.

The car was maroon, so dried blood would have been easy to miss if you weren't looking for it.

"Sheriff? This looks like dried blood back here, I thought James was inside the vehicle," said Catherine.

The sheriff moved quickly around to the rear of the car and looked closely.

"You sure you don't want to come to work for this department?" the sheriff mumbled as he looked at blood that had run from the edge of the trunk and onto the mangled gasket inside the protected area of the trunk itself.

He turned to his assistant and told him to go bring the detective as quick as he could.

"It might be from one of the crew that hauled the car out, but I don't think so," said the sheriff.

"You what? You're pregnant?" stammered Billy. "How do you know for sure?"

"I talked to the doctor, of course," said Sallee Mae cautiously. "You're not mad are you? Please don't be mad."

"No…, No…, course not," said Billy, rubbing his stubby beard nervously.

His mind ran back to what he was told about getting another house for them. Now he understood. But how could Miss Lyda know things like this ahead of time?

Then he remembered other things too, things he was trying to force from his mind, from his last visit with "Miss Lyda".

"I just didn't expect it, that's all," said Billy. "Looks like we gonna need a bigger house."

"Do you mean it?"

"Sure I do," said Billy. "I gotta hunt for a house for somebody else too. We'll look for 'em together, okay?"

"I know exactly which neighborhood I want to look in…," said Sallee Mae.

James left his mother and grandfather with the officers and went inside the Sheriff's Office. It looked like most any other police department he'd seen, and he'd seen the inside of plenty since he was a kid. He wandered around looking at busy desks, listening to some of the conversations and then to the front desk. In walked Deputy Floyd.

"My favorite person," thought James.

Floyd walked in and dropped a few items on his desk and went for coffee.

James watched him closely, noting how strangely he was acting around his fellow officers in the surrounding room.

He mused, "I don't know exactly what you had to do with everything, but you're guilty of something. If you're friends with Billy, I intend to find out."

There had to be something he could do to shake Floyd out of his comfort zone, maybe get him to make some mistakes. With only one viable asset, James plotted his first move.

He remembered the night of the crash, how it felt lying submerged under the weight of the car, unable to move anything but his eyes. The cold, tormenting agony of the pain....

Deputy Floyd was stirring his fresh cup of coffee, with a calm preoccupied expression as he sauntered back inside his cubicle.

Waiting there on his desk was the vision of a bloated, gray, mangled corpse staring him straight in the face.

In a heart shaking instant, his coffee went airborne as he stumbled backward, one hand grabbing for support from the cubicle wall, the other reaching for his gun. The wall wobbled at his falling weight and collapsed as James faded back to nothing.

With no one as a possible witness except the clerk or the sheriff, he scrambled on the floor, still fumbling for his weapon. But after a second terrified glance there was nothing to see. He blinked his eyes furiously, willing them to give him a true recollection of the last sixty seconds.

When nobody came to his assistance, he looked around to see if there were any witnesses to his collapse. The closest person was Jeanette and from her isolated room out front she didn't hear the commotion. Thankfully the sheriff wasn't in his office, not ten feet away.

Deputy Floyd scrambled to get up from his uncomfortable state and slipped on the coffee slick floor with his hard soled, department issued shoes. He tried to scoot backwards but only skidded, looking as if he were backpedaling.

Sheepishly he surveyed the area as he sat on the floor in his puddle of coffee soup. Once his heart had begun to slow, he stood up and looked at the mess he had made.

Still nervous and shaken, he looked around the office. It was a miracle that all the other officers were too busy to pay his calamity any attention. He was even more fortunate that the loosely connected cubicles didn't domino and cause a real catastrophe. This was going to be hard to explain as it was.

"What the *hell?*" whispered Floyd, taking a deep breath.

"Yes, what the hell," echoed James from behind him.

"Aaahhhhh!" gurgled Floyd, as he spun to see who was mocking him.

There was no one there, not even in the adjacent cube. He backed up slowly so he wouldn't end up on the floor in the pool of coffee again. Feeling his way backwards, he stepped to his desk and regained the few items he'd deposited and left the building, along with the mess for someone else to find and cleanup.

He knew what he'd seen and now he was hearing things. Had he been targeted? Had he been drugged like the Mastyn kid? His only option was to give Billy a call. This kind of thing fell under his jurisdiction. He didn't need this crap.

He raced off from the station, with James riding shotgun in his front seat.

Billy and Sallee Mae passed through *Natchez Under-the-Hill* and stopped for an early morning snack to appease Sallee's anxiety. The few houses lining the waterfront neighborhoods were nested among the various and sundry businesses. Most were substandard housing, but "Miss Lyda" had told him to find something near the water and something temporary.

Back on the main road, they skipped the entrance to the bridge into Vidalia across the river and continued on south into a dreary neighborhood. It had a bleak view of the water and the tall metal structure of the bridge in the distance.

"Why are we looking around here?" asked Sallee Mae. "I don't want to live down here. This is worse than where we are right now."

"Ain't for you," said Billy calmly. "Is for somebody else I'm workin' for, so never you mind. Your turns a comin' next."

Almost noon, after circling the same neighborhoods three times, Billy found a small two bedroom house and wrote down a number to call.

Sallee Mae was angry and worn out from driving around, her patience on thin ice.

"Why do we have to find this house first?" whined Sallee Mae.

"Because I have to, that's why," said Billy. "You need to grow some patience." Billy huffed out a long tired breath and remembered his employer's instructions, "Let's go and git you something to eat so you'll feel better."

Lunch. Several phone calls and a meeting with a landlord and he had rented a house for Lyda Brown.

Deputy Floyd was losing his patience with Billy. Against his better judgment, he had gone to Billy's house and found no one home. They weren't scheduled to have any contact for a month, but he couldn't wait that long.

The more he thought of what he thought he'd seen sprawled on his desk as well as memories of the final moments of the Mastyn boy, he didn't want to take any chances.

James wanted to increase the urgency and rattle Deputy Floyd until he began to second guess himself. He'd already scared him enough to make him search out Billy's house, which confirmed to James that he knew Billy well.

He moved into the back seat and positioned himself directly in the field of vision of the rear view mirror. Concentrating, James willed his hand to scratch slowly on the back of the car seat to get the deputy's attention.

From beyond the caged barrier, Floyd looked into the rearview mirror and saw a whisper of a glimpse of cold dead eyes staring back at him. Only a glimpse and it was gone.

The deputy could feel the vibrations of fingernails raking down the cloth covered seats at his back. Floyd was now becoming visibly shaken and nervous.

With the desired effect well in progress, James moved back up in the front seat. The radio blared out a call and the deputy jumped and swerved the vehicle.

James put his hand near the receiver and the voice came out as garbled static. He wanted no interruptions of his *special* time with the deputy.

It was late afternoon as the unlikely Poole couple drove back toward the neighborhood that Sallee Mae had been arguing to look in. They drove the few miles east of town when Billy saw flashing lights then the sharp sound of a siren behind him.

"Aww, not now," said Billy. "I didn't do nothing."

Regardless, he pulled over to the side of the road with his hand resting snugly into the grip of a pistol, stuffed in the crease of the seat behind his back.

The officer walked up to window and peered in. Billy was at first relieved and then worried as he saw the expression of the officers' face.

"What can I do for you Officer?" asked Billy.

"I need you step back to my vehicle for a moment please?" Deputy Floyd requested, trying to sound official.

As soon as Billy reached the back of the squad car, the deputy began a steady stream of talk.

"Billy, I got a problem…. A big problem. I'm seeing shit. I went to work this morning and there was that Williams kid squatting on the corner of my desk, all dead and bloated and looking like he just climbed out of the river. Then when I looked again, he as gone. You have to get me some help. You might be used to this crap, but I'm not. You got to make it stop and now. I'm even seeing stuff in my car."

"Relax, take a breath," said Billy. "I'll see what I can do."

"Well do it fast, I can't handle this," said Floyd. "I been looking for you all day, couldn't find you anywhere. I don't want to end up like Mastyn."

"You're acting like some scared sissy girl. Now calm down and I'll find out what's going on. You go back to what you're supposed to do and I'll page you," said Billy.

Billy walked back to his car shaking his head, leaving Deputy Floyd standing at the rear of his car in contemplation.

"What was that all about?" asked Sallee Mae.

"Just a warning," said Billy.

Toad was idling down the levee road slowly in his new three quarter ton Chevy pickup. It was several years old, but new to Toad.

He drove down the familiar path that he and his friend used to drive together to meet with the old woman. He was getting that queasy feeling inside that he always got before a meeting with the old hag.

The trees were getting more moss laden the deeper he followed the road. The truck came to a stop next to a pine thicket and as a matter of tradition he pulled out a bottle of whiskey from behind the seat and took a slug. He felt the familiar burn and ease of his nerves as he put the lid back on.

He walked the path and was soon standing on the creaky porch.

There was no familiar greeting, ordering him to come inside. It was quiet. He knocked on the door and listened. He could hear a faint shuffling inside, but could only imagine what was making it.

He knew that he was supposed to meet her today, but didn't understand where the old woman could be. Somewhat relieved he stepped off the porch to leave.

A familiar voice halted him, hoarsely rasping words coming from inside the shanty.

"Hello?" he called out.

Against his better judgment, he went to the door and pushed it open. There on the floor was the old woman. It appeared that she had crawled in from somewhere, filthy from head to toe and had ended up where she now lay.

He carefully walked over and prodded her with a finger to see if she was alive.

She grunted and he jumped backwards, nearly wetting his pants, which wouldn't have been anything new.

"Help me up," she wheezed. "Help me to my bed."

Toad looked at how much smaller she looked since he'd seen her last. He reached down and scooped her up and carried her through her curtained door into the back room, placing her on a small cot of a bed next to the far wall.

He couldn't help but notice the array of bottles and herbs and foul smelling items on shelves and in corners.

It was too late to leave; fate also had him cornered.

He looked for something to give her to drink and remembered that when the old two-room shack was pieced together, there was no running water of any kind or a "facility" to go to.

He went to the main room and looked in her food pantry. It was stocked full and there were several gallon jugs of bottled water, which was surprising.

All the supplies must have been Billy's handiwork. Billy was always the one coming to her beck and call, kissing her hindquarters whenever she needed anything.

He quickly quit surveying her goods and carried a cup of water into her room. She had rolled over with her back against the wall, facing him. He'd never seen Miss Lyda this debilitated before. Sure…, she was old and decrepit, but he never expected the evil inside her to allow her into an invalid state such as this.

There were other changes that he didn't have time to notice when he first walked into the cabin. Her hair wasn't gray and she had a full head of it. She somehow looked a little younger, despite her withered condition. If he didn't know better, he'd say this was someone else entirely.

He handed her the water which she drank down. Her eyes weren't as glazed looking as before. Several little things were different.

"What can ah do for you?" he asked. "What happened?"

She drank down the last of the water, then took the cup and threw it across the room smashing it to pieces. It was her all right. The old was still there under this new disguise.

"Nary a thing," she scowled. "Never you mind."

"You want something to eat? Or you just want me to go?" he asked, praying she would tell him to go."Naw…, just gimme a minute," she said. "Did you bring a truck like I told you?"

"Yep, got another one, exactly like you said."

"Look in that closet and git out some boxes," she ordered. "Put all this in them boxes and carry it all out to that truck of yours. Be quick about it. We be moving to town."

There were footfalls on the porch and Toad peeped through the hanging curtain to see who it was.

"Never mind who that is!" she barked. "You git to work like I tole you!"

Billy walked in as Toad was starting to fill the first box.

"What happened to you?" asked Billy.

"Why everybody so all-fired concerned what happened to me?" she asked.

"Okay, well…, I only came by to tell ya, I got you a house rented like ya asked," said Billy. "It's right close to the waterfront, two bedrooms and a garage to put yer stuff in."

"You git your woman a place, like I told you?" she wheezed.

"No Ma'am, I ran into that cop, Floyd. He got himself a problem you should know about," said Billy. "He's seeing stuff, all scared an shit. I told him that I'd ask you about it."

Billy shut up from the glare that she was giving him. He hadn't said anything to her about her loosing most of her youthful appearance, but his eyes were surveying every change.

"He ain't seeing thangs, they real," she explained. "It be that kid y'all ran off down the levee. That relative of Syrus Earl Ames. He gonna be a problem. All them Ames' need have an accident real soon."

"That's a bunch of accidents, Ma'am," said Toad. "There's a bunch of them Ames folks."

"What you care? You load them boxes an keep your trap shut!" she yelled.

"That boy done made a mess of things," she continued. "I'm gonna take care of him. Need ya'll to help wit the rest. Now leave that stupid cop out of your talking. He done served his purpose."

"Yes 'um," said Billy.

"They wanna war, they gone git a war!" she screeched.

Chapter 49

The disgruntled younger brother of James Earl had done everything except run naked through the old house in search of something to do.

"Mom, there hasn't been anything to do here all day," whined Sam. "I've explored the entire house, looked at every old artifact and ball of dust in the whole place. Can I please go outside and do something…, anything?"

"You took care of gramma this morning. I'll see if I can get a project for you to do for me," said Catherine grinning. "Something that will keep you busy."

"Awww, not a project," said Sam. "I mean something fun to do. There's a bike in the garage, there's acres and acres of land behind here and a pond to fish in…, or the river."

"I know it's boring right now, but you need to help me with everything around here until gramma gets better," said Catherine.

"Oh, let the boy run," said Martin, walking into the living room. "I'll take care of his gramma."

"Why don't you take Sam fishing and let me take care of the house and mom?" asked Catherine. "Maybe you'll catch something big enough to fry up for supper."

"What about it, Sam? I think the cane poles are still in the attic over the garage," said Martin.

"That's way better than a project," said Sam. "Sure, sounds great."

Both men had barely stepped through the outside kitchen door when Martiel stormed in the front door carrying several bundles of deli food in her arms.

"Catherine, can I have a word with you in the kitchen?" she asked huffing through the room, while handing sacks to Catherine.

Catherine followed a few steps behind her, "I thought I told you that I'd cook tonight," said Catherine.

"I know, I know and your cooking is fine, but we have things we need to discuss this evening and this will save us time. Can you see if Martin and Maime will keep Sam occupied this evening too?" she asked, blustering with the food.

"Is there something the matter?" asked Catherine. "I haven't heard from James, have you?"

"Not today, I thought he was with you…," she said looking concerned.

"He was until around noon, then he disappeared…, well maybe that's a poor choice of words, but you know what I mean," said Catherine. "Do we need to call him?"

"No…. No…, I don't feel that anything is wrong exactly, but my senses are going crazy like something's really off. I can't put my finger on it.

"Anyway, I need to give you an update on what I've been up to. I made arrangements and had James' grave done as we agreed.

"His new coffin and remains are now covered and encased in two feet of steel reinforced concrete, down in the ground. There will be a crypt erected *above* ground by tomorrow morning, made of whitestone blocks that will have the old broken coffin inside it. If anybody messes with the one in the crypt above, we know they're still around."

"How did you get that done so fast?!" asked Catherine.

"The same way I got your parents house repaired. Money talks and construction workers walk," smiled Aunt Martiel. "Plus I stood around and watched to make sure they finished the first part before I left."

"If James isn't back to report in by sundown, I want us to get together and call him again," said Catherine.

Deputy Floyd had shown back up at the office about a quarter of five and ready to go home. He hurriedly parked the car and slipped inside to find his broken cube walls removed and only his desk and furniture remained…, in the open.

Sheriff Howard peered out his window, surprised that Floyd hadn't argued about the changes in shift hours. His chief deputy was acting far stranger than usual, raising several red flags that were beginning to worry him.

Staring at the changes of his work area, Floyd was actually relieved that there weren't any walls to close him in. He didn't want to be alone even in that small amount of confined space. There had been noises and other strange things happening all afternoon that were driving him crazy.

He put down a few cumbersome items and began hurriedly to fill out his days reports, which were very few. Even with his back turned he felt eyes watching him and spun his head. Thanks to the missing outer wall, he saw the sheriff watching him through his office window. When their eyes connected, the sheriff poked his head out and waved toward Floyd.

"In my office in five," said the sheriff.

"Ahhh crap," said Floyd, looking around at his desk.

Not wanting to drag anything else out today, he quickly got up and hurried into the Sheriff's Office.

"Yes Sir," said the Deputy Floyd. "By the way, what happened to the walls of my cube?"

Feigning innocence seemed the easiest logical thing at the moment.

"Oh, that...," said the sheriff. "I came back in and the darn thing had fallen apart. The corners were broken, so I ordered replacements. Be about a week before they get in."

Deputy Floyd tried not to look too relieved at not being blamed for the incident.

"Thanks," he said. "What did you need to see me about?"

"I want to change your duties for the next couple of weeks, Floyd. I need you to report directly to Detective Mason effective immediately; starting first thing in the morning. You'll have to check with him for your hours. Any overtime has already been approved.

"I want you to be his *go to* man until we solve the Williams murder. You have more experience with the areas involved than any other officer I have at the moment and you have a better feel of most of the locals. This could be a chance for you to shine and even..., well..., we'll see. Make me proud, deputy."

"Yes Sir," he answered, while he really meant to say, "Oh, God."

"That's all...."

The sheriff turned his back, rifling through his filing cabinet while the deputy stood thinking for a moment. His mind swam through the roster of other officers to suggest for this special assignment. Then his mind cleared. He alone was capable of throwing all suspicions into wrong directions.

"Was there something you needed to tell me Floyd?"

The sheriff was suddenly looking at him oddly. Oddly was not good, not after the kind of day he'd had.

"Uh, no sir..., and thank you sir," said Floyd.

James was glad that no one could hear him laugh. The irony of this was too much for James to contain. Floyd was obviously trying to lay low and now he was the "go to" man for the chief investigator. It was going to be a pleasure to see how Floyd handled his new responsibilities while James devised more torments.

The deputy cleared his desk and by five thirty was walking out the door; with his next weeks' schedule in his hand.

When he left the station, the first thing that rolled through his mind was food and a drink. He really needed a drink..., or two maybe.

After he turned onto Main Street, James reached over and pressed the accelerator pedal. Not a lot, barely enough for Floyd's car to pick up speed. Floyd instinctively removed his foot and placed it on the brake pedal, which James held up.

The car was slowly getting faster as if the gas pedal was stuck. James pressed a little harder..., the car moved a little faster. The traffic was relatively light but Main St. was about to dead end at the coming intersection with Canal Street, which followed the Mississippi River's edge. More gas, a little faster.

Floyd was now actively pounding the frozen brake pedal, while ignoring the scores of cars he was flying past. He came to himself and stomped at the emergency brake. Immediately, the rear tires squealed, just as James let off of the gas completely.

The two back tires locked up solid, screeching loudly and causing the car to tailspin, stopping dead in the middle of the congested intersection.

When Floyd gathered his senses, there were several cars blaring their horns and stopped mere inches away in the road around him.

His hands were trembling and his face was red from embarrassment as he popped the release for the emergency brake. Prompted by a score of angry drivers, he pulled slowly forward, testing the brakes that were now working perfectly. After getting his bearings, the car eased into a parking area and Floyd let out a huge breath of relief.

"Who's doing that!!!!??" he yelled at no one.

Unexpectedly, a deep resonating voice answered, "Do you really want to know?"

The deputy bailed out of the vehicle and stood gawking inside at the empty seats like a lunatic. Instinctively he reached for his weapon, resting on his hip, ready to use it against his vehicle. The light had changed and he quickly looked around as the traffic resumed a steady pace. He could feel the heat on his face, as if everyone passing was looking at him. Back inside the car was nothing and no one that Floyd could see. Visions of what happened to the Mastyn kid rolled through his memory, along with the guilt of his more recent actions. Could a car be possessed? Was that even possible? He'd never even heard of such a thing.

As he thrumming heart slowed, he saw a local food joint within walking distance. He didn't notice the name of the restaurant, nor did he care; he needed to think. There were people congregating inside and he wouldn't be alone.

He shut and locked the car door, forcing his wary hands to throw it shut before trotting up the street, ignoring everything in between. As soon as he brushed inside, he slipped past the "please wait to be seated" sign and found a single dark booth next to the bar. Exhaling with deliberation, he picked up a menu and stared at words he couldn't read for his delirium.

An invisible James took the seat across from him.

Hardly a moment passed before a waitress came up to him, exasperated that he had seated himself, but after noticing his uniform, she let it slide.

Before she had a chance to walk away and let him *take his time*, he ordered food and two beers. *Take his time* meant she wouldn't return for at least twenty minutes of nervous fidgeting.

His beer arrived and he slunk down into the seat trying not to think about the days events. Only a few minutes passed before a woman in a short mini and halter top sat across from him in the booth.

"Hello Officer," she said, obviously on her way to intoxication and already looking for some early business.

"I really don't want any company tonight. Maybe next time?" said Floyd.

"I haven't even introduced myself yet," she said. "I'm Candy."

"Of course you are," mumbled Floyd into his glass of beer.

Just what he needed…, a hooker and she didn't show any signs of leaving any time soon. "Look, I appreciate the offer, but I'm a police officer," he said flashing his badge as if she couldn't see his uniform.

"Cops need love too. I saw the beer and thought you might be off duty."

"Look, I'm trying to be nice here, but I really want to be alone, okay?"

James brushed his hand lightly up the woman's leg and whispered, "Maybe later".

She jumped and almost tipped Floyd's beer over into his lap.

"What's wrong with you lady?"

"ME?! Nothing's wrong with me, you weirdo."

Candy quickly slid out of the booth, staring at him as she made her way around to the other end of the bar.

Floyd was finally alone now waiting for food and wondering if the whole world had suddenly gone insane. The food arrived and the waitress started setting his plates around.

Unsatisfied with the deputy's calm retreat, James slid the palm of his hand along the waitress's upper thigh nearest the deputy. She leapt backwards dropping his salad bowl on the floor with a loud pop. "Look, that's not part of the service here," she snapped, and picked up the plastic bowl from the floor.

"I'm…, I…, I…. What did I do?" Floyd stuttered horribly. "Whatever it was I'm sorry."

He raised both palms in submission.

"Well, don't try that again or you'll be wearing your food," she warned. "I don't care if you are a cop. I *could* fill out a citizens complaint on you."

Floyd sat there eyes bulging and mouth open, not knowing what to say. The waitress turned to go and James slapped her rear with a loud smack.

She fell forward from the unexpected nudge, then spun and slapped Deputy Floyd with a hard open palm, jarring his already jumbled senses. She walked off satisfied with the glowing handprint she placed on his left cheek.

Floyd's eyes blinked with uncertainty and shock. She struck an officer of the law…, but something had caused her to come off the rails.

"What the hell?" he whispered, on the verge of anger.

The waitress and the manager huddled behind the bar giving Deputy Floyd evil glances the entire time he was burrowed into his booth eating.

Floyd kept his head down until he finished.

The manager himself brought his ticket to the table and thumped it down with a stern look and a word of silence.

Floyd paid and left the premises.

It was almost dark when he walked outside the restaurant and struck a fast pace up the street to his vehicle.

He was going home as quickly as possible, with no intentions of going anywhere he didn't have to. He only lived about three miles south of the city limits and couldn't wait to get out of *Crazytown*.

By the time he parked in his driveway, it was good dark.

James heard a calling from his family and feeling proud of the day's events he decided to give Deputy Floyd a rest, for now.

Martiel was the person responsible for ending his pleasured endeavors with Deputy Floyd. However, he had barely missed Jolie according to his Aunt Martiel and she was very disappointed. His mother had offered excuses, telling Jolie that he was following someone to get information.

"That is what you were doing, isn't it James?" asked Martiel.

"I was with Deputy Floyd all afternoon right up until you called me here. I was giving him a taste of what it feels like to think you're going crazy."

"James, just because you can, doesn't mean that you should use your abilities like the invisible man. You're losing sight of who you are. Oh, I was afraid of this," said Aunt Martiel.

"You were afraid of what? That I'd want revenge for being murdered!? Well you're right. I do want revenge. I want to make them feel how badly they screwed up my plans for a life!"

James railed on until Martiel shut off his flow.

"James if you give in to this power craze your going to lose sight of who you are and those you love. Can't you see? You already missed Jolie. She still loves you James and you barely commented when I told you she was here. Wake up James."

"I am awake and…," James suddenly got quiet.

"…not alive, James. Don't you see why Syrus Ames hid those abilities deep inside each generation? He knew that the power would corrupt whoever possessed it, because it would eventually possess them."

"I don't need another lecture," argued James. "I'm going back to my fun. I'll be back in an hour or two."

Deputy Floyd went into his house, set his alarm clock, and immediately fell across his bed for a nap, exhausted. The day's events propelled him into deep sleep and he was snoring heavily in mere moments.

James remembered the annoying ticking sound that kept him awake for days on end, driving him to madness from lack of sleep. With patient anticipation, he began ticking his fingers on the wall about the headboard of the bed where his prey slept.

A nonstop maelstrom of tap, tap, tapping, continued until Floyd stopped snoring. James could tell that he was awake, but not moving; only listening. The room had become its powdery blue in his vision which meant that it was almost pitch black in Deputy Floyd's bedroom.

Floyd turned his head slowly and listened, trying to hear where the noise was coming from. James softly bounced the bed with his hands like steps moving toward the deputy. Floyd stumbled off the bed, knocking his wind-up alarm clock from the nightstand in a desperate attempt to turn on the lamp.

Intense light glared into the deputy's night attuned irises, blinding him for a moment. Floyd withdrew his gun from the holster by his bed and feeling stupid to have a drawn a weapon in an empty room, he put it back away.

The odd noise was gone and only the whir of the air conditioner resonated throughout the small house.

He crunched onto the edge of the bed and looked at the upside down clock on the floor. He must have passed out and with no intentions of going anywhere, decided it best to call it a day. Tomorrow he was the new "go to" man. How he hated that expression now.

Roused from his deep sleep, only a shower would trick his body into sleep again. He turned on the hot water and shaved while waiting for the water to warm up. Soon after the mirror above the sink had steamed up, he lazily entered the shower. With soap on his face and chest, Floyd had almost relaxed from the tension.

James grabbed one of his ankles and pulled the attached foot a few inches across the soapy slick bottom of the tub.

Floyd instantly had soap in his eyes and was desperately trying to regain his balance, clear his eyes, and see what caused him to slip.

He wished immediately that he hadn't.

Inside the tub stood the wet mangled body of James Earl Williams. Once again he appeared in the last throes of death, deformed and bloated from the crushing torment of the wreckage.

Floyd fell against the faucets and was hard pressed against the cold slick wall. Nothing rational was coming from his mouth due to the shock of the vision.

James reached out to him…, with an imploring blank expression. Demented by the carnage of his face and head, he began his performance.

"Guilty," James bubbled, gurgling red foam as he had the moment he was plunged into the river. Then he faded away.

Deputy Floyd crawfished, attempting to climb the slick wall and make an exit. The shower rod and curtain crashed down on Floyd's head from the frantic clawing. Now blinded, with his head covered in the paisley floral sheet, he fell from the tub onto the hard tile floor, gasping for breath as he stripped away the wet sheath. Water was still streaming, steam rising, as he ran in terror back into the bedroom.

Floyd was shaking uncontrollably now and looking in the mirror, he saw the face of hysteria - *his own*.

James spoke clearly now, "Tell them what you did and I'll leave you alone."

The deputy looked around for the source of the deep voice and once again reached for his gun.

"Confess and I'll leave you alone," James repeated.

The deputy pointed the gun at a new vision of what used to be James and emptied his Colt .38 service revolver into the wall.

"I'm not telling anything!" Floyd yelled.

"Fine...," said James. "Welcome to my hell."

True to his word, James returned home an hour and a half after he had promised his Aunt Martiel. Even when hard pressed he would not reveal his methods to get information from the deputy and omitted the fact that he was trying to get him to confess.

Catherine talked endlessly to him about right and wrong, reminding him of the summers he spent with his grandparents going to church, of his friend Granny Smith who spent hours instilling forgiveness and higher values in him.

James had already turned a deaf ear and was plotting his next expedition in terror, but after practicing his newfound revenge on Deputy Floyd, he had a different victim in mind.

Chapter 50

Pastor Milton, the younger version, was seated in his study memorizing his Sunday sermon, heavily laced with humility, servitude, and giving. All was quiet, no telephone ringing or outside interference at the late evening hour.

Thursdays were already his favorite night of the week, but after all the pain with the funeral, it was especially placid for him.

James came into the church through the sanctuary. There again was the unusual warm glow of light radiating throughout the room.

He passed through and sat on the front pew for a few moments. Looking up at the front of the church and remembering the earnest words of Catherine prior to leaving for this new destination.

He entered into the pastor's study much later, not realizing how long he spent in the sanctuary contemplating his tactics.

The pastor had finally put away his notes and was stretched in a recliner watching the end of the news on television. The small TV rested on top of a cabinet near the corner of the room allowing him to sit back in the recliner and relax.

The station blurred out for a moment and the face of James Earl, somber and gray, looked out on the pastor.

Pastor Milton readjusted his eyes and looked at the screen.

The visage of James spoke a garbled, "If you want to meet with the pastor, you have to fill out a card and get in line. Of course if the pastor is too busy with his neighbor's wife, he probably won't have time for you."

The TV screen blinked and was back to the local weather forecast. Milton looked at the screen in unbelief.

"That looked like that Williams kid," he said aloud.

He eased up from the recliner, walked over to the TV, and switched the channel to late night laughter.

He retrieved a cola from his refrigerator and sat back down. He was planning to stay up a little later than usual to have some private time.

The screen blinked once more revealing the same pale gray face of James Earl. A gravelly imitation of his own voice blared from the speaker, "That Ames family thinks they run this church. They should be put in their place."

The face of Archie Bunker blinked back on the screen yelling at his slow witted son-in-law.

Pastor Milton jumped up from his chair and looked out the window. He had heard about people capable of doing stuff like that to a television.

"Who's doing that!" he said loudly.

The telephone rang and he jumped around, staring at it for a moment. It rang a second time. Still he stared. The third ring was the charm that broke his fixation. He hurriedly walked over and answered it.

"Oh, hello, it's you," he said.

"Of course I'm happy it's you…."

"I don't know if it's a good night to come over…."

"Okay…, Okay fine. I'll be up late anyway…."

As he hung up the phone, the TV blinked again.

Superimposed over Archie Bunkers mouth movements were the words, "Adultery can be bad for your health."

"Who are you?" he asked again, gritting his teeth. "Show yourself."

"Oh, you don't want me to do that," the image quickly answered.

"Who are you?" he asked again, this time far more timidly.

"It's not God or the tooth fairy," said James. "That's your only clue."

Pastor Milton jumped over and grabbed his bible from his desk and shook it at the air, then at the image on the television, "Be gone spirit!"

"Not until I'm through with you," said James. It took all his restraint to remain in the realm of the unseen as he snatched the Bible from Milton's hand and placed it on a table.

"That's not a toy. Don't wave it around like a dishrag."

The pastor looked at his empty hand, wondering if he'd somehow dropped the limply bound black book.

"If you're not God…, who…, what are you?" asked Pastor Milton.

"Someone that asked for help, someone that you should have helped…. People need to know who you really are."

There was a long silence as Milton tried to sift through the long list of people he'd manipulated over the last several years. He shook his head; the list was too long and convoluted. He was beginning to feel foolish for falling for this pranksters trick.

"Ha!" said Milton in mock laughter. "You can't even show your face. How do you intend to expose me?"

"I warned you that you didn't want that. Don't tempt me again."

"Go away and leave me alone," he groaned, his eyes fixed on the wispy face on the television. "I don't scare easily."

"I know a secret," said James. "Something you don't know…, yet."

"You don't know Jack," spat the pastor.

"Fine, I'll let you find out the hard way."

There was over five minutes of complete uncomfortable silence as Milton was left standing maniacally in front of his hissing television set. Finally, he gave up, waiting for yet another odd manifestation. Even the smartest prankster fouled up and made some sort of mistake. Then he'd know who was behind this ruse.

The little black and white TV was now blaring some nonsensical commentary and he turned it off.

There was a knock on the door, followed by a muffled familiar voice, "Oh, Pastor Milton…, are you awake? Hey, Baby."

He hurried over to the door and opened it and Sallee Mae walked inside.

"You shouldn't be here tonight," said Milton. He was actually thankful for the company, yet terrified at the coincidence of her sudden appearance.

"You don't want me here?" she asked, almost pouting. "Since when don't you want *me* here?"

"It's been a really busy week and…."

Sallee Mae cut him short with a deep kiss and tight body hug that he couldn't ignore.

It had been quiet for long enough. The voice had to be some neighborhood kid that had rigged a homemade transmitter, or maybe it was only a dream and he had fallen asleep in front of the TV. He began to believe his own lies and relaxed to her insistent advances. Her kiss melted his fears and soon he returned it with his own and their hands began to grope.

"Wait a second," said Sallee Mae, as she gently pushed at his chest and whispered up at him. "I have some good news for you."

Sallee took a breath, still holding him close. She took both his hands in hers and placed them on her stomach.

"Guess what? I'm pregnant!" she exclaimed. "We did it!"

Pastor Milton jumped back and stared at her, "You're…, You're what? You're pregnant? How? I thought you were on the pill…."

Sallee Mae looked as if he had slapped her. She turned her back and sadness welled in her eyes at his reaction.

"I thought you'd be glad. You of all people. I thought you'd be…," she cooed.

"You're sure it's ours?" he asked. "Not your husbands?"

"Pretty sure," she said. "The odds are about five to one," she giggled childishly.

"Billy and I were trying for a year since…, well, before you and me…."

Sallee Mae Poole quickly altered her story when she remembered that Milton didn't know about the miscarriage of her first child.

"We been together since you came here…. I figured it was mine and yours…."

"What do you want me to do?" he asked cautiously.

"OH! Is that what you're worried about? I don't want nothing, I just wanted a baby. Truth is…, I don't know if Billy and I would have ever got pregnant together."

"You only wanted me to get you pregnant!" he said, trying to rationalize the situation. She was as crazy as she was insatiable.

"Well…, and the sex. Billy can't hold a candle to you," she said pulling him close to her again. "And now that I'm pregnant…."

She led him by the hand pulling him into his bedroom….

James entered Deputy Floyd's dark house again just after two o'clock in the morning. There were several beer bottles on the night stand, most of them empty and his alarm clock was still upside down against the wall, ticking away noisily.

Floyd had finally passed out either from exhaustion or alcohol while trying to deaden the effects of some poison he'd ingested from dealing with the Mastyn kid. It was the only rational explanation to the vivid hallucinations he'd endured that day.

He hoped this *bad trip* wore off before morning or he was going to report himself incapacitated and try to explain his theory to the sheriff without implicating himself. After all, the sheriff had witnessed him digging around in that truck the Mastyn kid was driving. Who knew it was contaminated with the same thing that…, killed the kid. Surely that would be good for some time off and excuse him from his new duties with Detective Mason.

To James, the deputy resembled nothing more than a drunk that had passed out. One dim light was still on in his bedroom, sharing its glow with the adjoining bathroom. Sleeping beauty needed a wake up call. James had another chore scheduled for tonight and needed to hurry this one up. He sat on the bed next to Floyd and played childish games with his face to try and wake him up, to no avail.

"Floyd," said James, into the deputy's ear.

"Huh? What do you want?" he asked groggily.

"Wake up. I need to know what your decision is."

"I'll file that report in the morning…," said Floyd, dreaming of some work effort.

"This isn't working," said James.

More and more comfortable with his physical abilities, James grasped one of the half-full bottles of beer and poured it on the deputy's face.

Floyd spat and jumped up off the bed, then tripped and rolled onto the floor; his heart fighting against the nearby cage of ribs.

"Wake up sleepy head. We need to talk."

"Not you again, ahhh nawww," he slurred his words.

"I need to know what you decided," said James. "Are you going to confess?"

"To what? To helping rid the world of a worthless little brat?! I'm not confessing to anything."

Even in this drunken stupor he was considering that this apparition wasn't something drug induced, but he had another plan all the same. If this really was that Williams kid's ghost, then Billy's *associates* could surely make it go away.

"Besides, I've got help that's going to make you go back to wherever you came from," he added cautiously.

Was this deputy somehow in league with the nightmarish witch woman? Was she somehow still alive?

"Be careful which side you choose Floyd."

Floyd stood on wobbly legs with a grin on his face. He'd rattled this thing, this specter or ghost.

"I've seen both sides. I have a pretty good feeling you'll lose."

Floyd did know about something about his adversary. If only he could read this man's mind.

"Tomorrow is going to be interesting for you, Deputy Floyd."

James saw that the lights were finally out in the parsonage of the Holiness Cathedral Church. This challenge had become a matter of pride for his family, even if the pastor wasn't involved in his murder.

Everything was becoming a matter of escalating revenge, but James was blinded by the escalating events. Now, James Earl had to visit this one last time, despite Catherine's warnings.

The naked, snoring body of Pastor Milton was almost more than he could endure. After a few quick adjustments to the bedroom, he scratched the walls until the pastor woke up.

"Sallee? What are you doing back?" he asked. "You decide to spend the night?"

"Well if it isn't the proud papa," said James.

Milton quickly sat up in his bed but couldn't see anything.

A gentle street lamp outside combined with the rising moon cast dim shadows through the curtains in his room. The quiet steady hum of the central air clicked off and left the parsonage in a sudden perfect quiet.

Milton could hear footsteps walking closer to the bed in the black of the room.

"I'm here," James whispered into the room, his voice echoing. The pastor reached for the lamp next to his bed, to turn on the light. It only clicked loudly, but offered no light.

"Did you like my secret?"

"Nothing I can't handle," said the pastor covering his naked body with the sheets. "Who are you?"

The faint voice of James Earl whispered once more.

"I have another surprise that's even better."

"I don't care," Milton said, looking around in the dark for the source of the voice.

Arnie Milton's voice was the slightest bit shaky. Talking to some unseen host was finally getting to him.

James laughed softly, "You will."

"Why don't you leave me alone!?" begged the pastor. "I haven't done anything worse than the rest of this bunch."

"When you confess your sins to the church," said James.

"So that's what you want?" he asked. "I'm no worse than half the members. If you only knew half the mess these people were in."

James reflected on this statement for several seconds. Milton was probably right. Churchgoers or not, they were all human.

"You lead, they follow," whispered James. "Isn't that your job?"

"No, I won't do it," he balked. "You can't do anything. You're only some spook or something, that's all."

"I wonder what Billy Poole would think if he knew," said James. "I promise he'll listen."

Sallee Mae had made it clear when the opportunity had first arisen with Milton, Billy wasn't the forgiving kind.

"No..., uh, no..., let's be reasonable here," he said spinning around in twisted sheets, still looking for the source of the voice.

"Confess," whispered James from another section of the room. "It's as simple as that. I'll leave you alone."

The pastor spun back in the other direction toward the voice.

"If I confess..., t...to the board..., and, and tell them I'm sorry, that it won't happen again, that it was a moment of weakness..., will you leave me alone?"

"Confess to what?" asked James in a monotone voice.

"Of the affair..., of..., what do you want me to confess?" he asked.

"Of being a fake, a snake oil salesman, an actor," hissed James.

"I can't do that! I need the job. I...," he replied.

James yelled into the emptiness of the house, "I'm tired of bartering with you! Don't you understand I'm not asking?"

In a sudden surprised rage, James lifted the bed the pastor was in and dropped it back down on the floor with a boom.

"You're going to lose your salary anyway," taunted James.

"What? How do you know that?" he asked, more terrified of losing his income than his good name.

"That family you degraded at the funeral...," began James.

"That Ames bunch? What about them? They're working trash like everybody else. They don't own this place," he barked. "I was trying to offend them, they need to leave. Why do you care?"

"They..., pay..., your..., salary..., entirely and always have," James said tiredly.

Arnie Milton laughed into the room, "Nonsense, the old man can't even afford a new suit."

Rage filled and tired, James Earl moved into the faint light coming through the window, his emotion causing him to appear. The wrecked and mangled corpse of his death wisped into clear view, giving Milton something fresh to consider.

Pastor Milton slid all the way up to the headboard of the bed and hit the wall with a slam.

"You're..., you're..., that kid..., that dead kid..., the one we just buried," he said, his voice huffing and squeaking.

His voice an unmetered blast, James Earl abandoned all restraint, yelling into the face of Pastor Milton.

"You've offended my family and you've offended me!"

"No...! Stay..., stay back..., get back.... Noooooooooooooooo!!!!!!!!"

Chapter 51

"Have you heard from Robert?" asked Maime Ames.

"He hasn't called," said Catherine. "I don't think he will."

"Well, if you ask me, you're better off," said Aunt Martiel.

"Don't say that where Sam might hear," said Maime.

"Oh, don't worry about that. Sam and Martin were up at the crack of dawn, cane poles in their hand, and headed to the back pond," said Aunt Martiel.

"I'm so glad. It'll be good for the both of them to get to bond," said Catherine. "Especially since he doesn't have James around anymore."

"Your daddy's really missing James Earl," said Maime. "He's closing up the garage you know. Said he can still see James working in there and cutting up with him and the "domino kings". It's too much on him."

Catherine and Martiel both gave each other quick glances at the mention of him "seeing" James, but quickly realized what she meant.

"He wants to sell the house over on Washington too. And so do I...," said Maime.

"How is your arm this morning, mom?" asked Catherine.

"It's much better. It throbs a little, but I can do everything I could before that...," she said becoming quiet, "the accident."

"Do you want to talk about what happened?" asked Aunt Martiel.

Maime Ames' face grew dark and distant. She shook her head "no" slowly.

"You need to get that old left arm back in shape soon. I for one, would like to have some of those wonderful buttermilk biscuits you make!" Aunt Martiel said cheerfully.

"I have another doctors' appointment today," she said. "I hope he'll let me get rid of this sling."

Sam burst through the door, dripping wet from head to toe.

"Somebody, help...," he said gasping for air. "It's grampa...."

Three officers were in the little makeshift corner office with Detective Mason standing near the chalkboard, waiting on a late arrival. Deputy Floyd walked in looking as if he'd been dragged through town behind a car.

The detective observed him strangely as he walked in.

"Okay, now that we're all here," he said glancing back toward Floyd. "I want us all to start from the beginning. If we follow this timeline of events and tie in all the little details, something will show up. We're missing something so completely; this ought to make it show up. I want each and every one of us to brainstorm all of the events together."

"First of all, here are the three names of graves that were robbed from both of the cemeteries."

Syrus Earl Ames
Captain Benjamin Morrison
Ellie Rosalie

"I need a volunteer to spend some time and see how they might be related," pointing to one of the officers.

"See if you can link them together somehow, by date, family, historical records. This is probably a stretch, but unfortunately Natchez has made the AP news along with a gang in New York that was just caught robbing graves and selling the bones to *Satanic Cults*."

Everyone in the room looked at him as if he'd fallen from the sky.

"Treat it as an angle so that we can be prepared in case someone asks. I *do not* want to start a witch hunt, but I don't want to leave any stone unturned.

"We don't want to be labeled with that kind of sensationalism so the sooner we rule it out the better. At all times gentlemen, keep an open mind. This isn't going to go away. I was just informed that the governor has the state police and the FBI watching what we do with this case. The Mastyn kid that died here in the jail crossed state lines in the commission of a felony which gives them the right to take lead, but they would rather play it down and let us handle it. People all over town are already spooked about this type of stuff and I can't say that I blame them."

The sheriff walked in the door and motioned the detective over to speak with him. After a few moments, he stuck his head back in the room.

"Why don't you men take a quick break and we'll meet back here in…, ten minutes, Okay?" said the detective.

Everyone filed out of the office and merged at the coffee pot and vending machines.

Floyd went to the restroom and splashed cold water over his face for the umpteenth time to clear the cobwebs. What a crazy night, hearing voices and seeing things. He had an entire wall full of bullet holes to repair as soon as he got home to show for it. If it hadn't been for the alcohol, he probably wouldn't have slept a wink, despite the slight hangover.

He got some coffee and walked back into the meeting. Floyd was the first to get back and sat in the front row, pouring down the hot coffee.

Suddenly there was the annoying sound of chalk scratching on the wallboard. It was moving by itself, which alone scared him fully awake, but when it finished, it read:

"ASK DEPUTY FLOYD ABOUT BILLY POOLE."

"No...," whispered Floyd to himself and jumped up to the board.

He quickly found an eraser and wiped out the incriminating text.

As he was erasing, the chalk began writing the same thing back as he had erased. He swatted the floating chalk with the eraser and it fell and broke on the floor into powdered pieces.

Floyd was still erasing the board when the Detective Mason entered the room.

"Have some ideas?"

"Uh..., yeah, but it..., didn't make sense after I thought about it, so I..., was clearing it off," said Deputy Floyd.

"Oh God...," Floyd thought, as he walked back and sat down, wondering if the chalk was going to repeat the performance.

Mason was watching Floyd carefully now, but nodding.

"Any ideas are appreciated, deputy. The sheriff says you should have a lot to offer in the way of local information."

"Confess," whispered James. "It's good for the soul."

Floyd shook all over spilling a little of his coffee on the floor, hoping no one would notice.

The room quickly filled but before they could resume, there was chatter and laughter among the officers.

"Man that guy is so lost."

"Do they know who he is yet?"

"Where did they find him?"

"Wrapped in a sheet, walking down the railroad tracks toward town."

"He doesn't belong here. They need to take him to the county home."

"Did you hear all that babble?"

"He was non-stop confessing his lifes story."

"Did you hear what he said about his last year in school?"

"Yeah, and taking candy from "Bobs Grocery" wherever that is."

"Who do you think Billy is?"

"I don't know but if he ever finds out that this guy got his wife knocked up...."

There was a round of laughter.

"What was her name...? Sallee something...."

"Oh and...,"

Deputy Floyd stiffened when he heard the names, Billy and Sallee in the same sentence.

"Who was this?" asked Floyd to the group.

"Some guy found wandering into town wearing nothing but a sheet."

"They just brought him in, you missed it."

Another round of laughter vibrated the air.

Floyd sat frozen, oblivious to the remainder of the comments.

"Okay that was your comic relief for the day gentlemen. Can we get back to business?"

Detective Mason barked at the group and didn't wait for them to settle before he continued.

"So the first thing will be a historical search. I need one of you to follow up on some new evidence that has been introduced. We have a clear fingerprint and a blood sample. The fingerprint was found beside the crushed brake lines near the frame..., here," he said pointing to a picture he'd just tacked to a corkboard.

"We need to do a search in the state and national crime database for matching prints. I went back to the crime scene and found two deep embedded footprints behind the car in the soil between the rocks. The footprints themselves are useless to match anything to except for the shoe size, but they still tell a tale. They were buried deep which means that the person was heavy set or he was lifting something big, like that car.

The Williams boy's family came by the other morning and noticed bloodstains on the back of the vehicle in the same approximate location that the footprints were pressed into the mud.

"I need someone to follow up and make sure that none of the emergency crew or members of the fishing boat that found the wreckage cut their hands, or stood around the back of the vehicle.

"If we can eliminate all of the workers, we might have our first solid lead and a positive blood sample of the suspect.

"People, listen up. I want your input first thing in the morning on the graves, the fingerprint analysis, and interviews with all the rescue crew members. Money is no object on this case.

"The Ames family has offered an open check for funding anything that is outside our budget to catch the murder or murderers. You will need to do the usual requisition and approval through me before spending, but it means that we won't have the usual red tape to get something rolling quickly. So if anything immediate comes to mind, bring it to me as soon as we're through here."

Floyd felt his heart beating so loudly that he could hear it pounding in his ears. His right arm was tingling all the way to his shoulder and his neck hurting. He quickly guzzled the last of the coffee in his cup, burning his throat.

"It would have been easier if you had confessed," whispered James. "It's too late now."

"What's wrong? What happened?" the three women asked in concert. "Its grampa, you need to..., you need to..., come and help me," said Sam, gasping for air.

Catherine ran on ahead with Sam, with Martiel scanning the area cautiously and bringing up the rear.

When they were in clear sight of the pond, there sat Martin Ames, his rear in the mud and feet dangling in the water.

"Grampa, I brought help. Are you okay?"

Martin was holding his head while spiting and coughing out residue of mud and water instead of answering them.

Aunt Martiel caught up with them and saw her brother sunk in the muddy pond.

"Grampa sent me over to that gully to dig us some more worms for fishing. I heard a big splash and when I got here, he was floating on the water," said Sam.

"He pulled me out," said Martin, still sputtering. "I would have drowned. I was standing right over there...," he said while pointing. "I had just hooked a nice little fish, when I heard running up the boardwalk behind me and I thought it was Sam coming to see. The next thing I knew I was dodging a club and someone pushed me in the back, off into the pond. Either he hit me or I hit my head on the bottom."

"Wait..., someone tried to hit you and pushed you into the pond?" spat Aunt Martiel. "Show me, show us."

Martin shook his head in aggravation, trying unsuccessfully to stand out of the sucking mud of the bank.

"Sam will you show them? I'm kind of stuck here..., could somebody help me up?"

"That's not a good idea. Whoever did it could still be out there in the brush somewhere."

Suddenly they all felt potential eyes watching them from every direction.

"Aunt Martiel, will you go call the sheriff? Tell them that we have an intruder, but stay out in the open where I can see you. Sam, help me get your grampa up to the house."

She looked at Aunt Martiel and whispered, "Where is James when we need him?"

A pair of eyes was indeed watching and learning how the Ames reacted to the situation; upset over the hours spent stalking their movements, and that the first attempt on their lives was fruitless. At least he'd accomplished one objective without anyone seeing where he came from or where he went. As they disappeared toward the front of the old house, the intruder finally retreated into the miles of untamed backwoods at the rear of the Ames property.

Chapter 52

Sheriff Howard and several officers were combing the area and Detective Mason had interview Martin and Sam before joining the group. Only Martin Earl had actually caught a fleeting glimpse of his attacker and there were a lot of tall fresh reeds on that side of the pond where they were fishing.

It would be easy to hide and not be seen or heard, especially for someone familiar to navigating outdoors or hunting.

The sheriff had heard the call come through and relayed the information to the Detective. They both agreed that it sounded as if it could be related and they responded as quickly as they could. Most of their unofficial task force was present; all except Deputy Floyd who had left for the day because of *personal reasons.*

The Ames family sat on the front porch reasoning through why someone would be interested in attacking Martin.

What could they possibly be after?

James Earl was dead, wasn't that enough? Then there was the tactics they were using, no gun or knife, but a simple elemental club for a weapon using stealth and surprise. If they had succeeded, Martin Earl's demise might have even looked accidental. An older man tripped on a loose board along their little pier and hit his head on the bottom of their pond.

Martin huddled alone with an old blanket wrapped around him, dried mud still stuck in his thick salt and pepper hair. He had a bruise on his forehead, of debatable origin.

"Good thing you made a big splash or I wouldn't have heard you," said Sam.

"I'm really glad you can swim. I'd still be bottom up in the pond if you hadn't jumped in when you did."

"When I heard the splash, I thought you caught a whopper of a fish," said Sam. "I never thought I'd see you out in the water."

The older man grinned at his grandson, "I bet the one I caught is still dragging my cane pole around the pond."

Sheriff Howard walked back up to the porch and sat down close to Martin.

"Hello sheriff," said Aunt Martiel. "I suppose I should apologize for my behavior the last time you were here. I wasn't myself, you understand. I was up all night and…."

"Please…, don't worry about explanations. I don't know what I would have done under the same circumstances."

The sheriff turned to Mr. Ames, "I've been talking to the Detective and we agree that there is the possibility…, well…, probability…. We both believe that whoever pushed you in the pond was related somehow to whoever killed your grandson. Now that is only speculation at this point, but we have to treat it as a genuine threat."

"You mean the creep that killed James has been watching our house?" asked Sam. "Great, we've made some kind of hit list."

Sheriff Howard grinned slightly, shaking his head, "Let's not get too imaginative young man, however we do need to discuss any family grievances or any incidents over the last few months or even longer if necessary.

"People don't usually target a family without some kind of motive. It could be money, somebody that felt wronged from your business, or even something as simple as a disagreement.

"Most crimes that involve murder or attempted murder are crimes of passion or greed. So you talk it over with your family here and if you can come up with even a few names, it would give us a good head start.

"Now let's talk about your protection. We'll have someone come by at odd times and stay close to this area. It's not like you're next door, you really are out of the way. That really bothers me the most.

"Is there any way that you can go back to your other house on Washington Street?"

Martin Ames explained that the house was still unlivable until the contractor and his crew of workers completed their repairs.

The Detective walked up, listening to the last of their conversation before he spoke to Sheriff Howard.

"We didn't find anything other than a few broken twigs of a trail. We believe that whoever attacked you thought that you'd drown before anyone could pull you out. You're really lucky to have a grandson that's a fast swimmer and saw you in time or…, well…, I won't try to draw any conclusions. Let's be thankful he did."

"What if someone breaks in during the night?" asked Martin.

"Do you have a weapon, a gun of some kind?" asked the sheriff.

"I have an old shotgun somewhere," said Martin. "I don't know if I have any shells for it though."

"I was hoping you might have something you were used to using," argued the sheriff.

"I do," said Martiel. "I have a pistol."

"You what?" asked Martin. "When did you get a gun?"

"I've had it for years. With all the traveling I do. Don't worry Martin, I have a permit for it."

"What kind is it?" asked the sheriff.

"It's a .25 caliber something," said Aunt Martiel.

"That's a cap pistol, get a .38, they make small ones for ladies and please…, throw that thing away."

The sheriff looked over at Martin. "You realize this is off the record. I really can't advise you about this. I'm only telling you what I would do if it were me or my family. Get some shells for your shotgun, don't take any chances."

"I don't like the thought of having to use a gun on another human being," said Martin.

Sheriff Howard nodded thoughtfully, "That's good. But remember, whoever this is wasn't shy about killing your grandson or showing up here in broad daylight to try and kill you. I don't want to get a call reporting a homicide from you or any of your family."

"You made your point. I've got to take Maime into town for her doctors' appointment this afternoon. I'll pick up some shells or maybe even look at something new," said Martin. "I never thought I'd see the day that I would need a gun for anything but bird hunting."

Deputy Floyd unwillingly spent the rest of the day with James. He had left early feigning sickness and ended up back at his house looking for a beer to end the day's misery. Unfortunately, he had cleaned out all his stock of alcoholic beverages the night before.

Floyd tried to call Billy several times and there was no answer on his telephone. Billy Poole promised that he would page him when he found out something, but never did, adding to a long list of unfortunate circumstances.

Everywhere Floyd turned James was there taunting him into a frenzy.

This unseen voice was coming from all around him, sometimes entering his thoughts as if they were his own.

"How long do you think it will be before they match your fingerprints with the ones near the brake lines? It's only a matter of time. I won't have to do anything but sit back and laugh."

"They won't find me!"

Floyd had resorted to railing into the air like a lunatic.

"I'm not in the crime database…, so, HA! What do you think about that?"

"Maybe a little bird will point them in the right direction. Maybe somebody will tell your friend Billy that you're going to talk and you'll end up like that Mastyn boy. Oh, yeah, I've listened in. I heard how he died. Do you remember? I understand you were there watching. How did it feel seeing a kid betrayed like some stray dog by his master? What makes you think they won't dump you in the trash too? Wasn't a pretty picture was it? As a matter of fact I could do worse to you if I wanted, but I'm not a murderer like you."

James continued in a stream of guilt laden pleasures, pushing at Floyd's mind, not allowing him any time to do anything other than listen.

"You can't do squat!" laughed the deputy. "I'll bet you can't…."

He began waving his hands in the air as if to fight off an invisible enemy, grunting with each swipe in the direction of the voice tormenting him.

A lingering memory floated in. One of James' last few hours outside the Hospital Emergency room, swinging his fists into the air in a final desperate attempt before his life's flame was doused.

James placed his hand near the chest of the deputy and felt it growing colder and colder as he pressed it into his chest.

Floyd stopped his acrobatics and grabbed his chest, his eyes bulged as he felt his heart thump, thumping from the ice cold that was gripping him from inside.

The cold inside his chest ached and he struggled to breathe. Every breath was labored and as he wheezed, he noticed his own breath escaping in a cold vapor, spewing from his mouth.

James removed his hand and Floyd shivered uncontrollably crumpling to the floor, "You're right, deputy. I can't do anything."

James Earl left him curled up on the floor sobbing and rubbing his arms.

"Where have you been?" asked Catherine. "We really could have used your help today. Someone attacked your grampa today at the pond."

James sank inside as he listened to the rants of Catherine and Martiel.

"Exactly what were you doing all day today?" she asked.

"I was trying to talk the deputy into confessing to his part," said James.

"I'll bet you were," said Martiel. "But would it be too much to ask of you to stay close for awhile, to make sure we don't have another day like today?"

"You act like it's my fault that this happened. I didn't ask for any of this. I wish I'd never come down here this summer. I might still be alive instead of…, of whatever this is I am now. Besides, I can't be in more than one place at a time."

"You're right," said Catherine. "I'm sorry James, but we came so close to another loss in the family. Don't you think that it scared us?"

"She's right," confessed Martiel. "I'm sorry James."

It was the first time he'd heard Martiel apologize for anything deliberately sarcastic. She had to be at the end of her rope.

"All right, I guess I can leave Deputy Floyd alone for a day or two," said James.

Fulfilling her promise to keep up a daily communication, Jolie and BeBe arrived at the Ames estate that afternoon. Catherine greeted them at the door and ushered them into their living room.

Catherine's parents and Sam had gone with Martiel into town for Maime's doctor visit, to make some unusual purchases and also to place a "For Sale" sign on their home on Washington Street.

Jolie and BeBe sat on the couch side by side in some kind of odd expectancy. BeBe looked around anxiously and Jolie was a little fidgety herself.

"Thank you both for coming," said Catherine, taking a seat in the chair nearest them. "Can I get you anything?"

BeBe skipped answering and jumped to what was on her mind.

"Something has changed," said BeBe. "I can't exactly say what it is, but there is a different presence here in the house."

Jolie quickly agreed, rubbing her arms. This didn't feel like James.

"That's what it is. It's the same as it was the last time, but, I don't know how to say it. It's stronger, I think…. Yeah, stronger."

"You're right," said Catherine. "It's James, only…."

"Maybe I should explain," said James. "If I can…, I'm not sure myself how to explain, except to show you."

BeBe jumped a little and snapped in the direction of his voice.

"We can all hear you?" whispered BeBe, looking at Catherine and Jolie.

"Yeah, that's what I was going to try to explain, but it's probably easier if James does," said Catherine.

James manifested himself sitting on the ottoman in front of them. They both inhaled sharply as he appeared.

"I had an encounter with the person that was responsible for killing me and it's changed me somehow. It was some old woman, trying to do black magic of some kind. I'd never even heard of anything like this before I saw it myself. I thought all this was only somebody's twisted imagination. Now it's as if I'm living some horror. Everything has gone crazy and nothing makes sense.

"I was able to resist her…, don't ask me how. All I know is that I fought back and got away from her.

"BeBe, you remember when the *Mambo*… or maybe it was *Dominique*… told me that I'd have to break the jar or pot. That's what I did. I broke it. There was a jar filled with all my relatives' spirits and all of them that were trapped went free. But somehow, I'm still here. I didn't get to go."

His voice seemed sad as he finished his short explanation. After a few moments of silence he continued.

"But now, I'm different. I can do things, hear things, go places, in the real world where you are…," he said quietly.

He reached out and touched Jolie on the hand and she took his, feeling his warmth radiating from this strange body.

"I can feel you, James!" said Jolie excitedly.

"Only when I touch you. I can feel you too, but it's different somehow, Jolie. It's something that I'd rather not try to describe for now. It's only one way, I can touch others but I can't be touched."

"Did you destroy her?" asked BeBe anxiously. "Did she die?"

"I don't know," said James. "She wasn't moving..., she fell to the ground after it was over. I couldn't tell. I was so glad that it was over."

BeBe looked at Jolie nervously with a quiver of the head.

"But at least now I can do things in the real world," James said excitedly.

"James, you are in the real world," said BeBe. "Where the living are is the temporary one. Don't ever forget that. Where you are is the permanent, real world. Everything comes from the spirit world. Just please remember not to corrupt yourself before you have the opportunity to move on."

"What do you mean, corrupt?" asked James.

"You must not use your new power to harm or do anything that is evil," she said. "You could be trapped where you are for...."

BeBe hushed suddenly as James lowered his head. All three could see the expression on his face fall cold.

"James? What have you done?" asked Catherine.

"I.... I've been trying to set things right. I didn't know. How was I supposed to know?" he raised his voice, looking from one to the other. "I don't know the rules here!"

"What did you do James?" asked BeBe, as calmly as she could.

Jolie stared at him in teary eyed silence.

"Oh..., I see how it is.... All of you are against me too!" said James. "You're safe and alive. I'm in this..., this damn dead place! Well if that's the way it is and I'm really stuck here, it doesn't matter any more does it? I can do whatever I want and it doesn't make a...," James stopped.

He saw the shock on Jolie's face and the tears on her cheeks.

"I..., I'm so, so sorry," he said. "I never meant to..., please..., wait...."

Jolie jumped up and ran outside the house onto the porch looking for some place of solitude.

Catherine's jaw fell slack and open, looking at the spectacle that was once her son. Her face was becoming pale and drawn.

"Mom, why are you looking at me like that?" asked James. "I'm still your son."

Catherine looked over at BeBe who was already hurrying to check on Jolie. James fled the room in a blustering exit. Chilled wind followed him, shaking the light fixtures gently to and fro. There was no telltale direction, only dread of what he might do next.

Catherine and BeBe sat on either side of Jolie, on the front steps. Catherine couldn't remember a time in her life when so much happened in a single day. Their lives had irrefutably changed by all that was happening.

Almost as if each circumstance was carefully planned, to keep them off balance and reacting to several things at once. Nevertheless, there didn't seem to be any way to stop the madness.

BeBe broke the silence that had descended on them like the evening darkness.

"Catherine, if James didn't destroy the evil, then it will try again," she warned.

Catherine shook her head dismally, "It's already tried again, today."

She went on to describe the near death experience of her father and how the perpetrator managed to disappear into thin air. BeBe listened closely and carefully, taking note of how disturbed and unequipped Catherine was for something of this nature. It was too late to distance themselves from the curses falling on the Ames family. The only thing left to do, the safest place to be was as close as possible.

"We want to help," said BeBe. "Would you mind if we stay?"

"You know that you are more than welcome to stay here for any reason, but are you sure it's safe to be here with..., Jolie?"

BeBe leaned against Catherine's shoulder in a deep sigh, "James needs our help. I don't know how quite yet, but we have to help him, even if he doesn't want our help."

"We have plenty of room," said Catherine. "I can guarantee that everyone will be happy to have you."

Chapter 53

The carload of Ames family members pressed through the front door carrying groceries and several boxed items.

Maime Ames had her arm in a much smaller sling and was excited to show Catherine that she was not only able to move her arm, but the doctor had encouraged her to do limited exercise each day.

"Look, mom!" said Sam bolting through the door. "Look what grampa got."

Martin Ames was pushing through the door with two long boxes in his arms. Sam sat down the heavy sack of groceries that he had been carrying and took one of the heavy boxes from his grampa's arms.

"I thought it was time to get something for the boy and I," said Martin. "I hope you don't care."

"That depends on what it is," said Catherine.

"Look, mom," said Sam as he opened the long box labeled *Remington* revealing a shotgun of some variety.

"Dad, you know how I feel about guns," said Catherine. "I don't think it's a good idea."

"Nonsense," said Martin. "I got one to match. Now that I'm going to have a lot of free time on my hands, maybe the boy and I can do some hunting together."

"Yeah, mom," said Sam. "And I bet that creep won't show his face if he sees these babies."

"He didn't show his face this time," Catherine reminded him. "Neither of you saw him."

Sam fell into a grim state as if he was about to hear another speech he'd heard a thousand times.

"Only if your grampa is with you when you use it," said Catherine, looking sharply at her father.

"Oh don't get your feathers too ruffled," he said. "You were his age when I taught you to shoot a gun."

Catherine stood silent remembering how the world had so drastically changed since then. She had enjoyed those few times with her father, shoving the long heavy gun to her shoulder and pulling the trigger. It was the first real blast, the ringing of her ears, and the huge hole in the old rusted jalopy that taught her the true nature and responsibility of a firearm.

"Well do me a favor and put them away," said Catherine. "We have company coming to stay for a day or two and I don't want them to get the wrong idea about our family."

"Who's coming?" asked Martiel, from the kitchen.

"BeBe and Jolie wanted to help with…." Catherine froze mid-sentence, not knowing how to proceed with her statement.

"Help with what?" asked Maime, looking concerned.

"Well, BeBe was telling me that Jolie was having a hard time with everything that's happened and I invited them to help with a few things around here. It will only be in the evenings after they close their Café and Jolie won't go to an empty and quiet home. I assured her that we have plenty of room."

Catherine saw that she had opened up a can of worms for speculation as to her motives.

Martiel spoke up, "Oh, good! We'll have some competition for bridge or canasta."

Maime looked concerned, wiggling her sore fingers, "I love company. But do you think it's wise with all the trouble we're having?"

"Oh it'll be fine," said Martin. "It's exactly what we need…. We need some life around this place."

Sam had been listening intently at the conversation and hoping that his mother would convince them to let their friends stay, especially Jolie.

The telephone rang and Aunt Martiel picked up the call in the kitchen, which seemed to be her favorite hangout of late.

"Martin, it's for you," she sang out.

Martin picked up the receiver and talked for what seemed like forever. When he hung up, he had almost everyone at the kitchen table eavesdropping.

"It was one of the board members from the church," he said quietly. "Something happened to Pastor Milton and we have an emergency board meeting tomorrow."

"Is he sick?" asked Maime.

"You could say that," said Martin. "They found him walking down the train tracks toward town, wrapped only in his bed sheet. They said he was naked as a jaybird underneath. But that's not the worst of it…. They took him to the county nut house."

"They what?" asked Maime. "I don't understand…."

Martin seemed lost for a few moments.

"They said he was jabbering on about stuff that he did when he was a kid, right up to…. Maime, do you remember a young woman from the church named Sallee Mae?"

James was in a fury. Now he was damned if he did and damned if he didn't. Maybe literally. He was tired of watching everyone going about their merry lives as if he had never existed there with them.

Forgotten. Oh, they remembered him from time to time in conversation, but for the most part, he was a "dead" subject.

Already!

What if he *was* cursed to stay here in this limbo for eternity?ames stalked the upstairs bedrooms and hallways, invisible and silent to everyone that had always mattered most to him. He felt the same as when he had been deserted by his parents, back when he fought the *Hand* years ago. Abandoned by everyone and accused. He did feel accused.

The pressure mounted on his thinking, escalating until he could hardly contain himself. He heard footsteps in the hallway as he made the sixth or seventh trip from one end of the upstairs to the other.

He turned and saw no one. It had suddenly become silent. He turned and walked toward the stairway at the end of the hall and the same footsteps seemed to be following him again.

It was his own.

Surprised, he walked a few steps and could hear the weight of his steps pushing on the wood flooring and pattering out the sound of his feet.

Some metamorphosis was still taking place and drastically. The more he gave into his anger, the more solid he became. James gently pushed at one of the empty bedroom doors, this time without having to concentrate his efforts. It was a door that he had walked right through many times since his returning here. It slowly creaked and moved at his touch. He relaxed and pushed it open. Against his mother's wishes and with this new found knowledge, he felt the urge to pay another quick visit to some of the living that he knew.

Billy and Sallee Mae Poole had spent the day viewing nearly twenty scattered houses all over Natchez and still hadn't found what Sallee Mae wanted.

Billy was tired of looking, but remembered to have patience; his employer had *ordered* him to help Sallee find what she wanted. That wasn't something that he took lightly.

He drove slowly across the railroad tracks east of Natchez and was going to cut around town to the highway. This was a faster way back into town to their apartment.

After crossing the railroad tracks, Sallee Mae instructed him to turn into a neighborhood she knew very well, very well indeed.

Billy was nervous at the prospect of her looking in a neighborhood so near the church and Heavens' Gate cemetery; in fact he had purposely shunned the entire area all day.

After a few turns they ended up on a dead end street and decided to turn around at the end of the road.

"Look!" said Sallee Mae. "That house is for sale! Stop!"

"I don' think this would be…," said Billy.

However, before he could even finish his sentence, she had exited the car and was walking up to the front door of the vacant house.

She walked around toward the back of the house and saw the flower gardens beginning to recover after the horrible storm. A small vegetable garden out back that looked like it had been recently abandoned, begging for attention.

There was a terribly big hole in the back yard, possibly where a tree had been ruined by the recent storm, from the looks of all the wood chips. In the dying shadows of sunset she also noticed a brand new back porch added on to the big old house.

She was elated at the size of this place and the hominess. It would be perfect for raising a kid, her kid.

Sallee strolled around the entire house, back toward the driveway and saw another small porch with an entrance door and a window. She peered inside with the innocence of a child watching rain from a schoolroom window.

It was a kitchen, a big one, and there was a nice table already inside and a new fridge. She hoped that it would come with the house.

Billy was still inside the car, sulking, with the engine now turned off as his wife continued on with her annoying exploration.

She ran almost skipping, back around to the front porch and peered into the window of the living room. It was filled with nice furniture.

"Oh, please let this stuff come with the house," she thought.

Sallee Mae walked back over to the *For Sale* sign and plucked it up from the ground and threw it inside the car.

"Don't you think we ought to talk this over before you get too happy?" asked Billy sullenly.

"I love it!" she exclaimed. "It's perfect. It looks like it has four bedrooms and it's full of furniture! Can't we please call and see how much they want for it? You said that I could have any one I wanted as long as it wasn't too expensive."

Billy cranked the engine and motioned with his head for her to get back in the car. She squealed with delight as they backed out and drove toward town.

Inside the house, a pair of eyes glared from the darkness of the far end of the hall, waiting for the setting sunlight to dim.

Deputy Floyd was anchored in his favorite chair in his living room. The television was blaring loudly and he was well on his way to being completely wasted.

A case of beer was in a large cooler sitting beside his reclining chair within easy arms reach. Several empties were parked in a neat pattern on the other side. Floyd thought that it seemed only right that if he was going to go crazy, he'd do it drunk as hell.

The little bastard that had been tormenting him couldn't wake him from a drunken stupor and he was headed for one great stupor tonight. It was a weekend, with Saturday off and he had a good idea that he could probably stay drunk all that next day without a problem.

Cablevision had finally made it to his neighborhood and there was some great stuff on HBO. Floyd was flipping through a multitude of channels when James arrived.

"You back again?" asked Floyd. "Here have a beer!"

"I'm not old enough to drink," said James. "I'm old enough to get murdered by a jerk like you, but I can't have a beer."

"Suit yourself. I believe I'll have another."

James was enraged and swatted the beer bottle from Floyd's hand and it hit the wall like a missile.

"Hey! That's a waste of a good beer!"

James sat in silence for several minutes watching Floyd as he reached for another and popped it open.

"I'll make a deal with you Floyd," said James. "Are you interested?"

"Nope, not interested," said Floyd, slurring his words slightly as the alcohol began its duty.

"You have two choices," said James. "You can accept my deal or I'll finish you off tonight, right where you sit."

Floyd's eyes bulged out as if on stems considering his options.

"I'm listening," he said, drunkenly interested.

"You're not worth my time, Floyd," said James. "I don't even think you have the ability for an original thought. Tell me, what did they offer you to help get rid of me?"

"It wasn't near enough. I can tell you that!" chuckled Floyd, as he slapped the arm of his chair.

"What was it?"

Floyd got up and staggered over to a cheaply constructed cabinet near the doorway into his kitchen. He opened the door and dumped out a small bag from a ceramic jar.

"Here, you can have it, for all the good it's going to do me."

How could something so small be worth anything, "What is that?"

"Twenty Spanish gold pieces, in mint condition," said Floyd. "A collectors dream. I did my homework on those. Hammered in 1728, almost pure gold."

He tossed them over to James and they fell at his feet on the floor.

"How would you like to make a hundred more like that?" asked James.

Floyd waddled back over and fell heavily into his recliner. He sat quietly and reached for his remote, killing the sound of some movie about to begin.

"Not inshurested," he slurred matter of factly. "That's what got me in this predicament right now."

"So you prefer the other option...?"

Despite the stern finality in James Earl's voice, Floyd seemed uninterested at any forthcoming wrath.

"What's the catch?" asked Floyd. "I'm already cooked, right?"

"You can come out looking like a hero Floyd, but you have to do exactly what I tell you to do. Do you agree to my terms?"

"Do I have a choice?" asked Floyd.

"Sure, you can join me or..., you can join me," James said with an evil joyful tone that made Floyd cringe inside.

With their tentative covenant settled, James left Floyd to his weekend binge, but warned him that he expected a sober deputy by Monday morning. He even arrived back at the Ames Estate in time to watch everyone clustered around the large kitchen table.

Aunt Martiel seemed unsettled as she gazed around the room despite the clutter of conversation. She could sense something different and went to check the doors to make sure they were locked. Through all the years, she hadn't felt any fear when visiting the old mansion, never locking the doors. The very presence of all the past Ames ancestors was not only a comfort, but an active alarm system that never slept. Most of the time, the doors weren't locked even at night.

Satisfied that the house was safe or at least would offer some resistance that could be heard if there was an intruder, she relaxed a little.

Her own words returned to bite her as she whispered, "There's safety in numbers."

Back in the kitchen there was a lot of bluster as to whom they could get on short notice to take the place of the pastor for Sunday service.

James merely looked around and listened as they droned on, taking note that there wasn't a mention of his name or any sentiment of his absence. It had only been two days since the funeral; you'd think that they would at least....

There was a knock at the front door and Catherine got up to go let their guests inside. Catherine had second thoughts as to who might be at the door as she walked the last few steps.

Was it someone from the Sheriff's Department coming to tell her that they had caught the villains that had destroyed her son? The son that she had completely misinterpreted his whole life.

Her guilt of not listening to the cry for help from her son was ever present on her mind and eating her like a cancer now that he was dead. Especially, after reading James Earl's last journal coupled with the soul wrenching confession only a few nights ago.

She opened the door to the smiling face of Jolie, with BeBe standing behind her, holding a few small items of baggage in her hands.

Catherine led them into the foyer and talked in muffled tones below the hearing of the others in the kitchen. She had to know about James.

"Yes, he's here," said Jolie. "I can sense him.... He's close but not here."

"Is he still sulking?" asked Catherine quietly.

Jolie shook her head, "I can't tell. Not without being close to him."

"Who is it?" asked a voice from far back in the kitchen.

"It's our guests!" said Catherine. "Give us a second. Sam, would you come here, please?"

Sam sauntered from the kitchen, to the front door. His demeanor changed as he saw who was standing inside the house.

"Sam, please take their bags up to the second room on the right upstairs," asked Catherine. "They're going to be staying a day or two with us."

"Cool!" said Sam. "I mean that's great," he corrected himself, embarrassed at his own outburst.

He hurriedly took the bags that BeBe offered him and disappeared up the stairs two at a time.

"He looks so much like James, it's scary," said BeBe.

"What did I tell you?" asked Jolie grinning.

They walked to the door of the kitchen and Jolie softly nudged Catherine's arm to let her know that this was the room that James was hiding inside.

Supper came and went with small talk. Sam spent the entire time stealing glances at Jolie, trying without success not to be noticed. Catherine and BeBe were the first to sense that Sam was unusually silent and seemed preoccupied with either his plate or doodling with the food on it.

James noticed. James noticed every last detail.

At first, James denied his jealously by listening in on the rest of the family conversation. It was actually amusing that his little brother would think that his girl friend was hot.

Then he noticed that Jolie had returned a few of Sam's flirtatious glances with her own. His brother was alive, living, breathing. James was..., what he was.

He had to be honest with himself. He had no right to hold her back. She deserved a life, but his brother? How could she be cutting glances at his little brother? So soon after his leaving, unless he hadn't meant anything to her in the beginning.

Maybe he was only a project to her..., an experiment. Testing her own gifts, after all she had dreamed that she would meet him that day in the library. She told him that herself.

And Sam, after all the times that James had saved his skin. After protecting Sam for years from things too evil to imagine; things done to him instead.

The more he mused the more heated his jealousy burned.

Martiel excused herself and looked around the room trying to sense exactly where James was as she walked out.

Afraid of being detected, she walked up to her room and closed the door.

"James!" she said angrily, while pacing the room. "James, you get yourself here right now!"

James was still fuming but felt a quivering inside him and then heard his name being called.

"What?" he asked as he appeared before Martiel.

The air in the room snapped with his entry.

"What do you want from me? Another lecture? Something else that's my fault?"

"What do you think you're doing?" she asked. "Do you realize how loudly you're thinking in a room with two people that can hear your every unguarded thought?!"

"I was at the point of blushing from your arrogance. How dare you accuse Jolie of flirting with your brother Sam? He's only a kid. She knows that. If you weren't so busy accusing her of being human, you would have heard her trying to talk to you the entire time. What's wrong with you, James?"

"If she was talking to me, then why couldn't I hear her?" he argued.

"You have to learn to listen or you're going to have lots of problems," said Aunt Martiel.

"I don't know how," said James. "I just…. I saw them looking at each other…, almost like she used to look at me and…. I don't know, what was I supposed to think? I lost it."

"Well quit listening with your emotions and start using those abilities of yours. Come here," she ordered.

Aunt Martiel sat on the edge of her bed and James stepped in front of her.

"Now, this is going to be strange, but you have to relax and calm yourself. Now sit down in my lap like you did when you were a little boy," she said slapping her legs with her two hands.

"Come on," she ordered.

James sat down where it would have been her lap, but went on through to the bed. The sensation was strange, just like she described. He was almost merged with his aunt.

"That feels nasty!" he said jumping up and turning around.

His Aunt Martiel was visibly shaken from the intrusive experience but recovered after a few seconds.

"Don't do that," she scolded, sounding winded. "That was awful. You have to remember to move slowly or you can hurt us flesh and blood people."

"Well I didn't like it either!" said James. "What the heck is that all about anyway?"

"Try again and it'll save me an hour of trying to explain, okay?" she asked. "Slower this time."

James sat slowly back where he had been, merging with his Aunt Martiel.

"Now sit back," she demanded, "and try to relax."

James was fully merged with his aunt and tried to remember to quit letting his thoughts run away with him.

Suddenly it was if someone had turned on a light bulb. He could see into his aunt's mind. Images and thoughts of her childhood began racing by, then..., others when she was married to her husband that had passed away a few years back. The joy when he was with her and the sadness of his passing.

Suddenly he could hear her thoughts as clear as a bell ringing in his head. He was reading her thoughts so vividly that he could almost see the imagery and reality that she did.

"Okay, that's enough," she said. "Now *slowly* stand back up please...."

James did as he was told, feeling electrified at the experience. His aunt was however visibly drained at the experience.

"James that was awful," said Aunt Martiel. "Normally, it tires the visitor a little to be inside a host, but I'm the one that's drained. I'm not sure I understand that."

"I feel like I was plugged into the light socket," said James excitedly.

"It's only inexperience on your part," she said. "What I wanted you to learn from the practice is this.... If you're clouded with emotions and can't hear the thoughts of others, you have other options. After more practice, you can simply place your head inside someone else's and hear and see their thoughts. If you're good enough at it, they will never know that you were there.

"Later on, you won't even need to be near them to listen in. Now the reason I let you know this isn't for you to run off and intrude on people, it's so that the next time your emotions are running wild and you can't hear what they're thinking, you can listen in and find out what's going on.

"Just so you know," she went on. "Jolie was asking me for help, because she could feel and hear your anger. You need to apologize."

Martiel walked out of the room and went back downstairs to let her nephew stew over her short training session.

"I know what I saw," said James, still blanched and angry. "But that will come in handy."

The telephone rang downstairs and Maime picked up the phone, while the others were setting up a game of cards and placing snacks on the table.

"Why, yes it is for sale...."

"We only put up the sign a few hours ago...."

"Of course. You can see it tomorrow.... Yes, most of the furnishings go with the house."

"And your name is?"

"Oh..., I see. I'll tell my husband...."

The conversation ended and Maime hung up the telephone. The perplexed look on her face followed her all the way back to her seat at the table.

"That was a call about the house," said Maime. "Somebody already wants to buy it."

"That's wonderful," said Catherine. "I can't believe someone ran across it so soon, you just placed the for sale sign in the yard."

"Yes, wonderful," she said dryly looking over at Martin. "Do you remember what the church board meeting is about tomorrow, Martin?"

Years of being married and knowing each other's thoughts and expressions paid off as she began hinting that she was worried about something.

"Oh, yes, getting an interim pastor," said Martin.

"Well, that young girl involved with the situation...," said Maime, quickly being cut off.

"Oh just spit it out," said Martiel, walking in the door. "You've got us all on the edge of our seats."

There was an uproar of laughter around the table.

"The person that wants to buy the other house.... It's Sallee Mae Poole," said Maime. "I don't know what to say to her. As a board member I can't break confidence and let her know...."

"Know what?" asked Martiel, getting impatient.

"The girl's pregnant. Possibly by that no-good Pastor Milton of the church. We need to avoid a scandal. It could really hurt the church."

"The Pastor!" said BeBe.

James laughed.

Everyone in the room stopped stark cold still and looked at each other.

"Did you hear that?" asked Martin, jumping up.

He walked into the living room and unboxed one of the shotguns that he and Sam had picked out earlier.

"Sam, where did you put that sack of shells?" he asked.

Martiel hurried to the adjoining doorway, "Now Martin, you need to settle down. You know how this old house echoes."

"I know what I heard," said Martin Ames. "I'm going to have a look around outside."

"Sam, go with your grampa," said Catherine. "Now, keep your mouth shut and your ears open."

"James, did you have anything to do with Pastor Milton?" asked Catherine.

"I paid him a visit…, or two," he said sheepishly.

"What did you do to him?" she demanded.

"Nothing that he didn't deserve," snapped James angrily. "He's the one that was messing around with Sallee Mae. At least that's what she said. Don't you remember who she is?"

James grew agitated at yet another scolding.

"Her husband is Billy. The one that was with the guy that killed me. He might be the one that attacked grampa."

"So you thought you'd play God and take care of the situation?" she asked.

"I don't see anybody else doing anything about it!"

"James I really think that you should let the law take care of catching these people. I didn't raise you to be like that."

"You're right about one thing," he growled. "You didn't raise me. You didn't listen to me, you…, and dad… never listened to a word I said."

Catherine stood quietly, assessing the accusations that had hit her in the heart.

"I'm…. I'm sorry, James. I can only say I'm sorry so many times," said Catherine quietly.

James hovered near for several moments, wishing he could retract his words. "I shouldn't have said that."

"And you're right. I'm going to let the law finish what they started," he said, smiling to himself.

The old mansion was quiet and most everyone had retired for the evening. Jolie was seated in the front porch swing listening to the sounds of the early summer. A few mosquitoes were buzzing around, repopulating after the serious rains. Her time in the soft breeze would have to be short or she would be eaten alive and carried away by the insects.

"Hello James," said Jolie. "Sit beside me?"

"I'm here," said James. "It's best I don't show myself, or grampa might try to shoot me."

"There's so much anger in you now. Why, James? Being…, being dead is one thing, but you're becoming different altogether. You're changing."

"I have changed," James admitted. "I don't like who I'm becoming, but I'm losing my patience. Nobody's doing anything about the thugs that killed me and now they show up right here, trying to hurt my family."

"That's not all that's bothering you James," said Jolie. "I tried to talk to you tonight. You wouldn't listen to me. Tonight I was noticing how much your brother Sam resembles you. I tried to point out the similarities and differences to you, but when I tried to hear you, all I got was some kind of jealous rage."

"I didn't know," said James. "I assumed that..., well, you know."

"Yes I do, and that's wrong too, James. Sam is just a boy. All I wanted to do was have some fun and talk to you."

"He might be a boy, but he's...," said James, ignoring her explanation.

"He's what?" asked Jolie. "He's your brother. And what if I talk to someone else? Are they going to have an accident, or run off wrapped in a sheet like that goofy man from the church?

"James, I will always love you. I will always be your friend, but...."

Suddenly he'd been reduced to the "Friend" category, the relationship death sentence. The vacuum between them began to ache.

"Please, don't say anymore," said James. "I don't know if I can take any more of this. Everybody is telling me what I should and shouldn't do. How this is wrong and that's wrong. I'm tired of all the rules. I have to start making my own rules."

When Jolie didn't respond as quickly as he thought she should, he pushed off the porch swing in a huff, "I need to think."

In less than a heartbeat, he was gone to parts unknown.

Jolie walked upstairs to where BeBe, Catherine and Aunt Martiel had congregated.

"You were right, he's gone," said Jolie. "You want to fill me in on what's going on?"

Chapter 54

The church was vacant and quiet. Only a few safety lights dotted the sides, illuminated the sanctuary and the surrounding grounds.

James sat on the church steps in a melancholy retrospect.

"Granny Smith, I need you," he said. "I need somebody to tell me what I should do. I've never really asked God to help me. It looks like it's too late for that anyway."

James sadly mulled over his situation. It was one thing to recognize that his mood was darkening day by day, hour by hour, and yet another to realize that he was helpless to change directions. It always seemed like the right thing to do at the time.

"The Cemetery," said James, in a sudden burst of inspiration.

In the span of thought, he was standing on sacred ground.

A car drove by the entrance to Heaven's Gate Cemetery and flashed its lights before turning the corner and speeding off crazily.

James leaned against the heavy iron archway and peered inside wondering what was in store. It wasn't fear that he felt, as much as it was hopelessness. Shouldn't he see someone else stuck in the same situation as he was? Was he so unique that there was no one else like him? How could that be?

He took a step inside and waited. Nothing happened to him, no hidey-behind to grab him, no dark sinister monster like the one he faced at his grandparents' house.

The darkness of the night gave way to his smoky blue-gray vision, the deeper and farther he walked away from the small street lamps near the entrance.

Luminescent fireflies played dots and streaks on his field of vision. There was constant movement in his peripheral vision, but when he looked, there was nothing to be seen. Dark shifting shapes jumped into and out of his field of vision almost playfully.

Nothing was hidden from his sight despite the near total darkness engulfing the cemetery. It was no more than an overcast day to his unusual vision.

The night air was peacefully still and only a few crickets chirped in the distance. As if drawn, he hurried on toward the place where he felt most duty-bound..., the place where he was buried.

There was no longer the small tombstone. In the place where James' body was laid to rest, there was a huge stone memorial.

Inside was a crypt where the coffin was encased, sealed with a brass plaque memorial to him. It looked oddly bulbous and out of place with the older variety memorials surrounding the area.

He waited longingly, brushing his fingers over the surface of the plaque. Did he dare look inside at the now rotting corpse of himself?

No, he didn't need a reminder of the state he was in. He was constantly reminded of who and what he was by all of his friends and family that knew of his extended existence.

Still…, some odd curiosity was pulling him closer. Was there something that could be learned? Would he become trapped inside, alive, thinking, waiting? Would he sleep?

These thoughts haunted him as surely as any demon that could have crept up on him in the darkness.

He stilled his ethereal nerves and listened, trying to remember every lesson that his Aunt Martiel had shared with him, coupled with his own experiences. James pushed himself ever so cautiously into the crypt where his coffin rested. Then onward, on into the coffin itself.

James jumped back out in terror. There was nothing there. There was no body, no rotting cadaver stiffly staring into the black darkness.

Even the steel nerves of vengeance could not steady his emotions. The night enclosed on him, on his thoughts and soul, suffocating him. He remembered the feeling of cold water being drawn into his lungs as he desperately tried to drag life into his body after the crash. The taste of the mud mingled with his own warm oxygen fresh blood.

James moved back out of the stone memorial as quickly as he could before imaginary tentacles could affix him inside. The coldness that followed him for days after the crash tried once again to crawl up his legs and into his loins.

He pushed it away and began walking through the rest of the stone littered property. He stopped at a gravesite familiar to him and read the name.

Wema Smith.

James quieted himself and mourned her passing, as he stood transfixed.

There was that irresistible urge again pulling him to do something that he felt warned against. Nevertheless, he pressed into the earth, down into the grave. He had to know.

New tree roots and earth rot filled his sense of smell. There was the coffin. He pressed himself inside to find…, the grinning corpse of Granny Smith.

He flung himself upward to the top of the ground, panting as if he had actual breath to spend. Reflexes from life made him gasp, even though he could no more take in a breath of air than he could take a leak, or eat a bite of food.

Where was *his* body?

Out of the corner of his eye, there was movement and James snapped around defensively. On top of a tombstone sat the gray outline of some bygone rebel in his stately uniform. His face was downcast in a mournful demure stare.

James spoke to him, but there was no response. Either he could neither see nor hear James, or years of sitting here trying to communicate with passers by had rendered him totally and completely insane.

Was this his fate? Was he once like James, able to move about without anyone to hear or understand him?

Suddenly, the graveyard came to life with the dead. None seemed interested or aware of each other, but seemed to be taking some strange interest in him.

James could feel unseen hands brushing at the sides of his feet and legs, moaning voices beckoning him to stay and join the throng of the silent.

Then it happened. Something took hold of his ankle and held fast. James kicked upward and extracted a ghastly corpse from its resting place. It flung up on top of the ground, flopped aimlessly and then began to stand.

James was petrified at the hollow eyes that walked toward him.

"Master?" spoke the ghoulish remains of the unidentified resident.

"No," whispered James, looking around.

The ghoul stopped its forward motion and waited as if for instructions.

James moved to one of the other graves and reached down. A hand met his and as he pulled, another wanton dead rose and joined the first, also awaiting instructions.

Not every grave responded, but James found that several were available and willing to be his servants. With each new prize he felt a surge inside, a collection of power.

As if instinct was taking over, he stretched out his arms to the ground and commanded....

"Rise! Rise up!" he shouted.

There was a swimming of power unlike anything he had ever imagined and it pushed into the ground surrounding him with a rumbling.

A dozen graves nearest him burst alive with new slaves awaiting orders from their commander. There were all walks of life before him. Soldiers seemed most prominent, but death was not picky in its horde. There were men, women, and one young child, all of whose genders were discernible only by the partial remains of their garments.

James felt forever changed. How could he go back to the mundane? There was unbelievable surging, intoxicating power here. He knew at once that this was another piece of this mystery that would complete him.

He regained control of his mind and momentarily understood another part of what the *Bokor* was after. She wanted power over the dead, all dead, it was a heady prize and it dizzied him.

James felt like a kid with the whole candy store at his disposal, not knowing where to begin, but tonight was not the night to test this newness.

Intuition of his new skill filled him as he ordered the mass of the dead to sleep in their resting place once again. They each obeyed, sliding back into their earthen graves and all was silent once more.

As the power subsided, excitement and fear began to push James along quickly and he decided to leave this place of the dead.

Things were somehow changed now, he was changed somehow, and the thirst for power had begun a willful tugging at him with the strength of the tides.

Miss Lyda Brown along with her helper, Toad, held lanterns and searched inside the ceremonial cave. The item they were desperately looking for was hidden securely and rendered the old *Bokor* helpless to force James Earl to appear before her.

Decades of searching for the right bones, the right answers from the dead, all wasted with one little sniveling snot of a child. Wet behind the ears, but empowered far beyond his own understanding.

Toad was getting more and more afraid at what she might do to him, should they not find the item she needed. The skull of Syrus Earl Ames was hidden well, in a place neither of them could reach nor discover.

Her screeching and clamoring could be heard echoing all the way out to the entrance at the rivers edge.

She picked up a piece of the urn that James had broken, which had contained the spirits of his ancestors, now forever safe from her reach. She hurled it into the rock face of the caves' wall and it shattered into fragments. There would be another time, another place; she vowed that this war was only beginning with every step she took. She had to get the boy back before he awoke to his full potential, her potential....

No, she would not, could not allow that day to arise.

She vowed that there would be dry thunder when she boiled the remaining dead flesh from James Earl William's bones.

There would be no more waiting. She had been so close to completing her task. Already she'd had a taste of what it was like to be young again. To feel like a woman again, with desires and pleasures of the flesh. The thought of all she had lost was too much to bear, ripping away all restraints. No matter what it took, no matter who had to suffer, she would not lose this battle.

"Load it all up and burn the rest!" she screamed at Toad.

Bitter anguish and tears of catastrophic failure followed her as she stormed outside to stand on the shores of the Mississippi River. After decades of collecting rubbles of bones, searching for the right person to capture, and decades of listening to her *familiar*, instructing her step by step – all for nothing. There was still a portion of her power hiding in one of the living Ames ancestors. One last throw of the dice, it could all be hers.

James still had a full dose of frustration boiling inside him. He had seen his potential end, in its many forms, and now some new heady potential power. He could either end up as the insane soldier mourning for eternity while resting on a headstone, or be something so much more.

Where were the rules? He had no idea how long he could exist like this or what his ultimate end would be. Was there a heaven or hell for him? Where were the lines?

There was an evil that James felt associated with the power he found, but it was his for the taking. It somehow rightfully belonged to him. There were too many choices with unknown consequences and confusion filled his mind.

That awful pull was still there, drawing him to some enormous unknown, something so vast the very hint of it was overwhelming.

A glint of sunshine caught his attention as he sat on the front steps of the Ames Estate. Life was simple for yet another moment and he knew the family would soon awake on this bright Saturday morning.

James remembered the warmth of other Saturday mornings from his childhood. Of brotherly fights with Sam, but most of all, those mornings at Earl's Garage working on his car, these last four summers. Those were his true memories from life and the ones he chose to hold close.

James remembered his grampa's patient instructions guiding his hand to restore a discarded classic vehicle, into a thing of beauty.

He sat and watched the sun quivering above the horizon as he heard familiar sounds beginning to stir inside the house.

Uncontrollably his mind delved back into the past in an invasion of thoughts. He wondered what his life would have been like had he not been forced to endure the hardships of gangland or a life of disregard by both his parents.

James was tired of thinking, tired of whining and mourning his misspent youth and all of its could-have-been scenarios. The repetitions of his solitary thoughts were driving him to the edge. James could hear the voice of his High School counselor, "Where do you see yourself in five years, James?"

"Not dead," he whispered to himself.

Chapter 55

SNARES

Sallee Mae waited anxiously on the hood of her truck for the arrival of the owner of the house on Washington Street. She had walked around the house almost a half dozen times in the last thirty minutes, taking note of anything that might need to be repaired. Begging to find any small bargaining chip against what she knew would be an expensive home. She couldn't find anything that was of consequence.

The house looked very well maintained and even had a relatively new coat of paint and shingles. The older style counter-weighted windows were caulked and seated, no dry rot to be seen in the windowsills.

A truck pulled into the driveway and two men stepped out. Not the owners. They were workers, asking her to move her vehicle for the truckload of dirt about to arrive, to fill the massive hole from an excavated tree in the back yard. There went her last hope of reducing the price of the house unless it had something wrong inside. She knew it didn't. Her intuition told her that the inside would be as clean as the outside of the house.

A few minutes afterward, a late model BMW pulled in beside her. A lady of obvious means stepped out of the car.

"Probably a realtor," sighed Sallee Mae. "She really looks familiar. Where have I seen her?"

"You must be Mrs. Poole," said Martiel and extended her hand. "My name is Martiel Ellington. I represent the people that have the house for sale."

Martiel fixed the oversized sunshades on her nose and the floppy hat covering the specks of gray in her hair.

Sallee Mae lost all hope of buying the house for anything less than top dollar. Nevertheless, she at least wanted to see inside the house, and extended her hand in greeting. The subtle disguise and changes to her appearance seemed to be working for Martiel. She was pleased that Sallee Mae didn't readily recognize her from their brief meeting at the funeral home.

"Do you have children?" asked Martiel.

"Oh, no Ma'am, but we're hopeful." She carefully patted her stomach.

"Well, this has plenty of room for a family; it's a four bedroom, two bath…."

Martiel went on to list all the amenities as she jingled with a ring of keys.

She opened the door and ushered Sallee Mae into the living room. The delicate furniture was still intact and there were several nice antiques. Martiel quit talking shop and let the young woman look and ask her questions about the house. Martiel pointed out two or three heirloom pieces of furniture that would not be staying, but for the most part everything in the house was included unless it was unwanted.

Sallee Mae assured her that she would like the furniture to stay and then came the moment that Sallee Mae dreaded - the price.

"You came at the right time to buy this one," said Martiel. "The elderly couple that owned this just moved and are willing to owner finance to the right kind of person or persons."

She told Sallee the price and the expected down payment and the young blond smiled inside and out. Billy had told her the limit that she could spend and the limit for the down payment and this odd woman almost matched both exactly.

Martiel gave her the phone number and address of their lawyers in downtown Natchez so that she could go by and finish the deal with them.

Martiel smiled as she drove away with the house sold to Sallee Mae Poole and her husband. Secretly gloating, "What a better way to keep up with your enemy than to have them sitting in your own house."

"Now see, James. That's the way it's done. I wanted her to buy the house. I also wanted to get every red cent that I could for the down payment. That money probably came from whoever hired Billy to kill you. That money will be forfeit if they terminate the loan, which is likely when Billy finally goes to prison. But frankly, it isn't about money, it's about justice."

"What if he doesn't make it to prison?" asked James darkly.

"Now James, don't you go and do something you'll regret. But if he doesn't make it..., well, we'll have to cross that bridge when we get there. Personally I think it's more than coincidence that she found that house to buy. I don't believe in chance, but I do believe in providence.

"So, I've made arrangements to keep Sallee Mae and Billy from finding out that the house belonged to the Ames family, as long as they don't dig too deep. It's all nice and tidy."

The new housekeeper arrived soon after Martiel and her invisible passenger arrived back at the Ames Estate. Martiel received heaps of criticism for hiring a full daytime housekeeper, but everyone reluctantly agreed when she pointed out that the woman was in dire need of a steady income. Martiel didn't feel the need to point out that there were seven living residents swarming about the house and none of them had the time to deal with some of the regular day to day chores.

The cleaning service that had been taking care of the large house had gone through it hurriedly to clean away the dust and cobwebs several days back, but there was still the daily light cleaning, laundry, and maintenance duties that needed ongoing attention.

Margie seemed the right choice for the job.

As soon as their new helper was introduced and pointed in the right direction, everyone dispersed for their Saturday routines.

BeBe and Jolie had left early for the restaurant. Catherine and Maime were taking a tour of the rooms upstairs where most of the fine furniture had been shifted over the years, discussing possibilities of rearranging some of the downstairs rooms.

She and her mother were also making use of the time by having the mother/daughter talk about her situation with her husband. Robert still had not called, since he and Catherine fought and he stormed out the door with baggage in hand.

Martin Ames and his grandson Sam, fully stuffed from breakfast, gathered their new hobbies in hand and each of them placed a box of shotgun shells in the pouches of their new vests.

They walked a sufficient distance from the house almost to the pond where Martin was attacked. Sam was teeming with youthful overconfidence that the person who had been so bold the day before would not dare try the same tactic with two armed men.

The sun was already producing heat enough to generate a sheen on both their foreheads from the steady pace. Sam stopped behind his grampa in a small open draw, which had a single old rusted car sitting up on blocks.

It was riddled with holes of all sizes and random patterns on its surface.

"This is where my daddy taught me to fire a gun," said Martin. "It was also where I taught Catherine and James to shoot a gun. So I guess it's only fitting that you get to get to plug some holes in this old jalopy too.

"Now this type of shotgun is called a pump," said Martin, as he began the task of showing Sam how to load and unload, as well as the safe operation.

Sam stood with the gun pulled tightly to his shoulder and once again fired the shotgun into side of the car. He had fired over a dozen times in the same area, producing a hole his grampa described as the size of a small frying pan.

"One thing about this gun, Sam. If someone hears the sound of a shell being loaded into its magazine and keeps on coming, he wants to die."

After both boxes of ammo were mostly spent, the two of them walked back up to the house side by side. They clamored on about how the guns performed and the younger of the two was rubbing his right shoulder while the older laughed at him.

Two eyes angrily watched on as the two men had taken turns loading and firing their guns. He'd have to pick his chances better or like most predators, find a weaker target.

James postponed his desired trips for the day and decided to stay around the home as guard dog. He watched Jolie leave with her aunt earlier that morning. His desire to have only a moment alone with Jolie was denied him. He felt a deep unexplained compunction forcing him to apologize and beg Jolie not to judge him too quickly.

The sudden desire to desert his post of duty came with an opportunity to get away from the house with his Aunt Martiel. His trip to and fro his grandparents old home with her was a genuine learning experience, but she was still teaching him as if he were still alive.

Did she still expect him to take over the family business? Or was Martiel babysitting him to keep him from doing something all the status quo disapproved of? And if she still had expectations, how was he supposed to manage any dealing?

"Hello, I'm James Earl Williams. Pay no attention to the fact that I'm really dead."

It was either laugh or cry and James had the desire for neither.

As soon as they arrived back home, James heard the sounds of gun fire far behind the house. His reticent memory drug up images of his first summer with his grandparents. His grampa walking beside him, while carrying an old shotgun that weighed a ton, made him feel ten feet tall.

James snapped back to where an old rusted shell of a car sat, almost covered in weeds. There stood his brother Sam and his grampa taking turns plugging holes in their wounded target.

James sensed something strange, but passed it off with indifference as he chose instead to reminisce his trips here from his own past. He remembered the smell of the gunpowder and the kick of the gun that always left his shoulder sore.

There it was again….

James didn't know what it was but instead of ignoring it this time, he relaxed and flowed with the sensation, pushing his feelings outward. There…, it was a movement, somewhere in the distance, in the overgrowth. James focused his attention and instantly arrived hovering over the face of a young scraggly man that appeared awfully familiar to him.

It could be some random kid that heard the same gunshots as he did, coming to investigate. Several towns' people wandered across the deserted Ames property to hunt small game year round.

One way to find out. James moved around behind him and slowly transposed his head into the kids, remembering what his Aunt Martiel had shown him.

His vision was instantaneously the same as the kid, watching his family.

Then the intruder's thoughts began to seep into his own. Vile thoughts. Images of places and things…, the old woman! He saw Billy and the old hag together! Then James remembered this kid in the vision while on the porch swing. It was dark when he had seen him before. His vision bounced back to the night in the truck, with Billy. Was the old woman still alive? Somehow it didn't matter.

This was him, *the one*. The end of his searching. He was peering into the mind of his killer!

James slowly exited their merger, hoping to not alarm his intended victim, while cruel desires and plans filled his thoughts.

The man swatted at his ear cautiously, hearing a buzzing in both his ears and searched around himself, then finally back to James' family.

Martin and Sam had stopped their warfare on the jalopy and were headed back to the house.

James felt the steam of hatred rise inside and a sudden need to make an end of all the trouble. How sweet it would be to cause him to….

James stilled his emotions before he transfigured himself and was discovered.

Here was one more piece of the puzzle. James had to make sure that this encompassed the entire group being used to harm his family. If he put this one to rest without finding out if there were more, then they would still be in danger.

If only he knew how long he would remain as he was, or how long he would be able to affect the world of the living. Was his condition permanent or was there some time limit he was unaware of? His Aunt Martiel was treating him as if he was eternal, but there were no assurances, no guarantees.

She also assumed that the family ghosts would be captive counselors until she ultimately joined them, adding her experience to the lot. That assumption was faulty, leaving her with many unanswered questions.

James sat patiently until the man began to move backward through the brush. He gingerly stepped through the mass of tangled growth, over obstacles and brush that gouged and tore at the kid's clothes.

Snakes looking for a cool place from the mounting heat of the day slithered past his feet. This path was obviously not new to him and seemed to know the territory quite well.

James could easily jump back in the house and alarm his family members, the ones that knew of his existence. Then the police would arrive a half hour or more later, blaring lights and noise, and his enemy would fade back into this wilderness unseen.

The temptation to take matters into his own hands and crush his enemy was almost unbearable.

After circling around the rough wilderness in a wide arc, they ended up less than a few hundred feet from the north side of the house, which was opposite the driveway and main entrance. And there he sat, unmoving for hours, James by his side.

"Margie, you don't have to take on the entire house all at once!" said Martiel. "We want you to stay around a while."

Margie had an oversized bundle of sheets in her arms, which she could hardly see over to navigate.

"It's okay, I'm trying to get it all sorted out," came a muffled reply.

"Why don't you put that down and come take a break with me? You won't be any good to anyone if you pass out."

Maime and Martiel were seated in the kitchen with tea in hand when Margie entered the room. She was obviously trying to make a good impression and was perspiring from her efforts.

"Here, come sit down," said Martiel. "We don't expect you to do the whole weeks work today. You take your time and we'll let you know if you need to do something extra, all right?"

"Thank you," said Margie. "I only want to make sure that my work is satisfactory."

"Well you have," said Martiel. "Now sit and have some tea with us."

Margie's clothing as well as her quiet character spoke of the hard times she had most likely endured. The lines on her face and hands, as well as her graying hair, aged her well past her actual years.

"Do you have family in Natchez, Margie," asked Maime.

"Oh, heavens no. Not any more. As soon as my children, I have two — a boy and a girl, as soon as they were of age they both married and moved east. I haven't heard from them in a couple of years. It's just me now."

"That must be hard, not hearing from them in so long," said Martiel.

"Oh, I suppose it was at first, but they can't stay tied to the apron strings forever, can they? As long as they're happy and well, that's all a parent can wish for isn't it?"

Margie grew quiet and the two women felt a change of subject was in order.

"Margie, how would you like to stay here on the premises?" asked Martiel. "It would take me a couple of days to get the "little house" out back up to standard, but we won't charge you to live there."

Martiel wondered that she may have crossed some unknown line of pride from Margie's expression alone.

"I couldn't do that…, I'd have to pay my way. I don't believe in charity, not anymore."

"Nonsense," said Maime. "That can be part of your wage, consider it a raise."

Pride succumbed to necessity and she accepted their offer.

Martiel was surprised at the turn of events. She had already decided not to press the issue with Margie for fear of running her off and yet she had accepted Maime's persuasive argument.

"Learn something new every day," thought Martiel.

"Good, I'll have the old servants quarters…, I mean the "little house" cleaned out spic and span in a day or two," said Martiel.

The mention of "servants" bounced from Margie's thoughts to Martiel with an evil she had endured many years ago. Martiel liked the term "little house" better anyway.

"Before you get back to your duties, I have some things I'd like you to take a look at," said Maime getting up from the table.

She led Margie into one of the downstairs bedrooms and opened the deep closet.

"I have some things here that look like they might be your size, if you're interested," said Maime.

Before Margie could answer or refuse, Maime reached inside, took out several dresses, and matched outfits, and stretched them out on the bed.

"Oh, I couldn't," said Margie.

"Sure you can. These haven't seen the light of day in a couple of years. If you think they're too outdated, put them over there in that chair and I'll find someone else that might want them." Martiel pointed to a chair in the corner and began to mill through a line of clothes.

Margie put aside her pride for the day and decided on them all. She picked one of the cool summer dresses and upon closing the door, exchanged it for the clothes on her back that reminded her of hard times, pitching those into a waste basket in the bedroom.

The entire family had a quick afternoon lunch together and went their separate ways. Martin and Maime had their begrudged church board meeting to attend and shortly afterward, drove away. Sam had found some adventurous oddities in the attic to ponder through and Catherine had given him several odd jobs to complete.

Catherine and her aunt took the opportunity to seclude themselves for updates on James and the family estate. It seemed that it was more and more difficult to find a time or place suitable for a private conversation lately. They both expressed concerns that James would take matters in his own hands and do something that they would all regret. James was still young in mind and experience and his actions could easily cause repercussions on the family. He was obviously not adjusting to his new existence, which was something that neither of them could lend any advice toward nor blame him for. Martiel assured Catherine that it would all most likely work out for the best with a little patience. With the help of BeBe and Jolie, maybe James could be taught to control himself.

James was paralyzed with boredom. The only thing that had happened was someone leaving in a car, which went practically unnoticed.

There was motion from the back of the house and the scraggly boy James was watching noticed it instantly, crouching down further. Out of the back door came a woman carrying several blankets and walked around beside one of the small servant houses to a clothesline.

She began to throw them one by one across the taught rusty wires. This lady was wearing a light yellow floral dress that James remembered his gramma wearing many times in the past.

The stalker now backed up into the cover and moved to a closer vantage point to the woman. There was something not quite right. There was no way his gramma could use her left arm yet, but this..., this was the housekeeper. Of course. But to his shallow minded enemy, this was only another Ames.

He drew a knife from a scabbard on his leg and began to stalk toward his victim. James sensed that he wanted this to be up close and personal, to make a violent statement.

Hatred and intent rose from the young man like heat from a glowing coal. James had to decide quickly, whether to protect the woman and reveal himself, or improvise....

Margie had thrown the last of her load across several lines of wire. The hot sunshine would give them a freshness that the electric clothes dryer couldn't. She took a few steps over to one of the "little houses" her employers had promised to clean out, smiling inside at the prospect of some relief as she looked through one of the windows.

She had no real transportation and was burdened to pay a neighbor for a ride to her new daily job. It would truly be a relief in so many ways to live within walking distance, but she also knew from past experience that it would also make her too accessible and her privacy might be an issue.

She turned to go back inside and get one more load of blankets, when suddenly there before her was an apparition. A person so transparent, that he wavered with the heat of the sunshine, yet solid enough to describe.

James purposely stood directly between her and her unknown assailant so that she would not readily see the danger. James was met with a surprise when he discovered that in the direct sunlight, his power was diminished and his purpose of appearing solid was a distorted see through version of himself.

Nevertheless, his distraction was sufficient enough to complete his diversion. Unknown to her, the would-be assailant waiting for an opportunity, had slid back into hiding.

Margie chirped a scream and bounced toward the safety of the rear entrance as James faded back into vapor.

Chapter 56

Twelve people perched solemnly around a table, weary at the situation they now faced. Martin and Maime Ames sat listening to everyone's concerns about the pastoral vacancy.

Just last year Martin had relinquished the role as head of the church board and was quietly thanking God that he had. He knew that the decisions made among this well meaning group were seldom unanimous. Not everyone would see the situation with the same optimistic viewpoint as the chairman did in most situations.

This meeting was somewhat different, in the argument that they had never lost a pastor under these circumstances before.

Their previous Pastor Baskin, had retired only months ago and had been with the congregation for years. Nothing of any moral consequence had ever come up.

The only items where the church board was convened usually involved food drives or building programs and church socials.

Now they had a pastor that had fallen completely over the ledge of sanity, and had confessed to too many eager ears of his true commission at the Holiness Cathedral Church.

Many blasphemous things about church members, his true feelings toward some of the board members, the Ames included, had been scattered. It was only a matter of time before half the town referred to Holiness Cathedral as a joke.

The most damaging confession which overshadowed them all was Milton's illicit affair with Sallee Mae Poole right under the noses of everyone including her husband.

Temporary damage control was in place and no one outside of the church board and a few members of law enforcement heard the complete list of sins that he was abhorrently spewing out for anyone willing to listen. But they all knew how gossip worked.

It was a child's game that they all had played at one time or another. Sallee Mae had not been informed of the slanderous remarks at the chance that Pastor Milton had gone insane and was rambling on about his fantasies instead of actual events.

The eventuality of the situation was such that even if everything he said was a lie, it would still taint the community's mind toward the church's reputation.

Martin and Maime felt compelled to share the fact that they were selling their house to the alleged other half of this potential scandal. Their recommendation was to try to keep a lid on any loose comments and get a temporary pastor in place as quickly as possible.

For once, the entire board agreed that a scandal would only hurt the confidence of any new members and converts in the church.

One suggestion was that they give a call to the old pastor and see if he would agree to cover the position only until they could find a suitable replacement. Everyone thought it would be agreeable with the exception of Martin Ames.

"I know that Pastor Baskin would be more than capable, but he has earned his retirement," he argued. "As long as we make a quick decision in the replacement process, then I won't have a problem with it."

⁂

"Miss Catherine," said Margie, grasping at Catherine's hand. "I..., I..., just..., saw something.... I think it was a..., a ghost."

"What in the world are you talking about?" asked Catherine.

"In the back yard. I was..., there was this man..., then I ran and he faded away, right in front of my eyes! I know that sounds crazy, but you *have* to believe me."

"Let's go take a look," said Catherine, pulling Margie beside her.

"Oh, NO! I don't want to go back and look," said Margie struggling. "I don't think that's a good idea."

"Nonsense, I'll be with you the whole time," said Catherine. "I won't leave your side. Hurry."

They rushed outside and found exactly what Catherine was hoping for. Nothing.

"Where did you see this..., ghost?" asked Catherine. "Was it over here?"

Catherine pointed toward the side of the building.

"No it was.... He was..., right here," she said, pointing down at the ground in front of her.

"Okay, I believe you. Why don't we go back inside now," said Catherine. "I'll fix you something cool to drink."

"James, I hope you know what you're doing," Catherine said to herself, gritting her teeth.

Martiel Ellington met them as they hurried in the back door, "Whatever is all the commotion?"

⁂

His prey was moving faster than James thought humanly possible through the thickets and bramble. Toad was barely making a sound as his body bobbed and weaved, throwing aside limbs.

The afternoon sun was beating down on him and the pollen and seeds from the abundance of grass and weeds were littering his damp clothing.

375

James made an occasional noise to keep his quarry moving as fast as possible. He didn't want this boy to have time to stop or rest and think about where he was going.

Push.

He wanted to push his murderer the same way Syrus Earl Ames was pushed in his dream along the banks of the Mississippi, before something crushed the life out of him and made him drown in the muddy river water. It was the same way James was pushed down the river levee, beaten and crushed inside his car and drowned in that same water.

Almost two miles at a dead run and panting, the boy stopped on the edge of a stream only for a moment to catch his breath. He had used this trail before and easily found a felled tree to use as his bridge across the snake infested creek below. Not a hundred feet further was his truck parked in a thicket beside a dirt farming road.

The new murky red truck was well on its way to the same mud encrusted look as the old one, but it cranked in an instant.

James rode silently inside the filth ridden vehicle back into town, until they were about to leave the city of Natchez. Natchez Under-the-Hill sped past. He turned off the main highway and drove into a neighborhood on the bluff south of the bridge.

When the truck died, the boy let out a long tired breath and went directly to the door of a small house. After using his key to a single lock on the door, James looked on in shock as he saw a most unexpected face.

It was the old woman that had been in the cave. His last memory of her was shaking a rattle at him and cursing him, and then her wilted body on the floor of the cave. She should have been dead, but here she was, her expression still full of evil and venom.

The old woman looked up and screamed at Toad, "You dang fool! You done brung a hitchhiker home with you!"

She looked directly where James was in the doorway. James backed quickly out of the house onto the covered porch. His last experience with her was not one that he wanted to repeat. No matter how much hate he had reserved for her, he had not forgotten all the fear she had orchestrated upon him and his family. He had to go, but not before he made a statement of some kind. She needed to know that he wasn't totally powerless any longer.

"I set them all free," shouted James. "Just leave us alone."

Fear reared its ugly head when he remembered how his powers wilted in the sunlight, especially now that the old woman was staring at him.

The same croaky voice blazed back at him from inside the house and echoed into the street, "I ain't leaving nothing behind that's mine! I'll be coming for you, an every one of your kinfolk too!"

James had stayed by the door too long. The familiar wrinkled face shot out the door and glared at him. She swung a crooked black stick at James and growled something under her breath.

James felt pain shake throughout his body. An almost unbearable memory of the moment of his death flashed through him. Every piece of him felt torn and broken.

"I see you got some flesh and bones feeling's about you now," she cackled.

James' anger rose within him and he pushed the flood of pain from his body.

This was *HIS* body now.

Her eyes grew wide with shock and hatred. She retreated into the recess of the house as James shoved his fist at the wall beside the door where she had been standing.

Splinters and siding flew in an explosion as his hand went completely through the wall. The force rocked the entire house and blew a hole through the wall the size of a small window where he stood.

It was deathly quiet inside the house now. James Earl stood in complete shock, looking at his hand, as well as the damage he was responsible for. The shade of the porch had afforded him a demonstration of power without allowing her the knowledge of his daylight weakness.

His body was wavering now. He felt drained and before she could mount another wave of unbearable pain or conjure some evil to follow him, James left to fight another day, on his terms.

The sun was sinking below the horizon and darkness descending. Dug into his foxhole of a drainage ditch for hours, within close sight of the enemy's house, James sat plotting.

How had he turned his fear into the force of a jackhammer? It was like spiritual adrenaline with no instructions how to use it.

There was no time to revel in this personal discovery. Too much was at stake for spending time in trial and error, and with no one to teach him the basics of his existence, he might as well be walking around blind.

The old woman knew what she was doing. He was as far on the other end of the spectrum from the *Bokor* as Deputy Floyd was from him.

Was the old woman indestructible? He was sure he had watched the life float out of her and into the jar in the cave, or *was it her life*? It must have only been a piece of what she was or even another imprisoned spirit. If that were true, then how many more were inside her, keeping her alive?

The clay jar…, it must still be there! She must not know that it still held that part of her that the conjure had ripped from her. She had looked helplessly dead back then, lying on the dirt floor of the cave, but certainly not now.

He had to go there and find out; to destroy whatever was residing inside that clay urn. Sadly and once again, James found himself in his usual situation of needing advice, but there was no time and no one to turn to.

He had to return and destroy it now, not later. What if the spirit he had seen enter the urn wasn't some trapped benevolent soul? What if destroying the urn only released some vile evil back into existence? It could make his problem worse, much worse.

His power was once more becoming tangible inside as nightfall approached and he could feel it coursing throughout his ethereal self. He walked back along the highway, weighing his options and once again trying to calm sudden extremes of fear and rage. Oblivious to their horror, traffic along the highway flashed their lights and swerved past him, brushing past some sort of misty form in the road.

Aided by a dead calm, fog was rising above the Mississippi River and was drifting east over Natchez as the night took on a familiar mugginess.

James decided to make at least a quick trip home, even if no one there could offer any help, he was duty bound to make sure they were all safe. By the time James reached the highway to the Ames home, the dying moon was all but occluded by the density of the white blanket.

He waited outside the Ames home listening to the sounds of clatter from the day. The family supper had already come and gone, and they had congregated in the living room. James entered as quietly as he could, but did not go unnoticed by several spiritually trained senses.

Jolie looked him right in the face as he entered and her eyes widened immediately. She excused herself and met James on her way out of the room.

"I can see you James!" she said in a whispery voice. "What I mean to say is…, I think that everybody might be able to see you."

"We don't want that do we?" asked James curtly. "I need to talk to your Aunt BeBe and my Aunt Martiel as soon as possible. Do you think you can arrange that?"

Jolie noticed the coldness and desperation in his voice, but pretended not to.

"James…. I'm really sorry for how I reacted to you…," said Jolie.

"No. Before you even start, it was me Jolie, all me. I have too many things bothering me. There's too many to tell you about. In fact, the less you know the better. There's so much I still have to learn and don't know about. I don't know the risks, and I don't know what might happen. Jolie, I want you to know that whatever happens, I did love you."

"*Did* love me?" asked Jolie, shocked instantly to the point of tears.

"I can't let myself love you right now Jolie, it could hurt you even more. I shouldn't tell you any more tonight. I'm afraid for you. Can you please get our aunt's together for me? It's really important."

Jolie stood in silence looking at him.

"Hold me James, please," she asked.

"You know I can't...," said James.

"Yes you can," she said. "One more time..., please."

James released his emotions for Jolie and stood almost solid before her. She reached out into the warmth of his body but it wasn't the same for her. The scent of his body, the roughness of his face, solid arms that she craved weren't there.

She withdrew and stood with her arms folded.

"You really don't love me anymore do you?"

James started to speak, to tell her the honesty of his heart, but held silent for a moment.

"Jolie, I..., I could never *not* love you," said James.

He circled around behind her fighting familiar urges to embrace her in a kiss. She stood still as he held her, giving in to desire. The beating of her heart began to vibrate with his ethereal body, pulling him, drawing him to merge himself with her and moments later they stood together as one person.

Jolie gasped at the flood of emotions inside her. James let his true feelings flow to her, through her. In an instant, Jolie knew everything she needed to know about his true feelings for her, quieting her every fear.

James could also feel her love, and something deeper, as her body shuddered and connected to his soul.

This need and desire was too much for him. He couldn't allow himself to give in to her right now. He slowly stepped away from Jolie letting her adjust to his absence.

Jolie was breathless for a few moments and flushed from the gift of his presence. Suddenly drunk on the emotional electricity running through him, he was unable to hide the rush received from her.

"Jolie? Do you want to play cards with us...?" came floating in from another room.

"Oh..., not now," she hissed gutturally, looking up at James as he spread his warmth around her once more.

"I need to talk to our aunts," he quietly reminded her. "I have some unfinished business tonight."

"You have unfinished business right here," she smiled. James felt like a thief using her affections so selfishly. There had to be a way to remedy this.

While holding her at arms length, he spoke carefully, "Jolie you have to be out of your mind. Look at me. This is all that I am. I'm not even sure what this is anymore. You don't want this, you can't. You're holding on to something that..., could have been. I can't let you do that to yourself."

Slowly he forced himself to fade from her view.

"James?" whispered Jolie. "James."

BeBe and Martiel both sat quietly and listened to James explain his dilemma. There was a part of his story that he could never share with them and could never allow them to probe.

Raising the dead was not something that would set well or be encouraged by his dear Aunt Martiel and he was sure that her experiences would not include waking ghouls from their graves.

He limited his tale to the experiences with his murderer at the Estate up to the point of discovering the house where the *Bokor* was and what he felt he must do.

Neither of the women had a suitable answer except that he must learn to listen to what his gifts were telling him, what his heart was saying.

He told them where he was going, what he had to do and why, and fearing the worst, told them that no matter what happened to let Jolie and Catherine know that he loved them.

Chapter 57

Revelations

Providence brought James once again to the entrance of the old woman's cave. He'd been here many times, both in dreams and as an ethereal entity and it only held reminders of horror.

The cave was all but empty. The altar and its heap of sacrifices were completely removed. The ground was hardly disturbed from traffic back and forth from the cave except for a small heap of ashes near one wall.

He was too late. He looked around horrified..., the urns were gone also. An empty feeling came inside him and he raced to look at his hiding place high above the cave ceiling in a seep hole, still leaking water.

It was still there! The skull of Syrus Earl Ames.

He rose from the floor and took the skull, dropping neatly to the cave floor. He sat holding the skull in wonderment. What could be so important that the she-devil could want it so badly?

He held it up at face level and peered into the lifeless eyes.

"If you could only talk," said James.

There was a moment of uncertain epiphany inside.

James held the skull facing forward and slowly merged himself with its shape.

In a kaleidoscope of light and sound, he was transported to another time and place.

Time itself seemed to stand still as James began to relive some of the experiences in the life of Syrus Earl Ames. The information was flowing faster and faster into his mind. Mysteries began to fall into place.

The education and gifts his Aunt Martiel had struggled to explain became clearer as if his own nature. Their origin was clear also.

He learned that Syrus had a lover. James was shocked to awareness of her familiar face. The beautiful young woman that James had seen in his dreams, had seen in the circle, and had appeared as the dark old woman. Here she was, suddenly alive in the memories of Syrus. Syrus truly was never married, but she was his lover and that was his ultimate goal.

Her name was Ellie Rosalie. She was as light skinned as an islander, but she was nevertheless a quadroon. Their union was not at all accepted at the time. She accompanied him to functions in pretense of French heritage, but for the most part had to keep the quarters of a servant. They truly loved each other, but Syrus had a serious problem.

He was a gambler to the point of compulsion and made his meager living at games of chance. His abilities did not match his enthusiasm and he was always indebted to someone.

Ellie's desire for them to be together was more powerful than her judgment and she went to a woman she had heard of, a powerful Voudun woman, named Lyda Brown. Miss Lyda was what everyone called her.

She was someone that could change Syrus' luck and get them away from the trap of the Mississippi Delta.

James was shocked…, this was impossible. The woman she went to visit looked exactly like the old hag he had first seen. Was she that old or was she something else? James didn't question, but watched on as it was demonstrated how Syrus had a change of luck.

The Voodoo woman worked her conjure, but the price of this new ability was beyond evil. The old woman required the first-born child of Syrus and Ellie as payment for her dark magic.

Driven by desire, it seemed a small price to pay so that they could be together and wealthy for the rest of their lives.

Ellie kept this secret transaction from Syrus, only showing him how to use the gift she had bargained for.

Almost immediately, Ellie became pregnant and Syrus acquired a lucky streak that was unstoppable.

James saw a replay of his dream, of the night Syrus was on the riverboat, the pinnacle of his career. It was the same as the night he dreamed of Syrus Earl Ames and the beautiful woman at his side.

The victory Syrus won that night was over a powerful land magnate, which had the similar uncontrollable vice of gambling.

Syrus could see into his mind, hear his thoughts, his plotting, and there was no gambling in the truest sense of the word.

Syrus cleaned the table and the other gambler let his pride become his downfall. He couldn't stand to lose, so he bet everything he owned as a rebuttal.

Syrus won the same as in the dream. The man devoid of all his and his family's fortunes could not return empty handed and in a drunken stupor, jumped under the riverboat to his own death.

James took a moment, trying to comprehend all that he was seeing and hearing.

There were rumors of war over territories which Syrus now held the title to. Syrus took almost all that he earned and sold it off in exchange for Spanish gold.

James recalled the gold pieces that were used to pay Deputy Floyd.

Syrus hid two of many large bags of gold in a cave, the cave he was sitting in. He and Ellie were now destined to make a trip to New York.

They booked passage north on a steamship to escape the prejudice of Southern customs where they could finally be together and live as man and wife.

It was then that Ellie Rosalie revealed the price she was to pay and the full extent of the bargain she had struck with the Voudun.

Ellie cried bitter tears to Syrus and begged him not to give up their first child still in her womb.

Miss Lyda, divined that they were plotting to renege on their promise for her evil demand and called for Ellie to come see her.

Then everything changed.

Syrus found Ellie butchered and robbed of her unborn child lying on his doorsteps the day before they were to leave.

James had to take a moment to regain control of his emotions at the visions he was presented with, but they were moving faster still.

Syrus was devastated and heart broken. His Ellie, his love, had been butchered like an animal. He swore revenge on Miss Lyda, giving no thought to who and what she was.

He took the fortune in gold, gathered a few parcel land titles in Natchez as well as a plot of land in the coastal town named Biloxi and delivered it to his elder brother Samuel Earl Ames.

The fully disclosed secrets were known only to Samuel Earl himself.

Throwing caution to the wind, Syrus paid a surprise visit to the voodoo woman and confronted her with the death of his lovely Ellie Rosalie.

Armed with hatred and vengeance, Syrus shot the old woman in a heated confrontation, believing that he had killed her.

Before he left her, he found the tiny remains of his unborn baby she had stolen from Ellie. It was so beautiful, so perfectly formed and helpless.

Syrus wrapped it up, reverently. The baby should be buried with its mother, not desecrated by some old witch.

He scattered and tore the old woman's house of evil and set it afire. He stood and watched as the smoke and sparks flew upward.

An ember from the fire popped near to his feet and Syrus picked it up clutching it and crushing it in the palm of his hand.

"For Ellie," he said as his hand scorched in excruciating pain. He'd never be able to hold a deck of cards again or his Ellie Rosalie. A power surged through him, a living power as he was vindicated for his loss.

James felt a sudden surge of power as if it were him and felt the burning coal in his hand. The memories were identical to the burn of the brand on his foot. It was almost as if he had shared and relived some of the pain and torture of his long past relation.

Syrus fled upriver, but unknown to him, the Voudun woman was very much alive. She crawled from the ashes and sent out a dark evil thing to crush Syrus.

James stopped and reflected at what he had been shown in the last few moments.

The dream of how Syrus had died was almost the same as what came next. The intensity was also as real. Syrus had relived and regretted the winnings from his gambling and the death of the magnate, almost to the point of insanity, right up until his death. The condemnation was killing him already.

The body of Syrus Earl Ames was discovered before the old woman could get her clutches on him. A fishing boat found him and his package wrapped in cloth. Syrus was found face down still holding the premature infant and had written "Ellie" in the hard packed sand.

But something happened upon his death, he didn't pass on immediately. He found his brother Samuel, appeared to him in a vision, and told him the full extents of his tragedy.

Samuel his brother buried Syrus Earl Ames in the family ground, but Ellie Rosalie was buried in another place, in a public graveyard.

James snapped to attention. She's using Ellie Rosalie to destroy the Ames family! The names! He had to check the names of the other grave robberies to be sure. But what did the *Bokor* want their child for?

The woman he watched wisp into the urn, which was now missing, held the key. Did he need to set her free and let her spirit go to Syrus? If that was all it was to this, then the old woman already had that. No, it was something more. Syrus had taken more from her than the child. James had something she still wanted, whether it was spiritual or physical, he could not tell for sure, but she was willing to kill his entire family to get it.

James was filled with strange sensations. He stood up and carried the skull of Syrus back to its refuge. His senses ached from having merged with the memory of Syrus.

Even with a clear understanding of who he was fighting, he still needed help.

Several hours had passed, but the fog was still present as he left the cave and it was much lower and thicker now.

James walked past the inlet where the big truck had been dumped, past where he died, and up the highway toward home.

There was the sound of his footsteps, solid as any man carrying weight. The sound kept him company as he mulled over the new information. The fog lit in a hazy yellow for a moment as a car appeared, swerved and honked its horn. He was losing his ability to hide unless he concentrated. This could prove to be a problem if he couldn't control his emotions; after all, they seemed to spark the visibility of his ethereal body.

A misty dew began to collect on his body and he felt the dampness of the night air. James couldn't understand the changes in himself. It was if he was real some of the time and a phantom the rest, and losing the control of an in-between.

Near daybreak Sunday morning, James arrived at the driveway of the Ames Estate. He jumped inside the house waiting for someone to wake that could listen to his new madness. He settled himself in a chair in Aunt Martiel's room waiting for her morning vigil.

He watched her sleeping and longed for rest himself. He was truly weary and tired, but there was no sleep for him. With eyes perpetually open, and the silence of the estate, he waited.

Chapter 58

Tricks and Traps

Martin Ames poured his first cup of coffee of the morning and walked to the front door. The light coming through the glass panes seemed tainted somehow, reminding him of a time when he did not like the estate or anything in it. That was a time when all he wanted to do was get away from it; always catching something moving, barely a wisp in the corner of his vision. Something that he didn't want to see…, refused to see.

Since moving back, since these last few days at the family estate, Martin had lost his fears and that indescribable feeling. Until now….

He opened the door and leapt backwards.

Hanging from the eaves of the porch, above the steps, was a dozen black chickens.

All dead. All headless. All bloodless…, wings spread and limp.

The steps were covered in carnage and foul odors.

On the front door, the porch, were smears of red swirls and patterns. It appeared to be some kind of sick art or symbols painted with the blood of these vile dead animals. A stench was already rising from the forming blood rot as the sun began to heat the carnage. Hordes of flies were collecting.

He rushed back inside shutting the door and snatched up the telephone. Martin Earl refused to let anyone go outside the front of the house despite their heated questions. The scene was too ghastly for any normal person to have created.

"Let's get ready for church and let the law handle it," he said fearfully.

Sam, full of curiosity, managed to sneak out the door connecting the kitchen with the garage to take a quick look at the butchery his grandfather had only hinted of. His stomach rolled over and he heaved a dry constriction at the sight of the blood and carcasses. He should have listened and stayed in the house.

The first law officer arrived in less than five minutes, but it was much later before Detective Mason, Deputy Floyd and two other officers arrived. The first officer had only made sure that no one walked through the scene.

"This confirms my suspicions that this is some kind of cult activity," said Detective Mason. "I guess that story from New York wasn't as far fetched as we believed. This changes everything."

Deputy Floyd was jotting down notes and looking busy.

After hearing the turmoil from his grandfather and sensing activity downstairs, James left his sleeping aunt and cautiously made his way to the front of the house. The sight of the evil inflamed his anger but after he began observing the details none of the others could see, his curiosity went into overdrive.

Upon each of the art forms was a little chalky black demon watching patiently and slashing out at each of the people that came within its reach.

Each photographers flash at one of the swirly art forms, *vèvès*, caused its personal little imp to hiss and slash at him, barely missing his legs. Invisible to everyone else, their demonic presence was in plain view to James. His between-worlds visage shook him back to his hard personal reality.

On the porch, on the door, on the steps and in the yard, black entities perched, waiting. Another officer stepped up to the edge of a *vèvè* nearest the steps and scuffed at the red crusty-dry blood with the toe of his polished shoes and was met with a precarious slash.

Jumping backwards he swatted vigorously at his pants legs swearing. Upon raising his pant leg, there was a whelp from something like a bee sting swelling on his calf.

Martin Ames was standing perilously close to one of the markings and the demon was feverishly slashing out in the air in his direction. Just a few more inches closer and it would be able to reach him.

As James approached, all the impish guards saw him and snapped to attention, perching on their clawed feet. Their legs were chained and shackled to the bloody art, unable to leave their post of duty. Their fetters allowed them only restricted movement.

James moved in close and knelt down near the *vèvè* on the porch nearest the door. It had lost the determined interest in gashing at his grandfather.

This was the largest and most vicious looking of all. It extended its teeth from its gums and lips in a drooling snarl and pushed venomous looking claws from sheathed fingertips. It was clearly not afraid of any of the humans walking around it, but was terrified of James, frantically pulling at its restraints to back away.

The imp's charred cadaverous body was heaving in breaths of air, flexing and exposing the crisscrossed bones of its ribcage.

"Aren't you an ugly little thing," said James, which earned him a vicious hiss of sulfurous fumes and drooling spit from the demon.

It reached down and yanked at its own chain feverishly trying to release itself. James slowly reached down and took hold of the chain where it was attached to the symbol and yanked on it.

It broke as easily as a dry twig and he stood holding the end of the chain, now a convenient leash. James arose and moved backwards slowly while tugging on the brittle leash.

The imp growled and whined and fought against him as it moved perilously close to the bloody edge of its predefined territory. Extended claws dug deep into the wood porch, just as James gave it a sharp yank.

The demon screamed, burst into a ball of smoke and disappeared.

"Crap!" said one of the officers. "Did you see that? Come here and look at the marks on the porch. I was looking right at it when these scratches rolled up on the wood."

While the others carefully gathered around to look at the sideshow, James went to each of the *vèvès* and performed the same procedure sending all the little dark terrors back to their origins.

He knew exactly whose handiwork this was, but needed to find a way for the law officers to link them to the old woman and her helper.

"Shows over..., get some pictures and look around for anything else out of order. Can one of you find out who might sell this variety of chicken?" asked the detective. "These are the biggest black hens I've ever seen."

"I've seen these symbols before," said one the officers. "I was in New Orleans with friends one year after Mardi Gras. We got lost in an old section of town and these symbols were all over this particular house. There were lots of people walking the street, but the locals wouldn't walk on the sidewalk or even look over at the house. We heard it was a Voodoo curse on the people that lived there."

"So the symbols looked like these?" asked the detective. "Make sure we get pictures of all these and you see if you can track down what they mean. That's a really good start."

"Don't tell me you believe in all that voodoo stuff," grumbled Martin Ames.

"No, but somebody does," said Mason. "And here's the proof."

He waved his hands pointing around to all the gore displayed on their home.

"None of you heard anything, even though this mess is everywhere?"

"Any idea when we can get this off our house, detective?" asked Martin, covering his mouth with his shirtsleeve. "It stinks to high heaven."

"After we get pictures of everything, we'll have someone take the birds down and bag them. Probably by this afternoon," he answered.

"We're going to church. We'll leave the house open. Would you lock up everything before you leave?"

BeBe and Jolie left for their home, at the recommendation of both Aunt Martiel and Catherine. This was too close and personal and the implications were too obvious that something bad was destined to anyone inside the house.

However Catherine's warnings were useless. Both women said that they would not run from the scare tactics and would be back later to help remove the bloodstains.

Aunt Martiel skipped church in lieu of making a trip to her home in Biloxi, which she had all but abandoned these last few weeks. The evil from that mornings' surprise prompted her need to hire a guard for her beachfront property.

James surveyed the damage and took his time looking at the bloody symbols. He remembered some of the same had been displayed in the cave, and on the clay *govi*, by the hand of the old woman.

His thoughts of failure began to overtake him once again.

These people probably drove right up to the front of the house sometime after his encounter with her that past evening.

Why didn't he come straight home? He could have been here, but he had been out of place again, away from where he was needed. Had they already committed these atrocities before he arrived at the estate last night? Or did they occur afterward while he waited at the bedside of his sleeping Aunt Martiel?

He could already hear his Aunt Martiel and mother scolding him no matter the vandalus timing.

Even after the priceless information he'd received from the skull of Syrus, his first priority was his family. They were all in church now, and everyone including Jolie and her aunt were scattered in several directions. He should have followed them.

With the estate emptied of his friends and family, he managed to get Deputy Floyd alone.

"Hello deputy," said James. "Glad to see you could make it."

He did his usual spin and duck at the sound of James' voice, but didn't acknowledge him.

"We both know who did this," said James. "I saw them late yesterday."

"I've already got one heck of a hangover," whispered Floyd. "Please…, give me a break."

"You work for me now, Floyd," said James. "No more breaks. No more alcohol. I had planned on giving you everything you needed to get started Monday morning, but today is just as good. Come take a walk with me around back."

Reluctantly the deputy strolled around the side of the house where he could talk more freely.

"Look Williams, if that's who you really are. I don't want any more trouble with you. Why can't you leave me alone?"

"I thought we had an agreement, Floyd. Do you need to be convinced again that it's to your benefit to help me?"

"No…. No…, I don't need any…," muttered Floyd.

"We're wasting time then. The guy that did this came through here, behind this little house out back."

"How do you know?" asked Floyd.

"I followed him yesterday - all the way to his truck and then all the way to his house."

"Why didn't you take care of it yourself then?" asked Floyd.

"That's your job..., from now on. Instead of what you've been doing, you're going to be Mr. Perfect. Look back here and follow the trail. If you get lost, all you have to do is ask me and I'll nudge you in the right direction."

"So what if I do help you? Aren't you going to kill me afterward?"

"Don't be stupid. If you do a good job and you're believable, then we'll see. But if you don't..., well..., there are worse things than death, Floyd, and I've met them."

"Detective!" yelled Floyd nervously. "Come look back here. This might be the trail they took.

James bumped and nudged Deputy Floyd through the overgrowth and wooded terrain until the trail was obvious enough even for Floyd and his hangover. He couldn't afford to make any more mistakes.

The time was now to do some damage of his own.

Chapter 59

Holiness Cathedral Church was full and the music was somehow alive this Sunday morning. The usually complacent congregation was standing and clapping with their songbooks in their hands.

Too many funerals had recently frequented its walls.

When it was announced that their old retired pastor would be temporarily serving the congregation, he was met with loud approval from most everyone.

They told the church that Pastor Arnie Milton had suddenly taken ill, that he wouldn't be able to continue and needed their prayers.

After a short fiery sermon and the traditional altar call, Pastor Baskin announced that there would be a dinner provided immediately after dismissal in the recreation hall.

Sallee Mae looked around desperately during the start of the service for the face of Pastor Milton. There were whispers and a few sharp glances her direction, but for the most part she had no idea where he was or what had happened.

As soon as the service ended, she hurried home, especially when no one seemed inclined to tell her what had happened.

Her spirits were not dampened by the sudden coldness of some of the church members. She had been given approval that Saturday evening to begin moving into her new house only a short distance away.

James sat hidden across the street from a house on Riverside Drive, a road on the bluff above the Mississippi River. It had a piece of plywood covering a conspicuous hole in the wall beside the door. Something he was quite proud of.

The window beside the door was spidery with cracks in several places, no doubt from the impact of his rage. He sat patiently watching and waiting for movement. An hour passed without any commotion whatsoever. James was about to go up to the house and search it out for signs of life, when the front door opened.

Out walked the kid, which he heard the old woman loudly refer to as Toad, closely accompanied by the old woman. She could have passed for any elderly senior citizen as she nimbly made her way to the truck.

James was reminded of Granny Smith and how reticent her efforts were, as she would make her way alone up her street with a cumbersome walker. He wished in that moment that he had made the time to walk her all the way to her house those few Sunday mornings that he had seen her.

His thoughts of benevolence were interrupted by the whirring of the engine of Toad's truck. They drove off up the street and out of sight.

James wasted no time in hurrying over to the porch of the house. He tried to step inside through the door and found himself facing outside walking away from the house. He walked to the shattered window and pressed through into the room and once again ended up walking away from the porch.

It was the same experience that James had encountered at his grandparents' house only in reverse.

It must be a conjure or spell of some kind. The one at his grandparents' old house was a trap, while this one was somehow repelling his entry. He had defeated the one at the other house, but he needed some time to figure this one out.

He thought back sadly on the family ancestors that had been trapped for so long and so many generations in the Ames family house. What a price to pay for gifts and wealth. He thought it interesting that it was almost as if they had been collected over the years.

James looked for a weakness around the house and each entry point returned him to the front of the house walking away. A light of memory, his or someone else's, flashed inside him.

He stood at the door, turned around, and backed into the house. Technically, he was leaving, so it admitted him inside.

The house looked like any other normal household of an elderly person. He walked from room to room and found nothing of substance. It was when he entered the short hallway to the garage door when he saw it.

Two peering eyes blinked open and closed, then became still. There was a predator awaiting its prey. If there was a guard dog, there must be something to guard inside.

James tested his adversary and placed his hand on the wall leading to the entryway. It remained still. Step by step he moved forward slowly, waiting for a reaction. It didn't appear to be like the sticky trap thing that had infested the grandparents' house, so what was its specialty?

James didn't really want to find out. Carefully, he collected his thoughts. Fear and emotions could either help or hurt him in almost every circumstance that he faced lately.

His daily existence was still trial and error. Any error here might be the end for him or more importantly his family.

He placed his hand flat on the wall and stood still, feeling, sensing his enemy through the structure of the walls.

There was intelligence in the darkness around the corner. Very base and simplistic, but dangerous. He could try going into the garage from the outside, but backing in could leave him exposed to some unspoken horror if there was another of these.

He placed his hand more firmly against the wall and concentrated on the coldness that had permeated his being when he first crossed over to this world.

The brittle cold traveled the surface of the wall, creeping toward the inanimate darkness. The creature stirred uncomfortably. Then he sensed something of its instincts. The creature was a kind of fear, fear itself, like a spirit.

James pulled from his resources and listened to his heart. The opposite was courage, faith, belief.

It could be that simple, or that quick an end. Either way it was time for action not procrastination.

James pressed the cold into the wall further to drive his enemy out into the open. He suddenly felt the creature reaching out to him, but for what? He got the answer to his question as he stepped closer.

The figure of his mother appeared before him and was in obvious pain and suffering. He watched as her body twisted and contorted into agonizing positions no human could endure. Her voice called to him for help. A simple plea.

James laughed at the transfigurations lie and stepped forward. The face of his mother changed into the gaunt face of Jolie, emaciated and weeping. James took another step and faced his enemy. It seemed to be warning of future events, almost a threat if there were some unseen lines that were crossed.

James allowed his rage to emerge with his own threat, slapping the wall with his hand. He screamed a warning as if scaring a dog to run. The creature receded back into a dark recess, skulking and watching.

Warily he passed, with a cautious eye on the creature as he entered the garage. There was the altar, with its multitude of candles and mound of offerings, the sweetness of rot and carnage filling the air. On the altar were pieces of clothing, hair, small pieces of jewelry, probably belonging to his family members.

Effigies of her intended victims were lying bound and blindfolded.

Then he sensed movement in the room. Several more entities, hideous and tortured souls that looked like the ghouls from his graveyard experience, stared at him and began stalking him and surrounding him. Time was running out.

He looked around the room and saw several urns resting beside each other near the opposite side of the altar. As he hurried to the altar, he instantly became cut off from any retreat by one of the ghoulish human like creatures.

He slapped at some of the putrefying offerings and sacrifices, sending them flying into the center of the room with a meaty plop. Their attention turned immediately and several began to try to ingest a freshly rotting meal.

James slid to the urns. Which one? He placed his hands on them one at a time feeling and listening. Then he remembered the oak plug that he had placed into the opening of the one that contained his quest.

He slid the urn in front of the altar with its tiered candles casting a grim illumination in the room. There was still the sound of slurping and other gastric noises where he had thrown the elements of the altar.

He spun the lid of the urn slowly, praying that this wasn't the biggest mistake that he had made to date. The cap released with a low resonating sound - poooh....

Remembering the tale of Syrus Earl and his loss due to the cursed *Bokor* that had killed his Ellie Rosalie, he hoped and prayed this was her and not some evil entity. It was too late now to change his mind, the lid was open.

Slowly a wisp of dust swirled up from the mouth of the urn.

The woman he had trapped inside, formed in front of him with a rage in her eyes. James didn't notice that the creatures in the room cringed and removed themselves to the farthest recesses of the garage in fear.

His eyes were transfixed on the person that solidified in front of him and looked deeply into him. The rage and anger disappeared and she extended her hand to James.

Some strange look of recognition filled her face and eyes.

"Syrus? Where is our child?"

She carefully clutched her stomach with her other hand.

James put out his hand in consolation to hold hers.

"I'll help you find her," said James without hesitation. "I'll help you."

This wisp of Ellie Rosalie leapt inside James with a force. The unexpected jolt left James nauseated and dizzy in an instant. Then waves of raw power began to ebb and flow inside him. The feelings were strong as water flowing from end to end captured inside a vessel.

He turned and raked the altar clean with a sweep of his hand, destroying the effigies and desecrating the offerings of the *Bokor* to her evil *Petro Loa*.

The room was instantly dark except for the flickering light of a few candles, which rolled to a stop and began pooling wax on the floor.

Everything whether living or nonliving scattered at once, cowering in the recesses of the corners.

James was yet again reeling and wavering from the increased sensations. How could she be inside him, spirit within a spirit?

He felt the inhabitation, but there wasn't time to explore the changes, he knew he had to leave, as quickly as possible, now.

He walked to the garage door and hit it full force, with an explosion of splinters and frame. Sunlight filled the garage, wilting the specters inside into swirls of rising dust and ash.

Something was wrong though. He was solid. What had she done to him?

He looked down at himself..., at least he was clothed.

Oh, this was bad... Or was it? Oh yes..., this was bad. He could already imagine the look on his family's face. They had already buried him, had his funeral.

"You would rather not be seen?" asked Ellie with a kind Southern drawl.

"It would be better," said James. "For now at least."

He faded back into transparency and slowly disappeared.

"That was good work, deputy," said Detective Mason. "I believe this was the entry route for sure. You must be part blood hound."

There were now two cars sitting on a dirt farm road on the other side of a creek about two miles from the Ames house. There was a single set of tire tracks other than the ones made by the Sheriff's Department.

"Looks like it was a truck," said Deputy Floyd. "By the type of the tread."

"I think you're right," said the detective and then he pointed over to one of the officers and motioned for them to take pictures.

"You're doing good so far. What else do you see?" he asked.

"I don't see anything else, no footprints of any kind, but we'll look around," said Floyd, bilking the limelight for all it was worth.

BeBe walked from the stock room, sweaty and tired. She and Jolie had unboxed their Sunday afternoon deliveries of supplies for the next week and placed them in their freezers as well as on the storeroom shelves.

At least one week a month she and Jolie would take over the responsibilities of stocking and taking a quick inventory of their operating supplies, letting her family workers have time off.

She also felt that this way she would stay in touch with the day to day activities of her employees. She sat down in her office to file the freight receipts when she heard the tiny front doorbell jingle.

"Hello?" she asked, but there was no answer. "We're closed."

After remembering that Jolie had locked the front door when they arrived, she got up and peered into the restaurant. It was dimly lit from the few lights near the kitchen.

"Jolie honey," said BeBe, looking around, then stepped fully into the dining room. "Jolie?"

She hurried to the front door, which was locked. She turned and listened, but the only sound she heard was of her own heartbeat. BeBe listened intently with her senses to locate her niece and felt her whimper..., and then nothing. It was gone.

BeBe ran and opened the front door, looking into the early night. The street was completely quiet except for one lone car which had stopped and was calmly idling at the corner traffic signal a block away. It took off slowly after the light switched to green.

There was very little pedestrian traffic of any sort. It was after all Sunday evening and downtown was deserted, which was the main reason that they didn't open on Sunday evenings in the first place.

"Jolie!" she called into the night.

She returned inside quickly and went to the back door where the freight trucks delivered and the pull down door was still latched and locked. There were no other exits.

Something wasn't right, she felt it inside. Jolie was no where to be found. She ran back to her office and called the sheriff.

Floyd sat quietly at his desk making notes of the day's events and organizing the evidence they had collected at the Ames family residence.

"You did well today," boomed a voice from behind him.

Deputy Floyd spun and dropped a handful of papers on the floor, in nervous terror.

Sheriff Howard quickly apologized, "I didn't mean to scare you, Floyd. I came by to check on what was being done on the Ames case."

Floyd was visibly relieved and bent over to scoop up the papers he had scattered.

"Detective Moore said you were instrumental in helping today. I knew you'd be a great help Floyd."

"Thank you. I mean, I'm glad," said Deputy Floyd. "I was just lucky I guess."

"Oh, I think your luck will hold out," said Sheriff Howard. "A little bird told me you'd be the right man for the job. Well, I see that you have everything in good order, so I'm going to lock up and go home. See you bright and early in the morning."

The sheriff walked over and clicked the door lock on his office and left for the evening, with the deputy alone in the office area.

The night clerk was busy talking on the phone with the night dispatcher. Other than their usual chatter, he was alone.

"I see you're making yourself useful," said James.

The deputy came unwound once again, but didn't make quite the same mess the second time.

"Don't DO that!" said the deputy into the air. "And I hate talking to myself."

James let himself materialize into flesh before the deputy.

Deputy Floyd turned white as a sheet and scooted backwards against his desk chair.

"You.... You.... You...," stammered Floyd.

"Yeah, I'm real," said James and he patted the deputy on the cheek with his hand. "You told me you didn't like talking to air. Which do you want?"

"I..., I don't want either!" said Floyd, flustered.

"Well, get a hold of yourself, we need to talk. I found out some information you need. You might as well take a seat and listen a few minutes.

"I know where these people are staying. Your friend Billy Don Poole has some connections to two really bad characters. One is an old woman that is bad as the devil himself and another stays with her like some tick and drives her around. He's another kid that she calls 'Toad'. Now Toad is the one that ran me off the levee and killed me."

"You mean to tell me that you met the person that did that to the Mastyn kid?" he asked quietly.

"More than once I'm afraid. They're staying in a house over on Riverside Drive, up on the bluff by the river. Do I need to write this down for you?" asked James. Picking up a pen and paper, he wrote down the address of the house. "Here, so you don't get lost."

"What if.... I don't want to have anything to do with her," said Floyd. "I don't mind telling you, from everything I've heard and seen, she scares me."

"More than me?" asked James.

"Oh yeah..., way more than you. She doesn't care who she hurts or how bad. I don't want to be on her shit list."

"I can keep her off you," said James. "As long as you do everything I tell you to do. I've been stirring her kettle for a few days now.

"Oh, and one more thing Floyd. If you do happen to hear from Billy, it's not a good idea that you tell Billy about his wife and her little bastard baby. I'll explain later."

The night clerk came storming through her door into the officers' area.

"I received a call from The Cajun Café a few blocks from here. This lady says her niece is missing and the woman's frantic. Can you take the call, deputy?"

"Isn't there anybody else on call tonight?" asked Deputy Floyd.

"Yeah, but they're handling a ruckus down near the docks," she said. "Looks like you're it. By the way..., where did your friend go?"

Floyd looked around the empty room and shrugged.

BeBe was seated on the curb outside her Café frantically waiting on someone from the Sheriff's Department to arrive. The wind rose and fell at the arrival of James.

"What happened!" he asked excitedly. "Where's Jolie?"

"She's gone. We were doing our usual unboxing and stocking and I turned around.... James, I'm really scared."

"Did you see anything..., anything at all?" asked James.

"Nothing, I only heard the front doorbell jingle, but it was locked. That's when I went to look for her, but the door was locked, James."

"They wanted you to know she was gone," said James angrily. "I'll find her, don't worry, I'll find her."

They could see a car coming up the main street with colored lights blinking on the top.

"That'll be Deputy Floyd. Tell him everything you can." BeBe shook her head in confusion, "But he's one of the people that…."

"Trust me, he works for me now. If he does anything you don't like at all, tell me…, and I mean anything."

Chapter 60

Sallee Mae Poole parked in the driveway to her new house. Her house, not some rented junky place in a rundown neighborhood. That neighborhood, where anything not nailed down outside was gone by the next day's dawn. For the first time in ages, she smiled at the potted flowers on her front porch. For the first time in forever, it felt like home.

It wasn't that she was uppity by any means. The life she had lived with her parents in a poverty stricken area had taught her how to make do with what she had been given.

She had seen her mother "invent" meals out of whatever varied items were available in the pantry on many occasions. As a little girl she remembered weeks of beans, mustard greens, ketchup sandwiches; all something to fill her growling stomach. And glad to get it.

Her father had been a farmer most of his early life, but after several years of failed crops he ended up working as day labor for other farms in the area. His desire to give his wife a better life had driven him into depression and alcohol. He died when she was fourteen years old. They said he fell from the seat of a tractor and into the shredder following behind it. Most likely he was drunk.

Her mother gave up after the accident. She still lived in a county home somewhere in Louisiana, not really remembering who she was or anybody else for that matter.

Sallee pushed the thoughts aside hoping for something brighter to fill her mind. She wondered from time to time where Billy came up with the wonderful 'deals' and fast paying jobs, but she didn't ask questions. He liked it that way and when it came right down to it, she didn't care.

Her truck was loaded with mostly clothes and food items. There wasn't a stick of furniture that Sallee Mae wanted to bring with her to her new home. It would only remind her of the rat nest she was leaving behind.

She grabbed several items in her arms and opened the front door with the key. Her key. The sound of the click of the latch gave her a thrill and she stepped into the warm light of a lamp in the living room.

She went through the front of the house flipping on light switches and admiring the brightness of the house.

An hour passed by with a steady stream of trips and finally the truck was emptied of its load into the living room and a few items littering the front porch.

She wanted to go through everything once more to make sure she wanted to keep what was here.

Sallee Mae stacked up a small pile of clothes that she wanted to wash before they were put away, then neatly hung the rest in the main bedroom.

She had never seen such large rooms and the house was enormous to her. How could anybody ever leave such a nice cozy home?

Maybe they fell on hard times.

Music. She needed some music to clear the cobwebs of her thoughts. There was no reason to keep going back to all those dreary things and digging up old bones.

Sallee locked the front door and flipped on the air conditioning, no more sweltering nights with that tiny overused window unit.

She found her little transistor radio and set it up in the living room and as soon as it flipped on it began blasting out a tinny *Delta Dawn* lightening her mood.

Everything was put away now in its own place and she scooped up the armload of clothes and walked down the hall to the back of the house where the washroom was.

She couldn't help feeling an uneasy rolling in her stomach as she neared the end of the hall. Although the light was on, it still seemed dark back here. She shivered as she past the back bedroom door, even though she was perspiring from her hurried pace.

Once inside the washroom she noticed that everything was brand new except for the washer and dryer. But they were still a far cry better than having to go to the neighborhood laundromat every week.

There was the smell of new wood and paint and everything looked so clean it made her smile. She shoved in her first load of laundry and suddenly felt a little out of place like some servant doing laundry as a housekeeper.

The switch popped on and she happily listened to the whirring of the water filling the machine. She flipped off the light and a new vapor light in the back yard filled the room with soft friendly light through the large windows.

Giddy with excitement, Sallee Mae hurried back inside and fell across her bed. There was no good reason to leave, so she decided not to go back over to her old house tonight.

She had two more days to vacate the tiny apartment and could easily get the rest of their things in one trip tomorrow morning. Tonight she would stay in her new home.

She relaxed across the comfortable mattress and lightly dozed.

Click... click clik... Click click click...

She woke with a start, the washer was making a funny sound and she jumped quickly and hurried down the hall. The load had gotten unbalanced and it was thumping gently against the side of the dryer. She shifted the load and waited until it was finished, then moved everything to the dryer.

A thrill raced through her again at the new surroundings and she was enormously pleased with herself.

The hall light still seemed dim to her and she decided to get a brighter bulb to light it up. She had bought several with her, robbing them from other fixtures of the old house. After scratching through a box, she picked a hundred watt bulb and carried her short step stool down the hall.

After removing the old bulb with a cloth, it became unusually dark down the hall. She fumbled with the new bulb until it finally turned in the socket, light shocking her eyes. It blinked to life and she backed down and away from the fixture.

This light seemed even dimmer. She held up the bulb she had removed. A hundred fifty watts was stenciled on the glass.

Click..., clik. Clik. Click....

She heard a noise from inside the back bedroom. It was quiet in the house other than the gentle whirring coming from the dryer in the back washroom.

She opened the bedroom door and flipped on the light switch. What a nice room. She propped the door open to let the room air out. It obviously hadn't been used in some time, because it had a musty closed in scent to it.

It would make a great nursery. It was perfectly situated and the morning sun would pour in one of the windows.

But that planning would have to wait. She was worn out and it was time to rest. It was evident that she would get plenty of that tonight. That weasel of a man she had been visiting for so long, bolted like a coward after he found out that he had potentially fathered a child.

Without so much as a goodbye....

"Ha!" laughed Sallee Mae to herself. "Good riddance."

It was cold..., so cold. Jolie woke up in complete darkness and up to her waist in water. Her jeans were gone and she was left with only panties and the t-shirt she had worn that day.

Suspended by her hands and wrists, which were bound high over her head, Jolie slowly tried to move. Her ankles were bound tightly with something that felt like duct tape.

There was a crooked springy limb behind her head, twisted around in front of both underarms forcing her head and neck forward.

After swallowing painfully, she tried to clear her aching head.

It was painful to move and she was dangling on her tiptoes in mud. The water around her seemed to be moving back and forth, maybe from the river or a cove.

Her head began to pound and her wrists were aching from the cord that had her suspended. Something warm was sliding down her forehead and onto her nose. She couldn't rub or scratch it or turn her head against her shoulder to remove it.

"How did I get here?" she moaned into an echoing void.

Her voice seemed to die and she yelled hoarsely, despite her chin digging against her throat, "Can anybody hear me!"

There was nothing but the muffled sounds of tree frogs chirping their mating calls into the night. She was inside something, some hollow enclosure, everything echoed.

Jolie bounced up on her tiptoes to relieve her aching wrists and neck. Her hands were numb from the constriction. The longer she pushed up with her toes; the calves of her legs began to cramp, amplified by the stress and the cold.

One continuous echo of lapping water filled the deep silence. It sounded as if she was in the middle of wherever this was.

"Hello!" she yelled again.

That evil stick behind her head was making her dizzy and it hurt her throat to yell.

The ooze that had rested on her nose now made its way slowly to her upper lip and hung stickily in place. She pursed her lips and blew at it to remove it and some dripped into her mouth, yielding a familiar metallic taste.

It was blood, her blood.

Her head was still pounding and unclear but she knew that she couldn't last much longer here. If this was the river, there were snakes, bugs..., there were also alligators.

A mosquito landed on her left eyelid and she batted her eye frantically to remove it.

How long had she been unconscious?

"Help!" she yelled again, and suddenly it was almost impossible to breathe.

The sound of her own voice hurt her ears in the enclosure. Her head ached and she drifted toward unconsciousness.

Slowly a full understanding of her situation rang clear; this could be the end for her. She wasn't being held here. She was being disposed of. Her bare toes pushed down in the silty mud to lift the weight from her aching arms, again creating a knife stabbing leg cramp. The pain was jolting up her body as she tried to bend her knee to loosen up the muscle.

The rope ground into her wrists again. It was almost a crucifixion.

"James, find me James," she whispered as she drifted into her own darkness.

"I'll be with you soon."

BeBe sat fidgeting in the most uncomfortable chair she could remember inside the Sheriff's Office. Sheriff Howard had been with her since five o'clock and attempting to orchestrate a search for her missing niece.

Catherine and Martin Ames arrived a short time earlier and Martin was explaining to Sheriff Howard how he and James had removed almost five pounds of sugar from her gas tank only days ago. How he believed that Jolie's disappearance was related to what was going on with his family.

The sheriff had tried to console BeBe, telling her that this kind of thing sometimes happened. Jolie had lost her friend James, and it was possible that she needed to be alone for a little while as a process of grieving.

BeBe had violently assured him that Jolie was not like the usual girl, which is why Catherine and Martin were also present.BeBe had tried to reach both her mother in California and her father on the east coast, but there had been no answer from either of them.

It was now well past six in the morning and Deputy Floyd had found his way to his desk after only a few hours sleep. He had passed off the search to the previous shift and Sheriff Howard.

BeBe refused to go home and get some rest, determined that her presence would force some type of results. Catherine had been instrumental in calming her down from the frenzy of her worry, but it was like two mother hens trying to calm each other.

BeBe was staring coldly into nothing and then she looked up at Catherine.

"She's alive," said BeBe. "She's blood of my blood and I can feel her. But there's no way for me to tell where."

James was listlessly searching through town following every possible route from the café. There were dozens of possibilities to anywhere.

"Jolie, you have to call to me."

He had checked both residences, which were vacant, the city park, the cave was deserted also.

"Ellie, can you help me?" asked James in desperation. "I don't know what else to do."

"Only if you can calm yourself," she answered from deep inside him.

"How can I? I can't shut off my thoughts."

Ellie Rosalie's voice seemed to soothe him as her voice lulled forward in his mind, "Let me do the work then. Let me come forward and you get quiet."

James felt the same surge of power he had before. It began to overwhelm him and it was if he were floating in that warm place in his dream, almost like being back in his mother's womb.

"See her with your heart. Feel her with your love. Call to her."

James pictured their first meeting and Jolie's tormenting gait as he followed her across the street from the library that first day.

Suddenly the euphoria left him. He felt cold and wet and his body was hurting all over similar to the night he wrecked. He was filled with sensations of the water lapping on his body and it was all he could take.

"I can't do it. It's like I'm dying all over again."

"Relax James," said Ellie. "That's not you that you're feeling, it's her."

"But it was so cold…, is…, is she dead?"

"No or you would not have found her."

The hazy light of dawn was burning its way into the night sky as James walked southward along the riverside. There were boats docked along the banks in various places and stages of repair.

"She is very near to us," said Ellie. "Hear her with your love."

"Where are you, Jolie?"

The night began to evaporate into a dark brownish-green haze. Morning sun trickled in from some tiny crevice, shooting a dart of light into the murky water.

Jolie could no longer feel her shoulders or arms. Searing numbness governed her upper body, but there were yet angry tingling feelings in her legs and feet. Her head could no longer lift against the cruel stick and her voice was barely a hiss.

The water had risen to a level above her waist and there was no longer a reason to push up. Something slid by her leg, slick against her skin, circled, then ended up back by her feet where it stopped.

"Help." she whispered hoarsely, a final plea.

She begged with the last of her strength, "Please."

Something nibbled at her little toe and it stung past the cold numb. She curled her toes under tight, causing her calves to cramp severely into knotting flames.

"Oh, God help me," she whispered as she closed her eyes.

There was a thudding above her. Thud and slide. Her world seemed to move and her body shifted positions like a pendulum.

She tried to cry out, but nothing came from her tired constricted lungs. Her breathing had been too shallow to supply any more oxygen than to keep her barely alive.

The little monster that had nibbled her toe was back. It swam and slid its slick body across her foot. Then came back and swam between her legs, getting trapped for a moment because of its size. Two sharp spines on pectoral fins gouged her inner thighs and gouged their way through. It was a huge catfish, ready for supper and she was its menu.

There was a loud cracking noise from above and light blinded her swollen eyes, just as she sank into a final delirium.

James saw the partially sunken fishing boat among several overturned skiffs. Its lower belly was buried in the mud but still yawing side to side with the current of the river. There was life here, somewhere. The trapdoor to the lower cabin was jammed shut and a new shiny brass lock in the hasp. This had to be it.

He knew he had to hurry. He boarded the vessel, dragging a large dislocated board with him. One good slam and the lid exploded into rotted splinters leaving the brass lock and hasp still fast in its place.

There below in the darkness was a body.

Jolie was unresponsive, her limp frame suspended from the cargo pulley. She was dangling in a slow spin from the motion of the rocking hull, a cruel crooked stick jammed behind her neck.

James panicked.

She looked dead and the water was swirling and sloshing beneath the surface, around her body. The hair on her head was a matted bloody glob hanging to one side and a visible knot behind her ear.

He jumped into the water beside her. The other end of the rope holding her hostage was spun around an open eyelet on the ceiling beam.

He snapped it apart carefully. It was not tied in any elaborate knot. Whoever did this did not expect her to be found or for her to put up a struggle.

James gently lowered her body and the curved stick fell free into the water as he untied her wrists. Her arms and hands were almost blue, and her body cold and limp. How could anyone do this? Who could be so cruel?

A rage built in him that made the water boil and quiver around him. The catfish that had stopped its frenzy was looking for an exit, banging its flat head against the rotted hull of the boat.

James felt electricity exploding inside him from his anger as Ellie inside him offered her calming presence. He lifted Jolie's body in his arms and walked up the steps from inside the hull.

There would be no mercy for whoever did this, no forgiveness.

He heard a gasp of breath from Jolie and felt her body shift.

Her wounded arms were flopping lifeless from the hours of tension. The side of her face was bruised and clotted blood was pasted around her cheek and neck. Both legs were bleeding from open gashes as well as her feet. The panties and thin shirt, left on her by her attacker, were covered in slime.

With her limp body cradled in his arms, he carried her to a safe and secluded spot in the warm sunlight.

BeBe had gone with Martin and Catherine to the Ames house to try to get some rest. She had refused sleep and was parked in a chair drinking coffee with Catherine when the telephone rang.

Martin answered the phone and stammered a few seconds in jagged conversation.

BeBe arose from her chair, her heart stood still hoping it wasn't bad news.

"It's for you," said Martin Ames, pointing at Catherine. "I think its Robert."

Martin handed the receiver to Catherine and sat down in a slump. BeBe could tell that something had upset Martin Earl terribly. His face seemed to pale and he hurriedly took a few sips of his cup of coffee.

Catherine spoke in cryptic banter for several minutes, then hung up the phone.

"BeBe, can you go with me?" asked Catherine. "We need to run a quick errand. Daddy, we won't be gone long, can you stay by the phone in case the sheriff calls?"

BeBe started to object, but saw the urgency of Catherine's request.

A few miles south of Natchez, there was a brush-hidden cove where abandoned boats of all calibers had been dumped. James was standing out in the open on the dirt road that circled the cove as BeBe's car approached. His mother had followed his directions quite well and they had made good time.

Not waiting for them to arrive, he turned quickly, cradled Jolie's fragile body in his arms, and hurried their direction. The car slammed to a halt inches from him.

Catherine wasted no time in getting out and throwing open the back door to help Jolie inside.

"Is she alive?" asked Catherine in a low voice.

"Barely," said James. "I was afraid to move her."

BeBe rolled out of the car and met them, frantic from the pale dead look of her niece.

"My baby. Oh Jolie!" she whimpered. "Where did you find her?"

Catherine was astonished at seeing James in the flesh and alive as he had ever been. Her eyes battled on whether to look at Jolie or her son.

"James…, it's really you. You look older, different," said Catherine. "Handsome," she whispered to herself in a painful swallow. "I might not have recognized you if I didn't know it were you."

BeBe broke her stare at the odd miracle and threw herself on Jolie again, "Oh, God. What did they do to you?"

"Let's go. We can talk on the way," said James. "She's alive, but she's barely hanging on."

Jolie mumbled as if in a fitful sleep as James slowly rubbed the circulation back into her arms and hands. BeBe handed him a blanket and crushed the accelerator almost to the floor.

"She needs a hospital, but not in Natchez. They can't know she is still alive. Do you understand? They left her for dead. They never expected her to be found. Take her to Vidalia or some other place close by."

"What about the sheriff's people that are looking for her?" asked BeBe.

"Only tell the sheriff…, Sheriff Howard, what you've done…. Let him know Jolie's alive and he'll know what to do."

Sixteen minutes later, after breaking every speed limit along the way, BeBe drove into the emergency parking at Vidalia Memorial Hospital.

"I'll see you later tonight. I have something I have to do," said James angrily, he leaned over and kissed Jolie lightly on the forehead and vanished from the car.

"James," said Catherine, but he was already gone.

The air was still and quiet inside the river cave where James sat.

Ellie Rosalie had helped him save Jolie and he needed to keep his promise to help her. His only hope of finding her child, which was cut prematurely from her womb, was to get Syrus to help.

He performed the same eerie steps as before. As he held the skull in his almost transparent hands, and readied himself for the coming transition. It was almost physically painful, enduring Ellie's morbid loss and sadness for her child. He raised his hands and slid the skull into place inside his own head, merging all three of them together.

There wasn't the immediate rush of power, but a reserved flux of energy. James understood in a moment that Syrus and Ellie were reunited for the first time since before their deaths.

He wanted to go hide and give them privacy from their intimate meeting, but realized that he must be the key to reunite them. They could not do the same physical things that he was gifted to do.

Ellie could not have placed the skull of Syrus within her as James had done, nor could she manifest without a host. Their union was complete and James could feel their love emanating throughout himself. It was peaceful and overwhelming.

James thought of Jolie remembering his love for her and how it had deepened, yet he had no clear understanding of his future with or without her. Maybe when this ended he would not exist any longer.

"Don't ever think like that," said Syrus booming from inside him. "You have a future as certainly as we do. You're not finished with your business here on earth. Always remember James Earl, love is the key. What you are fighting is pure hatred and evil and greed."

"How do we find your child?" asked James.

"All in good time," said Syrus. "We need to make sure the threat to our family is removed forever."

"I was hoping you'd say something like that," said James.

Ellie's peaceful voice chimed in, "James, don't give in to the hate. You don't want to be trapped here until judgment day."

"I want the ones that killed me, that stalked my family, that tried to kill Jolie to pay for their crimes," said James angrily. "But I can't fight the old woman on my own."

The cave echoed with his voice as if someone had spoken aloud during a dream.

"So do we, but make sure that you don't end up filled with hate like the ones you seek," said Syrus.

"What do we do now?" asked James sharply. "Do we wait for them to hurt someone else?"

"Oh no…, you don't understand. You've unlocked two of the three keys to ending all this by joining Ellie and me," said Syrus cheerfully.

"Keys?" asked James. "I don't understand."

Why did they have to speak in riddles?

"Oh, you will!" said Syrus. "As soon as you learn your true potential."

James left the cave in an explosive blast of wind and was instantly standing in front of the Ames home, not visible to the human eye, but reeking of power. Gazing down, even the blades of grass were leaning toward his feet where he stood.

"If you're going to do something like that again, would you please tell me next time?" asked James."

"Well I don't know who's giving you advice like that, but I wish I had him as a deputy," said Sheriff Howard. "Consider the matter taken care of. I'll make a statement to the paper that she's missing, or a runaway, which is probably what they want us to think. I believe whoever this is, wants us all chasing our tails looking for your niece, while they pull another stunt. Do you have a safe place to stay, BeBe?"

"She's going to stay with Jolie," said Catherine. "There's a hotel a block away with a room that's already been reserved for her. The name listed is "Ellington." You can reach her under that name."

"I have a personal friend in the Vidalia Police department that can watch the room," said Sheriff Howard.

"Martiel has already hired a person from a security firm to keep an eye on BeBe and Jolie," said Catherine.

"Sounds like you've got everything covered," he grunted.

"No we don't, sheriff," said Catherine. "We still need your help. It was too easy for them to simply walk up and take Jolie. My other son, Sam, is only a few years younger than James and I don't know what I'd do if something happened to him."

"I've got approval for two more deputies on my payroll after this last incident. They've already transferred in from another town, but it's going to take me a day or two to get them up to speed.

"I understand you live somewhere in the northeast. Could your husband watch Sam until we get a handle on this?"

Catherine blushed, but was candid with the sheriff, "I..., haven't heard from my husband since the funeral, I don't think that's an option."

The sheriff's phone rang and he turned away from the two women in a hushed conversation. He hung up and the grim look on his face betrayed his emotions.

"Well, it seems that we can add another murder to the list of the attempted murder, and kidnapping. Officer Greene, the one they attacked when they broke inside the pound, just died."

"From all they can tell, these people walked right up and took Jolie from the restaurant, daddy," said Catherine. "All I'm asking you to do is to stay close to mama and Sam until they are caught. That's not too much to ask is it?"

"I think we're blowing this all out of proportion," said Martin. "All that voodoo junk was probably somebody's idea of a nasty prank. I'm sure there are people around here that don't like me for one reason or another. They probably heard about what happened to James and want to rub salt in our wounds, that's all."

"Martin Earl, where is your mind?" asked Maime. "I've never heard you back down from anything before."

"I uh..., I don't think we should do anything to provoke more activity, and they'll go away," he said. "By the way, what did Robert want on the phone this morning?"

"Oh, that...," said Catherine trying to think up a good answer.

"Now you leave her alone about Robert," said Maime. "You know they're having some problems right now. He's probably upset about losing his family *and* James Earl."

Catherine managed to remain silent after being spared the necessity of making up a lie to tell her father.

"It's amazing how much he sounded like James," said Martin, looking provokingly into the face of his daughter.

"Like father, like son," said Maime. "What did you expect?"

The front door burst open and there was a rustle inside the living room.

"Anybody home?" yelled Martiel. "I could use a little help here."

She hurried into the dining room where everyone was seated holding several bags in her arms.

"Well! Who called this meeting?" she asked.

Chapter 61

Deceptions

Sallee Mae was making a salad to go with their meager supper when her husband Billy walked in the door. His face was exhibiting the results of burning a black candle from both ends. Drawn, tired, and in no mood to quibble over his day's troubles.

"It's about time you decided to come home," said Sallee.

"Don' start on me woman," said Billy. "You didn't mind using the money I made to buy this new house."

"Clean up and come eat," she said. "I'm sorry I bit your head off. I'm tired too. I just moved all our stuff over here."

"I need to just crash," said Billy, breathlessly. "Can I pass?"

"You'll feel better if you eat something before you go to sleep."

"Okay, okay, you win," he said dragging himself to the bathroom. "You done a real good job on the decorating."

"Thanks, but I didn't have to do a lot, most of the stuff came with the house! Can you believe it!?"

The door to the bathroom closed and by the time he walked to the kitchen table, Sallee Mae was already in the middle of supper. The towel wrapped around his waist barely covered his short stocky body.

"I started without you…, sorry…," she said. "Your clean clothes are on the dryer. I was just about to put them away."

"Where is the dryer?" asked Billy.

"Oh, sorry. I didn't give you the tour. The washroom is all the way down at the end of the hall. You can't miss it."

Billy sauntered out the door and flipped on the hall light.

The dimness of the expanse didn't catch his attention, not right away. He walked out into the utility room and found his clothes folded and in a neat stack. He slipped on some shorts and t-shirt while viewing the room. It was nice. It looked new and had new paint, new windows, new…, everything.

He turned to walk back into the hall and thought he caught movement in the corner of his vision and snapped around.

Nothing. It was nothing. It was the grueling thirty straight hours of unmentionable drudge without any sleep. He carefully shook his head side to side as he started back to the kitchen. The hue of the hall seemed dimmer somehow, as if the steps before him dragged on into a dark tunnel, stretching out. Taking a deep breath, he swallowed and plodded forward.

As he passed an unknown door on his left, the light bulb ahead of him blinked out, leaving him at the mercy of the glow from the open bedroom down the hall on the right and the kitchen light, even farther on the left.

Billy felt a sudden chill, but brushed it off. While staring at the floor for courage, he hurried back into the kitchen where his supper awaited.

"Light in the hall burned out," said Billy, cramming a fork load of food into his mouth.

Sallee Mae was already through eating and had her back turned, while busy at the sink washing dishes. Billy stared at her slim figure as her hips rocked from side to side in her blue flowery shift. Even barefooted, she made the cheap little secondhand dress look special. He finished his first bite wondering what a good looking woman like her could possibly see in someone like him.

"That's weird. I put a new bulb in only a few.... Oh that's what's wrong," she said. "I used one of the old bulbs from the apartment for the replacement. I have a new one here if you don't mind putting it in for me. Please?"

She patted her hands dry and reached in a box on the counter then pulled out a new bulb and set it on the table.

"Dang woman," he said agitated. "Can't I eat first?"

"Don't care what you do," she said sloshing another pot down into the sink. "You always do what you want anyway."

Billy fidgeted with a pack of cigarettes and lit it up.

"Not in the house!" said Sallee Mae. "I don't want no smoky smell where the baby will be."

Billy was tired and in no mood for a fight, not tonight - any other night. He needed sleep. He glared at her and obediently tamped out the glowing end of the cigarette on his plate.

"I ain't fightin' you tonight, woman. I'm tired," he whined.

Sallee Mae clanked and sloshed the pans in the sink mumbling to herself. A cold beer and..., she thought about Arnie Milton. Well that won't be happening any time soon. Maybe never, unless....

She giggled to herself.

As if waiting his turn in her thoughts, Billy said, "I hear tell that our little counseling preacher man done high tailed it out of town. You hear anything about that?"

Sallee gritted her teeth and started violently scrubbing the bottom of her last pan.

"All I know is he wasn't at church Sunday and the old man is back," she countered.

"Rumor around town is, he had him a woman on the side," said Billy, filling his mouth back up with food and chewing noisily.

"Would you throw me a beer?" he asked.

"Git it yourself," she spat back. "I'm busy here."

"Yeah, you're always busy, ain't ya?" he said, slamming down his plate.

He crept over and opened the fridge, opting not to mention how new and clean it was, getting out a cold bottle of beer.

"She wants a fight, she's gittin' a fight," thought Billy.

He rested the edge of the bottle cap against the counter top and slapped down hard popping the cap off. Sallee Mae spun and jumped, sloshing dishwater on the counter top. The bottle cap tink-tinked around on the floor and spun to a stop by his feet.

"Don't do that to my counter top!" she pleaded. "You'll mess it up."

"What's the matter? Did I touch a sore spot? You know about messing up things don't ya?"

"What are you talking about?" asked Sallee Mae turning back around to her last pan.

She didn't want this argument to go this direction, not now, not in their new home. This wasn't the happy reunion she had pictured in her mind, the images of a fresh start with this brute of a husband.

"Look, Billy, I'm sorry I yelled at you," she said coyly. "I don't want to fight either."

Billy's glazed eyes were already locked on target, and his tongue loaded with venom.

"See…, there's some loose lips around town saying ole preacher man was blabbing like a choir boy at confession when they found him."

Billy took another drink of beer while quietly Sallee rinsed the last pan and set it aside in the drain. She pulled the plug and wiped her hands with a towel. She didn't want to face Billy about this. How could that loser have blabbed about her…, about them? A real man would have kept his mouth shut.

"Yep, he was a talking from both ends at the same time," gloated Billy. "Mentioned a name or two, I hear tell."

"What are you getting at, Billy?" she barked back at him.

Billy was through playing cat and mouse with Sallee.

"How can you stand there so proud, when it could'a been one of his ass-ended sperm that got you pregnant?" spouted Billy.

"How dare you accuse me…," she growled, throwing the towel she was knotting to the floor.

She closed the distance between them and raised her hand to slap him, but he caught her wrist and popped her across the cheek with a loud smack. Sallee Mae saw stars for a few seconds and went weak in the knees.

Cautiously Billy let go of her wrist, his mission accomplished. In an afterthought, he ambled calmly back over to the fridge and pulled out two beers. He opened both of them and handed one to Sallee Mae, who was now seated in a chair cupping her face in both hands.

Sallee felt the heat building against her trembling palms. That was why no one spoke to her Sunday morning. That was why they cast her deep broody glares and refused to answer her questions. Her secrets were all exposed.

"Didn't accuse you of nothing. Just telling you what the gossip is around town," said Billy tiredly. "Besides, I ain't no saint of a husband."

Bang, Bang, Bang, Bang! There was a loud knocking at the front door.

"Who the...?" asked Billy. "Go away!"

Bang, Bang, Bang, Bang! Came the second round of knocks.

"Why don't you go and see who it is?" asked Billy snidely, taking another long drink.

Sallee Mae looked up with teary mascara running down her red swollen cheek.

"You're right. You made your point," he said with a sigh, getting up from his chair.

He opened the front door ready to pummel somebody. There was no one at the door or on the porch.

"Stupid kids," said Billy and walked back into the house after locking the door.

He had only taken a single step from the living room back into the hall, when....

Bang, Bang, Bang, Bang! Another round of irritation rattled the glass in the front door.

Billy jumped back to the door and fumbled to unlock it, turning on the porch light. Nothing but the street lamp and the sound of crickets were around.

Billy walked out to the edge of the porch and yelled into the night air, "I'll stomp a hole in you if I catch you!"

He was waving his beer bottle around in the air for emphasis. There was nothing but silence and he began to rail like a mad man. He looked over at the vacant house across the street. The yard was overgrown with weeds in the middle of a host of flowers.

He couldn't help but feel as if someone was watching him. He spat in the direction of Elberta Straw's old house and threw the empty beer bottle into her front yard, listening to it shatter in the distance.

Billy walked back into the house with James behind him.

The only thought clear in the mind of James was justice, until he saw Sallee Mae's bruised cheek, and it quickly turned right back to revenge.

Sallee Mae scurried into the bedroom and locked the door. Billy followed close on her heels and jiggled the doorknob but heard water running in their bathroom.

"To hail with you! There's three more bedrooms, I'll take my pick!"

Drunk from the alcohol and lack of sleep, all he could think of was many hours of downtime. He opened yet another bottle of beer, killing the light in the kitchen and stumbled down the hall toward the last bedroom. He flipped the light switch in the hall, and then groaned remembering that the bulb was blown.

Everything seemed so dark.

He scooted down the hall, beer in hand using his shoulder to guide him to the door facing. After flipping on the light in the bedroom, he staggered the rest of the way to the bed. There was a lamp on a small square desk which he flipped on. Off went the ceiling light and on went the fan. Billy was ready for twenty hours of sleep as he collapsed onto the bed.

James Earl waited patiently at the entrance to the hallway. The oppressive black trap was still planted on the walls and ceiling leading back to his old bedroom. James could also feel that same type of base intelligence waiting, hidden somewhere either in the hallway or the room itself.

Rather than risk getting caught up in the trap, he decided to agitate the predator that laid it. James started ticking his fingers on the wall.

Tick. Tick, click, clik…clik.

James could hear a scratching noise at the end of the hallway. It was hardly worth the effort, Tick..tick Click clik, clik, tik, tik. He could already see the outline of black shifting back and forth from the end of the hall and back into the bedroom. It was slow, but with a little patience and a few more seconds of his annoying tapping, his efforts would pay off.

He began another regimen of clicking and ticking until there was a frenzy at the end of the hall. The black hearted creature which had tortured him and wounded his grandmother was severely agitated. The dark monster charged up the hall toward James, but James stood his ground and clapped his hands running it back down the hallway and into the bedroom. There was some clamor for a few minutes and then….

"Sallee Mae, leave me alone! I need some…, Oh Hail!!!"

There was instantaneous thrashing and banging noises from the room. Out came Billy Poole barreling down the hall toward James. Immediately he met an invisible wall of James and slammed backwards onto the floor in the darkness. But that unknown was still hot on his trail. There was an unmistakable scratching and clawing noise advancing behind Billy. He spun and backed up against an immovable wall of legs and could move no further. Out of the black hallway came the hideous face of darkness. Two glowing white eyes and a mouth full of pointed gnashing teeth were drawing down on Billy.

"See what can happen when you keep the wrong company."

Billy, too afraid to turn around, looked up from his seated position on the hall floor.

"It's…, It…, It can't be you," said Billy. "You're dead."

"And who would know better than you, Billy."

"It weren't me! It was Toad that run you down, not me!" he yelled. "I didn't…."

"No, but you like to hurt women don't you Billy…," said James. "Smack 'em around a little, keep 'em in line, right?"

The scratching and clawing was getting closer and Billy tried desperately to scoot around James, backwards, even if it was only a few more inches.

"You like to tie 'em up and leave them for dead, don't you? That was you…. That's your style, isn't it?"

"I was only doin' what I was told. She'd kill me if I didn't do what she said."

He didn't even bother denying his part in capturing Jolie, in carrying out the old woman's plans. Deep inside James wished for strength not to do what he wanted at that moment, strength not to dishonor his family.

"So it was you and Toad that tied up that girl and left her for dead, wasn't it?"

"Yeah…, yeah…, so what. We done it," he confessed. "Worse would've been done to us if we didn't. She must have done something to deserve it."

These were not the right words to obtain mercy from the person that could grant life or death.

"And what about me? Did I deserve to die too?"

"Listen you. Move out of my way you little…," said Billy as fate grabbed one of his feet and pulled, stretching his kicking leg out behind him.

James inched away and the back of Billy's head banged on the floor. The dark predator pulled Billy closer to itself despite screams of unanswered help. His other leg kicked and thumped against the floor but was soon trapped and the thick body of Billy Poole started sliding down the hall into the darkness. Flailing arms desperately sought purchase along the baseboards. He spun for one last plea of help from James.

James had returned to the grotesque visage of his mangled corpse watching Billy in a dead stare. Billy's tired grunts of anguish, turned into a blood curdling scream as he slid the rest of the way into the back bedroom.

Finally, there was silence.

An unblinking eye was peering through the keyhole from the master bedroom door. Witness to the testimony and confessions of her husband and also witness to a living dead man. Sallee Mae was shivering uncontrollably with fright and blubbering nonsense.

What was that *other thing*?

It was in her house. Well it wasn't her house any more, she was leaving.

Sallee set two of the largest boxes she had onto her bed and began throwing all her clothes into them, her arms a windmill.

When she was satisfied that everything was quiet, she unlocked the door and peered slowly into the hallway. In less than five minutes, both boxes were thrown into the bed of her truck. She shot backwards out of the drive, bowling over Elberta's old white picket fence, then rebounded forward, tires screeching.

"I want them bones!" yelled Lyda Brown.

She swung her black, lightening struck stick in angry circles, yelling her demands toward Toad once again, "I want them now!"

"I'll go right now. I'll go right now and get 'em," said Toad, shaking violently.

The old woman had been inconsolable and vile all afternoon. Something had gone wrong and she refused say what it was. Her helper and driver had cleaned up the carnage inside the garage, all of which had been scooped and sacked in garbage bags. He assumed that one of the family members she was at war with had committed the act in retaliation to their skulduggery.

Toad had been seated in the truck, while Miss Lyda and Billy butchered and hung a string of black hens across the porch in the wee hours of the morning. But that hadn't been enough to satisfy her anger. That was when they followed the woman and the girl into town and kidnapped the girl.

Toad took a deep breath. Leaving that girl tied up like that was sick, even to him. What a waste of a pretty girl. He still couldn't figure out why the hag was so put out about a broken jug. He had no idea of the vital importance of the *charmed govi* where her altar had once been.

Now, he and his mistress were back where they started. The old woman was sitting in her shack with all that was left of her bones and effigies. Years of preparing destroyed.

There was still time, if she could make it happen. If she could get her hands on James Earl Williams' bones, she could take back what rightfully belonged to her.

Toad was tired and needed rest in the worst way. Even a young man has limits to his endurance and he was at the final point as he wearily gathered a few tools and threw them in the back of his truck.

It was after eleven o'clock at night and Toad had driven past Heaven's Gate Cemetery for the third time. The police cruiser left its parking place in front of the main entrance only moments earlier.

He drove away deciding to come up the miles of dirt farm road from the rear of the graveyard as they had when the three of them robbed Syrus' grave.

It was only him now, Billy didn't answer his phone and he didn't dare tell the old woman no. As riled as she was, it would mean a death sentence.

The rough road would have been impassible for a car and left most trucks stranded in some of the ruts that Toad was guttering through. The fatigue was setting right down into his joints. Fighting a steering wheel through twelve-inch ruts was work all its own. It was too easy to get trapped in the wrong set of tracks that pull you into a bog or runoff, much like Toads life.

He steered the truck into a familiar spot, a short walking distance from the broken down wall of his destination. With several tools and a cloth bag swung over his shoulder, he pushed through the heavy overgrowth.

The old woman had supplied him with a foul smelling ointment to stop the thicket of poison ivy from taking over his body. It stunk, but it still wasn't as bad as what would happen with his allergy to three-finger-ivy.

Toad walked up to where the grave was supposed to be, ready to spend the next hour digging alone. There was a whitestone walk-in monument where the grave was supposed to be. He dropped his tools and flicked on his flashlight.

"No digging tonight boys!" he exclaimed excitedly, slipping on a pair of leather gloves.

The opening of the crypt almost smiled at him and he broke out a two-pound sledgehammer to do the work instead of his pick and shovel.

A couple dozen smacks with the face of the hammer around the edge of the crypts seal and he could drag out the coffin and be out of this nasty place.

Instead, he went for destruction. The old woman would be proud of him for his extra effort. He pounded away at the end of the vault until the freshly set rocks lay in crumbled pieces on the floor of the crypt. He dragged the casket out of the sanctity of its final resting place grinding past the jagged opening in the stone wall.

The casket hit the ground with a smash.

There was a look of satisfaction on his face, which only a deviant could twist into an expression.

"Got to crash you twice in one lifetime," said Toad chuckling. "My lifetime...."

All that was left was to chop the head off the body and leave before someone caught him.

He had to be more careful this time as there was no rainstorm or law officer to obliterate his activities.

Toad kicked open the already broken lid and..., it was empty. Toad began to swear under his breath, then peered into the lower end of the casket as if the body could have shifted and hidden in that small an area.

He looked over the crypt and there was only room for the one casket. But where was the *BODY*? Where was...?

He cursed into the air and began kicking the casket over and over again, then raised the shovel and started slamming it against its top. The handle of the shovel snapped off evenly with the blade and it made a *tonking* sound off across the stone floor.

The most prevalent thought that entered his mind was, "What am I gonna tell Miss Lyda?"

It was the truth of course, but he wouldn't have the Ames kid's head she had demanded and she would take it out on him.

He could get another skull…. No…, she'd know…. He had to tell her the truth.

He picked up all of his tools, releasing a long string of loud profanities. He didn't care if the whole world heard him. Jail was better than facing Miss Lyda empty-handed, especially with the mood she was in.

He walked back the way he came and he was getting more nervous with each step. Everything flew into the bed of the truck with a loud banging noise.

He opened the door and pulled out his half-empty bottle of hooch, and killed most of what was left. What was he to do?

Leave before he was caught and think about it on the way. The trip out took longer than the same route getting there. He was looking for every possible explanation and excuse. His story had to be perfect. She'd know if he was thinking about lying as soon as he walked in the door. He turned up the bottle and emptied it in one breath as he veered onto the paved highway.

Behind him came a vehicle with its lights off following at a distance. It had the Adams County logo of the Natchez Sheriff's Department on both sides. Toad didn't see it following him due to his preoccupation with getting his facts straight and the alcohol in his already sleeplessly thinned blood.

Lyda Brown was in such a fowl mood. Could he go back there tonight? Could he face her?

He drove all the way across town and out onto the highway. He was already past the state line; knew he should keep going, but some inexplicable urge told him to turn around. It was better to go and face her. An hour later, he turned off onto the dirt road and passed through the "State Access Only" cattle gate onto the Mississippi levee; unsure about what he would say when he reached the old woman's shack.

Deputy Floyd had waited patiently as the truck reappeared from the dirt road that led up behind Heaven's Gate Cemetery. He thought it was ironic that he would now be following one of the people that he had helped protect. What a strange turn of events.

The Ames woman had been certain that they would go after the body of her kid. So certain that they planted an empty coffin in a big ugly vault and told them to watch who showed up. Why did it have to be his turn to sit and wait tonight?

Floyd stayed over a half mile behind the truck, unwilling to risk being seen in case the old woman was with the teenage boy. It wasn't hard to follow from this distance because of the truck's height and unique taillights. It was already caked with mud and almost a twin to the other big 4x4.

His orders were only to follow and see where the truck was going while staying out of sight. That was absolutely fine with him. He had no desire to meet Billy's "people" as he had often referred to them.

And where *was* Billy? He had promised to call him long ago and still hadn't seen or heard from him. Maybe he had someone else in the department feeding him information and they knew the heat had been turned up to locate them. Maybe Billy had left the state after all the gossip about him and his wife drawing so much attention.

The truck turned up the dead end road to the North Levee Access gate.

There were places that he knew he couldn't follow in his car, but he determined to maintain his distance until the road got too bad to travel.

In less than a minute, the road was destroying the front end on his state issued vehicle, but the big truck was moving too fast to follow on foot.

Several miles going to nowhere, the truck disappeared and everything got deathly quiet. Deputy Floyd pulled off the road into a patch of high grass and killed the engine.

He couldn't hear anything other than the usual night noises along the river. Its waters were virtually silent with only a gentle murmur of gurgles rolling up the slope of its banks.

Floyd checked his gun and re-holstered it. He turned down the volume on his police radio to a whisper and called into the station to let the dispatcher know approximately where he was located. The reply was somewhat garbled with static and he hoped desperately that they heard him correctly.

A wave of nervousness began to overwhelm Deputy Floyd as he walked up the eerie dark moonlit path. He kept telling himself that he was only there to observe, not engage. The dirt along the seldom used road was soft and siltish giving his footsteps a silent crunch. Several hundred feet later he practically stumbled over the big truck secreted off the overgrown road.

Floyd panicked and froze in his tracks. He could hear someone talking in the distance, nothing more than a mumble.

He strained his eyes, but couldn't see anything as he slowly eased forward through a heavy bed of pine needles covering the ground. Led only by the sounds of voices, he carefully walked into almost complete darkness.

Floyd didn't dare turn on his flashlight. He wanted his hands free and was now frequently testing the feel of his service revolver, reassuring himself that he was protected. There ahead in the darkness was a dim flicker of light coming from inside a shack.

He moved in a little closer and then froze as the conversation inside took on a different perspective. The mumbling conversation became abusive and yelling arose to a violent pitch. One voice was that of a quiet male and the other…, he couldn't really tell. It was like the voice of a raspy, belching foghorn.

It boomed into the silence. He could only make out some of what the conversation was about. The loud voice was not happy about something. It was obvious also from the sound of that voice that something didn't go well and a punishment was forthcoming.

The male voice climbed in pitch and was begging, "Please, please no. I'm the only help you got. You know I won't cross you on purpose."

The sound of the two voices and the ensuing argument became deathly quiet.

"You done it again," she whispered. "You brung another hitchhiker with you."

"Aww, no *Ma'am*. I was real careful," he begged. "Weren't nobody there to follow me."

"Something outside right now," she said quietly. "You sit on that floor right there, and keep your trap shut."

She rose from her chair and instead of putting out her single candle she was using for light, she picked it up and stroked it and talked to it like a pet or a lover.

Using a crusty fingernail, she began to scratch patterns into the body of the candle, scrolling wax onto the floor.

Toad watched silently, not daring to do anything to get her more agitated at him. Through all the times he'd helped her, this was the first time he could remember where the old hag had let him watch while she worked some strange dark magic.

When she was obviously satisfied, she took some spittle and began to stroke the candle, base to tip, mumbling. Her hand movements were slow and sure, progressing to something vulgar and erotic. The flame of the candle rose like an oil lamp with its wick exposed too far.

Quickly the flame rose to over a foot high and wax began to pour down its own shaft. She threw the candle into her fireplace and it burst into a ball of flame, which ascended into the chimney.

Floyd was still outside at a safe distance, propped against a thick pine tree, as he watched the window of the shanty cabin flare with light. His eyes already accustomed to the darkness, stung for a moment from the glow.

He saw yet another burst of flame erupt from the top of a chimney on the far side of the house. It reminded him for an instant of the blast from a burn-off pipe of a gas well.

The blinding glare lit up the entire area like a flare exposing the outline of the shack and the heavy moss hanging from all the trees. He covered his eyes with his forearm and looked away, feeling the heat of the blast.

Then..., it was silent and dark. Darker than he could ever remember in his entire life. He looked around for the dim flicker of light from the house and found none. Something strange must have happened inside the cabin.

He looked back in the direction where he had entered the hollow of the moonlit trail. Then blinked his eyes upward into the trees begging for starlight; yet still no light flickered onto the retina of his eyes. He pulled out his small flashlight and flicked it on and off in an instant.

Nothing happened.

He moved his hand frantically in front of his eyes and..., unless the flashlight had gone dead in the last twenty minutes..., he was blind.

Floyd panicked, but kept his wits and remained quiet. He tried to remember his position and began to backtrack out of the woods at a slow quiet crawl. The thick bed of pine needles would afford him a small amount of stealth if he could only maneuver the right direction.

There..., in the darkness he heard a rustle of leaves. Ever so softly. It was several feet away, but still, something was there and getting closer.

Pictures of the Mastyn kid flashed through his mind and he swallowed a hard knot of air down his throat. His most evil nightmares as a child, of the scratching in his closet, under his bed, at his windowsill, readily flowed into his mind. Yet none of them came close to the terror that was inching into his thumping heart.

He couldn't fight what he couldn't see.

He couldn't see to run.

He couldn't run for fear.

Floyd took a slow breath and tried to listen. Again, he heard a rustle on the ground, or was it higher up in the trees? He couldn't tell for the disorienting blackness of his vision. His mind raced, thinking, what would a blind person do?

Swearing at his own stupidity, he realized that a blind person wouldn't be here in the first place. He loosened the clasp holding his revolver in its place and slowly pulled it free. Floyd knelt carefully and began to slowly shuffle in the direction his mind assured him was the way out.

He didn't hear any more noises for the moment and his heartbeat slowed.

Then terror erupted. The door of the shack flapped open loudly and smacked a couple of times until it rested. Deputy Floyd flattened himself on the ground, waiting and listening. The noise was not in the direction it should have been, he was turned around somehow, slightly, but enough to get him in more trouble.

"I know you there!" croaked a loud raspy voice.

His heart leapt in his throat like a terrified child and he cursed himself for listening to James Earl Williams.

There was that shuffling noise again. It was getting nearer, but he couldn't see which way to run.

Deputy Floyd had already decided, "I'm going to die out here."

He felt a deadening weight fall on him and a hand clasp over his mouth shutting off all air to and from his already panting lungs.

"No, you're not going to die," whispered a voice.

It was so soft that he wasn't even sure that he had heard it.

"If you die it'll be me that gets that pleasure."

The hand moved from over his mouth and nose and he drew in a cold breath of night air. The pressure of the weight lifted from his body and pulled him carefully up to a crouched position.

"How...," the deputy began to whisper, and again a hand covered his mouth.

"Don't talk or think, she can hear either one. Take my hand and get ready to run," said the familiar voice. "Don't let go."

Letting go was the last thing on Deputy Floyd's mind. He put his gun back in its place, afraid that he would shoot himself while trying to run.

There was another rustle, closer by and the steps were heavy. Heavier than any man should have afforded.

At that moment, he felt the hand gripping his, tighten painfully and his entire arm recoiled like a rubber band pulling him into motion.

In an instant, all six feet two inches and 220 pounds of Deputy Floyd left the ground. When his two feet finally hit something solid, he was already pumping them furiously to keep up, never uttering a single complaint. He felt like a three year old being pulled furiously beside their parent with his steps scooting along.

There it was again, that sound behind them now, running heavily and pounding the ground like a two legged horse. Brush and bramble was giving way for their unseen pursuer and it seemed to be gaining on them.

James threw Floyd into the squad car in the same instant as their enemy cleared the tree line behind them. The deputy's blind eyes grew wide as fear overtook him. A wispy cloud formed into a mutating black shape outside the window of the vehicle, pulsing and vibrating in the light breeze.

There was some harmless looking flap of skin over the deputy's face and eyes, but he appeared safe enough for the moment and James let go of his hand. It was time for James to meet his destiny.

"NO! Don't go!" shouted Floyd. "I can feel it right outside."

As Floyd gave into his fear, the shadowy evil outside grew in enormity.

"I'll be right back for you. I can't let them get away. You'll be safe in here."

James let go and Floyd groped at him for safety. His failing grasps melting right through James' body. Still a mystery to James why he could be a vapor to others, yet they were solid to him.

James sped from the car back toward the cabin. He could hear a loud shriek of "Noooo!" coming from inside the car.

He turned and watched the car rise nearly three feet into the air and drop onto the ground with a loud bang as one of the tires exploded.

James grinned facetiously, thinking that Floyd probably deserved anything that happened to him. Floyd's head hit the ceiling right before rebounding into the floorboard in several harsh repetitions. He looked something like a bug shaken in a jar.

James quickly found his way to the cabin barely in time to see flames engulfing the roof. He pushed forward toward the flames when he heard another loud crash. Maybe Floyd wasn't so safe.

The deputy was now whimpering like a child as the car bounced in the air and fell repeatedly to the ground. There was a moment of silence and he immediately scrambled his large frame into the floor, reaching under the seat for something to hold onto. An earsplitting boom hit the roof of his vehicle and glass showered in all directions.

For a moment he remembered that he was a man, a manly man, a man among men. Floyd screamed. It was a manly scream, for his life.

James grasped his wrist and pulled Floyd free from the creatures' advances, through the passenger side of the car. It seemed content on assailing the car and had enough fear-fuel from the deputy to go on with its sadistic pleasure for some time.

Having fled with the childlike Floyd once again, James made the decision to leave his pursuit of the others to save the wailing deputy.

There was a screeching yell from somewhere in the distance and the loud banging ceased. Barely a moment later, a crashing sound erupted right behind them. Floyd was leaving a scent trail of fear behind him and his personal monster was locked onto him.

"It's gaining on us," thought Floyd. "I can't last much longer."

As if on wings, he was lifted into the air with a violent snap of his arm and air began to rush past his ears until they almost popped. Deputy Floyd tried to heave air into his lungs but found none as the world around him accelerated beyond his understanding.

He fruitlessly gasped into an unseen vacuum as his mind closed into complete darkness....

"Preston Floyd, can you hear me?" asked a gentle voice from somewhere far away.

"Mr. Floyd you need to try and wake up," said the voice, louder now.

It had all been a dream, some demented concoction of his imagination.

He opened his eyes slowly, expecting the comfort of light, but there was nothing but pitch darkness.

Floyd jumped up and flailed his arms as if terrified and two other sets of arms quickly restrained him.

"It's okay…. It's okay Mr. Floyd, you're safe," said the kind voice.

"Where am I?" he asked in a raspy voice. "What happened to me?"

"Sheriff Howard found you on the steps outside his office. You lie back and relax," said the voice. "You're here at the county hospital."

"I can't see," said Floyd. "I can't see anything at all. What's wrong with my eyes?"

"Would you go tell Sheriff Howard that he's awake?" asked the voice.

Chapter 62

From the river, it looked as if there was a small war about to take place. There were emergency lights reflecting across the water and searchlights illuminating the entire east bank of the Mississippi River a few miles north of Natchez.

The potential forest fire had been contained, while copious amounts of smoke drifted along the top of the water. The orange glow was beginning to die down among the treetops as the remains of an unknown shack burned its last dry stick of lumber.

All available manpower from the Sheriff's Department and a State Trooper with a K9 unit were searching the area for two suspects.

Deputy Floyd's vehicle was exactly where he had told Sheriff Howard it would be.

"They probably used one of those flash grenades, like the ones used in *'Nam*," commented Detective Mason. "This place wasn't much more than kindling; it could have backfired on them and caught everything on fire. We were lucky to contain it to this area."

"Floyd said that something was chasing him…, it's a shame it was too dark for him to see who or what it was," said the sheriff. "Would you look at this car…."

"And how exactly did your deputy say he got all the way into town?" asked Mason. "Didn't you say he was blinded?"

Deputy Floyd had neglected to mention that his car probably looked like it had been trampled. All the glass was scattered around the car and huge pummeling marks pushed deeply into the metal body and frame. One wheel was sunk in the ground on its bare rim, with the tires' location unknown. The upholstery and dashboard were scattered in pieces inside and out, and electrical wires strung about like entrails. The vehicle was thoroughly trashed and ready for the wrecking yard.

Sheriff Howard was standing off in the distance watching the efforts of his men.

The trooper, whose polished name tag read 'Calvin Johnson', walked up to the sheriff, "We've circled a hundred yards from this place as well as the vehicle. The dogs are coming up with nothing. It's like there's something in the air that's confusing them. And, that car…, they're scared of it, they won't go near it. Take a walk with me and I'll show you what I mean…."

The two dogs pulled violently at the length of their leashes in front of the trooper as he and Sheriff Howard walked to Deputy Floyd's ruined car.

As they neared, the dogs rebelled and squatted on the road.

"Watch this…," said the Trooper, bending over and picking up a piece of the shredded upholstery. "Whatever did this, had to leave a scent of come kind."

He put the piece of vinyl covered foam near one of the dogs' noses and it jumped back and cowered down, whimpering loudly while wetting the ground.

"There are claw and bite marks all over this, like some big animal," he continued. "Are there any reports of a rogue bear around here?"

The sheriff looked at the size of the tear marks and on the ground with his flashlight, but didn't answer. The grass was pounded flat, with no discernible tracks to be gleaned.

Trooper Calvin Johnson looked at the sheriff, expecting some kind of response, "Well, whatever did this made puppies out of my two best hounds. Maybe it's the smoke…, I don't know. I've seen a grizzly maul a truck up in Idaho, but from the looks of this car, I honestly don't know. I don't have any answers for you."

He moved the search back to the cabin after the dogs had proven their uselessness around the wasted car.

Another trial run around the perimeter proved that once again any evidence had been destroyed with the fire which was now little more than a smoldering heap of coals.

Early the next morning, Catherine sat quietly talking with BeBe in the hospital room. Her niece Jolie was resting quietly. She had regained consciousness a couple of times since being admitted through the emergency room.

Jolie was awake long enough to let them know that she didn't get a glimpse of who had abducted her. She had received several stitches to her scalp, legs and the last joint of her little toe on her left foot was gone, eaten by something, probably fish. The scars on her wrists were beginning to heal.

"Your niece is precious and very pretty, BeBe," said Catherine quietly. "I can see why James fell for her. I wish things had turned out differently."

BeBe looked carefully over at Jolie's tiny frame, "I only hope that there isn't any permanent scarring. If James hadn't found her, she would be dead right now. I don't know if I could have lived with that kind of scar on my soul."

Then she understood what Catherine must be feeling from the loss of her son.

"I'm so sorry, Catherine. I didn't think before I said that," she said.

"BeBe, I don't know how to accept that James is gone, and yet I don't understand how he's still here. I mean, the selfish part of me is glad that I can still talk to him, but isn't this is all wrong? Shouldn't he be at peace by now and not out chasing his killers?"

"If James hadn't been here, more of your family might be dead right now, as well as Jolie. Time will tell what's right and wrong. I believe there must be a purpose to this."

"I hope you're right," said Catherine. "This life is hard enough without living like James. It's not some grand adventure for him. He's so different now, something that I didn't know was there. I'm not sure I like it."

A nurse came in the room and motioned for them to step outside.

"You have a phone call at the nurse's station," she said. "I was instructed not to send any phone calls into the room."

There was a tall slender woman with shoulder length brown hair, seated watchfully in a chair outside the door, sipping a cup of coffee. She was dressed in a casual gray business suit, flipping through a newspaper. When BeBe and Catherine walked out, she stood and nodded, appearing to stretch. Her jacket swung open slightly revealing a holstered gun, which she quickly covered with a pull of her clothing. BeBe was glad that there was a guard, but never expected to see a woman.

At the desk, the floor nurse handed the telephone receiver to Catherine.

"They took the bait," said a nervous voice over the phone. "I felt like they would, but never this quick."

"Aunt Martiel, is that you?"

"Who else would it be?" she smarted back. "Your favorite aunt used her wily skills and a varmint fell in the trap!"

Martiel explained that the sheriff had just called her, who also explained that someone had destroyed the crypt where the empty casket of James lay, like cheese on a trap.

She told them both to be careful and not go anywhere alone.

James Earl was in a stew of agitation. He had lost their trail all to save the life of Deputy Floyd. Now all he faced was the smoldering ashes of the shanty, wishing that he had never given Floyd his word that he would protect him.

He had outrun the demon that the old witch had sent after them, but it hadn't been easy. And now, looking at the devastation of the car, James felt outmatched. He had obviously underestimated her, wondering what other kinds of evil the old hag had up her sleeve.

He had one last obligation. Floyd was still blind, he was sure of it. James focused on the hospital, and disappeared, leaving the burned remains of the cabin in a violent rush of air.

In a few moments, he was in the hospital emergency room. He entered the private room and found its lights dimmed down.

Floyd lay in a fitful sleep, moaning and twitching from some mental torture. When James looked at him, he almost felt sorry for him.

Still covering his face was a gray skeletal form in the shape of a man's large webbed hand. The parasite pulsed and ebbed with Floyd's shallow breathing. This thing was trying to suffocate him as well.

He probably should have removed it when he left him on the steps of the Sheriff's Department earlier. Now it had developed curved hooks extending from each of the appendages that were digging into Floyd's forehead and face.

James carefully peeled the little terror from Floyd's face, and flung it toward the window. It rolled into a ball and disappeared like vapor through the glass and into the early morning sunlight without as much as a sound.

Floyd stirred from his sleep and gasped in a deep breath, trying to sit up in bed.

"You!" he said with a shouting whisper. "You almost got me killed!"

He eased himself down to a lying position.

"Can you see okay?" asked James.

Floyd rubbed his eyes coarsely for a few moments.

"Yeah, I can see fine…. I guess I'm supposed to thank you, even though I don't understand why you saved me. What do you want me to tell the sheriff?"

"Anything you think he'll believe is fine with me," said James.

"Boy? If you ever let yourself be followed again, I'll make you wish you was never born."

The old woman turned and stared out the passenger window of Toads truck. Toad already wished he'd never been born. He was so tired. More than he could ever remember. He tried to tell her that he was too tired to drive, but her words echoed through his mind over and over.

"You can rest in hell, you working now," she had said.

Toad had seen the flash of light as it left the open fireplace and swept upward. He heard that cop screaming somewhere outside and assumed that he had been eaten alive.

Now he was driving his truck into a stiff south wind, heading toward familiar territory.

He spent most of his life in New Orleans and some of the islands. In and out of foster homes and the juvenile system, this was where he met Roger Mastyn. Roger was always the slow one, but good to take the fall whenever they pulled a job.

Toad had shot a gas station attendant, from their last money run, right between the eyes - all for thirty-two dollars and a full tank of gas.

Later he handed Roger the gun, which he shot into the air with excitement. His own fingerprints were obliterated, should they get caught.

Those were the good old days. Running free and doing whatever they wanted. But now..., now he was neck deep in the pit of hell and couldn't see a way out.

Toad was wondering what had happened to Billy. He hadn't heard from him and strangely, his companion hadn't said anything about Billy or asked about him. Toad thought it was peculiar that she didn't ask him why he didn't take Billy with him to raid the grave of James Earl Williams.

She knew something, but she wasn't telling him anything.

The old woman beside him was sleeping, but he was fully aware that if he stopped or made a wrong turn she'd wake up and..., well he didn't want to think that far ahead.

It had been almost two days since any visits or attacks against the Ames family. James still blamed himself for not getting back in time to follow the two people inside the shack.

"None of this should have happened," he murmured to himself pacing around in his aunt's room.

With Jolie in the hospital, and the guards doing their job, James was getting restless.

"This waiting is driving me insane. I want to go find them myself and take care of the problem."

"And how do you intend to go about that? They could be miles from here by now," said Catherine.

She and Aunt Martiel had been at this for an eternity and all three were tired of the conversation getting nowhere.

"If everybody had left me alone...," he said snaking his eyes over at the two of them. "My instincts tell me that those two are waiting somewhere close for another chance. Then who will it be that gets hurt? I'm not willing to risk another family member, are you?"

"Then your instincts must be clouded by emotion. Because I don't feel anything of the sort," argued Martiel. "And if you disappear to Lord knows where and we need you, we might not have a way to summon you James."

"I don't know why I bother," he said. "My own father hasn't called to check on you and Sam. My grandparents and Sam have all but forgotten me. And..., even Jolie doesn't seem to want to talk to me. All I wanted to do was talk to her and that aunt of hers rushed me off from the hospital room."

"*Jolie needs her rest*," he mimicked BeBe almost exactly.

"She's only looking out for Jolie," said Catherine. "And BeBe's very grateful for you saving Jolie."

"Yeah? Well I wish someone had been looking out after me!" he yelled.

"Please...," whispered Martiel. "You don't want to alarm the whole house."

"*OH, NO!* Let's not do that," snipped James, lowering his voice to a mock whisper. "Then they'd have to remember me."

"Why you selfish brat. What do you think would happen if your grandparents or Sam knew what we know?" asked Martiel.

James was quiet for a few moments....

"Yeah, of course you're right.... You're always right, aren't you?" sneered James, flustered and ashamed of his outburst.

The curtains in the room twisted and lifted as James stormed from the house into the humid evening air.

"What are we going to do?" asked Catherine. "What's happening to him?"

Martiel ignored her comment with a furrowed brow, "Didn't James say there were two more somewhere out there? I thought there were three?"

Chapter 63

Richard and Wanda Mills were driving their station wagon along Hwy 555 toward Natchez. Richard had insisted on the 'scenic route' much to the repressive looks from his wife.

She hadn't argued.

This was the first time Richard had offered to take all of them with him on one of his business excursions, turning it into a working vacation in Atlanta, Georgia.

He was a part time journalist and freelance writer for several publications in the Southwest. He and his family received the needed break from the usual routine and were now on their way back home to Texas.

The sun had gone down only minutes earlier and their two children were getting restless for yet another unscheduled pit stop. Five year old Melissa and her younger brother, Bobby were pinching, prodding, and kicking each other to get one another in trouble.

It was working.

Richard had already reached around swatting at his two children. He didn't really care which of the two got the swatting tips of his fingers, so long as he had the satisfaction of reaching them.

Wanda was as tired as the children, though she didn't admit it. They had been driving since five that morning and she felt as if parts of her were growing to the vinyl front seat. Richard was pushing the car well over the speed limit to get to Natchez and any restaurant or motel that might be open.

Once again, there were keening high-pitched screams from the back seat and Wanda pressed her head to the seat's headrest and closed her eyes for only a moment.

Her husband's arm swung in an automatic arc of response and twisted in his seat to correct the kids, causing their car to swerve slightly onto the right shoulder of the road.

"Richard!" she yelled. "Look out!"

Richard snapped to attention barely in time to glimpse the young man walking not fifteen feet in front of the path of the station wagon. There was no time to swerve at the speed he was driving. Nevertheless, his reflexes and adrenaline forced his foot deep into the brake pedal and snapped the steering wheel to the left. The heavy vehicle, not made for high speed maneuvering, pitched and yawed with the inertia.

The young man on the edge of the road turned instantly and looked right into the headlights of the oncoming car and instead of pounding into the front bumper and hood; he simply passed right through the car…, watching the occupants fly past.

The car continued to wobble violently. One of the hubcaps flew high into the air with a buzzing report and began running along the center of the highway.

Richard regained control of the station wagon and brought it to a complete stop as quick as he could.

"Are you kids okay?" whined Wanda.

Both of the adults were trying to regain their senses, and the kids were looking out the back window at the man that was still walking off into the darkness.

"Mommy, did you see the man?" asked Melissa. "He flew by me…, he flew right by me!"

"I'm scared!" said Bobby, whimpering in his usual high pitch.

He had slid down as far as his seat belt would allow.

"Ewww…, what's that smell?" asked Melissa. "Bobby peed his pants! Pee-cat! Pee-cat! Pee-cat!" she began chanting repetitively in her similarly shrill voice.

Richard nervously drove the car out of the middle of the highway, over to the shoulder and stopped. He and his wife looked at each other without a sound and both got out at the same instant.

"What the heck was that?" she asked, her voice shaking, almost in tears.

"I've heard about that kind of thing before," said Richard. "But I'll be hanged if I've ever seen anything like that in my life. If I had been alone…, I don't think I would have told you about it."

"I wouldn't have believed you either," she confessed.

"It'll make one heck of a story," said Richard.

James barely noticed the station wagon that had run him through. The kids were mildly amusing with their wide eyes as he flew past them inside the car.

He had much more difficult things mulling around in his head than to worry about some guy that couldn't drive.

All memory of life as a young man was melting like ice cream on a hot summer day. His mind was digging deep into a rut of confusion about who and what he was.

Then there were all the secrets that he was keeping closely guarded from his family. These secrets were for their own good. After his last conversation with Martiel and his mother, it was evident that they may never be able to handle the truth about him or what he'd learned of their family.

Then there were his inhabitants to consider. The constant whispering conversation of Syrus Earl and Ellie Rosalie in the back of his mind was maddening enough, but concentrating on a single personal thought was almost impossible now.

Keeping them quiet around Martiel and BeBe was also a near impossibility. There would be no way he could explain all the events making it necessary for them to be using him as a safe harbor.

He knew that he could probably ask them to leave, but where would they go? They all needed each other and he needed their power should he have the opportunity to face the voodoo woman.

James felt drawn toward familiar territory if only to ease his mind temporarily, for a few moments of peace. He took his time walking the rest of the way to the front steps of the Holiness Cathedral Church.

The neighborhood was quiet and peaceful, and exactly what James was hoping for. The church had its familiar warm glow from inside the stained glass windows. He sat down on the front steps of the church and his mind found a few moments rest.

Down the sidewalk came a shadowy figure of a man, walking slowly toward him. James could hear the quiet rhythm of his footsteps and even the sound of his beating heart inside him. The steady rhythm sounded somehow comforting to James as the man came closer. He looked down at the steps to avoid any confrontation.

"Can I help you?" said the voice of an elderly man.

The question was neither gentle, nor was it angry..., completely neutral in its tone.

James was startled for a moment and decided it was best to disappear back into his own unseen world.

"You sure do look familiar somehow," said the man. "My name is Timothy Baskin."

He offered his right hand to James, who halted his exit and stared at this fellow's hand, not knowing what to do. James was obviously visible, but had no way of knowing if he was viable enough to shake hands. Up until now physical strength only came with his emotions, especially anger and the results weren't for the faint of heart.

The gentleman lowered his hand and sat down on the steps where James had been moments earlier.

"Might as well sit back down with me," he said. "It's a really nice evening..., unless you have some place you need to go."

James sat down slowly and removed his gaze from the man's eyes.

He looked considerably older than he sounded and the light from the street lamps played on his aged features. James recognized him as the previous pastor of the church, Pastor Baskin. He had always been nice to James during his summer visits. It was a miracle that he didn't recognize James Earl outright.

His shirt was starched white, stuffed inside pressed slacks and a pair of well-polished black shoes sticking out of from under the cuffs.

James' eyes wandered back across the street into nothing....

"You seem pretty troubled," he said softly. "Is there anything you want to talk about?"

"Nothing that you'd understand," said James. "My problems aren't of this world any more."

"Ah, I see...," said the pastor. "So what you're facing is pretty unique. Most people your age are worried about some girlfriend..., or job...."

"You couldn't possibly understand what I'm going through," said James with a hint of resistance, "Unique is an understatement only the living are capable of."

"Hmmm..., you seem pretty satisfied with settling your hearts argument on your own," he said standing laboriously. "If you ever change your mind, I'll be right here. Okay young fellow? You sure do look familiar," he said walking on up the steps to the door.

"I..., I guess I do need help," said James quietly. "It's just..., I just...."
James couldn't make up his mind to tell the truth or merely let him go on his way.

"What if the old codger has a stroke, when he finds out that I'm a dead man?" thought James.

James sat back down. The old pastor slowly unlocked the door to the church and turned around.

"You say that your problems aren't of this world, eh?" asked the pastor. "I specialize in questions that aren't of this world."

James waited a few more moments while he made his decision. If the old man wanted a heart attack, then so be it.

"I'm a dead man," said James.

Sincerity followed the pastor's eyes, which had darkened at James' odd statement.

"There's no other way to describe my situation, Sir."

"Someone is trying to hurt you?" asked the pastor. "Why don't you come inside and let me see if I can get you some help?"

James was becoming frustrated and the peace and quiet of the church was disappearing quickly.

"No," said James. "They already did that."

"Are you hurt?" he asked sincerely, inspecting James for wounds.

"It's time for me to leave," said James, at the length of his patience.

"Why don't you come inside and sit for awhile then. I'm a good listener. No one will hurt you inside here."

The last thing James wanted to do was relive the events, up to and after, the death of everything he understood. This pastor reminded James of Granny Smith, caring, patient. He had that same persistent way of giving him time to choose what he wanted to do.

"You remind me of someone else I knew once," said James smiling slightly.

"What did you say your name was?" asked the pastor.

"It's not important," said James, not wanting to disgrace his grandparents' family name.

"Sure it is," he said. "Names tell us who we are, what we can become."

James laughed heartily and looked back at the old kind gentleman. He was a carbon copy of the heart of Granny Smith.

"You haven't heard a word I've said have you?" asked James. "You're a good man, not like that counterfeit that was here before. I shouldn't bother you any more."

"Please do," he said.

One last time James tried to help him understand without causing him distress, "I don't know how to make you understand what I mean when I tell you, I'm a dead man. You see..., I'm buried right back there in Heaven's Gate Cemetery."

The old man chuckled at James' answer and opened the door shaking his head as he stepped inside the church. He turned to let James in, but he was gone. The pastor leaned back out the door and looked around, but didn't see his visitor anywhere in sight.

"I'm down here," said James. "Don't be scared."

Pastor Baskin jumped and turned around to see James sitting on the front pew of the church near the center isle, several feet from the door.

"You pulled a fast one on me, young man!" said the pastor.

"I have that effect," said James. "But, you don't want to see my encore."

Their drawn out conversation was becoming a game of chess, each taking turns with their cryptic move.

"I can't tell you who I am," insisted James. "It would only make matters worse. Who I am doesn't matter anyway. It's not like I can come back to life."

James had almost convinced the old fellow of his current condition. Pastor Timothy Baskin was now seated on the altar directly in front of James with his hands folded and his face a pale white.

"I don't sense evil from you exactly. But if you're not evil, why are you still here? Are you an angel?"

James laughed at the thought of himself being an angelic being.

"You find that funny?" asked the pastor.

"Ironic, but definitely not funny," said James smiling. "I don't know what I am. Let's cut out the details of who I am, how and when I died and get to my problem."

The old fellow seemed to miss the point, still mesmerized by the young boy seated in front of him, "I hardly think you're a demon spirit. I doubt seriously you'd be sitting right here on the front pew talking to me if you were. Have you seen God or been in His presence?"

"The only thing I've met so far is pain, death, and evil. But honestly, that was true my entire life when I was alive."

His expression changed to one of utter insanity and he let out a few barking laughs. After a few moments, he settled back into the train of thought with the pastor and continued.

"I think I met someone like a devil. I've seen things I won't repeat to you. Things I…, wish I'd never seen myself".

James left out the fact that he'd done a few things that weren't too saintly either.

Very quietly, the pastor spoke his thoughts, "Then it's possible you're on a mission." Then as if in an epiphany, he seemed excited, "Or a transformation!"

"More stuff about responsibility…," groaned James. "I've about had it with gifts and responsibilities…."

"What gifts?" asked the pastor.

"That's a long story," said James. "It's not like any I've ever read about in your Bible. In fact I've seen things, I sure wasn't warned about in Sunday school."

"Most people don't want to be taught those things, son," he said. "They want to hear about God's love, but not His wrath or the consequences of evil. There is an evil that is ever present, even in the choices that we make, every moment of every day."

"A sermon," thought James. "I should have known."

As soon as his frustration vented, the pastor's words rang true. He sounded like Granny Smith.

"You think I'm being preachy, don't you?" asked the pastor.

"I think you are a good man…, and sincere," said James. "A good man that doesn't have a clue how to help me."

James stood and paced the front of the church where he had walked many times before.

"It's time that I leave," said James, frustrated. "Please forgive me for taking up your time."

"I'll keep you in my…."

A rush of wind whistled past the ears of Pastor Baskin as he sat on the front pew of the church. His visitor was gone with no trace of his ever being present before him.

"…prayers."

"Maybe I am evil," thought James. "Maybe I'm so evil that I didn't deserve a mother and father when I was alive. So evil that I didn't deserve a perfectly innocent girlfriend, without a bad thought inside her. I was so bad that I didn't deserve a normal life. I was destined to be tortured my entire childhood and end up dead and *still* tortured now."

Self-condemnation fueled his fury and it rose and fell like the stormy flow of angry waves trapped inside him. The trees along the road bent and quivered at the violence captured there. One thing was for sure, he was becoming a force to be reckoned with, and the power was becoming intoxicating as he gave in to the unnatural urges.

"Now I'm even tortured by my own off balanced virtue of right and wrong," continued James. "Am I evil? *Am* I evil?"

He stopped where he was, lost and looking around, on the corner of some neighborhood street he didn't remember. Beautiful quiet homes, with carefully trimmed lawns and large shade trees were on every corner. His loss became more than he could tolerate.

"I am evil!" yelled James, quivering inside from the pain.

The grass around him broke free of the ground, uprooted and spun into cyclonic vortex around him. The trunk of an oak nearest him crackled and twisted like a match stem.

Its solid trunk yielded to a force more sinister than the many years of storms that had raged against its strength. Over two hundred years of solid mass crumbled inside with violent pops and snaps, finally lowering its branches to the ground.

James hurried away while clutching himself across his chest, in fear of what he was becoming, and in awe of what he was.

Billy Don Poole lay on the floor of the hallway of his new home. Having crawled the length of the expanse, he made it to the living room door before collapsing there, mouth open and staring at the ceiling.

He didn't know how he had escaped. He didn't care. He was alive - alive and out of reach of the clawing toothy monster cowering down at the end of the hallway. It was still staring at him. Patiently. Waiting for a chance to reclaim its victim and finish what it had started.

"I can't feel my legs," thought Billy. "I can't feel nothing."

Billy couldn't make himself move. Parts of his body were silently numb. Painfully he forced his head to look at his lower extremities hoping that everything was still attached.

"If I ever get out of here...," his words echoed in the living room. "I'm gonna hunt down that kid.... I'm gonna hunt him down and finish the job I started..., him and his whole family."

"And my wife Sallee Mae..., she'll be next," he thought.

His legs twitched involuntarily at the nerve damage from the puncture wounds of long slender teeth and raking claws.

Billy looked up and spat down the hall toward his enemy in bitter anger.

"I think that all of you are making way too big a deal out of all of this," said Martin Ames. "The sheriff thinks that those hoodlums have skipped the country and won't ever be back."

"You sure are putting a lot of faith in him all of a sudden," said Maime. "There's a sweet little girl lying in a hospital right now that would disagree with you."

Martin ducked his head in remorse and had no reply. They weren't allowed to visit Jolie for fear of leading some unknown deviant to her location.

Maime continued to try and talk some sense into her husband, "If I recall, it was only a few weeks ago...."

"I know, I know," said Martin waving a hand up and down. "Maybe I did go off the deep end now and then, but Howard is doing his best. I think it's about time that we started acting like a family again, instead of like we're in some prison. I only want everything to go back to normal, is that too much to ask...?"

"Is it because you haven't been back to your garage?" asked Maime.

Sam sat at the table watching the two of them dueling while he ate his breakfast. Catherine had cleared the table and was washing the last few dishes, staying as far away from the conversation as possible.

Her father certainly didn't want to hear her opinion on the matter. If she had her way, the windows and doors would be nailed shut until their enemies were caught.

Besides, her parent's exchange sounded far too familiar to one of the hundreds between her and Robert, only theirs always escalated into a shouting match with him storming out and leaving, ...for days at a time.

It didn't help matters that even though James was now cowering upstairs in her Aunt Martiel's bedroom, he could still hear everything that went on in the entire household. Something else that was new about her son James Earl – something else to worry about.

"Maybe you're right about me missing the garage. I don't know if retirement is right for me," said Martin. "What if we took a vacation together? Just me and you."

Martin pushed the death of James farther away from his memory. He had been responsible for his grandson and the weight of the boy's death was eating him one piece at a time.

"Can you give the authorities a few more days?" asked Maime. "It will probably only be a few more days until we know something. I'll even consider the vacation idea."

James was crouched down in a corner of a room upstairs, staring blankly into space, listening to the conversation in the kitchen, the ongoing conversation with Syrus and Ellie inside him, along with his own ramblings. Every once in a while, either Syrus or Ellie would emerge and offer some consolation or advice, but for the most part it was like two people long separated and catching up on one another's lives.

James had told them more than once to "get a room," until they casually reminded him that *he* was their *room.* But for the most part their conversations were congenial.

The only thing James didn't like was the fact that their recalled memories seemed to be his own from time to time. It was confusing and disorienting on a constant basis like a radio with its volume turned low, playing several stations all at once, and he couldn't turn it off.

He had replayed the activities of the old woman and Toad repeatedly in his mind, trying to thresh anything - however small - that might let him know where they could be. His only thoughts lately were to dispose of the two of them quickly and efficiently, the same way they disposed of him.

He had to admit, he enjoyed conversing with the divisive Pastor Milton and tormenting Billy Poole had brought him much satisfaction. He couldn't understand why he didn't get the same redemption from tormenting Deputy Floyd. In fact, Floyd might even prove to be an asset to the human race after he was through with him.

He longed to see Jolie, but after his childish tantrum, and her aunt asking him to leave, his pride shut that door to him. He was closing a lot of doors lately, barricading himself from those whom he loved and respected.

Around and around these same thoughts cycled through his memory to the point of insanity.

"Why can't I make it all shut up!" groaned James. "I can't rest - I can't sleep - It's always noisy - I have to get out of here!"

Aunt Martiel had visited most of the reputable clothing stores all morning long with a final destination of the local grocery.

One store to the next was her perfect idea of a Friday morning. It always made her feel young again. Natchez was nothing like Biloxi or her frequent trips to Houston or Atlanta as far as the list of retail stores, but she managed to find items for the entire family.

She was especially happy at some of the things that she had picked up for her great-nephew Samuel Earl. He had begun to follow her around like a puppy lately. He even seemed to like the Southern drawl in her speech. It had become a common point of contentious fun for her as well, teasing him about his odd northern dialect, coupled with *cool, bad,* and *far out,* at every opportunity.

She was winning the contest as he slowly and unknowingly lost his accent to parroting the host of family members; all reinforced by both his parents' genetics.

As much as his father hated to admit his heritage, his early childhood was anchored in the Deep South as well, but now he hid that fact as best he could. It was not popular in his circle of business acquaintances *or* a certain female companion that he had attracted over the last few years.

His recent promotion to the Boston branch of his elite Investment Firm had been largely influenced by a certain Victoria Plainsfield, who was applying pressure on him to leave Catherine and *her* troubled children.

"It's the family," Victoria admonished him. "There lies the problem. You can't expect to get canaries out of a sparrow."

This fact had not escaped the watchful eye of the Private Investigator that Martiel employed since she had heard about Roberts long "work" days away from his family.

Her "archive" of family advisors, previously trapped in the Ames Estate, had insisted she hire an investigator to protect their family's assets. Unfortunately, they had been right.

Aunt Martiel was still in a position where she would not interfere with Catherine's marriage unless her niece decided to seek divorce on her own.

Then Martiel would happen to have pictures and surveillance information on his lengthy rendezvous of infidelity.

Aunt Martiel loved being the family watchdog from time to time. Following every member's activities and casting a protecting eye whenever necessary.

Her biggest achievement and disappointment had been James Earl. She wasn't prepared for what had happened. How could she have been so blinded with glib anticipation of his overwhelming abilities? He hadn't had a clue of how much potential he had possessed. Now it was all a big mess.

She had no family ancestors to ask advice from; they were forever gone to their eternal reward. And now she was incapable of introducing James to further pursuits with his constant preoccupation with the family's mysterious enemies. Most of all, she feared that James was most likely losing his sanity.

If only she could reach him....

Martiel had been tutored by her late father, John Earl Ames who had been the family heir apparent with the responsibility of passing down the torch. Neither her brother, Martin Earl nor their sister Bethany had shown any propensity to the family "gifts" whatsoever.

Martin Earl spent most of the time haunted by the unseen presence of his late family members. He could sense their presence, glimpse a wisp of their faces, but nothing else. Her belligerent older sister Bethany passed it all off as bosh, and closed any doors that may have been open to her.

Martiel on the other hand had vivid experiences, which she confided to her father, at a very early age. This had been a disappointment to their father who wanted his only son to carry on as guardian.

Martiel had resisted her appointment ferociously at first. She'd been as adamant as James Earl in disavowing her initiation to the gifts. She didn't want the duty or the lifelong responsibility of babysitting the family or the estate. It was a heavy ball and chain to be strapped with as a child.

James was exactly like her. It was how she knew that he would be magnificent, as soon as he understood the perks of the job. She had looked forward to relinquishing her responsibility, now everything had radically changed and she was in completely uncharted territory.

Amazingly, she still had her gifts, only without her repertoire of advisors. It was clearly a mixed bag.

Martiel was still in the process of her great escape, threading through racks of clothes instead of her heavy thoughts. When she became bogged down with regrets and memories, her favorite diversion was to shop 'til you drop.

It somehow cleared her head. Today had been no exception. She had a premonition early that morning and was formulating a plan..., it was brilliant and she was dancing like a schoolgirl inside at the very inception. It had a few glitches however..., it could be the end for her if it all went south and depended entirely on someone she had secretly come to adore, but knew very little about.

Chapter 64

"Have you seen this morning's paper!" barked Martin Ames. "Some traveling kook wrote an article about seeing a ghost out on the loop. It says the whole family saw some young kid walking…, aw, this is ridiculous. This ghost-person floated right through the car.

"The stuff this paper puts on the front page is beyond me. It says they're inviting anyone with similar experiences to call the Gazette and tell them their story. Well…," Martin slammed the paper down on the table. "They've gone from bad to worse, now we have our own local tabloid."

Catherine poured her father another cup of coffee and picked up the paper. She casually skimmed the story. "James…" she thought to herself, shaking her head. Should she go find her son and ask about this, or simply let it drop?

James was wandering throughout the house, drifting from seen to unseen without any forethought or care of who was around him. The power that he could summon within himself was becoming addictive. Of all the drugs that James had been around as a child, he had never seen or heard of anything that could equal the rush of energy or the feeling of invincibility that was building inside him.

The air yielded to him, anything physical was like putty to his will. But yet he still couldn't control it or make use of it with any precise measure. It was *all or nothing* and that made him nervous. It was almost as if this power was controlling him.

What if his family was too close when he had an outburst of energy? Would the same thing happen to them that happened to the huge oak? Would they be twisted into a pulpy mass?

The nearest sensation he could relate was the satisfaction of feeling his fist connecting to a cheekbone, or the grit of his knee against the groin of his opponent while in a fight.

After the experience ended he had felt…, dirty…, like he had delved into something that was wicked and stuck to him somehow. But it was almost worth the hours of soul searching and contrition it took to purge his conscience.

James was allowing little bursts of power as he meandered through the upstairs rooms, getting used to more and more energy flowing through himself.

He stole away like a thief in the room where BeBe and Jolie had spent their short stay. Beside the door which opened into the hall, was a small table with miscellaneous items as well as stationery. James lifted a pencil in his fingers and rolled it back and forth, sensing, more so than feeling it's smooth surface and texture. Then he began loosing a gentle trickle of tingling energy. He felt electric as his entire body and the surrounding air began to vibrate with its flow. The pencil swelled and contracted with that same vibrating ebb and flow.

Outside the door James heard a gentle gasp for breath and a bump on the floor.

Margie had made her rounds downstairs and had only two rooms upstairs left to filter through. She was getting tired and the two turns of stairs leading to the second floor didn't help matters any.

The armload of linen she carried prevented her from brushing away the wisp of hair that was teasing her forehead and eyes. Reaching the top of the stairs, she swung her head to the side in a futile attempt to stop the torment.

Her heart was silently appreciating the thoughtfulness of the Ames family as she trudged down the hallway. They never made a mess or threw heaps of items on the floor to be sorted through like the last home she worked.

Even when some person or apparition had terrified her, Martiel had personally talked her into staying. Soon she would be living in her own separate quarters out back.

Her thoughts snapped back to the ugly names that her last employer's family had called her. She had categorized them as spoiled rich trash. They threw away more in a week than her and her children could have used in a month. They never paid her on time. They treated her like....

Her sullen thoughts broke off like a dry twig as she passed the door to the middle room upstairs. Margie stood still for a moment while watching the little hairs on her right arm stand to attention.

It reminded her of the feeling she got when she would walk into her house late at night looking for the light switch - that feeling of vulnerability and weakness from some dark unknown.

As she raised her hand to look at her arm and at this strange feeling, goose bumps rippled up and down her spine and the loose hairs from her bangs stood out straight as if pulled by an unseen hand.

Margie dropped the linen she was holding, flipping at the rigid halo of her hair while every strand continued to disobey her grooming. Suddenly she felt cold, light headed and breathless, gasping for air and then everything went dark.

"How exactly do you track a ghost?" asked Detective Mason. The room became deathly quiet as his team stared blankly.

"Deputy Floyd almost became our next victim…, and why?" he continued. "He didn't wait for backup. He went in alone and unprepared. We have to work as a team. These people know how to work as a team and they've proven it over and over by staying one step ahead of us."

He paced the room like a staff sergeant for a few moments longer, then focused one of the fold out tables.

"This is our evidence. Do you see anything wrong with this?" he asked. "It's nothing but artifacts. There isn't enough here to identify anyone other than the blood samples from the car. We need to establish a motive. Motive will make their actions predictable. Think outside the box, people."

The sheriff entered the room and sat down quietly. The rest of the officers sat up and feigned a sharper attention to their speaker.

"These people, whoever they are, are doing something that we aren't. They are thinking *and* using the clock against us. I want double shifts, two on, one off, for the next two weeks."

There were soft groans among the three officers.

"Does that include Deputy Floyd?" asked one of the officers dryly.

"Yes…, and it includes myself," said Detective Mason, ignoring the intent of the comment. "These people have committed almost every crime between dusk and dawn. We've been responding to these hours already, this will give every body a chance to be fresh more often. See me for your assignments."

"Sir, what do you suggest next?" asked another.

"Daylight hours for two of you will be at the burned shack and vehicle. I want you to sweep the area clean and go over what's left of the vehicle slowly and carefully. No sloppy work, take your time. Night shift will be responsible for follow up and research."

"Sheriff, do you have anything to add?" he asked.

The sheriff stood and faced everyone.

"We have two dead, one missing, another attempted murder. One of the dead is our own. It could have easily been one of you instead of Officer Greene. I have reason to believe that the Ames family will be targeted again. Call it a gut feeling, I'm usually right. I'll be coming in with the graveyard shift, but I'll be spending time with all of you to keep up with your progress."

He looked at everyone in the room.

"We're a small team, but I expect progress. We have two weeks left before we'll be forced to turn it all over to the FBI."

He turned slowly and walked out of the room.

Catherine wound her way up the L-shaped stairway. She found a semi-folded pillowcase on the top step and casually picked it up. When she turned to the hall, she found Margie lying on the polished hardwood floor. There were sheets and pillowcases strewn down the hall.

Her first thought was "James, not again."

She and her Aunt Martiel had smoothed over the first incident with James in the back yard, but…, she shouldn't jump to conclusions.

Margie was breathing, no obvious injuries…. Catherine sat with her on the floor calling out her name for a moment.

Margie slowly turned onto her side mumbling and talking to someone. Catherine placed the back of her hand on Margie's forehead to check for fever and the woman took a slow deep breath. Then, Margie opened her eyes and sat up with a start.

"Oh, I'm so sorry, Ma'am," she said. "I was suddenly sleepy, or…, I can't quite remember."

"It's okay," Catherine reassured her. "You were lying here in the hall. Did you faint? Are you feeling well?"

Margie sat up straighter checking herself. "My arm. It has given me trouble for years."

"Is it hurt? I can take you to see a doctor." Catherine hurried to stand up.

"No, you misunderstood me, look…."

Margie extended her arm and bent it this way and that.

"It doesn't hurt any more," she exclaimed and then stood.

"You must have landed on it oddly and pushed something back where it belonged. Are you sure you don't want me to take you to see a doctor?"

"No…, I don't think so," she answered strangely.

"Why don't you take the rest of the day off and get some rest. We can take care of whatever is left. You've overdone yourself."

"Oh, no…," said Margie. "I couldn't, besides I feel great. As a matter of fact I feel better than I have in a long time."

"If you change your mind, you don't need to explain. You take off, okay?"

"I really don't know what came over me, but thank you for your concern."

She nimbly moved around and gathered up the linen on the floor, hurrying on to the room at the end of the hall.

Catherine stood watching her walk away in amazement. Then she noticed that the tiny hairs on her arm were standing to attention and the ends of her fingers were tingling. She quickly opened the door beside her and walked in, closing it just as quickly behind her.

The room looked empty.

"James," she whispered loudly. "Where are you?"

"Over here," said James, perched on the edge of one of the beds.

She rushed over to where he sat, "Did you do something to Margie?"

"Not that I know of," said James defensively. "Why does everyone always expect that I've done something wrong?"

"Shhhh…. You didn't do anything wrong. At least I don't think you did."

"What do you mean, think? I was in here by myself…."

"Were you near the door?" she asked.

"Well…, yes, for a few…. What does it matter where I was?"

Catherine's questions seemed to be forcing him into defensive mode.

"Margie was on the floor outside this bedroom door, passed out."

"I didn't touch her. I didn't see her. I didn't let her see me. I…."

"Just settle down a few seconds…. I'm not accusing you of anything. Do you remember what you were doing?"

"Of course I remember. I'm not senile; only living people can be senile."

Catherine entertained the thought that it might be the insanity Martiel spoke of, not senility, but quickly dismissed it. She had James to recant his exact movements and thoughts while alone in the room as she sat taking mental notes.

Catherine nodded and stood quickly.

"Come with me James. Bring that pencil with you."

There was a knock at the door just as Margie entered the room.

The pager set to vibrate on Deputy Floyds' waist was grinding a tune. His first few hours back on the job and he was still thinking about everything that had happened to him.

No one would have believed the truth or anything that didn't sound logical, so he had converted the weird happenings into something that was vaguely correct, but not misleading.

The last thing he wanted to do was cause more suspicion toward himself.

He looked down at the number displayed on his pager and both hands began to quiver nervously.

It was Billy Poole. He looked around the office using jerky eye movements.

"If I call him, and someone finds out, then they will know that I am…, I was…," he corrected himself. "Connected to all this. It's murder-one now, not only conspiracy. I have to find Williams and tell him, ask him what he wants me to do."

The problem was…, James had always contacted him and not the other way around. If he didn't call Billy soon, then the man would know that something was wrong.

The hospital in Vidalia was bustling with usual patient activity. The guard outside Jolie's room attracted a few strange looks from time to time. But even the nursing staff had come to accept showing their badges going in and out of the room. The two alternating guards eventually memorized faces and accepted the polite offers of coffee and snacks from the nurses' station.

"Tell BeBe what happened the same way you explained it to me," said Catherine.

Jolie lay sleeping in the hospital bed, still recovering from the effects of the ordeal she had experienced. James looked at her quietly. It was as if their love for each other was some long, distant experience. Emotions and memories began to flood in and take over, but they seemed as surreal as something from a long past life.

"James?" said BeBe. "You do know you're visible. One of the nurses might come in."

"I asked for some privacy for an hour or so," said Catherine. "It'll be okay."

James looked somberly at BeBe and retold part of his earlier experience. When he was through, Catherine finished where he left off.

"Do you think it's possible that James had something to do with her arm?" asked Catherine.

BeBe only shrugged, "I've heard of rare cases where people of different faiths could do something like that, but I've never met anyone like that."

"Would you be willing to try it…, here and now?" asked Catherine.

James interrupted, "No way. I don't think this is a good idea at all. I'm already responsible for her being here."

He tried to push away memories of the torrent of power that had flowed through him nearly destroying a city block.

Catherine seemed even more anxious, "Is there something else that you haven't told us?"

"No…."

The answer was too quick and too short and BeBe's head was beginning to hurt while trying to penetrate into James' thoughts.

James actually had told Catherine everything about the day's events, but wasn't about to tell her that loosing this unexplained power had crushed the core of a tree like a twig. And all he had to do was let his emotions run free.

Jolie touched the deepest emotional part of him that could be provoked. Allowing that vast amount of love to take control…, the thought terrified him. If he explained his fear, the issue of good vs. evil would raise its ugly head again and he didn't feel like having that debate repeated.

BeBe urged him from his quiet stupor, "James?"

"Okay, I'll try. But don't say I didn't warn you if something unexpected happens."

Catherine and BeBe hurried together pressing their backs against the door, away from James as he stood at the window near Jolie's bedside. He did his best to isolate his feelings and thoughts while focusing on one little pencil he was rolling between his finger and thumb.

The sensations of the pencil helped him focus away from Jolie and concentrate as he had earlier. The fluorescent lights flickered odd hues in the room and the window blinds swayed slightly, but nothing remarkable occurred to speak of.

Jolie was in a peaceful sleep and didn't stir at his small exhibition of power.

BeBe urged him on, "James, its okay to think about Jolie."

He prayed that nothing bad would happen to Jolie, something that he hadn't done since before his death. James looked at Jolie tenderly and continued to focus on the smooth texture and feel of the pencil which began to expand and contract, contorting its shape involuntarily.

Jolie stirred in her sleep and a slight frown played on her facial expressions. The fluorescent lights in the room began to glow brightly until a bluish sheen filled the room. Catherine and BeBe looked for the source of the glowing brightness, but everything including the walls seemed to be radiating that same soft aura.

The outer covers on Jolie's bed whipped softly as if driven by waves of water and the hair on her head floated to attention.

Jolie convulsed upward suddenly and gasped as if starved for air then fell back on the bed in a deathlike expression.

James jumped away, dropping the pencil on the floor.

"I told you it was a bad idea…, I told you…," he whined, as he vanished out of the room in a gust of wind.

Catherine and BeBe rushed over to the bedside where Jolie lay. When she didn't respond, BeBe froze in horror as Catherine rushed from the room to call a nurse.

Trapped on his own bridge in time, James Earl prayed for death, but not only his own, as he began a slow trek over the River Cities Bridge, back into Natchez.

Car horns blared, as he indiscriminately walked on and off the shoulder into the sparse traffic, visible and unconcerned of the consequences. The river far below looked both peaceful and foreboding as if it were trying to speak to him.

James was a knot of emotions and knew it had been a bad idea to hide the truth about himself. He did try to tell them, didn't he? The girl he had loved, did love…, what had he done? Wasn't she recovering on her own, with the best doctors money could buy?

His anger rose again not knowing how to quell the see-saw of emotions.

How could his powers be anything other than evil or destructive? He was a dead thing and left here on the earth to dispense that very thing. He had been violated by power and corrupted by its thrust of energy.

He resolved himself to what he could do best - inflict fear and pain on anyone in his path.

The huge iron bridge creaked and swayed under his feet as he paced the last few steps onto Mississippi soil. He forced his senses to float out for several miles around himself, which returned in a mass of gibberish. It flew at him in a maddening turbulent flurry that was indecipherable.

He heard one plea that he recognized. It was the distress of Deputy Floyd, yet again. What could this weak man possibly need now?

James split the air in a thunderous roar in the direction of Deputy Preston Floyd.

Floyd was waiting nervously outside on the front steps of the Sheriff's Office, smoking a cigarette. Something that he had quit almost a decade beforehand.

James appeared in front of him, slapping the cigarette out of his mouth, leaving a trail of red sparks dancing along the sidewalk.

"Don't you know those will kill you?" bleated James.

"Why do you have to do that!? Hurry, follow me."

"This had better be important, I have better things to do than...." started James.

"I got a page..., from Billy. What do I do?"

James smiled despite his foul humor, "He's alive? Let's pay him a visit!"

Deputy Floyd sensed the intent in James and countered, "Wait, you can't hurt him. He's the only one that might know where the others are. Don't you see? If I can bait him and tell him everyone left him without a trace, he might know where they went."

James grunted at Floyd's reasonable idea.

Floyd continued, "He's used to dealing with that..., that..., woman, that Voodoo woman. Billy Don won't cave in."

James remembered how Billy was cursing him the last time he saw him, even as he was being dragged down that dark hallway into what used to be his own bedroom.

"We'll do it your way," said James. "But if he gets the least bit out of line, I'll crush him like a bug."

As the visual of the statement sunk in Floyd assured himself - This kid was insane.

"Don't worry Floyd. We'll make it look as if you and the sheriff solved this entire thing all by yourselves."

"Will I have to deal with any more of whatever it was that chased me?"

James shook his head, "It was your fear that was chasing you, stupid.

Weren't you ever a kid? Don't you remember the monster in the closet and under the bed? Remember how big they got the more you were afraid?"

"Well, yeah…, but they were my imagination, they didn't pick up my bed and slam me around the room like a basketball. That thing almost killed me."

"Almost…," said James. "But it didn't, did it? We're wasting time. Get your car and let's pay Billy a visit."

Chapter 65

It was a nice little house, miles from any close neighbors. White sands and saw-grass littered the yard surrounding it. The sturdy walls and structure sat high above the ground and it looked as if it had survived a few high winds in its short history.

The "For Sale" sign had fallen over months earlier and now was lying on its face in the tall grass by the roadside. No one but a derelict would consider a vacant house like this except maybe someone like Cambii.

He had walked all afternoon up from the Grand Isle, with everything he possessed on his back. Miles of swamp and crunchy road lay behind him and before him. The heat had been suffocating, but it was cooler now, inviting the mosquitoes to come out and feast.

Not much work for a cook or dishwasher around there. Too early for crops, "everything is seasonal," he was told. At least he wasn't turned down for ethnic reasons, someone with a funny accent. Most people had found his Jamaican speak colorful. Even though Cambii was young, he was strong and experienced in most anything that required the use of his capable hands.

He had earned enough from a few odd jobs to get him into the big city, if he was careful with his money.

It was nearly dusk and he had already explored several little half-paved roads off the highway, but this one had stubble from the last year growing high, right down the middle.

There was no traffic here and no one to send him on his way if he had to camp for a night or maybe two.

In the high grass at a turn in the road stood some refuge. The house was completely dark from the outside and he cautiously moved up to take a better look.

"Chicken merry, hawk deh near," he rehearsed a warning that his ancient old Memaw had taught him.

"If it look too good...," his voice trailed off to a whisper, not finishing the sentence.

He eased closer to one of the rusty screened windows and pulled himself up, but everything was dark inside. He made his way around the back and there sat a red truck parked deep in weeds.

Even in the dusky light, he could see the grass was freshly mashed from the tires.

He eased back toward the front of the house as quietly as possible. Someone had beaten him to this sanctuary and it was always best to beat a hasty retreat.

A noise of some sort issued from inside and against his better judgment, he stopped and listened. Somewhere inside the house was a hoarse voice - chanting. Instantly, his hackles rose. He had heard something like this before, from a *mambo* in Trinidad, where he was raised.

"Time to go," he thought nervously. "Walk all night betta than sit here."

He shifted the load up higher on his back and was quickly gaining speed as he neared the front of the house. The front door popped open and a scraggly young man with long stringy brown hair stepped out front.

"What's the hurry?"

"Wrong house…, I be on me way," said Cambii, his feet still moving.

"Naw, you're at the right place," said the man. "My friend wants to talk with you."

"No tanks, man…, the road be calling me name," said Cambii, feigning a smile.

"I weren't asking."

Cambii's worst nightmare appeared in the form of a raised handgun pointed directly at him.

"Don't want no trouble, man," Cambii said.

His raised hands were beginning to tremble, his legs still backing up at a slow steady pace. A few more feet and he would be able to turn and sprint down the overgrown road.

Cambii knew that he couldn't outrun a bullet, but he had enough junk on his back to stop a small caliber shot. He had been showered a couple of times from the small pellets of a shotgun blast, but a pistol was different, especially if this guy got lucky or new how to shoot.

The dirt on the ground beside him exploded and his ears rang as the man fired a round from the gun not twenty feet in front of him.

Cambii's eyes grew wide and he began waving his hands back and forth, "Don't want no trouble. You can let me be on me way."

He heard every warning his old Memaw had told him since he was a little boy and swallowed a gulp of dry terror.

"Get inside," he demanded, waving the gun toward the open door.

"Who's your friend, Toad?" asked a croaky voice.

Deputy Floyd pulled in to the rear entrance of the city park.

James looked at the swaging moss and remembered several intimate visits here with Jolie.

"If Billy takes the bait, you need to give a message to my Aunt Martiel. Let her know that…, one of her investigators is taking a trip for the next few days, following up on something. That's all she needs to know."

Floyd nodded discretely as they got out and walked down the winding trail past a bench that was even more familiar to James.

"Now keep quiet and out of sight," grunted Floyd.

"You do your job and I'll do mine."

A stocky man stood in the shadow of a lamppost with a cigarette glowing in his left hand. Floyd recognized him immediately as Billy, but he looked rough and battered.

"Billy Poole," said Floyd, stepping up closer. "Where have you been? You never called me back."

Billy snapped his head looking left to right, "No names…, you know that."

"I was beginning to think you left town," said Floyd. "You told me you were going to page me days ago, what happened?"

"Don't be worrying about me," said Billy impatiently. "I need to know a few things."

Floyd told him only enough to make him believe that the police were clueless, and that it was believed the others abandoned town leaving for parts unknown. Which wasn't entirely a lie.

"Where do you think they went?" asked Floyd. "I could use another paying job."

"Don't you worry. We'll be back in business before the end of next week."

It wasn't like Billy to brag unless he already knew something was on the horizon.

Floyd decided not to bring up certain facts about his wife Sallee Mae. If Billy didn't already know, he needed to stay ignorant for the time being. The last thing he wanted was for Billy to get distracted.

Billy took a long drag on his cigarette, thumped the stub to the ground and started to walk off without so much as a "see you later".

"Are you going to page me when you get back?"

Billy waved a hand over his head nodding as he walked off into the shadows.

"Remember what I told you," whispered James. "I'll keep in touch."

James fell in step behind Billy Poole.

Cambii sat on the floor in the corner of a small vacant room in the center of the house. All of his personal belongings were strewn inside by the front door, so if he had thoughts of leaving, it would take him a while to get his small world back in order.

"Whut kinda name is Cambii?" asked Toad, scraping the bottom of a plate of cold pork and beans. He dabbed the plate with a piece of light bread, then farted as he sat down in the corner grinning proudly.

Cambii just sat quietly. Anything he said was ammunition for whatever they had planned for him.

"Sounds like a girly name if ya ask me," said Toad, chewing while talking.

Cambii kept his thoughts silent, "You don't have that gun, me show you girly."

The old woman was busying herself with several items and slowly drawing intricate designs on the floor with flour, while mumbling softly to herself.

"You done struck a nerve," she said looking over at their guest.

Cambii understood that the old woman was listening to his thoughts and became deathly afraid. She was something else, maybe *Bokor*. No true *Mambo* would do something evil unprovoked.

She stood up straight in the last of the evening light, admiring her handiwork. She was wearing something like a sheet and a wrap delicately wound around her head.

"Git my bag."

Toad put down his plate quickly and did as he was told.

That spoke volumes to Cambii. This man had the gun but he was obviously respectful or afraid of the old woman. Respect or fear, either was bad news for him.

"What you do with me?" asked Cambii cautiously.

The old woman spoke up quickly, "I got a use for you...," she raised her chin and sighted down her nose at him. "You look like a strappin' young man, plenty of git left in you."

"Give the man a plate of those vittles," she said swinging her arm at Toad. "He be needing his strength."

Toad reluctantly fixed a plate of beans and threw two slices of bread on top. He handed Cambii the plate and stabbed a plastic fork in the center.

The old woman got out a bottle of rum from her bag and poured a cup full. She secretly spilled a small portion of clear liquid from a tiny glass vessel and mixed it in the rum where no one could see.

"Here, hand him this," she ordered. "Man need something to drink with his vittles."

Cambii stayed there on the floor with the plate in his lap looking warily at the two strange people. He slowly took a few bites and a sip of the drink. It was hot rum and not bad either. The food slowly disappeared and so did most of the rum despite every warning going off inside his head.

The old woman had Toad drag one of several large boxes from an adjoining room. The old woman pilfered through its contents and pulled out several candles and a few other devices. She placed the candles one by one in strategic locations on the floor of the room.

Cambii was finished with his food and could see where this was heading, but didn't like it. That rum was giving him a buzz like no other he'd had in some time and he silently cursed his pangs of hunger and thirst.

The old woman began a low growling chant and lit one of the candles. The little hairs on Cambii's body rose to attention.

He had witnessed other ceremonies similar to this as a baby boy, during Carnival. His Memaw had *wailed* on his behind when she found out that he was peeping in on them, but he was a curious child.

She lit another candle and started a singsong chant and Cambii's head began to spin.

"Why did I drink that rum?"

Toad found a corner that kept him farthest from what the old woman was doing and slunk into it.

Yet another candle flared up, this time on its own, and the woman placed a bowl in the middle of the floor. She began to set what was left of her *govi* – her clay pots - near the bowl.

She disappeared into the back room and came back with a sack of salt.

"Here Toad, got a job for you. Go make a line around the house on the ground with this and come back here."

Toad didn't waste any time running out the door into the dark and in only a few moments he shot back inside the door, looking half-crazed.

"See something?" she laughed. "...called darkness. Gonna git lots darker."

Cambii tried to stand and run out the door while Toad was performing his duty outside, but his legs would not obey him.

His arms and legs felt unbearably heavy and his mind was getting more and more clouded.

He looked up again and all of the candles were lit, glowing in a foray of rainbow hues through the skewed lenses of his eyes. He could hear the beat of drums echoing in the nearly empty house, his heartbeat almost in tempo with the wild hammering. The old woman was in a trance and her face was shifting into many expressions as she walked and chanted her song.

She spun and began to rattle her *ason* in the direction of Cambii and chanting. Cambii's body flew to a standing position in front of her, against his very will. She backed away and he followed her, while barely this side of consciousness, into the middle of her circle of candles.

She softly shook the rattle in little short bursts toward his arms and he watched in drunken horror as they obediently levitated out in front of him. His mind was working, his mind was telling him to run for his life, but why wasn't his body following his instincts?

From out of nowhere, she pulled a knife and cut slashes from his wrists right down to the palms of his hands. Deep stinging cuts gaped open and began to spill out a river of his blood into the bowl on the floor beneath his hands. He stood before her shaking, helplessly watching as he slowly lost consciousness.

The *Bokor* reached down and took the hem of her clothing and dipped it into the bowl of blood and wiped it sparingly on her forehead. She chose a decorative *govi* and began to wipe it down and bathe it in blood..., Cambii's blood. Filled with power from the sacrifice of his spilled blood, her chant changed.

She changed.

Elberta Straw had been in a secluded room, much to her protesting for several weeks. Her son Johnny brought her here and abandoned her. He abandoned her to a life of solitude, exactly the same way as before.

Johnny, his wife, and their baby girl Bridget - her only granddaughter, never came to see her, and now she was a ward of the state, trapped and alone.

Her memories of how she arrived in this awful place and her present state faded like mist in the air. She didn't like being alone, not since that dreadful night when those evil kids came over to her house.

Why had she trusted them? No one had been in her house for years..., then she decided to open her arms to help that awful boy.

They brought something with them that wouldn't cease from its banging and tormenting her. Once again, she quickly pushed the nightly fears from her mind, afraid that somehow whatever that thing had been would find her.

She hated being alone most of all. She didn't feel safe when she was alone.

Green Oaks was a nice enough place, if you were hooked on drugs, alcohol, or just plain crazy. It wasn't a nice peaceful nursing home for the aged or handicapped. There was plenty of noise and happenstance at all hours of the day and night.

Elberta somehow found comfort in the fact that someone was awake and on call just in case..., just in case.

She sat in her lonely solitary room with the TV on, watching some game show re-run. It didn't matter. Her mind was far away from where she sat, caught in another one of its re-runs of her childhood. Another, running to things she regretted, doors she should never have opened. She looked at the pinpricks on her aging fingers, scars from opening her blood to things she could never speak of to anyone.

The lock on her door clicked shut with a loud snap and she barely noticed. The TV hissed and snapped, then went black.

Barely waking from her stupor, she blankly picked up the remote and clicked it several times; tapping it on the arm of the chair she was seated in.

"Cheap batteries," she whispered.

She was about to go press her "call button" and get someone to fix the problem, when she heard a tap, tap, tapping. She raised up from her chair quickly and went to the door. It wouldn't open and her knuckles turned white as she bore down on the knob with all her strength.

"Elberta...," whispered a raspy voice from behind her.

She spun and placed her back into the corner next to the doorjamb.

In the room was the figure of a person. Only an outline, wispy, floating and faceless. After helpless recognition, Elberta banged her small hard fist against the door, but no one answered.

"What..., what do you want!" she wailed, cowering deeper into the corner. "I didn't call you. Why don't you leave me alone?"

"All I want is to talk to you Elberta. You remember me, don't you?" said the apparition.

"Oh, yes..., I remember you."

Elberta was whimpering, her heart pumping like a teenager.

"Tell me what I want to know and I'll leave you alone," rasped the voice.

Elberta stood staring in unbelief. This was the very reason she didn't want a room by herself. Now they would really think she was nuts, like some loony old woman trapped in her vivid imaginations.

"Tell me about the Ames..., they were your neighbors," it inquired.

"I don't understand..., what is it you want to know?"

"Who's in charge? Who makes the decisions?"

"I.... How would I know...? The only ones I know are my friends Martin and Maime."

"NO! Not the old man and woman.... I know who they are..., who else?"

"I..., I..., I think they have a daughter..., and there's that awful boy, that grandson..., he comes to stay sometimes..., James Earl. And there's a younger one, but I don't remember his name."

Elberta had no knowledge of James' death or any other recent events.

"You're useless to me!" said the apparition and it moved closer to Elberta.

"No..., wait.... I don't know what it is you want," she cowered down further. "Please don't touch me..., not again."

"Who has the power!" it growled, and the air crackled with the anger.

"Power?"

Elberta knew this entity was going to kill her.

"Who's the seer? Who knows things, you stupid old woman!"

The bed flung itself against the wall, clearing the night table of her precious few framed pictures as it passed. The room was tiny and there was no space for escape.

Elberta banged on the door once again with her open palm, but could only squeeze out a tiny, "Please…."

The sinister shape leaned toward her, listening.

"I…, I don't know. Maybe Martiel, Martin's sister?"

"She's the seer? The one that's been hiding from me?"

The question hung in the air uncomfortably long.

At this point, Elberta would have told this thing that the Pope was living next door if it would save what little life and sanity she had left.

"I…, don't know, maybe. She seems to know a lot."

"Miss Straw? Elberta? Are you alright?"

A somewhat kind voice floated through the door, just before the doorknob ratcheted back and forth.

All Elberta could do was pound lightly against the door.

"You better be right, or I'll be back to see you soon," hissed the specter.

Elberta was crumpled flat on the floor in the corner as the door clicked open. The evening nurse saw the condition of the room as she opened the door. The door was blocked and she squeezed inside to find Elberta behind it in a fetal position, whimpering.

"Orderly!" she yelled. "I need help."

"Get rid of this," she waved tiredly at the shill of Cambii's used body.

Blood had covered the floor in a paper thin red pool, soaking the flour-drawn lines. Cambii lay motionless and cold, his pale eyes were frozen open in a perpetual stare that followed him into death. His long, carefully plaited hair, was beginning to congeal and matte together in a deep black-red paste.

Toad hefted the limp remains of Cambii over his shoulder and staggered out the door and into the woods.

"I dig 'em up…, I bury 'em…, I dig 'em up…, I bury 'em…."

Toad complained every step. He dropped the body of Cambii beside a swampy slough behind the house, grabbed his shovel and began his toil.

He could hear the old woman ranting like a fool inside the house, then cursed himself for even listening.

"I be like a god!"

The old woman had caught a glimpse of her future as she felt her strength returning.

"I has my powers and be rich and young t'boot." She danced a little foot scooting jig and then began casting out handfuls of flour into the carnage to remove the bloody evidence.

"We needs to pay us another visit…. I got what I need…. It's high time I put this all to rest."

The sun was shining bright and clear, with the hospital window shades drawn and open wide. Jolie was sitting up in her bed eating her last meal in the hospital, while BeBe and Catherine walked outside in the morning air.

"Catherine, how do we explain Jolie to your family?" asked BeBe.

Catherine had spent the night at the hospital, keeping BeBe company. Jolie had gone into a convulsion, but when she recovered, she was clear-minded and strong. She had no recollection of the incident with James.

"We simply don't," said Catherine. "When Jolie is released, you take her to a safe place and keep her guarded. No one needs to know where she is, or her condition. The guard outside will go with you wherever you decide. Did you manage to contact her mother or father?" she asked.

"Neither one, but that's not unusual, her mother is always gone somewhere out of pocket for weeks at a time. I've never talked to her daddy that I remember, but that's another story. That's one of the main reasons why Jolie moved here with me. She didn't like staying by herself all of the time. You know that they're divorced, right?"

"I suspected as much," nodded Catherine.

She wasn't in a position to judge. Divorce was inevitably on the horizon for her and Robert.

They walked back inside to the hospital room to find Jolie standing by her bed and inspecting her arms and legs.

"Look at this! The bruises, the tears, they're almost gone. Look at my legs, I was so afraid to look at them. I just knew they would be scarred and ugly for the rest of my life."

Jolie sat back on the edge of the bed and lifted the hospital gown exposing the insides of her thighs and calves. There was only some discoloration, but the gouges and tears were all gone.

Only the tiny haired ends of the stitches remained as evidence of her ordeal.

"James had something to do with this, didn't he? I dreamed about him all night. He was at the cemetery..., and...."

Jolie stopped talking and looked at both of the women.

"I'm sorry, I.... It's just that it was so real. All of us were there with him. Something evil was there. I can still see this awful face, all wrinkled up and...."

The nursed knocked on the door and walked in with her dismissal papers.

"How's my...? Oh, my goodness. You're so much better today. The doctor told me to get your paperwork to release you, but I thought you were being transferred, not released," said the nurse. "I can't believe you're already up and around."

"That's what the doctor said too," said Jolie. "I'm glad they did such a great job."

She smiled and glanced over at BeBe and Catherine, prompting them to join in on her revelry.

"Can you take these stitches out before I leave?"

"Oh, no. Those have to stay in until…."

She casually looked down at where Jolie's legs had suffered the most damage.

The nurse stopped mid-sentence and looked up at Jolie, "I swear…, I've never seen anything like this…. I cleaned these stitches myself only yesterday."

The nurse looked over at the two women with a fearful questioned expression on her face.

Aunt Martiel was getting in her car to leave the Ames Estate when one of Natchez' finest pulled into the driveway behind her.

Deputy Floyd's face beamed as he got out of his newly issued Crown Vic with the improved 351M Engine. He had been surprised by the news that they were finally getting rid of the older worn out Plymouth Grand Fury's as they fell out of service.

His had fallen out of service several times, all in one night. He grimaced inside as he recanted the ordeal in his mind.

"My, my, aren't we steppin' up in the world," said Martiel with her usual warm drawl.

"How are you this morning, Ma'am?"

Deputy Floyd hurried to Martiel's car.

"What can I do for you…, *Deputy*…? *Floyd?*" she asked, somewhat wryly, after recognizing the nametag on his uniform. Her expression changed immediately and Floyd noticed the transition.

"I came by to deliver a message from one of your investigators. He said to tell you that he would be out of town for a couple of days to do a follow up on something…, he didn't say what."

Floyd became noticeably tense.

"Which investigator did you say told you this?"

"I…, I'm not sure what his name was…, it was a young guy. He said you would know who he was. I really don't know any more about it. He was in a hurry to leave and asked if someone would bring the message to you personally."

"I see…," said Martiel, looking down at her hands for a moment.

Martiel's mean streak began to emerge, knowing that this man had played a major a part in James' murder.

"I really don't recall anyone that was supposed to be going anywhere…," she said slowly, looking deeply concerned. "What exactly did he look like?"

"I, uh…, I didn't really pay that much attention. Dark hair, probably 6 feet or so…."

He was really struggling for an answer and fidgeting to leave.

"Hmmm…, so this man that you barely remember, asked you to deliver a message to me, telling me that he was going somewhere you don't know of, to follow up on something that you don't know about," she said in summation. "I don't recall anybody working for me that looks like that. Sounds like a *ghost to me*."

With emphasis placed on her last few words, she looked at him with daggered eyes, "But I guess we all have our ghosts to deal with…."

Deputy Floyd wondered exactly how much this Martiel Ellington really knew. Martiel sensed the deputy's frustration rising as she continued listening in on his thoughts. She eased her purse to where she could have easy access to her handgun.

"Sometimes I wish my ghosts would cut me some slack," said Floyd, trying his best to relax.

Martiel eased her purse back down in front of her, realizing that he was testing her to see what she knew as well as hinting for some help.

"I guess that would have to be between you and your ghost, now wouldn't it? Now if you will excuse me, I have some rounds to make in town Officer Floyd, and thank you for dropping by."

Chapter 66

Billy Don Poole was one strange and creepy individual to spend this much time with. Stopping every hour to take a leak and load up on more beer or soft drinks.

He didn't seem to be in any hurry to get anywhere in particular. James was hoping that this wouldn't turn out to be a wild goose chase. Cigarette smoke filled the cab and the truck was closing in on him as they passed through New Orleans heading south on Hwy 1.

Billy had taken every rat trail, back road on the map; it gave new meaning to the childish phrase, "Are we there yet?"

Finally, he exited the main road, and began driving down side roads, one at a time. He took every dirt and half-paved road that he passed. It was obviously somewhere that he had been once upon a long time ago and was having trouble remembering exactly where.

Suddenly, Billy spun the vehicle around seeing some familiar landmark. This had to be it. James got out of the truck and stood in the road unnoticeable to anyone. He didn't want the same mistake from last time. The old woman could tell if he was close - how close he didn't know.

He made sure that the truck stayed in sight as it drove down a deserted road, littered with weeds. The truck stopped suddenly and there was a small deserted house in the marshy bottom. James came as close as he dared and remained still, listening.

"Home sweet home," said James to himself. "I could save everyone a lot of trouble if I went in and smacked the house down on top of them."

Quietly, Syrus reminded him of the pointblank gun shot he had leveled on the old woman years ago and the fire when Syrus was sure he had destroyed her.

A man with deep olive skin approached him from up the road by the house. James didn't see where he came from, but he was obviously lost. Long tight coils of hair hung down his face, swinging side to side, matching his gait.

He was wearing baggy jeans and sandals, no shirt; his hard V-shaped chest told of many years of steady labor. James remained still, not wanting to be distracted from his sentry duty.

The fellow stopped in the middle of the road near James, turned, and faced him, looking him right in the eyes. James was spooked, but met his gaze directly. The color in the man's eyes were washed out, dead fish pale and skimmed over.

"Which way New Or-leans?"

His accent was colorful and pleasant, different from anything James had ever heard. This could be bad. The man could see him and the others might be able to also.

He disappeared right in front of James, simply faded away.

Taken by surprise, James looked every direction and he wasn't anywhere to be seen. This was the first person like him he'd seen walking in daylight.

"The dead walk around here?"

James sighed and answered his own rhetorical question.

"Guess so…, I'm here."

Again, the man appeared near the house walking up the road toward him. When he got near James, he asked the same question, but before James could answer or talk to him, he disappeared.

"Oh great, a broken record."

James moved to the other side of the road for a better vantage point and to avoid *Mr. Repeat.*

Sure enough, like clockwork he came walking up the long path again, but this time he took the shortest route, right toward James.

"Which way New Or-leans?"

James pointed north in answer to the redundant question and as he turned that direction, he disappeared.

If the old woman was there, she would see him walking out to meet James. He had to do something about this ghost.

There was movement at the house and three people walked out the front door. James got down under cover of the brush beside the road.

Sure enough, there were two men, the scraggly guy called Toad, Billy Poole…, and *her…,* his true enemy.

The deceiving appearance of the feeble old woman fled away as she hefted a large box and threw it into the bed of a truck with a thud.

She stood transfixed, scanning the area and James did his best to turn off all his thoughts and remain motionless and hidden.

In her hand was that same black, tortured, lightning struck stick that had sent shards of pain through him at their last meeting.

She bent over, doodling and scratching the end of the stick on the sandy ground beside the house, when the repeating man appeared once again, and began walking toward him.

James did everything he could not to panic and send up a beacon, as her watchdog came slowly up the long overgrown drive.

The three of them loaded up in the two trucks while she barked unpleasant sounding loud orders out the window to Billy, alone in his truck.

As they started up the driveway James used the distraction to back far away to remain undetected, far enough to keep his quarry in sight.

A new dilemma presented itself as James watched them approaching slowly up the road, with the *Jamaican wonder* following close behind. He couldn't risk riding with either of the vehicles for fear of being discovered.

They drove past slowly and turned onto the dirt road, only a few miles to Hwy 1, back to New Orleans and ultimately Natchez.

Moments later, he had to begin pursuit to keep them in sight. Daylight hours didn't allow him the same sweltering power as the hours starting immediately after sundown, but he should be able to move along at their pace without being detected.

Here came *Repeat* walking up to him and stopped. James expected the same question to fall out of his mouth. Instead, he reached out, grasped James on the wrist, and held fast.

There was no pain associated with his grip, but James could not pull free. James unleashed a whipping fury with his arm, desperately trying to free himself.

Another trap. His enemy was still full of surprises.

"Let go of me!" yelled James, as he continued to shake and hit at the man. His body flung violently and loosely, a rag doll in a child's grip.

The *repeating man* held on silently as he continued his duty.

James stopped pulling when he remembered how daylight sapped his energy. Daylight and the fellows' grip was draining his strength and this leach of a friend was gaining a tighter grip.

"Fine. Then you're coming with me."

James began to walk, dragging his ball and chain along with him. At least that was the plan. When he reached the edge of the road, his ball and chain became a leash that stopped him in his tracks, unmovable.

Another surprise.

Martiel Ellington stopped humming to the tune on her radio for a moment, taking pause at the intersection while looking at the beloved home place of her brother and sister-in-law at the end of the street.

She received a call from her lawyer in Natchez, who informed her that the first payment was late on the Ames home purchase. The down payment was received and the contract of sale was signed by Billy and Sallee Poole, but no one had been able to contact either party to get the agreed upon first payment.

Schuler and Ross had been the Ames family's law firm for many years and regularly handled all of their particulars for them, mostly by telephone. Martiel had informed them that she had a special interest in this property and its new owners. Against her lawyer's advice, she volunteered to go by and check on the property herself.

As she neared the end of the street, the first thing she noticed, indeed anyone would have noticed, were two black streaks of tire tracks scorched onto the pavement leading from Elberta Straw's front yard. Dirt and grass were sprayed into the road, thrown from two deep ruts and her already scraggly picket fence was smashed flat at the origin.

"Somebody was in a big hurry," whispered Martiel.

She stopped across the entrance to the driveway and noticed that the front door to her brothers' house was standing wide open. The screen door was barely hanging by the bottom hinge and the entry door pushed all the way inside.

Against her better judgment, she cautiously got out of her car and looked around outside. There were no vehicles in sight and it didn't appear that anyone was home, however there were a few pieces of clothing dotting the ground.

She eased up to the front steps and peered cautiously into the living room, illuminated by the afternoon sun that was filtering inside. The house was harshly quiet as she continued onto the porch, finally closing the gap up to the broken screen door. She wiggled it and it fell off its bottom hinge with a tumble, landing in a clamor onto the porch.

The noise startled her and she stepped back while looking around her, fighting the urge to turn and run to her car..., run and get the hell away.

Something wasn't right, other than the obvious vacancy, the obvious damage. Maybe the Poole's had already left the country and this was the end of the story.

Martiel felt differently. Never had one of her premonitions lied to her in all her years..., but that was before James..., before all her advisors left her to her own resources.

Her steady breathing restored, a hand to her chest, she leaned forward peering into the doorway.

"Hello..., is there anybody here?" she asked loudly.

Her voice echoed inside and she heard the barely noticeable hum of the air conditioner.

Martiel almost expected the cheerful voice of Maime or Martin to ring out and welcome her inside for coffee or to discuss some travesty in the day's newspaper.

She placed her right hand on the door facing leaning further inside and jumped back immediately.

"Oh my God!" she said loudly, snatching her hand from the facing.

She looked at her hand and wiped furiously at some unseen filth that didn't want to release itself. She felt weakness in her legs for a moment and staggered backward off the porch, down into the crunchy freshly cut grass.

Something was definitely not right.

She trotted to her BMW as quickly as she could, leaving everything exactly as she found it.

Cambii's blank stare told him that any conversation might be out of the question but James felt that he needed to know more about his ghostly trap.

"Where you from?"

Repeat turned and looked at James with his scaled rheumy eyes. Something resembling tears were flowing down his cheeks, but he didn't answer.

James started noticing particular details of the fellow's appearance. He had a crazy tattoo circling the back of his neck, hair matted with some kind of…, it looked like paste. No…, it was blood – pasty, matted, sticky blood. His other hand…, no…, *both his hands* were leaking something onto the ground and it was then James understood how the man must have died.

There were deep gaping wounds splayed open from both his wrists all the way down the palms to his fingers. The middle finger of his left hand was dangling by a mere piece of meat or tendon.

James felt something more than nausea; he felt a sudden wave of urgent and deep compassion for the man. He was a perfect stranger. Why should he care? He had much bigger problems to take care of.

James turned away, trying to focus on some way of escape. An unusual dry sound guttered from the walking corpse.

"Me… name… Cambii. Where… me… at?"

The speech was slow, growly, articulate, and gut wrenching.

He felt that whoever this was… needed the truth.

"You're dead…," said James as easily as he could.

The man raised his free hand looking at his wounds as if remembering something and screamed a slow, dusty, blood-curdling scream.

James bounced backwards and stared. What this person must be feeling…, James knew exactly what he was feeling.

"Who did this to you?" asked James, even though he already suspected the answer.

"She…," he began, "…only want me blot."

James didn't understand him, but then it hit him what he was saying. She bled him. She wanted or needed his blood.

But for what?

"Why did she bleed you? What did she do to you…?"

"She work a conja," he wheezed dryly, and dropped his head to his chest.

"A conjure," whispered James.

Suddenly he knew that his family was in danger, that she was going back for them to finish her job.

"I have to go…," said James to himself.

"She make me," said what was left of Cambii.

"She made you what?" asked James, getting his answer as Cambii's grip became more intent.

Cambii was her slave and he was obeying her command. It was like something out of a nightmare. That compelling was back, brick-loads of compassion. Despite his urgency, somehow he had to help Cambii.

He was torn, his need to get to his family was bearing down on him like a weight, yet his sympathy for this man was relentless.

No…, he had to go. This poor soul was already dead, but his own family was still alive.

It was hours until sunset, when his power would rejuvenate and most likely he could break free, but he didn't have time to wait for the earth and sun to complete their daily rituals.

Instead of pulling to leave, James began dragging the man Cambii behind him, back toward the house.

"She killed you, there must be a body. We're going to find it. Come on…, you don't have anything better to do," griped James, as he yanked at the corpse's arm.

Cambii resisted, but followed mindlessly in a dead stare.

James went past the front of the house, his intentions leading him toward the back overgrowth, when he spied one of the old woman's drawings in the sandy driveway.

"This must be yours," said James. "I see what she was doing with her ugly stick."

In the middle of the drawing was one of the little steaming demon creatures staring bug-eyed and hissing at the two of them. It too was chained inside the *vèvè*, and there were spots of blood in places where it was traced in the sand.

James reached to get the farthest end of the chain when the little creature hissed smoke, baring its venomous looking teeth.

It lunged at James' free hand. An involuntary pull from Cambii, who was still latched on to his left arm, pulled them both away from the imp.

James turned and looked angrily at Cambii.

"Look, I don't have time for this game."

He swung the dead weight of Cambii forcefully around the edge of the *vèvè* to be a distraction, then snatched the imp's chain loose from its anchored spot on the bloody drawing with his free hand.

It broke clean with a snap and James pulled both of his leashes backwards until the screaming imp popped in a burst of black smoke.

Immediately, he was also free from the grip of *Repeat*, his Jamaican trap. He was free now and desperately needed to get home. James began to focus his will to transport himself home but found that he no longer had the strength. He yelled a few choice words in disgust at the situation and looked back around to *Mr. Repeat* to exact his revenge.

Cambii was standing motionless at the marshy edge of a scope of trees looking down at a shallow, freshly covered grave. All the hatred and frustration drained from James in an instant.

James hurried near Cambii.

"Is that you?"

"Is me," Cambii nodded sadly, pointing downward at the grave.

"How can I help?"

Cambii's blind eyes gazed up at James.

"You're like me. Nobody can help you, can they?"

"Make Cambii sleep." He pointed at his grave once again in desperation.

James remembered putting the spirits in the graveyard back in their graves after they had risen at his command.

"Go…, Cambii, sleep."

There was no response to the kindness in his voice.

"Go!" James spat the order as angrily as he could, pointing to the fresh grave.

Obeying the authority of the command, Cambii slowly slid to the ground and lay down on top of his grave, then silently disappeared downward to his body.

James was overcome with a deep sadness for the man Cambii.

"I wonder if you had any family…," said James. "Somebody should know what happened to you."

He wept dry tears that he didn't understand until the moment passed.

James refocused his thoughts on how to get home as quickly as possible and started up the dusty road to Hwy 1, north. When he reached the first intersection, the concept of the time he had wasted hit him like a wedge.

The sun was almost at the horizon and his oppressors had several hours head start. There was no way to find them or even tell where they were headed for the night. Until darkness filled the sky, he would still be too weak to travel.

The old woman's trap had worked perfectly and he was yet again overcome by her experienced cunning.

He had the option of getting home the old-fashioned way…, hitchhiking.

He reached the highway and there was steady stream of traffic from the South moving into New Orleans. Along came a car going the same direction and he jumped inside… then fell back out, flat onto the ground.

This couldn't be happening to him.

Just like everything else in his life, whenever something good happened, it was snatched away. He cursed at the car, picked up a stone and threw it. It dribbled to a stop a few feet in front of him.

This was a nightmare.

His enemies would be back in Natchez hours before he could get there and there was no way to warn his family or the police. James looked at the lowering sun and wished for nightfall, maybe another hour…, but another hour might be too late.

Saturday night there was little traffic through the town of Natchez. The two trucks carrying James' enemies had separated and rejoined at the railroad tracks on the other side of town.

A quick stop to discuss arrangements and they left together.

Billy's new house was the same as he remembered it. Dark and terrifying.

He stepped out of the truck and waited in the street by the mailbox. Toad drove by slowly and parked in the driveway across the street at Elberta's empty home. He was virtually hidden by the overgrowth in her front yard.

An odd couple of figures ambled across the street toward Billy.

"I ain't goin' inside that place until you do some exterminating," said Billy quietly, although their closest neighbor was a several city blocks away.

Toad stopped nervously. He had never seen Billy afraid of any man or beast.

The old woman seemed put out at Billy, shaking her stick at him.

"Pshaw! Never in my life I seen two grown men a feared of the dark."

"The dark ain't what I'm afraid of," said Billy. "It's your damn pet."

She laughed at Billy and walked through the door looking around. She stomped the floor twice and recognized her own handiwork shuffling at the end of the dark hallway.

A smoky black figure eased up toward her, stark white eyes blinking in recognition to its master.

Billy had bravely walked behind her, but seeing the evil that had almost finished his existence, he backed out onto the porch.

"What house you say this was?" she asked, finally understanding where they were.

Billy, still refusing to enter the doorway, answered from outside, "The one that Sallee Mae latched onto, wouldn't have no other."

"It'll do right nice," she said walking on inside. "Yep, right nice."

The nearer to Natchez James got, the stronger he became. Walking didn't rush the sun's departure from the sky, but it made him feel like he was at least doing something.

Blessed darkness finally came and he could feel strength roiling inside him like water again. Moments later, he was standing in his family's front yard.

Even though there was no obvious commotion, he quickly surveyed the household for anything or anybody out of sorts. All was quiet and the family was humming about, doing nightly chores.

He could alarm them later, first he needed to check in with his unwilling partner.

With a turn of the head toward downtown Natchez, James disappeared.

The Sheriff's Office was its usual afternoon hustle of shift changes, but Deputy Floyd was nowhere to be found. He didn't have time to go hunting for someone that was supposed to be working to help him.

After the disappointing excursion of following Billy and the all day affair of getting back home empty handed, he was getting weary in his mind.

It didn't help that the noises were back.

Since he had hit Natchez dirt, the voices of Syrus and Ellie had come alive in his head mumbling an irritating drone. On the fringe of his ability to comprehend them, their return of clamor was pouring salt into his wounded composure.

That same uncontrollable frustration was mounting again, pushing him to anger and retribution. This was, after all, the time that his power was at its peak, if he had to face his enemies, nighttime would be his best chance at being the victor.

Precious time passed wastefully as he searched the places where he knew his enemy had found refuge. The cave was the same as he had left it, the house on the bluff of the River was boarded up and empty, and the shack was totally gone. It was as if his enemies had disappeared once again.

He stopped in front of Deputy Floyd's house and there sat Floyd's car, trunk open filled with two large bags of clothes, presumably dirty and all the lights were on inside the house.

James watched on as Floyd busied himself with some frantic chore.

There were three small boxes filled with personal items taped shut and placed by the front door. James silently went inside and found Floyd quickly cramming folded clothes into two more containers on the end of his bed.

"What are you doing?"

Floyd spun around from his chore to see James sitting on his bed digging through the box of handiwork. He didn't reply at first, breathlessly staring at James.

"You look like you've seen a ghost."

"You..., you're back? You're back!"

For a split second, it looked as if Floyd would lunge to shake his hand in relief, then the moment passed and fear and shame stood in it's place. James felt disgusted for the deputy's sake, asking once again, "What are you doing, Floyd?"

"I'm packing," said Floyd, turning his back on James. "What does it look like I'm doing? I'm getting out of here."

He spun his head from his efforts and looked at James, "I didn't think you'd be coming back..., ever."

"I thought we had an understanding."

He snapped in front of Floyd so quickly that the man fell backward a step. Surprisingly, Floyd rushed up to face James, knowing any aggression was futile on his part.

"So did I, until I met that aunt of yours," barked Floyd. "She knew exactly who I was and if I'm not wrong, she knows a lot more than she should. Why can't you let me go?"

"What if she does?"

Floyd flopped down on the edge of his bed near James.

"If the whole world knows, why don't you go ahead and get rid of me now? If they arrest Billy, he'll tell how I was involved in all this from the start. I don't see a way out of this for me no matter what happens."

"Why don't you let me worry about Billy? We only needed him to lure the rest of them back in town. Which is why I came to see you…. They killed another person…."

James didn't expect his voice to turn so sad, "Don't you think they'd kill you too if they thought you'd talk? The old woman knows stuff, Floyd…, sees stuff…, and I'm surprised she doesn't know about our agreement already."

"My point exactly!" said Floyd. "I'm as good as dead right now no matter what I do. That's the reason I'm packing, or don't you get it?"

"I'll find a way, somehow," said James. "Even if I have to kill them all myself."

"What if you can't kill them? Maybe you can't kill anybody. Is that it? You're just a spook making a lot of noise and I'm on the wrong team."

"Don't press your luck Floyd. I only spared you by request. Someone thinks you might have some redeeming quality, which is beyond me. Besides, you really don't want me to start proving my capacity to kick your butt again, do you?"

Once again, Floyd stood and pressed in close to James, filled with fear induced adrenaline.

"I think you're nothing more than a little spoiled kid with a gun…, aren't you? In fact, I'm pretty sure you're insane."

James effortlessly picked Floyd up by the neck and raised him off the floor. Floyd gripped at hands that weren't there, kicking his feet in the nothingness of air.

It was worse than a hangman's noose; his hands passed through his oppressor, grasping vapor. His face turned red and shades of blue as James carried him to the door of his bathroom and dropped him down.

"No," growled James in a violent fury. "I'm a pissed off dead kid with one thing on my mind and that's to get rid of everyone involved with ending - my life - my hopes - my dreams. I was nothing but a kid and you helped kill me!"

His voice had slowly risen to a resounding boom inside the little bedroom.

"The only thing keeping me from killing all of them including you is something that you obviously can't understand – Right and Wrong. And the difference between Right and Wrong is wearing really thin right now."

Floyd fell backwards from the force and will of James' voice through his bathroom door. The resounding vibrations cracked the cheap sheetrock on either side of the door with shards and spider trails.

James tipped over one of the boxes of Floyd's clothes on the bed in anticlimax and took a seat.

Floyd regained his composure after several minutes.

"I should have started packing earlier. If you don't kill me, they will. If they don't, I'll go to prison. I don't really see much of a future for me, do you?"

"Give me *some* credit. I don't want to have this same conversation again, do we understand each other?"

James looked around at the empty room, shaking his head.

"So you were going to take the coward's way out, huh?"

Floyd's hoarse voice answered quietly, "What don't you understand? I thought you were gone for good. Without you here, I wouldn't have a chance in a whirlwind! When you left I began to think about what all she had done and…, did you think I should stay here and become another one of her martyrs like the Mastyn kid?"

Even though James was angry and weary, he didn't disagree with Floyd. Everyone was in danger from the evil this *Bokor* possessed, and she always seemed to be just one step ahead of everyone.

She was the real evil, not Floyd.

"No," said James quietly, reflecting on the morbid end of Cambii.

The wayward stranger had been an innocent homeless person in the wrong place and at the wrong time.

"I don't blame you."

Floyd stopped whining his case long enough to listen.

"Unpack your bags, deputy, you aren't going anywhere. She is."

"No, you still aren't getting it," begged Floyd. "I've thought over every possible angle, every possible outcome. I'll hand in my resignation and start over somewhere else. Maybe not in law enforcement…, a regular job. I thought I'd go stay with my sister in Oregon until I can get on my feet."

"I need you to watch my family, Floyd. I can't be everywhere. You might be a greedy bastard, but I think that somewhere down the road you had your head in the right place when you started to work for the Sheriff's Department. Anybody can get off track and I think that's what happened to you."

Deputy Floyd stood speechless for several minutes. Was this the same venomous kid that was ready to squash Billy Poole like a bug not 24 hours ago? Or him only minutes ago? Now this boy was standing before him acting as if he had a conscience.

"Floyd? I can't control my anger. It feeds on itself and I get trapped by it."

James had read his thoughts, and finally Floyd understood the futility of what he was up against.

"I just thought you should know."

The deputy cursed under his breath and began slowly taking his clothes from the box on his bed and placing them back on his closet shelves.

"Maybe I'm the one going nuts. I can't believe I'm letting you talk me into staying. This is such a bad idea."

"I know it is…, but it's the right thing to do, and for the record, I'm the one that's nuts."

Floyd tossed one of the empty boxes to the floor at the foot of the bed.

"You have a sister in Oregon?"

Chapter 67

Billy Poole slept on the couch in the living room, with the light on all night. If sleep is what you would call it. With every creak and unusual noise, he bolted upright to make sure the old woman had control over her pet.

The glow of sunlight was slowly entering the southernmost window of the room and Billy needed the bathroom terribly. He looked down the hall and everything was quiet. After weighing his options, he ran down the hall, jumped inside and locked the door, feeling the safety of the smaller solitary space.

Billy looked in the mirror at his aging face. Two days without shaving or a bath and he looked like warmed over crap.

He dug around in the cabinet beside the sink and found it completely stocked with everything that most normal families use, including a new pack of razors. Freshly folded towels lined the cabinet shelves. Clean smells. The handiwork of Sallee Mae.

He cursed bitterly under his breath, both at the loss of her touch and her infidelity. Why? But he already knew the answer to the questions pouring into his mind. Some husband he'd turned out to be.

He turned on the hot water and began his morning ritual....

"They're back..., I'm not sure where, but they're back."

James was hovering at the side of his Aunt Martiel's bed trying to rouse her to consciousness.

"What..., What time is it? Who's back?"

"Didn't Floyd deliver my message?"

Martiel rolled over and looked at the clock. It was merely ten minutes before six that morning. Sunday morning. She sunk back into her pillow trying to decide whether to wake up and listen or to pull he covers up and make James go away.

"Are you even listening? All three of them are here somewhere."

"All three?" asked Martiel groggily. "Floyd..., yeah..., good old Floyd."

Her last few words were muffled by the pillow she was hiding in. Martiel was already leaning toward covering her head and ignoring the impatient spirit causing her grief.

"This is great! Did you even know I was gone?"

Martiel decided that the talking alarm clock was not going to shut off and scooted up in her bed with her back against her pillows.

"Eight o'clock." She sounded tired and annoyed.

"Eight..., what?"

"Eight o'clock. That's what I had my alarm set to. It's the only day that I let myself sleep in."

She yawned painfully, letting her eyes droop closed. Her vision was bleary from the early hour and trying to look at James only amplified the problem.

"I can't believe you. Didn't you hear what I said? Those people are somewhere in town."

"James, how long do you think your condition is going to last?" she asked.

"My condition? What does that have to do with any of this? I guess until..., I don't know how long."

"Pretty long, James. You are going to have to learn to be patient. Chasing problems is only going to drive you insane and make you do things without knowing if it's right or wrong. Problems will always find a way to come to you. If you're prepared, you can handle them. But, if you spend all your time and energy chasing them down, you won't have time to think and prepare. Time is the one thing that you have over every one of us, James. Think about it. The most important thing I learned over the years from our departed family was to think the situation through from several angles. Then decide on the best possible one. Then you pick the right time and act on it."

Her eyes were open now and she sighed deeply before she started again.

"What happened to you when you were gone?"

James was tired of the lesson and was anxious to give an account of his travel experiences.

"I followed Billy down to where the other two were hiding in a house. That's what I did. I also found out that she killed another person and did some more of her mumbo-jumbo."

Martiel waved a hand to urge him on, "Then what? Please continue...."

Her usual smart-aleck drawl was all she could offer as she slid back under her covers.

James didn't want to admit that his enemy had outwitted him once again.

"I found out that the daylight makes me weaker, and if I hadn't..., if I hadn't got back when I did, I couldn't warn you."

"Where are they now, James?"

"I don't know, they got ahead of me.... I kind of got trapped and I couldn't follow fast enough. I didn't even think I'd get back in time to tell anyone."

His irritation was mounting with every nuance of the conversation.

"Tell anyone what? That you were gone off chasing someone that was bound and determined to come back and finish what they started? That you risked getting stuck somewhere and not ever able to find your way home? And what did you accomplish James?

"You know they're somewhere near, at some unknown location. Basically you ran your little hiney all over God's creation and you have exactly what you started with and risked yourself doing it."

"That's not true! I..., that is, we..., aw, this is crazy!"

"We? Who is *we*?"

"The person she killed, she did something to him, he was all butchered and..., I don't know..., empty in the head. I had to help him. I couldn't leave him there."

"Where is this person now?"

How did Martiel do it? He didn't want to talk about how he had been tricked and trapped by the watchdog spirit of a dead man.

"In his grave. He was dead. What was I supposed to do? Bring him here?"

"Oh James..., humor me for a minute. If you had stayed here, would they still be here now?"

"I..., I don't know, I guess so."

James was beginning to feel like he was being interrogated.

"And what about where they are. Would you know that if you'd stayed here?"

"At least I tried! It's more than anybody else is doing."

"Let me explain a few things about patience. I'm trying my best to help you understand if you'll only listen. We sold Billy and Sallee Mae the old house. They don't know it belonged to the family. Whether it was a stroke of luck or divine providence, they found the house. Billy is a greedy man or he wouldn't be working for a greedy person like this voodoo hag.

"He wants fast money. He lives for fast money. He isn't going to give up that huge down payment without a fight. He had to come back, it's in his nature. If I was a bettin' woman, and I am..., that's where you'll find them hiding. She won't go back to the shack, it's burned down. She won't go back to that rent house, you saw to that.

"She's an old woman, where do you think she'll go? More than likely the path of least resistance. What's available? Billy's place," she stopped to let everything sink in.

There was one thing Martiel had left out, "What about Sallee Mae? I doubt Billy tells her what he's doing for a living."

"Yeah, well what about Sallee Mae?"

"What about her? She's probably all the way to New Mexico by now. Do you know how I know that? No, you probably don't. She didn't show up to make the first payment on the house that she dumped every last cent of her money into. I happened to go by there yesterday and found some of her clothes on the yard and skedaddle tracks leaving the house."

"You're only guessing at all this," said James.

Martiel yawned once more and took in a deep breath.

"You're right. It is a guess…, an educated guess. If you'd stayed here with me after you and your deputy friend had your little pow-wow with Billy, I would have explained this to you. Patience is a virtue."

She was finished, hoping that some of her experience sunk into him.

"I'm listening," said James tired of arguing. "What's next?"

There was a knock on the bathroom door.

"You fall in?" asked Toad. "Miss Lyda wants to talk to you."

Billy heard the door open and close across the hall in the main bedroom. He had been finished for quite some time, but needed the solitude to think some things through. The problem was…, there were no solutions the deep chasm he'd managed to dig for himself.

He peered out carefully, then scurried across the hall.

"Come here," she said.

Billy walked in to find the old woman sitting on the edge of the bed without a stitch of clothes on. He quickly noticed that Toad was back asleep on the other side of the bed and from what he could tell, in pretty much the same condition.

Billy quickly turned his face to go back out, having seen far more than he anticipated for one day.

"What's wrong with you?" she snapped. "Come on in and sit."

Billy did as he was told, but sat sideways in his chair facing away from her, not wanting to look at what time, age and evil had done to her body.

"You sure didn't mind sharin' my bed when I had Ellie's body on."

The old woman cackled a dry laugh to embarrass him further.

"Where's your little honey at?"

Billy grunted, "Gone, an glad of it."

"So you think that preacher man did all the work makin' her a baby?"

"Fraid so."

"Ain't true," she said. "Kid is your kid, not his. They was just pokin' fun."

She cackled another crude laugh.

Billy sat there in the chair, trying to absorb the new information and feeling like the fool he was. He wasn't the most faithful husband himself. The old woman had made sure of that.

"How you know?"

"I know. Jus' do."

Billy had to find a way to appease his guilt, directing it toward a different source, "She wouldn't have run off if it hadn't been for that Ames kid showin' up."

"Come on over here and sit beside me," she said, patting the bed. "We'll work it all out."

Martin Earl Ames rattled his newspaper angrily, "They've had over twenty people call into the Natchez Gazette that say they've seen a ghost out on that highway and over the River Cities Bridge. One person said it looked like the picture of our James! They saw his picture in the obituary. This is slanderous!"

Martin was standing now, ready to go to war with some unseen newspaper editor.

Martiel sat quietly drinking her coffee, waiting for her brothers' blood pressure to drop back to normal. Maime had already read the article and was making herself scarce in anticipation of his reaction.

"Isn't there something we can do about this?"

Martin Earl glared at his sister, "You're the one with all the legal know-how. This has to stop."

He tossed the paper in its entirety on the floor by the trash.

"I guess we could buy the newspaper out," said Martiel jokingly.

He left the kitchen in a huff, headed to his favorite thinking place on the front porch swing.

"We've already used most of our influence by keeping everything else out of the paper," she answered.

Martin grumbled all the way through the living room, "It's not right..., it's just not right...."

"I'll call Schuler and Ross first thing Monday morning," Martiel sang over her shoulder, "But all they'll do is print a retraction and that'll get even more attention. Is that what you want?"

The front door banged shut as Martin walked out onto the porch. Catherine and Sam walked in the kitchen, glad the storm had passed.

"What's up with daddy? I heard him all the way upstairs," yawned Catherine.

Martiel pointed down at the Natchez Gazette and shrugged her shoulders.

Sunday evening was coming down hard on Sam. Church wasn't so bad, and dinner in town was great, but now he was going through the shelves of the family library and stacking all the books down onto the floor.

His mother had given him the chore of cleaning and rearranging them by author. So far, there were about 22 stacks of books that were from knee to waist high and a couple of pounds of dust to match.

He was wondering why he didn't go back to camp and finish out the summer. At least there, he could sneak the girly magazines from the other guys and get a real "balanced" education.

It was a bummer that his brother was gone. His dad was probably with the bimbo he'd seen, one of the several times he had to go with him for the weekend. A "friend" was what his dad called her, but friends don't touch or look you in the eye the way she did his dad. It was a cinch that something was up because his dad hadn't so much as called to find out about him or his mother.

Was he waiting for his mom to apologize? He was the one that had freaked out and left at the first excuse. In fact, it was as if his dad had planned the fight with his mother.

He missed James. When he was bored, James would always find something that needed doing that was a kick in the pants. Not sorting stacks of dusty books…, and the attic was next.

This house was ancient, there had to be something cool to do around here.

Catherine had once again given Sam some busy project so that she could try and talk sense into James. She hurried upstairs quietly and found James in Martiel's room, sitting very still and quiet with his back to the door.

"Hello, mom." He didn't bother to turn around, "You've got Sam busy with some boring crap, right?"

"You shouldn't sit with your back to the door, what if it hadn't been me? You are visible you know."

"I'm practicing. Aunt Martiel gave me a list of exercises. At first I hated it, but…, now that I'm getting the hang of them, well…. Let's just say I should have done these before now."

"What…, kind of exercises?"

"Listening, for one. I knew it was you coming up the stairs…, actually I knew when you made up your mind to leave Sam in the library."

James was listening to more than the thoughts of the inhabitants of the house. Syrus and Ellie were still chattering away inside him, including him in their comments from time to time. At least they were consoling him, trying to offer some comfort to all his misguided efforts.

James had actually enjoyed the peace of not hearing the constant mumbling inside him while he was trying to concentrate on his own thoughts. He was learning to push them down and away, but it took so much….

"You do know that Sam is about to go stir crazy, right?"

"Yes, I do. So am I. But there's only so much I can do to occupy him while he's inside the house and I'm running out of ideas for jobs."

"Why don't you let me take him on a ghost hunting expedition?"

"No, James! Don't you dare!"

"Oh, it would be fun! I promise not to scare him. I'll move a book here or creak a door or wiggle a curtain; that kind of thing. Sam would eat it up."

"Your grandfather has just now accepted living back in this old creepy house. The first thing Sam would do would be to tell him about it and…, well it might not be good for him."

"If Sam knew about me…, it might actually be fun again. I miss that you know…. I miss a lot of things."

There was an uncomfortable silence for a few moments as Catherine gathered her thoughts.

"I did some reading in the family ledger of Aunt Martiel's. It says that I'm an "elemental". That means I'm quite human and not quite dead. I'm stuck somewhere on the bridge in between. It can be caused by the spiritual power that a person has while they are alive.

"It's funny. I never knew I was so *empowered* while I was alive. Some of the ancestors were stuck here too, but they couldn't do any of the things I can.

"I plan on reading the rest of it tonight while you all are sleeping. You know…, it's a killer being awake all the time while everyone else is resting. That's another thing I miss…, sleeping. Closing my eyes? That's useless, I can see right through them. Did you know that my mind never rests? It's a nonstop chatterbox."

James rattled on with morose confessions, while Catherine listened for hints as to the emotional state of her son. He seemed so much more level than he had the last few days. Maybe now was the time to tell him about Jolie.

"What about Jolie?"

James stood quickly, plopping down on the floor in front of Catherine.

"Is…, is she any better? I've been afraid to ask…. I know I can't go back there now," he said bowing his head on her lap.

"You can in time, James. She's almost completely well, you know."

"She's well?" he asked. "She's better? How? What happened?"

"You left in such a hurry that you didn't get to see the results of our experiment. The bruises are gone as well as the scarring everywhere."

"Everywhere?"

"Yes, everywhere…."

Catherine waited a few moments for James to rid himself of his guilt.

"I was afraid that I might have made her worse. Mom, you don't know half the things I'm capable of…."

James covered his face letting out a sigh of relief.

"Jolie left the hospital the next morning. I'm sure you had something to do with it James. No matter what bad you think you're capable of, you're also capable of powerful good. BeBe has her hid away for now. She might go back to stay with her mother for a while."

Catherine watched his reaction closely.

"That would probably be good for her," he said, sporting a cold stare.

"She wants to see you James. You know I couldn't stop either of you, but...."

"You want it to be my decision, is that it?"

"Pretty much. I want it to be both your decision."

Catherine got up and walked to the window and peered through the heavy curtains.

"It will have to be Jolie's decision then. The ones I make have flaws."

Trying to find a subject other than himself, "What about you and dad? I know what Sam thinks...."

"What does Sam think?" Catherine snapped back, suddenly turning around to face him.

"And she thinks I'm unbalanced," thought James. "I'm sorry mom, I had no right...."

"It's okay. Tell me, please," she said, turning her gaze back out the window.

"I shouldn't, oh, well.... Sam went with dad one weekend when he got called into work. There was this woman..., she was kind of hanging around, you know?"

"Is that all? Just hanging around?"

"Mom..., she was hanging around all over dad."

"Jerk," she said under her breath, resting her cheek against the cool windowpane.

She fought back tears of pain remembering every "emergency" he had been swept away to take care of. She opened the French doors to the veranda, letting the muggy air wrap around her.

"Mom? You okay?"

After several minutes of silence, James offered some advice to his mother, "Life's too short.... Take it from me, I know."

There was a soft thump against the bedroom door and footsteps bumping away.

Catherine snapped from her trance-like stare and sped to open it. There was no one in the hallway. She came back in and James was standing very still near the bed, listening to something she couldn't hear.

"He knows," said James, looking down at his mother. "Sam knows."

Monday morning, at five o'clock sharp, James sat waiting on the end of Deputy Floyd's bed. Floyd was covered to his chin in rumpled covers, with a leg and an arm dangling out in the open.

The resonating hum of the air conditioner was the only sound other than the steady rhythm of breathing. The alarm clock went off and his heavy right arm flopped over to hit snooze.

James waved the clock back and forth up in the air above the sleeping deputy, waiting for him to wake up.

Floyd slapped repeatedly at the nightstand, looking for someway to get five more minutes sleep. The twelve hour shifts were already killing him. He cursed sleepily, reaching all over the top of the nightstand.

James shut off the clock and set it back where it was.

"Come on Floyd, we need to talk," said James. "Wake up!" Floyd sat up quickly and instinct took over as he reached for the gun holster under his pillow. The room was still dark even though there were signs of hazy light from outside.

"Who's there?" barked Floyd.

"You know, I've never understood why someone would ask a burglar, who's there. It's not like they're going to tell you."

Floyd rolled out and crouched by his bed straining to see. He fiddled with the switch high up on the lamp holding his gun forward. Finally, he found the button and pushed it on.

James patiently waited for Floyd to find him seated in the only chair in his bedroom. The back of which, was draped heavily with folded pants and shirts waiting for a trip to the cleaners.

"Do you intend to shoot me with that?" asked James.

Floyd stalked over pointing the gun at James and lazily took a swing at his head, passing cleanly through.

"Feel better?" asked James.

There were several advantages of his physical reality being a "one way" relationship.

Floyd grinned as he walked back over to re-holster his gun and sat on the bed without saying anything. He wiped his eyes with the tips of his fingers and yawned.

"Would it kill you to knock or call before you show up and scare the hell out of me? I never know if the next visit will be you or something worse."

"Just trying to keep you on your toes, Floyd. You're mostly on your rear end."

"Don't tell anybody," Floyd said while walking to the bathroom.

"You need to get in gear. We have things to talk about before you go to work."

James chuckled when he heard the familiar phrase of his grampa come out of his own mouth.

"Someone paid it?" asked Martiel. "Who was the receipt made out to?"

"Billy…, Poole," staggered a tiny voice. The secretary at Schuler and Ross was dutifully letting her know that someone had paid the past due first payment on the Ames property.

"He came in first thing this morning with cash. Do you want to reject it and begin Breach of Contract proceedings?"

"Uh, no. No. Go ahead and accept it. I have a feeling that we'll have another chance soon, real soon. Thank you for calling."

Martiel didn't bother mentioning the problem her brother Martin had with the bad press they were receiving in the Natchez Gazette. It would only further to humiliate the family name to ask for a retraction. It was best to let it run its course and die a natural death.

The telephone on the kitchen wall didn't get settled before Martiel snatched it back up and dialed the number of the place where BeBe and Jolie were staying.

"Hello…, yes it is…. I think they did what I said they would…. No…, I think the law enforcement had their chance. I'll tell Catherine…. Okay, be careful."

Martiel hung up, gazing across the room thoughtfully.

"Who was that?" asked Martin Earl, walking in for a fresh cup of coffee. "Where is everybody?"

"It was the law office. They said I need to come by and sign some papers. As for as everybody else…, I can't answer for them."

"I'm going into town. I need to check on the garage. I hope the place is still there."

Martin's comment held a hint of vinegar in his voice.

"I wonder if Sam is awake? Maybe he'll want to go with me."

"Are you sure that's a good idea? They haven't caught those criminals yet."

"That's bosh…. It's broad daylight. The sheriff said that everything they've done so far has been at night."

Martiel tapped her fingers on the countertop, "Like pushing you off in the pond?"

Martin Earl set down his coffee cup on the counter near his sister, lowering his voice, "I know you're right. It might be dangerous, but I'm going crazy sitting around here, little sis. You of all people know how much I love my family. But I'm used to doing things with my hands, talking with customers and friends…, you know, working. Maybe retirement isn't cut out for me."

It had been ages since her brother referred to her as 'little sis' pushing her thoughts back to childhood. Martin was already moving full steam ahead before Martiel recovered enough to offer her rebuttal, following behind him, "I understand that, Martin, but…."

Martin was already several steps up the stairs looking for Sam. A few minutes later Catherine walked into the kitchen as her usual routine for a cup of her father's dark coffee, which was now his religious morning duty.

"What's with daddy?" grunted Catherine. "He seems grumpy again this morning."

"It's a long story. I can catch you up real quick if you have the time."

"Sorry…, I really don't right now. Today is mama's last doctor appointment and it's…, in about an hour."

"So you're going into town today too?" Martiel suddenly had a concerned look on her face.

"Unless you know of a way for the doctor to see her over the phone."

Catherine finished pouring her coffee, glancing over at her aunt.

"Now I know where James gets his attitude. It didn't fall far from the tree," muttered Martiel.

Catherine smiled, considering the compliment.

"Is there some reason why we shouldn't go?"

"It's what I needed to discuss with you, but you don't have time…."

Catherine glanced from the clock on the wall and back at the concerned look on her aunt's face.

"Let me go make sure that mama's awake and getting ready. I'll be back in a second."

Deputy Floyd walked outside the Sheriff's Office away from the usual traffic of the day's business.

"Billy is the only one who knows that you're the cop that helped them cover up, right?" asked James.

"He wouldn't even let me know who the other people were that were helping him. He was real quiet about everybody and everything. I asked him once about meeting them and he turned cold."

"Good. Then most likely the others only know that it's somebody in the Sheriff's Department. And that could most likely be anybody."

"Most likely," repeated Floyd, sarcastically. "That doesn't give me much hope."

"I needed to know that if anything goes wrong when they are arrested, that he is the one that needs to have an accident," said James.

He suddenly remembered the creature that he peeled from Floyd's face. There truly were worse things than death, yet he had no experience in creating the type of evil that the old woman could conjure up at will.

It was time to find out if he could actually trust Deputy Floyd.

"You remember where we used to live? That's where I think they'll be."

"Where? I can't believe that. Why of all places would they go there? Don't they know the house belongs to your family?"

"Just trust me. It would take too long to explain, but no…. Billy didn't have a clue and it was Sallee Mae that bought it."

Deputy Floyd seemed overtly relieved, "Great! Let's get the Sheriff and go arrest them. Then you can go your way and I can go mine."

"Arrest them on what evidence? So far, thanks partly to you, there isn't any hard evidence placing them near me, the house, or anybody else. You're going to have to start thinking, Floyd. They might be able to place that scraggly guy at the scene of the wreck with the blood they found, but what if it wasn't his blood?"

"I still say your messed up idea of morality is going to come back to bite you. You should go there and clean house."

James lowered his head in disgust, "My messed up idea of morals is what's keeping you alive at the moment, so don't be too quick to judge them or me.

"I don't believe that they came here for a place to rest. If my aunt is right, either tonight or tomorrow night, they'll try something.

"I have an idea of what that will be, but I still don't know for sure. We have to catch them in the act this time Floyd, we can't mess it up. I might be out of your life for good if everything goes right. I might really be gone...."

James heard a familiar voice call his name.

Sam had heard most of the garbled conversation through the door Sunday evening. He also heard what his mother said about him going straight to his grampa and spilling the beans.

"James is alive! How did they pull that off? Why would they fake his death? And why are they keeping it all a big secret? It's a mystery! Finally something was going on around this dusty old place."

One huge problem skewed his theory.... He had seen what he thought was the body of his brother fall from a broken casket at the funeral. He couldn't understand how or why they would do something awful like that.

Sam dropped another stack of books on the floor, "I know what I heard."

"Sam? Samuel Earl? Are you in here?"

Music was blaring from one of the shelves by the window.

"I'm here...." His voice turned to one of disgust as soon as his train of thought was broken.

Someone actually found him. He was back in the library, stacks of books everywhere and every shelf empty and washed clean.

His grampa walked in looking somewhat relieved, "I've been looking everywhere for you. Do you want to go with me to the garage? Good Lord son. What has your mother got you doing in here?"

"Cleaning and rearranging the library. The attic's next."

"Nonsense! I need you to run errands with me today. You can piddle with this tonight or tomorrow."

"Did you ask my mom?"

"I'm her *Father*, in case you've forgotten. You're coming with me."

Sam threw the filthy washrag he was holding into a pail of equally dirty water.

"Give me a minute to clean up?"

"You got ten minutes or both of us may be stuck here all day."

Sam hurried off upstairs to their bathroom to wash up and change clothes. Finally, things were looking up. The fact that James was still alive kept him awake most of the night with ideas of what might be going on.

That was James' voice he heard, he was sure of it. Now, of all times, he was going to spend the day away from this stuffy place, right when he wanted to investigate further.

He slipped past the kitchen door and heard his mother and Aunt Martiel quietly discussing something. He wanted to know what it was, but decided it could wait.

He was going to use their preoccupation to grant him a free pass upstairs and then out of the house with his grampa. Sam slid past the door and up the stairs he bounded as quietly as he could.

Five minutes passed and he emerged back out into the hallway clean and changed. Something sparked inside him and yet he didn't know if it was worth the risk.

Quietly he walked to the next door, which was his Aunt Martiel's room, where he had heard James and his mother talking.

He gently turned the doorknob, listening for any sounds inside the room. All was quiet. Maybe James was asleep or hiding somewhere?

Everything was immaculately placed around the room, typical of Aunt Martiel. He eased the door closed behind him and stood listening. He could hear his heart pounding in his own ears from the excitement. There was no one on the bed and no real hiding places except for a tall cedar wardrobe and deep walk-in closet.

The door to the wardrobe was slightly open and he peeped inside slowly, half expecting his brother to jump out and scare the crap out of him like the old days. Nothing there.

He had to hurry or his grampa would get impatient and leave him here to finish wiping down shelves, rearranging books and then there was the awful attic to look forward to....

He walked on to the closet and stealthily opened the door, peering inside at its dark secrets. A pull chain dangled against his face, attached to the porcelain light fixture on the ceiling, much like all the other closets in the house.

The huge closet was filled with stuffy old clothes and boxes of all shapes and sizes. Musty old shoes that should have been thrown away years ago, lined the back wall.

No James to be found.

The door to the bedroom opened suddenly and in walked Catherine, his mother.

He quickly turned off the light, pulling the chain out away from the porcelain base to silence the click of the switch.

He eased to the door, which had shut on its own after he entered. There was his mother in the room standing by the bed.

She looked impatient, rubbing her hands together and then walked over to the window.

"James? James I need to talk to you."

Sam was beside himself, "Good! Now I can see where he's hiding."

Catherine circled the room once again, "James," she whispered loudly.

From out of his field of vision walked his brother James. Alive!

"Thank goodness you heard me. Aunt Martiel wanted me to let you know that the law office called. They paid the house payment, which means that they are hiding over in…."

James held up his hand to quiet his mother from speaking. He looked suspiciously around the room and then toward the closet.

He looked at Catherine and then walked slowly toward the closet door.

"Oh, crap!" thought Sam as he quietly scooted backward into the darkest recess of the closet. "I can't let them find me here."

The closet door opened wide and the light switch crunched to the 'on' position.

Sam was behind a row of dusty clothes standing as quietly as possible, heart loudly thudding in his throat.

Without a sound, the clothes parted in front of him and there was the face of his brother James…, or was it. Something was wrong, different…, he could see…, right through him.

Samuel Earl slid to the floor with a thud.

James carried the limp body of his brother to the bed and lay him down.

"What do you intend to do about this? He knows for sure now."

"Why did you let him see you?" asked Catherine.

"Me?" spat James. "You didn't even know he was here. I was the one that figured out he was watching. By then it was too late."

"You're right…, I'm sorry."

"No, you're right. I'm the one that supposed to be so sensitive to everything in the house. I should have heard his thoughts."

Catherine was genuinely worried, "But what do we do now?"

Sam stirred on the bed and began to wake up, looking blearily toward the light from the windows.

There was a knock at the door, followed immediately by a face poking inside.

"Sam? Are you in here? There you are…. What happened?"

Sam sat up looking around the empty room and then to his mother. Catherine remained completely silent, not knowing what to say, in what was possibly one of the most awkward moments of her life.

"I'm coming grampa," said Sam. "I got a little dizzy, probably from the cleaner I was using on the shelves."

Sam looked over at his mother once again and stared her in the eyes.

"Are you sure you feel like going anywhere?"

"Sure, mom. Everything is fine…. I'll be fine."

Chapter 68

Martin Earl Ames did not expect the overwhelming flood of emotions that hit him as he unlocked the door of Earl's Garage.

Samuel followed him inside and squinted as his grampa flipped the switches and turned on all the overhead lighting in the office and garage bays.

There was still the silent boisterous laughter of his deceased grandson clinging to the walls inside. Martin could still hear the clicking of tools and the noisy air compressor out back replaying in his mind.

On the wall inside was a corkboard with a collage of the 1967 Mustang Fastback that he and James had worked on together to restore.

He stared at the broad smile of James' face standing next to the front of the car in the final stages of restoration. His eyes watered and he turned and walked away in pretence of checking the storeroom back door, leaving Sam to admire the photos of their work.

How could things turn out so wrong, so quickly? Maime had tried to tell him that there was something wrong. She had seen something the night she was hurt, in the very same room James was tormented.

Why didn't he listen to them? The thing that his wife described was unbelievable. But what could he have done?

He had searched the room afterward, while the ambulance crew was loading his precious wife onto a stretcher.

There was an eerie feeling to the room, but there was nothing that he could see, nothing he could lay his hands on.

Then there was the reminder of his haunted childhood at the Ames Estate where they were living now. Once again, he had that same identical feeling there. Something wasn't right, but nothing that he could see or put his finger on.

Sam walked in behind his grandfather as he was unbolting the door to the rear yard of the garage. Thoughts of James as well as what he'd seen back home were scrolling through his mind. They were right. He couldn't mention any of this to his grampa.

"We don't have to stay here," said Sam.

"Nonsense. There's good memories here and there'll be plenty more too."

He reached inside his back pocket and pulled out a folded piece of newspaper and handed it to Sam.

"Here take a look at the place I circled..., there."

Sam took the clipping without looking at it.

"James was about your age when we started working on that car of his. It's about time we started another project. Lord knows I need something to do and I have plenty of free time now."

Sam looked at a circle scrawled onto a list of ads. Someone was selling a 1955 Ford Pickup without an engine.

"Are you kidding me? Awesome!"

"Why don't we lock up here and make a trip over to look at it? We're not on any schedule."

"All right!"

"It's located over on the other side of Vidalia, but we can be back before it gets too late. We'll drive back by and leave a note to let the family know where we are, if we have time."

The two of them opened the bay doors and backed the tow truck out in front of the station. Martin tossed Sam the keys and had him to drive the other vehicle inside and lock everything back up.

Martin climbed up into the big cab of the wrecker.

"We might as well be prepared to bring it home if it looks good."

Maime walked through the house looking for Catherine. She could hear voices coming from upstairs. How she hated those stairs, not that she was feeble by any means.

Step by step, she began the march up the incline to the first landing. The polished rail squeaked as she slid her hand from grip to grip upward. It was such an accomplishment to reach the first landing in the staircase.

"Mama! Oh, my goodness," said Catherine, looking at her watch. "I'm so sorry. How long have you been waiting?"

"Only about ten minutes, but I think we need to go."

Catherine took her arm and helped her back down the set of stairs she had ascended only moments earlier.

"I don't know why we need to go see a doctor to tell me I can move my arm. I can tell by myself that everything's better."

Maime wiggled her fingers, "Oh, these stitches…. By the way, who were you talking to upstairs? Did Margie come in already?"

"No, it was only Aunt Martiel," said Catherine, hoping her mother hadn't heard the voice of James.

They walked out the door onto the porch and heard a faint voice calling from inside. Martiel was scooting along, trying to keep her heels intact, "Wait for me. I'm leaving too. I have to go into town for awhile myself."

Catherine looked inside the house one last time before she locked the front door.

Chapter 69

The Gamble

Summertime in the South can be the most wonderful time of the year for the young. There's summer vacation to enjoy and days that seem to go on forever. Life still holds untold possibilities of treasures, mysteries, adventures, places yet unseen and those are the ones left to the imagination.

Lazy cool mornings to wake up to while listening to birds fight over some prize bug or the steady hum of the neighbor's lawnmower. Days with friends or relatives in the hot sunshine, in the water of some lake or beach or something as simple as the spray of a water hose on the lawn.

And then there's summer nights…, the smells and sounds of food cooking, inside or out. Busy trails of kids, heroes and villains in an imaginary life and death struggle.

Summer for James was somewhat different than he had previously anticipated.

"What if this is the end for me?"

Once again, James was entertaining another morbid fantasy.

The sounds of a conversation, just out of the reach of clarity droned on as he struggled to hear what was being said. Two bees in a pickle jar could not have been more annoying than the constant mumblings of Syrus and Ellie inside his head.

Would there ever be peace for him again? Someplace where he could go and just turn off everything, all the noise, all the confusion, all the talking….

"Shut up!" he screamed.

His guests tried to tell him their conversation was of the most extreme importance as they moved further from his conscious thought.

For mere seconds it became quiet and then the noise slowly revived until it resumed its original gritty slide.

"This is insane," he groaned, ready to eject his guests.

Fear that he would lose all ability to protect himself and his family shook him back to reality. Still trapped.

Was his behavior abnormal? For the living, it would probably have some psychological term assigned to it, but for the living dead? Maybe this was completely normal.

Eternity. He quickly pushed that subject far from his thinking as fast as he could. The very idea of *forever* in his current state was beyond anything he was able to comprehend at the moment.

There were immediate problems to deal with.

He needed something else to replace his idle thoughts and occupy his time. He needed to focus. Sharing his feelings with his family was fruitless. How could they help? It would only heap more burdens on their already emotionally charred life.

One by one he had silently visited them, listening in on their thoughts. His guilt mounted with every person he visited. He'd been so incredibly wrong to believe he had been forgotten. Each missed him and felt some measure of responsibility for his premature death. The truth was, he hadn't listened to his own warnings, even the blatant warnings of BeBe's friends.

The next wave was loneliness as it began to wash over him. Grief and self-pity dug their claws deeply into his heart. He wept dry tears, but the pain coursed through him all the same.

"James?" came a familiar voice.

He ignored the summons. He was in no mood to visit with anyone.

"James…."

The same sweet voice called again, taunting his soul. It seemed near to him, far nearer than it should be. He shouldn't give in to this call, but felt a gentle pulling on his insides, it must be….

Jolie sat in a solitary room inside The Cajun Café with her Aunt BeBe. She had become a recluse since her release from the hospital. Her watchful guard sat eating out in the dining room, a mere earshot away from the slightest commotion.

James appeared in his usual style with a breeze stirring the air as he transfigured.

"You shouldn't be here," said James. "Didn't my Aunt Martiel call you?"

BeBe nodded, "She did. Some things are more important than safety."

She looked at Jolie.

James glanced around the room remembering somewhat better times while stocking its shelves with Jolie and her aunt.

"Hello, James," said Jolie with her usual heart-stopping smile. Her darting blue eyes pierced his heart and he performed the task of being seated in an empty chair at a table they had setup.

"Hello Jolie," said James, resisting the urge to touch her.

He smiled his best smile and could tell it had an effect on her as well.

"You look really good. The last time I saw you…, well you were pretty ragged."

"It was a miracle, James," she smiled. "I'm alive because of you."

Jolie held up her wrists for him to see little discolored rings where there had been nothing but raw flesh from the angry ropes.

James looked from her to BeBe.

"You must have a good reason for allowing Jolie to come here."

"I do..., we do. Several reasons...."

Jolie placed both hands on the table as an offering, "I've been having those dreams again. Ones like I had right before I met you for the first time. Only..., these are darker, evil. I'm afraid for you James. I felt that I needed to tell you to be more careful than ever. In the dream you're...."

"Wait," said James as he instantly disappeared.

A knocking came to the door and the voice of one of their employee's muffled through the closed door.

BeBe opened the door and let them in to pull a few items from the shelf and exit, but not before looking around at Jolie questioningly.

The door shut and BeBe slid the lock closed.

James reappeared in the chair, "I'm getting a little better about being surprised. You trained me pretty good."

"That's partly what my dreams are about..., being surprised, but not in a good way. In my dream...."

Jolie went on to describe the reoccurring nightly events that were troubling her. The dreams only reinforced James feelings of impending doom, which he hid from Jolie.

BeBe however sat probing her way into his thoughts and emotions as her niece painted a picture with her story.

When she was through, Jolie sat quietly waiting for some type of response from James.

BeBe didn't wait..., "James, just because you're afraid, doesn't mean that everything is almost over for you."

"I know," said James contemplating future events.

"Your gifts have matured drastically," said BeBe amazed. "I remember a time when you...."

"Could only think about Jolie when I was around? And I couldn't read your thoughts then either."

BeBe's face flushed and she smiled, "That too."

"It's a nuisance sometimes. If I focus, I can read the minds of everyone in your Café dining room, one at a time or all at once. It's maddening, I think sometimes that I'm going insane, if I'm not already. Other things have changed about me too. Things I won't let you read from my thoughts."

Jolie frowned and tapped the table, trying to get their attention, "Whatever the dream means..., I think that it's going to happen soon."

Her eyes sparkled like blue diamonds at James and he had to admit, she was still distracting as ever.

"So do I," said James. "Aunt Martiel doesn't think they'll risk getting seen or caught by sticking around much longer."

"We all agree," said BeBe. "Make sure you use those new senses."

"It might be nice if one of my abilities included reading the future," said James, somberly.

"They might," said BeBe. "Have you tried?"

"I don't know if I want to," said James. "If you could spend only five seconds, ten years in the future, would you? Would it be something bright and happy or the cold black of the inside of a coffin? Five seconds in heaven or five seconds in hell?"

BeBe sat quietly for several moments and then shuddered, "Why don't we look on the dark side?"

"I'm sorry, I don't have time for any other lessons or surprises right now. I have to use what I know, what I trust."

BeBe took one of Jolie's empty hands, "You do know that no matter what happens, you can't control everything. You're trying to take on the responsibility for everyone around you. You can't be in two places at once, you know."

The receptionist was getting tired as she made her last stand, "I'm sorry, but you're late for Mrs. Ames appointment. We'll have to reschedule unless you want to sit and wait for the next opening."

"How long will that be?" asked Catherine, feeling a sinking inside.

"It might be fifteen minutes or…, well it could take a while."

Maime smiled at her Daughter, "Let's wait. I want this over with."

She swung her cradled arm in its sling, "I'm sure it's fine. All I need is his okay to go back to living a normal life."

"We'll wait," said Catherine.

She almost laughed at her mother's comment about a "normal" life.

They walked back to the seating area and Catherine looked around to see if there were enough magazines to pass two hours of her time. Maime leaned over and mumbled where Catherine could hear, "Have you noticed that Martin Earl has been acting a little strange?"

Catherine grinned at her mother, "I think everybody has been acting a little strange lately. Is there something in particular you mean?"

They got up and reseated themselves as far as possible from a couple and their child with a continual hacking cough.

"He's been distant," said Maime. "And everything has him on edge. It's not like him. He has his moments like anybody, but it's almost a continual state now."

"You need to give him a little more time, mom. He hasn't adjusted to staying at home. I think when the police catch those people…."

"Oh, I'm so sick and tired of hearing about them," said Maime. "That's all anybody has on their mind lately."

Catherine slumped behind her two-year-old magazine, "You don't realize how desperate these people are. It's not worth the risk."

Maime darted around the open page to make eye contact with Catherine, "You seem to know a lot about those people. Is there something you haven't told me?"

Her mother always had found a way to get her to say more than she wanted even as a little child.

"I do know that they were willing to kill James," she answered. "And what about daddy? Then there's everything the sheriff's people told us."

"We don't even know what they wanted. I'm beginning to think Martin is right; they're probably long gone by now."

Catherine changed magazines and groaned inside. This was going to be a long wait.

Floyd sat at his desk nervously taking notes and watching the clock. It had been the -*same old thing*- type of meeting with Mason and his co-workers.

He had given the hints that he and James agreed upon to keep the group busy. Sheriff Howard seemed to be watching him closely and anticipating almost everything that he did lately.

Had his fingerprints matched the ones on the car? Was that what had the sheriff suspicious? No one seemingly had made that connection or they weren't telling him about it.

So far, there had been no connection made with the two names of the graves robbed from the public cemetery.

One was Ellie Rosalie, the other a Captain Benjamin Morrison.

There was no history to be found on Ellie Rosalie other than the fact that she was born in the year 1795 into slavery, owned by a French nobleman and with no record of her death.

Benjamin Morrison was a steamboat captain back many, many years, with an uneventful history.

Neither crossed paths with any historical information especially with the Ames family.

The other two graveyard vandalisms were written off as unassociated events for the time being, unless evidence linked them back together.

It was nearly five o'clock in the afternoon and the good Detective would be leaving the office soon. James had asked Deputy Floyd specifically to watch in on the Ames house this evening.

If he had to choose between irritating Detective Mason or James, it would have to be Mason that drew the short straw.

His pager went wild buzzing and Floyd jumped slightly turning it off.

"No, not now…," thought Floyd. "Why me?"

He shuffled a stack of manila folders, stamping them heavily to even up their contents.

"Is there anything wrong?" asked the voice over the cube wall.

"No, I'm finishing up some notes."

"By the way, I was impressed with your input in today's meeting," said Mason.

"Thank you, just doing my job," said Floyd.

"I'm out of here for the evening, but if the slightest thing turns up you be sure and give me a call," said Detective Mason.

"You'll be the first to know."

Floyd could hear the reeking sarcasm in his own voice.

"What perfect timing…," he groaned.

The pager was showing a familiar number, 666 1100.

Meet the devil at eleven o'clock.

Billy wanted to meet with him at the Heaven's Gate Cemetery an hour before midnight, just six hours, so if he could get in touch with Williams before then, he'd know what to do.

Deputy Floyd sat back in his chair, assessing his life, as the office grew busy from the shift change. Everything was getting too complicated and dangerous. He'd seen situations on his job that were potentially bad, but everything was starting to implode now.

He couldn't run from James or shoot him. Then there was Billy and his group of twisted killers. The words of James Earl Williams came back to him. Floyd remembered that he fit into the category perfectly; he was a greedy bastard. Why did he have to get involved with them? None of his little scams and skims compared to the hole he'd dug for himself. If he hadn't been caught, how deep would his involvement have grown?

"I can't unscramble eggs," mumbled Floyd, sitting up in his chair.

Maybe the Williams kid was right. He had lost the concept of *Right and Wrong* somewhere along the way. He had to face the fact that he was only doing the right thing now for fear of what might happen to him.

"Rule number *whatever*, the true criminal always regrets getting caught, but not doing the crime."

Floyd recited the ode that the academy had pumped into their heads.

This was what he wanted to do…, right here and this was where he wanted to be. There had to be a way to straighten things back out and get back on track, all he wanted was a way to get there.

Martiel arrived back at the house after a day of legalities and mindless walks through some local stores.

The house was extremely quiet. She heard the distant scratching of pans in the kitchen and walked in. She went through the foyer, living and dining rooms to the kitchen door and took a half breath to speak, but only exhaled.

She had expected to see Margie or Catherine, but there was only an empty room. She suddenly felt a chill as she looked around. There was a commotion from inside one of the lower cabinets and the door burst open, with Tommy spilling out.

Big lazy Tommy scooted and clicked excitedly around the floor looking for an exit, running from some imaginary villain. He spotted Martiel, fuzzed all the hairs on his body and ran for the swinging pet door to his outdoor sanctuary.

"Who's there?" asked a soft voice from an unidentifiable location.

"It's only me," Martiel answered after breathing a sigh of relief. "I brought home some burgers for supper. Where is everybody?"

"Mama's still taking a nap, so it's only us here."

Catherine's voice became clear as she walked through the door.

"How was the doctor visit?"

"You don't want to know. Thank God it's daddy's turn next time."

"Is she better or is something wrong?"

Catherine slumped against the countertop, "Oh, she's fine. No more sling, no more stitches, and one more follow up visit in a month. It's me that's worn out."

"Where is Martin?" asked Martiel, suddenly worried.

"I don't have a clue. He and Sam were going over to the garage to check on things, but he didn't say where they might go afterward. You know how daddy can get when he sees tools of any kind."

"Yes, but that's really close to the old house…. You don't think he'd drive by there for any reason do you? I mean after all, we know who's hiding out over there."

Martiel grabbed her keys and purse from the table and started for the door.

"Where do you think you're going?" asked Catherine.

"I'm not going to sit here worrying myself crazy. I should be back soon, but if not, you might give Sheriff Howard a call…, and make sure you talk to him."

There were no lights on and no vehicles parked around Earl's Garage when Martiel drove up to the gasoline pumps. She sat under the awning in the dark, wondering what to do for a few moments. After staring at the large plate glass window for several minutes, she got out and stood by the open door of her BMW.

Swallowing hard, her mind went over the premonition she had endured only hours ago. It was one thing to have a vision, but to watch it enacted without putting up some sort of a fight was suicide.

Inside her purse was her new "Ladysmith" - Smith and Wesson .38-caliber revolver, Sheriff Howard had helped her choose. It fit perfectly, but felt cold as she slid it into her hand. Hopefully her practice at the firing range in Biloxi would not have to pay off tonight. The last thing she wanted to do was shoot someone.

Her thoughts flashed back to Jolie and what had happened to her and she shuddered. Jolie had youth on her side. One of the many reasons she had survived the heinous ordeal. Martiel shook her head, she was no spring chicken, there was no way she would survive such torture.

Martiel lightly flipped the cylinder sideways and looked inside. It was full of five hollow point rounds.

Sheriff Howard had shown her which one to purchase, always good to have the law on your side. Her old pistol was resting on the bottom of the Mississippi River. She had taken the sheriff literally, when he said to throw it away.

It wasn't getting any lighter outside and the streetlight in front of the garage was already on. Martiel followed the procedure that was burned into her memory by her formerly enslaved relatives. She stood quietly and listened for…, stray thoughts.

A person could hide quietly and keep their mouth shut, but the mind was ever active. All was quiet and she breathed a sigh of relief. The gun slid easily back in her purse as she walked up to one of the bay doors and peered inside.

There was Martin and Maime's family car parked inside, but her brothers tow truck with "Earl's Garage" stamped on both sides was missing. That was good news. Her brother was on a mission of some kind.

The crunching of gravel woke her from her stupor and headlights blinded her as they came to a stop only feet from where she was standing. Her hand was already inside her purse and her heart was thumping.

"Martiel Ellington?" questioned the voice behind the bright lights.

"Who wants to know?" she asked, but her eyes readjusted to the light and she saw the light rack on top of the car.

"I'm sorry, the lights blinded me for a second," said Martiel. "Yes it's me."

She eased her purse closed hoping not to alarm anyone.

Sheriff Howard stepped out of his car and walked over to where she was standing. He stuck out his hand in a friendly gesture and she shook it.

"Is anything the matter?"

"Probably not. Martin and Sam…, my other nephew…, they're late coming home and I got worried. The big truck is missing and their car is inside here, so he's probably doing somebody a favor, you know him."

"You seem awful tense, is something else bothering you?"

"I guess so…. Nervous enough to have this thing with me."

She held up her purse and he understood the meaning.

"You know better than to be out here alone at night. At least bring someone with you if you're going to be out. Do you want me to escort you back home?"

"Oh, heavens no. That won't be necessary. I have a key to the station somewhere here. I'll turn on the lights for Martin and lock the door behind me. I think I'll wait around a few minutes and see if they show up."

"I'm off duty. I'll wait around with you for a while. That is if you don't mind the company."

"Of course not. Why were you coming around here? Being off duty and all."

"I stop by here most every day to make sure no one has broken in or vandalized the place. The last thing I need is Martin Earl getting on my case if this place was broken into."

The office phone began ringing loudly as they stood outside, breaking up their conversation.

Martiel hurried to the door, fumbling endlessly through a ring of keys. The sheriff offered his flashlight and she found it immediately.

"Thank you," she smiled, and unlocked the door.

She hurried to the phone moments after it quit its repetitive insistence. Too late.

Howard found the switch panel on the wall and flipped on the lights to the office and the overhead garage bays.

"I'll be right back." She got in her car and parked it closer to the building in front of the police car.

Inside, Howard was sitting in one of the more comfortable chairs in the office.

"It's my regular chair," he grinned broadly.

"You have a nice smile," said Martiel. "That is..., I don't see you smile very often.... It's good to see you smile...."

She shut up and blushed at her obvious confusion of words.

"Let me see if Martin still keeps the coffee hidden in the same place and I'll make us a pot."

An hour and a half-pot of coffee later, they had shared the short version of the last few years of their lives. Martiel's nerves had settled down even though she was still anxious over her brother's whereabouts.

There was a call that came over the police radio outside and when he heard his name mentioned, he jumped up to report in.

He returned a few minutes later.

"Got a call at the station from your niece Catherine. She was checking up on you."

"Oh, my goodness. I forgot all about the time. I told her to call you if..., well..., only in case I didn't come back in a reasonable amount of time. I'll give her a call."

Martiel picked up the garage telephone and dialed the house.

Another truck pulled up under the bright lights over gas pumps and stopped. The driver looked intently inside the office. The sheriff realized that Earl's Garage looked as if it was open for business and stepped outside.

The window to the truck crunched down and a raggedy man bellowed out the window.

"Y'all open?"

"All closed, just locking up."

The window slowly rolled back up and the truck shot off out of the intersection without another word.

"Weird people. Nice truck though."

The police radio belched out another call and he walked back to see what was going on.

Martiel finished her call to Catherine and peeked out the door.

"I probably should go take a look at this. There's a bad accident a few miles from here," he said apologetically. "So much for being off duty. If you want to lock up, I'll follow you part of the way."

"If it's all the same to you, I think I'll stick around for a few more minutes and see if they show up. Catherine knows I'm here so she can call…."

"I don't like the idea of leaving you here by yourself. I'll come back by here when I get through to check on you, if that's okay."

"I'll probably be here," she said mildly disgusted.

"Next time the coffee's on me, if that's alright."

"Why sheriff, I'd be delighted."

His car pulled away and sped off into the distance.

"Poor man doesn't know I'm three years his senior," she thought with a grin. "I guess nowadays it really doesn't matter."

Martiel relocked the door, filled her coffee cup and sat back down. After another twenty minutes of complete boredom and silence, a tour of the garage, and a bathroom break, she was ready to leave.

The phone rang and Catherine was calling again to check up on her.

Mid conversation a truck pulled up to the outside gasoline pump.

"I'm going to have to get out of here, the whole world thinks this place is open," she told Catherine. "Hang on just a minute."

Martiel waved them on and pointed to the sign on the window.

The occupants of the truck sat in the same spot looking inside the office.

"We're Closed," she mouthed as a grungy man got out of the truck.

"I swear. What stupid people."

Catherine was still waiting for her aunt to continue where she left off.

Martiel laid down the receiver to the phone and walked closer to the door and the man stood waiting right outside.

"We're Closed," she said loudly.

The man screwed his face as if to argue that he couldn't understand her.

She unlocked the door and cracked it open.

"I said, *We're Closed*," she said in as normal a voice she could muster.

"I know," he said back to her and forced his way inside.

"Aunt Martiel?" a tiny voice buzzed from the telephone receiver.

A gloved hand set the telephone receiver back in its cradle, terminating the call and the man walked out of the office carrying Martiel Ellington over his shoulder.

"Aunt Martiel?"

Catherine cried out, "Hello?!"

A dial tone signaled the end of the conversation. Something was definitely wrong. Where was James when she needed him? She immediately called the Sheriff's Office again.

"I need to speak to Sheriff Howard."

"Is this Catherine Williams again?" asked the desk clerk.

"Yes, it is…, can you hurry? This is an emergency."

"Sheriff Howard is responding to an accident. Can I refer you to one of the deputies?" she asked efficiently.

"No, I had explicit instructions only to talk to him. Can you please try and reach him?"

"Didn't you talk to the sheriff only an hour ago?" she asked rudely.

"Is there another emergency person I can speak to?" asked Catherine. "This is an emergency."

The clerk grunted and shook her head tiredly, "Just a moment. I'll try to reach him."

"It's going to be one of those nights," she grumbled to herself. She touched the button to talk to the dispatcher…, hesitated, then instead, pressed the blinking square on her switchboard.

"I'm sorry, but he isn't answering his radio. Can I take a message?"

Catherine hung up the telephone, mad as hell, and worried sick. She couldn't leave her mother at the house alone and she certainly couldn't take her along on what would most likely be a dangerous trip.

"James!" she yelled out, half running up the stairs.

"James!" she called out again as she shut the bedroom door.

"Where are you?"

James had almost spent the entire day with BeBe and Jolie discussing past events and his feelings. He was careful to keep his thoughts locked carefully away and closed to the part of him that had tortured two of the people on his death list. Milton, his third, he practiced on for principle's sake.

BeBe had shared the better part of the last two hours with James on exercises to focus his abilities.

Jolie was more interested in personal time with James, but today would not be the day. The purpose of their conversations could prove critical to the outcome of his family.

It was almost time to check in with Floyd and take their surveillance to the next step. James was looking for a way to break the news to his friends when....

"James...!"

"What's wrong, James?" asked Jolie.

"Someone is calling me..., my mother. Something's wrong. I have to go.... I have to go now."

James appeared before his mother with a turbulent entry. She was frantic and pacing the room when she saw him.

"It's Aunt Martiel!" said Catherine. "I think something has happened to her."

James took an instant to listen at the house, "Where is she? Where is everybody else?"

"I don't know.... Your Aunt Martiel went to look for your grampa and Sam. They haven't shown up either. It's just me and your gramma here at the house."

"Did you call the sheriff?" asked James. "That's what she told me to tell you if there was an emergency."

"Oh..., I did that. Those people are clueless! He's out of pocket and they can't reach him."

"Okay, do you know where Aunt Martiel was going?" asked James trying desperately to get some real information.

Catherine was fighting back tears, "I was talking to her on the telephone at your grampa's garage and the line went dead."

"Grampa's garage? What was she thinking?!"

"Call this number," he said, looking for something for her to write on. "It's a pager. Leave your number and when the person calls, tell him..., tell him to meet me...."

James stalled when he didn't know where to have Deputy Floyd go. "Uh..., have him come here to the house. I'll try to let you know where to send him by the time he gets over here."

James was about to blast his usual exit and he paused for a moment.

"Mom, if anything should happen tonight.... I mean..., well, if for some reason I don't come back, I love you, mom."

Before she could breathe the words..., he shook the house leaving in search of his aunt.

"I fully intend have your job over this!" shouted Sheriff Howard. "How long ago did Ms. Williams call?"

"Only about thirty-five minutes or so," said the night clerk nervously.

"Weren't you in the same briefing with everybody else? Any call related to the Ames family is to take top priority. Was that too difficult for you to understand?"

Sheriff Howard reigned himself back in to a resounding yell.

"Do you think you might be able to remember what Ms. Williams said, or is that beyond you too?!"

"She didn't say, she only mentioned that she needed to talk to you directly, and that it was…, an…, emergency," she said, her voice fading off.

"An emergency," he mocked.

"Call the Ames residence immediately. No, never mind I'll do it myself," he threw the microphone to the police radio on the seat beside him, flipped on the emergency lights and siren to his vehicle and sped off.

"Martiel…, I knew I shouldn't have left you there."

James was at Earl's Garage almost instantly and standing in the intersection.

His aunt's car was parked in front and all the lights were on in the shop. That could be a good sign, if the phone line had simply gone dead. James knew that wasn't the case as soon as he heard the total silence.

He hurried inside and found the place relatively untouched. The only thing odd was the family car sitting where the Tow Truck usually parked. He went to the back door and it was locked tight.

There was a noise out front and James ran to see.

It was Sheriff Howard pulling into the front of the garage. He had to stay at least one step ahead of the sheriff.

The old house, the one that Billy and Sallee Mae bought, they might be there. He blew out of the office in a gust of wind moments before a frantic Sheriff Howard ran through the door.

Martin and Maime's old house was completely black, not so much as a single point of light emerged from any window around the place.

If he was worried about being detected, it was far too late.

He went to the front door, which was standing open, pushed his senses inside finding only the singular thought of the night creature that had tormented him.

"I'll deal with you later."

The only other logical place he could think of was…. No…, NO…, not the cemetery. Thoughts and visions of what his dead friend Cambii had endured flashed in front of him.

"Aunt Martiel!"

Sheriff Howard ran yelling Martiel's name throughout the empty garage. Everything was exactly as he had left it, except for Martiel. She was gone. It had to be what Catherine was trying to tell the incompetent night clerk.

He flipped open a notepad and picked up the telephone.

"Catherine?"

"Oh, thank God you called," said Catherine, crying frantically. "I've been trying to get you for almost an hour now. Martiel was at the garage and something happened to her. I was on the phone and she was telling somebody that the station was closed and then the phone went dead."

"That damn truck," hissed the sheriff. "I'm so stupid."

"What truck?"

"It doesn't matter now. Do you remember anything else…, anything at all?"

"No, that was it. Sheriff, you have to do something. You have to find her."

"I'll do my best," he mumbled before hanging up.

Chapter 70

Split Die

"**Don't you worry yourself** none," said a scraggly old voice. "I ain't a gonna kill you right off. I gonna let you suffa some first."

Martiel came in and out of consciousness for a few moments. Long enough to see that it was dark and there were gravestones all around her. She was in a cemetery. It had to be her family's cemetery.

There was a hideous old woman standing over the top of her. She was securely tied on top of James' grave, inside the small crypt.

Candles were winking around her in the slight breeze, illuminating a deep red stain that was streaked everywhere. She felt lightheaded again, about to slip back into unconsciousness, then gave in to the fact that it was her blood that was painting the walls and floor.

This wasn't exactly how she pictured the last moments of her life, but her premonition had come true despite her efforts.

"Jolie...."

Martiel concentrated past the throbbing headache and tried to call out with her last strength.

"Jolie, I'm in the cemetery...."

James felt himself being snatched forward to the Heaven's Gate Cemetery. It wasn't the voluntary thrust of his own will that was moving him. Something was happening.

James landed in a pitch and roll on the ground, feeling a painful skidding against his ethereal body. He stood quickly and looked at a familiar sight. The ugliest person alive was standing over his Aunt Martiel and..., blood was everywhere.

Such carnage James had never seen, especially torn from the body of a loved one. She lay immobile, her lifeblood slowly draining away, staining the white stones above his body's enclosure.

Against her will, Jolie lay sleeping restlessly. Her reoccurring dream was playing in her mind once again and the agony was beyond her ability to remain asleep.

She jumped awake as soon as she understood that it wasn't a dream after all, this was real.

Jolie ran into the other room and found her Aunt BeBe.

"You have to call Catherine...."

Catherine was pacing the floor waiting. Waiting was something that she was not used to. Her life back home had been one of giving orders and having them carried out quickly and efficiently.

How far away that life seemed now. How trivial and meaningless. Finally, the phone rang.

"Catherine?" asked BeBe. "Are you okay?"

"No, Martiel is missing. I'm expecting a call any second. Is there something you need?"

"Jolie had a dream."

Oh God, now she wanted to discuss a dream of her niece.

"Is it something you can you tell me later, please?" asked Catherine her voice becoming shrill.

"No, this can't wait, just listen please," said BeBe. "Your Aunt Martiel contacted Jolie in this dream. She's at the Heaven's Gate Cemetery. And Catherine? I don't think she has much longer to live."

Catherine became frantic, her sobbing cry obliterating the conversation.

"You have to hold yourself together," said BeBe. "Is there anything that I can do?"

"No…, yes! You might try calling to James. He's not answering me either. I'm expecting a call from one of the officers any minute. I'll tell him where he should look."

Floyd looked down at his pager. It was the second time he'd been paged this evening and he didn't want to answer either of them. Both meant big trouble.

Now was time to make a decision as to which side he was on.

"Hello, I got a page to call this number?" said Deputy Floyd questioningly.

"You have to get to the Heaven's Gate Cemetery as quickly as you can," said Catherine frantically.

"Who is this?" asked Floyd.

"James gave me your pager number. Does that ring a bell?" she barked.

"Yes, Ma'am, it's ringing loud and clear. I'm on my way".

James faced his enemy squarely.

"You think you somethin' else don't you boy?"

The old woman's voice was smug and sarcastic.

"Whuppin' around on Billy, and chasing my little Toad here. We'll see how you like bein' whupped on."

She huffed loudly in a dry laugh.

All James could think of in that moment was her total destruction.

Apparently, his own bones held something he needed, because the closer he moved toward his grave the more energy rippled through him.

He raised his hand to point at her, but his strength faded like trickling water.

She shrieked and laughed at him.

"Can't use no power against me. Where you think it come from in the first place? And it's time for you to give it all back to me…, an then some."

"Syrus, Ellie, I could really use some help right now," thought James, stepping slowly backwards from the desecration.

Ellie Rosalie's voice suddenly came to life inside him, "My baby."

James had forgotten to help find her baby, the one promise that he had made to her.

She was crying now, "My baby is here, someplace near."

James felt her struggle to be free of him and find her baby.

Syrus held her tight, not letting her go to her child.

"Not now, please fight each other later. We need to stop this before my aunt dies."

The old woman seemed confused, "Who you talkin' to boy?"

James ignored her and tried to make sense of what was happening to him on the inside.

The old woman raised her hand, "Makes me no nevermind."

A sudden tempest rose as she lifted her thin arms and began to chant, sliding closer to the grave of James Earl. James felt what was left of his life draining from the inside. It was taking all his concentration to stand erect.

Blackened clouds began filling the night sky and the tops of the trees whipped and strained against the sudden velocity. An ugly vortex of wind began to spin, vacuuming in the muggy air from above.

Before all his strength left him, James fought to get away, begging for Syrus to tell him what to do.

"Tell me something, anything. This can't be all there is, not after all this time."

Haphazardly, his legs began to run through the graveyard, stumbling against stone after stone. Lightening erupted in the top of a tree near James and he cowered to the ground.

"That right! Run, run…!"

His enemy had begun laughing and taunting him to the edge of his endurance. James ran until his strength was all but gone. Close ahead was the broken stone of Syrus' grave and he fell down against a stone cross on an unnamed grave beside it.

"My baby! She's here! My baby girl!"

Syrus let go of Ellie and she leapt from James, falling into the grave beneath him.

"I don't understand. Ellie's baby is in this graveyard?"

Buried in a small unnamed grave beside Syrus Earl Ames. It was simply marked "Beloved Daughter" with a single date – 1824.

James rolled over to try to crawl further away from a nauseating pull on his insides. It was as if he was on a leash and it was being reeled in. Reminders of his dreams vomited up into his mind.

Unscheduled lightning flashed again, followed by a loud crash of thunder. His new efforts dragged his nearly lifeless shell only a few feet further. The ground began to shake around him and the earth rumbled beneath him.

At the end of his strength, his body began sliding toward his grave and his dying aunt. The earth split open over the grave of the child, while he was being dragged from off top of it.

Miss Lyda, *Bokor*, his enemy, was frantically chanting and pointing both her arms toward the ground where his body lay under the crypt. Electricity crackled the air, with sounds of arcing and snapping. The old woman was becoming a conduit for that energy and forcing it underground into his grave.

His insides gave another yank and he shook and quivered.

Closer, ever closer, it was the dream of being reeled in all over again. As his life ebbed, an oily sick weakness had him moving toward her.

Ellie emerged from the grave standing before James. A huge smile beamed on her face, glorious and radiant. She was swaddling the form of a tiny baby, pulling it near to her.

One last coherent thought, "At least something good came from all this."

Good. Could it all be that simple? Good versus evil?

Ellie reached down and took James by the hand and strength filled him. He stood, now able to resist the sickening pull on his insides.

"No! The power mine!" screeched the old woman.

Increasing her efforts, more power arced into the grave of James. The wind rose into a fury, pushing every piece of loose debris across the graveyard. Miss Lyda's arms began to glow from the power flowing between her and James' grave.

Syrus calmly spoke inside James, "One more thing to do for me. Put what's left of me, my skull back in its grave."

James gently extracted the skull of Syrus Earl Ames from where it was nested in his own head and pushed it into the earth of Syrus' freshly covered grave.

There was silence inside James, blissful silence and peace. His head was clearer now than he could ever remember, his senses running violently hot and cold.

Syrus and Ellie stood together before him holding their child, stolen before birth and endowed as a cauldron of power, a hiding place for the power of the age-old voodoo woman.

The baby was taken to refresh her youth, but it was hidden from her by Samuel Earl the brother of Syrus, buried in this cemetery, miles from her mother.

The three of them surrounded him with their bodies.

His body began to glow from the inside out - something inside him was changing.

"You have everything you need, right inside you…, right now," said Syrus. "The only battle that's left is in you. You have to let go…, believe James."

The words echoed in his mind, sounding like Granny Smith's Sunday lessons.

Ellie smiled beautifully, "You don't need us any more. It's time for us to rest. Thank you, James," she said, backing away.

The old woman turned from her efforts over James' grave and whipped out her knife. She took the point of the knife and stabbed her own hand with the point, piercing the paper-thin skin of her palm.

She walked in a large circle from gravestone to gravestone smearing it with her own blood. When she was satisfied of her work, she screamed a blood curdling howl.

"Giiit uuup!"

Waving her hands madly in an upward fanning motion, something began to answer.

The ground shook violently and dirt spit up in the air over each of the graves. Each one in turn gave up their dead and slowly stood over their resting places. Eyes void of understanding, their bodies reassembled to some vague appearance of humanity.

Their stench swirled in the air as she stood by his Aunt Martiel's limp body, in the center of an assembly of the dead. Lightening flashed again and its blue light cast eerie shadows around them.

Chapter 71

A pair of headlights pulled up in front of Heaven's Gate Cemetery. Floyd hurried out of his car, holding onto the door. "What in the heck is going on?"

He walked quickly into a torrent of wind as blowing debris began pelting him from every direction. He ran quickly following the sounds of yelling in the distance. His eyes were instantly on stems and he slowed his pace to a stop as lightning illuminated twelve putrid corpses standing around an extremely animated, dried up old woman.

The only thing he could think of was, "Wow, she sure is tall for an old woman."

Floyd froze in panic, not knowing what to do as the elements erupted around him and thunder crashed with an odd dying echo. The air was getting heavy and humid, night bugs stinging and pelting amidst the turmoil.

Floyd swatted at a passing swarm of mosquitoes attacking him like bees.

"Ain't you a little early?" boomed a voice from behind him.

Floyd spun around looking into the darkness, waiting for another stroke of lightning to illuminate the voice.

Some twenty feet away stood Billy.

Billy raised his chin, "You been a busy boy, ain't you? You're almost an hour early."

"I…, I drove by and saw the commotion…, what's happening here?"

"Nothing you'd understand probably, but why don't you stay, now that you're here?"

Floyd eased his hand toward his gun and slowly unsnapped its restraint.

"Uh, uh…," said Billy, producing his own weapon. "Why don't you drop that on the ground, real easy like."

"I cut the sacrifice! I put my power in that baby!"

It was hard to believe that someone that old could produce the volume of her threats, "It belongs to me!"

His body was suddenly dragged forcefully toward her, his feet sliding trails in the dirt.

"All I need is a little touch and it all be over! You be mine forever."

Her voice had turned into a growl, hatred flowing from her obnoxious speech. She spoke and the helpless dead obeyed her, walking toward James.

"Bring him to me!"

"On your knees, deputy," said Billy, waving his gun.

"What do you mean?" asked Floyd innocently.

Billy closed the gap quickly and smacked Floyd across the head, causing visions of stars and pain as he fell to his knees.

"That's what I mean," said Billy. "Now stay right there 'till all this is over and done with."

As his vision cleared, Floyd could see the silhouette of his gun only seven or eight feet away on the dark ground, but leaping for it would be fatal.

There was a loud snapping sound behind him and Billy fell down over his body and sank to the ground unconscious. Floyd spun his aching head around to find Sheriff Howard standing above him, holding his shotgun.

"Cuff him, to something solid," said the sheriff quietly. "Get your weapon and follow me."

Chapter 72

"Isn't it me you want?"** another voice boomed from behind Miss Lyda.

The old woman whipped her body around to face a new adversary.

"How…? Who are you?!"

"James Earl Williams and rightful heir to the family power."

The silhouette of a man eased closer, the voice was undeniably that of James.

"You a liar!" she yelled. "Ain't no two of you."

She raised her hand at the man, speaking her blasphemies and there was no reaction, her power had no effect whatsoever.

"You ain't him!"

She spun to look at James, still valiantly struggling to stand against her legion. The undead slowly stepped nearer and were almost within arms reach.

She turned back around and the other one was gone.

From another place behind her, the man taunted her yet again.

He held out his arms, "Test my blood, I'm James Earl Williams."

"Ain't got no blood, liar! You stay away or I kill this woman right now!"

"She looks dead already to me," said the man, stepping even closer.

The old woman whipped out her knife and stood only steps from Martiel in front of the grave. No longer alone and without any doubt that he had everything inside him he needed to end this, to end her, James Earl felt complete.

The only thing holding him back was his fear and it slid off him like a cloak. The minion of dead stopped their motion, staring with expressions as empty as the eyes trained on him.

"Git him…. I said git HIM!"

The unfaithful zombies seemed listless and undecided, unable to obey.

"It's me you want," said the other man again.

She twisted her head back and forth looking at the two figures of James Earl.

James heard a voice inside say, "Go ahead, touch her. Your enemy fears most what she uses to frighten you."

His helpers faded from sight, "You don't need us any more."

James walked toward the dead touching them one by one.

"Sleep!"

They each fell heavily over and disappeared back into the ground from where they had risen.

The old woman backed up, anger in her steps, holding her knife.

"We both know that knife won't cut me," said James as he stepped directly front of her.

"I bet it'll cut her real good."

Swiftly the knife dropped toward Martiel's throat.

James caught her wrist.

Lyda Brown screamed, her voice gurgling a foul stench from her lungs. Her eyes grew wide with shock and surprise.

"You wanted to touch me...?"

The old woman began involuntary jerks and twists as her body gave up its enormous glowing energy..., into James.

James began to shake and shiver, rivers of power entered him.

His spirit split from his own ethereal soulish body and he floated above near treetop level, looking down at the scene as it unfolded below.

From this vantage point, he watched strands of lightening stretch from him to the ground and strike his crypt.

He snapped back inside his visible self down below with audible crackling sounds around him, the residue of the power released and then thunder rolled into the distance.

The old woman lay motionless and withered on the ground, her body becoming parched and dry, only an empty shell.

There was an instant stillness and quiet.

"You're not going to leave me here like this?"

Billy begged the stringy haired boy while handcuffed to a wrought iron railing.

"You brought this all down on your own head," said Toad. "There's somebody coming, so it's every man for hisself."

"Get me out of these!" yelled Billy.

"Shut up, the whole damn world'a hear you. See ya in the funnies."

Toad hunched down and began to hurry off, just as Billy began to yell at the top of his lungs.

"He's over here! Hey, over here!"

"Shut up!" said Toad, spinning around. "I ain't doing time because of your loud mouth."

Toad put the end of his shotgun up to Billy's head. Toad's visage darkened, frightening Billy as he saw something unexpectedly different about him.

"Then help get me out of here with you," said Billy, frantically.

Footsteps began pelting the ground and getting close.

James felt his aunt and listened for life inside her. It was there but barely, her thoughts a mere whisper.

"If only...."

He untied her mangled wrists and legs as the other James approached, looking on.

He picked up the tiny lifeless body of his aunt and stood looking at a carbon copy of himself.

"How's it going bro?" asked Sam, sudden tears welling in his eyes.

"Sam..., it's good to see you," said James looking down at their Aunt Martiel.

There was a loud blast of a shotgun from somewhere behind them and they both turned to look in the direction. Shouts erupted all around them and the flicker of flashlights through the trees in the distance.

"It's the sheriff," said Sam. "Let them finish it."

Martiel stirred slightly looking up at the two of them.

"You can help me James," his Aunt Martiel spoke inside him, barely audible to his mind.

James closed his eyes and tilted his head upward to the sky.

Once again, he held her close and let his power flow through her, praying - something he was getting better at now that he knew someone was listening.

The hair on Martiel's head stood out freakishly in a halo of light. Samuel Earl staggered backwards slightly, the odd electricity making his body tingle. He watched on as his deceased brother James, seemingly alive again, stood glowing in the dark holding their aunt in his arms.

Martiel began drawing in violent gasps for air and fell still.

Sam backed up in horror, thinking that James had killed their aunt, but his brother only grinned at him.

"You can put me down now, careful now." said Aunt Martiel, stirring in his arms.

Sam was completely stunned by everything he had seen and stood helplessly watching his Aunt Martiel take to her wobbly feet.

"We need to have a long talk," said Sam looking intently at James.

"How did you know?" asked James.

"It was grampa's idea," said Sam, looking over toward the grave of Syrus Earl Ames.

Their grandfather stood in the distance looking down at the grave in silent reflection.

"When we got back to the garage, everything was open and the sheriff was there."

There was another well deserved silence as the two stood staring at each other in unbelief.

An engine cranked in the distance and raced violently as it sped away from the front of the cemetery. Instantly one of the Sheriff's Department vehicles' began pursuit, its siren wailing off into the distance.

James looked anxiously between Sam and Martiel then up at the sky.

"They don't have a good track record. I'd better lend a hand."

"James...," said Martiel in a whisper.

It was too late. A blast of air swirled around them as James disappeared.

The pickup was careening along, cutting through the neighborhood yards, its engine a whining roar. Toad had already managed to lose the flashing lights behind him. They weren't willing to take the chances he was. Of course, they weren't facing several life sentences, or possibly *the chair*.

The highway was the easiest way to get caught, but he had to chance it. It was the shortest route to his favorite dirt road to nowhere. He always kept a good supply of food and clothes for just such emergencies, hidden away in his wilderness hideaway.

If he could make it there, he could easily disappear forever into the wilds along the Mississippi River delta.

James Earl slid into the seat beside the grungy excuse for a man, called Toad. The smell of blood and death was heavy on him.

After taking a closer look, he saw pieces of bloody flesh on his pants legs. Then he looked deeper inside the man and saw that he reeked of something even darker, more hideous within him.

He wasn't alone, he was inhabited by something, something *familiar*.

Toad slammed on the brakes hard and readied the truck for the turn down a dirt road. James reached into the dash and pulled wiring loose by the handfuls.

Instantly, the truck began to sputter and smoke inside and it died, coasting to a silent halt.

Freed in his mind from the confusion of the last several weeks, James had lost his desire to kill this man, even though he was the very one that drove him down the levee to his death.

James jumped outside the truck and pinned the driver's door shut, the moment Toad leaned into it with his shoulder. He banged against it twice, then three times as hard as he could.

Toad slid across the bench seat to the other side of the cab and James quickly met his attempts again.

He was trapped inside.

In a frantic leap of desperation, he leaned back in the seat and raised his feet to the windshield, double kicking it out onto the hood of the truck. Smoke was filling the cab as he crawled out through his new exit, coughing.

"I know you're here! You git away from me!"

He rolled off the hood and onto the ground looking around desperately.

James appeared in front of him, blocking his path.

The young killer made a mad dash of an exit as an iron fist grabbed him and turned him around. James picked him up and tossed him bodily back inside the truck.

Toad began to swear loudly, his expressions changing.

"You get away from me or I'll hunt down every member of your family and kill them one by one," said Toad in an unusual gravelly tone.

"That'll be hard to do from prison."

"I won't be in no kinda' prison."

It was then that James fully understood it wasn't Toad that was speaking and his voice was becoming more robust and literate.

The new voice laughed, "If they kill this body, I'll find someone else to live in. It's nothing to me. I'll hunt all you Ames down, every last one of you."

Then mockingly the voice changed, "Then I'll git back what belongs to me."

"I'll be around for awhile too," said James.

"Let me go or you'll be watching your back and all of your family for generations," he said grittily. "There'll be no place to hide."

James knew he was telling the truth. It would be a full time job keeping his family alive. This night would be repeated generation after generation.

He searched his mind for any idea of what to do with this creature. He remembered what his Aunt Martiel said.

"Keep your friends close, but your enemies even closer."

James reached inside and yanked Toad from the truck. As he held him with one hand, he reached inside Toad and yanked out a very surprised dark creature from inside him.

It was the only forced exorcism James had ever heard of and he was performing it. The creature was flailing several appendages and writhing in its own steam. James recognized it immediately.

The body of Toad gurgled and yelled fainting to the ground, ripped and torn at the forced exit of the dark spirit.

It looked similar to the creature that had tormented him from the very beginning. Talon like claws, spidery legs, a mouthful of fanged teeth, and those glowing white eyes that could freeze blood still in the veins.

James looked the truck over and found what he expected to be there. In a wooden box was several of the clay jars designed to hold the trapped souls of unfortunate people.

He found the one that Ellie had been in and set it out on the ground. The little monster squirmed vigorously biting at the air, steamy smoke flowing off its black body, raking and snapping its claws over the vice grip that held it fast.

James uncorked the jar and took one last look at his enemy.

"You little murdering devil, here's you a new home."

"I'll be back, you'll see. You'll wish you'd let me go," hissed the spirit.

"Got a little liar in you too, huh?"

In a fleeting moment, the creature was incarcerated inside a *govi* prison, with the lid on tight. There was one perfect, dark, dank place to put it.

The sheriff or one of his men would arrive at any second and he didn't want to be seen. James looked down at Toad passed out on the ground, took the earthen jar and left, shattering the remaining glass in the truck from the wake of his exit.

Chapter 73

James met his family as they were exiting the front gates of the cemetery. There were several county vehicles swarming the area. Lights were flashing from crime scene photographers and official vehicles.

Catherine had arrived with her mother, against her better judgment and thankfully Martin had coaxed Maime from the car into the cab of his big tow-truck.

Sheriff Howard marched past and advised both of them not to stay while they cleaned up the area. Martin and Maime readily agreed and decided to go lock up Earl's Garage and un-hook the old Ford truck that was still attached to the back of its carriage.

"I guess I can be in two places at once," said James smiling.

"Only with my help," said Sam.

"Aunt Martiel…, how did you know that you would be taken?" asked Catherine.

"Sometimes I can see shadows down the road from my premonitions, but when Jolie told me about her dream, I knew it was more than a hunch. It was the real thing."

"Then it really is over?" asked Jolie.

"It's over," said James, with a soft touch of his hand. "The evil that started all of this locked away. I saw to that. You know, I didn't find where the old woman hid the gold coins though."

"It was blood money," said Martiel. "Good riddance."

Sam's imagination suddenly went into overdrive, "There was gold?! How much gold was it?"

Catherine looked at her youngest son and groaned.

"Martiel, you realize that you have a lot of explaining to do when we all get home," said Catherine, "You too, James."

It was Martiel's turn to moan, but there were no spooks left to object to the full knowledge being exposed to the rest of the family. The other members of the Ames family had fought together, as well as their adopted family of BeBe and Jolie.

Their family history was about to be rewritten and sealed once again for their eyes only.

"*Detective* Preston Floyd? Can I see you in my office?" asked Sheriff Howard. "That new title has a nice ring to it."

"Yes sir," said Floyd.

He stepped in the door, James silently in his wake.

"Come in…. Have a seat…," said the sheriff, motioning at one of the new chairs.

Detective Mason sat quietly balancing his cup of coffee.

"I have it on good authority that John Raymon, alias 'Toad' is going to get the chair. They're still making a list of possible murders he's committed. An anonymous tip led Louisiana Police to the shallow grave of a migrant worker also linked to him."

"I still don't see how you two put this all together," said Detective Mason.

"Mostly we were in the right places at the right time," said Sheriff Howard. "I was just lucky that my intuition coincided with their intentions."

James laughed to himself, "Does he even know what coincided means?"

EPILOGUE

The waves of the Mississippi River lapped lazily against the shores in perfect rhythm with the gentle currents and breezes of the hot August afternoon.

Just north of Natchez, deep inside a cave, free from the noises of life outside, a faint scratching and clicking was breaking the silence.

Peering into the darkness of its prison jar were two gleaming white eyes patiently waiting….

The End

ABOUT THE AUTHOR

David Pyle is the author of several supernatural tales and short stories with a library of information for new writers on his website – www.pentwist.com.

Other recent publications available through Amazon Books and Kindle:

Minutes

ISBN-10: 0615860516
ISBN-13: 978-0615860510

Pitre

ISBN-10: 0615877958
ISBN-13: 978-0-615-87795-2

www.ingramcontent.com/pod-product-compliance
Lightning Source LLC
Chambersburg PA
CBHW061505020726
47502CB00006B/1950